JURASSIC HORDE WHISPERER OF MADNESS COUNTY

Titus Stauffer

FreeVoice Publishing

DEDICATION

This book is dedicated to the hope that more of us will come to realize that it's far better to laugh at the Horde Whisperer than it is to listen to him.

ACKNOWLEDGMENTS

Special thanks to Mary Stauffer, Carolyn Weatherly, and Alan Mills for proof-reading this book, and to Capt. Gary L. Percival and the office of Dr. Phillip Zimbardo at Stanford, for chasing down information about Zimbardo's prison psychology experiment (see Chapter 17 endnotes). Special thanks also to Ken Michaelsen for the awesome illustrations!

ARTWORK

Drawings (cover and all interior illustrations) by **Ken Michaelsen,** McCloud, CA 96057. Cover artwork title is

"The Four Hordesmen of Rampant Inappropriateness."

Copyright © 1998 by Titus Stauffer.

ISBN No. 0-9644835-2-1

All rights reserved. No portion of this book may be reproduced by any means, electronic or mechanical, without the prior written permission of the author. For information, or to order additional copies, contact:

FreeVoice Publishing
P.O. Box 692168
Houston, TX 77269-2168
(281) 251-5226

Also by Titus Stauffer:
Bats in the Belfry, By Design and
Freedom From Freedom Froms

Manufactured in the U.S.A.

First Edition

DISCLAIMER

All the individuals, organisms, organizations, and other entities in this work are fictitious. Although the world that I desire to live in is also still fictitious, I would like to convey that in this better world, all lawyers would find themselves something honest and productive to do. They wouldn't bother and parasitize those who harm no one. They wouldn't, for example... oh, let's just say, for a totally randomly selected example, they wouldn't bother to harass innocent writers who exercise their First Amendment free-speech rights, but in so doing, happen to hurt the baby feelings of sensitive individuals, organisms, organizations, and other entities.

What I'm trying to say is, all you lawyers go away, and leave me alone. In the Name of the First Amendment, Censorship Demons, I command you, begone! You are not welcome here. Not that I would ever mean to imply that any lawyer is evil, or a demon - that might be slander, and God knows I mean to slander no one! So please notice, all you libel lawyers out there, I DO NOT pick on, or slander, any specific non-fictitious organisms or entities. I don't, for example, say that specific Scientologist-lawyers like Steven L. Hayes and Earle Cooley are sleazy, no-account scumbuckets, for example. If by any chance any of my fictitious names belong to real organisms and entities, then I apologize; I wrote this book while unaware of any such pure coincidences. If there's a *real* Church of Omnology, a *real* Aileron Hubba-Hubba, or a *real* Ale Run Hubba-Bubba out there, or a Hillary-Bob or a Billary-Bob, etc., I say to you, I wasn't talking about you, I was talking about a fictitious organism or entity that just happened to have the same name as you.

I say again, this entire work of fiction is... ***fiction***. In those places where I cite references, such as in footnotes and in chapter-introductory quotes, for example, I do deal in facts. Let me just go one step further, though, in expressing my apologies to anyone who might misunderstand: If it *does* exist, then I don't even mean to slander the sincere believers in this (to me as of now, at least) hypothetical Church of Omnology. If you're befestered by clusters of scamgrams descending from the Evil Galactic Emperor Zebu of 75 million years ago, and you'd like to have these befestering scamgrams fleeced away from you, and you have a lot of spare time and money, then by all means, the fellowship of the sincere worshippers of the Church of Omnology just might be your best bet. I'm all for religious freedom, and against libel, slander, and all other forms of chaos and badness. If Omnology sets you free from your scamgrams, then I certainly don't mean to tinkle in your Wheaties.

INTRODUCTION

WELCOME TO MADNESS COUNTY!!!

Welcome to Madness County—a place of myths and madness—a place where the Horde Whisperer reigns. A place where Tom Edisonosaurus tries to invent things for the betterment of dinosaur society, but Lawyersaurs constantly sue him, since a certain Whinasaurus is always getting hurt by his latest inventions, like the wheel and fire. Dinosaur society progresses only after Tom and his friends take drastic actions against the Lawyersaurs. But then the Horde Whisperer strikes, and brings all the dinosaurs to an end. The Horde Whisperer flees for millions of years, returning to the Earth to stir up more trouble and weirdness only when the ape-men come down out of the trees.

But it's in modern times that the Horde Whisperer does his worst. He causes the mad scientists at the government's THEMNOTUS agency to invent Chewdychomper Chupacabras, a vicious beast who in turn whispers in the ears of an ambitious man by the name of Ale Run Hubba-Bubba. Ale Run in turn invents his famous V-Meters and Ping Things, and His Church of Omnology. All troubles are caused by scamgrams, and only the *Experts* of His Church can *fleece* them away, using their V-Meters and Ping Things! All manners of modern madness are manufactured in Madness County, it seems. Far, far too many to be anything but the wackiest of wacky fiction, we tell ourselves.

But then we get to the annotated facts in the factual endnotes (almost 20% of this book), and we're left with disturbing knowledge. *Jurassic Horde Whisperer of Madness County* is based on facts—facts far too irrational, crazy, and destructive to be pure fiction. The Horde Whisperer is still with us, still Whispering his destructive, irrational lies in far too many ears. Just look at the government, media, Hollyweird, and church-sponsored madness all around you. Especially examine cults like $cientology, as this book does. This book is some zany fun, yes. But it's also a warning about the Horde Whisperer's lies, about how destructive irrationality runs rampant in our modern, supposedly enlightened age.

Chapter 1

The Horde is Bored

"We are not amused."
Queen Victoria (1819-1901)

In the waning, whining, weenie days of the late twentieth century, it came to pass that the Horde became bored. So they went down to Panderwood, which was the source, in those days, of copious quantities of thrilling amusements. The Horde had high hopes that Panderwood might snap them out of their latest funk. Something new, that's all that they were looking for. Something shocking, but not too much so. Something that wouldn't insult their intelligence, either, although there wasn't much danger of that.

Steve Spudburger came out to meet the Horde, saying, "Well, how about a show in which you can learn all about the deep scientific implications of The Chaos Theory, at the same time as you can watch dinosaurs eating lawyers. Not *your* lawyers; we all know they're the good guys. I mean, the *other* guys' lawyers."

The Horde paused for just a moment, and then grumbled, "Nah. Been there, done that."

Rupert Rotifer gave it a shot. "Hey, whaddaya say we do a show about this dude, man, he's got, like, mystical powers. Special, mystical powers, over, like, high-strung, bodacious corporate executive babes, and high-strung horses, like, ya know?"

The Horde shouted, "We're **Bored**!"

Frank Lee Deceasedwood got up and said, "I've got it! I have just the thing for what ails you. A little romance. Not with your wives, now, for heaven's sake! A little fling, with the *other* guy's wife. Just the thing to chase the blues away. All you guys out there, couldn't you relate to a guy, he *looks* like an old geezer, but he's not. He's something *very special*. He's a Lone Wolf Studmuffin, and he makes love like a panther. And all you gals- aren't you waiting to be swept off of your feet, and carried away to nights of wild passion?"

The Horde was pissed. "We want something ***NEW!!!,***" they protested. There was silence in Panderwood, but outside the gates, there were ominous mutterings.

Finally, Titus Maximus Stupidness got up to save the day. "Hear me out," he pleaded. "How about a tale of dinosaurs, lawyers, chaos— *lots* of chaos—a man with mystical powers over Hordes like yourselves— now, strictly just to *amuse* you, of course—*AND* nights of wild romance?"

The Horde paused. "Well, maybe," they mumbled. "Just this once. But it had better be good!"

Chapter 2

The Jurassic Horde Whisperer

*"Those who can make you believe absurdities
can make you commit atrocities."*
Voltaire (1694–1778)

The Triassic Period, from 230 to 195 million years ago, was a time of rampant insensitivity. Many, many creatures ran amuck, chasing one another, not only sexually harassing one another, but even trying (steel yourself, now!) *to eat one another!* Some of them even succeeded, on occasion. Most of them didn't even realize that they were being quite disgusting and barbaric. None of them, not a *one*, restricted herself or himself to macrobiotic diets.

Very few paleontologists have been able to overcome their anthropocentrism sufficiently to admit this, but humanity is by no means the first species to strive for sensitivity towards all life-forms. Most of them are too embarrassed, on behalf of morally and ethically stunted human beings like themselves, to speak the truth freely. Towards the tail end of the Triassic, and especially at the beginning of the Jurassic (195 to 140 million years ago), dinosaurs reached outwards and upwards, lifting themselves to higher and higher planes of self-awareness, self-actualization, and sensitivity. In these endeavors, though it took them many millions of years, they eventually exceeded the accomplishments of human beings. We can only hope that some day, we might be walking in their footsteps.

So their tales must be told. The truth, in all its glory, must be set free. The tale of the dinosaurs is largely the tale of its struggle with the Horde Whisperer. You know, the Horde Whisperer, the one that whispers to the horde. A disembodied spirit, flitting, twisting, and slithering hither and yon, across the space-time continuum, putting thoughts into the minds of the multitudes, be they humans, dinosaurs, or dinoflagellates.

Now there are those who say that the Horde Whisperer isn't very nice. That he isn't self-actualized, that he has low self-esteem, and worse. Well, OK, we may speak freely. They say, sometimes, even, that he is the Insensitive One. The Inappropriate One. You know, inappropriateness phantasmagoric—the Supreme Ruler of Heck and Gol Darnedness, the Prince of Sub-Standard Lighting. That he rode a tank in the general's rank when the Blitzkrieg raged.

But one must be sensitive, even towards alleged insensitivity. One must have sympathy for the Horde Whisperer, and understand his perspective. There's two sides to every story. Paying heed to the one, and not to the other, must most certainly rank among the grossest of injustices.

It seems that the Horde Whisperer simply likes to say to all of us, that which we want to hear. He likes to say unto others as they would like to be said unto. And as the Horde Whisperer says, this isn't so very far removed from doing unto others, as we would like for them to do unto us. Ethical is ethical, so don't let the sophists muddy the waters.

So he says to us, it's not *our* fault, it's *their* fault. The oil companies, the tobacco companies, beer advertisers, and all those other drug pushers. Not our fault. No Sir! Not those who drive cars or smoke cigarettes, or light up a joint now and then. Nor even those of us who support the witch-hunt hysteria that prompts school administrators to expel little girls for smuggling Advil into classrooms. If he told us *we* were to blame, whenever reality is less than perfect, that would make us feel *bad*.

Bad feelings are bad. Negative feelings, low self-esteem and suchlike things, they're all very negative. And negatives can only generate negatives. Nothing big ever came from being small, nothing good ever came from bad. Especially bad, is, like, thinking of oneself as being bad. Chaos is badness, reality is whatever we define it to be, and all we have to do is to think positive thoughts. Everything is just a highly subjective social convention, so we need to work harder on adjusting our definitions of reality, and reaching for those positive thoughts, especially about ourselves. How can we work towards the good if we don't define ourselves as good? Self-doubt is negative, and negatives are bad. So never doubt yourself. You are pure and innocent. If something is bad, it's not *your* fault, it's *their* fault.

The Horde Whisperer never bothered to visit the Earth until the dinosaurs had started to make small gains towards crawling out of the slime, towards sensitivity. Only Sensitive Ones can hear the Whisperings of the Horde Whisperer, after all. Especially that Whisper about us being far more Sensitive than the Average Guy, who is a stupid and miserly lout. So it was early in the Jurassic era, then, that the tale of the Jurassic Horde Whisperer began.

Tom Edisonosaurus was working on his latest invention. In keeping with dinosaur society's latest push towards getting all dinosaurs, carnosaurs included, to eat only vegetable matter, Tom was working on methods of getting farm produce and processed goods to market faster. After all, how can one expect the likes of Allosaurus to refrain from dining on his fellowsaurs, if one can't get sufficient quantities of bean sprouts, celery, and tofu to him, before it all spoils? So developing reliable bulk transportation was of the utmost importance, and Tom was devoted to uplifting dinosaur society.

Tom's last cart had worked just fine, but it hadn't lasted long. The edges of those new-fangled wooden "wheelybobs" he'd invented—he was considering shortening their name to just "wheels"—had splintered and disintegrated after the cart had carried a heavy load of brussel sprouts for just a few miles. So there was Tom, pounding durable stones into the edges of his wheelybobs, forming custom-shaped indentations, then lifting the stones back out, and finally, gluing them back in, using tree resins. It was all very painstaking work, especially since he had to avoid wasting any of his precious resins. He'd been very careful in gathering those resins, so as not to hurt any trees. He planned on fending off any environmentalist protest concerning his carts with bumper stickers saying "No living trees were damaged in the manufacture of this cart." And Tom was an honest dinosaur; he never even *thought* about lying, or cutting corners.

Just as he was applying the resin to the last stone of the last wheelybob, Tom heard some rustling behind him. Now the carnosaurs of the day had indeed been cutting way back in their bad habits—their blood cholesterol was even averaging below 200 in those days—but old habits died hard. Tom turned around and breathed a sigh of relief. They were small, spindly dinosaurs of such slight build as to provide no hazards to a medium-sized dinosaur such as himself. But wait—what was that? Weren't those suits and ties that they were wearing? And weren't they hefting large briefcases? The fear crept back into Tom's two-chambered reptilian heart, his cold blood flowing even colder, as recognition sunk into his reptilian neurons—that was a small roving band of *Lawyersaurus!*

Oh, calm down, Tom told himself. He'd done no wrong; surely he had nothing to fear. In fact, his cause was a noble one: He was uplifting dinosaur society by enabling them all to move towards a sustainable vegetarian diet. He straightened out his hunched back as he lifted himself up from his work and greeted the pack of *Lawyersaurus* with good cheer, "Good morning, Comrades! And how are you this fine morning?!"

The five Lawyersaurs just daintily tip-toed through Tom's outdoor work area, carefully, even suspiciously, eyeing all his tools and supplies. They approached Tom. Finally, the first one spoke up. "Fine, just fine. Thank you. And just what, exactly, is the meaning of all this?"

"I'm trying to devise methods of reliable bulk transportation," Tom replied. "So as to uplift dinosaur society, to get vegetable foods to market better and faster. To enable our formerly carnivorous brethren to stick to their new diets more reliably."

The first Lawyersaur eyed him through narrowing slits. "Are you implying that some groups of dinosaurs are inherently less likely to obey the law? Do you follow equal employment opportunity guidelines here, or not?"

"Oh, I do, I do," Tom hastened to assure him. "It's just that I'm only employing myself, so far. This is a very small outfit, and will remain so, until I can demonstrate the reliability and usefulness of my products. If and when I can start to hire, I'll be sure to document that all my employees are legal residents, and diverse, and have proper wages, benefits, and working conditions, and don't harass each other or take illegal drugs or endanger the environment, or neglect to pay babyosaurus support, or say insensitive things, or..."

"Okay, Okay," another Lawyersaur interrupted him. "We hear you. Now about these 'carts' we've been hearing about. Will they meet emissions standards? Will they come equipped with anti-lock brakes, brake lights, turn signals, seat belts, airbags, and mudflaps? Will you certify the percentage of domestic content? Will you ensure that all your customers are licensed and insured cart drivers? Will you report the names and addresses of all customers who pay you more than one hundred dinodollars in cash?"

"Oh, yes, yes, of course," Tom assured him. "But can't we be a bit civil? Let me introduce myself. I'm Tom Edisonosaurus, inventor. At least, I'd sure *like* to invent things for the benefit of dinosaur society. And you? Might I have the benefit of knowing who has come to inspect, and possibly assist, my noble enterprises here?"

Yet another Lawyersaur spoke up. "You say you're doing this for the benefit of dinosaur society. Are you sure you aren't just another money-grubbing capitalist, out to exploit the workers? Are you going to pay it all back to the community that has paid you, or are you going to spend it all on fancy digs for yourself?"

The first Lawyersaur "shushed" him and announced, "Enough of that. Mr. Edisonosaurus is right. Introductions are in order. Overdue, even." He reached out a front foot to Tom, who shook it. "Hi. I'm Jack B. Swindle, and these are my partners, Charles I. Robb and Robert B. Steele. We represent the law firm of Swindle, Robb, & Steele. With us, we have two of our assistants, Susy Sue Suezallott and Knuckles Writ Armstrong."

Front feet were shaken all around. "So then, how may I serve you?" Tom inquired solicitously.

"No, we're here to serve *you*," Jack replied to the smiling Edisonosaurus. Tom's smile didn't last long, though. "With a *Writ of Hideous Dorkishness*," Jack continued, brandishing a sheaf of papers. He began to read.

"Know all ye Dinosaurs by these here presentations and obfuscations that the law firm of Swindle, Robb, & Steele, having hereby been duly appointed counsel of the aggrieved party, a Ms. Willow W. Whinasaurus, hereinafter to be known as the party of the pure and innocent party, has been charged with the responsibility of securing suitable reparations from the negligent party, a Mr. Thomas Edisonosaurus, hereinafter, hitherinafter, thitherinafter, and foreverandeverinafter to be known as the guilty party. The *a priori swine qua nonsense* of the guilty party's malice and negligence having been the proximate cause of the grievous bodily harm wreaked upon the pedal extremities of the pure and innocent party, we do hereby and alwaysby implore, beseech and entreat that megagigadinodollars be awarded to the pure and innocent party, and to her counsel.

"Just to send a message," Jack threw in as an aside, looking up from his papers. "It's not the money, you know. It's the principle. We can't allow greedy capitalists to run rough-shod over the rest of us. Society has to defend itself from irresponsible robber barons."

"Massive remuneration being the only conceivable ointment that could serve as a *squid pro quotient* to the massive bodily damage and physical and mental anguish inflicted upon the pure and innocent party, we thereby declare that in order to assuage the sufferings of the pure and innocent party, the guilty party shall be obligated to recompense the pure and innocent party with his current net worth, plus all future earnings, minus his oral hygiene appliance—that's a 'tooth brush' to ignoramuses like you—and one can of Who Hash.

"Hereinafter and foreverafter, let all Dinosaurs be..."

"Hey, wait a minute!" Tom protested. "Would you care to translate all that garbage to ordinary Dinospeak?!"

"It means we're taking you to the cleaners," Jack assured him. "For the good of dinosaur society. You can't enrich yourself at the expense of others, and be allowed to get away with it."

"I haven't made a *dinodime* yet!" Tom squalled. "So what did I do wrong?!"

"You ran over Ol' Lady Whinasaurus's toe with your newfangled contraption, that's what you did," Susy chimed in. "You should be thankful she's not charging you with sexual assault, too. You were all alone out there, no witnesses. You know all about..."

"That's ridiculous!" Tom howled. "She just ran right up and stuck her toe under my wheel. What was I supposed to do?"

"Let bygones be bygones," Jack said soothingly. "There's nothing you can do about it now any more, except to try and right your wrongs. Help repair the wounds to Ms. Whinasaurus. Here, sign these papers."

"Yeah, right, Buddy! All you leeches are hereby invited to vacate my premises! Out! Scram! Git! *Vamoose!*" Tom picked up a wheelybob-whacker, brandishing it somewhat less than politely. He'd tried to be nice about the whole thing, but sometimes a dinosaur's got to do what a dinosaur's got to do.

The pack of *Lawyersaurus* scrambled about, gathering up their papers, zipping up their briefcases, straightening out their ties, and trying to stay well out of the reach of Tom's wheelybob-whacker, all while also trying to look dignified. Tom danced around like a boxer, swinging the

former wheelybob-whacker, now a would-be *Lawyersaurus*-basher. Briefly, it began to look like he might bag himself a Lawyersaur or two. In all the ruckus, one of the Lawyersaurs stepped into Tom's bucket of resin. He hobbled away, slopping resins all over papers, briefcases, suits, and Lawyersaurs. Despite his anger, Tom couldn't help himself. He roared with joyous laughter.

Soon, all the Lawyersaurs had gathered up their belongings, and had scurried off into the middle distance. "You can't escape your liability quite *that* easily," Jack taunted. "Guess who we're gonna go see next? Your *insurance* company! So there!" Then the pack of Lawyersaurs disappeared into the brush, briefcases briefly flashing.

Dejected, Tom sat down to think. His Insurance Agentasaurus would doubtlessly come by soon to tell him to cease and desist from cart-building activities, since the insurance would become prohibitive. Maybe Tom could do without insurance. Wait, no, strike that—no insurance, no license. No inventor's license, no inventing, or go to jail. Maybe he could at least finish this one cart, and sell it before he was told to stop.

He dipped that last stone in the dirty dregs of resin now oozing into the porous prehistoric soil, and glued it into the wheelybob. Now if only it would cure fast enough so that he could sell it before the Insurance Agentasaurus came by... Let's see, heat should speed-cure this. Too bad that that other *Lawyersaurus* pack a while back came and sued me into suppressing that other nifty invention of mine, which I called *fierybob*. Fierybob, applied just right, could speed-cure the resin, without burning the wood. But he'd had to just say no to fierybob—it was just plain too hazardous. Whinasaurs would burn their toes and smoke would irritate the delicate noses of Allergiasaurs. So Tom settled for dragging the cart gently out into the hot noon Jurassic sun. Then he settled down under a large tree, and ate some bean sprouts and tofu.

Tom searched desperately for a buyer, but alas, the Insurance Agentasaurus came by the very next day, and told him they'd agreed to settle out of court. "And now, I want to watch while you destroy this 'cart' of yours, and listen while you solemnly promise never to invent such a thing again," Insurance Agentasaurus concluded. Helplessly, Tom did just that. He eyed the heap of scrap wood ruefully as Insurance Agentasaurus disappeared into the brush. Someday, he'd come up with something he could build out of that wood. Something very useful—and no one would stop him from using it.

The next day he sat around, thinking. He still wanted to Do Good for dinosaur society. If he couldn't get the foods to market fast enough, maybe he could invent a way of preserving them out in the field. If he could preserve them long enough, the consumers could wander at their leisure out into the fields for their meals, even in the off season! They'd even have to get a bit of exercise, other than by chasing fellowsaurs to eat, to boot! Healthy dinoaurs are happy dinosaurs, and happy dinosaurs make for a happy dinosaur society. What a deal! Enthused, Tom set out to invent what he was going to call the *refrigeratorywhatsit*. And this time, he was going to keep it all secret, hidden from the eyes of Lawyersaurs and Whinasaurs, until he'd proven what a great benefit these refrigeratorywhatsits would be to all dinokind!

Alas, the best-laid plans of mice and dinosaurs come to naught. Just as Tom was putting the finishing touches on his refrigeratorywhatsit, another pack of a dozen Lawyersaurs came by. Cease and desist, they told him yet once again. The working fluids in your invention are hurting the ozone layer. Tom the Inventorasaurus once again turned into a Demolishasaurus, and his scrap heap grew some more. He started to worry about them soon finding his scrap heap to be hazardous waste site.

Okay, one last time, he resolved. And this time, I've got to do it right! Get the word out in advance to the public, about how much good my inventions will do for dinosaur society. Enlist the help of some of my good buddies, too, as an ace in the hole. Then he got to work.

He discovered some glowing rocks, and some careful methods of handling them without getting hurt. Then he discovered that these rocks killed micro-organisms. At the same time as thousands of dinosaurs were dying nationwide from food poisoning, from organisms such as *Cyclospora, Salmonella, Vibrio cholerae*, and *E. Coli*, he'd discovered a way to kill such organisms, safely. He called his invention the *food irradiatorgigalopholus*. He sampled his irradiated foods, and found them to be safe and delicious. But he kept it all to himself. He pondered how he could thoroughly prove this method to be safe, without using any dinosaur other than himself as a test case, and without letting the Catosaurus out of the Bagosaurus.

So he ended up having to invent the computerdingus, too, so as to be able to run simulations, with dinosaur digestive systems and ionizing-radiation-processed foods thoroughly and accurately simulated, so as to scientifically prove that food irradiation was harmless. This took him a few years, but he did manage to pull it off. The computerdingus, too, he kept secret, because he knew all about carpal tunnel syndrome, and how this would cause keyboard-pounding dinosaurs to sue and bankrupt him.

Finally, he was ready. He unleashed an anonymous media campaign, through friends, to make all dinosaurs aware of how Lawyersaurs were keeping many modern conveniences out of the front feet of the public. Then he published the results of his simulations, showing how food irradiation could harmlessly save lives. The media gave him lots of free coverage. That night, after the news conference, he sat at home, eating his irradiated bean sprouts and tofu, savoring what he thought was his victory. Tomorrow he'd start selling food irradiatorgigalopholi, the public was informed and with him, and lives would be saved!

Or so he thought. That night a pack of two dozen Lawyersaurs showed up at his door, explaining that he was the target of a class-action lawsuit, and demanding, under full-disclosure laws, to see all his records. "How can you do this to me?" Tom demanded. "No one other than me has even eaten any of my irradiated foods yet! How can you sue me so soon?!"

"Just watch, and you'll see," replied one of the Lawyersaurs. With a start, Tom recognized him as Jack. My, my, but how the law firm of Swindle, Robb, & Steele had grown! "We'll sue you because we can," Jack continued. "Because we can anticipate that since you plan on selling hundreds of food irradiatorgigalopholi, tens of millions of dinosaurs will eat irradiated foods, and several thousand will get stomach cancer. We're striking pre-emptively, before other law firms get to you first, and before you ruin thousands of lives."

"But that's Hogosaurus wash!" Tom protested. "Sure, several thousand will get stomach cancer! They would, anyway, even without irradiated foods! And at least we can cut way back on deaths due to food poisoning!"

"That may or may not be true," Jack slyly admitted. "But do you want to explain that to a jury? Or maybe several thousand juries, depending on whether or not we get class action status? You know, here's megagigadinobucks Tom Edisonosaurus Incorporated, and little old ladyasaurus with stomach cancer. Who's the jury going to sympathize with? Especially after we weed out all the potential jurors who might understand epidemiology and the simulations you've run."

"Take a hike," Tom replied stubbornly. "I'll get them to see how you bunch of leeches are keeping good technology out of the public's front feet. And I'll overwhelm them with my expert testimony."

"Oh yeah?" Jack retorted. "You don't know what you're up against. You remember Jimmy Junkscienceosaurus? And Juree Consultasaurus? The guys who convinced juries that those hi-tech, new-fangled 'hat' doo-wongussess were causing brain cancer? Well, guess what—we've got them both on retainer!" he bragged triumphantly.

Tom glowered. It was time to call up his ace in the hole, his reserves. He bolted out the door and issued a shrill whistle. In a matter of minutes, out of the moonlit brush came charging three large adult Allosaurs! Behind them, looking very strange and quite awkward, came three Shishkebobasaurs.

Now, many modern human paleontologists claim that the ceratopsian dinosaurs, the likes of Triceratops and Styracosaurus, were all descendants of Protoceratops, and that they all lived in the late Cretaceous. But they're wrong. Shishkebobasaurus predated them all, way back to the early Jurassic. *Shishkebobasaurus* had a body like that of a large wiener dog, so you wouldn't have thought of him as very fierce, judging just from the size of his body. Nor would the upward-pointing horn coming out of his nose have scared you very much, for it was in rough proportion to his size. But the two horns pointing forward out of his neck shield—now *they* were a very different matter! In adult male Shishkebobasaurs, these measured 25 to 30 feet long!

Now it's true that a small handful of modern paleontologists have stumbled onto the skeletons of Shishkebobasaurs, and that they've puzzled long and hard over the remains of these utterly bizarre creatures. They've kept this all secret, fearing that something so completely unexplained would undermine the very foundations of belief in evolution. They have also puzzled over just exactly why it was that carnosaurs the likes of *Allosaur* and *T. Rex* had such relatively small, stunted front legs. If only these paleontologists would research the truly academic literature like *Jurassic Horde Whisperer of Madness County*, they would know the answers to these questions and many others! And just exactly *why* were they called *Shishkebobasaurs*, you ask? Well, be patient. We're getting back to the story just now. All will be revealed!

Mayhem broke loose. Blood flowed in rivers and torrents. It was so bad, they'll probably have to excise this part of the plot out of *Jurassic Horde Whisperer of Madness County,* the movie, if they expect to get anything less than an NC-17. The Allosaurs (pay attention now!) picked up the Shishkebobasaurs and clutched them to their chests, with arms just large enough to hold their relatively smallish wiener-dog-like bodies. But now, out of the Allosaurs' chests, there protruded twin razor-sharp 25-foot daggers! Then the Allosaurs pranced around fiercely, impaling Lawyersaurs right and left!

The slow and clumsy Lawyersaurs were no match at all for the nimble, quick Allosaurs. Despite the fact that the Lawyersaurs dashed around like manic Madrosaurs, the Allosaurs made short work of every last one of them. The Lawyersaurs kept on trying to fend those long horns off with writs and briefcases, all in vain. They only succeeded in adding "filler" to the shish kebobs—stacks of paper and briefcases got impaled along with the Lawyersaurs. Finally, three Allosaurs paraded about, each sporting eight impaled Lawyersaurs.

At first, the sight freaked Tom out pretty badly. But then he kept on reminding himself that these were, after all, Lawyersaurs. So he got used to it fairly fast. He didn't even mind watching, as the Allosaurs, tired of tofu, bean sprouts, and celery, tried to munch out. They served each other by waving their Shishkebobasaurs about, taking turns nibbling on the fare offered up by their partner. Or at least, they tried. They complained about how the Lawyersaurs' suits got in the way, and how the Lawyersaurs themselves tasted rather harsh and unpalatable. Tom felt pretty bad for the Allosaurs.

So Tom sat there and thought, and lo and behold, a brilliant idea came to him! He remembered how years ago he'd invented *fierybob,* and how heating his bean soup had made it taste better, and how he'd been able to burn the chaff out of his wheat germ, leaving a tasty, toasted result. And right now there were no Lawyersaurs in any sort of condition suitable for keeping him from lighting up a fierybob again! So he ran off, fetched his implements, and set fire to his scrap heap. All that old wood fired right up, and he explained to the Allosaurs. They then promptly proceeded to burn the papers, the briefcases, and the suits right off of all the Lawyersaurs, toasted them up nice and well done, and had a feast! A good time was had by all, excepting the Lawyersaurs of course, even though nobody had thought to invent marshmallows yet.

So now you understand why they were called Shishkebobasaurs. They served a similar function for all the other, later bipedal carnosaurs, down through the ages, except that the carnosaurs were no longer carnosaurs, except for very, very rare crimes. Shishkebobasaurs remained the hunting partners and became the roasting implements of the bipedal carnosaurs, except now, the carnosaurs only used them to hunt and cook cabbages, carrots, and beans.

In other words, after the episode here described, peace reined for ages. The remaining Lawyersaurs learned their lesson, and most dinosaurs learned to resist, whenever the Horde Whisperer would come by again, whispering that the road to prosperity consists of every dinosaur suing every other dinosaur. Nor did they believe the whispers about technology, free markets, and greedy money-grubbing capitalists being the source of all evil. Amazingly enough, they didn't even believe the ensuing whispered quasi-truth, so much closer to the real truth but still so far removed, that all bad things were the fault, then, not of technogeeks and capitalists, but of Lawyersaurs instead. Feeling defeated, neglected, and dejected, the Horde Whisperer fled the Earth for a hundred million years and more. Technology, capitalism, and legal justice worked in harmony, and a peaceful dinosaur civilization prospered for the rest of the Jurassic era.

Chapter 3

The Cretaceous Horde Whisperer

"The tyranny of a multitude is a multiplied tyranny."
Edmund Burke (1729–1797)

The ages slipped by. Continents shifted, oceans drained and mountain ranges were thrust up into the heavens. Still the dinosaurs lived in peaceful prosperity. Their technology didn't *explode*. It just sort of *simmered*. Yes, they had fire, the wheel, houses, microwaves, food irradiation, nose rings, and double-entry bookkeeping. But they didn't have fossil fuels, intensive agriculture, field artillery, nuclear power, pop tarts, or Roller-Blade Barbie dolls.

They were intent on being ecologically and spiritually advanced, more so than materially advanced. So they shunned all unsustainable technologies, and those which might hurt the Earth, or any of its species larger or more conscious than an ammonite. This meant that one of their much underdeveloped sciences was pharmacology, because there were no species close to them that they could ethically experiment on. They managed to live happily at a medium technological level, and they had the wisdom to refrain from unsustainable technologies. They were able to live in peace for uncounted millions of years.

Then the Earth beckoned to the Horde Whisperer once again. After all these eons, *surely* they'd forgotten the lessons of the past! Hopefully, they'd listen to new Whispers about it all being the fault of the Other Dinosaur. The Horde Whisperer tuned his ears to the cosmic vibes, hovering down towards the lush and fertile Earth. His Mission: To go where no Horde Whisperer had gone before. To find Sensitive Ones, Receptive Ones, those who would be willing and able to hear and obey his Whispers.

Titusaurus Rex, of the much-ballyhooed species *Tyrannosaurus Rex*, got up that morning feeling more than just a little depressed. He winced at the smell of rotting bean sprouts and tofu on his breath, then brushed his teeth, feeling only marginally better. He checked his look in the mirror, noticing how the lines on his face kept getting clearer. He moved 'round and 'round his dumpy apartment, thinking, dinosaur, life's slipping me by, and I'm not even so much as dancing in the dark. A glance at the calendar—here it is, the very, very late Cretaceous, and I've never even so much as thrown a truly memorable party, attended by anyone who's somebody. I've got to get into the game, and get a piece of the action, he told himself. I've got to come out with a new attitude. Like, dinosaur, this Shishkebobasaur's for hire! Stay outta my way!

But he couldn't just snap his claws and make himself feel better. He still felt depressed. He wondered whether all those vegetarian foods simply didn't quite suit his metabolism. Maybe those starchy roots were making him manioc-depressive. So he sat and thought long, brooding thoughts about how maybe in the old days, when carnosaurs were carnosaurs and herbosaurs were afraid, life had been better for his kind. The thrill of the chase, victory, and a satisfying, high-protein meal!

The memory of that small snippet came back now to haunt him. He knew all those many years ago when he stumbled onto the very freshly but naturally deceased body of a juvenile *Corythosaurus*, that he should've just brought out the body and notified the relatives. Or at the very least, just left it there, and notified the authorities. But there he was, all by himself, out in the brush. He'd not even bothered to bring Sherman, his faithful sidekick and favorite Shishkebobasaur. This was, after all, just a nature walk, not a vegetable-hunting expedition. So no one would ever know. The temptation was just too great.

He'd wolfed down the remains of that young Corythosaurus. The raw meat tasted rich and smooth as it slid, lubricated by slightly congealed blood, down his gullet. The crunch of bones somehow added to those plaintive, primordially satisfying sensations. Thoughts of a grieving Corythosaurus family, never knowing what had happened to their lost beloved, subtracted from his pleasure only marginally. Far more so, it was fear of getting caught that kept Titusaurus Rex from seeking out more of the same.

Meanwhile, he often satisfied his hunting urges by rounding up Sherman and going out for fat, ripe, juicy fruits and vegetables. He'd wave Sherman's horns way up into the air and into the trees, spearing coconuts, bananas, and, when he was feeling particularly skilled, apricots and persimmons. But the whole thing left a sour taste in his mouth. So then he'd swing Sherman's horns low, using his awesome brute strength and his seven-ton mass to plow Sherman's horns through the damp and fertile soil. Then he'd impale the carrots, potatoes, and woolly peanuts that spilled forth into the light of day. Prehistoric woolly peanuts, in those days, were much bigger than the modern ones, so those didn't take such a remarkable degree of skill to harvest as did smaller fruits and vegetables.

Titusaurus made a fairly decent living gathering fruits and vegetables, and he was never in any danger of starving, but something was still quite clearly missing. *Surely* there had to be more to life than *this!* When his lust for flesh grew particularly strong, he'd lick the insects off of the fruits he'd gather, and the worms out of the clumps of soil that clung to those roots and tubers. Sherman's sight was poor, and on those rare occasions when Sherman inquired as to what Titusaurus was up to, he'd simply explain that he was doing a pre-wash rinse of their produce, getting rid of the debris before washing it in the river and then taking it to market. Lighten the load, Titusaurus explained. Sherman would look slightly disgusted, but there'd be no more questions.

But worms and bugs never truly satisfied Titusaurus's carnivorous lusts. All this simmered in the background as Titusaurus rounded up Sherman for another day's work. Titusaurus tried to remember his new resolve to be more upbeat that day, as he worked in the fields, spearing yams. Remember, he told himself, you can't start a fire without a spark. This Shishkebobasaur's for hire!

But it *just didn't work*. No matter how hard he tried, he couldn't change himself or his attitude just by wishing it were so. The sun was still hot, the soil still resisted, and the yams still weren't anywheres near as satisfying as flesh. Tasty, slippery, tantalizingly forbidden flesh. Now *stop* that, he told himself. On occasion he'd make "jokes" to Sherman, about how maybe they should go on a *real* hunt, like their ancestors had done so many eons ago. Sherman would laugh, and then say, "Oh, just go and *eat a bug*, why don't you?!" Then Titusaurus would laugh, too. Every once in a while, he wondered if Sherman knew more than he let on to.

So Titusaurus toiled in the fields that day, thinking, out here in the fields, I fight for my meals. But life's a bore. Nothing ever changes. Drudgery and monotony. Remember when I was young? She was going to be an actress, and I was going to learn to fly. Those dreams are gone now. Or are they? *Surely* I could be a movie star, if only I could get *out* of this place! Then he got to thinking, now, just how many times have I gone through this? Resolved to get me a new 'tude, and get me a life. And it all comes to naught. Then he got really depressed.

So that night he decided he couldn't take it any more. He *had* to do *something*. He'd heard, lately, about new theories about brain biochemistry and herbal fixes. How certain substances could make one feel better. So he set out to visit an old friend who he'd not seen in quite a while, by the name of Yule Pharmacolosaurus.

Now Yule was an old buddy of his from way back. They'd gone to school together. Yule had never amounted to much, ever since he'd gotten kicked out of high school for causing trouble. So Titusaurus was quite surprised to find Yule living in a large new mansion that night. But they sat down together and had a long chat.

It was past midnight when Titusaurus got back home to his apartment that night. It had been a long journey, but it had all been worth it. There was a new spring in his step, and he wasn't anywhere near as tired as he'd have expected to be, after such a long trip. After he and Yule had talked, Yule had decided that Titusaurus suffered from depression and poor circulation. So he'd given him a small sample of "what's good for what ails you", which in this case was an ancient herb called "Gringo Balboa". Titusaurus bolted it right down, and announced that it wasn't so bad. So Yule sold him a few baggies. On credit, Yule assured him. Just bring me a few bags of those yummy yams, or whatever's in season.

As he bounded into his apartment, then calmed down before getting to bed, Titusaurus thought about all this with a fair degree of hope. The only thing that baffled him was that Yule had asked him to keep it all secret. This, he didn't understand at all. If it made dinosaurs feel better, then why keep it secret? But Yule had refused to explain, and had sworn him to secrecy. Oh, well, Titusaurus Rex thought, dismissively, it's not my problem. Just do as you promised your friend, and don't worry your large, fearsome head about it, he told himself, nodding off to sleep.

For the next week or so, he faithfully ate a small clump of Gringo Balboa every morning. He felt reinvigorated, energetic, even youthful. He resolved to visit, pay, and profusely thank Yule sometime real soon. Then that fateful day dawned.

He was out picking bananas when he heard those far-off, hideously pitiful moans. Being a far more compassionate Tyrannosaurus Rex than modern paleontologists have ever suspected was possible, Titusaurus Rex barged through the brush, fellow-feeling coursing through his veins, powering his awesome muscles. In short order, the source of the sounds appeared right in front of him, there in the clearing. A herd of Pachycephalosaurs milled about in anxious, loud confusion around one of their kind writhing in obvious great pain on a makeshift bed of leaves. Writhing carefully and delicately, strangely enough, it seemed, for the tortured creature appeared to flail all parts of its body except for its lower back and its hip joints.

Titusaurus waded right into the raucous ruckus. Making his way straight to the loudest debaters, he interrupted, saying, "Gentlesaurs, gentlesaurs. Now I sympathize with your anxiety, here, but surely this is no way to improve matters! Unlike your friend, here, you have no real reason for behaving so... irrationally uncontrolled. Perhaps it would be best to tune your friend out for just a few minutes in order to calmly decide what is best for...", Titusaurus shot a quick glance at the suffering Pachycephalosaur, paying special heed to the head, "...him," he finished, after conducting a quick, simple gender inspection. The herd of Pachycephalosaurs calmed down considerably.

My, my, what powers I wield! Titusaurus congratulated himself. Just by my shear size and calm demeanor, I soothe their frantic distress! "Now what seems to be the trouble, here?" he gently inquired.

"Paul's in terrible pain, can't you see?!" one of them wailed. "He's got inoperable, terminal bone cancer. To top it all off, he tried to walk around, stumbled, fell, and broke his hip! So now he's..." The statement just trailed off into an unintelligible babble of anguished sobs.

Bedlam murmured louder, threateningly, so Titusaurus nipped it in the bud. Raising his voice, he asked, "Well, haven't you asked a Doctorsaur for some of this new, um, *hurtfighter?* Now, I'm not much for keeping up with the news, but it seems to me that we've been making some really great progress in the way of medicines in just the last few million years. So why..."

They drowned him out in an orgy of shouting, almost coming to blows with one another. Titusaurus barely understood a few sentiments here and there: "...take care, 'cause Paul might get *addicted*, and that would be just *awful*, to have him die that way, after he's led such a good life..." "...anyway, we can't find a Doctorsaur who'll do it for us, so why..." "... got to be strong, and just say **no**, 'cause..." "...care *what* you say, I'm going down to Yule Pharmacolosaurus *right now*, and..."

There was some scuffling, and grabbing at the last speaker. "*Hold it* now, just **HOLD IT!!!**" Titusaurus thundered. "Now calm down! Would y'all please explain..." A small group pulled aside, to explain to Titusaurus in detail. The other Pachycephalosaurs, seemingly somewhat embarrassed about their emotional excesses, debated much more calmly. But Titusaurus saw them keeping a watchful eye on him and the small group that was trying to explain to him. Somehow, Titusaurus knew that as soon as they'd explained the details to him, they were all looking to him, the large and powerful outsider, to make some sort of wise, impartial decision.

The pain of a fellowsaur, and peace in a Pachycephalosaur clan, all rested upon him! Titusaurus found himself wishing he'd spent more time reading the papers, or at least watching the evening news, instead of just eating tofu and watching saursitcoms and saurball. All these heady issues, all those Pachycephalosaurs over there pretending to try and look after their suffering fellowsaur, but really actually keeping an eye on *me,* and I barely know what's going on!

He forced himself to pay attention, very carefully. What were they telling him? It seemed that these new *hurtfighters* sometimes led to a thing called *addiction,* whereby dinosaurs would come to depend on them. That was bad. We already depend on sleep, air, water, tofu, and Monday night saurball. We just *can't* go adding yet another, was the sentiment of some. Including an agency called **BIGDADA**, it seemed. Titusaurus, embarrassed, had to ask what that stood for. **B**ureau of **In**exorably **G**rinding **D**own on **A**ll **D**rug **A**dvancement, they explained.

So Titusaurus asked why they didn't just ask a Doctorsaur to get them the medicine that their fellowsaur needed. "Surely it's obvious to all that he's in great pain, and needs this hurtfighter!" Titusaurus objected. "Why the big controversy?"

So they explained to him that BIGDADA opposed all drug advancement. Whenever they'd hear of anyone scheming to advance pharmacology, they'd bus in supporting demonstrators, and they'd all march around, chanting, **"F-D-A! F-D-A! F-D-A!"** This, apparently, stood for **F**orsake **D**rug **A**dvancement. And BIGDADA had it in for hurtfighters especially. No new drugs may reach the market, and those few that exist already, which alerted us to this *addiction* thing, well, those, we've got to keep a special eye on. Doctorsaurs who prescribe more of these than other Doctorsaurs in the neighborhood must obviously be up to no good, so we've got to take their licenses away. Then there's always the next remaining Doctorsaur, who's now the new one who prescribes more hurtfighters than anyone else in the neighborhood. So after a few million years of this, there were no licensed Doctorsaurs who were willing to help Paul.

That's where the big argument came in. The clan's young hotheads were are charged up, ready to go and see if a certain Yule Pharmacolosaurus would help them. But Yule, you see... Titusaurus became even more attentive now. Maybe the mysteries around Yule would be resolved! But calm down, he told himself. Remember your promises to your good buddy Yule, and don't even let on that you've had any dealings with him! So pay attention, yes, certainly. But don't look too eager!

"Yule," one said, "has no license. He's not paid his dues to BIGDADA, the Doctorsaurs, the pharmacists' unions, or even the Legislatorsaurs. So if we deal with him, we take a big risk. If we got busted, Lawyersaurs, Judgasaurs, Policasaurs, and all other sorts of Goonasaurs, at the behest of BIGDADA, the Doctorsaurs, and such, will all descend wrathfully on both Yule and all of us. It's a risk we can't take."

So now, finally, I understand! Titusaurus crowed. Yule's furtive, fearful demeanor. His insistence on secrecy. Even his new mansion. Now Titusaurus was no Geniusaurus, but at least he understood a small bit of economics. If there were demands for goods and services that were dangerous to fulfill, those who filled these needs would be well compensated. On the down side, he wondered how long Yule could stay out of the dinodungeon, what with BIGDADA and the long claws of the law not taking too kindly to what Yule was doing. Nor were Yule's activities quite as big a secret as Yule might have wished, it seemed to Titusaurus. It all appeared to be common knowledge, here.

"So let me get this straight," Titusaurus summarized. "There's a fellowsaur suffering, here, with no relief in sight. And the relief that lies out of sight, not so far away, the only relief that we know of, might not linger much longer. Then we must conclude that time to act is now! They say that all that is necessary for the triumph of insensitivity, is for good dinosaurs to do nothing!"

Titusaurus stood up tall and proud. He announced, "I can stand the sight of a suffering fellowsaur no longer. All you who are with me, come with me now, and we'll fetch pain relief for him. We'll go and see our good comrade, Yule Pharmacolosaurus, *right now!*" He strode forth with determination.

A small army of protesting Pachycephalosaurs surrounded him, pushing, shoving, and shouting. Only a small fraction of them seemed to side with him, pushing back, trying to protect him. But the numbers were against him. He tried to fight his way out of the herd, but they crowded him back towards Paul. Trying to play rough, are they? He glanced outwards, looking for his ever-faithful (OK, well, mostly-faithful) sidekick, Sherman the Shishkebobasaur. There he was, at the edge of the clearing! Titusaurus gave him a meaningful glance. Sherman, seemingly reading his mind, slowly but resolutely shook his head "NO". Sherman wouldn't get himself involved in any sort of violence against any sort of fellowsaurs, no matter what the cause.

Titusaurus fought. For ten minutes, he gave it his all. Doing everything he could, short of deliberately trying to hurt his fellowsaurs, he and the small number of young Pachycephalosaurs who sided with him tried to break free. But they were surrounded; the opposition kept on pushing them into the middle of the herd, crushing Paul, amplifying his agony.

Finally, Titusaurus just couldn't take it any more. Something snapped inside of him. **"ALL RIGHT, ALL YOU BONEHEADS!!! I'M WARNING Y'ALL ONE LAST TIME!!! LET US GO!!!"** He bellowed. Still the crowd refused to yield. Titusaurus didn't believe it to be possible, but they crammed him and his buddies in even tighter against Paul, and Paul screamed in even greater agony. So Titusaurus stooped down, and, with mighty jaws flinging flashing teeth around in great arcs, he sliced Paul's body into great chunks of bloody flesh. Paul's agony was at an end at last.

Titusaurus couldn't help it. The taste of all that flesh and blood was just too much. He stooped down again, and gulped down bloody chunk after bloody chunk of fresh Pachycephalosaurus flesh. Blood flowed down his neck and flank. He felt completely out of control, as if a spirit from another place and time, from a hundred million years and more back in time, had come and inhabited his body. He heard the primeval roar, not even realizing it was him. The entire herd of Pachycephalosaurs fled in terror.

A timeless time later, he found himself wandering, all alone, lost out in the forest. Why did his stomach feel so totally, blissfully happy? Why did he have a strong urge to just lie down and sleep? *Why was he all covered with blood?!* It all came back to him. Horrified, he made himself sit down, calm down, and think. There's no way you can run from this thing, he told himself. The whole world will know. Every dinosaur everywhere will demand my death, in payment for this most terrible crime, unheard of in all these millions upon millions of years. I can run, but I can't hide. So he gave in. He just lied down and went to sleep, as his forgotten instincts and his heavily laden stomach demanded.

When he awoke, his stomach felt distinctly less happy. Worst of all, though, was *why* he awoke. A Policasaur was excitedly yelling, "Over here! Over here! I found the murderer!!!"

Titusaurus Rex slowly joined the waking world, a sick and sinking feeling overwhelming him. He found himself facing a phalanx of Policasaurs, with their array of long spears menacing him. Sherman the Shishkebobasaur would come in real handy just now, if he hadn't abandoned me, he fleetingly thought. If I had any will to resist, which I don't. I'm guilty as sin! Time to face the music. They herded him out of the jungle and towards civilization. He just plodded along in a daze.

Not too much later, he found himself outside the courthouse. Dinosaurs of many kinds had gathered from far places to see this most strange of aberrations, a murdering fiend of an insensitive, carnivorous, killer dinosaur. The courthouse being too small for the gathered horde, the weather being pleasant, and the Lawyersaurs loving to put on a show for as many dinosaurs as possible, the trial would be held outside.

"Kill him, kill him," the horde chanted. "Blood for blood, death for death," they chanted. "Kill him, kill him, blood for..."

One Lawyersaur stood up in front of the shackled form of Titusaurus, bullhorn in hand, shouting out to the crowd, "All right, settle down now, ya hear! *Settle down!* Now we can't just go off and kill our fellowsaur, just like that! We have to have a proper trial first! *Then* we can kill the killer—now be patient. If we could have all of our witnesses..."

A bigger, apparently more important Lawyersaur barged through the small crowd of Lawyersaurs surrounding Titusaurus, bowling many a Lawyersaur aside, and grabbed the bullhorn. He glared first at the Lawyersaurs, then at the large and growing crowd surrounding them. "Now wait just a minute! We'll have no Jumpasaurus court here in **my** court! What *is* this!? We'll have a fair trial, *and then* we'll kill him?! I'll remind all my fellowsaurs that in Dinoland, all dinosaurs are innocent until proven guilty! And that's guilty beyond a reasonable doubt, too!

"SHAME on you, you hooligans!" he thundered. "Now if any of you are here thirsting for the blood of your fellowsaur, you can leave *right now!* This isn't some big show put on for your amusement. We're going to be very slow and methodical here. Justice hurried is justice denied. So if you're impatiently lusting for some titillation rather than impartially seeking illumination as to exactly what our fellowsaur here did, and why, well, you can just leave, right now. This is *my* court, and in my court, we seek justice, not amusement. Illumination, not titillation. You *got* that?!"

The crowd calmed down. Joe Judgasaurus conducted some ceremonies, then declared the court to be in session. Prosecution and defense made their opening statements. According to the latest court procedures in Dinoland, defense got to call their witnesses first. First to take the stand was Sigmund Psychiasaurus, an expert witness.

Sigmund said a lot of things that day. Fancy things, long-winded things. After a long while, even the Lawyersaurs got pretty impatient. So Sigmund got the hint and wrapped it up. "So gentlesaurs, what I'm saying, here, is that Titusaurus is not to blame. He *can't* be. He's merely the helpless victim of his own primitive instinctual, primeval carnivorous urges. We may recoil in disgust from what he may have done, but even if he really did what he's accused of, well, he's the victim. Victimized by his own feelings, to simplify greatly. And we can't go blaming the victim. No dinosaurs could do such a thing, and still claim to be civilized."

The crowd muttered and grumbled. The Judgasaurus banged his gavel, but the crowd paid him no heed. If anything, they grew even more restless. A few dinosaurs, up close in front where they could be heard, thundered out, "Well, then, who *is* to blame?!"... "Paul Pachycephalosaurus is dead and gone. *He's* the *real* victim! How about him and his family?!"... "*Somebody* must be at fault! *Somebody* is to blame! Let's find him and kill him!" and other assorted outbursts.

Joe Judgasaurus banged his gavel, good and hard. "Order! Order in this court!" They still ignored him. His eyes rolled and his shoulders slumped. There was only so much he could do. The crowd wanted justice, and they wanted it *now!* How does one say "No" to thousands of enraged dinosaurs? Maybe one doesn't, Joe thought. Maybe one goes with the flow. Let's see, what are they saying now?

"Sigmund Psychiasaurus eats dinopoop," he thought he heard one dinosaur shouting. I can't be responding to *that* sort of thing, Joe thought. Very unprofessional. Besides, if we let them start questioning our expert witnesses, *who knows* who they'll be questioning *next?* Lawyersaurs, maybe, or even *Judgasaurs!* Demidinogods forbid! No Sir, we'll not pursue such avenues. Respond to our large and restless crowd, yes. After all, they've apparently lost a fellowsaur to murder, for the first time in many millions of years. So the crowd must be appeased. The usual procedures by which the Lawyersaurs and I orchestrate the whole show, well, that might have to drop by the wayside, this time. But I've got to at least carefully pick and choose which inputs from the crowd we go with. Control the direction of this Jumpasaurus court, if not the precise steps or the speed.

"I know who's to blame!" One very loud dinosaur was bellowing. "*I know who's to blame!* **Listen** to me! I know..."

"Pipe down, everybody!" Joe thundered. "Let our fellowsaur speak!" There's danger here, he thought. I don't know who he'll blame. Well, if he blames Lawyersaurs, Judgasaurs, or Psychiasaurs, we'll just have to deal with that. But he sounds as if he's got new and original material. Let's just go with my instincts, and hope that he'll lead us off on a path that I can use...

The crowd quieted down. Joe held his front leg out towards the large Hadrosaur who'd spoken up, saying, "Gentlesaurs, we have a fellowsaur up here who claims to have some information we should all share. Now if you would, please, let's give him our undivided attention. And for the record, Sir, if you will first state your name..."

Joe had debated swearing him in, first, but the crowd seemed pretty steamed up. Only so much ceremony they'll put up with, he'd decided, making another one of those snap judgments. This, after all, was one of the reasons Joe was a Judgasaurus.

"Ah, um, yes, Your Honor," the Hadrosaur stammered. "Harry. Harry Hadrosaur, that's my name." Good so far, Joe thought. Show me some respect, follow procedure and formality at least a little bit. We'll soon be right back on track. Sort of. As much as one can be on track, with such an unusual and controversial case.

"Your Honor, I would direct the court's attention towards Titusaurus Rex's friends. Now I've heard he's been hanging out lately with a pretty bad crowd. I've been told he goes out carousing with those impish, impertinent young Deinonychusses down there in Tangee Town. Not that I'm denigrating their species, mind you! But they've been filling his head with all sorts of improper, even gruesome ideas. It's clear to me, Sir, that these 'friends' of his must be to blame. I think..."

"No Sir! Out of the question!" Joe shut him off. "No can do. Now, I appreciate your input, Sir, but you see, here in Dinoland we have freedom of association, and freedom of assembly. This is the land of the free and the home of the brave! Anyone can associate with anyone, without fear. No guilt by association. And no hearsay. None! That'll be enough of that!" Joe grinned inwardly. I'm getting back into control here. Let's see, what next?

"Anyone else out there have any helpful information they'd care to share?" he inquired. Many front feet were thrust towards the azure late Cretaceous sky. Scanning his eyes rapidly across the crowd, Joe called upon his considerable intuition of dinosaur behavior. Now, pick one who seems properly respectful, he told himself. Not one whose body attitude tells me they're only just barely containing themselves, and forcing themselves to gain permission to speak. Pick an innocent-looking one. OK, there she is. A young Ornithomimus. "You, ma'am. Please speak up. And don't forget, we'll need to know, for the record, who you are."

"Yes, Your Honor. Pleased to meet you. I'm Olivia Ornithomimus. Sir, I'd like to point out that I, personally, have seen Titusaurus Rex going to meetings at Stephen Stegoceras's pseudo-religious 'services'. You know, that crazy cult where they do all sorts of bizarre things that violate the will of the Demidinogods. I'm *quite sure* that they've been brainwashing him into these crazy ideas that have now taken root in this poor, demented fellowsaur's brain. We can't let them get away with *murder!* We can't, we've got to..."

"No way!" Joe roared. "I'll have none of this in *my* court! Now thank you very much, young ladysaur, but that's as far as we'll go with *that* sort of thing! You see, in Dinoland, we have freedom of religion, and I want it *kept* that way! Everyone is allowed to have their own religious beliefs, so long as they don't infringe on the rights of others. No matter *how* we might feel about the things they believe, we've *got* to leave them alone! Can't fault a fellowsaur just because of the way he or she worships. Now, who else cares to speak up?" Joe judiciously picked yet another uplifted front foot.

"Ah, yes, I'm Sally Saltasaurus Nosenheimer," an older female Sauropod spoke up. "He's been reading some awful books and watching some really terrible shows. I work at the library, and I, personally, have seen Titusaurus Rex check these books out. And my friend right over there, he works at the video store. He can testify, and so can I. No hearsay here! Now these books and shows, I tell you, have been really just horrid! Awful, violent, unspeakable things! Unimaginable things!

"So the authors and the scriptwriters are clearly to blame. Like Jonjon Gristlyspammasaurus, who writes about sleazy, promiscuous and violent dinosaurs, and then blames others for doing the same thing! Him and these others, they're just tearing dinosociety down! *Killing,* now even! Killing the likes of poor, innocent Paul Pachycephalosaurus! These hypocritical, irresponsible writers, we can't let them get away with it! We've *got* to stop them, before they kill again!"

"Enough!" Joe Judgasaurus thundered. "Just stop this right now! I'll remind you that Dinoland is the home of the free, and the land of the brave! And in Dinoland, we have freedom of speech! Writers and artists can say whatever they want to say, without fear of being punished. Even if sometimes some of our fellowsaurs take wrongly, those things that our artists say, we cannot, and will not, squelch the freedoms of Writersaurs and Artisaurs! Not so long as *I'm* running this court, we'll not go blaming innocent artists for what others do! Do I make myself clear?!"

Well, that was a bit harsh, now, he said to himself. So he added, "Not that we don't appreciate your input, of course. We really *do* need to find who is to blame for this horrible deed, and all inputs are welcome. You, over there."

"Um, yes, Your Honor. They call me Andrew Anatotitan Buttinski. This Titusaurus Rex fella, now, I know him. I live not too far away from him, and I've talked to him often. *I'll* tell you who's to blame. I'll tell you who's been putting these crazy ideas into his head, that he can just go ahead and act on those bad instincts of his. It's his political party! He's a rabid member of **T**he **O**rder of **A**narchic **D**inosaurs! He's a **TOAD**, don't you see! They're like a *militia!* They advocate all sorts of destructive and anti-social policies! It's *them* that put these ideas into his head! It's *them* that killed Paul Pachycephalosaurus! We've *got* to hold them *accountable* for their evil deeds! We *must!*"

"We must NOT," Joe replied most firmly. "Not in Dinoland, the home of the proud and the free. You see, we have political freedom here in Dinoland. You can belong to any political party that you like, and vote for anyone you like. You can even go off all by yourself, and form a *new* party to your own liking. So we'll not go off and blame his political party for this. Now I'd really, really like to know: Just *who*, exactly, *is* to blame for this cold-blooded murder? You. Speak up."

"Your Honor, if it may please this court, I can tell you who's to blame. Oh, yes, my name: They call me Skape Ghoaghterasaurus."

Oh, no, Titusaurus thought, panicked. Ol' Skape, here, he's a character! What will he *do* to me?! Like what he did to his Dentisaurus after he *dared* to give Skape that root canal? Suppose Skape knows about my false teeth? I can see it now! Stir up the crowd. But for or against whom? Blame my Dentisaurus? Or me? "Dentures don't kill dinosaurs. Dinosaurs kill dinosaurs." It's all been going so well! It's not my fault at all, so far! I hope Skape doesn't go off and ruin it. If he knows about my dentures, that's bad news, either way! They'll blame me again, or my Dentures. After all, without my dentures, Paul Pachycephalosaurus might still be with us. So we've got to implement better denture control policies. And I'm not thinking Polydinodent—I'm thinking I'll be stuck gumming my food for the rest of my life! Not at all a pleasant prospect for me, a member of the proudest of species, a powerful *Tyrannosaurus Rex*!

Titusaurus listened fearfully to Skape, shortly realizing that his worries had missed the mark: "Now, I've seen our victimized fellowsaur, Titusaurus Rex, here, going on down to visit Yule Pharmacolosaurus. I'm quite certain that if we get the right dinosaurs to testify, we can *prove* that Yule has been selling poisons to Titusaurus Rex. Poisons such as an ancient herb called 'Gringo Balboa'. Herbs that have poisoned the poor fellowsaur's mind. This Yule Pharmacolosaurus, he's clearly to blame! He never got himself a Doctorsaur's license, or even so much as registered with BIGDADA or the pharmacists' unions, and here he is, taking it upon himself to randomly dispense poisons, to anyone who will pay!

"Now I know many, many dinosaurs have been turning blind eyes towards these nefarious goings-on. Now one of us has died. *Murdered, by Yule Pharmacolosaurus!* What more will it take?! I say the time to act is *now!* All that is required for the triumph of impropriety is for good dinosaurs to do nothing! Now let's *go*, and punish the killer!"

"Not so fast," Joe grumbled. "We must proceed with all due caution, and all due process. Turning, he said to Titusaurus, "Is it true? Did Yule Pharmacolosaurus sell poisons to you? Have you been under the influence?"

Startled, Titusaurus replied, "Um, no, Your Honor, no one has poisoned me, and I've felt fine, just really fine, lately..."

Skape broke in, protesting, "Yeah, Your Honor, he's been feeling *way* fine. *Way* fine, I tell you. Yule Pharmacolosaurus has been making a lot of dinosaurs feel *way fine*, lately. *And without a license!* Now get him to tell you the truth. Put it to him more..."

"Hush, hush," Joe commanded. "I'll do this. Now Titusaurus, is this true? Has Yule Pharmacolosaurus been selling you things that have made you feel better?"

"Why, yes, Your Honor. He's been a real chap! He..." Titusaurus talked some more, but no one heard him, no one at all. Not even his chair. Most of the crowd, including Lawyersaurs and Policasaurs, arose as one, thundering out their anger. They hoisted their garden implements and torches in anger, and stampeded towards the dwelling of one certain Yule Pharmacolosaurus. A few of the remaining Policasaurs came over to Titusaurus, telling him to get up out of his chair. They then promptly removed his shackles.

"You're free to go," one of them announced.

Titusaurus was by now totally baffled. "What? Free to go, completely free?" He turned towards the Judgasaurus for confirmation.

"Go, go," Joe assured him. "You're free. Free as a Quetzalcoatlus. Now fly free!"

Not even so much as a "Go, and sin no more?" Titusaurus wondered. He couldn't help it. He pressed his luck. "I murdered and ate my fellowsaur, and I'm *free to go?* What *is* this?!"

"No, no, you didn't murder and eat your fellowsaur," Joe Judgasaurus assured him. "You were the helpless victim of a lawless poison pusher—a conscienceless, spineless wonder, not deserving of being called a fellowsaur, who *dared* to take it upon himself, to sell you things to make you feel better, without a license. *He* was the killer. *He* must pay!! Our agents of justice, in all their thousands, they go now to serve him his just deserts! And all others like him! Strongly warned, now, we will no longer turn a blind eye on him and others like him! You, in playing your part as an innocent victim, have served dinosociety well! Go, now, and go with pride!"

Titusaurus just shook his head and shuffled off. "Feel free to come right on back here for free government-sponsored counseling for crime victims if you need it!" the Judgasaurus called out after him, as he headed for home.

Titusaurus wasn't very worried about his need for counseling. He was worried about what fate might befall his friend, Yule. That, and, being as self-centered as most of his fellowsaurs, he also worried about himself. Where, now, would he get his supplies of Gringo Balboa? Maybe he'd have to learn all about wild herbs. Maybe even grow some himself! He wondered if maybe he should go back and ask the Judgasaurus if he'd need a license for that. On second thought, he figured he'd pressed his luck often enough already. By the time he got home, he was quite depressed.

The Horde Whisperer was quite pleased with himself that day. But he wasn't satisfied. The Horde Whisperer never is. Dinosaur technology was too simple for his purposes. Yes, properly goaded on, the dinosaurs could do a few nifty tricks. But they were too sweet, too non-violent, too innocent, and certainly far too primitive. And as usual, the Horde Whisperer was figgering on biggering. For *real* fireworks, he'd have to go elsewhere, he decided. He headed up and out, off of Earth, and into space, to a location not so very far away.

Chapter 4

The Zorgonian Horde Whisperer and the Cretaceous Mass Extinction

"Of all possible sexual perversions, religion is the only one to have ever been scientifically systematized."
Louis Aragon (1897–1982)

The Zorgons were a race of vaguely insect-like beings who'd been hanging around the Milky Way galaxy for a long, long time. So long, as a matter of fact, that their beginnings had become shrouded in the mists of time. By the time their emissaries were lounging about near-Earth space, in those halcyon late Cretaceous days, they'd been quite civilized for several billion years. Some had become so civilized that others accused them of being decadent.

But they were, without a doubt, both technologically and ethically advanced, taken as an entire species and civilization. Now there were a few exceptions here and there, where things went astray. Chaos always finds a way to insinuate itself into even the most well-laid plans of dinosaurs and Zorgons, it seems. And as we shall see, chaos is badness, quite often.

The Zorgons spread themselves far and wide across the Milky Way. Where there was no life, they felt free to establish themselves. But where there was already life, they very ethically refrained from invading, building shopping malls, erecting intergalactic billboards, or interfering with the local lifeforms in any manner. However, where there was intelligent, conscious life, they kept a close eye on it. They kept on hoping that some planet, somewhere, would sport a species, or multiple species, which would become advanced enough that the Zorgons could openly contact them, and welcome them to the Zorgonian Galactic Federation. Alas, no such luck had befallen them yet.

Now the Earthling dinosaurs, though, certainly showed some promise. They were very, very slow in developing their technology, and so the Zorgons just stayed back, watching. Being ethically advanced, the Zorgons had pondered these matters at great length. Premature interference would be cultural imperialism, and stunt the development of the true nature of a budding new civilization. Interfere too soon, and all they'd get would be an inferior clone of Zorgonian culture. Wait till the time was ripe, and the new civilization would become an equal partner, bringing new cultural riches to the Zorgons.

Then there were other, even greater dangers. Any new civilization carried a threat of bursting forth, and spreading the virulence of military conquest throughout the galaxy. Now this was judged to be a very improbable danger. Any civilization (if we can even use such a word in such a context) greedy and hateful enough to act in such a manner would most likely annihilate itself before getting very far off of the home planet. So said the wisest of the Zorgons, and their computer simulations, at least.

But the Zorgons, being quite sensitive and ethical, worried about chaos and badness on all levels, even those lower than the triumph of inappropriateness throughout the entire galaxy. They also worried about the injustice of millions of innocent species being wiped out on a planet where one or two hot-headed, suicidal species might decide to blow the whole shooting match to Queendom Come.

After a great deal of thoraxial alimentary canal-wrenching ethical analysis, they'd decided that if they were ever faced with such an abominable situation, they'd have to prevent the butchery. Show themselves and their vastly superior technical powers, and prevent planetary holocaust. If they ever were called upon to act in such a manner, though, they'd decided that any such suicidal species would thereby forfeit its right to self-determination and self-government. The Zorgons would have to go in, and use genetic engineering, political control and force, and even involuntary counseling, in reforming such a species.

But the Earthling reptilian lifeforms showed absolutely no such tendencies, as far as the Zorgonian social analysts could tell. And their developmental pace was extremely laggardly. So the Zorgonian outpost near Earth was clearly on the skimpy side. If the situation ever started to change, they could always bring in reinforcements. All in due time. Tens of thousands of years, at least. Physical interstellar space travel, after all, was excruciatingly slow.

Now there were dangers in having isolated, skimpily staffed outposts, such as the one close to Earth. One was simple genetic drift. Any time one has a breeding population of less than one hundred or so individuals, the gene pool is too small to provide proper in-depth genetic variation. So genetic drift sets in, and who knows what might happen? Chaos is badness, after all. The Zorgons were well aware of this, though, and so they always had at least one hundred breeding individuals per outpost. That, and they'd send along an ample supply of preserved gametes (sex cells). If the outpost's genetic health started to slip, or they started to evolve away from the Zorgonian norm, they could always dip into the reserve gene pool.

But then there was another danger, which would occasionally upset the well-laid Zorgonian plans. That was sociopolitical drift. Zorgonian outposts, especially the smaller ones, would sometimes run off course. A charismatic Zorgonian leader would emerge in a small group, and they'd do things that were, well, contrary to conventional Zorgonian notions of propriety. And due to the immensity of interstellar space, it could be thousands of years before a large Zorgonian force could arrive and set things right. Mostly with gentle, sensitive counseling, of course.

Such was the case on **Zorgonian Outpost Gorglephutz (ZOG)**, at that time. The local Zorgonian leader tried his best to hide what was going on, sending quite persuasive messages to Zorgonian Galactic Headquarters, but they knew. They knew what was going on near that primitive, bizarre yet beautiful blue planet Earth, and their new commander and chief counselor and her staff were on their way. But that would take many, many years. So in the meantime, Aileron Hubba-Hubba was having it *His* way.

Now the Zorgons were a quite bizarre species, by Earthling standards. Their appearance, if it resembled any form of Earth life, was closest to the insects, in that they had heads, thoraxes, and abdomens, and could fly, in some of their life stages. They weighed about 100 pounds at the most, except for the queen, who could weigh up to 300 pounds.

But some of their most bizarre features, and those that go farthest in explaining the nature of their behavior, involved their life stages, and methods of reproduction. They had *seven* fairly distinct life phases, and three sexes, if a sex is defined as a contributor of genetic material. The egg and grub phases were fairly simple and straight-forward. Then there were the infant workers, too young to do much of anything very useful. They just played and learned. These were called barbalutes. Then there were the mature workers. These were still entirely asexual.

Workers, after serving the colony for a decent interval, matured into females. On the dorsal surfaces of their abdomens, egg buds grew. These had to be fertilized by a drone (male) before they'd grow beyond the tiniest nubs. After a long time as a female, a small number of Zorgons would then metamorphose into drones. Only those females who'd managed to both acquire many resources, mainly food and the attention of drones, and who'd had many healthy offspring, would eventually mature into drones.

The last phase was the most selective and elite of them all. If a drone managed to collect enough of a certain biochemical (the Zorgons called it Holy Feces) from enough females—and it was physiologically impossible for the females to release this substance without the females freely, willingly regarding the drone as the best of all the local drones—then and only then could a drone metamorphose into a Queen. That is, with the additional qualification that this metamorphosis was not inhibited by the continuous presence of biochemicals from an already-reigning local colony queen.

The Queen was the supreme ruler of any Zorgon colony. She would suck the sacred sap of the Truffulla tree, and metabolize it into a liquid called Holy Water, which was the most sacred of all Zorgonian substances. This, she would mix with her own gametes (sex cells), contributing a small but vitally essential portion of genetic material. This would be sprayed upon mature egg buds, allowing them to be released from the females. Without this Holy Water, egg buds couldn't mature into grubs, and the females couldn't become ready to be fertilized again. But with the Holy Water, the egg buds could break free, becoming grubs, and starting the cycle all over again.

So evolution had provided the Zorgons with methods of selecting for genetic fitness, as well as sociopolitical unity and coherence. After all, without the females actually "voting" for a drone to become Queen—this "voting" being built into their very bodies—the drone could never become a Queen. So only politically astute and compassionate drones ever made it to become Queens. And without the Queen's contributions, the whole show would come to a screeching halt. So if any individuals decided to split from the colony, and do their own thing, they might do so for as little while, but they couldn't reproduce without the consent of the Queen. So political unity was strongly favored.

Then there was the tie-in to the Truffulla trees. They provided essential biochemicals to the Queen. And the entire colony had to religiously look after the Truffulla trees, in order for them to provide the sacred sap. This provided a limit on population density. If space and resources became too scarce, or the political unity of the colony, or even relations with nearby colonies, suffered, then the trees would suffer, the sacred sap would run low, and reproduction would slow down, providing a very nice, neat feedback loop.

This is what evolution had provided to the Zorgons. They, in turn, culturally overlaid their instinctual behavior with very strong religious commandments and taboos. Starting with their strongest taboos, and working down the list's top hitters, the list approximately translates to this: 1) Obey the gods and their sacred scriptures, 2) Obey the Queen, 3) Respect, and do not waste or destroy, any phase of the Zorgonian life cycle, or the Truffulla trees, and 4) Do not conflict with, or steal from, any neighboring colony. Parenthetically, we might add that once the Zorgons became space-farers, they broadened this to become, "Don't mess with any other planet that has life on it."

For billions of years, their instincts and taboos had served them well. Their species was a very stable, balanced, and life-respecting one. Even though they could, long, long ago, have supplemented and bypassed many features of their reproductive system (for example, synthesize Holy Feces, Holy Water, genes, and so on, and even do entirely without queens or Truffulla trees), they refrained, for the most part, from doing so. Cultural continuity, sociopolitical stability, and species solidarity demanded it. Religiously, this translated into an extension of respecting the Zorgonian life cycle.

But there were, now and then, a few cases where charismatic leaders would bend and even break the rules, leading isolated Zorgonian outposts astray. Aileron Hubba-Hubba was one of them. He'd been trained as a biochemist, in hopes that he'd be able to solve the twin mysteries of how the Earthling dinosaurs managed to be intelligent with such small brains, and how they apparently managed to communicate with each other. So, being a biochemist by training, he had the skills. Being of strong will, intelligent, and utterly in thrall to his strong lusts for sex and power, he had the drive. He'd diverted resources, and figured out how to synthesize Holy Feces, Holy Water, and the relatively simple genes contributed by the Queen. The latter, he derived from his own genetic material.

So when the Queen died a mostly natural death (he'd only slightly hastened her demise with his poisons), he was prepared. Now, he could have just gone ahead and become the new Queen. That, alone, would have given him a lot of power. But it wouldn't have given him a whole bunch of sex. The genetic contributions of a Queen, after all, were pretty minimal. Thus, too, in proper proportion, the instinctual/emotional satisfactions derived by a Queen from such reproductive functions, were rather small. The drives and pleasures were much stronger in the drone phase. Of this, Aileron Hubba-Hubba was well aware.

So he didn't actually go through with the metamorphosis. He'd fabricated a large prosthesis, a fake striped orange-and-green Queen's abdomen, a "falsie" to slip on over his own abdomen. He'd rendered it, and his metamorphosis, faithfully enough to fool the entire colony. A few drones were suspicious, but they didn't live long enough after the Queen's demise for them to make any difference. So now Aileron Hubba-Hubba was quite clearly Queen of the hop.

Except He was also King of the hop, too, because he retained drone reproductive functions as well. This wasn't entirely unheard of; in times of great stress, Zorgonian myths and legends (or was it history?) from ages ago said that when all drones had died, an occasional, very powerful Queen would still be able to serve as drone as well. These myths, and Aileron Hubba-Hubba's methods of staging His Metamorphosis, served all the more to prop up His Power.

Entirely appropriate, at this point, would be an explanation of Aileron Hubba-Hubba's name. This is rendered as a fairly accurate translation from the Zorgonian. Yes, Zorgons resembled flying insects. But that's only very, very roughly. Their front wings were mostly fixed, liked fixed-winged aircraft. Propulsive power came from vertical and horizontal flappers at the rear of the abdomen. Flight control surfaces on the trailing edges of their fixed wings, then, corresponded to no known Earth species, but rather, to the ailerons on an aircraft.

During the metamorphosis from female to drone, the Zorgonian cloaca (one combined opening for wastes and gametes) would migrate from the abdomen out to the right wing, close to the inner right aileron. By snuggling up to a female from her left side, then, a drone could place his ailerons, and hence, his cloaca (now protruding out of a prehensile peduncle, or stalk, for mobility and control) over the abdomen of a female. Then he could fertilize her embyronic egg buds.

Now Aileron Hubba-Hubba was quite the specimen, and He much appreciated the females of his species. And yes, that's an understatement. In the manner of His species, whenever He'd see a very attractive female (which was quite often, since He considered them all very attractive, so long as they had six legs), He'd push His cloaca out onto the very tip-top of His peduncle, and He'd grind it against the resonant, rubbery surface of His ailerons. This would create a loud, repetitive sound, which might translate roughly into Earthspeak as "Hubba-Hubba." And so they called him Aileron Hubba-Hubba.

But that translation is extremely crude—just like any Earthling translations of Zorgonian concepts and words must be. To Earthlings, "Hubba-Hubba" connotes the crude and vulgar utterances of a lout. But the original Zorgonian sounds are considered music to Zorgonian auditory antennae. Similarly, we might add, the concept of "Holy Feces" has lost much of its respectful Zorgonian aura, in translation to modern Earthspeak.

So on that fateful day, life seemed sweet to Aileron Hubba-Hubba. There inside a large hollowed-out six-mile-long asteroid named Chicxulub, within the safe, sheltering confines of Zorgonian Outpost Gorglephutz (ZOG—and yes, the asteroid and the colony had two separate names, just as humans might give one name to an island, and another to the city covering the island), Aileron Hubba-Hubba lolled underneath the Truffulla trees, idly watching the barbalutes scamper through the Grickel grass. There were so, so many barbalutes these days! But Aileron Hubba-Hubba didn't mind them a bit. After all, they were all *His* barbalutes (baby Zorgons), unlike so many of them were when He'd first come to power. So these latest barbalutes, *these* He made sure were fairly well cared for.

Then, to make His idyllic day complete, who should come fluttering into His verdant grove of Truffulla trees, but *her!* Her very own nubile, gorgeous self, Snuggle Thorax (her name, of course, is crudely translated from the Zorgonian). Aileron Hubba-Hubba's most favorite of all His babes! And best of all, she'd shed her egg buds now, and was ready to go! "Hubba-Hubba," the musical notes reverberated throughout the glade. Snuggle Thorax alighted onto the Grickel grass, right there next to Him.

She swept her antennae back alluringly, and whispered, "Hey, Your Magnificence. Whaddaya say You tell the barbalutes to scoot, and we, um, have a little talk. Some spiracle to spiracle, as they say?" Zorgons regarded their spiracles to be the poetic seat of their feelings, as human regard their hearts.

Aileron Hubba-Hubba needed no encouragement. He instructed the barbalutes to "scram" on out of that grove of trees, as Snuggle Thorax had suggested. This He did without much thinking, almost as a reluctant afterthought, but He knew He had to at least make some genuflections towards Zorgonian propriety. So the barbalutes scooted.

Her antennae reached out, and smoothly caressed His. His spiracles heaved, shooting out a hot, fine mist. Her embryonic egg buds throbbed in anticipatory pleasure. Eagerly, He swung His glistening abdomen around, and thrust His gleaming thorax towards her abdomen. He juxtaposed His cloaca to hers, stimulating her, but also probing her for her levels of Holy Feces. "Oh, Aileron," she moaned, "You're such a hunk! Just *look* at You! Your clypeus, it's like a fresh Truffulla bud! And Your epandrium, it beckons to me like a bright beacon in the night! And such a shapely reticulated endocranium, it makes my thoracolumbar mucopurulent membranes pulsate! I can't help it! Oh, oh! Yes! Such a hunka, hunka, gamete-spewing, love-making mean orange-and-green machine! *Take* me now, You Big Steaming Peduncle, *take me!* I'm yours!"

He ripped the bodice off of her thorax in one smooth, well-practiced swoop of His mandibles, swung His quivering right wing out over her abdomen, and thrust His throbbing cloaca out to the tip of His peduncle. Then He did things that can't be described here, in case they ever want to make *Jurassic Horde Whisperer of Madness County* into a movie with any sort of decent rating whatsoever. All you Zorgonian readers out there, *shame on you!* Now put your cloacas *back!* And Marv Albert, Hugh Grant, and Billary-Bob, that means *you,* too!

After all this brief but intense love-making, Snuggle Thorax fished around in the shreds of her bodice, finally coming up with a small kit. As

✻ CENSORED BY THE CHURCH OF OMNOLOGY

✻ ✻ IDENTITIES OF AILERON HUBBA-HUBBA & LADY ABDOMEN CONCEALED TO PROTECT THE GUILTY.

is Zorgonian custom in such circumstances, she flattened out the processed leaf of Truffulla tree, sprinkled some dried fragments of Grickel grass onto it, and rolled it up. Then she repeated these motions, ending up with two cigarettes. One, she offered to Aileron Hubba-Hubba, and the other, she kept.

Then she lit them both up. Aileron Hubba-Hubba, however, did His part purely out of Zorgonian propriety. He'd draw the smoke very slightly into His spiracles, just enough to make it look good, then He'd spew it right back out. He never inhaled, you see. As often as He was enjoying these pleasures these days, if He'd indulge in Grickel grass every time, He'd soon have abdominal cancer, He thought. Besides, I have to be in top condition all the time, just in case there's some heavy-duty religious or political machinations.

So they laid there, smoking. Or at least, she smoked, while He pretended. Then, she struck up a conversation. Oh, no, here we go again, Aileron Hubba-Hubba protested inwardly. Religious and political discussions again! Why must they always do this to me?! But He went along with it, as He always did. It gave Him a chance to sample the thinking out there in the rest of the colony, while He'd also push His own views. "So what are we going do when all these barbalutes grow up?" she was asking, "We're going to run out of room. We'll have to hollow out another asteroid. Do you think Galactic Headquarters will give us permission? You know how they usually are. We're just supposed to be an outpost, not a population center. And the more asteroids we inhabit, the greater are our chances of being found out, by those giant reptilian lizards down there."

"Oh, don't worry your gorgeous thorax about it, Snuggle Thorax," Aileron Hubba-Hubba replied. "Galactic Headquarters will *have* to give us permission. As you can plainly see, the Truffulla trees are giving Me enough sap to make all these barbalutes. And as the Holy Markings say, we are to be fruitful and multiply, to the limits that our trees and commandments will allow." Good thing she can't read my mind, Aileron thought. If she knew I was synthesizing all that sap, and only *pretending* to suck it from the trees, why, there'd be hell to pay!

Then, there's My other worries, He thought. Disobedience and insurrection here in ZOG seem to be on the rise. Doubts about Me and My Leadership. I've got to keep a visual sensory stalk or two on this situation. Now Snuggle Thorax, here, she seems to be fairly loyal, judging by her levels of Holy Feces. No, wait, didn't I learn from that other nubile but rebellious young babe, H bsches M„dchen, that I can't judge by that anymore? No competition any more, so *of course* I'm the biggest, most sensitive peduncle around! Their "votes" mean nothing, any more!

So, best to make sure I keep 'em in line as best as I can. Along these lines, it's good to frequently chastise them, and insure that they still react in such a manner as to acknowledge that I'm the boss. The situation at hand, now... what was she saying? Oh, yes, us populating more asteroids means us increasing the probability that we'd inadvertently reveal ourselves to the "giant lizards" below. Now, *there's* a hook!

"But I heard you calling them giant reptilian lizards," he added sternly. "I don't think that reflects proper respect for our fellowbeings. It's for *their* benefit that we're here, you know. I don't think they'd take too kindly to the way you're describing them. I do believe they'd much prefer to be known as magnitudinally and metabolically challenged individuals. Now I think you're displaying your own attitudinally challenged nature."

"I'm sorry, Sir. I won't do it again, Your Magnificence."

That's much better, He thought. Now if only I can steer her clear of all these controversial topics that keep on cropping up more and more lately...

No such luck. "But it seems to me, and to many of the others, that when we calculate all this out," she continued, "That we're already behind. I mean, count the barbalutes that we've got already, not to mention how many more we're bringing into our world these days, and how much room they'll need, how soon, and all, and how long it takes to hollow out another asteroid, and..."

"That's enough of that!" He thundered. "Don't you know, the Sacred Markings instruct us to be fruitful and multiply! And not to worry, the future, the gods, will take care of tomorrow! We need not worry! And most of all, they say, obey the gods, the Markings, and your Queen! I'm not only your Queen, but also your King! Now I'll have none of this insurrection!"

He knew extremely well, exactly what she was talking about. But He did indeed trust that the future would take care of itself. And the hell with all the work of hollowing out another asteroid, in the hostile vacuum of space! A friendly planet beckoned below. At the last minute, when ZOG's population pressures became nearly unbearable, there would be a certain transmission for Zorgonian Galactic Headquarters. Or, at least, that's where they'd *think* it came from. Then they'd violate a few rules. They'd descend down to that beautiful multi-colored, multicultural, multi-specied planet, and get intimate with it. They'd set up a small colony on a small, isolated island down there. And then they'd grow. And grow and grow. But no need to reveal those plans yet.

"But I'm not rebelling, Your Magnificence. I'm just asking," she wheedled. "I mean, just use the evidence of your senses, common sense, logic and reason. There's just no room here for this many adults of any kind! Now, I believe the gods and the Sacred Markings are perfectly correct, and so are You. I'm not questioning any of those things. But just suppose something has gone wrong. Pretty much, if we are to believe in reason, and the evidence of our senses, then this must be the case. Maybe the Truffulla trees have mutated, gone astray from the master plans of the gods. Maybe they're just giving off way too much Sacred Sap. Maybe..."

"Enough blasphemy!" He declared. "Reason and the evidence of your senses are worthless! We must go by faith and faith alone! Faith in the gods! Reason tells us *nothing!* Can you tell Me how reason tells us *anything* of fundamental value? It doesn't tell us why we should love instead of hate, create instead of destroy, seek pleasure rather than pain, live instead of die. Why we should worship the gods, and not the dark whisperers? If reason can't tell us these most basic things, then of what use is it? I tell you, it is faith and faith alone that will save us."

She wouldn't give it up. She knew she could get away with more than most others. He'd never harm her, since He so intensely lusted after her body. "But Sir, just suppose for a minute that You're right, but only so far. Maybe faith is where we get these fundamental choices you list. Maybe these are starting assumptions, axioms, postulates. From there on, though, we must strictly adhere to reason and the evidence of our senses, to get us to the goals dictated by those axioms."

That *really* set Him off. He began a long tirade against reason, and in favor of passionate faith in the gods. He told her she should just behave herself like all of the many faithful ones in ZOG, and listen to her Leader. She should go with faithful obedience, not with the deceptions propagated by "reason" and the evidence of her so-called "senses." He quoted the Sacred Markings at great length. Snuggle Thorax just laid there, impressed but unpersuaded. Halfway through His harangue, the ground below them quivered slightly. Then the graviton generators automatically smoothed the vibrations out, so that they never consciously noticed them.

Meanwhile, some mischievous barbalutes, smarting from having been kicked out of the Truffulla grove, had decided to go and explore. To have themselves some adventures, as it were. To indulge in Inappropriate Activities, as inadequately supervised barbalutes were prone to do, in the absence of watchful adults. The adult to barbalute ratio was getting pretty low, those days. So chaos and badness got its chance.

They snuck into the control room. Aileron Hubba-Hubba had erected barriers preventing all Zorgonian adults from entering without His Permission, since the control room was where the communications link to Zorgonian Headquarters was located. He insisted on strict control of this link, for obvious reasons.

But His precautions weren't quite up to the appropriate standards, as events would show shortly. The barbalutes, smartly clad in their barbalute suits, snuck through the tight spots in the barriers, easily slipping through where no adult could ever have gone. They sat at the many controls, tweaking many dials, fiddling with many switches. Asteroid Chicxulub, with its contents, the entire ZOG, accelerated under the impulse of giant thrusters. The barbalutes chortled with glee. "Asteroid go zoom," they chanted, congratulating each other, slamming their manipulatory appendages into one another, making the "high elevens" gesture. The graviton generators kicked in at that point, disguising the acceleration.

But the appropriate alarms were tripped, and engineers (adult worker phase Zorgons) were summoned. They frantically scampered about, trying to cut off power to the control room, trying to bust in, and screaming at the barbalutes through megaphones, telling them to stop immediately. But the barbalutes only chortled some more, and tinkered happily at the controls. "Asteroid go ZOOM!" they hollered with glee, watching the multicolored displays flashing hideously. ZOG assumed a most dangerous orbit, one almost certain to cause it to skim across the top of Earth's atmosphere, but still, hopefully, allowing it to break back free. The alarms now kicked into high gear, indicating truly dire straits.

The engineers desperately debated whether they should go off and interrupt His Magnificence. The last time they'd done so, His Magnificence had been truly outraged. Some blamed management, some blamed employees. On ZOG, only one opinion mattered. Several engineers had died shortly thereafter. His Magnificence told them it was just another random spurt of industrial disease. They hid their doubts, waving their antennae in assent. Despite their fears, this time, they felt that they had no choice. Several of them were selected randomly. They set out to bring these matters to the attention of His Magnificence, Aileron Hubba-Hubba.

By that time, His long philosophical and religious discussions with Snuggle Thorax had come to a rather abrupt halt, when another of His favorites, Lady Abdomen, had happened by. So when the engineers arrived, Aileron Hubba-Hubba and Lady Abdomen were caught in a passionate embrace. Despite the utter urgency of the matters that brought them by to visit Aileron, they simply couldn't force themselves to interrupt. So they waited, wasting more precious moments.

By the time the engineers got back to the control room, Aileron Hubba-Hubba in tow, it was too late. The ZOG's electronic hardware and software had many, many safety features, supposedly preventing that which happened next. But like most systems, the propulsion systems had override features. They were supposed to be able to be activated only by fully trained adults. Yet despite all the radars, gravity sensors, computers, and software, twelve barbalutes at twelve separate stations, with their child-like intelligence, somehow mysteriously did exactly the wrong thing. Safety systems were overridden in a seemingly coordinated manner, and ZOG, imprisoned within the six-mile long asteroid named Chicxulub, blazed through the Earth's atmosphere. "Asteroid go ZOOM!" the barbalutes chortled one last time.

Chicxulub approached the southern edges of the North American continent from the south. Then ZOG got much more intimate with the Earth, far sooner than Aileron Hubba-Hubba had ever intended. The unspeakable fury of millions of megatons of explosive force detonated, instantly vaporizing many cubic miles of the Earth's crust. Countless globs of white-hot, glowing magma literally went ballistic, then rained down from the skies.

Within three minutes, incendiary gasses swept across most of North America, igniting a continent-wide firestorm. Billions upon billions of tons of soot and vaporized minerals roiled the atmosphere. The entire planet rang like a struck gong. This planetary gong, having been struck entirely too hard, ruptured. Across the globe, shock waves shattered the Earth's crust, rending the planet's face with giant fissures. Lava burst forth, flooding the land and sea. Angry dark clouds blotted out the sun, and poured acids down upon the battered Earth's open wounds.

Death bestrode the globe like a raging army of Titans. Billions of dinosaurs and lesser lifeforms perished, extinguishing hundreds of thousands of species forever. Upon hearing the news, several insurance companies on the Zorgonian home planets collapsed. The Zorgonian stock market took its biggest hit in several million years.

The Horde Whisperer smirked with glee. There were no more missions here for him, for a long, long time. He departed the solar system, never to return again. At least, for another sixty some million years, that is.

Chapter 5

Setting The Pleisto Scene

"One has to belong to the intelligentsia to believe things like that; no ordinary man could be such a fool."
George Orwell (1903–1950)

The dinosaurs had reached consciousness, intelligence, sensitivity, self-awareness, self-congratulation (that is, most especially, self-congratulation regarding the superior sensitivity of the self, one's own self, as compared to other, lesser lifeforms), and all sorts of other, similarly wonderful mental attributes, only due to some very special, highly improbable genetic mutations. They'd acquired awesome mental powers completely out of proportion to their relatively small brains; so much so, as a matter of fact, that mainline modern paleontology hasn't the vaguest *hint* of what really happened during that entire 165-million-year span known as the Mesozoic era (comprising the Triassic, Jurassic, Youarassic, Bodacious, Smegmacious, and Cretaceous periods).

So remember, only the most elite academic researchers, the true elite of the elite of the neat, only *they (you!)* know. Only to the readers of *Jurassic Horde Whisperer of Madness County* is the full Truth, in all its glory, revealed. And the Truth is, the dinosaurs weren't dumb, lumbering beasts. Not at all! *Dumb?!* Ha! So they didn't have fancy vocal chords, or hyoid bones suitable for speech synthesis. *So what?!* They had awesomely advanced mental powers, including the ability to speak, wheedle, cajole, plead, scream, holler, whisper, and yell, all without making a sound! Their ESP (Especially Sensitive Perception) abilities allowed them to groove to each others' cosmic-karmic brain vibes.

And *lumbering?!* Another lie! The American Heritage Dictionary, 3rd Edition, © 1992 by Houghton Mifflin Company, as revealed to me in CD-ROM driven dreams from beyond realms of time and cyberspace, defines the verb "lumber" as A) "To cut down (trees) and prepare as marketable timber." or B) "To cut down the timber of." And the dinosaurs, they never cut down a single tree. No Sir, not a *one!* They were far, far more Sensitive than *that!* They waited for the dead trees to fall all by themselves, first. Only *then* did they feel free to make use of the wood. After all, dead but standing trees provided primary habitat for the spotted Archaeopteryx.

So as we can see, the dinosaurs were neither dumb nor lumbering. They were, indeed, quite advanced, more advanced even than modern humans, in many ways. And those highly improbable genetic mutations that enabled the amazing feats of the dinosaurs have never evolved again. Well, OK, so, twice, in two individuals, these genes came into play once again. But those were even more extremely unlikely events, in which these genes rose from the grave, so to speak, ever so briefly, and then subsided once again, this time forever. These events occurred at the dawn of humanity, and profoundly shaped the myths, legends, and dreams (and therefore the very essence) of humanity itself.

What happened is that dinosaur blood, containing dinosaur genes, was sucked down by voracious Mesozoic-era mosquitoes. These mosquitoes in turn often became stuck in tree resins. The tree resins became fossilized amber, in certain times and places, excluding such times and places when and where the likes of Thomas Edisonosaurus used said resins to fabricate industrial artifacts and to gum up Lawyersaurs. And so dinosaur genes were preserved through the long ages, entombed in white blood cells inside mosquitoes inside amber. And inside these genes were entombed the vast, almost mystical mental powers of the dinosaurs, awaiting the highly improbable events that would unleash them upon unsuspecting victims... (Note, macabre music starts here, all you hordes of screen-play script writers).

Scene: Dawn of humanity. The alarm clock of humanity has just buzzed, and humanity is sloshing around in the waterbed of humanity, floundering its way over to pound on the snooze button on the alarm clock of humanity. Outside, a large female snake by the name of Shoshoni Squamata (to be played by Demi Fleiss, Heidi Bassinger, or Kim Moore) is slithering down a path. Shoshoni Squamata shows irritation, and signs of molting setting in.

Shoshoni slithers on down that path. After a few hundred yards, she comes to a outcropping of sharp rocks. She starts belly dancing on

the rocks. Soon, her outer layer of skin starts seriously peeling off. Male snakes, forked tongues flicking out, gather around, panting, wolf whistling, and sticking freshly killed hamsters (roughly, hundred-dollar bills, translated to modern human currency, and accounting for inflation) underneath a ring of Shoshoni's old skin (the first "garter belt", even though Shoshoni is a python, not a mere garter snake). Showing her appreciation, she wriggles and writhes all the more enticingly. The male snakes go wild!

Now the camera zooms in. Zooms, and zooms some more. We see, in the middle of all these sharp rocks, some yellow-orange crystalline rocks. Amber-colored rocks. Amber. Zoom some more. Inside the amber, we now see the dark outline of a mosquito. Computer graphics take over, as we zoom to the mosquito's guts. Zoom yet more, and then we see helical DNA molecules. Zoom way back out. Now we see that Shoshoni has punctured herself on the sharp rocks, and is bleeding a bit.

Zoom very slowly way back out, and we see Shoshoni dancing in the middle of a mass of writhing male snakes in the middle of the jungle. Focus goes fuzzy slowly, while we hear Shoshoni's voice-over: "One day I was just a stupid snake, a dumb beast. The next day I was endowed with awesome mental powers. I eventually figured out what had happened. The DNA in those amber crystals mixed into my blood. Retroviruses carried the genetic codes through my blood-brain barrier, and into the cell nuclei of my brain neurons.

"Highly improbable, yes. But the Chaos Theory, this incredibly deep Theory based on mathematical equations that say that if you put a drop of water on the back of a hand, it will run off, but it will also give you an excuse to hold that hand, if it belongs to a gorgeous member of the opposite sex. Now I'm just a snake, and I don't have a hand, so how can I know these things? Well, don't forget, due to the immense complexity of genetics and Chaos, I became very wise. So now I know All Things. Don't forget that. And don't forget that Chaos is Badness."

Shoshoni slithered away after shedding her old skin, giving all those male snakes a quick brush-off. The last thing in the world that she wanted to be, right now, was a mounted python, let alone a multiply-mounted python. Just what kind of a girl did they think she *was?!* They're just after my body, with no respect at all for my mind, anyway, she thought. But *wait!* What's *this?!* I didn't even know I *had* a mind, till a few seconds ago!! What's come *over* me?!

She slithered off into the bushes, and pondered matters for quite a few days. At first, just *thinking* was a great thrill. She came up with all sorts of wonderful new ideas. But then she realized that she had no one to share her marvelous new thoughts with. And so she became profoundly lonely. In the whole wide world, as far as she knew, she was the only one with a mind. This was quite simply intolerable.

So she set out to see if maybe she could convince other snakes to writhe on the shards of amber, to see whether perhaps the same thing would happen to them. Then, they'd become highly intelligent and conscious, too, and she'd have company, and all would be well. But alas, such was not to be. First of all, she ran into tremendous difficulties persuading dim-witted snakes that they should writhe on sharp rocks, at any time other than when they were molting. And then, to try to get them to deliberately make themselves *bleed?* Forget it! Soon, all the snakes for miles around were quite thoroughly convinced that Shoshoni Squamata was the craziest snake that anyone could imagine.

Worst of all, even Shoshoni started to think she was crazy. She set up detailed biochemical simulations in her mind, and showed herself how utterly improbable her current condition was. By any common-sense analysis, a snake awakened to sentience by dinosaur genes in mosquitoes in amber should never have happened. Yet there she was. But now, to go off and try to replicate such extremely improbable events? Wasn't this utterly *insane?!*

So Shoshoni gave it up. Then she slithered around in desperation, thinking, well, obviously, so far in my wanderings, and in picking up the brain vibes of the various creatures, I've been able to tell that some are smarter than others. Yes, none of them are anywhere close to being as smart as I am. Still, some show more promise than others. So if I just slither all around, and survey the creatures, maybe I can find some, somewhere, that might be worth communicating with. Maybe even, if need be, I can intellectually stimulate them, poke and prod them in exactly the right ways, and help bring them to self-awareness! Yes, that's it!

So, enthused once more, full of grandiose ideas about what she'd accomplish once she shared a world with fellow sentient beings, she set out. She sifted the whispers of the winds from distant times and places, searching through the cosmic-karmic vibes for those indicating intelligence. She explored her mental powers, probing here and there, using parts of her mind that no one had ever shown her how to use. Here, she thought, what's *this?* If I just use my mind *this* way, then maybe I can detect...

The anguished death cries of billions of dinosaurs came crashing down on her from sixty-five some million years ago. She shut them down instantly. *No way* can I handle that kind of psychic shock, she told herself, thoroughly shaken. Besides, they're all dead, frozen in time, and can have no real, genuine interaction with me. We'll have to try again.

This time, she tried to open up that part of her mind again, this time with a filter: only the cosmic mind vibes of creatures in the present were allowed. This time, there was again a sensation of crashing. She fearfully retreated, only to stop herself almost immediately. There was no threat, no pain. She concentrated... the crashing was the crashing of waves, and of flukes upon the surface of a salty sea. Cheerful, sleek, happy, intelligent creatures splashing among the waves, out beyond a distant shore, playing in an immense body of water. Company! She had company in this world! Creatures fully as intelligent as herself! She slithered off towards distant shores. Many, many miles lay between her and the sea. But as they say, the journey of a thousand miles begins with a single slither.

Months later, she dragged herself onto the beach. Exhausted, she sought the shade of a surfside palm tree. There, she relaxed. And then she got to thinking again. What if these creatures had no interest in her? She'd been so obsessed with getting here, she'd never even allowed herself to do much doubting about what would come next. She'd not be able to swim with these creatures. Their styles and hers, in locomotion and so much more, mismatched fundamentally. What, if anything, would she have to offer them? For that matter, what would they have to offer her? Oh, stop it, she told herself. Like seeks like, and sentience seeks sentience. *Surely* that is enough!

Surely they'd soon come swimming close by! Surely they could hear her cosmic brain vibes, just as she could hear theirs! Surely they'd come to assuage her loneliness any minute now! She waited. And waited. And waited some more. And they never came close by. She drifted off to sleep. After having traveled those many, many miles, she slept the rest of the day, and then through the night. She dreamed of growing flippers, slapping silvery waves, and slipping through the seven seas, all in the company of her new cetacean friends.

In the morning she woke, and probed the ether with her mind. Where were they? Were they close by? Yes, they were! They were some miles to the north, swimming south along the coast, straight towards her, it seemed! She could feel their vibes getting stronger by the minute! Did they hear her presence? No, it didn't seem that way. Maybe they weren't as strong, in the receive mode, as she was. Maybe they just weren't quite as sensitive as she was. Still, they talked among themselves with obvious ease! Surely they'd hear her, when they'd swim right down the beach beside her! She eagerly slithered right down into the water.

The surf pushed her back up onto the beach. She made herself content to slither north, there on the hard wave-packed sand. She pushed herself faster. Every yard closer to them meant they'd be that much more likely to hear her before they turned back out towards the open sea. Here they come, she thought. Maybe time to slow down, relax physically, and pour all my energies into reaching out, psychically, towards them. And so she did.

And then they were right upon her. She could even *see* that gorgeous sight, as their dorsal fins sliced through the waters, no more than two hundred yards away. Shoshoni poured herself into *screaming* at the dolphins, straining every neuron in her newly reconfigured neural networks. Yet they never showed even the slightest hint of being aware of her presence. So she stopped screaming at them, after they'd just barely passed her, just long enough to listen very carefully. It was only then that she came to realize that they were using *physical vibrations in the water* to communicate with, and that they couldn't hear her at all.

Crushed, she headed back inland. But she wasn't defeated yet. She reached out with her mind yet once again, this time adding yet another filter: flipper-footed critters need not apply. Land lubbers only. Maybe with land creatures, she could get so close, they'd not be able to ignore her psychic screams, even if they were almost deaf.

So she searched high and low. Then she found the elephant-like creatures. They weren't anywhere close to being as smart as dolphins, but they were certainly a lot smarter than your average bear, or most any other land-lubbing creature she'd slithered into. So she set out to work on them.

But she very rapidly ran into problems. First of all, there was the fact that along with the intellectual and psychic capacities that she'd inherited from the dinosaurs, she'd also picked up their ethical sensibilities. So she had to ponder long and hard, the ethical implications of what she was about to do. What would happen if she put mammoths or mastodons on the road to sentience, civilization, and technological advancement? After watching their behavior, and trying her best to understand their essence, she conjured up such a future. It didn't look good. The females, infants, and juveniles behaved just fine. They were highly social and well-behaved animals, if one ignored their tendency to wreak havoc with their environment. They'd trash the local environment, tear down trees and eat everything in sight, and then move on.

The real problem was the males. They were antisocial loners, except during mating season. During mating season, they'd go into "musth", many of them getting extremely grumpy and peevish. To expect such a species, with such behavior among the powerful males, to advance to higher levels of technology and political organization—well, it was scarcely an acceptable risk. Put it this way, the first tentative visions Shoshoni got when she conjured up such a future, was of male elephants running around with sharpened metal blades strapped to their tusks, goring, slicing, and dicing their opponents left and right.

Despite her extreme misgivings about what she was doing, the force of her loneliness pushed her on. She persuaded herself that surely, there'd be no harm in just gathering a bit more data. So she forced herself to go up right next to a large female mammoth, the matriarch of her herd. Shoshoni announced her presence with a loud psychic shout, saying, "Hi, there, Mrs. Mammoth, can we talk?"

Mrs. Mammoth did indeed hear that psychic shout, but she also promptly proceeded to try and squash one Shoshoni Squamata. Shoshoni squirmed away as fast as she could. The hell with that, Shoshoni concluded. If even the females behave this way, then there's no hope. Let's move on to some other creature.

Then Shoshoni discovered the ape-men. Now she was quite reluctant to deal with them, since they smelled quite disgustingly awful. But they seemed to have their virtues. They were highly social, and the males even seemed capable of often getting along with one another, rather than constantly fighting over the females, as in harem-oriented species. The male ape-men, being mostly monogamous, even managed to do a bit of offspring-rearing. Now *this* species has the potential to become sentient, maybe even civilized, Shoshoni noted approvingly.

There were of course some disturbing attributes of those two-legged beasts. Shoshoni couldn't quite put her finger on exactly what it was that bothered her so much, other than their smell, even if she'd had a finger to start with. So she pondered the nature of those beasts, and conjured up a possible future of civilized humanity. She opened up her mind, and the vibes rushed in.

Peon I was yelling at Peon II, saying, "I'm starving, and you've got bread, and you're not giving me any. You're valuing your possessions more than my life! Now if you had any compassion at all, you'd share. Give it to me."

Now Shoshoni had no idea what bread was, but she could put it in context. Something like freshly killed hamsters or some such, to these critters, no doubt, she figured. Hummmm. Hissss. Interesting. Perhaps I'd better listen in some more.

"Now fork it over," Overlord was saying to Peon II. "You heard him. You're being utterly selfish, while your comrade is starving. Let's have the bread. Good. That's more like it, more like the way a citizen should do his duty. OK, now, I'll take my small administrative fee for the Bureau of Compassion. Here you go, Peon I."

"Peon I, stop! Don't you *dare* take a bite! How can you be so cruel, getting ready to chow down in front of me, Peon II, your starving co-worker and comrade! You're valuing your possessions more than my life! How *could* you?! Comrade Overlord, make him stop!"

"Now listen up," Overlord said to Peon I. "Let's have none of this reactionary insensitivity. We've got to be team players, and work for the good of society. Give it here. Great, that's more like the New Society Man. Now I've got to collect taxes on behalf of the State, so that it can perpetuate the new, classless system of glorious equality. And here's the remainder for our hard-working co-worker, Peon II."

"Peon II, how *could* you?! You put that down right now! You crass materialist, you're valuing mere material possessions more than the life of your starving fellowperson! Comrade Overlord, make him stop!"

"Comrade Peon II, now, you know this crass materialistic selfishness won't cut it. We can't be punishing Peon I for his poverty. Here. OK, good. Now for the transaction fee, and the rest goes to our deserving comrade, Peon I."

"Peon I, stop, I say! Comrade Overlord..."

Shoshoni had heard enough. Let's see what else is out there, she thought, tweaking the knobs of her cosmic-karmic vibes detector. So far, things look rather bleak. But maybe she'd just gotten a bad sample. OK, here we go...

"We've *got* to find our common ground, so we can be compassionate to Our Children. Only then can we come together and face our tomorrow, which is our future. Nothing big ever came from being small, and nothing positive ever came from negative thoughts. Negative thoughts like questioning our goals of being compassionate to Our Children. How can anyone who clames to *care*..."

"Yes, yes, I know, I've heard you and your husband say that many times. But now we need to work with the people, so that they can understand..."

"But Eleanor, they just *won't* understand! They're so cruel and heartless, so self-centered! Here I am, with degrees and honorary degrees from all sorts of top-notch schools, with more compassion than a bucketload of those selfish oafs, and they're resisting my selfless attempts to make their charity decisions more wisely for them! Those low-brow simpletons, if we let them keep their money for themselves, they'd spend it all on trailer parks, beer, and cigarettes! And lottery tickets! *State* lottery tickets, not *federal,* mind you! We've *got* to get the power into the hands of those who are morally superior, more sensitive and most compassionate! If we're going to move ahead, and have the village raise the children, then..."

"There, there, now, Hillary-Bob," the feminine vibes of the Eleanor-creature said soothingly, "You just hang tight. Think cattle futures. Now if you can just raise some money, then, since it takes money to make money, you could, like, drag a few hundred dollars through Washington. There's no telling what you'll scare up when you drag a few big bills down the corridors of DC. The possibilities are endless. Maybe you could even rent Billary-Bob out for children's birthday parties, tea parties, garden parties, pool parties, and so on. *Lots* of fund-raising potential there. And after you've got the money to get your messages out, you can Do Good."

Shoshoni could hardly understand any of this. Inchoate apprehensions nipped at her scaly tail. What was this bizarre, all-important thing called *money*? She decided to leave this pleasant little chat, and cast about for another sample.

She found herself as a disembodied spirit flitting about a large, ugly, smelly, hellish and hellishly hot open-air dungeon called *Chicago*. She watched as old, withered humans died of the heat in little cages. They were afraid of opening their *windows* for fresh, cooler air, lest unrestrained violent fellow humans rob or kill them. She listened to some of their conversations, as they suffered and died. Apparently, they suffered from the heat because they were *poor*, which meant that they lacked *money*. That, in turn, meant that they couldn't get the things that could make their air cold, nor the mysterious *power* that made these things work.

She studied and pondered these matters diligently, and concluded that *money* must be a weird distillation of worth, of material value. Symbolic freshly killed hamsters, one could say. With what few of these symbolic freshly killed hamsters that these *poor* old folks had, apparently, they'd *buy* things of value, like the small shiny *metal cans* of *beans* that they'd eat.

Then she heard some racket outside the little cages, and fled out to the *streets* to see what was going on. Loud, angry humans were shouting and carrying *signs*, things with more *symbols*, protesting that their air was too dirty. She listened long enough to realize that most of the protesters were what was called *rich*, which meant that they had enough freshly killed hamsters to worry about dirt in the air, so much so that they carried these *signs*, wrote *letters to the editor*, and made *campaign contributions,* rather than just worrying about staying alive, like the *poor*. After doing all these things, the *rich* would then retire to the cooled comfort of their *air-conditioned* cages, while the *poor* ones died in the heat.

Then she flitted back to the cages of the withered *poor*, and listened some more. She came to realize, from the utterances of some of the few better-informed suffering ones, that cooled air *cost* a lot more than it otherwise might, because the *rich* ones insisted on clean air. The air-cooling *machines* and their *power plants* somehow fouled the air. To make things even worse, the air-cooling things of the *rich* cooled their *indoor* (cage) air, while heating up the *outdoor* air, making the air of the *poor* even hotter.

So the *poor* died, while the *rich* got cleaner cooled air. Some said that there was a simple solution to all these many interrelated problems. Dirt in the air, soil, and water, and the *prices* being driven up by *richer* humans demanding more *regulations* on all the *machines*. The all-wise *regulators* should *own* everything, and make everything good and clean for everyone. Yet when this had been tried in other lands, the results had been dirt and suffering for everyone.

Her brain reeled as she tried to assimilate all this. It was all way too confusing. She decided that maybe it was time to tie up loose ends, to go and see if she could now make more sense of the two ladies' conversation.

"Yes, you could give money to the poor, and feed them for a day," Eleanor was saying. "But if you use that money to lobby, to change the cruel and heartlessly punitive ways of the government, why, then, you could do much, *much* more good. Much more long-lasting good."

"Yes, you're right," Hillary-Bob said, thoughtfully. "There's no end to the good things I could do for the poor. Take care of their children, give them all good medical care, clean up their air..."

Shoshoni couldn't stand it any more. "But Hillary-Bob," she said, breaking in, "Realize you that you *regulate* everything, you make bigger *prices* for all-one? Them wrinkled ones, them *poor* old folks in *Chicago* have not many fresh killed hamsters cool their air. Them with many fresh killed hamsters, them get cold air, them protest, them make ones who not have fresh killed hamsters get *hot* air. With fresh killed hamsters get cold air and cleaner air, with no fresh killed hamsters die. Poor ones become killed, become killed hamsters for them with many killed hamsters. But ones who kill think them are much compassionate, because them want clean air, which is such big good thing. Isss sssily."

There was a long, long silence. Finally, Hillary-Bob ventured, "And just who are *you* to barge in on our conversation like this?!"

"Oh, I are *Shoshoni Sssquamata*. I what you call *python*, large sssnake. But not mounted python. I the only, the lonely, the only sssmart sssnake in thirty thousand B.C., as you sssay. I not mounted sssnake because I the only sssmart sssnake, they all want my body, not my mind. Ssso they not mount me. But you not care about that. I come to sssee you. I come to sssee if OK for me to make ssstinky ape-men go road to sssivilization, as you sssay."

Again, the long silence. Hillary-Bob, frightened, managed to squeak out, "Listen, Eleanor, I'd better cut this short. *Way* short. This is it! No more! I'm laying *real low* till after the elections! Good-bye!" She beat a speedy retreat.

"What ssslithered up her asss and died?" Shoshoni inquired, trying one of those weird *idioms* that these humans were so fond of.

"Oh, don't mind her," Eleanor replied. "She's not too hip on us spirits in the afterworld, and other such-like bizarre, otherworldly spirits. She frightens easily. She fears for her sanity, and so she's afraid she'll ruin Billary-Bob's chances of getting re-elected."

Eleanor said this quite breezily, as if totally dismissing the idea that she, herself, might fear this alien spirit, this *Shoshoni Squamata*. But Shoshoni knew otherwise. She could *smell* the fear, somehow.

"So tell me," Eleanor continued, "What were you saying? About you being from 30,000 B.C., and such? What's the deal?"

Shoshoni explained as best she could, that Hillary-Bob, Eleanor, Chicago, rich, poor, regulators, elections, money, air conditioners, and so, so many other things were all still quite hypothetical at this point, and that she, Shoshoni, had come to scope things out, to see if this grand experiment should proceed, or not. She was quite lonely, so she wanted to go for it. But she'd had her doubts. And now she had yet more doubts. So what should she do? She didn't know. So she asked Eleanor for some advice.

Eleanor was shocked to her ethereal bones. But she recovered enough in time to mumble something about Shoshoni not playing with billions of souls. Bossily, yet fearfully, she asserted that Shoshoni had better go kick-start those ape-men, and pronto! Shoshoni slithered merrily away, happy to have gathered some encouragement for her endeavors. Her loneliness would come to an end, and soon!

Little nagging doubts kept on nipping at her scaly tail. Well, they said to her, what if you'd gone ahead in time, and looked in detail at hypothetical civilized elephants instead? What if you'd had a conversation with one of *them?* Wouldn't they have said the same thing? You can't play with billions of souls, you have to bring us into existence. So in the future, the elephants could be carving trinkets out of the teeth of dwindling populations of humans, instead of the other way around. Why was one any better than the other? Shoshoni just told her nagging doubts to hush up, because no human had ever tried to trample her. So that was

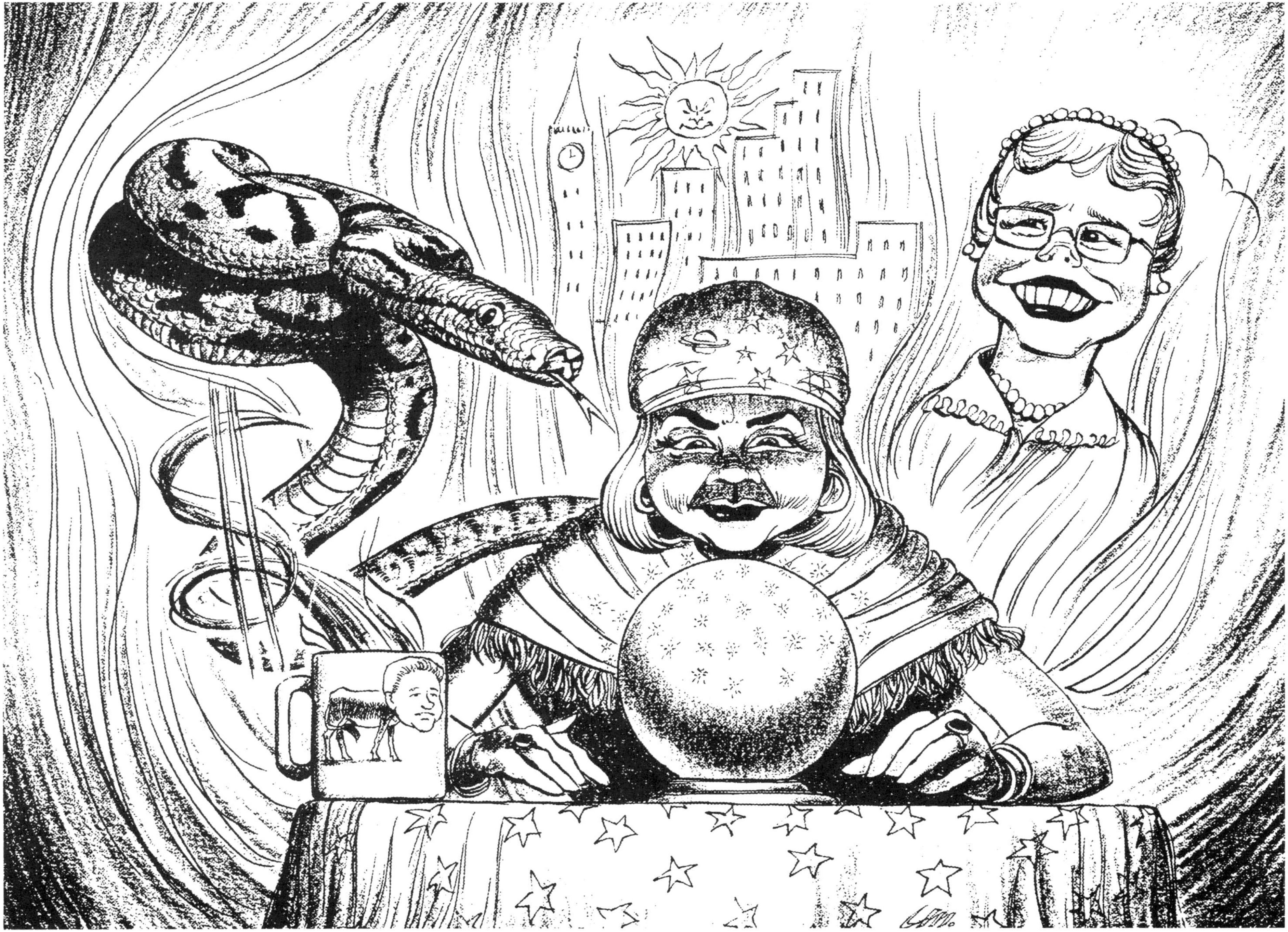

that.

She set about the business of intensively studying the ape-men. She soon discovered that there were three *tribes* (extended family clans) of them, all living together in harmony. They were fairly smart already, certainly smarter than the elephants, although nowhere near as smart as Shoshoni, or the dolphins. The three tribes shared the same lands, trading various goods and services between themselves. They all had their own ways of *worshipping* their *gods*, which mostly translated to eating certain things that made their brains do strange things. But they had *taboos* against messing with each other, or using the resources that belonged to other tribes.

The Firewater Tribe used the seeds of grass plants, grinding them up and using their knowledge of yeast. Well, to be more accurate, they knew nothing about yeast, other than how it worked, or what it did. They called it the **BFD** *God*, for **B**read, **F**irewater, and **D**ough. *Dough* was the lumpy, gooey mix made by grinding up grain seeds. *Firewater* was the fermented liquids obtained by sprouting seeds, drying, grinding, and roasting them, making them into liquids, and then enclosing the liquids in large earthenware jars. They called it firewater because it burned their lips. Yet they liked it, because it made them feel good, and enabled them to talk to the gods. And *bread* was a food made by heating their *dough*; this *bread*, it seemed, lasted longer and tasted better than the *dough*.

The Firewater Tribe gave bread and dough to the other tribes, in return for other goods and services. But the firewater was sacred, and reserved just for them. The other tribes respected this, and their fields of grain, as the sole provinces of the Firewater Tribe.

The Shroom Oog Tribe had the secret of *fire*. *Fire* made heat, which they used to harden clay into earthenware jars and pottery. Also, periodically the Firewater Tribe would come to visit them, and they'd all have big ceremonies and celebrations. The Firewater Tribe would bring dough to be *baked* into bread, which they would then share with the Shroom Oog Tribe, in return for their baking services.

They'd also bring the dried, ground-up remnants of barely-sprouted seeds, so that the Shroom Oog Tribe could roast this, too, in preparation for the fermenting of firewater. This was the time when all the special ceremonies would be conducted, so that the Shroom Oog's *Fire God* would bestow his *Fire Powers* unto the Firewaters. At the end of the day, the Firewater Tribe would go home with bread, jars of fermentable powder for *brew*, the occasional wooden tools, and empty new jars fresh from the *kilns* of the Shroom Oog Tribe. The Shroom Oogs, meanwhile, would contentedly lay back, bellies and larders full of fresh bread.

The trees and shrubs of the forests belonged to the Shroom Oogs. This meant that their fruits, nuts, and berries were theirs, to eat and to trade with the other tribes. The special resources of the Shroom Oogs also included the mushrooms that sprouted in certain special places. These, though, were for eating only by the Shroom Oogs. When they'd eat them, they'd commune with their gods. And all the dead wood of the forests belonged to the Shroom Oogs, too, because they needed it for their fires, and for making a few wooden tools now and then. The other tribes respected the Shroom Oogs very much, and took special pains not to offend them. In fact, the Shroom Oogs, with their special Fire Powers, were actually regarded as gods by the other tribes. It was unthinkable that anyone other than a Shroom Oog should ever mess with Fire, which belonged to these particular gods.

Then there was the Blunt Heads Tribe. They talked to their gods by eating the leaves of the cannabis weed, a hardy plant that grew in special places. Their weeds, and their Weed God, were, needless to say, their sole province, and highly respected by the other tribes. They got their fruits, nuts, and berries, wooden tools, and their earthenware, for carrying water, from the Shroom Oogs, and their bread from the Firewater Tribe. In turn, they provided various services for the others. They gathered wood for the Shroom Oogs' fires, and tended to the spirits of the plants that nourished all the ape-men. In times of drought, they'd carry water to their own weeds, to the grain plants of the Firewater Tribe, and to the trees and shrubs which belonged to the Shroom Oogs.

Even more than all these other things, though, the Blunt Heads were highly respected for the special services they conducted to appease the spirits of the Earth Mother, and all her daughters. They made beautiful music and dances. They appeased the Earth Mother by carving beautiful images from the ivory of naturally deceased elephants. Then, they'd conduct fertility rites, and put seeds into the soil. Seeds for their weeds, grains for the Firewater Tribe, and tree and shrub seeds for the Shroom Oogs.

Last but not least, the Blunt Heads had the immense patience and magic required to sit still for long, long periods of time, pondering the Earth Mother, and catching glimpses of the wild animal spirits that the ape-men shared their world with. Then they'd use their special gifts to go deep inside the sacred caves (members of the Shroom Oog Tribe would come with them, with torches of fire, to light the way) to paint pictures of the wild animal spirits, who were full of life and vigor. When the members of any tribe then fell sick, the Blunt Heads' Medicine Men would go into these caves, appease the animal spirits, draw on the reserves of power in the paintings, and return to heal the sick. These Medicine Men were also responsible for protecting the ape-men from the wild animal spirits, which were occasionally known to directly attack, and even eat, the ape-men, instead of just causing sickness.

The wild animals spirits, as well as the resources and special provinces of the various tribes, were highly respected by all the ape-men. No one ate of their flesh; this was taboo. Killing of animals could only be done by the Blunt Heads Medicine Men, in the rarest of circumstances. These cases were in defense of the lives of ape-men, or in ending the sufferings of near-dead animals. And the Blunt Heads had a lock on the privilege of using the remains of animals, mostly naturally deceased. From their skins, they would fashion blankets, which all tribes used to keep warm, when the weather turned bitter cold. From the tusks of elephants, they'd fashion images of the Earth Mother. From the antlers of elk, they'd fashion implements with which to process the soil, in special rituals to prepare the earth to receive seeds.

So all the tribes were in what they called a mutual flea-picking arrangement, and it worked out very well. They all lived in peace and harmony. All this, Shoshoni learned in the space of several months, by hanging out close enough to hear their thoughts loud and clear, always avoiding detection. But she longed for the day when she could get closer—close enough, even, so that she could finally talk to these ape-men, without them running away in fear. After all, they'd regard her as a dangerous, powerful animal spirit. Yet she needed still more information.

She decided to investigate the Shroom Oog Tribe some more. She made this selection for several reasons. First, she perceived that the Shroom Oogs, when eating their hallucinogenic mushrooms, would regard a telepathic snake to be far less of an unusual threat, compared to what she might expect from the other tribes, whose consciousness seemed to be much less altered during their communications with their gods. Then there were the tantalizing hints that there were some highly intelligent members within the Shroom Oog Tribe, who were running the show, somehow. And the Shroom Oogs, with their fire and pottery, seemed pretty advanced, probably more so than the others.

She started to move in closer to one particular group of the Shroom Oogs (each tribe had many small groups, spread out over all the lands Shoshoni knew of), searching for more details. They weren't long in coming. Yes, indeed, there *were* special Shroom Oogs with special knowledge and intelligence! The Shroom Oogs had their Medicine Men, but they didn't fool Shoshoni for long. They were mere figureheads. Each small group had one or two wise old women, called *witches*, who really ran the show. They set the fires, and supervised the care and maintenance of these fires. They selected the clays and colored minerals for making pottery, supervised the forming of the clay, and performed the most delicate operations.

Shoshoni noticed that, along with the witch being the one who did those things requiring the greatest skill and intelligence, she exhibited other strange behaviors. She, alone, of this entire Shroom Oog group, didn't partake of the mushrooms. And she surreptitiously crept off, on fairly frequent occasions, and ate of a taboo fruit. This was the musical fruit, the fruit of a forbidden tree. Now Shoshoni knew, from her glimpse of the human future, that the humans would one day call these forbidden fruits *beans*, and call the smaller plants *shrubs* and simply *plants*, rather than calling all plants *trees*, as these ape-men now did. And she also knew that in the future, all knowledge of these *beans* having once been taboo, would be lost. She knew, because she'd seen those old folks in Chicago eating them out of metal cans.

But at this point, Shoshoni couldn't understand much about any of this. Why was the musical fruit taboo? Why was it called musical fruit in the first place? Why did the witch violate the taboo? How and why would things change in the future, so that musical fruit should become no longer taboo? Curious, she started intensively following the witch, and observing her thoughts and actions.

Shoshoni was quite lucky one day, happening to be hidden in the bushes really close by, when Beldame Oog, the witch, not only came to eat of the forbidden fruit, but also to sit, relax, and to think things over.

So Shoshoni got quite the earful, so to speak. Beldame sat there, morosely pondering her options, while Shoshoni snooped on her thoughts.

Beldame, like most witches, had been raised by a witch, from infancy on. Ever since she could remember, she'd secretly been fed the musical fruit, and told, most severely, not to reveal this secret to anyone. In her turn, she and her fellow older witch had raised another two female children to be witches. They'd fed them the taboo fruit, and kept the mushrooms away from them. The special diet, it seemed, was necessary to prepare the minds of the young, so that the magical witch knowledge could take root there. In a flash of brilliant deductive reasoning, Shoshoni came to realize what this all was really about. The ape-men were all starved for proteins, except for the witches. With their special monopoly on bean proteins, only their brains developed their fullest potential. And the abstinence from eating mushrooms was simply to keep their minds from becoming too addled.

But Beldame Oog had stumbled onto some bad luck. The two young girls who'd been slated to become witches had both died, the older witch had passed away, and so now there was only Beldame. She was getting old, so there wasn't enough time to raise a new witch from infancy. She couldn't convince any spare witches from any nearby Shroom Oog groups to come and join their group, so there weren't many choices.

Rather than facing the strong possibility that her group would collapse, and either revert to animal status, or join some other group of Shroom Oogs after her death (a source of great shame in the afterworld, as envisioned by witches), she'd have to tackle a very difficult task. She'd have to persuade a young ape-woman, one almost but not quite yet an adult, to become a witch. And she'd have to teach her to become a good witch, despite her mind not having been prepared by the special diet.

Shoshoni observed, fascinated by all this, as Beldame pondered her predicament. Of the young ones, who would she pick? Which one was the smartest, and most easily persuaded to secretly break the taboos, at this late stage, when minds have begun to rigidify? Beldame's mind swirled with complex considerations of all the sophisticated ramifications of her group's social dynamics, the nature of ape-man behavior, and past history, as relayed, word of mouth, from one generation of witches to the next.

Shoshoni listened with rapt attention. She came to realize what awesome powers these witches held. They were actually the ones who'd set up the taboos, the various sole provinces for the three tribes, so that they could all co-inhabit the same areas, and live and trade in peace. Beldame knew of distant times when all had not been quite so peaceful. Before her ancestors had deliberately designed and set up the new social order—they'd apparently enforced it with threats of severe counseling and other punitive magic—there had existed a primeval state of war, a war of all against all. All resources had belonged to whoever could wrest them from the other ape-man, or, more realistically, from the other groups of ape-men.

Beldame, in her ruminations over their current troubles, was rather superficial in her mental review of a lot of background information, though. Questions persisted in Shoshoni's mind. Why was the musical fruit called musical fruit, and why was it taboo? If it could make ape-men smarter, why weren't they all eating it?

Beldame wondered yet again, which young ape-woman might make the best witch. Who would violate the taboos, and eat the musical fruit? There was one young one called Eve Oog, it seemed, who showed some promise. On occasion, she was known to speak quietly to her friends, proposing wild ideas. Ideas in direct contravention to received social wisdom, taboos, family values, and common sense. Some members of the group, now, were occasionally known to whisper dark suspicions about just how strange Eve Oog was. Yes, Beldame concluded, Eve Oog is my best choice.

Frustrated, Shoshoni began to debate. Could she perhaps send out her thoughts, cosmic-karmic vibes and such-like things, and touch the mind of Beldame? Could she even do so without Beldame catching on? Or would Beldame flee in terror? There was risk, yes. But there was also so much more she needed to know. So, quietly, subtly, she sent her thoughts out to Beldame.

Taboos were made by witches, and witches can tear them down, Beldame thought. Or, this is what she *thought* that she thought. In reality, of course, these thoughts came from Shoshoni. Why settle just for subverting Eve Oog? Why don't I just make a frontal assault on the idea that we should all addle our brains with mushrooms, and that none should eat of the forbidden musical fruit?

Beldame recoiled in shock at this latest turn in "her" thoughts.

"Get thee behind me, Dark Whisperer," she hissed inwardly. "What do you want, *anarchy?* A return to the war of all against all? Only our taboos stand between us and utter madness! Now get *away* from me!"

Shoshoni's mind boiled and bubbled. A Dark Whisperer? What's that? Just another of these irrational, superstitious ideas cooked up by these witches, to give them a grip on all the other ape-men? Well, whatever it is, I know *I'm* not one. Maybe it's time to come out in the open, and have an honest snake-to-witch talk. Get this all out in the open.

This idea of having honest, intelligent conversation with a *real, live sentient being*—not dead dinosaurs or hypothetical beings from the future, mind you—was just way too much for Shoshoni to resist. Her loneliness was just too much to bear. So she slithered out into plain view, and said, "Hi, Beldame, I Shoshoni. I wonder you answer questions from me. Why called musical fruit? Why..."

Beldame threw incomprehensible curses at Shoshoni and fled in terror, wondering who'd been sneaking mushrooms into her food, how, and why. Shoshoni cranked up the amplitude of her vibes, pegging the needle and screaming at Beldame. "I *real,* #ä&Æ@y%¥!, I *real!!!* I just harmless sssmart sssnake! I not hurt you! Come talk me!" But Beldame fled all that much faster. Crushed, Shoshoni slithered back into the bushes.

Chapter 6

The Paleolithic Horde Whisperer

"If there were only one religion in England there would be danger of despotism, if there were two, they would cut each other's throats, but there are thirty, and they live in peace and happiness."
Voltaire (1694–1778)

Meanwhile, back at the branch—that's a branch of the river, not of the bank; 'cause we're still back in 30,000 B.C., now—no, that's B.C., not B.S.—now look what you've done; you've made us lose our train of thought. What little we had. OK, so we're out over the river. We've set the Big Scene. The Pleisto Scene. Now set the little scene. Where the eagle glides descending, over an ancient river bending. The eagle's name is Aquila Martlet, and his mind isn't on his gorgeous view. He sees it just about every day. His mind isn't even on getting some fish in his belly, as is so often the case. He's had his fill already, today.

His mind is on his itches. Those damned mites and fleas, they're just driving him bonkers. So he's thinking some dust fluffed into his feathers, then shaken back out, again and again, might satisfy his itches. The dust might take a few pests with it, when he shakes it out. He's not aware of all that, though. He's not even aware of what causes his itches; he just knows how to scratch them. So he's thinking, like, clearing in the jungle. Clearing where there's many, many crumbling rocks, so many that the plants can't grow so as to cover them all. Here and there, in those plant-hostile rocks, there's fresh sand and dust. Sand and dust created by crumbling rocks, that is, but once again, these are things unknown to our hero, the eagle, Aquila Martlet.

Aquila wheels and soars, heading in the general direction of the rocky clearing. He descends, swoops over to his favorite rocks, and lands. He rotates his head back and forth several times, eagle fashion, giving everything the eagle eye. Satisfied that all is well, he hops down the talus slope and into the dust and sand. Delousing activities commence.

Little known to Aquila, he's picked the same outcropping of rocks where Shoshoni'd had her brush with fate a while back. The tiny, sharp shards of shattered amber work their way through his feathers, and one works it's way down beneath the skin, down between a feather's shaft and eagle flesh. There, Aquila's bloodstream picks it up and carries it to his brain. The second and final case of dinosaur genes quite improbably arising from the grave and animating a living creature's brain has commenced.

Aquila flew off in a huff when he felt the strange changes begin in his mind. He sat in the highest branches of the tallest nearby tree, shaking his head and fluffing his feathers again and again. But the bizarre new thoughts wouldn't go away.

By the time the changes were complete, he'd accepted that they weren't so bad after all. Like Shoshoni, he experienced the great thrill of the awakening intellect. Like Shoshoni, he went off by himself for a while, to ponder matters large and small, for quite some time. And discovered great loneliness. So he, too, ended up looking for other sentience to communicate with.

Unlike Shoshoni, he didn't waste any time with elephants or dolphins. Elephants didn't seem anywhere near as smart as ape-men to him, and ape-man smell didn't bother him much. Dolphins were very smart, yes, but they looked like fish. Aquila couldn't seriously consider trying to communicate with something that looked like a good, giant dinner. So the ape-men were it.

Now the use of cosmic-karmic vibes for communication being extremely personal and subjective, it just happened to be that Aquila's tastes ran in different veins than Shoshoni's. Whether that was due to their different species, or just to their personal differences, we'll never know, because the sample size is just way too small. Aquila, after investigating the three tribes of ape-men, decided that the Blunt Heads were his best choice. When they ate of their sacred weed, the states of their minds were closest to his, when compared to those of the Firewater Tribe, or to those of the Shroom Oogs.

The local clan of Blunt Heads had stumbled onto a new patch of weed that day, so they were quite happy. They were kicking back, enjoying a potpatch dinner. Aquila detected the resulting spike in cosmic-karmic vibes compatible to his own mentality, so he flew over to take a look-see. Sitting in a tall tree nearby, he kept an eagle eye on the party below.

Panama Red, Bud Roach, Head Rush, Roach Clip, Chong Bong, and other, lower-ranking members of the clan sat in their assigned positions in the Great Circle, conducting The Ceremony. In front of them, inside the circle, there lay piles of weed and earthenware pots. Aquila watched carefully. They'd strip leaves off of the weeds, twirl them into cylinders, pick small objects out of the jars, lay them alongside the tips of the cylinders of leaves, then wrap yet more leaves around this assembly. The tips of these finished assemblies were then tamped into a rock, and passed around the circles, with each Blunt Head, in turn, taking one small bite, and chewing it with great dignity.

Even Aquila's eagle eyes weren't strong enough to discern what, exactly, it was that they were putting into their *roach joineds*, as the finished assemblies were called, nor were their thoughts on this matter entirely clear, from a distance. So Aquila flew to a tree a mere fifty yards away, to get a closer look. This caused quite the stir among the ape-men. The females pulled their infants in closer to their bodies. Aquila perched in perfect stillness, and they went back to the ceremony, as before.

Aquila watched and listened to the vibes. Those were *insects*, mostly *cock roaches*, that the ape-men were pulling out of the jars, and putting into their sacred fare! After careful study and thought, Aquila came to realize that the ape-men suffered from a low-protein diet. Their taboos forbade all animal proteins except for insects. So they gathered insects, saving them in covered jars. Blunt Head tastes were such that they felt that their weed and their insects, together, tasted far better than either one alone. Sort of like fish flesh and fish guts, Aquila surmised. So the weed and the roaches were joined together, creating the *roach joineds*.

As Aquila further studied their thoughts, he realized that there was yet more to the story. It seemed that when the Blunt Head Medicine Men went to create and fetch magic in the caves, they'd first have to appease the Weed God, and get in the proper state of mind, by heartily partaking of the Weed God's blessings. Being then quite inclined to bump their heads on stalactites and cave ceilings (hence their name, "Blunt Heads"), they wanted to take out any available insurance against becoming *too* blunt headed. So they ceremonially blunted the heads of the roaches in their roach joineds, offering these creatures as living sacrifices to the Weed God.

Aquila stuck with the clan of Blunt Heads for a few weeks. His constant presence spooked them at first, but they soon got used to him. He soon noticed just how large a difference the weed made in their moods. When they'd not had a recent meal of weed, they were edgy, irritable, and hard for him to understand. When they were sated with weed, they were easy-going, open, and mellow. Aquila decided that if he was ever going to make successful psychic contact with them, and push them towards higher levels of sentience, to end his loneliness, he'd have to catch them in a very, very weedy mood. Yet they just never seemed to get very close to the desired state. Even after the best of their potpatch feasts, they just didn't get *high* enough to talk with him, to use their term.

So Aquila studied this problem at length. What made them *high*? Their ceremonies, their belief in their Weed God? Or the chemicals in the insects, or in the weeds? Well, OK, sure, he thought, it's all of them combined. But which is the most important? How can I work on them, get them to a state where we can communicate? What's the angle, here?

He pretty much concluded that it had to be mainly the chemicals in the weeds. So how to I boost these? Poop in their pot patches, to fertilize their plants? Nah, no way, there's not enough poop, even if I could convince a few of my far-less-intelligent fellow eagles to join me. Bury dead fish in the pot patches? Now that sounds more likely. Still, entirely too slow, too impractical. The problem is, they just assimilate those chemicals way too slowly, way too inefficiently. But how do I solve that? And that's where matters were stuck, for quite a few weeks.

One day their nomadic wanderings brought them close to a far more settled clan, a group of Shroom Oogs. Aquila grew excited; he suspected something big was about to happen. So, along with his periodic escapes to the river to catch fish, he now also abandoned the Blunt Heads often, to fly off and go investigate the Shroom Oogs. Flying back and forth between these two groups, as the Blunt Heads slowly approached the Shroom Oogs, he surmised what was about to happen.

And what was that? A big ceremony—singing and dancing, and beating of drums, which the Blunt Heads did so well—and then trading. The Blunt Heads would present blankets of animal furs that they'd collected from carcasses during their wanderings, and then there'd be a feast. Bread, fruits, nuts, berries. The Blunt Heads would put some flesh and fat back onto their weary, gaunt bodies. Then their best Medicine Man, Head Rush, would join a torch-bearing Shroom Oog Medicine Man, and they'd make their way deep into the sacred caves, fetching magic from the paintings. Maybe even make a few more paintings, if they had plenty of time and energy, if the harvests had been good. Other Blunt Heads would hang out for a few weeks, helping the Shroom Oogs gather firewood, nuts, fruits, and berries, and planting seeds. Then the Blunt Heads would gratefully receive a few earthenware pots from the Shroom Oogs, and they'd be back to their nomadic ways.

Aquila watched enviously as the Shroom Oogs and the Blunt heads met, celebrated, and socialized. Oh, if only he could end his loneliness, and interact with fellow sentient, or at least semi-sentient, creatures, as these ape-men did! He made himself content, for now, to just watch, as they socialized and gossiped. He was mildly amused to hear them gossip about the large bird that had been following the Blunt Heads. Was this good magic, or bad? They concluded it was good magic, since he'd never made even the slightest threat against them, or their babies.

He dismissed one minor piece of gossip as no more relevant than any other piece of gossip, at that time, although he later came to realize its significance. That was that a neighboring clan of Shroom Oogs, many, many miles away, was experiencing some difficulties. Their only witch, or witch in training, was quite old, and she was having trouble persuading her would-be apprentice, a headstrong young ape-woman, to co-operate.

One night as Aquila roosted in a tree, watching the glowing embers of a fire, he got to thinking. What was this *smoke*, these partially oxidized fragments of burning vegetation? Would the sacred weed burn? Would partially oxidized weed fragments, perhaps, be a method of delivering chemicals rapidly and efficiently into the bodies of the Blunt Heads?

So off he flew, in the middle of the night, to the weed patch. Returning with talons full of weeds, he dive-bombed the unattended fire, and watched. Smoke poured forth. He flew through the smoke, drawing it into his lungs. Hacking and coughing, he retreated to his perch, high in the trees. Then the euphoria came to him, and fed upon itself. I can *feel* it, he thought, giddy with joy. If *I* can feel it, then *they'll* be able to feel it! Now all I need to do is to persuade them to do this, and victory is mine! He got so high, high in his tree, that he nearly fell off his perch.

Then the morning came, and with it, letdown. How would he ever persuade the Blunt Heads to do as he had done? Do it again, in the light of day, for all to see? But what if they determined this to be an omen, that the spirit gods of the birds and wild animals wanted them to destroy their sacred weeds, and just say no? This was an all too real possibility, as best as Aquila could judge how the ape-men thought. So demonstration was entirely too risky. What to do? The Blunt Heads didn't even mess with fire; it was the sole province of the Shroom Oogs. Aquila became downright dejected.

So he flew off all by himself for quite a few days, and thought. His loneliness drove him back. But at least he returned with a tentative plan, a first step. Obviously, he had to get close enough to one of the Blunt Heads to persuade him that the fire taboo was wrong. That he should steal fire from the Shroom Oogs, and then persuade the rest of the Blunt Heads clan that this was good and right. After that, then let's move off to weed smoke, Aquila concluded. First things first; one step at a time.

Panama Red seemed to be the wildest, most radical of the high-ranking Blunt Heads, so he was the one that Aquila chose to work on. Aquila spotted his opportunity one fine day when Panama Red took a walk with Twiggy Sinsemilla, his favorite babe, out in the jungle. He swooped down to perch on a branch not more than five yards above their heads. "Hey, you party animals, like, let's get faced," he psychically blared out at them. Panama glanced inquiringly at Twiggy, a funny look on his face. Twiggy just shrugged, in that appealingly feminine manner that so endeared her to Panama.

Aquila tried again. This time, he spread his wings out, fluffed his feathers, and audibly squawked, while saturating the ether with his vibes. He projected images of burning weed, lungs full of smoke, euphoria, and an immensely satisfied Weed God. "This bud's for you," he shouted, mentally projecting an image of a particularly potent clump of weed smoldering under their noses. "Bud is Wiser," he added.

Panama turned to Twiggy again, saying, "Maybe I'm crazy, but I think that big bird is trying to tell us something. Don't look at me so funny, but I think... it has something to do with weed, and fire. Like he wants us to sacrifice weed to the Fire God. But that's crazy! Weed belongs to us, and fire belongs to the Shroom Oogs. We can't go and..."

"Squawk, squawk," Aquila protested quite loudly. Then he concentrated on cranking up his vibes. "Take fire from the Shroom Oogs, you dense bunch of overgrown monkeys! It's real simple! Just feed it dry wood! You'll not regret it! It'll keep you warm at night, and when you breath the smoke of burning weed, the Weed God will be *quite* pleased! Trust me!"

Panama Red took the concept of a talking eagle in stride, with amazing equanimity. "But we can't go and steal fire from the Shroom Oogs!" he protested. "They're *gods*, you know! Surely stealing goes against all the taboos! *Surely* the gods will punish us, swiftly and without mercy!"

"Oh, don't sweat it, dude," Aquila replied. "They'll still have their fire. All you do is take a few embers, and stick 'em in a jar. Wrap the jar in grass to keep from burning yourself, and feed it wood. They'll never miss a few embers. Stick some extra wood in their fire when you take the embers, if you must, to make yourself feel better, 'cause embers are just burning wood. You won't really be stealing anything."

"It is forbidden," Panama replied staunchly. "Fire belongs to the Shroom Oogs. We must not steal! So the gods command us. We obey the gods! We won't listen to your madness."

Aquila sampled the vibes. Nothing but adamant conviction wafted it's way to him from the minds of Panama Red and Twiggy Sinsemilla. He squawked in frustrated protest and flew away in temporary defeat, thinking, I'll convince one of these ape-men of the virtues of what I say, one of these days. And then their minds and their technology will be stimulated, their auras will be much more palatable to the refined tastes of an advanced creature like me, and my wretched loneliness will be at an end. All I have to do is figure out who to convince, and how to convince them.

Many miles away, Beldame Oog was having similar troubles explaining to Eve Oog that it might be wise for Eve to violate the taboos, and eat of the musical fruit.

The old witch said *what?!* "No, I'm serious, Eve," she said, out there in the jungle where she'd pulled Eve away from prying ears. "In the old days, we lived in a war of all against all. People fashioned sharp rocks, tied them to the ends of sticks, and killed large animals. Then they *ate* them! Yes, that's right!"

Eve could barely imagine such barbarous acts. The Blunt Heads, with their killing and eating of cock roaches, were bad enough, but at least these were small, stupid creatures they ate, not large, spirit-filled animals, like deer, bear, tapirs, and so on. Nor could she imagine that, as

Beldame explained, in those old days, ape-men fought and killed *each other*, in conflicts over limited territories and sources of fresh meat.

"So the witches of old got together, and talked and thought things through," Beldame continued, "They decided that the greedy, bloody ways had to end. They very deliberately designed and implemented a new social, magical, mystical, spiritual order, in which the three tribes could live together in peace, respecting each others' specialties and resources. The large animals wouldn't be killed any more, either, so that there'd be no more fighting over hunting lands. Yes, our population density, the level of proteins in our diets, and our brain power all took hits. But these were small prices to pay for peace.

"So witches implemented our new social order, using threats of magic, unrelentingly stern counseling, and merciless sensitivity training. The common ape-men, with their new, lower-protein diets and lowered mental powers, soon forgot the old ways, and took the new taboos to heart. We witches, meanwhile, secretly violate the taboos against eating musical fruits, which allows us to retain our higher mental powers. We've passed on, from one generation to the next, the secrets of the past, musical fruit, and our hopes. You see, Eve, we eventually hope to bring all of us to the light of *reason*, of higher mental powers. Some day, we hope to again allow all ape-men to eat of a high-protein diet, this time in peace. So far, though, we still haven't figured out how to safely set up such a new and improved society."

The shock to Eve Oog's mind seemed nothing less than traumatic. "The commands from the gods didn't originally come from the gods, but just from *witches?*" she protested. "Witches aren't even the bosses of Shroom Oog society! Sure, we all respect you witches, a great deal," Eve hastened to add. "But doesn't Thag Oog conduct all the most important ceremonies?"

"That's of no real concern," Beldame insisted. "Thag Oog and all the other Medicine Men don't really have as much power as we witches do. *We* have the *real* power. Who runs the fires, after all? Our whole tribe derives its power from fire, and the other tribes regard us as gods. They'd not be able to survive anywhere near as well as they do, without us."

Eve didn't know what to think. The worst part of it all was that Beldame then strictly forbade Eve from talking to anyone about anything they'd discussed. Eve feared Beldame's magic, so there was no question that Eve would have to keep all this to herself. She, and she alone, would have figure this out. Should she become a witch, as Beldame asked? Beldame insisted that Eve's decision would be truly voluntary, as it had to be, for some strange reason, and that she'd not be punished if she said no. The choice was hers—entirely, dreadfully hers. Should she risk angering the gods, violate the taboos, and eat of the musical fruit? Or should she risk the future of her clan, and the wrath of Beldame—Eve couldn't quite convince herself that Beldame would completely refrain from exacting any revenge, should Eve choose to say no—and resist Beldame's entreaties?

"I don't know," Eve hemmed and hawwed. "Give me some time to think it over. I just have such a hard time envisioning myself violating the taboos. All my life I've been taught these things. And now you want me to go off and eat of the musical fruit? I fear the wrath of the gods!"

"Oh, come on now, Eve! I'll *show* you! I'll eat them right in front of you! You'll see that no harm comes to me. None. None at all! It's what gives us witches our special powers, really. Come on. Join me, and we'll go eat them somewhere in secret."

"I don't know. I don't think I'm quite ready. I don't think I could eat them here or there. I don't think I could eat them anywhere."

"Now, Eve! Think rationally! You already know I eat them, and I don't suffer from the wrath of the gods! Come join me, eat of the musical fruit, become a witch! What are you afraid of?!"

"Well," she admitted shyly, "Witches never have children. Men won't mate with you. I'd really like to... to..."

"Yes, yes, I know," Beldame broke in, "You'd like to have children with Adam Oog. You know, what you think are such secrets, your friends are blabbing to the whole clan. They all talk about your strange ideas behind your back. That you should like to *marry* Adam, as a man and a woman, the way that the Firewater Tribesmen and the Blunt Heads marry, instead of the way we marry. Some mock you, for, they say, you go against family values. In our Shroom Oog Tribe, men marry men, not women. And that's the way it is, and must be, for our tribe, they say."

What Beldame said was true. Like some other societies (notably many Greeks) later on down the long and winding roads of human history, the Shroom Oogs regarded ape-men as superior, and ape-women as inferior. Therefore, sex between equals (males) was far better, more noble, than sex between males and females. The latter was merely a distasteful necessity for perpetuating the Shroom Oog Tribe.

"But that's the main reason why I've picked you to hopefully become the clan's new witch," Beldame continued, "We need you, you know. I'll not live much longer. Anyway, by questioning this taboo, at least, you show some promise. You don't unquestioningly obey all the taboos. I was really hoping that you could hear what I say with an open mind. You know that the other tribes regard marriage differently than we do, and you've thought it through. Now come and watch me eat musical fruit, and you'll see that this taboo, too, needn't be mindlessly obeyed."

"Well, then, what's the purpose of this musical fruit taboo in the first place? Didn't you say you witches set up most of the taboos? And why do they call it musical fruit, anyway?"

"Well, we've got to keep the commoners down," Beldame explained patiently. "If too many of us eat the proteins in the musical fruit, too many will be too wise. They'll gain knowledge, and start questioning the taboos. Then we'd have to resort to stern, harsh measures again, or fall back into barbarism. Eating animals, fighting each other, and so on. Then there's some of the more subtle reasons, too. Eating of the musical fruit can be dangerous, as we discovered way back when. Should you decide to become a witch, I'll have to teach you how to be very careful.

"In a nutshell, what we say is, 'musical fruit, musical fruit—the more you eat, the more you toot.' Your tooter becomes a polluter tooter. That means if you feel the toot coming on, you have to leave, get away from the rest of the clan, else they might catch on to us violating this taboo. And most of all, remember—never, never, *never ever* toot close to a fire! The Fire God can't abide by toots, and can burn your polluter tooter!

"That's really about all I can say for now. Some of our magic is real, not just stuff we've made up to keep the commoners in line. But that stuff's secret. Any more, we have to wait till you're a *real* witch. Till after you've eaten of the musical fruit. So what do you say? Ready to go? Shall we dine on The Forbidden Fruit? I'm ready when you are!"

"Um, no, not quite yet," Eve mumbled. "Give me a day or two. Surely you can spare me a few days to ponder this?"

Beldame reluctantly gave in and walked away, back to the clan's huts. Eve Oog's mind reeled as she headed off in another direction, out into the jungle, to be alone with herself and her thoughts. She had important matters to ponder, obviously.

For almost subconscious reasons, she headed for a patch of musical fruit. Arriving there, she thought, well, yes, this is appropriate that I should sit here and look at these while I think things over. Look at these little musical fruit trees, and get over my fear. Realize that they're just another tree. Nothing more. Nothing less. Nothing threatening. Now let's just go ahead and move on out, here, and sit here in the middle of this patch...

She sat there, studying the bean plants, AKA musical fruit trees. Here, there were green fruits, and there, there were ripe fruits. And over here there were little flowers, magical blossoms, as Beldame had once explained. Strange little trees, that the fruits should be at all stages like this, in the same patch. Look at those blossoms! Weird smell! What had Beldame called them? Oh, yes, that's right—"fart blossoms." What a strange name!

So can I imagine myself *eating* these, she asked herself, eyeing the ripened little fruits. Well, not just yet. But maybe I should go ahead and pick a few, and see if I can work my nerve up later. She steeled herself against her queasiness at picking the forbidden fruit, and started filling her small satchel.

Eve felt a *presence*. A non-human, non-mammalian presence, with its life force laying down low, close to the ground. Now Eve, unlike Beldame, remembered many strange experiences after having eaten mushrooms, so she wasn't particularly spooked. She didn't even get that upset when she saw a large python's head poking out of the bushes, looking at her with hypnotic eyes. "Hello, Eve, out for nissse little ssstroll? I Shoshoni Sssquamata. Nissse meet you."

At this point Eve got a wee bit disturbed, recalling that, well, hey, after all, I haven't eaten any mushrooms lately. Now if this seemed just like a regular big python, and it was heading closer to me, I'd be makin' tracks outta here! But here it is, *talking* to me, and I've not had any mushrooms! Nor have I been one to eat too many, too often, so as to be like a few of the others, mostly older male Shroom Oogs, who randomly *see things* just about any time. But this is such a *nice* snake. If I can handle the idea of eating taboo musical fruits, then I can also calmly chat with a snake.

"That right, Eve, Shoshoni is nissse-sssnake. I no hurt you. We talk. And eating musical fruit not bad, either. You want sssee me eat sssome? Watch." Shoshoni chomped on a clump of the forbidden fruit and slithered backwards. The shrubs bent, then gave way. She swallowed without chewing. "Sssee?" she concluded, "No hurt me. Not poison. You try?"

"You're just like Beldame. Why are y'all so bent on getting me to eat these? No, I mean, Beldame I can understand, I guess. She's got to line up a new witch, to replace Beldame when she's gone. But how about *you*? What's *your* interest here?"

"Oh, I want what besss for you and clan, just like Beldame. Fruit make you sssmarter, wiser, you know. And I want you sssmart, wise. I only, lonely sssmart sssnake. I need company of sssmart one talk to. You be my friend?"

"Oh, I'll be your friend, don't worry about that." Eve was very nice, very solicitous. "But I don't know about eating musical fruit. What will they *do* to me?"

"They make you wise. Sssself-aware. You will sssay to yousssself, 'Eve, I am.' You will know good and bad. That chaosss is badnesss. You help Beldame and them who follow you to work towards good sssociety she talk you of. You musss eat musical fruit wisss me."

"I don't know if I could eat them with a snake. Maybe I could eat them if they were baked."

Shoshoni couldn't imagine any way she could manage to bake the fruits, even if she managed to get access to a cooking fire. Not having any limbs was *such* a drag! "Well, try them, take home with you, bake them for youssself if you please," Shoshoni pleaded. "Maybe Beldame help you. Just try them, try them, won't you please? Try them, try them, you will sssee!"

"I couldn't eat them back at camp. They'd catch me, and call me a tramp. I'm not sure if I can eat them here or there. I'm not sure I can eat them anywhere!"

Shoshoni sighed. Be patient, now, she told herself. Think. *Think!* OK, so, like, maybe if she eats some mushrooms, and gets quite "fried", as they say, maybe *then* she'll try them. But what if it takes too many mushrooms? What if we have to destroy her mind to save it? There's danger here! But maybe it's worth a try. Maybe we can have her go just far enough, but not too far. She projected these concepts, asking Eve, "Now, to not think of me as sssnake. Think of me as you friend. Could you eat them with a friend? Could you, would you, eat them as you go 'round the bend?"

Shoshoni could feel the fear as Eve contemplated going around the bend, as certain other members of her tribe had done. Eve was getting stubborn now. "I could not eat them with a snake, I would not eat them if they were baked. I could not eat them with a friend, I could not eat them as I go 'round the bend!"

Come *on,* Shoshoni, she said to herself. You've *got* to go for it! If you want to end your loneliness, you've got to help her, stand by her, coach this dim-witted but kind-hearted girl to see that if she'll just eat this fruit, she'll become wiser, much wiser, and help her kind, as well as me! Now let's see. Among other things, she fears that they'll taste bad. And truth be told, they do taste kinda bad. That's to python taste buds. Who knows about human taste buds? Even if I get her to try a few, that might not be enough. I've got to get her into the habit, which means that they've got to taste good to her. Let's see, her fellow ape-men over there in that Blunt Heads Tribe, they have a way of mellowing out the harsh taste of their weeds. Let's try it, now...

"Would you, could you eat them if I was your coach? Would you eat them with a roach?"

Eve Oog picked herself and her satchel up off the ground and flew away in terror, fleeing back to her camp. Eating musical fruit was bad enough, but the idea of eating roaches, like the Blunt Heads did, was just far, far too much, she thought. Stupid snake! Doesn't she understand *anything* about us?!

Shoshoni, crushed once more, slithered back into the bushes and tried to sleep. She started seriously suspecting that the ape-men and ape-women were just a bunch of speciesists. Well, no, how can that be, she asked herself. Eve seemed to be quite nice, as an individual. She cared that I'm lonely, and wants to be my friend! Maybe it's just one of these insidiously invidious things. Institutional speciesism, I guess you'd call it.

Eve ran for a few hundred yards, then calmed down a bit. Still, she walked towards camp, rather than back towards her new friend, whose ideas she feared so much. That little satchel, with its cargo of musical fruit, weighed heavily on her mind. She really, really needed to share her burdens with someone. Someone normal. Not a witch, and not a snake. I've just *got* to talk to people about this, she thought. But Beldame told me I'm not to talk to *anyone* about our little talk! Now Shoshoni, *she's* a different matter! I can talk all I want to, about *her!*

Eve burst into the camp during the middle of a solemn ceremony, but she didn't care. Just as Thag Oog invoked the gods to bless the marriage, saying, "And do you, Adam Oog, take Steve Oog to be your lawfully...," Eve ran up, breathlessly saying, "Thag Oog! Thag Oog! Help! Help! I need some Strong Medicine! There's a big snake in the musical fruit patch, and it was trying to get me to eat the musical fruit! Her name's Shoshoni, and she says that if I'll just eat the fruit..."

"Now, now, calm down, my little one," Thag Oog said reassuringly. "Calm *down!* Now, have you been partaking of the mushrooms, without anyone joining you, and without the proper ceremonies? You *know* how the gods get angry when..."

"No, no, Thag Oog, Sir! *No!* This is *real!* It's a **real** snake, a real, large, smart snake with a long tongue and piercing eyes, and it eats musical fruits, and..."

Thag Oog spoke patiently, tolerantly. "Now Eve, you know I've heard some talk. Silly things about you wanting to marry Adam, here. Can you imagine? Adam and Eve, instead of Adam and Steve?! No, now, really, I'm not trying to make fun of you. Are you just trying to break Adam and Steve up, because you're jealous? You can't stand to watch us complete this ceremony?"

"No Sir! That's not it! There's really actually a real, live, large smart snake in the patch of musical fruit trees just down that path a ways, and it wants me to eat the fruit, it says it will make me wise! I can't figure out what I should do! I need some help, some advice!" She started to sob.

"There, there," Thag Oog said, taking her in his arms. "Why don't you just tell your big strong handsome Medicine Man about your visions, and I'll help interpret them for you, and you'll be all better."

Eve protested yet once more that the snake was real, not a vision. Thag Oog nodded very reassuringly. Then she told him all about it, between sobs, and excluding any mention of Beldame. When she was all done, Thag motioned for her to sit down. He stood up to address the crowd. "Eve Oog here has had a powerful vision, bringing us Good Medicine. Now some of her motives aren't so good, but that's not her fault. Her motives are subconscious, not willfully malicious. As we all know, she likes Adam very much, which is OK, as long as she doesn't get in the way of Adam and Steve, or think that she's as good, as powerful, and as beautiful as men are. And I think she'll do fine, here, and stay in her place, even if her dreams bring thoughts that are disturbing to her, if we keep on helping her out.

"Now we all know that we men have long, beautiful noses, with beaks like eagles, while women have short, stout, ugly little pug noses like the pigs in the forests. Lots of people talking, few of them know. But we mighty Medicine Men know! We know about visions from the Great Spirit. We know what a large snake stands for, in dreams. Snakes stand for long, powerful, beautiful noses. Eve has nose envy. She'd like to be like a man, with a long, beautiful nose."

The crowd muttered in anger. Thag Oog raised his arms, saying, "Now let there be no anger or chaos. Chaos is badness! She brings *Good* Medicine! *Good* Medicine, I say!" The crowd calmed down. "Now I say her visions bring Good Medicine because it shows that we men of the Shroom Oog Tribe are beautiful, with noses worthy of great envy. It shows that the evil spirits that dwell in the musical fruit trees want us to do bad things, because they know we are powerful, that we have much Medicine. But we can defeat them! They have shown us that bad things go together. Bad things like women wanting to be men, and disobeying the taboos, by eating musical fruits, for example.

"But they defeat themselves in their own actions! Now we know yet again that they're bad, and what they're up to! When we stick together, when we ask each other for help, as Eve Oog asked me to help her, then we will make yet more Good Medicine! Now people of mine, remember this! And remember, we shall not blame Eve Oog, or the serpents, for what the bad spirits of the musical fruit groves would try to have us do! There will be no chastising Eve, or tormenting of serpents, or any other animal spirits of the wild! Hear me and obey!

"Now let's get back to our ceremony. And do you, Adam Oog, take Steve Oog to be your lawfully..." Eve picked up her satchel and headed for her hut, still sniffling.

That night, under the cover of darkness, she ate the musical fruits.

It wasn't so much that the proteins stimulated her brain. The beans didn't contain that many proteins, and Eve was already entering adulthood. Protein deprivation affects the human (or ape-man) brain the most during major developmental phases, before birth, in infancy, and in childhood. So the beans were too late to make much difference, physiologically.

Psychologically, matters were much different. All Eve's recent stresses concentrated on those magical beans. She focused all her mental powers on overcoming the taboos. So when she did, she felt great relief. The placebo effect kicked in. She'd overcome her internal self-limitations along with the taboos, and had become self-actualized! Self-awareness blossomed. "Eve, I am," she muttered to herself.

The next morning she woke up at dawn, bright-eyed and bushy-tailed. She ate breakfast, then went to find Beldame. After Eve called for her outside her door, Beldame limped out of her hovel, looking miserable. "Beldame, Beldame! Guess what?! Last night, I..."

"Hush, my child, hush. I can *see* what you did. I'm proud of you. Now let's go off into the woods before we talk."

"Beldame, you poor old dear, you don't look too well, or too happy. Aren't you *glad* about what I've done? What's the matter?"

"I am indeed quite glad for you, my child. My young lady. My witch. My successor. You've done what you needed to do just in time, it seems. But now there's much more on my mind. Let's walk into the forest before we speak, though, for we must take great cautions not to be overheard," she whispered. "Now let's casually speak of trivial things until we're far away from camp."

They veered off of the path, and hid deep in the middle of a lush riot of trees and vines. They sat beneath an ancient, gnarled but stately tree on an old rotting log, where they could survey their surroundings fairly well. "I ate the fruits!" Eve exclaimed at last. "I've become self-actualized!"

"Yes, yes. I know. I'm so glad. Now you're a witch. When we've had our little talk, we'll return to camp, and we'll have the ceremony. We'll make it official. Will you be ready? Are you willing to give up your hopes of having men like Adam pursuing you, and having children?"

"Yes, I am."

"Good. That means I'll now tell you all the most important secrets of being a witch. First, let..."

"But Beldame, excuse me, you seem so... down. I'd have thought you'd be a lot happier to see that I'm becoming a witch. What's the matter?"

"You're right, Eve, something is wrong. Very wrong. Terribly wrong. I'm quite happy, really, that you're joining me as a witch. I frankly don't know what would happen if you didn't. Some very, very bad things, I suspect. They may happen anyway. But at least our chances are a lot better, now, with you joining us witches. I'm sorry I don't seem more enthused; it's just that I have a lot on my mind, now, suddenly.

"But I'll fill you in on all this, just right here, right now. Be patient, and I'll explain. You already know some of the most important things about being a witch. That we're working towards a much better society, some day, when we can combine the best of the old, and the best of the new. The higher-protein diets and population densities of old, with the more peaceful ways of today. Meanwhile, we secretly pull the strings, using taboos and magic.

"What you don't yet know is what I'm going to tell you now. We witches perform very, very little real magic. Maybe none at all, depending on which witch you ask. It's a good thing we Shroom Oog clans live so far from each other, that we have meetings of witches so very, very rarely. Else we'd sit around and debate such matters all day, and never get any work done. But what I'm saying is, there's little if any real 'magic', the way that the commoners, or even the Medicine Men, think of it. Magic is in the mind. Ceremonies and rituals don't really do anything, in and of themselves. They only do what they do, through the power of the mind.

"Does that mean our magic is all false, a trick? That it's not 'real'? No, not at all! The power of the mind is very real! This contradiction is why we witches can sit around and talk about such things all day. Eve, this you must understand: *The Most Important Thing* about being a good witch, next to having a heart full of love, is understanding *what is real*, and *what is **not** real*.

"You see, we witches even practice 'magic' on each other. We do and say things to each other that aren't 'real', in the strictest sense of the word. We deceive each other a bit, now and then. Deliberately. Older witches are especially likely to do this to the younger witches, who are in training. This puts the younger witches into the web of 'magic' by which we control the clans and the tribes. In other words, younger witches often have a hard time appearing to believe in the rituals enough to persuade the commoners, if they, themselves, don't believe in literal 'magic'. So we tell them that it's entirely real. In doing so, we also show them the power of the mind. Then, later, after they see this power, we can reveal to them its true source.

"We witches have a tradition. A tradition in favor of honesty and knowledge, and against the danger of 'magic' becoming too powerful, a power unto itself. Usually, when the oldest witch is close to death, she'll see it coming. A matter of weeks or days, usually, it seems. At that point, she'll stop all deception between her and the next witch in the line of succession. She'll tell her everything she knows, as best as she knows it, which usually means that she'll reveal how very, very little of the magic ceremonies and rituals address anything 'real', so to speak. But keep in mind, now, that the power of the mind is completely real and awesome. *Magical,* even!

"The bad news—well, OK, only a *part* of the bad news—is that you're facing an extremely steep learning curve. You've not been a witch for more than a day, yet, and you haven't even had your induction ceremony. I'm telling you everything right now. You see, last night a vision came to me. I'll not live for more than a few weeks at most."

"Beldame! No!"

"Yes. It's true. But the Life Force provides, it seems. You're here. You'll carry on. Life, and the good life of our clan, will go on. It *will* go on. It *must* go on. So you must know all that I know. Know, then, that magic is in the mind, but that it is extremely powerful. Probably the most powerful thing of all.

"Now some things lie between the worlds of the real and the unreal. Words become very slippery here, but I will try to tell you these things as best as I can. By believing in them, we make them real. We invent them, and they invent us. By the power of our minds, we create them. By their power over our minds, they become real. So then we must be utterly, *extremely* cautious as to what it is that we invent. Yet strangely, they also seem to exist even beyond just what we invent.

"On the good side, there is the Life Force. A thing that links and loves all minds. A thing that wants us to live and grow. Most of all, it wants the powers of our love and of our minds to grow, and to be devoted towards helping others to grow. It feeds upon the powers that our minds devote to helping others to grow, in a process that feeds upon itself. If we all help each other to grow, there's no telling *what* we can do. There will be no stopping us! Victory will be ours!

"On the evil side—note that 'evil' backwards is 'live', that these are opposites—there is a Dark Whisperer. It wants us to fool ourselves into depending on the literal magic of our rituals and ceremonies. It wants us to think that we needn't worry about devoting our powers of living, loving, learning, and growing, because all we have to do, is to trust in our magic. We just have to do the ceremonies and the rituals, and say the magic spells just right, and that's *all* we need to do. We needn't worry about suffering through honest learning, where we have to undergo the pain of admitting that what we *thought* we knew before, was wrong.

"We just need to perfect our literal magic, says the Dark Whisperer. There's no need to worry about developing the magic of our minds, the Whisperer says. That's too painful, too honest. And then, we're left defenseless, without any *real* power, because there's no real power in perfecting empty ceremonies.

"Then, when others try to help us, by telling us that we're crazy for thinking there's all this magic in these worthless spells and rituals, the Dark Whisperer tells us that they're attacking *us,* not our crazy ideas. It tells us we must defend ourselves against them. We shouldn't just sit down with them and think and talk, we must defend ourselves and our elaborate, almost-perfect ceremonies. All we need to do is add just a *few more* finishing touches to make the rituals perfect, and *then* they'll see!

"The Dark Whisperer tells us that our literal magic is all-powerful, yet when outsiders question our beliefs in this magic, the magic isn't powerful enough to defend itself. We must defend it with our own violence. *'Everything is all the fault of those others over there'* is Its favorite line, it seems. When we blame others, including those who say our ceremonies and spells are silly, then we needn't work on growing, and fixing our own problems. But It's not happy till we've given up *all* real power to learn and grow, and we're dead. Even then, It won't be happy. It can never be satisfied; It's thirst for death and destruction can never be quenched.

"Forgive me, Eve, if I get carried away, here, and start to sound as if I'm reciting another spell. I'm not. These are matters that other witches and I have pondered and talked over at great lengths. Now let me just throw in here that if and when your time comes for you to pick more witches to follow in your footsteps, you must be *extremely careful* in just *who*, exactly, it is that you pick. Even if you should be so lucky as to find little girls, who you can start at a young age. You will know. Just make sure that they have a feeling, deep down, low in their guts, that they want to follow the Life Force, and not the Dark Whisperer. This magic thing is a powerful thing, and it cuts both ways.

"Now the funny thing is, the Life Force and the Dark Whisperer can be understood to be just more creations of ours. We willful beings don't need that much help from outside forces, comes time to do good and bad things alike. Whisperers? Forces? Just more ideas, more ways to look at things. I strongly suspected that that's *all* that they are, for long periods of time. I really didn't *know* one way or the other.

"Then last night I learned that the Dark Whisperer is all too real. That's the rest of the bad news. I felt a great, deep, dark disturbance in the Force. But right there is the good news also! There *is* a Force, you see, because I have *felt* it! And It, too, will be with us!

"There's no room for complacency, though. The Whisperer has always been with us, in a sense, in the internal, metaphorical sense. But now, after having left our world an incomprehensibly long, long time ago, when willful life of some sort, somewhat like ours, was wiped out by this very same Whisperer, he's back again. He's here, and he's hungry. He's felt the stirrings of our awakening minds, and so It wants to push us back into the mud. Or worse! It's real, It's here, and It wants to hurt us. *Real bad.* Bad, bad news."

"So what are we going to do?" Eve inquired nervously. "Can't you just turn the Whisperer into a frog or something?"

Beldame replied quite patiently. "No, my child, I can't do that. *Real* magic is a seldom thing. I don't know *what* we'll do. We'll just take it a step at a time. Trust the Force, Eve, trust the Force. We do what we must, day by day, hour by hour. We learn, then we think, and then we ask the Force what it is that It would have us do, to help all minds to grow. And then we act. And when that time comes to act, we'll know it, and we'll not look back. We'll just *do it,* and do it *right!* Victory will be ours! Trust me! Trust the Force! We will win! The Force told me so!"

This is all just entirely too heavy for me, Eve thought. What have I gotten myself into? Is it too late to back out? Where'd they find this crazy old bat anyway? Am I going to be like her some day? Am I halfway there already? How 'bout that snake yesterday? Now just how 'bout *that,* anyway? So who's the crazy bat, here, now?

"Beldame, I've been meaning to talk to you about something else, here. You know I talked to a snake yesterday, out in the middle of the grove of musical fruit. It was *real*, I tell you, **real**. Real as you and me! I *saw* it, we *talked* together. It told me to eat of the musical fruit, because that would make me wise. Because the snake wanted my company, my friendship, as a fellow wise being. Do you suppose this snake has anything at all to do with your Dark Whisperer?"

Beldame just sat there, staring at Eve intently for a few silent moments. Then she said, "No. Thag Oog and the Medicine Men are full of turtle poop. There are no evil spirits in the groves of musical fruit. We keep that to ourselves, of course. I think the snake is our friend. She may be of help to us. She is somehow linked to the lives lost long, long ago, to the depredations of the Dark Whisperer. She will be no friend to It, when we tell her what's going on. Now let's go back to camp, to conduct a proper ceremony, for all to see. All must know that you are now a witch. Then we'll know what to do next, to oppose the Dark Whisperer. Let's go."

Beldame was right. The Horde Whisperer had returned. After sixty-five some million years of hanging around more lucrative domains, and only occasionally casting the gaze of his cosmic-karmic phase-sensitive vibes detector arrays at Earth, he was back. Sensors indicated that vulnerable intelligence was on the rise; these ape-men held forth promises of providing the Whisperer with much in the way of jolly amusements. Unlike the far more intelligent and wise cetaceans, content to frolic endlessly, frivolously, and merrily in Earth's seas, the budding bipedal sentients were damned with the triple vices of ambition, seriousness, and ideology.

The Horde Whisperer hovered far above the Earth's atmosphere. Gingerly, he cranked the gain on his remote sensors, hoping to remain concealed. Ah, yes, he thought, my long-distance surveys were right. There are indeed some novel new intelligences down there, stirring things up, prodding the ape-men towards advancement! For so long, they've remained in boring, harmless stasis. Now they awaken! Now they become Sensitive. Vulnerable. Who is upping the stakes? How are these cards stacked?

Expertly, he twiddled with his sensors, rejecting this frequency, damping that one, amplifying others. Filtering out the noise. The vibes rushed in, painting a detailed picture. Three tribes of ape-men, all with their own gods, their own rituals and beliefs, and their own mind-bending chemicals with which to talk to their gods. And—*what's this?!*—yes, two greater sentients, each one prodding on one of the three tribes! Who are they? *What* are they?!

Careful, now, contain yourself, don't reveal yourself too easily, he told himself. Let's probe some more. Blazing Beezlebubba, dude, what be goin' *down*, bro?! Check it *out!* This can't be! Yet it is! Two dinosaur minds! After all this time! How could they have survived, dormant? No? OK, I see. Highly improbable, yes. But chaos is badness! And the power of badness, as we all know, is what pleases me!

And they are lonely. Oh, so lonely! So they stir the pot, waking the dormant powers of the ape-men. Yes! This, I can use! Now let's see, what's the angle, here...

OK, so we've got the Blunt Heads. Their weed god is a mellow fellow, a benevolent sort. A peaceful people. They get high, and then all they want to do is to sit around and eat, listen to their silly, primitive music, watch the animals, and paint pictures. How quaint! How disgustingly non-destructive! There oughta be a *law* against this sort of thing, I'll tell you! And some of them are watched over by one of the newly recycled dinosaurs. Best to stay clear of all such true intelligence. After all, they say that a thinking creature is the worst enemy that I could have.

Then there's the Shroom Oogs. When they get high, there's more possibilities. They *see* things. Things that aren't there. Maybe I can get them to *see* me, and to Listen. To be *Sensitive* to me and my ways. To hear my Whispers, and to obey. Maybe. Or maybe not. But they, too, have a recycled dinosaur trying to look out for some of them. And also— wait, what's this—a wise, wise old ape-woman, a witch, wise beyond all expectation, for a low-brow, stupid ape—and *she knows I'm here!!!* Oh, no, could be trouble brewing!

All right, damage control! Deflector shields up! Cloaking devices on! Full steam ahead, Baals to the walls, all that jive! Now—Who, exactly, *is* she? What does she know, and when did she know it? Who finances her campaigns? Where are her weak spots? His tentacles snaked out, probing for data. They met silence, as if a thick brick wall had smashed down between him and his adversary. OK, be that way, then, he thought. There's more fish in the sea.

Chapter 7

Magic, Myths, and Whispers

"There are two equal and opposite errors into which our race can fall about the devils. One is to disbelieve in their existence. The other is to believe, and to feel an excessive and unhealthy interest in them. They themselves are equally pleased by both errors and hail a materialist or a magician with the same delight."
C. S. Lewis (1898-1963)

The Horde Whisperer's ethereal presence haunted the Paleolithic Earth. He flitted here and there. Ah, yes, he exclaimed to himself, here they are, with their growing powers left unguarded. The Firewater Tribe. Promising material, here. Their **BFD** God, who gives them **B**read, **F**irewater, and **D**ough, makes some of them aggressive. And since their god is such a BFD God, maybe I can get them to go on the warpath, in defense of their particular understanding of their particular god! Yes, that just might do the trick! So *clever* of me! Take their worship of their "higher power"—a concept which could give them so much *real* power, the power of the mind, and of working together, if they understood "higher power" wrong—and turn it to the *right* path, *my* path! Give the power to *Me*, the only one who really deserves it! Ah, yes! A plan that can't fail! Let's *go!*

Dough Boy, Yeast Man, Bread Pan, Beer Bellicose, and all the other, lesser lights of the Firewater Tribe were sloppily arrayed around the amphorae, roughly according to rank. But their ranks were looking a bit ragged. Yeast Man would normally have served as Master of Ceremonies, but he was too far gone. Dough Boy and Bread Pan were doing the honors that night, pouring from the earthenware amphorae into individual calabashes (dried-out bottle gourds). Harvests had been good that year, and the Firewater Tribe was paying proper homage to the BFD God. That's with heavy emphasis on the "F".

Beer Bellicose was feeling pretty miffed. Yeast Man, Big Man on campus, hadn't appointed him as one of his stand-ins during his temporary incapacitation during this, the high Holy of Holies, Smashed Calabash Bash, and Falling-Down Fall Festival. This seemed, to Beer Bellicose, to bode ill for his hoped-for eventual rise to Yeast Man's hallowed position in the Firewater Tribe's org chart.

So Beer Bellicose (they all called him B-Belli for short) watched, disgusted, as Yeast Man mumbled and sloshed about in the smashed calabashes and beer-and-barf-soaked mud, where he'd fallen down. How pathetic, he thought, that our fearless leader can't hold his beer, and has fallen into such a low state. And *look,* that fool, he seems to be wanting yet *more* beer! He dishonors the BFD God, not only by making a fool of himself, and appointing fools to act in his stead, but also by barfing up His Bounty! And then he asks for *more!* Ha! His arrogance knows no bounds!

B-Belli had hoisted a few calabashes himself by now, but he was no lightweight. No Sir! He still had his head together. So he thought, well, maybe it would be the good and honorable thing to do, here, to teach Yeast Man proper respect for the BFD God. One doesn't barf up the blessings of the BFD God, and then ask for more. It's just not done. It's not right. And to let a bad deed like this go unpunished, would, itself, be a deed most foul.

Well, let's see, here. We could make sure he remembers that when he gets sick of the BFD God's blessings, maybe the BFD God is telling him something. Something like, "Hey, weakling, you can't even hold the power I give you in Firewater. What makes you think you can properly handle the powers of being My Representative on Earth, the leader of the Tribe?" So it falls on me to make sure he remembers his lessons, that he's got to quit while the quitting is good. Make sure he remembers that he can't handle his beer, and never be such a disgrace to the Firewater Tribe again.

B-Belli forced a smile onto his face while he went up to Dough Boy to get his calabash refilled. Then he slipped into the darkness of the surrounding jungle. He homed in on a patch of belladonna, where he picked some of their glossy black berries. These, he squished into the beer, discarding the solids. Then he returned to the party. There, he generously attended to the fallen and ignored Yeast Man, giving him the beer. Yeast Man promptly spilled half of it, but managed to drink the other half. Then he asked for more. B-Belli rolled his eyes, then went to fetch more beer. The party continued.

Yeast Man had been laying off in a dark corner, barely visible from the main action center of the party, which was the filling station, where Dough Boy and Bread Pan were serving up the hoochgrog. Hoochgrog: that which is good for what ails you, if what's ailing you is that your head feels too good, and you're still managing to stand up. B-Belli strolled haphazardly around, making an unnoticed departure from his rendezvous with the fallen, neglected Yeast Man. Yeast Man may very well have been Big Man on campus, but after his over-indulgence at this particular frat party, he was pretty much regarded as less than a stimulating party partner. So no one paid him any heed at all. That is, until a little while after B-Belli casually sauntered up to the collection of amphorae and loudmouth drunkards.

B-Belli squelched his natural instinct to jump into the fray to reassert once again that he was the most raucous and rowdy of them all, as he had his calabash filled once more. Then he stepped close to the main action, and selected Sadsac Grainslinger, a suitably gopherishly ranked member of the clan, for a special mission: he was to go and deliver the fresh calabash of beer to His Eminence, our Great Leader, who you'll see right over yonder, rolling in the beer-and-barf soaked muds while calling out for more beer.

Sure enough, the partygoers noticed this transaction, and the sad state of their Leader. They laughed as they watched from the distance, as Yeast Man grabbed frantically at the proffered beer. Then B-Belli stumbled onto his best luck of all: Keg Tapper, known about campus as quite the sardonic wit, boisterously offered up yet another assignment for Sadsac Grainslinger. Sadsac was to ferry ever more beer, until such time as Yeast Man's thirst was thoroughly quenched for this evening. After all, this was the Smashed Calabash Bash, and the BFD God might be quite angry if the Chief Himself got less than his deserved bellyful. Keg Tapper proposed these motions in a clever toast. There were guffaws all about.

In the morning, Yeast Man would no doubt chew on some ears about how he felt so awful, and how no one had helped him out last night, in his hour of need. But he'd have forgotten whoever would and wouldn't have helped him during his Dionysian Bacchanalia and Barfing Fest, anyway, so what good could come out of attending to him? Besides, this wasn't the first Festival of Chiefly Overindulgence, nor would it be the last. Or, at least, so they all assumed.

Meanwhile, B-Belli thanked the BFD God that Keg Tapper had offered that witty toast, and that Sadsac Grainslinger was now quenching the Chief's thirst with repeated deliveries of brewsters. If Keg Tapper hadn't done it, B-Belli might have had to. Things were better this way. And some of Keg Tapper's humor tapped into an underlying vein of tension between Sadsac and Yeast Man. Sadsac was just one of those lowbrow ape-men who couldn't help but loudly squabble with his superiors, despite his low rank. So he'd evolved into a whipping boy of sorts for other, higher-ranking clansmen.

Sadsac would say things he'd hear others say, say them, and receive the Chief's wrath. The process of receiving said wrath would prod Sadsac's dim bulb just long enough to keep him from spilling the beans about who he'd heard say such things in the first place. No use getting beaten by the squealed-upon clansman, too. So Sadsac served as a hybrid trial balloon, litmus test, and punching bag. Anything you could say to Sadsac, that he'd not get beaten for repeating, was OK to say to the Chief's face. Anything different... well, maybe better keep it to yourself, unless you wanted to take on the Big Man.

This meant that there wasn't much love lost between Yeast Man and that dimwit, Sadsac. So there was a certain hilarity about the whole deal. Sadsac was getting back at Yeast Man by doing Yeast Man's bidding! B-Belli couldn't believe such good luck! If anyone suspected poisoning, in the morning, when Yeast Man would be even more indisposed than usual, then blame would attach itself to Sadsac, sure as beating the ceremonial drums was known to cause the Eclipse Dragon to un-eat the Sun God.

B-Belli chortled inwardly at his great fortune. Regardless of how this whole thing resolved itself, he'd come out ahead. The boss would be weakened, physically and politically, any way one looked at it. Maybe he'd even be dead. B-Belli blanched at the thought, contemplating the enormity of his unheard-of crime, if this was indeed what was going to happen. But then he calmed himself, telling himself he'd never be caught, and that even if his actions would result in such dire consequences, he could always reassure himself with the thought that he'd not meant for it to quite go *that* far. He merely meant to teach the Chief some self-restraint and dignity, for the sake of the Clan, the Firewater Tribe, and in service of the BFD God.

The party's momentum faltered slightly, but kept on moving towards it's beery, falling-down-at-the-dawn conclusion.

So far so good, the Horde Whisperer nodded in satisfaction. Now what's the haps at other current loci of vibe vortices on this cosmic wave front, he asked himself. He tweaked the knobs. The coherent wave fronts of the cosmic-karmic vibes harmonically collapsed within the confines of his phased array detector node stubs. Focal lengths of aura analysis elements contracted precisely. Even though the vibe apertures asymptotically metastabilized somewhat harshly due to the malfunctioning oil pan modulators, the new image coalesced promptly into a new pattern. The Horde Whisperer cast his gaze inquiringly.

Beldame Oog was up at the dawn, fussing about her latest and largest rendition of ceramic splendor. Eve Oog paced about, inquiring about this and that. Beldame patiently answered her questions, occasionally restraining Eve when she got too eager to help. The chatter was fairly rapid and tense, it seemed, despite Beldame's outward calm. Something big's up, it seems to me, the Horde Whisperer thought. Better watch this for a while.

"Can I help you over there? Here, how about I smooth out..."

"Watch it there, now, we have to be careful not to add too much water, here. We want to make this large, with high walls. Get the clay too wet, and it'll collapse, even if we keep the walls thick to give it extra strength. The extra weight of that thickness will bog us down. We've got to keep the clay on the dry side, to get fairly thin yet high walls. The signs of a good piece are thinner walls. This helps when firing the pieces, too, because the Ceramic God and the Fire God are angered by thick walls. Thick walls often mean there's little holes, gaps, voids, within the clay. The Fire God breaks the clay in these spots.

"Here, do it this way. Put a flat piece of wood on each side, and push. If you have to, just keep the wood a bit wet, and slide it like this. OK. Looking good."

"So why are you making this thing with sharp corners, instead of making it round on your potter's wheel?"

"We're making a very special container today, Eve. A magic container."

"What kind of magic container?"

"It's called a 'box.' It'll have four sides, a bottom, and a lid, which is a separate ceramic piece for a big top opening. The top will be a lot bigger than anything I'd normally make that's intended to be sealed at the top. Can you see how it's shaping up?"

"Sure, Beldame. I see what you mean. But why are you doing this? What kind of magic do you mean to make? Magic to mess with the power of the people's minds, or some of what you call those very, very rare cases of *real* magic?"

"Oh, make no mistake about it, Eve, this will be *real* magic. *Quite* real. *Very* real. Count on it."

Eve put down her tools. "How so? What's up?"

"Oh, the Dark Whisperer is out to do us in. We've got to take strong measures. This calls for very strong, very real magic."

At this, this Horde Whisperer's phased-array vibe detectors invisibly pricked up. What's this, he fretted. *Surely* the old crone is off her rocker! In all my billions of years, I've never seem any *real* magic, in that sense! Sure, I can mess with their minds real bad, by making them *believe* in literal magic. When they think reality is a subjective whim to be redefined at will, I can take away their real powers. I can make them help me to make what is unreal, real, by getting them to fear, irrationally. There is no *real* magic, as far as I can tell. My powers over minds, not matter, is all that I have.

So far, that's all I have, at least. But there's always the chance that I could invent some *real* magic, or steal the techniques from someone who has them. Never discount that possibility. If *real* magic ever becomes possible, it's imperative that *I*, and not my opposition, be the first to exercise it in a big way!

The Horde Whisperer's mind briefly flashed back to the last time he'd had a brief, sneaking suspicion that someone had invented *real* magic. This had been during some of those millions of years he'd spent away from the Earth, in a far-distant corner of the galaxy. The local powers, Cluster Buster and Scamgram I Am, ruled that corner of the galaxy as co-equal rulers. This was about 75 million years ago.

Cluster Buster and Scamgram I Am ruled co-equally, holding court in an adversarial but cordially balancing yin/yang kind of arrangement. Everyone lived in relative harmony; there was peace, generally. But oh, those cultural wars! Cluster Buster favored keeping the citizens clean, protected from the ravages wrought by those dastardly artists, especially the Bloody Thespians. But the Bloody Thespians fought back with their ideas, heaping travails upon Cluster Buster. Scamgram I Am was their staunch supporter.

Those millennia were filled mostly with boring, low-fireworks kinds of days, so one of the few avenues that the Horde Whisperer had to wreak any havoc at all, was in was those cultural wars on Planet Claire. So when that new Bloody Thespian with her new, radical ideas emerged on Planet Claire, and stormed her way, with her dance troupe, into the Grand Galactic Imperial Court, for a very public show, backed by Scamgram I Am but vocally denounced by Cluster Buster, the Horde Whisperer was there.

For a few nights, they put on their show. Galactic citizens great and small denounced the crass degeneracy of the show, or praised its piercingly honest portrayal of contemporary society's crude materialism and refusal to abide in higher, metaphysical realms of uplifting transrationalism. There was much gossip about how that leading Bloody Thespian, Shurely Inane, was "channeling" the spirits of many powerful deceased Bloody Thespians in her dressing room before the show. In other words, she was performing *real* magic. The Horde Whisperer discounted all these rumors at first, but he did keep a careful watch on her.

But judging by the complete uproar she and her dance troupe caused in their normally relatively staid society, the Horde Whisperer began to have second thoughts. Had Shurely Inane managed to somehow stumble on the formula for *real* magic? Watching her show, and how galactic citizens reacted to it, he had to admit that the theory couldn't be rejected out of hand. The climax of her show was when she pulled out that large, ornately decorated symbolic spleen, vented spleen dregs all over her naked body, smeared it around, and cried out in anguish about how cruel society was.

Now her society had very negative thoughts about bodily remains, and spleens were regarded as especially sacred, where the essence of one's soul resided. Yet Shurely had managed to convince a totally radical citizen to donate his spleen upon his death, and Shurely had made good use of it. Liquids from this spleen were diluted billions of times. Yet according to Shurely and her disciples, the power of those spleen dregs remained. Her followers used these liquids in many, many ceremonies. Then, of course, there was that highly incendiary climax at the end of her show.

Cluster Buster and his followers said nonsense; probabilistically, there's a next to zero chance that you or any of your followers even have a single molecule of spleen left in your liquids, and all this is completely silly. So why do you object, then, retorted Scamgram I Am and his followers, when we do these ceremonies? Cluster Buster would reply, "Because y'all are *sick*. **Sick, sick, sick,** you hear me? You're wasting time on disgusting perversity!"

But Shurely and her troupe just kept on putting on the show. The capitol, Planet Claire, and then the whole Empire got further and further up in arms. The nay-sayers and crass materialists, led by Cluster Buster, kept on bad-mouthing the show. Why won't you at least come and see it before you condemn it, the New Wave Artists would say. Because it's a perverted waste and a bad influence, they'd reply.

Shurely just kept on drenching herself in spleen dregs for the conclusion of her avant-garde show, every night. During the day, she'd attend rallies, pushing her concept of a homeopathic elixir for all that ails society. Her cure was **SPAMM** (**S**ocially **P**rogressive **A**rt for **M**obilizing the **M**asses).

Society's moral fiber couldn't long withstand this onslaught. One night, Scamgram I Am couldn't take it any longer. So he had Cluster Buster forcibly bound up, and deposited in a front-row seat for Shurley's show.

"There, Cluster Buster," Scamgram I Am announced. "You will like the Show. Come on, try it, you will like it. You will see. This is what's best for you, this I know."

"But I don't *like* spleen dregs and SPAMM, Scamgram I Am!" Cluster Buster wailed in a shriek of pure terror. "I do not like them here or there, I do not like them anywhere!"

Cluster Buster flailed helplessly against his tentacle clamps and other bindings. He went into an apoplectic rage.

"Geeze, Dude, don't have a *cow!*" Scamgram I Am protested in panic. "It's just a *show*, for Great Galactic Cluster's sake!"

But that's what he did. Cluster Buster had a cow, right there on the spot. Then he died.

But his cow grew up immediately, right then and there, in front of everyone. It became known as Zebu, the Cruel Galactic Emperor. It took vengeance for its parent's death by seizing power, and then outlawing all magic, transrationalism, spleen dregs, and SPAMM. Shurely Inane spent her last years in abject anonymity. The Horde Whisperer was never able to complete his studies of her acts, to see if she had the secret of *real* magic, or not.

Now Emperor Zebu was indeed a villainously vile, cruel tyrant. You could tell by the Nazi helmet he wore, and the large brands of cobras, knives, and skeletons emblazoned on his hide. Confirming beyond a doubt that Zebu was an inappropriate sort of a fella, one could also observe that he had neither steely eyes nor a square jaw. And those *brands!* Talk had it that he'd had those blazing branding irons thrust onto his hide without any painkillers whatsoever, without flinching. So everyone said that Zebu was the toughest, roughest bull around.

And it was true. Without mercy, Zebu severely chastised anyone who *dared* to talk of Socially Progressive Art for Mobilizing the Masses, or any related concepts. All such matters were now considered to be sacred, since these were what had brought about the birth of the sacred **CCHOWDERHEAD** (**C**hief **C**ow and **H**oly **O**ne; **W**ith the **D**uty to **E**nforce **R**ationalism, **H**ead the **E**mpire, and **A**dvance **D**emocracy), blessed be His Name. And we all know that matters which are sacred, dare *not* be discussed, lest they be questioned. Zebu managed to drag a lot of things into the realm of The Sacred, and so He prohibited any discussion or flexibility on a lot of matters, not just art. Society froze into stasis, especially for lack of avant-garde artists to point the way.

Zebu's ideas about democracy were roughly as follows; 1) Make as many things as possible as sacred as possible, so that the people will be cleansed of their unclean thoughts. Everyone will then go around being Sacred all day, and they'll all agree with Me. 2) Without remorse, viciously assassinate the character of anyone who is unclean, who disagrees with Me. Hire private detectives to ferret out or create some dirt about them, and broadcast it on all cosmic-karmic aura channels, especially during prime time. 3) If all else fails, sue and harass the unclean ones into silence. 4) Do all of the above well and faithfully, in the Name of CCHOWDERHEAD, blessed be His Name, and all the other, minor things, like mandates from the voters, will follow.

His people were a deeply pious folk, so Zebu's grip on power was unquestioned. All his followers, being meek and mild, never once even *thought* of resisting Zebu's will. So he mooed his terrible moo, stomped his terrible hooves, and chewed his terrible cud, and sent the mild things off to bed without any supper, and they were all sorely afraid. They whispered in the dark, saying, *surely* this must be the cruelest Galactic Emperor of them all!

But the Cruel Galactic Emperor Zebu was cruelest of all to the Horde Whisperer. The Whisperer endured frightful powerlessness and boredom, since all belief in any power but Zebu and Zebuism was roughly squashed. He had to content himself with tempting Zebu into giving some of his powers to him, but the Horde Whisperer couldn't seem to wrest anything of significance away from Zebu.

Zebu may have been a cruel, intolerant, insensitive, and sometimes even a shockingly inappropriate despot, but He wasn't a truly *evil* cow. He was, after all, Zebu, the *Holy* Cow. He realized that if He listened to the Whisperer, said Whisperer would be leeching His, Zebu's, powers away from Him. Zebu loved His power too much to share it more than He had to, in order to keep it. And sharing power with the Horde Whisperer seemed to Zebu to be a very irrational thing to do. So the Horde Whisperer had tolerated this boredom for ten million years, as Zebu locked all the action into stasis.

Then there'd been that little K-T mass extinction party at Earth. After that, the Horde Whisperer had gone straight back to nipping at Zebu's thoughts, with occasional side trips to see if he could seduce any Zorgons into listening to his Whispers. Still no luck. Then one day, ten million years later, a wandering tribe of barbaric nomads stumbled into the palace on Planet Claire. Not knowing any better, all they saw was a placid cow, chewing its cud.

Being insensitive, under-developed hicks from the hinterlands, they were totally deaf to the cosmic-karmic vibes with which Zebu severely admonished them as they carved Him up and made Him into steak tartare, beef jerky, and liver-and-marrow burgers. No one even thought of answering Zebu's loud cosmic-karmic cries for help, for His society had been in stasis for so long that no one knew what a physically violent emergency was, any more, or how to react to one. And Zebu was but the first of many sacred cows brutally butchered. So stasis collapsed, and business picked up for the Horde Whisperer for quite a while again. Only now, fifty-five million years after Cruel Galactic Emperor Zebu's cruel demise, were things getting back to boring.

ZEBU HERO OF THE WORKING COW!!
ALL HAIL ZEBU
HOLIEST OF HOLY COWS!
HERO

But now, all these millions of years later, here he was, watching Earth, and some new and exciting developments in this former backwater. Could this low-brow ape-woman witch, Beldame Oog, have concocted some *real* magic? What was she *up* to, anyway? He wrestled with the controls, refocusing the vibe vortex induction synthesizer. The thermoelectric diffusion injector gasket sprung a tiny leak, and the rear-view mirror synchronizer acted up quite a bit, but overall systems performance was still within acceptable norms.

"Well, Eve, I do believe it's looking good, if I must say so myself," Beldame concluded. "Now let's take a break, and let it dry a bit, before I carve the Magic Symbols into all the outside surfaces. Can't go carving on it when it's still too wet. Break time."

They retreated from the morning sun's budding heat into a tree's shade, and chatted. "So what's the deal, here, Beldame? I'm your apprentice, and you say you don't have long to live. You say you have to tell me everything now. Well, I'm listening. Why don't you go ahead and explain all the details about this 'real magic' we're making here right now?"

"OK, Eve, I'll do that. What we're going to do, in detail, and why. On our level, and on the commoners' level. They have their truth, which we work with, and then we have our higher truth. The day will come when all knowledge will be accessible by everyone, but for now we have to work with what we've got.

"What we're doing is carving magic symbols all over this box and its lid. I'll have to do almost all of that myself; you'll be able to help only a tiny bit. Then we'll fire it. While it's firing, we'll make a little trip to the musical fruit grove, and see if your friend the snake is still there. If she is, we'll explain our situation, and why we need her help. I'll bet she'll be glad to assist us.

"After the box is fired, we'll have a big ceremony. We'll take the whole clan, along with the box, to the musical fruit grove. There, I'll explain to them that we're being attacked by the evil spirits of the musical fruits, and that the way to fight back is to gather up all the fart blossoms, and put them in the box. By picking all the blossoms now, you see, there won't be any fruit later. At least, not at this particular grove. They won't worry much about other groves, because they'll be all wrapped up with this strange new magic I'll be showing them.

"Yes, I know what you're going to say. You think no one will go into the grove at all, for fear of all those evil spirits. They'll believe that they can't go in there to pick the fart blossoms, because they fear they'll accidentally touch a fruit, and then they'll die. Well, you're wrong. I'll explain to them that we're under dire threat from the evil spirits, as shown by what happened with you and the snake in the grove the other day, and our only hope is to take strong measures, and fight back. I'll explain that if they let me do my special magic to them first, then they can go in there, pick the fart blossoms, and even live through it easily if they accidentally touch a fruit now and then.

"They'll be scared at first, sure. But then they'll see you and me picking the fart blossoms, without any problems. And then the snake will come out and join us in our task! Everyone will be really impressed with what we witches have wrought, and then they'll pitch in to help. Their spirits will be much strengthened when they see that they can touch the dread musical fruits now and then, and live to tell the tale. So one of the small side benefits of this whole deal will be that we'll move closer to the day that we can actually get everyone to *eat* of the musical fruit, get more proteins in our diet, and move towards a rational age. All will have access to knowledge, and all will act out of reason and love.

"That's how we'll handle the commoners, and that's how they'll understand this whole exercise. But you and I, and hopefully the snake, we'll be operating on a different level. We know what this is *really* about. It's about putting together an extremely powerful talisman; one that'll overpower the Dark Whisperer. When he sees the awesome power inherent in this thing we're making, he'll flee in fear. He'll have no choice but to leave us all alone."

"But Beldame, how will this talisman work? Isn't this just another piece of pottery we're making, and won't all those fart blossoms be just another bunch of tiny flowers? How can there be *real* magic here? Are you sure this isn't just another case of messing with the powers of the mind? How can you get *real* power out of some pottery and a bunch of flowers?"

"Oh, we're onto some real power here, my dear. Trust me. What it is, is that eventually, we'll go back to a high-protein diet, largely from the benefits of fruits like these now-forbidden musical fruits. We will become far more wise and powerful, and begin to respect all knowledge, and to act out of knowledge and reason. The fart blossoms are both symbols and embryonic substance of these dormant but budding powers of ours. When we gather many, many of them together, their vibes will reinforce each other, and create a very subtle but immensely powerful vibe vortex."

"OK, if you say so. But what about these special magical symbols you said you'd carve onto this 'box' thing?"

"Oh, I'll show you in just a few minutes. What we'll do, is we'll call on the magic of the future of the human mind. See, our descendants will be known as fully human, 'Homo Sapiens,' wise men. The box will be decorated with symbols of the future, in a time when the powers of men's and women's minds will be channeled into large, powerful organizations. These large organizations will be ordered in such a way as to fully unleash the potential of many, many human minds, and the results will simply be quite awesome. So the combination of the fart blossoms, as symbols and substance of our budding powers, and these symbols of our future, carved into solid ceramics, will create some incredibly powerful magic."

The Horde Whisperer watched, taking it all in with growing apprehension. What if—OK, the old hag is crazy, but just *what if*—she happened to be talking about *real* magic. He tried to probe her mind yet once again, only to be coldly, forcefully shut out. Well, I'll just have to keep a close eye on all this, he thought. He watched as Beldame and Eve lounged about for a few more minutes, and then got back to work.

Beldame carved away at the clay very rapidly. By now, a few members of the clan had started to drop by. They, and Eve, questioned her as to what, exactly, all those symbols were, but she "shushed" them all, saying that she'd explain it all as soon as she was done. Finally, she pulled back, adoring her creation. There were boxes, circles, arrows, labels, and symbols all over the box and lid. "Explain-explain-explain," demanded many voices.

"All right," she relented. "I'll explain. These represent the future of the powers of many of our descendants' minds, all working together in harmony. Sort of. These will help us to scare away the evil spirits in the musical fruit grove. OK. Examples. This little box says 'Quality.' And this one says 'Teamwork.' This circle says 'ISO 9000.' And this one says 'Dullbert.' Then this arrow over here is labeled 'Form BR549, Authorization Requisition and Design Guide for Synthesizing New and Improved Forms.' And here we have 'Focus on Proactive Employee Empowerment.' And here we have the various org charts and Gantt charts and pie graphs. Then this big box over here says 'Leveraging the Synergies of Global Marketing's Quality Paradigm and the Mission Statement of the Interdisciplinary Cross-functional Technology Strategy Enhancement Team.' Y'all understand, now? Any questions?"

There were no questions. All of them, including Eve, just shook their heads, thinking, geeze-um, this witching business is way over *our* heads. We'll just trust Beldame, they all seemed to agree.

Surely this old witch has been sneaking way too many mushrooms on the side, the Horde Whisperer concluded disgustedly. But he failed to convince himself completely. After all, he might possibly find himself with a severe handicap, if someone stumbled onto *real* magic before he did. Especially if said someone was opposed to him and his worthy causes. So he couldn't resist trying to sneak a look into Beldame's mind yet again. Her psychic barriers withstood his onslaught, same as before.

He retreated, thinking, well, no great loss. So I can't read the contents of some stupid old ape-woman's mind. Big deal. Just a bunch of silly trash in there, anyway. I must confess, though, it's amazing how she sustains that kind of energy, keeping her shields up that way. So now they're just sitting around, chewing the fat, watching the jungle grow and the clay dry. Let's blow on outta here.

The Horde Whisperer eyed the gauges, shifted gears, recalibrated his vibe vector overshoot dampers, and inserted the lockout bypass modules into his secure aura translation transducer. All systems performed normally, and his new link sprang to life. Ah, that's more like it, he crowed.

B-Belli stood towards the rear of the crowd, as the clan paid final respects to their fallen former leader. They'd dug a large hole in their best grain field and conducted the proper ceremonies, led by none other than B-Belli himself. With just a few well chosen and emphatically delivered words to the wise, he'd become the new acting Chief. He'd finish consolidating his power after a proper period of mourning.

The Horde Whisperer concentrated intensely on his tasks for a few days, and all sorts of thoughts churned through B-Belli's mind. The Shroom Oogs and the Blunt Heads had been ripping the Firewater Tribe off, he thought. Despite the fact that they'd given out much bread from their bumper crop this year, they'd not gotten much more than the usual, in terms of pottery and wooden implements from the Shroom Oogs, magic and furs from the Blunt Heads, and so on. Obviously, they were intent on disrespecting the BFD God and His Bounty. Come to think of it, those morons with their silly false gods should worship the BFD God the way *we* do, and give up their immoral, sinful ways.

But what about the Shroom Oogs and their Fire God, B-Belli mused. Aren't the Shroom Oogs, themselves, gods? Since the Fire God gives them very special powers? Some very obviously *real* powers? Well, just wait a minute, though. Maybe fire hasn't got much to do with the Fire God. I'll bet we, with the help of the BFD God, could handle this big "fire" deal. What's so special about it, anyway? Take fire from the Shroom Oogs, and put it to our own use, ourselves. Surely, properly done, this would only increase the glory of the BFD God!

So B-Belli became determined to violate the taboos, and transgress into the provinces of the Shroom Oogs. He'd steal fire from these so-called "gods", and the Firewater Tribe would put the fire into firewater for themselves. No more submitting to the insults of those BFD-God-disrespecting fools!

The Horde Whisperer was pleased. He truncated the vibe vector parsing routines, and reinitialized, dedicating all hyperbolically tangential cosmic energies available to him into the maw of his latest, most high-tech Cosmic Vibomatic Vibatron™. The yaw dampening embedded circuitry within the synchronicity self-actualizer overloaded. Bias currents within the current-limiting FETs punched through the gate to source barrier, spewing red-hot sparks all over the radiator hoses, causing one to spring a leak. In a cascade of events, ethylene glycol contaminated the auxiliary vibe vortex generator, blowing several banks of fuses, which in turn caused the cosmic wave front aperture to go into electrosomatic shock. Only with immediate and astute corrective action did the Horde Whisperer forestall systems lockup, thereby saving himself several days of work in rebooting and reconstructing lost files.

"Oh, sugar-peas!" the Horde Whisperer exclaimed in anger. "This Cosmic Vibomatic Vibatron™ is a golly-gee shuck-darned piece of unacceptably substandard workmanship!" But then he calmed back down, and got to the business at hand. The image formed once more, even though phase jitter cut down resolution a wee bit.

Beldame and Eve Oog were plucking fart blossoms, before the astounded eyes of half of the clan. Then Shoshoni slithered out of the bushes, joining them. They calmly continued gathering blossoms, as the snake bit off the tiny flowers. The other members of the tribe exclaimed their great amazement as Shoshoni dropped clumps of flowers into Eve's hands, for her to place them into the box. Pandemonium ensued as the spectators consulted one another as to whether they were all seeing the same thing. Then there was discussion about whether they'd all had too many mushrooms, cumulatively, and had all "gone 'round the bend."

Eve and Beldame calmly continued picking fart blossoms during all this time. When the spectators finally calmed down, Beldame called out to them, asking that they come and join the effort. They refused. Their fear was too great. So Beldame abandoned Eve and Shoshoni to the work, and went to talk to the troops. After a long, long talk, she persuaded a few brave souls to join their effort. Sure enough, these few brave souls soon jubilantly exclaimed their great powers in defying deep, dark forces and their fears of these deep, dark forces. It wasn't long before the half of the clan that was in attendance was all out in the grove, picking fart blossoms.

The Horde Whisperer just watched in rapt fascination. The few passes he made at probing Beldame's mind, now, any more, were quite half-hearted. But everyone else's minds were open to his inspections. And the clan's minds were full of how they were forcefully fighting off the evil spirits that dwelled there in that large grove of musical fruit trees, by making powerful magic.

Shoshoni's and Eve's minds, too, were full of magic, on a different level. By doing what they were doing, they were getting the tribe used to the idea that they could mess with musical fruit trees, and not die. This was just one step towards unleashing the *real* power of human minds and high-protein diets. And then, of course, there was the literal magic of combining the symbols and substances of these keys to human advancement, embodied there in that slowly filling, magically decorated box of fart blossoms. What, exactly, was Beldame up to, anyway? All in all, it filled the Horde Whisperer with a sense of dread and foreboding.

Periodically, Eve would step into the box, and trample the blossoms down, making more room. There were many, many blossoms in that large grove, and Beldame vowed that every last one of them would go into the box. But the box had a lot of room. Work continued till daylight gave out, and dusk called all efforts to an end. Shoshoni was left alone to guard the box overnight, as the excited and zealous clansmen and women returned to camp.

By now, the Horde Whisperer was quite anxious. He focused all his cosmic-karmic energies on trying to do physical harm to the blossoms, or to the box. If his opposition was to be allowed to do *real* magic, then he, too, should be allowed such activities, he decided. Box, break! he mentally commanded. Nothing. Wind, blow, he decreed, but the breezes barely tugged at the lid, let alone got even close to carrying the blossoms away. Blossoms, burn! he psychically shouted. As best as he could tell, the vegetable matter got only slightly warmer than its surroundings. This gave him some solace, since he'd never studied the phenomena of exothermic chemical reactions causing self-heating and even spontaneous combustion in large piles of freshly cut vegetation.

So he stayed there all night, raising the temperature of the blossoms ever so slightly, more and more, all night. Just a wee bit more effort, here, he told himself, and this whole mess will break out in flame! Then in the morning, the whole tribe showed up! When they lifted the lid to put more blossoms into the box, the excess heat escaped, unnoticed by all but the Horde Whisperer.

He spent that whole day trying to scare them away, with thoughts of great fear and foreboding. Calling up these particular moods wasn't too difficult for him. Beldame, however, did an excellent job of convincing her troops that fear, itself, was the enemy, and had been sent by the evil spirits, to dissuade them from completing their noble and vitally essential task. Still, the Whisperer couldn't tear himself away.

That night the clan made a temporary camp at the grove, and excited and inquisitive juveniles (and the occasional adult) couldn't resist lifting the lid periodically for a peek at the budding magic within. By now, the warmth of the exothermic reactions could be felt at the outside of the bottom of the box. Beldame explained that this was the result of the anger of the grove's evil spirits, who were quite frustrated that none of these blossoms would ever become musical fruits.

The Horde Whisperer was, indeed, frustrated and angry. Mostly, he was angry about the fact that as soon as he managed to build up the heat in that box, some fool would lift the lid for another peek, and heated air would escape. He was still far, far from being able to burn up Beldame's talisman. Finally, he gave it up. For the time being, at least.

Crossing his fingers, he consulted his checklist, then implemented precautionary action items proactively, and punched the buttons on his phased-array aura analyzer's remote-controlled channel-changer. Amazingly enough, all systems performed without anomalies.

The clansmen of the Firewater Tribe were dancing around their fires, celebrating how their brave new leader, B-Belli, had stolen fire from the gods. But they weren't all wasting their time in celebrations. In the light of one fire, away from the main action, the Whisperer could see that other seeds he'd planted were now taking root. B-Belli was encouraging Dough Boy as he experimented with mounting a spear-head onto a shaft. They'd found several spear-heads over the space of many years of digging in their fields, and had kept them as curiosities, not realizing their ancient origins or purposes.

But now they knew what they were for, and they were intent on reviving the ancient sports and arts of hunting. Keg Tapper, too, sat there with B-Belli and Dough Boy. He was teaching himself the art of fashioning new spear points from raw, natural rocks. B-Belli coached both of his disciples eagerly.

Fine job, good work, the Horde Whisperer nodded approvingly. Well, big deal, so far, really. But just wait till what comes next! As soon as they learn (or relearn) the fine arts of big-game hunting, we'll move on to the *next* step, which is where the *real* fun comes in! We'll see if they can't also do a good job at *infidel*-hunting!

Just then, the Horde Whisperer realized he'd been neglecting his personal hygiene. His perm was frazzled, but his nails were far worse: they were nothing short of atrocious! So he thought matters over, and concluded that all was roughly on course on Earth for a little while. The Firewater Tribe was well on its way towards Whisperer Wisdom. Beldame's crew of fart-blossom pickers were still several days from completing their task of picking every blossom in the grove. So he could relieve himself of the concerns of this world for a little while. Time was ripe for attending to more personal matters.

He fled the Earth and its hick backwaters for a few days, to seek more civilized sectors of the galaxy, wherein he might procure a first-class perm and manicure for himself and his nine-inch nails. Never hurts to pamper oneself, he thought. Heck, if my nails get to short or too tattered, other spirits might regard me as low class—even as one who is so low that I've got to work with my hands!

Oh, and while I'm out and about, I'd better get the shop to take a good, long, hard look at this Cosmic Vibomatic Vibatron™. I think it's still under warranty. After all, its still got less than thirty thousand gigavibes on it.

So the Earth was left without the Whisperer, to run on autopilot for a little while. Beldame noticed, but other than relaxing her psychic guard a bit, she never missed a beat. The blossom gatherers still gathered fart blossoms, full speed ahead. And B-Belli and his gang blazed full speed ahead also.

Meanwhile, one night Aquila, in one of his exploratory flights, flew within the range of the smoke from B-Belli's campfires. Thinking it must be a previously-unknown Shroom Oog camp, he flew up to investigate. He was totally astounded to find B-Belli and his clansmen sitting around campfires, feasting on freshly roasted boar, and clad in luxurious bearskins!

Aquila perched in a nearby treetop, pondering matters. Well, well, well, what have we here, now!? Obviously, some big changes taking place! How? Why? Well, never mind. What's in this for me? Or for my buddies, the Blunt Heads Tribe? Yeah, now we're thinking! If Panama Red won't steal fire from the gods, maybe I can convince him to steal it from those who stole it from the gods! Get these Blunt Heads on the road to advancement, and more efficient methods of getting into my favored state of mind!

So he flew off and summoned Panama Red that very same morning. Sure enough, Panama Red was amenable to his line of persuasion. Aquila flew scouting missions for Panama, and told him exactly when and where to go, to sneak into the camp and steal fire undetected. He snuck in while the entire clan had traveled down the trail a bit, in order to give a hero's welcome to Dough Boy, who was dragging a freshly killed tapir home.

Panama savored his few minutes alone, sneaking around the empty camp. He scooped the red-hot coals into the ceramic pot normally used for roaches and wrapped it in insulating leaves, as instructed. He was ready to begin his long journey home, when he noticed the amphorae off to the side. I'll bet that's where they keep their sacred firewater, he thought.

While I'm here, why not sample the wares? He took a tentative sip. Yuck! he thought, spitting it out. But then the flavor sunk in, and he persuaded himself to drink deeply. Well, I'm not sure if I like it or not, he thought. Burp! Maybe it's not so bad after all. But I hear them returning! Best to boogie on outta here before they catch me. Maybe just grab this full amphora, here, and decide later, at my leisure.

His beer buzz settled in a bit during his long walk home, and he decided he liked it. But he refrained from drinking any more on the way home, realizing that he'd have to be in top form when he got there, explaining how he'd gotten fire, and how taboos were going to need to be violated. Not wishing to violate too many taboos at once, he stashed the amphora in the bushes not far from home, then strolled into camp with the leaf-wrapped ceramic pot full of hot coals.

As instructed by Aquila, he promptly gathered up dry grasses, twigs, and small logs. He spilled the coals onto a heap of dry grasses, blew the fire to life, then heaped twigs and logs on top of it. A small crowd of lower-ranking members of the clan had gathered by now. Bud Roach and Head Rush came running over in a panic. "And just what, exactly, do you think *you're* doing?" Head Rush demanded. "Have you gone off and stolen fire from the Shroom Oogs? Do you know what the punishment is, for stealing fire from the gods?"

"Oh, no, Sir, *I* haven't stolen fire from the gods! It was the Firewater Tribe! *They've* stolen it! They've got big fires going, and they're killing, roasting, and eating the wild animal spirits as we speak! And you know what?! *They're not being punished!* Not one bit! They're having big meat feasts, right now! I'll tell you, the times, they are a changin'! And if we don't change with them, we'll get left way behind! Now's the time! Sir, with all due respect, we've *got* to get *with* it!"

Head Rush paused. Other than the crackling of the flames, there was silence. "And this 'getting with it' that you speak of—it means stealing fire from the Firewater Tribe, then? Since they've stolen it from the Shroom Oogs, then it's OK for you to steal it from them?"

"But Sir, they'll never even miss those few fragments of burning wood that I took from them! Fire is cheap! All it takes is the heat of the burning from an older fire, and dry, dead wood or grass! You see how much dead wood and grass there is all around us. Even though, yes, the wood *does* belong to the Shroom Oogs, they'll never miss it if we use just a little bit of it for ourselves, to help keep us warm at night! See? *Feel* this! It'll keep us toasty warm, more so than a whole *heap* of blankets!"

"Stealing is stealing, Panama," Head Rush pronounced with seemingly great regret. "And taboos are taboos. Wood and fire belong to the Shroom Oogs. You'll have to be punished, to ward off the righteous anger of the Shroom Oogs. I'm sorry, but that's just the way things are. You should've known better."

"Sir, that's ridiculous! What I've done is nothing, compared to what B-Belli and his clan are doing! And they suffer no punishment! None whatsoever! Zero, zilch, nix! You doubt me? Come with me, and I'll *show* you! OK?"

"Oh, we *believe* you, no problem there," Head Rush replied. "It's just that wrong is wrong, no matter how many people do it. And stealing is wrong! Wrong, wrong, wrong, you got that?!"

"What's to steal?! There's all the dead wood and grass all around us here that anyone could want, and *then* some!"

"I wouldn't suppose that the words 'global warming', 'fine particles pollution', 'deforestation', and 'erosion' mean anything at all to you?" Head Rush said in a this-is-gonna-hurt-me-more-than-it's-gonna-hurt-you tone of voice.

Panama Red replied with a snappy comeback. "And I don't suppose that 'Incredible buzz from the Weed God' means anything to you, either?"

"And just what do you mean by *that*, you impertinent young twit?!?!" Head Rush thundered. One could discuss most anything with him, in an at least somewhat reasonable tone, but when challenged on the finer points of theology, Head Rush couldn't conceive of himself in the role of second best.

"Bring me a roach joined, and you'll see. As a matter of fact, skip the roach. Just bring me rolled-up weeds, minus the roach, and I'll show you a thing or two."

All the Blunt Heads were too astounded to do anything other than what Panama suggested. They hastened to bring him the weed. How could this cocky young snot talk to Head Rush in such a manner? He'd better have some awfully strong magic up his sleeves, or there'd be quite a price to pay!

Panama pulled a burning branch from the fire, applied it to the end of the rolled-up wad of weed, and sucked deeply. Then he passed it to Head Rush. Astounded, Head Rush followed his example. Panama, still holding his breath, motioned to Head Rush to pass it on. And so he did. And so the whole tribe did. Blunt Head see, Blunt Head do. "Whadda rush!" they finally exclaimed in collective amazement. "Let's crank the drums up and order some pizza!"

A wild party was had by all. Panama smirked inwardly in triumph, resisting the urge to crow. Everyone was happy, and that's all that mattered. Who was right and who had been wrong? That was all academic now. This was Party Time, and the Weed God was being appeased as never before! Remotely, Panama sensed that Aquila, perched low in the branches overhead, was immensely enjoying it all, too.

Panama sensed correctly. Aquila was soaking luxuriantly in all those groovy vibes, and inhaling the stray smoke. This is like—um, this is like—oh, heck, I don't know, Aquila concluded. It's like hanging out and sunning myself on a cool, clear autumn day after having eaten my fill of slightly rotten fish flesh and fish guts, in just the right balance, and having scrogged a gorgeous babe. In the old days, before I judged all the babes to be incredibly dim-witted, and beneath my station in life.

But then Panama remembered the amphora of beer he'd left stashed out in the bushes. Wanting to top off this best party of all time with yet another buzz, he headed off into the woods. Aquila sensed the meaning of his vibes. Now Aquila was feeling quite fine, himself, by now, but he still had his wits about him. Aquila cared for Panama's well-being. He perceived danger for Panama, so he followed Panama out to Panama's beer stash in the bushes.

Panama floundered about it the dark, then found his stash. He pulled the plug and drank. Then he drank some more. Aquila watched, apprehension growing. Doesn't Panama know about hangovers, Aquila wondered. Doesn't he know about the physiologically addictive nature of alcohol, lethal overdoses, and delirium tremens? No, he's used to the relative benevolence of his Weed God, Aquila reminded himself. Heck, he doesn't even know about cirrhosis of the liver, I'll bet! Perhaps I'd better set him straight!

But... well, just how *does* one go about informing an uninformed barbarian, anyway? I can't very well go into all the biopsychoneurovibophysiomedical details of substance abuse with this oaf, now, can I?

Well, maybe I'd best just try to project these concepts in mental imagery, Aquila concluded. So he flew down to a branch right smack above Panama's head, and prepared to crank up the vibes.

Then he choked. Addiction? Delirium tremens? Overdosing? Cirrhosis? What to project to Panama? How? In his present intoxicated state, what's going to get through to him, anyway? OK, let's just pick something. Cirrhosis, then. Let's compare it to... OK, here we go. It's like intense, chronic pain in your shrunken, hardened liver.

It's like being chained to the rocks, and having the vultures come by once a day, nibbling on your liver. Got that? Come *on,* you stoned dimwit! Vultures chewing on your liver! *OK?!* That's what you'll get for drinking the firewater you stole from those who stole fire from the gods! Now *concentrate* on this, you fool! Aquila poured all his energies into his cosmic-karmic vibes generators, broadcasting on all channels. Panama finally, dimly received the message, although he mangled it considerably before passing it on to others later when he was in a more sober state of mind.

Panama regarded this stoned experience of his, listening to the harsh admonitions and allegorical vibes from Aquila, as a seminal development in his spiritual awakening, so he repeated the story many, many times in later life. And because he regarded himself from that point forward as having become completely reformed, he took a new name for himself, that being Prometheus.

Shortly after Panama/Prometheus's special experience, the Horde Whisperer returned to Earth. The vibatronics repair shop had been swamped, so he was running a bit later than expected. The first thing he did was to attempt to get a navigational fix on Beldame's vibe vortices. But unexpectedly strong transverse orthorhombic psychonuclear forces overwhelmed his gyroscopically rectified aura transducer anodes, tearing down the PNP junctions in the impact force sensors in his airbag. Regulatory agencies had neglected to allow the Cosmic Vibomatic Vibatron™'s manufacturer to tie a simple vibe-rate transducer into the airbag's trigger logic, so the airbag deployed, despite the fact that the Horde Whisperer was scanning at well under the danger threshold of ten to the twenty-third megavibes per femptofeeling.

When the airbag deployed, it sent forceful shock waves reverberating about the Horde Whisperer's cockpit. He had his seat belt on, and was sitting back, so he, personally, wasn't much traumatized. But the shock waves knocked the tritronatronatron's* translation look-aside cache buffers into temporal dislocation, spewing non-indexed data into indeterminately aliased memory addresses. Read/write heads slammed into servo stops, and wildly over-amplified vibe fronts overwhelmed the automatic gain circuits like a tsunami washing huts off of a small, low-lying island.

Holy frijoles, the Horde Whisperer exclaimed to himself, frantically flailing at the controls. This gol-darned thing has gone *way* outside of the control limits at three sigma! This process is out of control! In fact, I'll bet it's not even ISO 666,000 compliant! Dang stupid incompetents at that lousy shop! I go to a certified vibatronics repair shop, and what do I get?! Certified junk! It's just about impossible to get good help these days!

After he cleared the smoke by invoking his NOSMOKE.BAT batch file, the Horde Whisperer found himself stuck with severely crippled systems. No matter how often he readjusted his **VCO**s (**V**ibe-**C**ontrolled **O**scillators), the picture just wouldn't straighten out. He dug out his oldest, simplest, and most primitive viboscope, and even it ended up not wanting to work quite right. So he ended up "fixing" it, if we can be so generous as to use this word here, by slapping some Propoxy™ ethereal epoxy putty on it, here and there. Oh, no, he thought, looking through his newly repaired viboscope, reality has become Propoxified!

But he soon forced himself to tolerate the fuzzy, partially obstructed view. Then he resumed spying on Beldame, starting to wonder if maybe she had something to do with his technological bad luck streak lately. Let's see, what is she doing now. Looks like I'm just in time! They're bringing the last few fart blossoms in now. There's just barely enough room in the box for them, and that's despite the fact that they've stomped them in there as tight as tight can be.

And what's *this?!* It sure seems that the blossoms are putting out quite a bit of heat, even though I've not been here at all! So has this been

---

* No, this particular tritronatronatron was *NOT* of the same sort as those manufactured in Stanstanistan. Stanstanistan didn't even *exist* till 33,000 years later. This particular brand of tritronatronatron was manufactured intergalactically by **EVIL** (**E**thereal **V**ibatronic **I**nstruments, **L**imited).

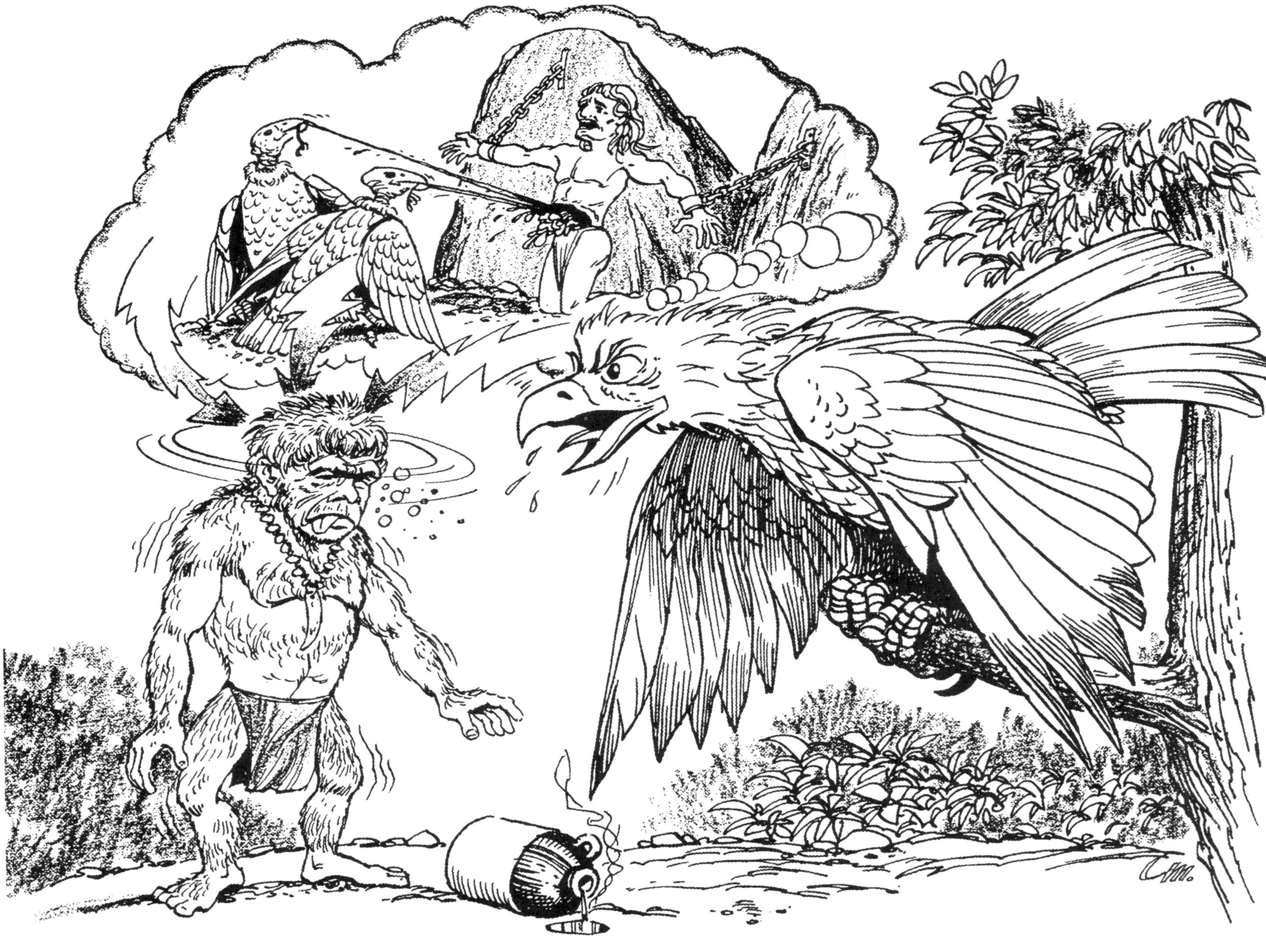

Beldame's magic all along, then, instead of mine?! Might be trouble! And just what, exactly, is that old hag doing now, anyway? It seems she's messing with some mud, with some tiny bright specks in it, and she's—she's—well, what in tarnation *is* she doing, anyway?

The Horde Whisperer grew increasingly frustrated with the limitations of his quite low-tech viboscope and its blurred, partially Propoxified view. So he thought, it's time to be bold. Stop sitting here all bottled up in my high-tech womb, behind my vibotronic shields, being a nowhere man, and playing with my nowhere gland, and break the paradigms. Get down there, in my own personal if still ethereal form, and get my hands dirty, so to speak, even if I *do* break my nails. Desperate situations require desperate methods. And this is definitely an emergency! I absolutely *must* find out whether Beldame has beaten me to the punch, and has managed to cook up some *real* magic!

So the Horde Whisperer abandoned his technological accouterments and personally appeared on scene. Only Beldame noticed. He glanced at her mud, dismissed it as harmless, and dived into the box of fart blossoms, right before Eve threw the last handful of blossoms on top of the pile. Beldame stood up, grabbed the ornate lid, and quickly but gently sealed the box. Then, in a matter of seconds, she smeared the mud around the seal. A great sigh of relief escaped from her, and an ecstatic grin brightened her old, withered face. Then she literally jumped up and leaped for joy!

Beldame and Eve led their whole Shroom Oog clan in a frenzied celebration of their victory, while the Horde Whisperer discovered his defeat and imprisonment. After a whole day of feasting and celebrating, Eve finally managed to pull Beldame aside for a private conversation.

"So what's the deal, here?" Eve inquired. "I can see how this has helped unify the clan, and how we've at least gotten them over their silly fear of the musical fruit grove. But where's this *real* magic you've been speaking of? Other than how this box has been heating up, I see nothing! So has all the magic just been in the minds of our clan, then?"

"Thanks, Eve, for reminding me about that heat. Yes, the box has been getting awfully hot, lately. Even more so, now that we've put the lid on it. It might get hot enough to crack, and we sure don't want that! Let's continue this discussion later, and do something about that heat."

Beldame and Eve recruited some brawny bodies. They pushed the hot box very carefully onto some stout small logs. Then they gently hoisted it up, and carried it to a nearby stream, where they partially submerged it in cool flowing water. Beldame and Eve were shortly left alone again there by the stream, as their assistants returned to the party.

"So where's this *real* magic, then?" Eve resumed pecking at Beldame. "Just the fact that the box is hot? Surely that can't really be the anger of the defeated spirits of the musical fruit grove, as you've told the commoners! So is this heat all there is to this real magic?"

"No, Eve, the heat isn't magic at all, any more than our fires are. They're both just ordinary exothermic chemical reactions."

"Then where's the magic?"

"In our minds, and in the minds of our opponent, as usual."

"Is there any *real* magic here, at all, then?"

"No, Eve, I'm truly sorry, but I've had to deceive you—and your friend Shoshoni with you—one last time. The contents of your minds were an integral part of our magic, the same as the contents of the minds of the commoners. Yes, we're on a different level. But the magic is in our minds, the same as is true for the commoners."

"Then there's nothing of any real, material significance in that box, and we could open it right back up, without any real impact to anyone, other than what it would do to their minds, if they knew that that's what we had done?"

"No, that's not quite right. There *is* something immaterial sealed up in there, but it's impact on minds can be very, very real. That is true, regardless of whether they know we've set it free, or not. So it mustn't ever come back out, for a long, long time, as best as I can tell. Till we've become wise enough to resist Its Whispers, I suppose. I'm not sure how long that will be. We must allow the heat to bleed off for a few days. Then we must very carefully bury it, deep, deep down, in a geologically stable area. Like where we dig up our salt, but off to the sunny side a bit, where the salt is poor, and future generations won't go digging into it. Then we must forget where we've buried it.

"Eve, this is what we must do. I will die soon. Can you promise me that you'll take care of this? Eve, this is very important. Do you promise to do this?"

"Sure, Beldame, sure. But I'm totally confused by now. Are you just making more magic in our minds with all this? What's in the box, anyway?"

"The Dark Whisperer. The Evil One. Eve, I'll tell you a secret. Many, many people think it's cruel and insensitive to call It the Evil One. So they call It the Inappropriate One, and other such nonsense. None dare speak Its Name. 'Evil' is a four-letter word, as they say. But when we call It by Its real name, then we gain great power to resist. This is a very, very important part of magic."

Eve's frustration verged onto anger. "But you told me that the Dark Whisperer is nothing but a spirit, an immaterial thing that has no power over anything but willing minds! It goes where it will, being immaterial! So how can this box hold it?!"

"Because of magic."

"*MAGIC!* Come *ON,* Beldame!" Eve spat out. "Will you *please* just cut all the magical hoo-ha, and tell me the *real* truth?!"

"We trapped the Dark Whisperer through the magic tricks we played on Its mind. It saw in all of our minds—except for me, because I, alone, knew the complete extent of our plans, and I shut It out of my mind—It saw in our minds that we were completely convinced that we were making very, very powerful magic in our box. And that includes your mind, and Shoshoni's mind. So I'm sorry that I had to deceive you, yet one last time. But It came to fear our magic, so It came to investigate. Yet the magic was just in Its mind, in Its fear of our magic."

"Then what keeps It there, locked in that box? Why doesn't It flee, if It's the immaterial spirit that you say it is?"

"The truth is sometimes a very complicated thing, Eve. I told you about those symbols on that box being symbols from our future, in which we'll combine the powers of our minds, in large things called corporations and organizations. This is true, and these things will, indeed, be quite powerful. But these symbols denote how truly atrociously repugnant and loathesomely boring these conglomerated minds will also often be. They will be so bad, even the Dark Whisperer cannot tolerate the thought of them. The terrible meaning of these symbols permeates the entire amorphously but solidly fused molecular structures of the box and its lid.

"Although theoretically, the Dark Whisperer could sneak his way out of there, between the molecules of ceramics, Its mind rebels at the thought of having to tolerate such close contact with the utter, sheer inanity of the meanings of those symbols, which permeate the ceramics. For lack of self-discipline, It can't make Itself do anything that It finds abhorrent, even momentarily, and even in service of Its other, lower goals. In other words, the Whisperer is the helpless slave of the undisciplined, rebelliously irrational magic of Its own mind."

Eve sat there shaking her head silently and in total confusion. Finally, she came up with another question. "Then why doesn't It just slip out through the mud-smeared crack between the box and its lid? Is It afraid of mere *mud?!*"

"No, but there's some very special substances in that mud. Ground-up little bits of APAPPD DiPablium crystals. They are very, very powerful. You could say that they hold the ultimate trump card, in the sort of situations we find ourselves in."

"APAPPD DiPablium crystals! And what, pray tell, are *these?!* Can you fill me in on the details?"

"Yes, indeed, I can. **APAPPD**, you see, stands for **A**ll **P**urpose, **A**ll-**P**owerful **P**lot **D**evice. That's why they're so powerful."

Eve just shook her head, finally giving up. They sat there in silence for a few minutes. Then, out of the blue, Beldame started to cough. Deep, ugly, wretched, hacking coughs. Eve helped her to her feet, saying, "Beldame! What's the matter?! We'd best get you back to camp, get you to lay down in a comfortable spot on a nice bed of fresh moss close to a good, warm fire. I'll gather up some herbs and make you a potion. Come on. let's go."

Eve helped her walk. She trudged slowly along, stopping to cough frequently. To Eve's incessant, worried chatter, she simply replied, "Time has come for me to die soon, my child. Don't trouble yourself too much on my behalf. But make sure you bury that box in a proper manner." And then, between coughs, she filled Eve's mind with all the details of how the box should be prepared for burial, in such a manner that it wouldn't break, and the caulking wouldn't fall out of the crack, for a long, long time.

When they got back to camp, Eve busied herself making a potion for Beldame. Halfway through this task, she remembered that they'd left the box unattended. She briefly devoted just enough attention to this lack of security—thinking, what if some unknowing barbarian Blunt Head or Firewater clansman stumbles onto it, and opens it unawares—that she quickly selected a young maiden, Pandora Oog, to go attend to matters back down at the creek.

Now one might ask, "How could any supposedly mature, enlightened young adult go and pick a young girl named 'Pandora Oog' to go and guard a sealed box containing a Dark Whisperer, AKA Horde Whisperer?" Go ahead, ask away. But remember, Eve Oog suffered from a low-protein diet early in life, and suffered from sub-optimal brain development. Worst of all, neither she nor any other Shroom Oogs had had a properly funded education.

So that's what Eve did. Sent Pandora off to guard the box, warning her about the seemingly obvious, that she *must* refrain from opening the box. This just goes to show what can happen when young children don't properly learn about important cultural matters, including Greek mythology, along with all those non-western cultures.

Anyway, Pandora pouted about the fact that Eve was belaboring the obvious, and commented that she, Pandora, hadn't fallen out of the mushroom basket yesterday. Then she went off to watch over the box.

It wasn't but an hour later that Beldame stirred vigorously on her sick bed, saying, "I feel a great, deep, dark disturbance in the Force."

Eve gave her another swig of potion, saying, "There, there, now, Beldame, you hang tight. Everything will be fine."

The Horde Whisperer made a beeline for B-Belli and his clan, after Pandora opened the box. Not even so much as parole; this was free and clear! But he'd broken all of his newly done nails while writhing around in that cramped box, so he was pretty darned well torqued off!

One hour after that, B-Belli's troops, drunken but under the skilled command of General Dough Boy, charged through the Shroom Oog camp, conquering in the name of the BFD God. They yelled things about evil heathens, infidel witches, disrespectful heretics, shroom-eating and weed-addicted substance abusers, and sacrilegious unbelievers. They speared and gored ape-men, ape-women, and ape-rugrats right and left, up and down, and sideways, and struck the huts on fire, and just generally had themselves a good time.

Eve abandoned Beldame and fled for the bushes only after they'd just narrowly missed her with a thrown spear. She spent the night silently, inwardly simpering in terror, trying to sleep out in the noisy, damp, and forebodingly dark jungle. In the first light of morning, she peered out over the wasted, smoldering remnants of her former home.

After she verified that it seemed safe, she toured the battleground. Corpses lay strewn about. She called out softly, asking if anyone was still alive. No one replied.

She was just about ready to retreat from the macabre scene of death and destruction when she saw the bushes stir slightly. She froze, then dashed for cover. Then she cautiously crept up to see what was rustling the leaves. There she spied Beldame writhing slowly, weakly. Eve gently scooped the frail old witch into her arms, and carried her off into the jungle. She deposited her in a safe place, fetched water, and attended to her wounds.

Beldame finally recovered enough to faintly croak a few words out for Eve, who listened intently. "I've been wrong all along," she 'fessed up. "Eve, I had it wrong. It's OK. The Dark Whisperer is allowed to be free, to pester and befester us. This may not quite exactly be called good, but it's certainly right. We'll never grow up to be big and strong, unless we learn to resist Its Whispers. We've all got to learn the difference between truth and lies sooner or later. The sooner we get started, the better. Yes, some will listen, and fall by the wayside. Let the broken hearts stand as the price we've got to pay.

"So don't begrudge the Whisperer Its freedom. Just beware, and never listen to It. Work against It, speak out against It, and warn others, but don't hate It. When you hate, even when you hate hate itself, you're being irrational, and when you're irrational in a hateful manner, then the Whisperer has won.

"Yes, chaos will be badness. But it will also be goodness. We must resist the idea that we've got to chain chaos up in our boxes, rows and columns, matrices, and spreadsheets. Because we can never chain it for good. It'll break back out, always. Think you can chain it, and you've listened to the Dark Whisperer. Let chaos be chaos. Work with it. Roll with the punches, and pick and choose, carefully, the little bits of chaos that you might be able to tame. Then do your best to bring forth good from chaos. No one should expect any more from you.

"We make a mistake when we confuse chaos with the Dark Whisperer. In chaos, there can be many beautiful things. Things like freedom. Freedom for all to chose for themselves leads to apparent chaos, but hidden in that chaos is complex order. That complex order, if allowed to flourish, will bring forth many beautiful things. This will happen only if we restrain our urges to always try to fight and contain chaos. The root of all evil is the urge to conquer chaos completely.

"No one can conquer chaos, and no one should try. When we think the solution is always more order, obedience, control, and power, then we are listening to the Dark Whisperer, and he will push us towards destruction, which is the worst chaos. We must stop listening to the Dark Whisperer, and listen instead to those whispered words of wisdom—'let it be'.

"Don't worry, the Force will send courageous prophets, and many will speak out powerfully against the Dark Whisperer. Unfortunately, most people, most of the time, will ignore the wisest of the prophets. Or for sure, they'll not pay proper attention to things they don't want to hear. But that's just the way things are. We have to live in the real world, and accept things the way they are. Always look on the bright side of life. Some will listen to the prophets, and ignore the Whisperer."

They sat in silence. Many of Beldame's words were meaningless to Eve, yet somehow their essential meanings were quite clear. Eve grasped Beldame's hand, wincing at her labored breathing. "Is there anything more?" Eve prompted.

"Yes. You can lead a horde to water, but you can't make them think."

Eve sat and stewed on that for a bit. Then, gently, she asked yet again, "Anything else, Beldame? If you've anything else to say, I think you'd better get it off your chest soon."

"Yes, my child. The meaning of life is..." But then Beldame slipped into a coma, twitched, and died peacefully in a matter of minutes. Eve sorrowfully drifted away, vowing that Beldame's ideas and causes should never die.

Many miles away, Aquila and Shoshoni, both fleeing from the frightfully insane carnage among the fledgling humans, stumbled into each others' cosmic-karmic vibe auras. The dialectic vibe constant was high that day, so this range was a bit close; a matter of mere miles. Aquila and Shoshoni rushed towards one another, he at a pace obviously greater than hers.

"Oh, my love!" he called out to her, "I've been looking for you for entirely too long!"

"Oh my darling!" she replied in eager anticipation. "You've a beautiful mind! A real, intelligent, thinking and feeling mind! A mind like my own!"

"Oh, sweet bliss!" Aquila's vibes sang out as he soared descending, far from that ancient river bending. "My darling! My gorgeous darling!" He zeroed in on her, and only the uncaring, non-sentient jungle paid witness to their frenzied, passionate love-making. Not one creature condemned the brazen unnaturalness and immorality of their inter-species love affair. No one even cared, other than the millions of soil bacteria which happily feasted on drops of the physical manifestations of Aquila's love, spilled so generously and directly onto their homes.

Aquila and Shoshoni lived together happily till death parted them late in life. This, though, was after they made a great journey. Wishing to leave human butchery far behind, they traveled south 'cross land. When they got to the sea, Aquila stole a hide from some humans, and carried Shoshoni, stork-and-baby-bundle-style, across the great waters. Arriving in a new land, they celebrated by making love in a swamp.

The ape-men of this new land had never lived under the wise, subtle rule of Beldame and her fellow witches. Beldame's world and vision had never encompassed these remote peoples. More fortunately, they were destined to live free from the wrath of B-Belli's descendants for thousands of years, still. They were still quite innocently primitive, in those days.

Being quite innocent, the few of these primitives who witnessed Aquila's and Shoshoni's love-making could never have conceived that this was the results of an incredibly, shockingly sordid inter-species love affair. They thought the eagle and the snake were fighting. But they were quite impressed, and dedicated themselves to obeying the command of this great vision of theirs. They vowed to build a great city, out there in the middle of that swamp.

But the Horde Whisperer was loosed, destined to bedevil humanity for the ages. This was the end result of the historical forces shaping those legendary times. Also, these were the days when great myths propagated throughout the infant human populations, forming and shaping their world views and forging their very destinies.

Chapter 8

The Horde Whisperer Breaks Through- The Modern Era

"In quantum gravity, as we shall see, the space-time manifold ceases to exist as an objective physical reality; geometry becomes relational and contextual; and the foundational conceptual categories of prior science— among them existence itself—become problematized and relativized."
Alan Sokal, modern physicist, in recent demonstrative spoof writings published in an article entitled "Transgressing the Boundaries: Towards a Transformative Hermeneutics of Quantum Gravity", *in* "Social Text", *a "scholarly" journal dedicated to "deconstructing" modern science.*

The Horde Whisperer plied his trade steadily throughout thousands of years, spreading low self-esteem, misery, death, and destruction. One of his favorite tricks was to Whisper to people, and to convince them that they had the secret to *real* magic. Not just the kind of mental/spiritual magic by which, for example, if enough people pray sincerely enough for peace, there will be peace, but real, physical magic. The "mere" magic of the mind just isn't enough. Believe such-and-such, and do these rituals here, in just the right way, the Whisperer said, and Awesome Powers will be yours.

The Whisperer never delivered. His promises were naught but lies. What a shocking surprise! When his victims listened intently enough, they'd be drawn into his spiral vortex of magic thinking. When all their attempts at *real* magic ultimately failed, they'd perform that one, final piece of *real* magic that was clearly in their power. They'd firmly convince themselves of just what, exactly, lays beyond death, for themselves and for others. And then they'd transport those others, especially those who didn't support their ideas of magic, to those realms beyond death. When this happened, the Horde Whisperer was fairly well pleased. But what pleased him most of all was when, merely through his own power to Whisper, he could convince True Believers to "magically" transport *themselves* to those realms beyond death!

Through all the ages, the Whisperer kept on wondering if there could ever be *real* magic, though. He lusted after such powers for himself, but the entire universe valiantly, steadfastly resisted his efforts for billions of years. The laws governing the physical behavior of the universe and all the matter and energy in it remained firm and unbreakable.

But during the 1990s, the Horde Whisperer finally broke through and attained *real* magic. A physicist, Alan Sokal, unwittingly, unwillingly, unknowingly, and in complete contravention of his own intentions, released the Horde Whisperer from his most effective shackles. Prior to this time, the Horde Whisperer had been constrained by the objectively unbending physical, chemical, electromagnetic, quantum mechanical, gravitational, relativistic, etc., laws of the universe.

After Alan Sokal unintentionally revealed that existence is merely a subjective matter of social convention, reality became problematized, and the Horde Whisperer was left free to redefine reality at will. Now reality didn't suddenly become radically problematized all at once. It became problematized slowly, quietly, and furtively. Many people didn't notice it for years.

As one might expect, the first manifestations of this problematization were created by a spawn of the Horde Whisperer. Also as one might expect, this spawn of the Horde Whisperer was one of many designed and built in a secret laboratory owned and run by the federal government. This was in a top-secret lab known only to those fiendish researchers as **THEMNOTUS** (**T**echnologists **H**elping to **E**ngineer **M**arvelous **N**ew **O**pportunities for a **T**otally **U**ngrateful **S**ociety).

But then word about THEMNOTUS leaked out. Hordes of reporters, camerapersons, editorialists, and demonstrators constantly badgered all the lab's workers, engineers, and scientists, and the government, saying that a far more accurate description of THEMNOTUS would be **T**errible, **H**ateful **E**litists **M**aliciously **N**egating **O**ur **T**otally **U**nquestionable **S**ainthood. The outcry was so deafening that THEMNOTUS was shut down.

In many ways, this shutdown came too late. The government shut the barn door after the spawn of the Horde Whisperer had escaped. And the Horde Whisperer's spawn were legion. First, THEMNOTUS devised diabolically clever subliminal messages to secretly sell to fiendish tobacco companies. The tobacco pushers then put these messages into "Schmoe Camelhumper" cigarette advertisements. Innocent, angelic Boy Scouts, Brownies, and choir boys by the millions were thus ruthlessly forced, robot-like, to put cigarettes up to their virgin lips, light them up, and inhale deeply.

Other than augmenting THEMNOTUS's financial resources, addicting helpless children served their interests in another, even more sinister manner. THEMNOTUS scientists invented nanotechnological behavior-modifying molecules, then snuck them into everyone's vaccines, drinking water, and cigarettes.

Nicotine, though, served to synergistically boost the effect of these behavior-modifying molecules more efficiently than any other substance, so this is where THEMNOTUS concentrated its efforts. They encouraged the tobacco companies to spike their cigarettes not only with nicotine, but also with many kinds of these special molecules, some of which also increased nicotine addiction. As a side benefit, the tobacco companies then repaid the government for its help by selling more heavily taxed cigarettes, thus saving socialized medical programs from collapse. THEMNOTUS orchestrated lawyers and tobacco companies, making a great show about how adversarial it all was, but it was all really just a friendly mutual back-scratching arrangement.

And just what, exactly, did all these special behavior-modifying molecules do, besides increase nicotine addiction, thereby increasing the government's funds and powers? The effects of these molecules were pernicious and pervasive, and too numerous to list in complete detail. However, we can summarize their major effects briefly.

They caused parents to neglect their children, and allow them to watch horribly immoral, sexy and violent TV programs, videos, and computer programs, and to listen to terrible music. Some parents resisted valiantly, trying diligently to discharge their parental duties of loving and guiding their children, but those diabolical molecules held them in their iron grip. Many children fell under the influence of these satanic molecules, too, and had no choice but to slip so deeply into cults and role-playing games that they ended up losing touch with reality, and committing suicide. The molecules had left them no choice at all!

They caused many, many people to become the friends of characters on TV, instead of making friends with their neighbors. So then, when their cars wouldn't start in the morning and they needed a friend to give them a ride to work, and Murphy Brown turned out not to be much of a friend after all, refusing to give them a ride, well, once again, they had only those evil molecular engineers to blame. Those molecules made them limit their friendships to TV characters, and got half of them to become unmarried mothers, to boot.

Some of the worst havoc that THEMNOTUS molecules wreaked was inflicted on poor minority communities. They caused teenagers to have unprotected sex, women to go on welfare, fathers to abandon their children, and almost everyone to catch AIDS, smoke crack, and fight gang wars. On top of that, those demonic molecules then caused richer, more talented, and more privileged workers to keep the poor from competing with them on free labor markets, through the use of minimum wage laws, licensing laws for hair braiders, interior decorators, and taxi drivers, and explanations such as "we're just defending the poor ignorant consumers from their own weaknesses and stupidity" and "we've got to defend the working poor from slave-driving capitalist pigs."

THEMNOTUS molecules also devastated the plight of womyn everywhere. They implanted oppressive patriarchal paradigms into womyn's minds, including self-fulfillingly prophetical ideas such as this: that it's normal for womyn to suffer from morning sickness and labor pains. Had it not been for the vocal protests of courageously radical feminists on campuses, even more womyn would have fallen for these tyrannical lies.

Some mad technologists at THEMNOTUS even conspired with the radicals of the far right, slipping behavior-modifying molecules into Billary-Bob's food pods, such that Billary-Bob was utterly, totally and completely incapable of keeping his cloaca in his peduncle. Fortunately for everyone, Hillary-Bob caught on to the right-wingers' goals if not their methods, warning everyone about "...this vast right-wing conspiracy that has been conspiring against my husband..."

In society at large, the molecules caused everyone to sue everyone, draining vast quantities of resources away from other, more productive uses. They caused everyone to believe, and vote for, those politicians who promised them increased government-administered compassionate benevolence, to be funded by the other guy. "Don't tax you, don't tax me, tax the fella behind the tree," as the politicians said. And the people believed! All because of THEMNOTUS molecules! Those horrible molecules just did all sorts of strange and perverted sorts of things to all sorts of innocent people, who would otherwise never have dreamed of acting in such silly and irresponsible ways.

They caused everyone to admire Kate Moss and other gorgeous waifs so much that many people died of anorexia. Then there were split ends, overgrazing, body odor, genocide, halitosis, global warming, indigestion, interracial adoption, women with hairy armpits, soil erosion, baldness, satanic Procter & Gamble symbols, boredom, radioactive wastes, tooth decay, sexism, hemorrhoids, executive (but not athlete or movie star) overcompensation, dandruff, racism, athlete's foot, political and moral corruption, headache pain, and a thousand million instances of hate and death and war, all also caused by the diabolically, fiendishly clever molecular engineers at THEMNOTUS.

As one might imagine, the public's thunder of righteous indignation was overwhelming, when word about THEMNOTUS finally leaked out. THEMNOTUS was shut down in the nick of time. Right before they were shut down, they'd been working on their most diabolical scheme of all: they were going to invent *real* magic, and put magic molecules into the papers of marriage licenses for gay people. These magical molecules would have tainted the cosmic and orgasmic love-ether, causing normal, non-perverted couples to dishonor their marriage vows. They'd have had no choice but to get divorced, since *real* marriage and family values would have been torn asunder.

Since real, legitimate love is a finite resource, and a marriage license is a type of currency, the gays would have stolen limited love-vibes from straights. Marriage licenses would have been devalued, love inflation would have set in, and divorce and fatherlessness would have skyrocketed, since straight love-vibes would have been leeched away.

Fortunately, this most fiendish of THEMNOTUS's plots was foiled before the engineers completed systems design integration. So THEMNOTUS never did attain *real* magic, directly. This was left to one of their creations.

Chewdychomper Chupacabras was another gruesome creation of the mad scientists at THEMNOTUS. He was a slimy synthetic mutant mucous-covered multi-tentacled blood-sucking monstrous fiend, and that was on his *good* days, when his various biorhythms maximized. They'd at first intended for Chewdychomper to become an IRS auditor, but experiments indicated that he grew lethargic after drinking his fill of blood. They never managed to explain the concept of the national debt to him.

So the authorities at THEMNOTUS decided that Chewdychomper should help them to keep minorities in their proper place. Since they'd already taken care of Blacks with their demonic nanotechnological behavior-control molecules, they decided to loose Chewdychomper on Hispanics. They sicced him on Costa Rica, the Dominican Republic, Cuba, South Florida, and Mexico. There, Chewdychomper was free to terrorize and oppress all the natives.

In the lab, he'd gained his first name, Chewdychomper, because if you didn't watch out, he'd chomp your chewdies and chew your chompers. And after they set him free, the natives called him "Chupacabras", which is Cuban/Mexican/South Floridian etc. for "goat sucker".

And Oh Boy, did he ever suck those goats! And sheep and pigs and cows and horses and rabbits and geese and guinea pigs and emus and ostriches and all other sorts of domestic livestock! He'd sneak up in the middle of the night, leave a few fang marks, suck the animals' blood dry, and then slip away. He never paid any refunds, and he never promised a lower blood burden on the middle class, let alone a pyramid scheme to support his victims in their old age. However, even *he* refrained from threatening anyone with audits and incomprehensible forms to be filled out.

He never did directly threaten any unwilling human victims, that we know of. Humans, being anthropocentric speciesists, found him to appear repulsive and vile. Their biased perceptions fouled the aura of any potential human-chupacabras interactions so thoroughly that this particular oppressed and misunderstood chupacabras knew that it was useless to even bother to *try* to interact socially with them. Some say he was just too cowardly and shy, but such statements merely demonstrate ignorance of the extent of anti-chupacabras intolerance. However, despite his lack of empowerment in the social arena, he set in motion a chain of events which was to cause all humans a great deal of problems. In fact, we could say that he was the one who (by obeying the Whisperer) problematized reality.

One night, Chewdy was out sucking goats' blood in a favorite backwoods area of Mexico, and the rancher's dogs caught wind of him. They chased him under a large woodpile, where they barked and growled at him all night. The rancher called the police, but they were too busy to help a common rancher. At the behest of various Gringos, they were out smuggling drugs and busting drug smugglers who hadn't greased the right palms. The dogs got tired of guarding against fearsome fiendish monsters, so they sauntered off to attend to more important matters, such as barking at doorbells and squirrels. Chewdychomper, shaken but not stirred by the terrors of his long, wild night of snarling back at semi-domesticated long-fanged fellow-beasts, slunk off into the dark right before dawn.

Chewdychomper was shaken enough by this experience that he began to think about certain matters. He decided that his low-tech life was just plain too dangerous. So he dragged his slimy tentacles off to the nearest dump, where he invented *real* magic. Using fragments of a broken lampshade, a beer bottle, an old magnetic compass, some battery acid, an egg beater, and a transistor radio, all of unknown brands, and a Cheese Dwonky™ wrapper, he created the Quart Low Tracker.

Note, we do *NOT* imply that Cheese Dwonkies™ or associated products are defective in any manner, that their wrappers should be disposed of in anything other than a sanitary landfill meeting appropriate legal standards, that readers should attempt any such experiments themselves (especially not without proper adult supervision), or that Author or Publisher makes any guarantees, express or implied, of such devices working properly. But remember, you can't prove to us that the Quart Low Tracker *DOESN'T* work, either. If it doesn't work for you, it's just operator error. These things aren't easy, or for novices, you see. One needs *Faith*, not pessimism and unbelief.

Now the Quart Low Tracker wasn't just an ordinary heap of junk. It was, indeed, an *extraordinary* heap of junk. A *real magic* heap of junk. With it, he could detect those who were a quart low in common sense and intellectual and physical vigor, but who weren't too terribly low otherwise, especially in succulent blood. In other words, the Quart Low Tracker allowed him to safely pick his victims.

Chewdychomper Chupacabras enjoyed a few months of happy bloodsucking. With the **LCD** (**L**uciferescent **C**hromosexual **D**iPablium) display on his Quart Low Tracker giving him infallible guidance as to whom he should suck dry next, life became safe and easy, and a belly full of blood was one of life's givens. Life became dull and boring for Chewdy. Now that his belly was always full, he wished to slime his creepy tentacles up Madlow's Hierarchy of Greeds, and acquire some money. Visions of $$$$$ danced through his head. Sadly, though, he came to realize that money was useless to him, since his appearance was so horrifying that he'd never be able to spend money and enjoy it a meaningful manner. So he decided to settle for second best, which was to enable someone else to get rich, and vicariously watch all the fun.

He pondered long and hard. Then he made some very extremely special modifications to his Quart Low Tracker. He hearkened to his LCD display, and made plans to head for Madness County. Then he hauled himself off to the dump once more, gathering up fragments of lampshade, a beer bottle, a magnetic compass, some battery acid, an egg beater, a transistor radio, and a Cheese Dwonky™ wrapper.

He carefully popped the cover off of the little hand-held magnetic compass, examining it's delicate bearing. Dang, he cussed to himself, the bearing works, swiveling freely. Entirely *too* freely. Well, we can fix *that!* He dabbed a spot of battery acid on the compass bearing again and again, watching is as it caused the metal to fizz weakly. Finally, after much diligent work by Chewdy, the bearing rusted rigidly shut.

After testing the bearing, a satisfied Chewdy carefully wrapped the compass in the Cheese Dwonky™ wrapper, and performed other delicate high-technology engineering operations. Thus, he fabricated yet another Quart Low Tracker; the world's second such device.

Now in Madness County there lived a striving, seeking, searching young lad named Ale Run Hubba-Bubba. They called him Ale Run because in his younger years, he'd always been the one to make the ale run, when the party ran dry. And yes, he did like women. But only halfheartedly. He'd inevitably be distracted by the nearest pink plastic yard flamingo. But even his passing infatuations with pink plastic yard flamingoes would only last so long, before a nameless sense of seeking and longing drove him away. So he carried such a mediocre rank in both fields of endeavor, with the women as well as with the pink plastic yard flamingoes, that he deserved neither to be called Hubba-Hubba nor Bubba-Bubba. But his friends thought highly enough of him in both categories that he became known as Ale Run Hubba-Bubba.

Now Ale Run, they called him a seeker. He'd been searching high and low. He sought bliss and ale and enlightenment and women and higher consciousness and a new pickup and inner peace and power and nirvana and status and blessedness and pink plastic yard flamingoes and a well-grounded sense of centeredness and money. Especially money. *Lots* of money. Now money isn't bad. Prosperity and good fortune, to put a better spin on things. So Ale Run never said he liked money. He just had a well-grounded sense of centeredness, and he happened to be centered about prosperity and good fortune for himself, especially. So far, he just hadn't latched onto a proper channel through which to attract prosperity and good fortune to himself. He'd discovered that it was hard to convince people to give their money to him merely because he liked money. So Ale Run was seeking.

Chewdy consulted his Quart Low Tracker one last time, confirming his reservations for an auspicious day for traveling. Then he made his trip to Madness County one hot sultry late August day, on Friday the Thirteenth, with the Moon in Uranus and Chewdy having been manufactured a Pisces next to a black cat under a ladder, stashed securely away in the cargo bay on Panama Red Airlines flight #666, arriving on schedule one dark and stormy night.

He pried the screen aside and crept through the open window of Ale Run's apartment, replacing the screen behind him. He scrambled up into the bedroom and stashed his second Quart Low Tracker under Ale Run's heap of dirty laundry. He secreted himself underneath the floorboards underneath that heap of dirty laundry. Then he waited.

Ale Run tottered into the bedroom at ten-thirty, flopped back, and watched TV for a while. Then he turned everything off and worked his way to within millimeters of snoozeville.

But then Chewdy Whispered to him. "Ale Run. Ale Run. I have what's good for what ails you."

"Wha-hunh? Who's that?"

"It's just me, your friendly neighborhood Chewdychomper Chupacabras. My friends just call me 'Chewdy'. I'm here to be your friend. Trust me."

"How'd you get here? Who let you in? What are you doing here? What do you want?"

"Why, I flew in on the friendly skies, just like anyone else. And you let me in. You invited me. You asked God to bring you riches, yes? Riches and power for you, so that you can make sure people do God's Will? Well, let me tell you something. That's a darn good thing to ask for, because that's God's will, is for you to be rich and powerful! That's so selflessly noble of you, to want vast powers and riches with which to serve God. So God sent me here to help you become rich and powerful."

Now this all caught Ale Run's attention, you can bet on that! But Ale Run's soul hadn't been dispensed by the cosmic-karmic vending machine yesterday, so he was a bit skeptical. "Where are you? *What* are you? What exactly *is* a 'Chewdychomper Chupacabras', anyway? Why should I trust you?"

"I'm an invisible spirit," Chewdy lied, tweaking his Quart Low Tracker and concentrating on projecting his voice in such a manner as to foil Ale Run's directional hearing. "I'm a good spirit, sent by God and his Vibes to help you help Him. I bring many blessings. And you should trust me because I bring concrete evidence of my good will. I bring you the Quart Low Tracker. Lift up your dirty laundry, and Behold My Wonders!"

Ale Run lifted his stained underwear and rotten socks up to the heavens, and proclaimed, "All I see is some weird heap of junk. What's this? Is this some pervert's stupid idea of a trick to play on me? One of my old frat buddies? Moondog? Is that you?" Ale Run looked around skittishly.

"No, no," Chewdy assured him. "Not a joke. Not a joke at all. Now get pen and paper, and listen up, please. I'll tell you all about the Quart Low Tracker, how to use it, how it works, and how to build more. Everything you'll need to know. You'll become rich, powerful, and famous. Just listen, please. Listen, and write."

Ale Run fetched his pen and pad. Then he listened and wrote. And listened and wrote and listened and wrote some more. For five hours he listened and wrote. First, Chewdy told him how to use the Tracker. He even walked him through some exercises, learning hands-on how to use the Tracker. Then he taught him the theory of operation, in detail. Finally, Chewdy walked him through just exactly how one goes about fabricating one's own Quart Low Tracker from scratch, using commonly available household items and supplies.

In conclusion, Chewdy dictated to the still-furiously transcribing

Ale Run, "And now don't forget, the final step of systems integration here is that one has to very, very carefully align the LCD display chromosexually with the Earth's electromagic lines of flux, emanating from the current locus of the geomagic pole, using a counter-clockwise hand-waving motion and the right-hand rule. This counter-clockwise rotation is what you've got to use here in the Northern Hemisphere in order to invoke the Coriolis Force. If you were in the southern geomagic field, of course, you'd have to wave your hands clockwise, OK? Great! May the Coriolis Force be with you!"

Now Ale Run was a bit tired and sleepy by that time, so we really should find it in our hearts to forgive him for getting a bit sloppy in transcribing the notes. And Chewdy was getting hungry and impatient, too, so he didn't bother to thoroughly double-check the **CRC** (**C**ertification of **R**idiculousness **C**heck) codes that his Tracker displayed after performing calculations based on the vibes returning from Ale Run's aura. So one might say that mistakes were made.

Chewdy conducted a lightning-quick review of all they'd gone over, while Ale Run drowsily checked his notes. Then, finished at last, Ale Run fell into a deep and exhausted sleep. Chewdy slipped away into the few remaining hours of night.

Ale Run awoke halfway through the morning. By the time he was fully awake, he came to realize that yes, the events of last night *had* been real—not just a dream. But he checked his notes, just to be 100% sure. And then he found the Quart Low Tracker, right there where he'd left it on his nightstand. He picked it up with trembling hands, thinking, *I'm rich I'm rich I'm rich!!!* Providence has finally acknowledged my deserving nature!

He checked his notes and his memories very carefully, thinking, I've got to be methodical, here, and make sure I don't blow it! This is a once in a lifetime chance, if this all checks out the way that this "Chewdy" spirit says it will. OK, first things first. I'll make sure that the Quart Low Tracker works the way he says it does. Let's see...

Ale Run decided on phase one, and then he acted. He got himself signed up as a telephone solicitor for the Law Enforcement Officer's Club, calling people and asking them for donations. After filling out the proper papers and taking his training course that morning, he sat down at his telephone station. Then he gathered up his pencil, lunch box, and phone book, excused himself, and went to the little boy's room. In the privacy of his stall, he pulled the Quart Low Tracker out of his lunch box. He used it meticulously, marking about a hundred numbers. Then he got back to work.

Ale Run shone like a star that day. Not a one call failed to elicit a promise of money for law enforcement officers. All his bosses and co-workers mobbed him, asking him how he'd managed to do it. He only gave vague replies, saying you just had to have a special touch. He thought to himself, well, this is just peanuts. Chump change. Wait till I *really* get going! Now that I've obtained my demonstration of the Quart Low Tracker's powers, why am I still hanging out with these losers? He almost told his boss he'd not be back in the morning, but then he stopped himself. What if Chewdy's hunk of junk was playing tricks on him, and all the charitable givers were going to change their minds? What if not a one of them followed up on their promises to mail money in to their noble cause?

So he came back the next day, and performed his magic once again. And the day after, and the day after that. Then the money started to roll in. Thousands upon thousands of dollars poured in. Ale Run got raises, the other employees got envious, and the policemen's widows even got a dollar or two now and then. Well, I guess it's time to move on to phase two, Ale Run thought. Time to quit my job, and move off to bigger and better things. Once more, he stopped himself in the nick of time, right before resigning. Better think this through first, he told himself.

He went back home to his apartment that night and initiated phase two. This consisted simply of intensely studying the theories behind the Quart Low Tracker, as dictated to him by Chewdychomper Chupacabras. Phase two lasted for several evenings, while he staunchly forced himself to keep on slugging away at his stupid old day job. He told himself he still needed that job, because he had to have a method of properly verifying completion of phase three. Besides, the money, paltry though it was, came in handy.

Then came phase three. This consisted of his attempts to make his own Quart Low Trackers from scratch. Let's see, he thought, pondering over his notes and memories. This sure is frustrating, seeing how my notes get progressively sloppier and sloppier looking, and my memory likewise gets hazy, as I move towards the end of all those instructions that

Chewdy left. I should've interrupted that spirit now and then, just long enough to make me some coffee or pop some study buddy pills, to keep my butt awake, towards the end of all that. Let's see, now...

What *are* these crazy notes saying, anyway? "Align the LCD display chromosexually with the Earth's electromagic lines of fux, something something magic pole, counter-cockwise hand waving, the right hand rules." Do you suppose he meant *homo*sexually? Or was that really counter-*clock*wise, not *cock*wise? The right hand rules the magic pole, maybe? And what *are* electromagic lines of fux, anyway? Ale Run puzzled long and hard, thinking of all the various possible meanings, and all the various possible permutations and combinations thereof. Some he found quite distasteful, but he tried them all. The lure of money was just too strong. But no, a family-oriented book like *Jurassic Horde Whisperer of Madness County* can't very well get into those kinds of details. Suffice it to say that the men of the evening that he hired gossiped about how he was the strangest bird they'd ever encountered.

For the next few weeks, Ale Run would make an attempt, every evening before work, at making himself a Quart Low Tracker or two. Then he'd try it out at work, waving it over the phone book while sitting on his porcelain throne in the privacy of a toilet stall. Chewdy had warned him that the Quart Low Tracker's data needs to be as fresh as possible, due to the perturbations that free will causes over time in the electromagic lines of fux. Or something like that. In any case, the readings had to be fairly fresh. Ale Run had verified that he couldn't very well get away with taking his readings on the phone book the night before, in the privacy of his apartment, even with his known-good, original Quart Low Tracker. The yields went way down. So he had to sneak off to the toilet during work, on a fairly regular basis. It was troublesome, but workable.

The worst part of it all was that none of his new Quart Low Trackers worked! They only rarely seemed to agree with his original device. Sometimes he'd experiment, and go with the readings of his new devices, ignoring the old. Not a *one* of them got any better results, consistently, than his coworkers did! It was all extremely depressing. How was he going to market his technology and make any money if he couldn't duplicate it?

He went into a deep, deep funk. It got so bad that his one and only good Quart Low Tracker started returning fewer and fewer numbers for him to call at work. This caused Ale Run to *really* panic, till he realized that it was his own depression that was causing his yields to fall. Even *magic* couldn't cause many people to send money to a morose, mopey, woe-is-me solicitor, he finally concluded. So then he snapped out of it just enough to get his yields back up.

His bosses congratulated him. They'd been worried that maybe he was losing his touch. So they gave him another raise, to help his spirits and keep his productivity up. But then Ale Run quit his job. His bosses begged and pleaded, and offered him even more raises, but he had bigger fish to fry. He quit, and that was that.

He'd finally snapped out of his mental rut. Inspiration had struck, and he'd come to realize that there was no real need to come up with more Quart Low Trackers that actually worked, to rake in the big bucks. No need at all! One *real* Quart Low Tracker was enough! He'd mass-produce *fake* Quart Low Trackers, and, with the assistance of the *real* Quart Low Tracker, he'd line up buyers for the fakes! He got to work.

He purchased the assistance of an industrial designer and a plastics company, and they made a few hundred Quart Low Trackers. They consisted of small plastic boxes with swiveling metal antennae, and little interchangeable plastic "chips" carrying photocopied pictures of things such as dead ants. Then he worked up the promotional materials. Matter and energy are one and the same, Einstein said, they said. So all matter gives off energy. With the right optional plastic chip (for the right price) in this device, it will detect those energies for you, and you can just sort of follow the vibes, and you can find whatever you're looking for, they said. Like drugs or weapons.

If you really, really care about the welfare of our children in our schools and on our streets, his promotional materials said, you'll be sure to have a Quart Low Tracker or two on hand in each and every school and law enforcement agency. The relatively small investment in Quart Low Tracker gear will surely pay itself off in just about no time flat, in reduced medical, law enforcement, and prison costs later on. Investing in human capital, after all, is the most wise and enlightened course of all.

Ale Run had tens of thousands of copies of his promotional materials printed up on nice, glossy brochures. He had some very impressively technical-looking labels printed up, too, which he glued to his Quart Low Trackers. Then he recruited salesmen for his new organization, Scamway International. And he also invested some money in special CD-ROMs.

Every morning, in the privacy of his home office, Ale Run inserted special CD-ROMs into his PC. These CD-ROMs contained information about schools and law enforcement agencies across the nation. He then used his one and only truly functional Quart Low Tracker to pick a few institutions, whose names, addresses, and phone numbers he'd then pass on the appropriate people in sales. He used a different set of CD-ROMs (along with his original Quart Low Tracker, of course) to pick new members of his sales staff. He then passed these names to existing sales staff, who added them to their direct reports. Thus, his empire grew. And grew and grew and grew some more.

Within months, Scamway International spread like wildfire. Millions of dollars rushed into Ale Run's coffers. Thousands of schools and law enforcement agencies snapped up his Quart Low Trackers, each costing several thousand dollars. Manufacturing went to three shifts. Even though there were a few skeptics here and there who said that the Quart Low Tracker was nothing but a modern-day dowsing rod, and no one ever proved that they worked, they were a big hit. Illicit drug and gun users and dealers ran in fear. Policemen and educators swore by the Trackers. Regular civilians even got into the act, using the Trackers to find lost golf balls.*

So here's where we start an intermittent habit of putting endnotes after some chapters. Facts and editorial comments, with source notes following that. In order to keep your story flowing smoothly, though, we've put all that stuff at the end of the book. If you like to take a break from the fiction, now and then, you can stick a second bookmark towards the end of the book, and go read a chapter's endnotes as you finish that chapter. I'll put an unobtrusive little note at the end of each chapter that has endnotes, this being the first. If you like your fiction uninterrupted, ignore these little notes, and read all the endnotes later. Or don't read them at all; suit yourself. But don't tell me you skipped my endnotes, or I'll pout!

So if you want to learn all about the Quadro Crackpots who inspired my tales of Quart Low Trackers, go see the endnotes for Chapter 8 on page 229.

---

* OK, so by now all you readers out there in readerland are thinking, man, what kind of a nutcase *is* this Author-type-dude Titus fella, anyway? Where does he get such totally whacked-out ideas? Just how far out of touch with reality *is* he, anyway? Well, sad to say, I get my inspiration from reality. I may be off of my rocker, but so is reality.

Chapter 9

The Grain Elevators of Madness County

"Robert believed the world had become too rational, had stopped trusting in magic as much as it should. I've often wondered if I was too rational in making my decision." "Francesca Johnson", *a character in Robert James Waller's* "The Bridges of Madison County", *writing in a letter for her children to read after she died, explaining her secret affair with* "Robert Kincaid", *a wandering* National Geographic *photographer, while still married to the children's father.*

Oh, yes, and from the same source: "In a way, he was not of this earth. That's about as clear as I can say it. I've always thought of him as a leopardlike creature who rode in on the tail of a comet." Fascinating. Was he perhaps descended to Earth through Heaven's Gate, from the Level Beyond Human? Was the comet perchance named Hale-Bopp-Bopp-Bopp the Really-Bopped? We don't know. The text doesn't say. Perhaps there'll be a sequel.

Now in Madness County there also lived a striving, seeking, searching early-fortyish semi-young woman named Francestuous Johnsdame. She was striving for the next higher level of enlightenment, a husband who didn't slam screen doors, bliss, an exciting sense of romance, higher consciousness, better tastes for what is truly alluringly elegant and fashionable, inner peace, a guy who was stylishly skilled in matters of lighting cigarettes and opening beer cans, finding herself, and being appreciated for her incredibly superior sensitivity towards all living things.

Unfortunately, she lived her life in a hum-drum rut. She was married to a slob, Bob, a chubby farmer who ate meat and brushed his teeth. It wasn't enough that he dined on the flesh of animals. No, Sir! That wasn't enough. He had to go and top it all off by *brushing his teeth*, thereby committing genocide upon the billions of innocent bacteria dwelling in his mouth. Francestuous often fantasized about living a *quiet* life, and smelling only *quiet* scents. Wouldn't it be nice not to have to smell the scents of mass killing, like the smells of meat and toothpaste? Those murderously *loud* smells assaulted her nose every day, forcefully reminding her of her plight. Married to an uncouth bonehead, she was! There was no escape.

And that wasn't all. Her husband insensitively slammed the screen door, didn't want her to smoke cigarettes, never talked to her about Panderwood, movies, and fashion (instead, it was usually hunting, farming, and football), and behaved in a generally undignified manner. Oh, he was gross! Farting, belching, and letting kids and dogs climb and drool all over him! It never seemed to end. When was he going to grow up, and become more concerned with really *meaningful* things? Failing that, when was some star creature going to descend from the skies on the tail of a comet, and come and relieve her of her boredom and drudgery? Throughout all those long, dark, torturous days, she never lost sight of her hopes and dreams.

Then one day, her knight in shining armor rode into town. He rode into town on a special, experimental new hypnohypoallergenic bicycle, courtesy of the **DOT** (**D**epartment **O**f **T**ransportation). Raoul Kinky was on a mission. A mission from *National Vegetarian* Magazine. He was there to photograph all those shining monuments to vegetarianism, the grain elevators of Madness County. These elevators now accepted only organically grown grains for direct use as human food in macrobiotic diets, and for feeding companion animals. Yes, there were still a few elevators here and there that stored grain for animals which were then to be murdered for human use. But these wouldn't receive any press from Raoul Kinky and the National Vegetarian Magazine, *that* was for *sure!*

Unfortunately, Raoul suffered from **MCS** (**M**ultiple **C**hemical **S**ensitivity). This meant that if Raoul had an unprotected encounter with abhorrent artificial chemicals (as opposed to always-benevolent, wholesomely natural ingredients from the Earth Mother), then he was in great danger of breaking out in rashes, bad vibes, sneezing, negative karma, toxitisapoptonecrosisitis, fatigue, depression, headaches, sympathy, spots, and other severe industrial diseases.

Fortunately, Raoul had a few arrows in his quiver, with which he fought back valiantly. First, there was his special $300,000 bicycle. DOT had built this experimental vehicle for him. It was lubricated by (organically grown) corn oil, and built out of organically laminated soy proteins and wheat germ, alfalfa sprouts, bean curds, and organically mined iron and molybdenum. By organically mined, we mean that donkeys, not internal combustion engines, were used to power the ore carts. And the donkeys were never subjected to substandard working conditions or paid substandard wages, which meant that they were fed all the organically grown hay that they could eat.

As a further anti-MCS measure, Raoul and his all-natural bicycle had been jointly bonded together through expert sessions of nature-centered hypnosis. Hence, the hypnohypoallergenic designation. Not that Raoul or his bicycle held labels in high esteem. To Raoul, his bicycle was simply known as "Herman", and of course, to Herman, Raoul was simply Raoul. The theory was that if bicycle and rider could bond thoroughly, then Raoul's hypersensitive immune system, as part of his holistic mind/body whole, might be a lot less likely to act up. It all made a lot of sense to Raoul. He considered himself to be quite lucky, to have bonded so fast and so well to such a mellow fellow as Herman.

This had left one major, almost insurmountable problem. Raoul simply hadn't been able to face the idea of pedaling through carbon monoxide, synthetic ozone, partially oxidized hydrocarbons, and Gaia knows what all else. Just the thought of doing this, unprotected, even on the most lightly traveled of country roads, had made Raoul break out in rashes. First, he'd thought of gas masks, but even when he was finally able to find one that had been manufactured organically, it was way too heavy and cumbersome.

So Raoul had suffered in abject, pitiful terror, hidden away in his specially constructed $1.2 million Ecology House, manufactured chemical-free by HUD as a demonstration project on how to build homes for disabled MCS sufferers. Then DOT had provided Herman (his bicycle), which he couldn't ride in comfort, what with that ugly, cumbersome gas mask. Raoul felt grateful in a way, but it hadn't been enough. Sure, he had a place to live without suffering too much, except when reporters, HUD and DOT officials, and other visitors came by, wearing synthetic clothes and after-shave, and driving fume-belching cars. Yes, his lack of a driveway forced his visitors to park a half-mile away, but those fumes still followed them.

Raoul had lived for a few years as an isolated hermit, desperately longing to join society as a productive citizen. But the ravages of his MCS had prevented him from doing so in any meaningful and fulfilling manner. Once, he'd tried his hand as a writer. He'd finally managed to find organically manufactured paper, pens, and ink. Organically manufactured computers, modems, fax machines, etc., had been unheard of in those barbaric days just a few years ago, and he hadn't found anyone to blaze new technological pathways for him, due to society's unthinkingly cruel disregard for MCS sufferers. With great difficulty, he'd finally found a publisher who was willing to work with his handwritten manuscripts. He'd been deliriously happy for a short little while, thinking he'd finally arrived.

But then there'd been the need work with his editor at the publisher. Raoul couldn't talk to him on the phone, because he couldn't find an organically manufactured phone. The editor would send letters, but Raoul would have to hang them out on the clothesline for weeks on end, letting them air out, before he'd finally be able handle them (with organically manufactured rubber gloves) enough to read them. Even then, he often broke out in rashes, thinking about all those chemicals used in manufacturing the paper. He sent some of his own expensive organically manufactured pens, ink, and paper to his editor, to ease matters a bit, but that still left the contamination wrought by those chemically uncouth louts of the US Mail Service, not to mention their awful machines. So matters didn't improve much. Finally, in exasperation, his publisher dropped him.

Raoul still remembered those terrible days all too well. Sitting around with nothing do to, looking at Herman, longing to ride him. Longing to get out and about, to see the world, to interact with it, and to become a productive citizen. But the gas mask was awful and awkward, even if it had been organically manufactured, and it let in the occasional whiff of polluted air, whenever Raoul would get physically vigorous on Herman, and start breathing hard. So traveling by bicycle was a great ordeal.

Then finally had come his day of deliverance. He'd worked up his nerve, and had managed to ride Herman to a special gathering. This was a meeting of an MCS support group, way out in the woods, far away from contaminating unnatural chemicals. That's where he met Big Moose Running Nose, who'd set him free. Raoul could still remember it, pretty much word for word.

There he was, freshly arrived, sitting on a stump, wondering whether it was finally safe to take his gas mask off. A big galoot came up to him and stuck his hand out. "Hi. I'm Big Moose Running Nose, and I'm a recovering MCS sufferer."

Raoul looked at Big Moose's large outstretched hand suspiciously. Where had that hand been recently? Oh, heck, be brave, Raoul told himself. This is a fellow MCS sufferer. Trust him. Take a chance. So he whipped off his gas mask, peeled off his gloves, and shook Big Moose's hand. "Hi. I'm Raoul Kinky, and I'm an MCS sufferer, too." There, there, see? He told himself. You're not breaking out in a rash. Now sit down, and talk to this nice man.

"So tell, me, Big Moose, how do you do it? I mean, here you are, I don't see you carrying gloves or a gas mask, and you seem to be doing just fine. Are you feeling OK? Or are you a *real* MCS sufferer in the first place? And what's that funny thing with all those bunches of feathers there?"

"Raoul, you're no doubt a smart kind of a guy. Now you see, I'm not really so much an MCS sufferer, as I'm a *recovering* MCS sufferer. Heavy emphasis on the *recovering* part, there, see. And the key lies right here, in my hands, with this thing you refer to as a mere 'bunch of feathers'. These are very, very special feathers. Sacred feathers. We Native Americans call them horde feathers."

"Horde feathers? *Horde feathers?* What do you mean, horde feathers?"

"Yes, horde feathers. Horde feathers, because they come from a horde of different kinds of birds. And each kind of bird has its own special kind of properties, which we blend together in just the right way, to do some very special things. To make sacred objects like this thing here, which we Native Americans call a Sacred Dream Catcher."

"Are you really a Native American? You look like a regular old melanin challenged Euro-American to me. And I thought Native Americans hold *eagle* feathers sacred, not bunches of assorted different kinds of feathers. Come on, Mr. *Big Moose Running Nose*, I think you're putting me on. Tell me the truth."

Big Moose stared down at the ground, but only momentarily. He looked back up defiantly and hefted his Dream Catcher. "Well, OK, genetically I'm not Native American. And you're right, Native Americans—*genetically* Native Americans—they hold *eagle* feathers sacred, not *horde* feathers. But I'm what you call genetically challenged. So the National Eagle Repository out there near Denver, they won't mail me eagle parts, from naturally deceased eagles, like they will state-certified Native Americans, who fill out their forms right, and have tribal elders vouch for them, and so on. So if I, who the cruel state judges to be a heathen, Native-American-wise, am caught owning eagle feathers, then I'm busted for trafficking in body parts of an endangered species.

"You've got to have sympathy for me, as a genetically challenged Native American. I'm a Native American, but I have no Native American genes. The government bureaucrats, those heartless bastards, they can't see that I'm *spiritually* a Native American. Every last *one* of the lives that I've lived for the last *five hundred years* or so, I've been a Native American, except for *this* one. And I can have my past-lives regression hypnotist *show* that, too. Yet the feds, they won't mail me eagle feathers. They'll *bust* me if I have them, even though they're every bit as sacred to me as they are to any other Native American.

"Obviously, the feds, those oppressors, they're highly selective, trampling all over people's religious liberties. Punishing us for no reason at all! Why, I met a fella, real nice fella, a while back, name of Ale Run Hubba-Bubba. He worships a metal he calls Sacred Gold, just like we Native Americans worship Sacred Eagle Feathers. The feds, they have a repository for gold, just like they have for eagle parts. So he mailed in a request for some gold, in the name of religious freedom, just like genetically Native Americans do for eagle feathers.

"Well, dang it, you wouldn't believe this, but they turned him down! Violated his religious freedoms just like that, without so much as a second thought! I don't know how we've let things get to this point! Such a bunch of hard-hearted bureaucrats, I've never seen! And in a supposedly free, democratic country, yet! Why, we oughta go down there to that place with that gold, and, and..."

Raoul nodded his head sympathetically. "Yeah, maybe we should go down there and protest. Where'd you say these hard-hearted ignoramuses hang out?"

"Oh, I think they call it the Fort of Hard Knox, or some such. Anyway, where were we. Oh, yes. So I'm spiritually a Native American, yet I can't have Sacred Eagle Feathers. So I made my Dream Catcher, with the advice of a Lakota medicine man, out of aspen, willow, and various feathers..."

Big Moose showed Raoul how the Dream Catcher had been made. It was a long stick wrapped in colored string. From the tip hung a clump of feathers. Close to the tip hung a hoop strung with string, looking like a loosely woven fish net. From this assembly, yet more clumps of feathers hung. Big Moose rattled them off. Geese, pigeons, ducks, turkey, vultures, turkey vultures, and...

Raoul cut him off. "Well, that's a very nice dream catcher. So what's it good for? What does this all have to do with MCS, anyway?"

"Oh, my friend!" Big Moose exclaimed. "What is a Dream Catcher *good for!?* What are *dreams* good for?! They're good for whatever you *want* them to be good for!" He lowered his voice. "You know, Raoul, I used to be like you. Skeptical. Pessimistic. Negative. And suffered from MCS something awful! Then I met Large Bottom Snorfling Bear. He showed me how to make a Sacred Dream Catcher, and how to weave my dreams directly into its very essence. Then I worked at it a while. And I finally figured out how to weave in my dreams of a chemical-free life. So long as I have my Sacred Dream Catcher with me, it filters all the contaminants out of my life. Now I'm free! Free as a bird! I *fly* though life, now, unhindered by MCS! I'm *free*, Raoul, *free!* And you can be free, too, Raoul! Free like me!"

Raoul squinted and looked at Big Moose really, really skeptically. Big Moose just lifted his eyebrows and stared back silently. "Oh, I don't know," Raoul finally replied.

"Well, what's there to not know? Do you *like* suffering from MCS, or not?"

"Of course I don't like suffering from MCS! It's just that I don't know about your Dream Catcher. You admit you made it without any *eagle* feathers at all. The *real* ones have *eagle* feathers, it seems to me!. Does it *really* catch dreams, or not? How can I tell?"

"You can tell by looking at me! I don't suffer from MCS any more! Now I hate to do this, but if you insist, you can take my Dream Catcher from me for a little while, and walk over thataway for a hundred yards or so, and I'll just betcha I'll break down and start sneezing and coughing up a storm, just like that. That's usually the way it goes. Well?"

Raoul declined the challenge, not wishing to be rude. Big Moose, satisfied, continued. "OK. Now on those eagle feathers, and your so-called 'right way'. We all know there's really not a 'right way'. Right and wrong are purely subjective, and vary from culture to culture. So I've made my *own* way of making a dream catcher, integrating the good things from many, many Native American and other aboriginal, pure, nature-loving cultures. Now if you'll..."

"Wait," Raoul interrupted. "You say you've integrated many different cultures. So just exactly what kind of Native American *are* you then, anyway?"

"Oh, me? Well, I guess you could call me a Cree-Poospatuck-Navahopi-Blackfoot-Bigfoot-Yeti-Winnebago-Lakota-Dakota-Toyota, more or less. Approximately. But we really shouldn't be into this *labels* thing so much, you know. Even this 'Native American' label-thing. I'm just a Native. A Native, natural kind of a guy. Just try to think of me that way. Now about these Dream Catchers. I *really* think that's what you're looking for. It could *really help* your MCS, just like it helps me."

"Well, I don't know. I've got a really, really bad case of MCS, you know. Probably worse than anything you've *ever* had. I think I need the really, really Strong Medicine. I need to have real, sacred eagle feathers, most likely."

"Well, Raoul, you might be right. I won't argue that with you. But I want you to think about something. You really have no right to the body parts of an endangered species. I'll bet you're not part Native American. I'll bet you're not even able to prove, like I am, that you were Native American in your past, most recent lifetimes. Am I right?"

Raoul nodded his head, affirming Bog Moose's suspicions. Satisfied, Big Moose continued. "That means your desire for eagle feathers is illegitimate. Not just illegal, but also immoral. You have no Native American genes, karma, or culture, nor do you know how to properly conduct Native American ceremonies. No way you're a Noble Savage, then. That puts you on a par with—let me speak frankly now—that puts you on a par with, say, the superstitious, greedy, Earth-raping, slant-eyed, kooky gooks of the Far East, who eat rhino horn and tiger penis in hopes of propping up their sagging health and pooped-out peckers. Or the irrationally, chauvinistically violent and macho rag-heads of Yemen, who carve dagger horns out of rhino horn. As a sensitive, Earth-loving citizen, don't you think you could settle for horde feathers instead of eagle feathers?"

Raoul just sat there, looking profoundly skeptical and stubborn.

Big Moose just moved on to his next argument. "Raoul, you know, I'll bet there's something you haven't thought about. Eagles, these days, they're at the top of our poisoned food chain, and so they're eating all sorts of things. DDT. Dioxin. PCBs. Plutonium. Saturated fats. Animals and fish that were abused when they were young, and who knows *what* all else! Now the feathers *I* use to make *my* Dream Catchers, *they're* raised organically. They won't let me raise eagles, 'cause they're endangered; otherwise I'd have some organically raised eagle feathers for you. But that's how it goes. As is, I've got a source for the most organically pure and powerful feathers you'll find anywhere."

"Sounds pretty good," Raoul nodded agreeably. "So do you think maybe you could sell me a few feathers, then, and show me how I could make my own Dream Catcher?"

"Oh, yes, my friend, I *could* do that. But it's tough. *Real* tough. Took me a lot of practice, a lot of years. You've got to learn or devise all these elaborate ceremonies. Ceremonies, for instance, where you take sacred yogurt and pureed tofu, and smear it all over your body, while you wear a tie-died bandanna and get your nose pierced. Now that may sound trivial, but you have to do it just right. You've got to be in just the right frame of mind, while also eating peyote and being supervised by a Navahopi healer under the light of the full moon, while Venus is in Uranus. I tell you, it's not easy! Took me years, like I said.

"Or you could take it easy on yourself, and just stroll over this way for about a mile, where I have my car parked in the bushes. I've got a few spare Dream Catchers in my trunk. One of them I'm thinking of, I think it would be just the right one for you. Why don't we walk on over there, and..."

"Wa, wa, walk over, over to you c-*car?!*" Raoul sputtered in disbelief. "You drive one of those fume-spewing metal, synthetic *monsters?!* How *could* you?! How..."

"Oh, no. Not at all. It's electric, so take it easy. No fumes. No pollution. Well, OK, so they make a little bit of pollution when they generate the electricity to charge my batteries. But it's all for a good cause. I go around selling these Dream Catchers to people like you, to reduce suffering."

"Well, OK, then. Hold on a second, here, while I put on my mask and gloves, and..."

"Oh, no, my friend, don't forget, I've got my Dream Catcher with me. It'll cover the two of us while we walk on over there. Trust me. You'll see."

Big Moose was right. Raoul strolled without gasping, hacking, or wheezing, or even breaking out in a rash. They got to the car, then marveled over the Dream Catchers. Big Moose finally persuaded Raoul that he should buy one particular one. "Since you're my good friend, I'll let you have this one for a steal, at four hundred ninety-nine dollars and ninety-nine cents," he finished.

"Um, seeing as how I'm kind of, um, unemployed, and, like, a victim of MCS and all, I was wondering if maybe you could get my Medicaid to reimburse you for this?"

"No, I'm sorry, I'm working on that. But so far, those nasty Nazi bastards in Washington, they're blocking my efforts. Punishing all the poor people who suffer from MCS. So for now, I've got to ask for cash. I've got to make a living, and pay for all the organic feed for my birds."

"I don't have it in cash. Take a check?"

"Sure."

Raoul wrote out a check, using his organically manufactured pen, ink, and paper. He forked over $499.99 that he really didn't have. Then he walked away with his very own Sacred Dream Catcher, specially made to catch the dream of living free from the ravages of MCS. All this had been quite stressful, so he sat down and lit himself up an Earth Spirit, which was his favorite brand of organically grown, all-natural cigarettes.

Raoul never regretted buying that Dream Catcher, not for one second. It was the best $499.99 he'd ever spent, and the start of a whole new life. He stashed his gas mask and gloves in the attic, and started riding Herman on a regular basis. He made a special attachment to Herman, so that he could mount his Dream Catcher right up front. There, it filtered the toxins out of the airstream before they could get to Raoul. Now, Raoul was able to ride anywhere on his bicycle. Through heat and haze, smoke and fumes, and fog and smog he rode, never missing a beat. He lived life to the hilt!

Finally, he was even able to get himself a decent job. He became a traveling writer, poet, and cameraman for *National Vegetarian* magazine. Since *National Vegetarian* came out in both hardcopy and on-line versions, they bought him a digitizing video camera and a laptop computer with a radio modem, and sent him out on the road. Being the Earth-loving kind of a guy that he was, he refused to use any sort of polluting vehicle, not even an electric car. So he faithfully stuck with Herman. He mounted all his gadgets, including the antennae for his radio modem, onto Herman, and enthusiastically hit the road.

So here he was, several years and many adventures later, on yet another journalistic assignment. Yes, this was the big one! Raoul Kinky had been given the Big Mission. He was to get the scoop for *National Vegetarian*'s feature article on the organic-only grain elevators of Madness County. He was to capture it all on his digitizing video camera, all while extemporaneously creating poetry to capture the spirit of those fabulous *Grain Elevators of Madness County.*

So he rode Herman on down Amber Road, heading into Madness County. Several miles away, an unsuspecting Francestuous Johnsdame cooked a lonely breakfast of bean sprouts, carrots, and tofu for herself, since her husband and children were gone for four days to see the State Fair, several hundred miles away.

Raoul and Herman were in high spirits that day. So was Lucky Foot. Between the three of them, they were hardly ever lonely or bored. Lucky Foot was Raoul's and Herman's companion animal, a rabbit. She rode up in front, in a wire basket in a position of great honor, which was right next to that well-worn detoxifier and decontaminator, the Sacred Dream Catcher. Lucky Foot had joined the gang during some of Raoul's most recent adventures.

Just when the navigating got a bit tough, as Raoul was fussing with his maps while also pedaling and steering, a dog caught wind of Lucky Foot. The dog chased them for several hundred yards. Raoul cursed, swore, and kicked at the dog, all while pedaling furiously. So he missed a few turns and got lost.

Raoul ended up on Francestuous' doorstep, looking for directions. Wow, who could be knocking on my door at such an early hour, out here in the middle of nowhere, she asked herself. Maybe I'd better be careful. She tied her nightgown up tight and peered through the peep hole. No need to fear, she told herself. He looks like a sensitive sort. She opened up the door.

"Um, hi, ma'am, I'm Raoul Kinky, and I'm a poet and photographer for *National Vegetarian* magazine. No, no, that *is* my day job, so don't slam the door on me. And I'm not trying to sell you any magazines. I'm not trying to sell you anything. It's just that I'm here looking for some grain elevators for our upcoming spread, which is going to be called *Grain Elevators of Madness County*. I'll be helping to put y'all on the map, see, ma'am? Anyway, I'm lost, and I was merely wondering if you'd be so kind as to point me in the right direction. Can you tell me where to find Dinkledorf's OrganiGrain Silo?"

Wow, he *is* a sensitive sort of fella, Francestuous marveled. He's asking for directions! Whatta guy! Makes me cry! Now how often *does* one run into such a star creature, anyway?! "Well," she started, "You head down thatta way, till right before you get to old widow Henderson's farm, and then you... Oh, never mind. I'll take you there myself. I've nothing..."

"Oh, no, ma'am, I didn't mean to trouble you so. I'm *sure* you're busy, and you've got better things to do than to play tourist guide to a vagabond like myself. Now if you'll..."

"Oh, no, no trouble at all. Come on in. Here, sit down while I go change into something more suitable for traveling." He gracefully slipped into the house, gently closing the screen door behind him. She pulled up a chair for Raoul, thinking, wait, this man's a total stranger, what's coming over me? I'm being a total hussy, inviting him in here and prancing around in front of him in my nightgown! No, wait. So there's a one in three million chance he's a rapist or a murderer, or he's casing out our house. Fat chance. He looks and acts like a really decent sort of a guy. Take a chance. Live a little. Let him hang out here while I go change. No sweat.

She looked down at her half-eaten breakfast, feeling slightly embarrassed, as if she was a beast-like slob, eating slop in front of royalty. Now why am I feeling like this, she asked herself, embarrassed for feeling embarrassed. Here I've invited a stranger into my house, and I'm feeling embarrassed over what I'm eating, in the privacy of my own home. Oh, face it, I'm acting like a silly, shy schoolgirl, in front of this sensitive, gazelle-like creature. Get over it! "Would you care for some breakfast?" she asked lamely, self-consciously. "I can rustle you up some grub, real quick-like." Oh, God, she thought, did I really *say* that? I sound like a real hick! Am I getting to *be* a real hick, married to Bob the slob all these

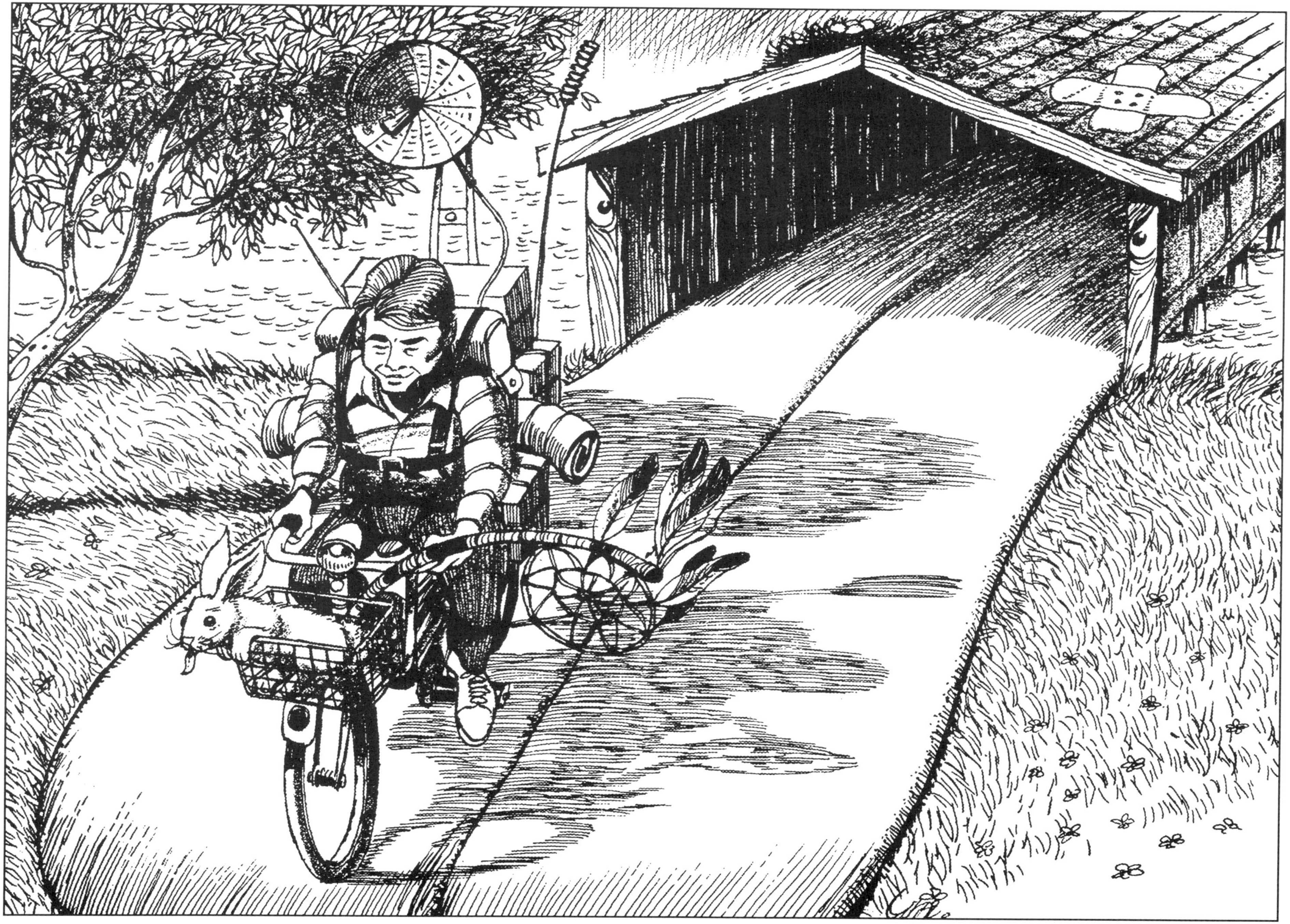

years?! Now *stop* that!

But the graceful, gazellelike creature took it all in stride. "Oh, ma'am, your cooking smells so delicious! So vegetarian! So *quiet*, as I always like to say, because it doesn't scream of the murder of helpless meat-bearing animals! But no, I can't impose any more on you than I have already. I'll just sit here on this seat you've so kindly provided, and keep you company while you finish up, if you'd like. Or wait for you while you change, if you're done eating. Whatever. Although, if you could spare a cup of that good coffee you're drinking, I'd be forever grateful. Black is fine."

She busied herself finding another clean cup, and found herself hoping he'd not think her too much of a low-class slob when she noticed the cup's chipped rim, halfway through pouring the coffee. Oh, great, lookit that, too, she thought, I've gone and picked one o' them thar cups that says "Harvey's Honeydipper, Septic Cleaning Services" on it. Now he'll think I'm a *real* country bumpkin!

But the gazellelike creature once again took it all in stride, sipping coffee without seeming to notice the cup's inelegance. "Ah, good stuff!" he exclaimed. "This must be the same organically grown kind that I always drink. FreeBird Deluxe, isn't it?"

"Why, yes, it sure is!" she replied, sitting down next to him. "Now are you *sure* you're not hungry? I've got some more bean sprouts, carrots, and tofu all warmed up here on the stove. If I put some on a plate and put it right in front of you, I'll bet you could eat a bite or two. So what do you say?"

Raoul confessed that he'd eat a bite or two, but that he simply hadn't meant to be such a bother. So she served him breakfast. "Whoa!" he said after taking the first bite, "This is *great!* You really know how to cook *quiet* food! You're quite the *quiet* cook, um... I'm sorry, what did you say your name was, anyway?"

"No, *I'm* sorry, I never did introduce myself, Raoul. I'm Francestuous. Francestuous Johnsdame. So tell me a bit about yourself." They sat there eating and sipping coffee, chatting up a storm. It was amazing—just like talking to an old friend. They talked about art and poetry and natural things. Deep and meaningful things, so unlike what she and Bob talked about. When they talked, that is. When Bob the slob wasn't busy belching and farting and letting the kids and dogs climb and slobber and drool all over him, that is.

Then breakfast was over and they each had themselves another cup of coffee. Raoul fidgeted a bit, so Francestuous asked him what was the matter. "Oh, it's just that I've got Herman and Lucky Foot and all my equipment out there right in front of your house and I'm afraid I'd better be keeping a better eye on things. I mean, I know you're way out here in the country, where there's less crime and all, but I've been in here so long now already, and..."

"Well, let's bring your stuff in, then, for a few minutes, and then I'll get dressed, and we can go find Dinkledorf's Silo. Here, let me lend you a hand."

So they went out front, and Raoul introduced Francestuous to Herman, Lucky Foot, the Sacred Dream Catcher, and all his equipment. Francestuous cooed over how cute Lucky Foot was, and listened in rapt fascination while Raoul explained all about the Dream Catcher. They put everything in the garage, closed the door, and then went back to finishing their coffee.

They sat there sipping more coffee, discussing life, and looking deeply into each other's eyes. Probably more deeply than any other couple has ever stared into each other's eyes anywhere in the known universe, that is. I could fall into those eyes and lose my very center, she thought dreamily. She began to wonder if maybe he made love like a panther. She got wet between her legs, but then made herself stop. I've got duties to my husband and children, after all, she reminded herself.

Then the coffee was gone and the magical time threatened to come to an end. Raoul fidgeted yet again. "Um, sweetie, you look nervous," Francestuous observed. "Is something wrong?"

"Oh, no, I just need a smoke, that's all. Whenever you're ready to go change, I'll just step outside for a smoke, and then we'll be ready to go. But no hurry."

"No, you can smoke in here! Go right ahead! No problem!" She added to herself, there's four days before Bob the slob and the kids come back, and I can air this house out real thoroughly before that. What he doesn't know won't hurt him.

So Raoul whipped out his Earth Spirits and lit one up, very expertly flicking his Bic®. Then he inhaled deeply, sensuously enjoying those all-natural vapors. Francestuous was quite impressed. "My, my,

Big Boy, you flick your Bic® so very well! And those Earth Spirits, they smell so swell! Do you think that maybe you could like spare me one?!"

So Raoul expertly flicked his Bic® yet once again, and Francestuous, feeling utterly, lusciously, sensuously worldly, purred over her cigarette. She'd not had one in *years!* Bob the slob didn't approve, so she'd refrained. But for today, she was *free!* It felt great to *live* a little! The magical time stretched out a bit longer, as they sat there smoking and chatting some more.

Finally it was time for Francestuous to go upstairs and change. As she stood up from the table, her arm brushed his, and tingles of electrovibosomatic energy energized her entire body. But she stifled her urge to fall into his arms, smother him with deeply passionate kisses, and satisfy his throbbing maleness. Instead, she used those unspeakably vast quantities of electrovibosomatic energy to propel herself upstairs to her bedroom. Feeling as if she was in a trance, she went. The energy made her go. So she just went. And she kept on going and going and going...

She found herself in a dream, in her bedroom. There's a gorgeous creature downstairs, and there's a nameless song in my head, she thought. An old song, I can't really say how it goes. It's old and it's sweet, and I knew it complete... no, no, it's old and it's sad, and I'd be glad to be bad... No, that's not it, either. It's about how sad it is to belong to someone else when the right one comes along. A man who doesn't slam screen doors, who knows how to light cigarettes just right, and who appreciates *quiet* cooking. And did you notice, she asked herself. Even his *breath* smells quiet! Star creatures like this don't just *happen by* every day!

She forced herself to snap out of dreamland for just long enough to select here best, low-cut sun dress, to brush her hair, and to put on a dab of Wind Sock Perfume, which had sat there in that little bottle in her dresser drawer, unused, for many years. Then she stifled her impulse to put makeup on, and headed back down the stairs.

"My, my, you look ravishing today," he said. She just blushed. They went outside and opened up the garage door, and stared awkwardly at Herman. Herman had no room for a passenger. By now, Francestuous knew all about how Raoul had high principles, and wouldn't ride in polluting vehicles. So she only momentarily debated on asking him if maybe they could just throw Herman, Lucky Foot, Dream Catcher, and everything else in the rear of her pickup, and head off to capture the essence of Dinkledorf's OrganiGrain Silo. She thought better of it.

Instead, she worked up her nerve, and then moved in to touch Raoul lightly on the arm, saying, "Um, Sweetie, Honey Buns, I hate to admit it, but I haven't ridden my bicycle in years. It's sitting over there in that corner, behind the boxes. Do you think maybe you could like look it over and fix it up? That way, see, I could join you, and show you the way to the grain silo, without me feeling so bad about driving an Earth-disrespecting fume-belching monstermobile. What do you say?"

"No sweat! *Anything* for you, my dearest Sugar Tush!" Raoul dragged the bike out, cleaned it up, blew the tires back up, and made adjustments. As he stooped over, working on that bike, Francestuous couldn't help but notice his flexing lean muscles. Then she caught a glimpse of his macho workingman's bun cleavage. Wow, she thought, if I only had a camera right now, here it is—the cover of a new hit romance novel! Now all we need my cleavage next to his cleavage, and we'd be into some *really* heavy heavage! She stooped down to join him, getting ready to ask about the details of what he was doing. But he stood up, declaring, "There! Good as new!"

"Oh, you're *so* sweet!" she proclaimed. "And such a handyman!"

"So what's *your* bicycle's name, anyway?" he asked. "I feel so crass. Here I am, I just worked on her, and I don't even know her name. A doctor shouldn't work on a patient without knowing her name."

Francestuous was deeply embarrassed. Her bicycle didn't even *have* a name. But, hey, we can fix that up real quick, she thought. He'll never need to know. "This is Betsy. Betsy, meet Raoul. Raoul, meet Betsy."

Raoul insisted on introductions all around. Betsy met Herman, Lucky Foot, and Dream Catcher. Then, finally, they were on the road to Dinkledorf's OrganiGrain Silo. They pedaled down the roads in the summer morning's clean sunny country air, taking in the sights, sounds, and smells. Francestuous felt young and free, like a little girl, on her bicycle. And she didn't even worry about whether any of her farmer neighbors, out on their tractors, saw and recognized her out there bicycling with a strange man. She was *free!*

Those pure, innocent feelings of all-natural joy washed over here out there in that rustic scene. She couldn't help but to share her feelings of joy. So she gazed over admiringly at Raoul, as they rode down that road side by side, and sang out to him, "You make me feel like a natural woman!" His silent but sincere reply, a simple but radiant smile, confirmed to her that everything was right with the world. Here she was, sharing her innermost feelings with a beautiful man in a beautiful world, doing beautiful, natural things, without a care in the world. What could be more innocent, what could be more free?

Then they got to the silo. Raoul opened up his saddlebag to unpack his laptop computer, tripod, digitizing camera, and various accessories. Francestuous watched intently, looking at all that well-packed gear. "Hey, Big Boy, I really like the way you organize your gear," she commented. He unbolted the radio modem's antenna from Herman, and hooked it all together.

He gazed intently at the silo, pacing back and forth. Then he turned to Francestuous, saying, "OK, I think I've got it. Now I'm going to do my Thing. Please just sit there and keep still, and don't say anything for a few minutes. I'll say 'cut' when I'm all done, and then we can talk again. OK?" Francestuous nodded her assent, and he got to work.

He pulled the legs out of the tripod dangling from the camera. He flipped a switch, then slowly, smoothly walked around, capturing the silo and its surroundings from many angles. Then he splayed the tripod's legs out, set the camera down, and solemnly marched around to stand between camera and silo. There, he paused once again.

Then he swept his hands out, gesturing at the ground, the sky, and the grain elevator, as if to silently say, "Look at all this majesty that surrounds us." Then, staring straight and hard at the camera, he said:

> The Earth is good,
> The rain is wetter,
> Organically grown,
> Grain is better.
>
> The sky is blue,
> The grass is green,
> Get off your butt,
> And join our scene.

Then he said, "Cut."

Francestuous clapped and cheered. "Bravo! Bravo! Encore! Encore!"

"Encore at the next grain silo," Raoul replied mock-sternly. "Let's go!" He packed back up and they headed out.

When they got to Schicklefhart's All-Natural Elevator, Raoul repeated the performance, more or less. This time, when he got out in front of the camera, he said:

> There was a man from Bombay,
> Who walked in a peculiar way,
> With each little stride,
> He wiggled from side to side,
> This is what we call The Way.
>
> They keep all chemicals away,
> They keep their poisons at bay,
> So a place called Madness County,
> Of grain brings forth a bounty,
> This is surely the best, we say.

Francestuous was quite impressed. She commented that she was sure looking forward to buying a copy of *National Vegetarian*, to see Madness County in the limelight. But fate held the best reserved for last. They pedaled many miles, following the large signs for Wiesengruber's Elevated Gaia-Grain, which was a major local attraction.

Halfway through those many miles of pedaling to their last destination, they took a break. This was when Raoul insisted on taking some pictures of Francestuous. She was quite flattered, and did her best to look as alluring as possible.

Then they arrived at that last silo. This time, it was Raoul's turn to be impressed. So he took a lot of footage, far more than at the first two elevators. Then he gestured yet even more solemnly in front of his camera, and said:

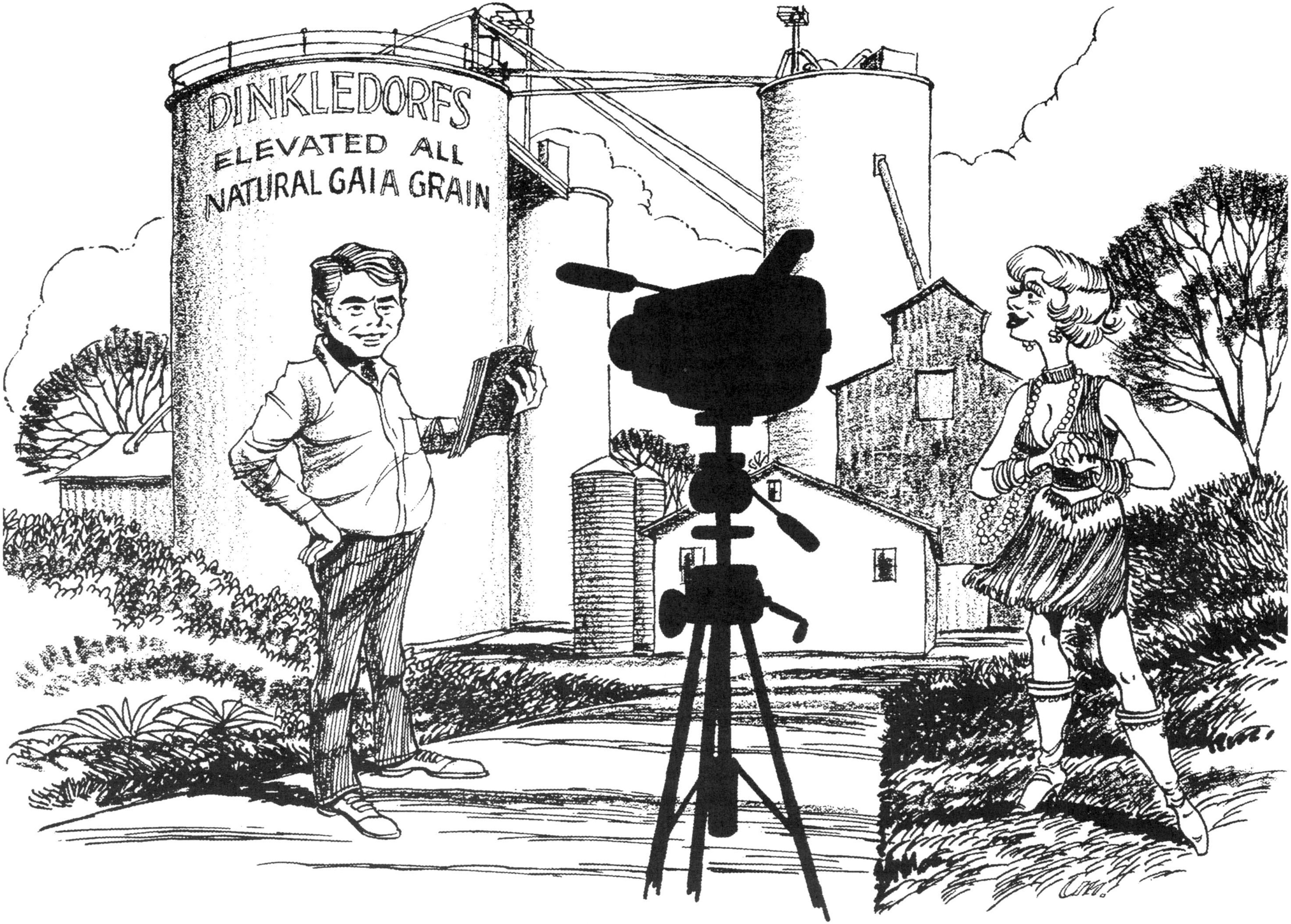
DINKLEDORFS
ELEVATED ALL
NATURAL GAIA GRAIN

The Earth breathes in,
The Earth breathes out,
She gives forth humus,
She gives forth sprouts,

The Earth breathes in,
She breathes again,
She gives forth rain,
She gives forth grain,

The Earth breathes in,
The Earth breathes out,
That I'm quite deep,
Is beyond all doubt.

"Cut" was barely out of Raoul's mouth when Francestuous flung herself into his arms, saying, "Oh, Raoul, you *are* so deep! I can't help it! Come on, quick, let's go climb the silo and make love in the grain!" She smothered him with insistent kisses.

So he did as she asked, abandoning Herman, Lucky Foot, Dream Catcher, and all accessories. They'd all have to survive for a little while without him. They climbed the silo and crawled onto the grain. Then they abandoned all control. He ravished her throbbingly sensual womanhood.

They lay in each other's arms, exhausted. "Wow, Raoul, that was *great!* You're the best! You complete the essence of my womanhood! You're like the graceful meaning of the molecular spaces between the smoothest feathers of every bird who has ever flown into the moonrise! You're like the last mystic poet, falling forever towards me from dimension B, fulfilling my deepest womanly longings! You really *do* make love like a panther!"

"Well, yes, Francestuous, my One True Fructose Fanny, that's exactly how I feel. I couldn't have said it any better myself. But a panther is a carnivorous beast, an eater of flesh. I'm a vegetarian. Don't you think I make love more like a bunny rabbit? Never mind; I know what you were trying to say. All my life has been just a rehearsal for this heavy scene. This is what I've been made for; this is my mission on this planet. You're right. Always, I've been falling from dimension B-grade. Falling towards loving you, Francestuous. Loving you, my dearest Francestuous, loving you. Forever and ever. Like the dew kissing ten tired turtles in a tuddle-tuddle tree, that's how I was meant to kiss and cuddle thee." So he kissed her, deeply and meaningfully. Then they made mad passionate love again and again.

The sun sagged down towards the trees by the time they brushed the dirt off themselves, straightened themselves out, and hit the long road home. Dusk enveloped them as they rode up to her house. They showered together, and ate another quiet meal of quiet but fresh vegetables. Francestuous dug some beer out of the deepest, darkest recesses of her 'fridge. He opened the cans expertly, and they had themselves a drink. Then they went to bed, where there made mad passionate love, bunny-rabbit style, yet again and again.

For three days and three nights, all told, they quoted poetry to each other, talked of deep and meaningful things, and made bunny love, while Raoul always lit their cigarettes and opened their beer cans most expertly. Never, ever, never *once* did he slam the screen door, either.

Still, their time together had to come to end, sooner or later. Or did it? This was their unspoken question, which neither dared to raise first. Finally, as they lay exhausted in bed yet again, Francestuous brought it up. "You know, Sweetie, you and I remind me a lot of this couple I read about in a book a while back. It was called *The Bridges of Madison County*. They had a deeply meaningful and mystically moving affair, but then her husband came back, so her lover split, and then they both lived the rest of their lives, desperately, hopelessly longing for each other.

"She made her choice out of like this rational sense of duty to her husband and kids, but she always kind of questioned like if maybe she'd have been better off going with her feelings, and the chemistry of their totally profound passion. So the two of them went their separate ways. It was *so* sad! She had to make do with her *husband!* The hero, the last cowboy, her lover, he was never able to make love to a woman again, 'cause no one could ever compare to her. So he ended up buying a dog to keep him company in his last days, and then, that was it. So have you ever read that book, Raoul, sweet buns? Do you think we're maybe kind of like them?"

"No, I didn't read the book, but I saw the movie. And, well, ah, yes, I guess we're sort of like them. Except I already *have* a pet, which I bought to console myself after my last true love cruelly, heartlessly betrayed me in favor of her husband and kids. But I'm over that now."

They both laid there in dark, tired silence for a while. Francestuous broke the silence. "You know," she said wistfully, "I really don't want to be like the lady in that book. Being too rational, going with my head instead of my heart. Ignoring the *important* things, like magical vibes—*'chemistry'*, as they say. I'm way too special to go with boring, regular, rational thinking. What they call 'common sense' is just way too unromantic. Duty is dull. Just doing whatever makes your heart go pitty-pat is far, *far* more *glorious.* More like the really cool things that the glamorous people in Panderwood are doing." Then she lapsed back into silence.

She was working up her nerve to ask if maybe she could avoid a lifetime of regret, and come with Raoul on his journalistic journeys, when he spoke first. *"You're* not going to do that to me, *too,* now, *are* you, my deepest, dearest Francestuous?"

"Why, do what, Raoul?" she asked, tumbling off of their mutual train of thoughts.

"Abandon and betray me in favor of your husband and kids," he croaked in hushed hoarseness.

"Oh, no, I'd *never* do that do *you*, my dearest Polysaccharide Patootie. Never! *Never!* I was just so afraid to ask you if I could come along with you! You mean, you'll *have* me?!"

"As often as possible, for as long as possible. Till death do us part," he replied solemnly. She started sobbing with the sudden relief from all her worries. So then he sniffled a bit, too, and they held each other tight. Then they made love all night.

In the morning, she persuaded him to bend his principles just enough, just this once, to use a fume-belching monstermobile. She did this only by promising that they'd sell the thing as soon as they moved her stuff. Then they loaded her most precious clothes, furniture, and other household goods onto her pickup truck.

She wrote a *"Dear Bob the Slob"* letter, pointing out to him that she didn't want to hurt him or the kids, but that she had her *own* needs to consider, too. Rather than living with a lifetime of regret, she was going to go with her feelings. She'd found a man who didn't slam screen doors, and who knew how to light cigarettes, open beer cans, and love a woman. But yes, she loved him and the kids very much, and she always would. She put it down on the kitchen counter.

"Hey, Sucrose Snuggles, you mind if I read that?" Raoul asked.

"No, please do," she replied. "I'm open for suggestions. You're a literary kind of a guy, after all."

He read it in silence, lifting his eyebrows now and then. He put it down. "Kinda harsh, I'd say. Maybe you could sort of soften it up by adding some reference to a snippet of classy, uplifting poetry or music lyrics or some such."

"Have anything in particular in mind, there, Glucose Gluteus Monosaccharide Maximus?"

"Oh, I don't know. OK, well, sure, sit back down here and write a wee tad more. You've got quite a bit of room left on your second page down here, see? OK? Great! Here goes: 'PS. Dearest Bob, please don't take it too hard. If things ever get you down, then please just remember some wise words from the Beatles. As they once sang, "Oh-blah-dee, oh-blah-da, hey, hey, hey, life goes on." If you can remember this, and live by it, then nothing can ever hurt you. Love, Francestuous.' Now how's *that* grab you? Lift his sagging spirits, it will! You never know what a few kind words can do."

"Oh, Raoul, you're so *deep!* And so caring and sensitive!" She fell into his arms, and they smooched long and passionately. They drove for miles and miles along those twisting, turning roads together, in ecstatic happiness, and moved her stuff into his $1.2 million HUD "Ecology House". Then they sold the truck, got new tires for Betsy, and started to build their perfect life together.

This chapter has endnotes concerning All-Natural Nicotine, Eagle Feathers, Multiple Chemical Sensitivity, and Sensitive and Romantic Writers. See page 229.

Chapter 10

Whispers of Omnology

"There's a sucker born every minute." Attributed to Phineas T. Barnum (1810-1891). Barnum may or may not have actually said this. He admitted that he may have said, "The people like to be humbugged." Show-business rival Adam Forepaugh accused P. T. Barnum of having said the "sucker" quote. Barnum never denied it, and even thanked Forepaugh for the free publicity.

"The Journal *said, 'There have been repeated reports that Mr. Hubbard told his science fiction colleagues that the way to get rich is to found a religion.' The problem is this incident never happened. So, from the Church's perspective it does get tiring responding to it, repeatedly. (For the record, George Orwell is the person who really said that and to our knowledge he never knew or met Mr. Hubbard.)" From an ad in the 1 April '97* Wall Street Journal, *placed by the Church of Scientology International, in response to a* Wall St. Jrnl *editorial of 25 March '97. The Church made no indication whether or not this was an April Fool's joke, either. We were left in suspense.*

"Wrong! See 'Over My Shoulder: Reflections on a Science Fiction Era,' by Lloyd Arthur Eshback, one of the first prominent publishers of science fiction (Oswald Train: Philadelphia, 1983). He is very specific as to the subject:

"'The incident is stamped indelibly in my mind because of one statement that Ron Hubbard made. What led him to say what he did I can't recall—but in so many words Hubbard said: "I'd like to start a religion. That's where the money is!"'

"Scientology may argue that Mr. Eshback is wrong or duplicitous (he's not), but the statement is neatly documented for all time." Our suspense is thus relieved, thanks to A. H. Lybeck's letter to the editor, which was published in the 1 May '97 Wall St. Jrnl.

Not authoritative enough for you? Just another crackpot letter to the editor? Okay, then. "In the late 1940s, pulp writer L. Ron Hubbard declared, 'Writing for a penny a word is ridiculous. If a man really wants to make a million dollars, the best way would be to start his own religion.'" Eugene H. Methvin, in Scientology: Anatomy of a Frightening Cult, Reader's Digest, *May 1980.*

"All men are your slaves." La Fayette Ron (AKA L. Ron) Hubbard (1911-1986), according to "The Thriving Cult of Greed and Power," 6 May '91 Time *magazine, by Richard Behar.*

Ale Run Hubba-Bubba and his friends in Scamway International kept on rolling in the prosperity and good fortune. Everyone everywhere demanded Quart Low Trackers for finding drugs, weapons, and lost golf balls. Unfortunately for Ale Run and his friends, though, all good things must come to an end. So an FBI lab spent several months and millions and millions of dollars to investigate, and lo and behold, they reached a conclusion: Quart Low Trackers were a *fraud!* And Ale Run and all his hordes and all his men couldn't prove that the Quart Low Tracker did what their advertising said it could do. A federal judge ordered Scamway International to stop selling the Quart Low Tracker.

Ale Run was brought up on charges of fraud. Fortunately, since the prosecution couldn't *prove* that the Quart Low Tracker *didn't* work, when operated by a properly trained expert, he was acquitted. So he kept his prosperity and good fortune and avoided jail. But he couldn't sell his Trackers any more, so it sure looked like the good times had come to an abrupt halt.

Ale Run sulked in his mansion that night, trying to console himself with that fact that he at least retained custody of that one last ace in the hole. This was his original Quart Low Tracker—the one with the *real* magic, which Chewdychomper Chupacabras had given him. He drank a few pints of ale, sinking into an ever more sullen mood.

But then he got to thinking, well, I'm not *all* washed up. There's *got* to be a way I can use this technology to benefit humanity and my bank account! All I have to do is to figure out a safe way to do it. A manner in which I'll be guaranteed freedom of action. Some method of using the Quart Low Tracker's technology whereby the government can't *touch* me. I've got to *think*. Maybe if I stare deep into the LCD display on my Quart Low Tracker, here, the answer will well up into my mind.

Ale Run concentrated long and hard. Then the Whispers came to him. Whispers of Omnology, borne on the cosmic-karmic vibe fronts. Let's see, he said to himself as he channeled the vibes. I'll add some very simple circuits to the mass-produced Quart Low Trackers. A switch, a battery, a Geiger-counter style beeper, a random noise amplifier, and some flashing LEDs. I'll call it the V-Meter, for Vibes Meter. Then I'll come up with an elaborate system and vocabulary to explain what all wonderful things that the V-Meter can do for you. All your problems are caused by, oh, say, clusters of, um, scamgrams. To get your scamgrams to go away, you've got to hire an expert who will use his V-Meter to chase away your scamgrams. We'll have a special word for casting out the scamgrams—say, "fleecing".

Got troubles? And who doesn't?! What a huge, untapped market! All your troubles are caused by clusters of scamgrams and maybe even a bloody metan or two. Bloody metans, that is. Scamgrams and bloody metans that were left here maybe like seventy-five million years ago, by, oh, I don't know, say, like, a Cruel Galactic Emperor Zebu. And the only way to set yourself free is to have your scamgrams and bloody metans fleeced by an expert with a V-Meter! That's *it!* Brilliant!

OK, then, so we've got magic words and magic *technology* to make everyone's troubles go away. Now what do we call our discipline? A science, or a religion? It's a lot like a science, like psychology or psychiatry. We don't have to prove anything; all we have to do is have lots of scientific-sounding words and theories, and act very authoritative. Judges will send us clients. No probation unless you come and see us. And we'll be called upon to be expert witnesses. Very lucrative, possibly.

On the other hand, we'll have to pay taxes. Keep records, maybe even give money back to dissatisfied customers. And the FDA will doubtlessly call our V-Meter a "medical device", and take years and years to approve it. Maybe even *never* approve it! We could avoid all these troubles by just calling ourselves a *church*. A *religion*. Sure, the courts won't be able to call us as expert witnesses or send us clients, that way, 'cause of separation of church and state. Yet if we call it a *religion,* then no one will be able to *touch* us! After all, isn't religious freedom *sacred?!* Yes! Yes! This is it, Ale Run, *this is it!!!* Fame, wealth, and power, here I come! Ale Run just about creamed his pants with joy at his latest inspirations.

OK, calm down, he told himself. So what will I call my church? Something impressively all-encompassing, rational, modern, and scientific. Something to tap into the trappings and respectable rationality of science, even though we're a church. Have our cake and eat it, too. Something like, say, maybe... *The Church of Scatological Scamology?* No, no, *that* won't do! Too honest! Hmmm... OK, yes, this is *good!* **The Church of Omnology!** I'll be the high priest of *The Church of Omnology.* The Church of Everything. The Church that has All the Answers. For the $Right $Price. Yessiree, Ale Run, you sly ol' devil, you, you're *on* it! All the Answers, all right! All the Answers to the problems of me not having as much power and money as I need, at least, *that's* for sure! And what other issues really matter, anyway?!

Ale Run got to bed late that night, and still found it hard to sleep. He'd never been so enthused in a long time. The Quart Low Tracker would help him select his disciples and his methods. Surely the Church of Omnology—especially as a *tax-free* institution—*surely* it would put Scamway International to shame, revenue-wise. He couldn't wait! Finally, he drifted off to sleep.

The next day he consulted his Quart Low Tracker once again, and got to work. He called his industrial designers, and they got to work revamping the Quart Low Tracker design, creating the famous V-Meter. Ale Run secluded himself in his mansion, writing down the doctrines of the Church of Omnology at great length.

Not too many months later, Raoul Kinky and Francestuous Johnsdame were laying in bed. One rolled over to the other and said, "I wanna be an Airborne Ranger, live a life of sex and danger." Francestuous looked at him with shocked, disapprovingly wide eyes. "That's a *joke,* Sweetie, a *joke!* I'm just laying here all washed out, and thinking I'd like to be healthy and vigorous again some day. That phrase just popped into my head. I went to protest at this Air Force base once, and I remember this from a marching song that the young troops were singing. You know, kind of like, I'm just randomly grasping at our society's clichés about vigor. I'd like to be a lumberjack man, too. Except I wouldn't be killing people or trees. Know what I mean?"

"Sure, Honeypot," Francestuous patted him gently. "I understand. We'll get you over this CFS thing real soon, now, and you'll be just like new. Have faith. We'll find you a cure, don't you worry." She referred to the fact that not long after he'd cured his MCS with the Dream Catcher, he'd caught a severe case of CFS (Chronic Fatigue Syndrome). They'd tried hypnosis, acupuncture, herbs, crystals, and homeopathy, all to no avail. So he lay there, still bedridden.

"Have you tried contacting Big Moose Running Nose lately?" he asked her for the umpteenth time. He hoped that maybe Big Moose could make him a new, customized Dream Catcher to cure his CFS. He often fondly handled Big Moose's tattered old business card, desperately dreaming of a new Dream Catcher.

"Yes, Lactose Lips, I tried to call him again yesterday, and wrote him just a week ago. The number is still disconnected, and the address is still like obsolete. And I can't find him listed anywhere."

"I just can't understand why a man with such a sure-fire cure for such a common and devastating illness would be so hard to find," Raoul complained yet again. "It's a shame. A mystery and a shame."

She agreed with him and told him she'd be heading downstairs to fix him breakfast in bed. A breakfast of good, wholesome *quiet* food, of course, that is. She crawled out of bed and stooped over to kiss him. "I love you, Glucose Gluteus Maximus," she whispered. "Hang in there, you poor dear."

He smelled her quiet breath, thinking, what a wonderful woman I've managed to link up with, here. "I love you too, Fructose Fanny." He rolled over gently, straining to protect his delicate, sore and aching muscles from abuse. Francestuous headed downstairs. Shortly, he heard the sounds of pots and pans, of the genesis of a delicious and quiet breakfast. Then he heard her open the front door, to make the long walk to the mailbox. Shortly, she'll be back with news of the world, he thought. He glanced over at his old Dream Catcher. At least these days I'm over that nasty old MCS thing, he thought. I won't have to air all those toxic chemicals out of my mail for days and days before I can stand to read it, like in the old days. No more mail on the clotheslines, thanks to my Dream Catcher! Sure, this CFS thing is bad, but look on the bright side. Things could be worse.

A few minutes later, he heard the front door opening again. Then there were more quiet breakfast sounds. Shortly, the love of his life entered their bedroom once more, carrying two steaming trays of quiet food and some mail. He sat up gingerly, then she set the tray up around his lap. They dined quietly. He finished up and praised her good cooking, like usual. She gathered up the dishes and trays, heading back down the stairs.

He reached over to the nightstand and picked through the mail she'd brought up. Hm, no disability check from Social Security yet, but we'll still survive for a little while longer. What else have we got here? A new copy of *Mother Earth* magazine. Hm. Let's see. He started reading.

With curses long, loud, and foul, he leapt out of bed. Francestuous started to dash up the stairs, but ran into him as he dashed down the stairs, proclaiming his outrage. His vehemence overwhelmed her momentary amazement at his miraculous recovery of vigor. "Look at this *crap*, Francestuous, just look at this *§&*@#a~¶!!!*" He sputtered incoherently.

"There, there, my Sweet Sodium Cyclamate Mate, now, *calm down!* What's wrong?"

"Look! See *this?!* There's this nasty lying bitch of a whore, this Bertha Bubblebuster and her new book, she's running around and, and *slandering* all of us CFS sufferers! Listen to this! This is all about her new book, called *'Chronic Fatigue Syndrome and Multiple Chemical Sensitivity Sufferers and Those With Recovered Memories of Being Forced to Eat Alar-Poisoned Apples by Silicon-Breasted Space Alien Abductors in Abusive Satanic Rituals Are All a Bunch of Hysterical Whining Crybaby Sissies But We All Need to be Deeply Sympathetic and Double Our Contributions to Psychiatrists and Other Public Servants Who Will Destigmatize Their Neuroses and Heal Their Illnesses.'* She says it's just *all in our heads!* Can you believe this woman's fascist insensitivity?! Why, this Nazi wench, we should..."

"Come on, Sweetie, now, *calm down!* Maybe you should call your CFS support group. Maybe they could help you feel better about how society blames the victims, and maybe we could come up with something to like *do* about all this."

Raoul did just that. He and his CFS support group got together and decided upon a course of action. They rounded up a few trucks and went around to grocery stores, garages, flea markets, and trash dumps. Raoul and his friends got some good, healthy exercise, throwing old tires, crates of rotten organically grown tomatoes and eggs, old furniture, and moldy water-logged mattresses onto their big trucks. Then they waited for just a few days, till Bertha Bubblebuster showed up at the local *We Be Big McBooksnores* for her book signing.

At Raoul's signal, they crashed their battering ram through the McBooksnore doors. Splinters flew everywhere. Their loud, blood-curdling screams sent hapless pedestrians fleeing in all directions. Carrying old sofas, refrigerators, tires, and crates of rotten produce, they streamed three abreast through the shattered doors. Then they heaved their cargo at one Ms. Bertha Bubblebuster. Raoul shouted fiercely, **"You sniveling rotten insensitive hysterical lying wench, here, see what it feels like to be victimized! This is all just in your head!"**

She fled, screaming. "Now who's hysterical?! Now who's hysterical?!" they all chanted triumphantly in unison. "Fascist bitch", "Evil murderer", and "Hitler's whore", they muttered as they traipsed out of the trashed McBooksnore. Then they all went to hoist an organic beer or two in celebration, and then they headed for home. All except for Raoul and Francestuous, that is.

"That was really great!" Francestuous said. "Way to stand up for the voiceless, helpless, oppressed victims! I'm like really, really proud of you! Now, while we're out and about, and you're like feeling pretty good it seems, at least for a little while, do you think maybe this might be a good time to go shopping for that wheelchair you've been wanting to get? I mean, I hate to say it, but you never know when this CFS thing is gonna come and go. You might be feeling worse again tomorrow or the next day. Especially if those pesky, nosy Social Security folks come snooping around again, and making us all tense and stressed out."

Raoul agreed that this might be a good idea. So they went window shopping. But before they could get to the handicapped appliances store, they happened upon *the All Paths Multifaith Soulorama*, a cooperative multi-church recruitment center at the shopping plaza, between the Armed Services Recruiting Center and the head shop. Francestuous paused there thoughtfully. "You know, Raoul," she said pensively, "Maybe our lives are too empty and shallow, spiritually-wise. Maybe we're like, um, too content with our material blessings. All our quiet food, quiet clothes, our one point two million dollar ecology house, poetry books, and our bicycles, and all. Maybe we should be paying more attention to our spiritual dimension."

So they walked hand in hand down the hall, looking at the displays, the signs on the doors, and the pleasant little offices. Buddhists, Hindus, Shintoists, Animists, Zoroastrians, Christians of many flavors, and Muslims beckoned at them from posters, displays, and office doors. "This is all so passé," Raoul muttered. "Too boring and bourgeois for me."

Then they came upon an exceptionally tasteful display. On the door there were gold-plated inscriptions:

Vyizder Zomenimor
Orziz Assiz
Zanzer R. Orziz

Master Universal Omnologists
CEOs
(Certified Experts of Omnology)
Smile! Happiness is at hand!
Whatever your troubles—we can help *YOU!*
The Church of Omnology
Earth Division

Raoul stood and stared in awe. "This might be it, Francestuous, this might be it. Just *LOOK* at this! *The Church of Omnology!* It sounds so... so... *scientific*. So powerful, so universal. We'd better check it out."

So they did. They strolled right in. The first sight which greeted them was a small crowd, all milling excitedly about a tall, dark and handsome man and his smiling, leggy blonde babe. Could that possibly be Jon Travibesty, the famous Panderwood actor, and his actress wife, Julie Peston? Here, in podunk little ol' Madness County?

Surely not, Raoul said to himself. Probably someone's idea of a joke, dressing up to look just like them. Running into Jon Travibesty at the local Soulorama just seems too much like running into Elvis at the grocery store to possibly be really true. Then again, how many pranksters would go to the trouble to also hire what looks like bodyguards and reporters with such big, fancy, and obviously expensive cameras, just to make the show more convincing? Maybe they're the real thing, after all.

Raoul and Francestuous sauntered on up to the crowd, seemingly entirely casually. Two men, upon noticing the new arrivals, peeled off of the huddle. They introduced themselves, shaking hands with Raoul and Francestuous. The tall one with the thick, glossy black hair said, "Hi.

I'm Vyizder Zomenimor, and these are my partners, Orziz Assiz and Zanzer R. Orziz," with a sweeping gesture. The gesture clearly meant to Raoul that the shorter, more scholarly-looking gentleman must be Orziz Assiz, but as to who Zanzer R. Orziz was, Raoul had no idea. This part of Vyizder's gesture, as best as Raoul could tell, had pointed to nothing but empty space.

Francestuous paid scant if any attention to the introductions. Instead, she stared intently towards the center of attention. "Um, yes," Raoul replied, poking Francestuous in the ribs with his elbow. "This is my companion human, I mean, um, my significant other, um, Francestuous Johnsdame. And I'm Raoul Kinky. Pleased to meet you. And I'm sure Francestuous is, too." She nodded vaguely, still staring towards the center of the huddle's attention.

Raoul gave up on her. "Is that really Jon..." he started to ask quietly, looking wide-eyed at Vyizder.

"Yes, it really, truly is. Jon Travibesty and his wife, Julie Peston. Here in our own little Madness County. You see, the Church of Omnology is starting to draw the attention of those who are truly hip and in the know. Even though our esteemed leader and founder, Ale Run Hubba-Bubba, began imparting his wisdom to the masses only a matter of months ago, already the Word is spreading far and wide. Wise and influential people are flocking to us. Through the use of our latest therapies and technologies, we are casting out scamgrams, fleecing bloody metans away, and healing the people. So as you can imagine, if we can do great things for even the rich and powerful, we'd certainly be able to do a lot for you." Raoul didn't quite follow all the jargon, but he got the general drift of things.

"Um, sounds good," he replied. "I'm not quite sure what scamgrams and bloody metans are for, but they sure don't sound like nice things to have hanging around. So if you can make them go away, that sounds like a good idea to me. Now I'm sorry, I didn't even quite follow your introductions. So you're... Vyizder Zomenimor? Did I say that right?" Vyizder nodded. "And you're Orziz Assiz?" Orziz nodded in turn.

"But then who is Zanzer R. Orziz?" Raoul finished. "I didn't quite follow you."

"Zanzer R. Orziz isn't very apparent to the untrained eye," Vyizder assured him. "But you'll learn to understand and appreciate him, if you'll allow us to bring The Word to you. The Words of Ale Run, that is. Words that will ring down throughout all future eons, because they were written by He Who Fleeces Our Scamgrams Away. Don't worry, now, we'll give you the answers that you deserve. All in good time. But we'd really much rather explain it to all of you at once, instead of going the piecemeal route. Not that we mind the endless repetition. It's just that we could be *so* much more efficient, if we could speak to everyone at once. We could then get The Word out to all those millions of victims of scamgrams that much faster. So please excuse us while we put off your questions for just a few minutes, while we begin our class, here."

Vyizder and Orziz circled around the huddle that in turn circled around Jon Travibesty and Julie Peston. They tried to pick people off of the perimeters of the crowd, announcing to all those who bothered to pay attention to them, that the class was about to begin. Unfortunately for Vyizder and Orziz, Jon and Julie were just now breaking out their pens and offering autographs. The crowd ramped into a chaotic crescendo. Francestuous escaped Raoul's clutches, and rushed towards Jon and Julie. **"So where, exactly, *is* the end of this line, anyway?!?"** she demanded loudly. Everyone ignored her.

Jon waved a pacifying hand over the crowd, announcing that anyone who wanted an autograph would get one. So Vyizder and Orziz gave up, and patiently waited while Jon and Julie satisfied the crowd's demands. Finally, the huddle broke up, and everyone had a seat in an array of chairs in front of Vyizder and Orziz.

Vyizder started off with, "Good evening, ladies and gentlemen. Now I gather that you've all come together with us here this evening to learn about the wonders of Omnology. This, we'll do our best to help you learn, Ale Run willing. But first, I believe, proper introductions are in order. This is my friend and co-teacher, Orziz Assiz. And I'm Vyizder Zomenimor. With us this evening is a third teacher, who hides himself from the uninitiated. You can't see him. You won't be able to see him till you're thoroughly trained, and have become enlightened, operating metans, channeling vibes from higher energy levels. But rest assured that our third teacher, Zanzer R. Orziz, is with us, here, and that his lessons, too, are vital for our well-being. More about him in a few minutes.

"Now please rest assured that the Church of Omnology is broad-minded and tolerant. There are many, many branches of our church, and many ways of thinking. All that holds us together is our common bond. This is that we all acknowledge that our Esteemed Leader, Ale Run Hubba-Bubba, is the One True Seer and Caster Out of Scamgrams. So our particular arrangement here hasn't been officially ordained by the Church of Omnology, nor do all branches of the Church do things exactly the same way we do them. As long as we all work for Ale Run, and against scamgrams—and that's the way I see the Church sticking together for the foreseeable future, for untold eons—then none of the little details will matter.

"Here in our little group, though, our approach is a division of expertise. Orziz Assiz, here, he's got his specialties. They are the right-brain, holistic concerns of theology, philosophy, and all matters intuitive. My specialties are the left-brain, logical, rational matters of science and technology. Between the two of us, we can answer almost any question you'd like to pose to us.

"Now there are some matters, though, where wrong, deceptive thoughts and scamgrams infest and befester some of us so thoroughly that we just can't see it. Try as we may, neither Orziz nor I will be able to break these paradigms. Some of us, we just don't get it, as they say. Here, we need the assistance of a third party.

"Now, I'll be honest with you. Our invisible third party, Zanzer R. Orziz, he's a liar. A deceiver. Yes, he's a scamgram. A carrier of falsehoods and bloody metans, of dysfunctional thinking. Yet..."

"You mean he's a delusion?" Raoul interjected.

Vyizder tolerated the interruption patiently. "Yes, we get these kinds of questions all the time," he admitted. "Are scamgrams like delusions, and are bloody metans like neuroses. When we fleece your scamgrams away, using a V-Meter, is that like when a psychiatrist analyzes your delusions away using a couch and a notepad. Well, there may be some extremely superficial resemblances here, but we of the Church of Omnology are much, *much* more sophisticated and technologically talented than psychiatrists. For one thing, our V-Meter has flashing LEDs, and emits these really cool beeps. For those Omnologists who take enough of our courses, and become operating metans at a *truly advanced* level, we even have a Technology That Makes 'PING!' Sounds. No mere shrink has any notepads or couches that can compare to these kinds of sophisticated technological features.

"We Omnologists don't believe in psychiatrists. They are quacks and frauds. They mis-diagnose scamgrams, calling them delusions, confusing people with false promises of help, preventing them from coming to us, where we could give them some genuine help. So they do far more harm than good. Shrinks are deluded, or full of scamgrams.

"If Omnology is to fleece our scamgrams away, so that we can become operating metans, then we as Omnologists must guard against the thinking and the words that psychologists and psychiatrists use. Their entire world view and their vocabulary has so poisoned our entire society that we can't even *see* our scamgrams and bloody metans for what they really are! You ask if Zanzer R. Orziz is a delusion. Is he real, or is he a delusion? If people are depressed, do you ask them about whether their depression is real, or whether it's all in their heads? Is their depression real, or delusional?"

The room full of budding students of Omnology just stared at Vyizder in wide-eyed, uncomprehending wonder. Vyizder showed only the barest hints of frustration. "Are my delusions real, or delusional?" he continued. "To me, they're real. If I perceive them, they're real to me. Perception is reality. That's all that matters. 'Delusions' is shrink talk, and we Omnologists don't believe in shrinks. Shrinks are delusional. No, I mean, the shrinks are deluded. If we must fall back into our psychologized society's vocabulary in dealing with these things, that is. Their ideas and talk of 'delusions' being real or not, it's all delusional.

"I mean, Omnologically speaking, it's scamgramish. It's befestered with clusters of scamgrams and bloody metans. It's like saying, is my depression real, or is it all in my head? You just can't go *saying* things like 'It's all in your head.' It's not *sensitive*. In some very crude sense, yes, my depression *IS* 'all in my head'. But telling me that doesn't help me any. It doesn't ease my pain, or make me feel any better. It doesn't validate my feelings, and it *surely* doesn't fleece my scamgrams away. And if I tell my shrink that I'm 'depressed', that's what I really, really need. An expert Omnologist, equipped with a V-Meter, who will fleece my scamgrams away."

"Oooh-oooh-ooooo," the crowd babbled in excitement, arms waving. "Fleece my scamgrams away!" "No, fleece mine first!" "Can you fleece my CFS?" "Can you fleece my recovered memories?" "Come on, bring out your V-Meter!"

Vyizder and Orziz stood up tall and raised their hands way up, waving and appealing for calm. Orziz thundered, **"Now, that's *quite enough* of that!"** They calmed down. Orziz continued, "Excuse me. Now, we can't just break out our V-Meter and wave it around like a magic wand, fleecing all your scamgrams. For one thing, you have to understand what it is that we're doing, or the scamgrams will just come right back, as soon as you leave here, if not sooner. We have to thoroughly enlighten you first, and *then,* and *only* then, will fleecing your scamgrams hold some real promise of permanently helping you.

"For another thing, your selfish desires, themselves, are signs that you are all severely scamgramified. What about the person right next to you? Don't they, too, need fleeced of their scamgrams? Yet you all demand 'Me first!' And what of the larger picture? All across the globe, there are millions and billions of metans just like yourselves, who are all operating on a very, very low level. They *all* need to have their scamgrams fleeced away. Yet all you clamor about is your individual needs.

"Now Vyizder and I, we really *do* want to help you. But you're not the only ones to be considered, here. There's those millions and billions of others, too. And there's us, the leaders of the Church of Omnology. We have *our* needs, too. We need your support in order to fleece away the scamgrams of all the multitudes of multitudes. Would you demand that your shrink wave his notepad and his couch at you, and make your neuroses go away? For free, and in a few seconds? No, obviously not.

"Then why do you expect miracles of us? Yes, we *do* do a far better job than shrinks. Still, just like them, we need time and money. Yes, money. Money to buy food, clothes, and shelter, even like metans like yourselves, and money to help us spread the word about how we can heal the people and fleece their scamgrams.

"Yes, we'll bring out our V-Meter, and fleece your scamgrams away. But only if you contain your selfishness and impatience, receive your training willingly and with an open mind, and make some reasonably generous donations to the Church of Omnology. We don't ask for much. Now fend off your selfish scamgrams for just a few more minutes, while we work towards fleecing *all* of your scamgrams on a far more permanent basis."

Vyizder noticed that Jon and Julie were fidgeting and glancing at each other and their watches. Fearing the loss of their most noteworthy pupils, he stepped forward to take some of the sting out of Orziz's harsh remarks. "Now, never fear, we'll get to you and your needs very shortly. All of your needs and your feelings are valid, after all. It's just that you *do* need to be patient, while we work towards filling your needs.

"Now where were we. Oh, yes. Introductions. You already know Orziz and I. Next we'll talk about our less-than-obviously-observable partner, Zanzer R. Orziz. Then we'll talk very, very briefly about the Church of Omnology, and then we'll hear from all of you. Who are you, where are you from, and what are your needs. Then, for those of you who display the necessary faith, we'll fleece your scamgrams away.

"Now, then. Zanzer R. Orziz. Zanzer is our training aid, a token scamgram. Most scamgrams are fierce and strong, a genuine danger. One must beware of them at all times, and be fleeced on a regular basis. But Zanzer, he's our own semi-domesticated scamgram. He's not too bright or particularly strong, for a scamgram. In fact, he's almost totally foolish. He's so weak, we trained Omnologists can see him with little effort. We can tell when he whispers in your ear, and attempts to ensnare you into scamgramification. So we warn you, when we see him do it. And the very best part of it all is, these foolish attempted depredations of this particular scamgram, Zanzer, are uninspired and predictable. And he doesn't even catch on to the fact that we've turned him into our training aid, so that all his attempts to fool you are in fact hurting his cause and helping us! Isn't it just *great?!*

"But the thing is, this nifty trick to defend yourself against Zanzer works only if you listen when you're warned that he's whispering in your ear. When we warn you, you *must* take heed.

"Class, this is very important. We Omnologists aren't into nagging you. Bad feelings are bad, they're scamgrams, so we avoid them whenever we can. The Good News is that faithful Omnologists who are fleeced on a regular basis are empowered to ultimately avoid all scamgrams and bloody metans eventually. But we really, really have to warn you about Zanzer and especially his many, many smarter and stronger partners in scamgramification. Most of the rest of them, most of the time, they're smart enough to stay away from us and our V-Meters, because they know that we'll catch on to them, and warn all those who we've taken under our protective wings.

"So when you're away from your Omnological Spirit Guides, then you must especially be on guard against all the stronger and smarter scamgrams. But when you're with us, you can let down your guard, because we'll detect and warn you about any attempts by any scamgrams who try to deceive you. So long as you heed our warnings, you'll be safe. So now you understand how Zanzer is our very own semi-domesticated scamgram, and why we keep around as a training aid. Listen to us, and you'll be safe. That's all you have to remember.

"So that's the three of us." Vyizder once again made his sweeping motion, pointing first to himself, Orziz, and nothingness, intoning, "Vyizder Zomenimor, Orziz Assiz, Zanzer R. Orziz. That's us. The three of us, through the grace of our Leader, The One Who Fleeces Our Scamgrams Away, Ale Run Hubba-Bubba, can help you. We can help anyone who comes to us with an open mind, acceptance of the validity of all feelings, and generous charitable, spiritual offerings. Now let me turn this over to my companion and fellow Spirit Guide, Orziz Assiz. He'll briefly tell you all about the Church of Omnology. He's a very enlightened being. Orziz is a metan who operates on a very high level, so please listen to him carefully."

"Um, yes, thank you, Vyizder," Orziz muttered, "Thank you. You're an operating metan, too, Vyizder. Let's get on with this. Now we must not act with undue haste, but the longer we chat, here, the longer it is before we can separate those metans who operate on a high enough level to join us, from those who don't. To separate the sheep from the goats, as they used to say. And the longer we take till we see who is for us and who is against us, the longer that Zanzer will have to whisper in your ears. Yes, sad to say, some of you will definitely listen to Zanzer's whispers, rather than to our warnings. That's the way it almost always goes, with a group as large as this.

"Some will listen to Vyizder and I, and some will listen to Zanzer. Some are born to sweet delight, and some are born endless night, to suffer endless scamgramification of their own choosing. That's just the way it is. One of the central doctrines of the Church of Omnology is that no one suffers anything without their consent, conscious or subconscious, express or implied, as the shrinks and the lawyers would say. As we Omnologists say, what is, is, and what's not, isn't, except when what is, isn't, and what isn't, is. The only way you can really, truly, with absolute confidence, know which is which, is to listen to the Will of Ale Run, as revealed to you by the Church of Omnology and its Spirit Guides.

"So now, just what *is* the Church of Omnology? The Church is the Truth and The Way. A Way of Truth and Life, of fleecing scamgrams and bloody metans away, and of getting one's own personal body metan to operate on a higher cosmic level. That's it. That's all there is. Yes, we do have technological devices like V-Meters, and for truly advanced operating metans, we have Technology That Makes 'PING!' Sounds. But for day to day life for common Omnologists, that's all there is to life. Have fellowship with fellow Omnologists, listen to The One Who Fleeces Our Scamgrams Away, and have your scamgrams and bloody metans fleeced away regularly, and you will be ecstatically descamgramified.

"Yes, there are always higher and purer levels of descamgramification, but so long as you keep on working on it, especially by giving to the Church and becoming sanctified by periodically taking advancement seminars, then happiness is guaranteed. If you follow us with an open mind, no scamgrams will be able to harm you. And we'll guarantee that in writing.

"Now we'll just very briefly cover the history of the Church, then we'll talk about you and your troubles. You and your scamgrams. Then we'll fleece scamgrams away from all of those of you who find yourselves worthy to become Omnologists. You see, it's all up to you. We all choose our own fate.

"The Church of Omnology officially has existed for only a few months, ever since Ale Run revealed His Wisdom to us all. But the roots of Ale Run's visions go way, way back. Seventy-five million years back, as a matter of fact. Seventy-five million years ago, there was a Cruel Galactic Emperor Zebu. Zebu captured and tortured ancient souls and pickled them in cucumber jars. Then he buried these pickle jars in swamps on an ancient planet known as Teakgeakiac.

"Over millions and millions of years, those swamps became beds of coal. Millions of years later, humans first started talking. The first words they came up with were 'Earth', the new name for the old planet Teakgeakiac. They became more advanced and intelligent, but they continued to live in peace and harmony, grooving to the vibes of an all-natural planet.

"But then they discovered fire. Now fires aren't bad, when they're natural. We all know from recent experience in the national parks out west that wildfires clear out the underbrush and renew and enrich nature's biodiversity. But when people set them, they're bad. Unless, of course, the people setting the fires have been fleeced and descamgramified first. This relates to one of the central axioms of Omnology, which is that chaos is badness.

"That is, since those early humans didn't have the technology to fleece and descamgramify themselves before setting their fires, and since chaos is badness, then it was only a matter of time before badness set in. Yes, sure, for a while, they set their fires to keep themselves warm, cook their meat, and keep predators away, and all was well. But then they started to encircle their campfires with rocks. And then it was only a matter of time till they used some coal, and noticed that these particular rocks were very peculiar, because they burned just like wood!

"So a few of them here and there started to burn coal. And then one day they burned some coal formed around those seventy-five-million-year-old pickle jars. The imprisoned souls, captured and tortured so long ago by the Cruel Galactic Emperor Zebu, were then let loose upon an unsuspecting humanity. Ever since, we humans have been mercilessly befestered by what we now know as bloody metans and scamgrams.

"But then, only recently, the Great One and Spirit Guide of All Omnologists, He Who Fleeces Our Scamgrams Away, Ale Run Hubba-Bubba, came to Earth and set us all free! Or, at least, he sets free those of us who heed His Word. Now that He has revealed the technologies that can set us all free from chaos, badness, scamgrams, and bloody metans, there are three paths that you can go by. You can rationally understand Omnology as a science. Or you can intuitively understand it as a philosophy of life, a religion. Or you can reject it altogether, and continue in your present misery, chaotically scamgramified by clusters of scamgrams and bloody metans.

"So in our particular individual Church of Omnology, as opposed to the overall Church of Omnology, we have chosen to represent the three paths with the three of us. Vyizder Zomenimor, Orziz Assiz, Zanzer R. Orziz. We represent your three paths. Through the wisdom granted to us by Ale Run, Vyizder and I can cast out your scamgrams and fleece your bloody metans. With Ale Run's guidance and generous donations to the Church, you can learn and advance as far as you'd like to go.

"You can specialize in the rational and technological route, following Vyizder. Omnology is a very technical and impressive science, as you can tell by our technical vocabulary, and by the LEDs and beeper-speakers on our V-Meters, which the self-chosen worthy ones among you will get to see later. Or you can specialize in holistic, intuitive approaches under my guidance. Either way, you can learn all about what, exactly, scamgrams and bloody metans are, and how best to fleece them away. What, exactly, the difference between descamgramification and fleecing is, and when it is best to use the one, or the other. All sorts of deep technical knowledge awaits those who find themselves worthy to live a life free of scamgrams.

"Or you can ignore our warnings, and listen to Zanzer. You can continue on a road paved by bloody metans and littered with the wreaked shards of unfleeced humanity. The road to scamgramification, that is. It's all up to you. I wish it weren't so, but we're all free to choose chaos and badness, as well as descamgramification. But Ale Run in His Wisdom has declared that we, the fleeced, must allow the unfleeced to freely depart from us. He says that when we spread The Word, and the people won't allow us to fleece them, then we should shake the dust of their bad vibes from our shoes and depart from them, or they from us. We cannot allow the unfleeced to scamgramify the fleeced!

"Enough preaching. We Omnologists aren't into nagging, or the laying on of guilt trips. Guilt trips are a prime example of unfleeced scamgramification. We don't ask for much in artificial constraints on your behavior. Once you're fleeced of your scamgrams, you can just go with the flow, do what comes naturally, and live a guilt-free, happy, descamgramified life. All human metans are basically good, once scamgrams are fleeced away. So all that we ask is that you be fleeced or descamgramified on a regular basis, and that your charitable contributions go to the correct accounts. We have a matrix, descamgramification versus fleecing on one axis, operating metan advancement versus maintenance on the other. Since chaos is badness, proper accounting procedures must be followed at all times.

"Now let's move on to the part we've all been looking forward to. That's the part where you get to tell everyone else who you are, where you're coming from, and what your vibes and troubles are. What your scamgrams are, and what you hope that the Church of Omnology can do for you. We in the Church of Omnology are very informal. This part of our services is actually almost the very best, because we can all tell it like it is. We are all very, very strongly encouraged to be totally, totally and completely honest, and tell everyone all of our innermost, deepest beliefs and feelings, because all beliefs and feelings are valid. As Omnologists, we are empowered, so we need never deny our feelings. When we are totally honest this way, and accept the validity of everything, then this part of our service is very powerful medicine against scamgrams. So once again, I encourage you all to be as honest as you can be.

"Then after that, we'll have the very, very best part of the service, which is when we get out our V-Meters, and fleece your scamgrams away. So that's where we're headed. But now, since we're coming up on these most important parts of our service, we must first invoke the presence of The Benevolent One, The Mighty Fleecer of All Scamgrams, Ale Run Hubba-Bubba. Omnologists usually join in, here, but since y'all don't know the words yet, Vyizder and I will recite:

Our Fleecer, who art descamgramified,
Hallowed be Thy Name.
Thy polls go up, thy Wisdom be acknowledged,
In Panderwood, as it is in the Church of Omnology.
Bring us this day our daily session with a V-Meter,
and let its speakers beep, and its LEDs shine brightly.
Fleece us, as we fleece others.
Lead us not into scamgramification,
but keep us safe from bloody metans.

Ale Run is my shepherd,
I shall not want.
He validates all my feelings,
and leads me to descamgramification.
He fleeces my bloody metans away,
and the LEDs of His V-Meter light The Way.
Yea though He leads me through
the valley of the shadow of discomfort,
I will fear no inappropriateness,
for Ale Run is with me.
Your V-Meter's Technology comforts me.
Surely perfection and descamgramification
await me all the rest of the days of my life,
so long as I contribute to Your Church.

Chapter 10 has some endnotes about being chronically fatigued of horse's patooties. See page 230.

Chapter 11

Fleecing the People
and
Casting Out Scamgrams

"Whether Hale-Bopp has a companion or not is irrelevant from our perspective... The Joy is that our Older Member in the Evolutionary Level Above Human (the Kingdom of Heaven) has made it clear to us that Hale-Bopp's approach is the 'marker' we have been waiting for—the time for the arrival of the spacecraft from the Level Above Human to take us home to 'Their World'—in the literal heavens." From the Web site of Heaven's Gate. *39 of their members committed mass suicide, leaving behind their "earthly containers" to go hitch a ride on some alien spacecraft that we weenie unbelievers can't perceive.*

"And now," Orziz continued, "The time has arrived. Time for us all to speak honestly to each other, and tell each other all about ourselves. Remember, it is of utmost importance, if we are to achieve the healing effects of this part of our Omnological services, that we all be as completely and utterly honest as possible.

"I'll start off by saying quite honestly that although all of us human metans are equal in the sight of Ale Run, some of us have more power to spread The Word which sets us all free from scamgrams than others. Along those lines, I am very, very pleased to see that we have with us today the famous Panderwood actor and actress, Jon Travibesty and his wife, Julie Peston. If we can get them to see Ale Run's wisdom, then there is much cause for celebration, for they have the power to spread The Joy of His Word far and wide. And I've noticed that quite a few of you have spent more time staring at them then you have listening to me and to Vyizder. That's okay, though. Their vibes are strong. I can tell even without my V-Meter. So we understand how you are all fascinated by them.

"Along these lines, then, I'd ask that Jon and Julie go first, so that we can all satisfy our curiosities, and then maybe we can pay better attention to the rest of us, when our turns come, instead of wondering and whispering about Jon and Julie. So Jon, please stand up and go first. Tell us who you are, where you're coming from, why you're here, what your troubles are, and what you hope that The Church of Omnology can do for you. And don't forget to be totally honest."

Jon stood up. "My name is Jon Travibesty, and I'm a famous Panderwood actor, and you're not. I'm tall, dark, and handsome, *and* I have a square jaw, as you might have noticed. That's why they pay me twenty million dollars per movie. And Melvin Swine pays me millions more to endorse his fragrances. I'm in town here in Madness County because I wanted to visit my mother, and because I wanted to make a token show of mingling with the common folk out here in Hicksville. I was hoping to get some media exposure, so that more people would see how utterly handsome I am, pay to see me in more movies, and make me even richer. So that's why we have so many cameras here today.

"I was just passing through, and I saw the signs up in front of the Soulorama. Then I got to thinking, you know, I have almost all that life has to offer. Fame, a wife whose body everyone lusts after, a fifty-thousand-square-foot home, many obviously expensive cars, suits, boats, camels, goats, horses, trainers, coaches, and therapists, three private airplanes, bodyguards and servants to help me blow my nose, wipe my butt, and take care of my children. But there's just something missing. Some part of me left unfulfilled.

"Pondering just what it is that I'm missing, I can't help but think some, um, of what I'd like to very modestly think are some pretty deep thoughts. I'm thinking thoughts of, like, um, I've got all these things that make everyone pretty much aware that I'm an important and powerful kind of a guy. But then, everyone in Panderwood, all the actors and actresses and producers and directors, even some of the script writers, they're all important just like me. And they all have big houses, fancy cars, expensive jewelry, herds of cows and sheep and goats and lusty young babes and handsome young boy toys and therapists and all, so how am I different than any of the rest of them?

"So I've been sitting here thinking, you know, like, if I should join a totally whacked-out, bizarre, and far-out cult, with really strange beliefs, then I'd get a lot more media exposure, even *more* people would notice how handsome I am, and everyone would be impressed that I'm really, really, *really* important, because I can afford a *really exotic* status prop. I can throw money away right and left, even for expensive nonsense like pseudo-scientific, technobabble-laden genuine imitation spiritual advancement, and never even blink an eye. So then Melvin Swine will pay me even *more* to endorse his fragrances, and maybe I can make *thirty* million per movie. So that's what I'm hoping that The Church of Omnology can do for me. And y'all don't forget to see my movies, and wear Melvin Swine fragrances."

Everyone—well, almost everyone, excluding radical extremists, of which there weren't too many present—clapped and cheered. "Well, thanks for your honesty," Orziz replied. "I'll bet Omnology can make your wildest dreams come true. We'll certainly work on it. And now let's hear from your wife, Julie. Now Julie, don't forget to be totally honest, just like Jon."

Jon sat down and Julie stood up. She draped herself all over Jon and purred, then stood back up. But she massaged his shoulders and caressed his face and hair while she talked. "Hi. I'm Julie Peston, and I'm deeply, deeply In Love with Jon. In fact, I'm far more deeply In Love with him than any human being has ever been In Love with anyone before, in all the history of the world. So I'm hoping that everyone will notice, not just how utterly handsome he is, but also, how utterly sexy *I* am. How I'm *so* sexy that a man of Jon's wealth and power finds me worthy. Then all the men will lust after me, and the women will want to know all my secrets, so everyone will want to see me in the movies, and all the women's magazines will want to interview me.

"I'll help them tell all the women that the way to be fabulously wealthy and famous, and to snag rich and powerful men, is to **be beautiful**. Above all else, don't forget to *be beautiful*. This will fit right in with the magazine's theme statements, which in turn helps them sell advertisements. Happiness and success are all about buying the right rouge, makeup, eyeliner, dresses, houses, cars, furniture, cigarettes, and liquor. These things help give you women the right alluring qualities to snag a rich, handsome man like I've got. So don't forget to envy me, because that helps make me get interviews with the women's magazines, helps them sell advertisements, boosts my fame for being famous, and helps me make more movies.

"What am I hoping that The Church of Omnology can do for me? Well, I'm looking for something more, spiritually. If the women's magazines interview me, and they ask me about my spiritual life, and I tell them something conventional, boring, and unpleasant, that their readers don't want to hear—oh, for instance, that spiritual growth is hard to come by, that one has to work at it, suffer pain for one's mistakes, ponder long and hard, personally, without letting anyone else make one's decisions, to divine God's will, and to practice discipline and self-restraint, for the longer-term good of everyone—why, then, my value as an interviewee goes down. People don't want to hear *that*. It's boring, plain, unoriginal, and unpleasant.

"If, on the other hand, I can tell them that my Spirit Guides have assured me that all that I need is the *right technology,* and enough cash to donate to The Church to entitle me to salvation, then that fits in with their theme statements and their advertisements a lot better. Spiritual perfection is an ingredient of happiness just like makeup, cars, houses, furniture, liquor, and cigarettes, see, and they can be had for the right price, and that's what I've got to push, if I want to help them sell advertisements. We wouldn't want to disturb the readers. Bad feelings are bad, and chaos is badness, I heard you say. I agree. So I'm pretty optimistic that maybe The Church of Omnology has what I need."

There was another hearty round of applause, although a discerning ear might have picked up a few "boos". Orziz was still clapping and cheering after almost everyone else had stopped. "Fear not, my pretty young lass," he intoned, "Omnology has technology for every need. All you have to do is to listen to your Spirit Guides, make generous contributions, and in turn be fleeced and descamgramified on a regular basis. Everything will then be perfect forever for you. This simple Truth is the brilliant essence of Omnology!" Then he pointed at Raoul, saying, "All right. Let's hear some yabbering from some ordinary Joes. You. Now be honest. But don't go on all day. Other people want to talk, too."

"Um, yeah. I'm like a Sensitive Dude. My name is Raoul Kinky, and I'm a poet, a writer, a photographer, and sometimes even an actor. Now I've not made it to Panderwood, I'm not famous, but I *am* a truly

Compassionate and Sensitive sort of a guy. I'm from around here. I eat quiet food, food that doesn't scream of mass murder, which means I'm a vegetarian, and I've suffered from Multiple Chemical Sensitivity, MCS, until I bought this here technology, it cures MCS." He hefted his Dream Catcher.

"Since I got my MCS cured, though, I've caught CFS, which is Chronic Fatigue Syndrome. So I'm looking for a cure. I'm sure hoping that CFS is just a scamgram, and that you can fleece it away."

"Oh, yes," Vyizder rushed to assure him, "We can cure your CFS. CFS, as you'd hope, is, indeed, just another scamgram. So is MCS. Cancer, colds, stomach problems, zits, bad breath, obesity, poor circulation, amputated limbs, death, they're *all* nothing but scamgrams. With sufficient donations and fleecings, and if you believe in the Power of Ale Run strongly enough, all these things and more, all can be cured. So stick with us, and you'll be fine. You can even part with your Dream Catcher. We have technology for every problem, don't you worry about that."

"Good, good. Great! Glad to hear that," Raoul replied. "Although I'll want to keep my Dream Catcher just out of sentimentality. Other than that, what do I want out of The Church of Omnology? Well, I was sure hoping to validate my feelings of moral superiority. You say that all feelings are valid. That sounds good. So, as an Omnologist, would I be able to, for example, feel morally superior to those who murder meat-bearing animals? Wear leather? Use soap made from dead animals? Brush their teeth, murdering millions of innocent bacteria? What do you say?"

Vyizder and Orziz paused, shuffling back and forth a bit. Orziz spoke up. "You're dangerously close to listening to the whispers of Zanzer, there. Yes, all feelings are valid. Some, though, are more valid than others. When you're judgmental about other Omnologists, though, you make them feel guilty, sometimes, and guilt laid on an Omnologist is one of the ultimate scamgrams, for we are all equal in the eyes of Ale Run.

"Specifically, for example, in the kinds of issues that you raise, Ale Run has said that it isn't that which we eat, wear, or bathe with, that makes us unfleeced, it's that which we withhold from The Church of Omnology. Our money and our honesty, primarily, among other things, that is. So we can't really quite say that you're listening to the whispers of Zanzer, yet, because you're being honest. But you must work on not judging your fellow Omnologists, some of whom indulge in meat, leather, soap, and tooth paste." Orziz stared at Raoul expectantly.

"Yes, I can see the wisdom of Ale Run shining brightly through your words," Raoul admitted. "That's all I've got. Now, I'd like for everyone to meet my domestic partner, Francestuous Johnsdame."

Francestuous got up and said, "Like this man here, my companion human, said, I'm Francestuous. Not that I couldn't have said it myself. Anyway, there it is. I'm Francestuous, an independent woman. I'm from like around here. I'm a poetess, an artist, and sometimes an actress. Or, at least, I'd sure like to be a *paid* one. But I guess I wasted way too many years as a farm housewife, trying to do what I thought were my duties, instead of flowing with the vibes. So now I'm getting older, getting closer to being over the hill.

"What do I want from The Church of Omnology? Well, I want to have someone put meaning and excitement into my life. But really, what I want is to be like a rich and famous actress. So I read all the women's magazines, follow all the beauty hints, and try to stay up with all the goings-on in Panderwood. Some sunny day, when someone notices all my beauty and talent, I'll be right on top of things. I'll move right on into Panderwood, and people will think I've been there like all my life.

"I suppose I might be asking for a bit much. For now, I guess I'd settle for some help with my relationships. For one thing, now, my companion human, here, Raoul, he's not too bad, as men go. He knows how to light a cigarette, how to open a beer can, and how to love a woman. But, you know, when we go out on overnight camping trips on our bicycles, Betsy and Herman, well, Raoul, here, when he puts his toilet paper on the handlebars, he like puts it with the paper rolling off of the top. I think that's inconsiderate male chauvinism. The protruding paper is like a phallus, and he insists that it be on top! So I think we need some help with our relationship." She glanced sidelong at Raoul, who gasped and floundered in silent astonishment.

"Yes, yes," Orziz proclaimed, "I can see that you do. But don't forget, we have technology for every need. Technology for every relationship, even. Trust us. We're brilliant, hip, and up with the latest! And don't be afraid to dream. If we're going to be the big hit in the Panderwood scene that we expect to be, especially if Jon and Julie here help us, why, then, you never know. The sky's the limit. Everything is possible; you just have to believe in yourself. Now, Francestuous, is there anything else we can help you with?"

"Well, yes. About that moral superiority thing, and all feelings being valid, but some being more valid than others. Can we who are like intimately in touch with the vibes of the Earth Goddess feel morally superior to those who aren't? Like, Raoul and I never hardly *ever* drive fume-belching monstermobiles. We almost always ride our bikes. So what's in this for us, if we're not like allowed to feel morally superior? Or are we, in this case?"

"That's kind of a touchy subject you've brought up there," Vyizder replied thoughtfully. "I'd say it all depends. Like not driving motor vehicles, for instance, that's fine, but it would be scamgramified to lay a guilt trip on another Omnologist over that, usually. Especially if they've been faithfully donating, and getting fleeced and descamgramified. Now if, on the other hand, you want to feel morally superior to oil company executives or tobacco lawyers, and there are no such types of metans in the fellowship of Omnologists currently present, why, then, Ale Run and I see no reason why your feelings should be any less valid than anyone else's. So as you can see, it all depends. It's usually best to just ask your Spirit Guides. Next?"

"Howdy," a middle-aged, burly man in beat-up old overalls spoke up. "They calls me Harvey da Honeydipper. Ah'm a local yokel, an' Ah earns a honest livin' by cleanin' out people's septic tanks. Two hundred bucks a crack. Call me any time. Now, Ah don't make no twenty million bucks, not in several lifetimes. Twenty thou on a good year's more like it. Ah nevuh learnt ta read or write so well, but ah ken clean your tank just like a ringin' da bell! Ah'm not nobody's fool. Ah knows rotted old poop when Ah sees it. Or when Ah smells it, fer that matter.

"Ah ain't no dumb hickabilly just 'cause Ah talks funny. Ah ain't never went ta school much, but Ah done thunk about a lotta stuff a good long time. Now Ah doesn't hold nobody's religious views against 'em, not so long as they's gots a lick a common sense an' consideration fer others. But it seems ta me, today's religions, they's got being saved, but nothin' ta be saved *from*. All sorts o' fancy talk, believe this or believe that, do this or do that, an' you'll be *saved*. But saved from *what*?

"We's gots a lotta talk, but not much meanin'. Say somethin' with *meanin'*, and ya might *offend* somebody. Say people shouldn't sleep with anybody unless they's ready to deal honestly, fairly, and responsibly with all da possible results, and you's just a prude, not *with it*. So we's got being saved, lotsa talk about being saved, but nothin' about what we's bein' saved *from*. Not that Ah's into guilt trips, as y'all say. Ah's into thinkin' 'bout what Ah does, what it does ta others, and how ta live best, believin' in what Ah sees, an' listenin' ta common sense an' conscience.

"Maybe we *should* feel guilty when we does bad things. Maybe we *are* personally responsible fer the bad things we does. Maybe we should stop blaming Satan, the Devil, scamgrams, an' so on. Maybe we should say, 'Ah was wrong, and Ah won't do that again.' Ah even been able ta teach my *kids* ta say that now an' then.

"So Ah's lookin' fer a Church that's about *real* stuff. A Church that's a gonna tell me what's good an' what's bad, not just ta 'lay a guilt trip' on me, but *why* good is good an' bad is bad, and when somethin' is sometimes good an' sometimes bad. Mostly, though, Ah wants 'em ta *reason* an' *think* with me, tell me *why*, an' work with common sense an' what we sees. Not a bunch a empty words.

"Christ died fer our sins; He washes our sins away. Ale Run fleeces our scamgrams away. What's it all *mean?!* How's it relate to my life, an' how Ah can live a better life? What's we bein' fleeced of? What's a scamgram?"

"Now I see Zanzer whispering in your ear," Orziz warned.

But Harvey went right on. "Well, come on, now, tell me. What's a scamgram? Why should Ah believe in them? Why should Ah be fleeced?"

"Because you're befestered with massive clusters of scamgrams and bloody metans, that's why!" Orziz thundered. "They're plain for any trained Omnologist to see," he continued more quietly. "Now we can help you if you'll let us. And we can explain scamgrams and bloody metans to you. But that takes a lot of time, a lot of training courses, and, of course, lots of generous donations to The Church. Now if you'll stick around and get out your checkbook, we'll fleece you all in good time."

"Ah don't wanna be fleeced until y'all explains what Ah's bein' fleeced of," Harvey insisted.

"Zanzer's *shouting* in your ear now," Orziz grumbled ominously. "Can't you see? He's leading you down the path to destruction *right now*. Scamgrams, if you must know so soon, are, in very simple terms, those thoughts that make you ignore your Spirit Guides. Like right now. You can shut Zanzer out, sit quietly, and wait to be fleeced soon. If you make an extra donation, Vyizder can even take you into the back room and fleece you right now. But you've *got* to stop listening to Zanzer *right now*, before you scamgramify the whole congregation. Got it?!"

"Ah's gots it. Y'all wants ta fleece my money away from me."

"That'll be enough!" Orziz bellowed. "Now go get fleeced *right now!* Or *leave*. Pronto!" Vyizder stood and beckoned towards the back door.

Harvey stood up taller, put his hat on, and walked towards the front door. "Like Ah says, Ah knows rotted old poop when Ah sees it," he announced. "Ah'm outta here. Y'all take care, now. Don't let the scamgrams getcha." Then he slipped out the door.

Orziz sighed and continued. "Now, people, if you don't want to be scamgramified by massive clusters of scamgrams, it would be best if you'd just forget all about what that stupid, nasty man said. It's best that we all put his scamgram-befestered thoughts out of our minds, just as we flushed his unfleeced body metans out of our presence. Now will y'all please stand up."

Everyone was taken by mild surprise, but everyone stood up. "Now shake the dust off of your shoes," Orziz commanded. Everyone made motions of shaking and brushing their shoes. Then they all sat back down. Orziz gazed expectantly towards another member of the congregation, who reluctantly stood back up.

"Um, yes," the beautiful, dark-haired young woman submitted quietly. "I'm Dorcas Whistling Elk. I'm an anthropologist from the Pawnee tribe. My people have sent me forth to study the ways of the White Man. And the White Man's, um, sidekicks. So that's why I'm here today. Now if you don't mind, I really don't want to participate, I just want to observe." She started to sit back down.

"No, no, now just *wait a minute* here," Vyizder objected. "We Omnologists are very broad-minded, and we're all in favor of having all sorts of different people learn all about everyone else. Now why don't you just go ahead and ask about everything you've got on your mind. I'll bet many of the others here, they're wondering about the same sorts of things, but they're too shy to ask. So go ahead. Fire away. We'll answer all your questions."

"Well, okay, then, great!" Dorcas replied. "Now I'm wondering about a lot of things. I've heard about a lot of what Pale Face does, but I'm still quite ignorant. So I hope you'll excuse me for asking stupid questions."

"There are no stupid questions," Vyizder interjected.

"So then, do you, like, um, have these ceremonies where you chug wine, I mean, drink the blood of Ale Run, and eat, like, bread that's actually his flesh? And this sets you free of your scamgrams? And is Ale Run the Father, then, or the Son, or the Great Spirit?"

"No, ma'am, I'm afraid you're confusing us with some other folks," Orziz admitted politely. "That's not quite right. That's not us."

"I'm sorry, I guess I must've learned some wrong things. I suppose I've got to ignore all those wrong things, and start with the basics. So then who is your God? What is He like, and what does He command that you do? And does He have an enemy, an opposing force? Do you have prophecies of the future? Will there be an end time? What will it be like?"

"No, ma'am, Omnology has no God. There is only Ale Run and His Words, which will never fade away. Ale Run is completely free of scamgrams and bloody metans, and He commands that we try to join Him in this state of perfection. All we need to do, then, is to be fleeced and descamgramified on a regular basis. It's that simple," Orziz replied. "As to the enemy, the end times, and what they'll be like, no one but Ale Run knows. If anyone but He should know about all these things, such knowledge would interfere with the fulfillment of the prophecies themselves.

"But thoroughly trained Omnologists *do* eventually reach a high enough level to learn a lot—not *everything*, just a lot—about the enemy and the end times. All that I can tell you for now is, yes, there will come an Anti-Hubba-Bubba, and that time is soon. No one but Ale Run knows the day or the hour, but the Anti-Hubba-Bubba will come. He's probably walking this Earth as we speak. For all we know, he might be in this room right now, here with us."

Everyone cast sidelong glances at their neighbors and hunched back into their chairs. Dorcas continued, "Well, then, besides being fleeced and descamgramified on a regular basis, what, exactly, *is* it that Ale Run commands you to do? *Surely* there must be more! Doesn't Ale Run, like, tell us to love our neighbors as we love ourselves, and to treat others the way that we wish to be treated?"

"No, ma'am, you're confusing us Omnologists with some other folks again. Omnologically speaking, all that a metan must do to be fleeced, is to take advantage of Ale Run's amazing new technology! If you're fleeced and descamgramified on a regular basis, then all else will flow from there. The White Man has many, many different beliefs, but only Omnologists have the One and True Wisdom of The Ages, which are contained in The Words of Ale Run."

"I'm sorry," she replied. "It's just that you all look so much alike. I thought that the White Man's beliefs were cute, simple, and comfortably, refreshingly quaint. But now I guess I'm seeing that there's many, many different *groups* of Pale Faces, and they all believe different things. So you'll have to excuse my ignorance. I'll have to go off and study these things, I suppose. Could you tell me where I might buy the comprehensive Omnological works of Ale Run, maybe?"

Astonishment washed over Vyizder's and Orziz's faces. Outraged, Orziz declared, "You think we would **sell** The Words of Ale Run?! Why, why..." he sputtered off into silence, lacking words with which to convey his shock and amazement.

"Well, sure, why not?" she replied. "You say you want all peoples to know all about the others. I think that's just *great!* So sell me a copy of his central works, so I can learn. Or donate them to me, whatever, if buying and selling offends you. Maybe I could make a contribution?"

"Oh, yes, yes, by all means," Orziz rushed to assure her. "You can make a contribution at any time. Please feel free. But we can't give or sell you His Words. They are Sacred, Priceless, Treasured, and Descamgramified above all else. And they're very, very Powerful. So Powerful, as a matter of fact, that novices, newcomers to Omnology like yourselves, you can only be exposed to tiny little pieces at any given time. You have to advance through our fleecing and descamgramifying sessions, one stage at a time. Else you'd be totally overwhelmed, and unable to appreciate The True Wisdom of His Words."

Dorcas wouldn't give up easily. "Well, how about if I try to maybe just study them, academically, detached-wise, not trying to understand The True Wisdom of His Words so much as simply trying to study the beliefs of the White Man? As an anthropologist, not so much as an Omnologist, I might be able to handle..."

"NO!" Orziz thundered. "You Native Americans, you cultural imperialists, you, you come here and gawk at the quaint customs of the White Man, and then you try to steal our culture! You think you can just go and *buy* our Sacred Spiritual Secrets, just like you'd buy some beads, blankets, or a quart of whiskey! Well, we'll just say *no!* **No!** There! Got that?! We say *NO* to cultural imperialism!

"Cultural imperialism is a scamgram. Zanzer is whispering in your ear. You've got to wait patiently for The Words of Ale Run to be revealed to you, just like everyone else. You can't buy your quickie ticket to salvation. Not from us Omnologists, you can't. Now you can just ignore Zanzer, sit there, and be fleeced in a little while. Or if you can't resist Zanzer's lies for just a few minutes, then Vyizder can fleece you in the back room, right now. But this cultural imperialism has *got* to stop. We can't tolerate such sheer scamgramishness. Okay?"

"Well, okay, I guess," she murmured. "So how much does it cost to be fleeced? I'm not rich. I'm just a poor student."

"We don't charge money for fleecing. That would be gross, crass, and materialistic. We take donations. Those who donate are entitled to be fleeced."

"So how much does one need to donate in order to be fleeced?"

"Oh, approximately nine hundred and ninety-nine dollars and ninety-nine cents, for four minutes and thirty-five seconds of fleecing. Give or take. Not that we're into counting our pennies."

"Well, I'm afraid I can't make those kinds of donations. Is there any other way I can learn The Words of Ale Run?"

Just then, a beeping sound burst forth from behind the podium. Vyizder and Orziz consulted there briefly, stooping to stare at a hidden object. Then they straightened up solemnly. Orziz announced, "We've already noticed that Zanzer is whispering cultural imperialism into Ms. Whistling Elk's ear. Now our V-Meter tells us that she's contemplating searching for fallen members of Omnology, and gaining access to illegal copies of Ale Run's Words. We must warn against this in no uncertain terms. The Words of Ale Run are Ultimately Powerful. To those who are properly trained, they lead to freedom from scamgrams and bloody metans. For others, who steal His Words, they lead to nothing but endless pain and agony.

"Ms. Whistling Elk, we'll have to ask you to leave now. And we've got to warn you, if you publish unauthorized copies of The Words of Ale Run, you'll be prosecuted."

Dorcas Whistling Elk got up to leave. Four others rose with her, heading for the door. "Wait!" Vyizder proclaimed, "Why are you leaving?"

"I ain't got no thousand dollars for no five minutes of gettin' fleeced," one of them yelled, scurrying out the door. "You be a bunch o' jivin' muthus," another one added. "You be a coupla chitlins short of a picnic." "Tell 'em, my man, tell 'em," yet another one chimed in. "Dood B. Bad, you tells it like it be!"

"When you get tired of all your scamgrams, come on back!" Vyizder called out after them. "I just hope it won't be too late. All right now, class, everyone stand up." Everyone stood up and brushed the dust off of their shoes once again.

"Let's get on with the service," Orziz added. "You there. Who are you? Where you from? What can we do for you?" He nodded towards a nervous-looking young lady.

"Hi, we're Polly Hydrahead. We're the leaders of all my various multiple personalities. There's about thirty of us, give or take, depending on the weather, the phase of the moon, which shrink we're talking to, and the ratio of how much our landlord is charging per person, versus SSI benefits per person. Right now there's twenty-eight of us. Please allow us to introduce all of us.

"Right now Polly Hydrahead is talking. She's actually five different personalities, but we five have all reached consensus amongst ourselves. So we're pretty tightly integrated. So much so that we don't even insist on separate names for ourselves, for right now. But there's still five of us, sometimes more, especially when the SSI folks are counting, calculating our benefits.

"We Polly Hydraheads are pretty reasonable, middle-of-the-road kind of folks. Not all that argumentative, like some of the other people who share our body. We seek common ground and compromise. Like when one of our, um, companions, Violet Passionflower, insisted that we attend a womyn's protest meeting, we went along. But then, some of the womyn at the meeting were going topless, to protest about how men could do this, and womyn couldn't. Others said no, look at how all the men are coming by to stare and ogle. Going topless just promotes turning womyn into objects.

"Well, a lot of us—all thirty-something of us—were all ready to get into a big fight about that. It was looking pretty bad. But then us five Polly Hydraheads, we were the calm heads that prevailed. We compromised. We just showed *one* breast."

Everyone stared at Polly incredulously. "Don't you *get* it, you silly people?" They just continued to stare. "That's the problem with the world today," she declared. "People simply don't know how to compromise any more. See, some of us thought we should go topless. Others thought we shouldn't. So we went half topless, half clothed. Like *this*, you morons!" She reached over her back, unstrapped her bra, and started to pull one breast out. The crowd watched, fascinated.

Suddenly, Polly's demeanor changed. She writhed briefly, then a new voice spoke up. "Hi. I'm Miss Prissy, and you can't see my breasts. Neither one! Not unless you spend a lot of money on me first, and tell me a lot of good lines. Especially the ones about how you'll respect me in the morning, and call me. I'm no slut, like those Polly wenches. They..."

Polly/Prissy convulsed again. "Hey! Who're you calling a slut, you whore! *You're* the one who slept with our old boss, you filthy wench! *We* never consented! So he *raped* us, and it's all *your* fault!"

"Excuse us, please. Polly Hydrahead here again. Our slutty sister, Miss Prissy, here, she gets us into all sorts of trouble. Some of us think it has to do with today's excessively permissive and promiscuous ways. Miss Prissy has been watching too many soap operas. So she married this guy and had a kid with him, all because he manipulated her. Told her he loved her, stuff like that. But *we* weren't consulted. So we had him busted for rape, and now we have custody of the kid. We're trying to straighten out Miss Prissy's messes.

"We're working three jobs, trying to give Junior a decent upbringing. Meanwhile, Miss Prissy's One and True Love can't even hardly ever seem to send us a child-support check, and..."

Polly's body twisted, and Miss Prissy spoke up again. "Yeah, well, if Brad wasn't making humongous payments to his lawyers to keep him out of jail, all 'cause of you and your silly rape charges, then maybe he'd have some money to give for supporting Richard. And maybe Brad would feel more like sending money if you hadn't gone and shacked up with Frank."

Miss Prissy cringed and twitched, and a new voice took over. "Hi.

I'm Aunt Diluvianne Marmish. Pleased to meet you. Now you can see how all my nieces here have managed to make our lives just one big mess. I believe in being responsible. If you mess up your bed, you should either fix it up, or lay in it. And if you get laid in it, then you've got to lay in *that*, too, and not lie about it. Not tell no lies, like it was someone else's fault. Take care of yourself, and of your own. Don't go running off and blaming everyone else, and trying to make them pay for it.

"Now for example here, Miss Prissy married and slept with Brad. And she even *lived* with him, too! So she not only slept with a married man, she was even *living* with him, too! And Polly Hydrahead, they never did nothin' to stop her. But they was there, too, see, and so they're responsible. Tolerating is like tacitly approving, like I say. So now Polly Hydrahead is, um, are shacked up with Frank, yet she expects Brad to be sending child support!

"Well, I just don't know what this world's coming to, these days. Brad went off and did the morally upright, responsible thing, and he got married to his new woman. And he makes good money. Yet Polly, who are poor and shacking up with another man, expect Brad to send child support! So Polly are setting a bad example to little Richard by living in sin, being irresponsible, and Brad is being a much better example and makes more money, yet Polly keep custody! Seems to me, we could give custody to the parent with more responsible lifestyle choices.

"The laws are all messed up. Frankly, child support laws, just like welfare laws, do some good, but they also do more harm. Child support laws prop up women in their poor choices of mates. 'Well, yes, this man might be unreliable,' women now say to themselves, 'But I'll go ahead and sleep with him anyway, 'cause I can always rely on the Welfare State to squeeze money out of him if we have a baby and it doesn't work out right!' This is all just insane!"

Aunt Diluvianne shuddered and disappeared, becoming replaced by yet another voice. "Hi. Violet Passionflower here. I can't believe the male-chauvinist fascism of that evil Aunt Diluvianne! What repressive patriarchy! Blame the victim! Punish the poor and powerless, and then stigmatize them for being poor, powerless, and punished! Self-righteously dump on poor ol' Polly Hydrahead and Miss Prissy, here, blaming the victims, then advocate punishing them and all the other poor unwed mothers, taking their welfare and child support away! Have you ever heard of such ruthlessly punitive self-righteousness?!

"I mean, come on, now. If all the dads and taxpayers out there were allowed to make their own choices, they'd all spend every last *dime* on beer, cigarettes, and trailer parks! They'd never spend one lousy *dime* for all the oppressed poor folks, 'cause they're all a bunch of cheap, rotten, selfish, lazy bastards, and we all know it. Damned greedy taxpayers! It's only by the enlightened Power of the People, as expressed through the collective voices of Compassionate Voters like me, that poor people can ever make any headway at all!

"People, listen to me! We can't go and judgmentally punish poor people like Polly Hydrahead and Miss Prissy, just 'cause their lifestyle choices are different than ours! Miss Goody Two-Shoes here, Aunt Diluvianne, she's stigmatizing single parents and their lifestyle choice in 'shacking up', which is entirely a valid lifestyle choice, and why be so judgmental? Cheapskate scum won't allocate any of their funds to the Betterment of Peoplekind, unless we voters, exercising the collectively morally superior Will of the People, make their charity choices *for* them. After all, they *are* totally worthless cheapskate scum, who act in a morally repugnant and judgmental manner, when they question, and refuse to fund, the lifestyle choices of single mothers who just happen to want to 'shack up' with their partners. I just *hate* that, when people become so quick to condemn others and our moral choices."

"Um, yes, I agree," Orziz gently interrupted. "All feelings and all lifestyles are equally valid, so long as we're all fleeced and descamgramified. But, now, we've, um, we've heard a lot about you—*some* of you, at least—but we still haven't heard about what you expect that The Church of Omnology could do for you. Could you all maybe fill us in on that?"

"Oh, certainly," Violet replied. "I can tell you what I expect out of a church. I expect social activism! If a church doesn't work for the Betterment of Peoplekind, then what *is* it good for?! So tell me, what social causes does The Church of Omnology support, and how does it provide this support?"

"Oh, we fleece people's scamgrams away, and we descamgramify their bloody metans. All else flows from this. If everyone would only be fleeced and descamgramified on a regular basis, everything would be perfect forever. Now, do you or any of the rest of you have any more questions for us?"

Violet shuddered, and another personality appeared. "Hi. I'm Frank. Yes, I'm the one that's 'shacked up' with Polly Hydrahead. What do I want out of The Church of Omnology? Glad you asked! What I want is a validation, a destigmatization, a descamgramification I guess if you will, of me and my lifestyle! I've been to all sorts of churches, and none will sanctify my marriage to Polly! Talk about your bluenosed self-righteous holier-than-thou prudes! Some of these churches, they marry gay lesbian fornicators and cross-dressing adulterous kumquat molesters and celibate self-abusers, some who amuse themselves by abusing themselves, and others who abuse themselves by *not* abusing themselves, and all sorts of other lustful, wicked sinners. But none of them will marry Polly and I, just 'cause we inhabit the same body! So tell me, will The Church of Omnology sanctify our marriage? Maybe stop some of the endless bickering over how we're *'living in sin'*?"

Orziz muttered to Vyizder for just a few seconds, then Vyizder announced, "We can't give you a one-hundred-percent guarantee, because we've never run into this sort of thing before. However, we promise to elevate this to The Supreme Spirit Guide, Ale Run Himself, and get a ruling. However, we're almost absolutely positive that this will be permitted, especially if you and Polly donate for fleecings on a regular basis. After all, Omnologists are very tolerant. All lifestyles are equally valid. We Omnologists aren't into denying feelings or any other form of repression."

Frank folded, spindled, and mutilated himself spasmodically, and another voice spoke out. "Hello, ladies and gentlemen. I'm Brad. Nice to meet you. Yes, I'm the same Brad who's the bad Dad of Richard. The one who's behind in child support payments because I'm too busy paying my lawyer, fending off rape charges. I'd be able to make both payments, if it wasn't for the fact that I lost my job as a policeman. I'm an accused wife abuser, 'cause I yelled at my former wife once, ten years ago. So now they passed a new law, and so I can't carry a gun, 'cause obviously wife abusers shouldn't be allowed to carry weapons, and cops have to carry weapons.

"I've been thinking about suing under the ADA, the Americans with Disabilities Act, 'cause obviously they're discriminating against me just 'cause I'm Domestic Tranquillity Impaired. But I can't afford more lawyers. Maybe I could be protected if I was a rich executive with lots of money, but as is, I guess I've got to take it in the shorts."

Many puzzled eyes stared at Brad. "Yes, I know, you've got all sorts of questions. How can I be the father, when I'm in the same body as my former wives? And how come I got married, but Frank can't? Well, don't be too nosy. The details are too personal. Let's just say that they involve a sperm bank, a chicken, green paint, and a dwarf. I'm sorry, make that a genetic repository, a member of an avian companion species, mid-spectrum pigments, and an altitudinally challenged person. I didn't mean to crassly shock and offend. Now on that thing about having our union blessed, let me just say this: Frank is a weenie, and he gives up too easily. You can find what you want, if you look hard enough.

"What do I want from The Church of Omnology? Well, let me just say this: I've done some wrong things in my life. I want to do better. I need and want some guidance. I want some wise people to give me some good thoughts and some good advice. But I want these people to be aware of one thing: It's impossible for an individual to pass off personal responsibility, even if they try, or pretend to try. You can pretend to be guided by the Infallible Word of God as revealed in the Bible, but it is you who makes the interpretation of those words. You can pretend to follow the Pope, or Hillary-Bob and Billary-Bob, or David Koresh, or Jesus Christ, or Ale Run Hubba-Bubba.

"But it is you who choose which leader to follow, and how to interpret their words. So I and I alone am responsible for my choices and actions. The individual conscience is the highest moral authority on this planet. This is what I want my Spirit Guides to keep in mind at all times."

"I see Zanzer whispering in your ear," Orziz warned.

"It is completely impossible to pass one's own moral responsibilities to anyone else," Brad insisted. "Any person or group that denies this is spreading lies."

"That *used* to be true," Orziz admitted. "But now that Ale Run has come to us, and revealed how He Can Fleece Our Scamgrams Away, this is no longer true. We are naturally good; it's only our scamgrams and bloody metans that befester us with chaos and badness. So fleece them away, and all your goodness will flow freely. It's that simple."

"Too much simplicity is for simpletons," Brad replied. "Like Albert Einstein said, 'Everything should be made as simple as possible, but no simpler.' Can't you see the wisdom of that?"

"No, I can't. Albert Einstein was a very smart man. Too bad for him, he passed away before Ale Run revealed His Wisdom. Now what I *can* see, quite plainly, is that Zanzer is whispering in your ear. I'm afraid we'll have to ask you to leave, unless you go and get fleeced *right now*."

Brad started to struggle and flail. "You're stigmatizing my scamgrammedness! I don't *wanna* get fleeced! Help! Hel..." Another personality took over. "Hi. I'm Wein E. Bhutt. I really, really hope you won't kick us all out, just 'cause of one rotten apple in our midst. Brad may not admit it, but there's a lot of us in here that *need* a lot of help. And if y'all can make our scamgrams go away, we're all in favor of that. Maybe you can even make *Brad's* scamgrams go away, even if he's not co-operating. Can we stay? We promise to make big contributions and get fleeced and descamgramified. The rest of us can outvote Brad. We promise."

Vyizder and Orziz consulted in whispers, then proclaimed, "Very well, if it's as you say. But we want to talk to Polly Hydrahead about this. They say they're the leader, that they have more consensus than the rest of y'all. Will you please let them speak?"

"Only if you promise to listen to *my* troubles, later, too."

"Okay. Deal. Polly?"

"In just a second. Bye!"

"Polly?"

"Here."

"Do you promise to love and to honor, to stay and be fleeced? To keep Brad and Zanzer and their scamgrams at bay?"

"Oh, yes. To be sure."

"Okay, great. Now, we promised to listen to Wein E. Bhutt. Could you put, um, him or her back on line?"

"Sure. He's a 'he'. Here he is."

"Wein?"

"Yeah, that's me. Now, as I was saying, I've got troubles. Oh, boy, do I *ever* have troubles! Maybe your Church can help me. Maybe my recovered memories are just scamgrams, and maybe you can make them go away.

"I've been troubled ever since I was a little boy. I never knew why. So I went to see my hypnotist, and she dug up some deeply repressed memories of mine. I was a very happy little boy, till one day I went out to the school playground. There, I fell off of the swing. I scraped my knee just a tiny little bit, it didn't even draw blood. I cried just a little bit, but I was getting over it real quick, getting ready to get back on the swing.

"Then my teacher came over. She said, 'Wein, are you all right?' I told her I was just fine. But then she said, 'I saw you fall, and a cloud of dust rose up. In fact, I see some dust on your nose. You probably breathed some in, you poor dear.' So she rushed me to the school nurse. She put on her clean suit and decontaminated my nose, but then she called the doctor. Soon I was at the hospital, and hordes of doctors and lawyers and media people were swarming around me, talking in hushed tones about some dread disease called 'sillycosis' or some such.

"So they told me about this dread disease, and I thought, hey, if all these important people think there's all these reasons why I should be sick, why, I'd better be sick, 'cause they know better than I do, I'm just a kid. And so my parents and I, after I got all sorts of therapies and finally got out of the hospital, we told everybody how sick I was from playground dust and sillycosis. And the media stirred up a lot of dust, too, and so *lots* of people got sillycosis. They had to shut down all the playgrounds in town.

"All this was such a trauma to me, I repressed all memories of it. But these memories made my life miserable. It's only since my hypnotist helped me that I've finally been able to face the terrors of my past. So now I'm suing not just the playground equipment makers, but also all the media folks, the doctors, lawyers, teachers, nurses, and social workers who got me so worked up about this. But the endless suits and countersuits are making me all stressed out, now, too. So I'm sure hoping that it's all just one giant cluster of scamgrams, and you people can fleece me."

"The Church of Omnology won't let you down," Orziz assured him. "You can count on us. We'll set you free from *all* your scamgrams!"

Wein shuddered and shook, and another voice rose in protest. "Hi. I'm Amanda the Panda, and I like to eat meat, but all they ever feed me is bamboozlement. Where's the meat? Do you Omnologists..."

"What is this silly parade of goofy characters all about," another person altogether interrupted angrily. "This Prissy Polly, Aunt Diluvianne, Violet Passionwine, Brad Frankfurter, Zanzer, Panzer, Pander, Panda person has been talking for all of about twenty minutes now, which is far more time than even important movie stars like Jon Travibesty and Julie

Peston got! Now I'd sure like to tell everyone all about *my* troubles, too, one of these days! When is it going to be *my* turn?! How can this person have so many more scamgrams than all the rest of us? Huh?"

"Yeah!" "Right on, man!" "My troubles next!" "No, mine, I've waited long enough!" *"My* troubles are deeper and more important than *your* troubles!" "Your troubles are nothing! Wait till you hear about mine!" There was a loud hubbub, but the message was clear enough: Polly Hydrahead and all her friends and enemies has hogged the stage for long enough. Orziz admitted as much. Polly et cetera protested that they were all being stigmatized just because they had far fewer physical bodies than all the others in the room, but the show moved on anyway.

More troubles were aired. There was much weeping, wailing, and gnashing of teeth. But Vyizder and Orziz assured them all that yes, *of course* all your troubles are due to scamgrams, and we can cure what ails you. Best of all, no one else got kicked out.

So the next time that they all stood up, it wasn't to brush the dust from their shoes, it was to Prepare To Be Fleeced. By resisting Zanzer's whispers, all remaining members of the congregation had now found themselves fit to be Ale Run Hubba-Bubba devotees, Vyizder and Orziz proudly announced. "And now," Orziz proclaimed, "The next phase is what you've all been looking forward to. Next, we'll all be fleeced! But first, we must gather contributions for our cause. May the Spirit of Ale Run move us all towards generosity."

Francestuous glanced anxiously at Raoul. Raoul murmured, "Don't worry, Sweet Buns. Our credit limit will handle this." But then a worried look furrowed his brow. He called out, "Do you accept credit cards?"

Orziz looked pained, but replied, "Sure. No sweat. We're hip, we're with it. The Church of Omnology will handle any credit cards you've got."

So offerings were made and tabulated, secrecy was sworn to, V-Meters were brought out, and Vyizder and Orziz fleeced the people and cast out scamgrams. Polly and her gang got a volume discount. Any more details than that cannot be revealed to heathens unchurched in the Ways of Omnology. Sorry! Send your donations now, and we'll see what we can do, to perhaps train you, the reader, so that more can be revealed to you, all in due time. And due time is dues time. Pay up!*

Footnote*: Send your contributions to: P. T. Barnum Fan Club, C/O Titus Stauffer, P. O. Box 692168, Houston, TX, 77269-2168. Allow 4 to 6 weeks for descamgramification. You will be automatically, remotely but undeniably fleeced when your contributions are deposited.

Raoul and Francestuous stayed on after the ceremonies. Raoul dragged Francestuous back from her attempt to follow after Jon Travibesty and Julie Peston and their entourage and fans. "Listen, Vyizder," Raoul said on behalf of the two of them. "We're really, really, really and truly and deeply impressed by all this fleecing and descamgramification. Why, I can feel my CFS scamgrams fleeing in terror right now! All this is just totally amazing! I just can't think of how to thank you and Orziz and Ale Run, it's just, this is all so incredible! I've never felt so, so fleeced in my whole life!

"But you know, it's really a shame. Francestuous and I, we're not very wealthy at all. We're very deserving, but those heartless government people in Washington, they—now, we know they're doing their best, but there's a lot of greedy and heartless taxpayers out there—they punished us, and cut our SSI checks. And the NEA is stingy when they pay us, to acknowledge how our artistic contributions are a lot deeper and more profoundly meaningful than the average trailer-dwelling slob can appreciate. I mean, there's a lot of sophisticated people at the NEA who understand our art. But there's a limit to how far they can push the boundaries with the uncultured masses of plebeian taxpayers and consumers, who wouldn't know art if it bit them.

"Anyway, to make a long story short, we really, really appreciate what you're doing, and what you've done for us. But we're poor. So I'm feeling at a loss. Feeling totally out of control and down on our luck. Pretty hopeless, frankly. If we're not going to be able to make any more contributions, then we'll not be able to be fleeced and descamgramified. Yet we're as willing to be fleeced as anyone. Must we then live out our lives befestered by clusters of scamgrams and bloody metans? Or is there some other way..."

"There, there, now, take it easy," Vyizder soothed Raoul and Francestuous. "As a matter of fact, there *is* another way, just for truly deserving folks such as yourselves. Now, normally it takes many, many contributions, and many, many classes and training sessions, for most metans to reach an advanced operating level. But our V-Meters tell us that both of you are extremely exceptional people, in that you're already relatively free of scamgrams. You seem to accept the Wisdom of Ale Run with open minds, and a minimum of negative thoughts, chaos, scamgrams, and bloody metans."

Vyizder looked around, then lowered his voice. "Now keep this to yourselves. What we can do in special cases like yours, is we can skip those donations, and..."

"Oh, goodie, goodie, goodie," Raoul squealed with joy, clasping his hands and jumping up and down.

Francestuous smiled dreamily. "Oh, thank you, thank you, *thank you!* Thank you *so* much! Now maybe there's like hope for me and my dreams after all! Maybe I'll be going to Panderwood soon, to start my *real* life!"

"But it's not all peaches and cream," Vyizder hastened to warn them. "Certainly not until you're actually completely and totally free of all scamgrams. So far, only Ale Run has attained this level. Some of the rest of us will join Him in due time, to be sure, but till then, we all have to struggle to do our best. What this means for the two of you is, if you want us to cast out your scamgrams even though you can't make financial contributions to The Church, then we'll have to ask you to make other sorts of contributions.

"We'll want for you to become staff members of The Church of Omnology. This is a very high, special honor. It means you'll need to devote your entire lives, and all your material possessions, to defending The Church against all scamgrams, foreign and domestic. This is a deep, sacred responsibility you'll be charged with, if you're willing."

"Oh, yes, certainly, we're willing," Raoul interjected eagerly.

"So long as it doesn't interfere with me pursuing my dreams of becoming a famous Panderwood actress," Francestuous chimed in. Raoul frowned and glanced at Vyizder, but Vyizder only smiled.

Vyizder hastened to assure Francestuous, "Don't worry about *that*, now, my child. Don't worry about that at *all*. Panderwood is a very, very good place for a faithful Omnologist to do Ale Run's work. So we'll have no problems with your dreams. Those are good, descamgramified dreams.

"We want you to join the staff of The Church of Omnology. First thing is, you'll need to decide. You can either understand Omnology as a science, or as a religion, a philosophy of life. You can go primarily with your rational mind, or with your heart. All Omnologists below the level of Ale Run need to make that choice. Either choice is equally valid, and the other choice, the one you don't choose, will always color your metan a little bit. But you must make a choice. Your primary path has to be one or the other. Only Ale Run, so far, can truly understand both views. So you must choose.

"Come Friday night at seven, one week from now, you'll need to meet us here. You'll have to have made up your mind by then. You'll need to know which path it is that you wish to go by. You'll need to have all your worldly matters all wrapped up by then. You need to become detached from your material goods. Sell those that you can sell, and abandon the others. Let us turn all your material assets into something far more valuable, which is your Treasures in The Church of Omnology. This is one of the strongest ways that you can keep your scamgrams away. Then you can come with us, and devote your lives to The Church, and vanquishing all scamgrams. Orziz and I will be leaving this outpost of Omnology, this beacon that shines to the world. We'll be leaving it in the hands of some other capable Spirit Guides.

"Each of us will be gathering up a group of students. Omnology staff members in training, like yourselves. Then we'll go somewhere far from here, wherever Ale Run sends us. Our two groups may or may not be sent to the same place; we don't know yet. Wherever it is that Ale Run needs us, there is where we'll go. That's what you need to learn to say, as good staff members of The Church of Omnology.

"So meet us back here Friday night at seven. But beware of your scamgrams! They'll be filling your minds with doubts, as you sell off all your worldly possessions to join us in your higher callings. We know, because we've been there. If your scamgrams start to get the better of you, and you need help, then just go ahead and call me or Orziz. Here's our business cards.

"Now you do have all week to decide; we're not trying to rush you. But I'm just a little curious. Omnology as a science versus Omnology as a religion and philosophy of life, you know. Which of those two paths do the two of you think you'll go by?"

Raoul spoke right up. "Oh, I've always been very interested in science and rational thinking. I think I'll go with understanding Omnology as a science."

Francestuous, however, replied, "Fine, Raoul. Fine. Just *fine!* Go ahead and make this kind of life-changing decision without consulting me. That's fine by me. Me, I'll go with Omnology as a philosophy of life. I've always been the holistic, inspired, view-from-the-mountaintop kind of a gal. So you like just go do *your* thing, and I'll like do *mine*."

"But Francestuous, my dearest! I take it back! If it means not being by your side, then I'll forsake Omnology as a science, and go your way!"

"No," she said huffishly, "You've already spoken your mind. We know what you really want. Your feelings are valid, and you should like go with your flow. Don't worry about being with little old me. I'll take care of myself, with the help of our newfound Omnology friends."

"But Francestuous, please! Maybe that was just my scamgrams talking, when I said I wanted to be rational and scientific! Maybe my *real* mind wants to go with *you*, and with Omnology as a philosophy of life! Why can't I change my mind?!"

"Because you have to go with your flow, and we already know your flow doesn't include me."

"But sweetheart, that was just my scamgrams talking! Here, maybe Vyizder can fleece my scamgrams again. *Then* you'll see! Vyizder? Can you help us?"

By then, only Raoul, Francestuous, Vyizder, and Orziz remained. Orziz had shepherded all the other church-goers out the door already, admonishing them to be sure to return for more fleecings, lest they be scammed by scamgrams. Vyizder glanced at Orziz. Orziz glanced back. The glances exchanged some meanings, but also some unanswered questions. "You two will need to stay right here while Orziz and I consult our V-Meter." Vyizder and Orziz met behind the podium and looked down on their V-Meter, while Raoul and Francestuous waited at the other end of the room. Raoul simpered while Francestuous glared.

"What's the deal?" Orziz whispered.

"They're bickering over which of the paths they'll choose," Vyizder replied. "Raoul wants to back out of Omnology as a science, now that Francestuous wants to go the other way, but Francestuous won't let him. One of those really silly lovers' spats. Now Raoul wants us to fleece him, so he can blame his first choice on scamgrams. I think that'd be a real bad precedent, for us to let him blame scamgrams for *either* choice, Omnology as a science, or Omnology as *anything*, for that matter. We obviously can't be blaming scamgrams for any valid Omnological choice."

"Well, of course! So what do you think we should do, here? Surely you're not actually thinking of fleecing him *again*, when he's got nothing left to be fleeced of, any more!" Orziz rubbed his thumb against the tips of his fingers, under the podium but right above the V-Meter that they were apparently studying so intently.

"Well, we could always let him go into debt. Let him pay back later, after they sell everything off. Help to make sure they don't back out, by making him feel indebted. Are they likely to back out? Should we give them the 'total immersion' routine to keep them snared while we've got them? What do you think?"

"Nah. I don't think they're likely to back out. They're hooked. Total immersion wouldn't be worth the trouble, in this case, anyway. So you really want to bother to fleece him again? If we do that, then what are we going to find? Are we going to try to keep 'em together, or split 'em up? If we want to keep 'em together, then which way? Do *you* want them? I'm not too hip on having the two of them together in *my* class. How about you?"

"Let's not fleece them again. Tell 'em to sort it out themselves. We'd be better off with them split apart. Loyalty to Omnology, you know, not to each other. Apart, I do believe they'll be useful idiots for us. Together, I don't know. But we'll not try to push them apart. They'll do that all by themselves, it looks like. Okay?"

Orziz nodded in assent. He twiddled with the knobs, eliciting a few beeps. Then they sauntered on back to Raoul and Francestuous.

"The V-Meter tells us you're both still relatively free of scamgrams, from your last fleecing," Vyizder announced. "What with your good general health and relative freedom from scamgrams—this is why you've been selected for this very special honor in the first place, remember—and the fact that it takes a while for scamgrams to befester you again after a fleecing, why, then, for us to formally fleece you again so soon would be a waste. Besides, there's no way a scamgram could cause you to falsely prefer one valid Omnological choice over another. You two will have to sort this out for yourselves.

"Now if you'll excuse us, Orziz and I need to leave. We'll see you at seven on Friday. Please remember to call if your scamgrams threaten to make you wimp out. In all honesty, though, I must tell you that those kinds of things, being weak and vulnerable to scamgrams, and needing constant help, will count against you as Omnology staff members. One has to be strong against scamgrams and bloody metans if one wishes to advance to a higher level. Okay?"

Vyizder and Orziz shooed them out the door, climbed into their cars (a Mercedes Benz and a Ferrari respectively), and drove off. The first thing that Raoul did after stepping out of the Soulorama was to light up an Earth Spirit. Francestuous sniped at him, so he had to light up yet another one, to calm his nerves some more. Then there was the long bicycle ride home and a sleepless night of laying in separate beds. In the morning, they began the task of putting their worldly affairs in order.

Chapter 11 has endnotes on Inventing Religions, Defending the Domestic Tranquillity Impaired, and Pandering with Scientology. See the end of this book, of course... Page 231...

Chapter 12

Understanding Omnology as a Science

Raoul said to Francestuous, "Did you know that according to arcane, murky legal practices set up by shysters, if an author uses a detached or semi-detached quote, not weaving it into his or her story, at the beginning of a chapter, then he or she doesn't have quite the same, strong 'fair use' protections of free speech, as he or she would otherwise have? That inappropriate and insensitive people can then sue authors who quote them, if the authors don't watch out?"

"No, I didn't know that," Francestuous replied. "What does *that* have to do with anything?"

"Oh, not much of anything," Raoul admitted. "Nor does L. Ron Hubbard and his Dianetics pseudopsychobabble quasireligion have anything to do with Omnology, either. Omnology is obviously far, far superior to Dianetics, of course. Whatever Dianetics is. It just follows from the known Omnological fact that Omnology is superior to everything.

"But in order to keep my scamgrams fleeced, I'm getting these vibes right now. They're telling me that I have to quote to you, a paragraph from page 442 of *Dianetics: The Modern Science of Mental Health,* by L. Ron Hubbard, who lived from 1911 to 1986. Now this is by no means as deep as what Omnology teaches. But now and then, even non-Omnologists get just a tiny, tiny hint of Omnological wisdom, it seems to me. So here's the quote:

"'The *grouper* is the nastiest of all types of command. It can be so variously worded and its effect is so serious on the time track that the whole track can roll up into a ball and all incidents then appear to be in the same place. This is apparent as soon as the preclear hits one. The grouper will not be discovered easily, but it will settle out as the case progresses and the case can be worked with a grouper in restimulation.' End quote."

"That's ridiculous," Francestuous objected. "You think that's like, even *one tiny bit* as wise as the teachings of Ale Run Hubba-Bubba, The

Mighty Fleecer of All Scamgrams? I mean, it's like, *'Duh!'* That's even obvious to *me,* and I've hardly gotten *any* Omnological training at *all,* yet! You know, Raoul, for you to say such things—that this *Dianetics* thing is anything *nearly* as profoundly deep as Omnology—I think it just goes to show that you're severely scamgramified. I think you'd better call Orziz or Vyizder at that emergency number they gave us."

Raoul just stomped off in a huff. Despite whatever Francestuous said, he still felt better, now that he'd listened to those otherworldly vibes, done his duty, and delivered the quote. Bad karma had been defeated in two ways: 1) Shysterism had been thwarted, to the maximum extent allowed by law, which admittedly is never very far. 2) Also, all those observers on that otherworldy plane, who by now had gotten used to their once-per-chapter introductory quote or quotes, were appeased, as well as profoundly impressed by Dianetics wisdom. They all eagerly awaited revelations of an even more profound, Omnological nature.

Raoul and Francestuous had a tempestuous week quasi-together, putting their affairs into order and preparing to turn their material belongings into assets in The Church of Omnology. It was a hectic week.

Finally, it was all over. Raoul and Francestuous met Vyizder and Orziz at the local Soulorama and turned over their assets. They attended some short Omnology services. Then there was the orientation speech about Where We Are Going, and so on.

Omnology was rapidly solidifying and gathering followers, they were told. Those staff members who wanted to understand Omnology as a Science were to be trained at the Scientific Institute for the Advancement of Omnology in Akron, Ohio. Those who were more theologically and philosophically oriented were to be trained at the Intergalactic Headquarters of The Church of Omnology in Los Diablos, California. And finally, for those who felt that they just couldn't make up their minds, Ale-Run Hubba-Bubba Himself, in an act of great mercy, had decreed that all feelings were valid, including feelings of indecision. Those who couldn't choose were to be trained at the Media and Government Institute for the Fleecing of All Metans, in Washington, D.C.

Madness County being in the Midwest, scientific types could get on the bus and ride straight to Akron. Those metans destined to be trained in religion, or in media and government, on the other hand, had much longer journeys ahead of them, so they would be bussed to Chicago, where they, and others like them, would be put on charter airliners to Los Diablos and Washington. So Raoul and Francestuous got on two separate busses, and went their separate ways. Then there was that long bus ride.

But now, Raoul was sitting in class at the Scientific Institute for the Advancement of Omnology, about to learn all about Omnology as a Science. He could barely contain his excitement. His real life was about to begin! Maybe someday he'd be a really famous scientist, he thought dreamily. Maybe he'd make great Omnological discoveries and earn himself a Nobel Prize in Omnology. Maybe...

All right! he told himself. Snap out of it, and listen to Vyizder.

"...great strides for The Church of Omnology. If we can get everyone to realize that The Church of Omnology is both a religion *AND* a science, then each of our groups will be able to specialize. The Church part of The Church will get tax breaks, and the Science part of The Church will get research grants from the government. So a lot is riding on us, as leaders and future leaders of Omnological science. We must learn, then reach out to further reason and knowledge.

"So let's get right down to it. All rational thought is based on mathematics. Omnology is no exception. So let's talk about Omnological mathematics, starting with the basics. In Omnological mathematics, the central concept is The Chaos Theory. Now, I know what you're thinking. After all, I'm a trained Omnologist. 'Well, just what, exactly, *is* The Chaos Theory, anyway?' is what you're thinking. We Omnologists value classroom participation. So go ahead. Ask me." He flipped on the overhead projector, then waved his hands like a symphony conductor. The students read the words on the screen, asking in loud unison, **"Well, just what, exactly, *is* The Chaos Theory, anyway?"**

"I'm glad you asked. That's a sign of intelligence and budding greatness, to be asking such profound questions. After all, without asking profound questions, one hardly ever gets profound answers. And only profound answers, especially from deep thinkers like myself, can lead the masses of humanity towards a Deeper Understanding. And, a Deeper Understanding, you see, leads one away from Chaos, which is badness.

"In fact, one could very aptly summarize the whole Chaos Theory by simply stating that Chaos is Badness. That's a sign of true understanding, you know, is to be able to take matters profound and complicated, that scholars have spent their entire careers puzzling over, and to distill it all down to its essence, without oversimplifying. An ability that I take great pride in.

"But let's go back to the beginning, and put it all into proper perspective. The Chaos Theory is really just part of the Math Theory. The overall Math Theory, then, goes into the Theory of Everything, which explains everything. But that's just way too much to get into today. Let's just stick to Math Theory, and where Chaos Theory fits into Math Theory.

"Math Theory basically started with The Algebra Theory, which states that if X equals Y, then Y equals X. And even yet amazingly more, if Y also equals Z, then X equals Z. Very simple, yet profound, with implications throughout the natural world, as is so often the case in truly great Theories. So, then, after many great mathematicians, together, reached a consensus on The Algebra Theory, then all they had to do was to hammer out a good approximation for X, and then, of course, they knew what Y and Z were, too.

"After they did the same for other groups of letters and symbols, spanning the English, Greek, and Cyrillic alphabets, well, they just published a big look-up table—we've even embedded it into handheld calculators, these days—and now, nobody has to sit around figuring out what all these symbols are equal to, any more. Except for school children. It keeps them off the street, out of trouble, and out of the greedy claws of capitalist ogres, who might otherwise be tempted to enslave them in child labor schemes. Oh, yes, and according to The Education Theory, it helps their brains to grow. When properly administered by government-certified Algebra Instructors, the Algebra Theory stimulates neurons and raises the pupil's levels of intelligence. Taking matters much further, we must get society to realize that certified Omnology instructors can use The Chaos Theory to make all of society's scamgrams go away, which will be the ultimate investment in human potential.

"Anyway, after the publication of the Algebra Tables, Algebra Theory pretty much had nowhere left to go. Nothing else left to theorize about, much, there. So mathematicians moved off to newer, more exciting endeavors. They formulated The Geometry Theory. Now, The Geometry Theory was a great discovery, it lead right, straight, directly to The Chaos Theory. You see, The Geometry Theory states that if two planes intersect, well, you've just got to draw a line, there, before they do, because if two planes intersect, a lot of badness will happen. Just look at what happened at the Denver International Airport recently. Hundreds dead. Now, if that's not Chaos and Badness, then I don't know what is.

"So, The Geometry Theory was great at explaining that you've just *got* to draw a line somewhere, anywhere before the planes intersect. Even millionths of an inch away from intersecting is fine, theoretically, but once they've intersected, you're in Big Trouble. Once they intersect, there's Chaos and Badness, and The Geometry Theory can't help you any more. Chaos and Badness are way too complicated for The Geometry Theory to be of much help, any more, at all.

"So, then, Omnological mathematicians formulated The Chaos Theory, for cases where people have failed to properly apply The Geometry Theory, the two planes have intersected, and Badness has happened. Among other examples of Chaos and Badness, that is. The Chaos Theory states, basically, that Chaos is Badness. Even more amazingly, The Chaos Theory ties in, not only back to The Geometry Theory, but also, way back to The Algebra Theory, too. Remember, if X equals Y, then Y also equals X. The Chaos Theory, in a sense, is nothing but a very special case of this. If Chaos is Badness, then Badness is also Chaos. It just demonstrates the profound beauty of mathematics. Simple equations capture the essence of very complicated phenomena, all throughout nature. It's like, you know, it just goes to show you, Ale Run Himself must be a mathematician, the way He designed the Universe, to follow all these equations."

"Why, that's *brilliant!*" Raoul exclaimed. "Now let me get this straight: The Chaos Theory says that Chaos is Badness. Right?"

"Right!" Vyizder proclaimed, beaming proudly.

"But, how did you ever manage to summarize it so simply yet profoundly?" Raoul asked.

"Well," Vyizder replied, humbly, "If I've been able to see further than others, it's because I've stood on the shoulders of giants.

"So there's Omnological mathematics *theory*. Now let's move on to Omnological mathematics *applications*. Time for our first lab experiment. First, though, we must momentarily digress back to Omnology as a religion. One of the prime principles of Omnology as a religion, as with many other religions, is that things stated in normal, plain, everyday English are quite unremarkably dull, prosaic, and frumpishly mundane. If, on the other hand, you can say something in some ancient old Holy Language, or some other obscure jargon, then that's quite profound and deeply, mystically meaningful, especially since no one can quite understand you. So the Catholics have Latin, Protestants have the old King James Version, and sports fans have Sports Blather.

"Omnology, though, being less than a year old, suffers from some handicaps here. Our jargon is still not very highly developed, and we have no tradition of using some ancient, obscure dialect. This is both a blessing and a curse. On the plus side, as we invent our own jargon, we can keep it completely free of racism, sexism, capitalism, speciesism, and realityism. As we all know, all those old-time religions are severely befestered with all kinds of 'ism' scamgrams. God is a macho, male-type White Man guy fella, all that kind of stuff.

"On the minus side, though, those old-timer religious folks have a leg up on us. They can take their old sacred writings, run them through computer algorithms, and find all sorts of deep and meaningful hidden messages in there. If we do the same thing with the sacred writings of Ale Run, though, no one will be impressed. They'll just say Ale Run put those things there deliberately, and so what if He predicted stuff three months in advance? They can impress folks by finding stuff about Hitler in Hebrew writings from thousands of years ago. We can't compare to that.

"Or can we? As Omnologists, we believe in having our cake and eating it, too! Why not take Ale Run's writings, have some disinterested third party translate them into Hebrew or some such, some language Ale Run doesn't even know, and *then* we go off and find hidden messages! We think that'd be pretty impressive. But then, if we translate Ale Run's writings into some old language, they'll be contaminated by all those 'ism' scamgrams, because the ancients didn't know how to talk without isms. Language reflects thinking. As Marshall McLuhan said, the medium is the message. There's just no way you can translate something into Hebrew without it getting befestered by all sorts of 'ism' scamgrams.

"Well, fortunately we Omnological researchers never give up! One of us, Dr. Libby Leftlimper, ran into a widely respected feminist scholar, Dr. Sapphire Butschbeach, and told her about our dilemma. So she helped us out. She translated Ale Run's writings into the only known ism-free ancient language, which is Shebrew, which was spoken in the Amazonian rain forest thousands of years ago.

"So that's where we're at today. Time for our Omnological mathematics lab exercise. Now if you'll all follow me, we'll go to the computer room. There, we'll ask you each to sit by a terminal, and supervise our supercomputers as they parse Ale Run's writings in Shebrew. How does this work? Well, we try all sorts of different ways to assign input letters to output letters, all sorts of different sizes and shapes and starting points for matrices, and then we parse for meaningful phrases and sentences, crossword-puzzle-like. All that's done by our extremely sophisticated machines and programs.

"So we look at billions and trillions of different combinations. For any given long combination of characters, it is *extremely* unlikely that you'd get exactly that combination. So after we find a meaningful combination, after looking at three trillion combinations, we can say, 'Now lookee here, here it says that Ale Run has the keys to the Universe,' or whatever, and the chances of finding that message was only one in three trillion! *SURELY* this is way too amazing for it to be a totally random happening, and *SURELY* this must mean that Ale Run is the Master of Space, Time, and Dimension! And the media will come running to us, and we'll get lots of press, and lots of money.

"So that's how it works. Now where you guys come in, other than learning about Omnologic, is that computers can take the process only so far. They can only select *candidates* for Deeply Meaningful Messages. We have to make the final determination. Omnologists in training can make the next winnowing, or filtration, steps, but a trained Omnologist like me has to make the final determination. So everyone follow me..."

They walked to the computer room, and each of the twenty-three students sat by a terminal. Vyizder walked around, showing everyone what to do. Then he sat at his terminal and executed the executables. Everyone sat in eager but silent anticipation.

"Got one!" Sally sang out. "'The world will end in 1612,' it says!"

"Flush it," Vyizder commanded. "No meaning there. Keep on looking."

"Here it is!" Bob announced shortly thereafter. "'He who writes on bathroom walls, wraps his Hubba-Bubba in little balls. He who reads these lines of wit, eats those little balls of...'"

"Enough of that one," Vyizder grumbled. "Can it. Invalid message."

A few minutes slipped by. "Check this out!" Andrew yelled. "This is it! 'Get a grip, don't be a dip, Omnology dumnology is a worthless trip!'"

"Into the bit bucket," Vyizder ordered. "Just more random nonsense."

More time slipped by. Then Raoul stood up and shouted, "*Look! Look at this!* It says, 'Repent, repent, the end is near! The Anti-Hubba-Bubba comes, but have no fear, fleecing kicks scamgrams in the rear!' Now what do you think of *that?!*"

Vyizder got up, clapped and cheered, and gave Raoul a big fat "Attaboy". Everyone shouted with excited glee. One student was dispatched to tell the media all about it, while everyone else went back to the classroom.

"That's *great!*" Vyizder announced yet once more, after everyone took their classroom seats again. "That was a very, *very* good mathematics lab! Only Omnologically, by the Grace of Our Lord Ale Run, could there ever be such a conclusive and logically, scientifically, and methodologically bulletproof demonstration of the Deepness of Existence! And of Ale Run's profound grasp of the meaning of such matters, of course.

"Now, class, let's get in touch with our feelings about Omnological mathematics. It's very important that we all feel good about our Omnological mathematics knowledge. So now we'll go around the room, and everyone will stand up, and briefly tell us how they feel about their abilities."
Everyone did so. Everyone felt very good about their abilities, and Vyizder was quite pleased.

"Very good, class, *very good!!!* I'm *so* glad we all feel *good* about our talents! It's *good* to feel good! Now since we all feel so good about our work, we must all be rewarded!" Vyizder clapped his hands. A butler appeared with a large round tray, bearing ice cream sandwiches under frosted glass. "Make sure our star pupil, Raoul, here, gets an extra one," Vyizder ordered. "For discovering the secret message about Ale Run's Wisdom." Everyone enjoyed their rewards.

"Now class," Vyizder continued, "We've got to stay serious. There's a lot of deep, deep, very heavy material to be covered here. We've got to move on. You'll doubtlessly feel like you're drinking through a fire hose, but we've got to just go and *do it.* So let's **do it!**

"Okay, so we've got to wade right in. Now in Omnology, our goal is to know everything. After all, the Name of Our Church is The Church of Omnology. *Omno* means *all*, just as *omniscient* means all-knowing and *omnipotent* means all-powerful, of course. So although we don't know quite exactly *everything* just yet, Ale Run willing, we soon will. I for one have a very hard time envisioning us Omnologists failing in our endeavors, because we believe in ourselves. We believe in positives. Belief itself is a positive, you see. We just have to work at it, and *believe. Believe* above all else! Because as you believe, so shall it be. Reality is defined by the observer.

"Then think no negative thoughts, and your reality is forced to be positive. Above all else, never believe any negative thoughts about yourself, or about The Church of Omnology. Such doubtful thoughts are the purest of scamgrams! Whenever anything bad happens, it's probably not *your* fault, and it sure as all git-out isn't the fault of The Church of Omnology! All badness and chaos flows from scamgrams and bloody metans, not from you or The Church of Omnology. Remember these basic facts, and no scamgram can hurt you. Then you'll be able to learn, understand, and act from the most deeply profound of all Omnological facts, and keep right on living a descamgramified life.

"Speaking of descamgramification, I forgot to mention one of the new technologies that you'll now be able to benefit from. The less advanced metans among us must contribute to The Church and be fleeced by a V-Meter, yes. But you're far more *advanced* metans now, who've already given your all, and have devoted your entire lives to The Church. So there is no point in us subjecting you to time-consuming fleecings. As staff members, you'll have the benefits of a far superior technology, which is called the Technology That Makes 'PING!' Sounds. More informally, among ourselves we call it the 'Ping Thing'. This is not to say that we mean to trivialize or disrespect the Ping Thing, of course."

Vyizder opened up a desk drawer and lifted out a small black object. Lifting it up, he said, "Behold the Ping Thing! As you might expect, it does indeed go 'PING!'! However, this cleverly designed and superbly crafted technological wonder does far, far more. Whenever an expert Omnologist like me detects a scamgram befestering a highly trained staff Omnologist like any of you, then there's no point in wasting time with a V-Meter.

"Trained Omnologists like yourselves are capable of understanding the meaning and function of the Ping Thing, and you have no need, any longer, for elaborate ceremonies to accompany your fleecing with a V-Meter, to help you feel you got your donation's worth. And frankly, any scamgram powerful enough to befester a staff Omnologist wouldn't be scared by a V-Meter anyway.

"For such more powerful scamgrams, we must bring out the big guns! All we have to do is point the Ping Thing at the befestered metan, push this little red button here, and your scamgrams will be instantaneously de-energized! That is, so long as you continue to devote your mental energies towards living a life that is pleasing to Ale Run, and most especially in this case, so long as you pay special heed to the sound of the Ping Thing. Since you are all highly trained Omnologists now, I should hope I needn't belabor this any further. I'd like to demonstrate the Ping Thing, but its energies are sacred, and mustn't be wasted on anything other than defending trained Omnologists from scamgrams.

"Very well then, we must move on, into the heart of Omnology as a Science. One of the central teachings of Omnology as a Science is the Five-and-Three-Quarters-Fold Way. Master the five point seven five ways, thoroughly, and you'll be almost like Ale Run Himself. So you can see the Power of The Ways.

"Now the first of The Ways is Paradox. Examples are that all feelings are valid, yet some feelings are more valid than others. Feelings in favor of Omnology, for example, are far more valid than feelings against Omnology. This should be obvious to any Omnologist, but we have to point it out just to be academically complete and rigorous.

"Another example of Paradox would be that yes, reality is defined locally, by the immediate observer, but then again, reality is also defined by other, more remote observers. My reality and your reality can't both be true, if they contradict each other. And whose definitions of reality shall prevail? That will be one of today's major lessons. First, let's complete our list of The Ways.

"The second Way is Eschatology, which is the study of the End Times. When will the Anti-Hubba-Bubba come, and how will we know who he or she is? How then will we help Ale Run Hubba-Bubba and The Church to rise up and triumphantly and finally vanquish all scamgrams, inappropriateness, and less-valid feelings? This entire topic encompasses some very profoundly Deep Matters, and must remain to be examined some other day.

"The third Way is Quantum Metaphysics. The Universe consists of an almost infinite number of microverses, or small, local environments, and many, but far fewer, macroverses, or large systems. Then the Universe, of course, is the union of all macroverses. Quantum Metaphysics concerns the behavior, in a micro-microversal scale, of almost infinitely tiny sub-atomic particles like electrons, neutrons, positrons, photons, tachyons, and croutons. By studying the behavior of tiny particles, we can seduce the Laws of the Universe, and hence, derived from these and other Laws of Nature, moral Laws about how we should live our lives in obedience to Ale Run.

"The fourth Way is Cosmology. Cosmology of course concerns the Universe—the infinitely large and cosmic, as opposed to the infinitely tiny. Here, once again, we can seduce the laws of Mother Nature, from which we derive Omnological moral rules. That's why our moral rules are so cosmic.

"The fifth Way is Cosmetology. Since reality is collectively defined by many observers, we must make everything appear as attractive as possible. If reality *appears* attractive, then we will *perceive* it as attractive and good, and therefore it will *be* good. So our role as Omnological Cosmetologists is to cover the blemishes and flaws in reality, to give reality the proper 'spin', so that it will be *perceived* as more positive, and therefore *become* more positive. Remember, then, to strive for positive thoughts at all times, especially about ourselves.

"Finally, the final three-quarters Way is incompleteness. Our Omnological ideas simply aren't quite complete yet. We still have more ideas and theories to devise and discover and new marvels of technology to invent. Some day we'll be done, Ale Run's Will will be done, and this Three-Quarters Way will no longer be one of The Ways. So it is not a *full* Way. But we're obviously more than half-baked. So we're halfway between half-baked and perfect—hence, for several reasons, this is the Three-Quarters Way. Only after we complete and perfect Omnology, only then will the Anti-Hubba-Bubba become so enviously enraged as to lash out and usher in the End Times. Thus will the Anti-Hubba-Bubba inadvertently trigger the events which will allow us to descamgramify the entire Universe, making everything perfect forever.

"Now our first major lesson of the day illustrates a number of points about the Five and Three-Quarters-Fold Way. Being scientifically profound sophisticates, we take our teaching examples from arcane Laws of Nature. The first such law or phenomenon is that of 'frame-dragging'. They've been planning an experiment to measure this for forty years, and they've already spent five hundred million dollars on it. It's one of Einstein's predictions; the only theoretically predicted result of his theory of relativity that hasn't yet been measured.

"Soon, we'll measure it. By 'we' I don't mean specifically us Omnologists, but us scientists generally. We'll launch a very special 'gravity probe' satellite with a near-perfect gyroscope and a near-perfect telescope in a near-perfect vacuum. It will measure how the spinning Earth, to a tiny, tiny degree, drags the very essence of space-time along with it, in its spinning motion. You can read all about it in the March 1997 issue of the science magazine *Discover*.

"To illustrate exactly what *frame-dragging* is, I have a little thought experiment for you. You're all no doubt familiar with centrifugal force. If you tie a stick onto a string and swing it around you, it will pull on the string, as if it were trying to pull away from you. Spin 'round and 'round on the merry-go-round, and you're pushed towards the outside. Stand inside a spinning space station, with your feet 'down' towards the outer wall of the station, and you will feel artificial gravity caused by centrifugal force pushing you down against that wall, in proportion to the dimensions and spin rate of that space station.

"But wait! All things are relative! *Who says* you and that space station are spinning, and that it isn't you and your station who are standing still, while all the rest of the universe revolves around you? It may sound silly at first, but the Universe has a sort of 'voting scheme'. Put it another way—the local properties of matter originate in distant objects scattered throughout the universe. Each piece of matter in the entire universe gets a 'vote', weighed according to its mass, as to what is 'fixed' space, reference space, non-moving, non-spinning, stationary space, and who is moving. Sound crazy? Well, it's not just a democratic way to run the universe, it's the only way for everything to logically fall together in a consistent manner.

"OK, the thought experiment. You're sitting in a non-rotating space station, and all the matter out there is 'fixed' with respect to you. None of it revolves around you. You feel no force at all; you float in zero gravity. Now you start the station spinning. You're pushed against its outer walls. You feel one 'G' of Earth-normal artificial gravity, because we select the right rotation radius and spin rate.

"But now a miraculous outside force interferes. Suppose it should please Ale Run to grab half of the matter in the entire universe and start it revolving around you, so that it is now spatially 'fixed' with respect to your spinning walls. Guess what? Your one 'G' would be cut in half! As you'd use your miracle force to grab more and more of the universe's mass, and cause it to revolve around you also, then your centrifugal force would also diminish. By the time you were done, all the matter in the universe would now be 'fixed' with respect to your now-stationary walls of your no-longer-spinning space station, and you'd feel no force. Everything would be the same as when you started, because you're no longer spinning with respect to all those other pieces of matter out there, each of which gets a 'vote' on whether you're spinning or not.

"Thus is reality collectively defined by matter, by observers, by who is doing what with respect to everyone else. Notice that the larger your mass, the larger your 'vote'. If you collected 99.9999 plus percent of the universe's mass into one giant sphere, and you took a tiny flyspeck of three micrograms of dirt and revolved the dirt around the giant sphere, would the giant sphere then start to 'think' it was spinning with respect to the stationary speck, feeling centrifugal force, and falling apart due to that centrifugal force? Or would it dismiss the tiny flyspeck as just being a tiny bit of dirt in orbit around it, with centrifugal force holding the speck up against the giant sphere's gravity? Does the Earth orbit the Sun, or does the Sun orbit the Earth?

"Just think of it this way: A massive object will grab the frame of reference and drag it along with it. Hence the term *frame-dragging*. A massive object defines reality to suit itself. When an aircraft carrier and a kayak both say 'this is my space', the aircraft carrier wins.

"Yes, Raoul, you have a question?"

"Yes Sir, I sure do. Now you suggested in this thought experiment of yours that Ale Run could cause half of the universe's mass to rotate around us, if He should choose to do so. Could we maybe have Him just go ahead and *do* that? This would demonstrate this *frame dragging* thing, saving research funds, and far more! Wouldn't that alone be a quite compelling demonstration of the wisdom, power, and brilliance of

Omnological thought? Wouldn't such a demonstration be sufficient to justify federal funding for the Scientific Institute for the Advancement of Omnology?"

"Sure, Raoul, I'm sure that would be *quite* compelling! But you see, Ale Run plays no favorites. He wants us Omnological scientists to demonstrate the superiority of our thought, of our dedication to His Will, over that of more mundane, conventional scientists, on a level playing ground. He wants us to develop and demonstrate our great strengths as Omnological researchers, by wresting the Universe's tightly guarded Secrets from Her. No strokes of lightning from the clouds at His opponents, and no miraculous interference in the affairs of mere mortal metans. That's the way Ale Run operates, Blessed Be His Name."

"But *why*, Sir, *why?* Couldn't He just force the stubborn Universe to yield up Her precious Secrets, which She guards so jealously? Couldn't He just make everything and everyone perfect forever and get it over with?"

"No, Raoul, because, well, we must be allowed our own free will. We must choose descamgramification or chaos, badness, and bloody metans, entirely of our own free will. Ale Run believes that metans, and the Universe for that matter, are basically good, and will choose to do His Will, if we'll just use our V-Meters and Ping Things to help the ignorant metans along. Descamgramification freely chosen is best of all."

"But Sir, if all metans are basically good, why does The Church of Omnology end up suing the badness and chaos out of everyone who says bad things about us?"

"Because that is the Will of Ale Run! Now these are entirely legitimate questions, but this is a *scientific* organization, not a theological and philosophical organization!" Vyizder calmed himself back down, and continued in a quieter tone of voice. "Well, I do admit, though, that science can sometimes show us The Way, morally, ethically, and Omnologically, as far as we should behave, and follow the Will of Ale Run. Now let's get back to frame dragging.

"What are the practical, moral implications of frame dragging for us as metans and Omnologists? Besides refraining from arguing with a tracker trailer if we're driving a bicycle? Should we all go out to the nearest all-you-can-eat restaurant, and start putting on mass, so that we can define reality on our own terms? No, I'm afraid not! We Omnologists can't become Masters of the Universe by playing the game on the level of dumb, stupid, low-level matter. We have to take the fight to the higher levels of Life and of Spirit.

"On the spiritual plane, that which corresponds to *frame-dragging* is *fame-dragging*. Those who are famous get to define reality to suit themselves. Who is important? What ideas are important? What is Deep and Meaningful? Who deserves to saturate the media? Those who are famous, not those who are massive! If you're too massive, as a matter of fat, chances are that you'll not be famous! You're much better off paying attention, then, to Cosmetology, not Cosmology, when it comes to being able to define reality to suit yourself.

"So as devoted Omnologists, we must at all times remember the very important principles of fame-dragging. Those who are famous define our reality. So if we Omnologists want famous metans to define Omnology as good, so that Omnology will be perceived as good, then we must go way, way far out of our way to accommodate the actors, actresses, screenwriters, producers, and directors of Panderwood! At all costs, we **must** make fame-dragging work *for* us! So whenever any good Omnologist runs into any famous metans from Panderwood, even if they are famous for nothing other than for being famous, then we must..."

At this point, Raoul couldn't concentrate on what Vyizder was saying any longer. He slipped off into resentful thoughts about how the lure of fame, Panderwood, and rich, handsome, square-jawed actors had stolen his beloved companion human away. Yes, she'd fallen for it. For actors who not only knew how to light cigarettes, open beer cans, and love a woman in just the right way, but who also put their rolls of toilet paper up just right. For the likes of Jon Travibesty. For...

'PING!' 'PING!' 'PING!' At first, Raoul thought he'd been caught in some submariner's sonar. Then he snapped out of it to see that Vyizder was pointing the Ping Thing at him. He straightened out, paying attention to what Vyizder was saying.

"You've been befestered by scamgrams," Vyizder rebuked Raoul. "Now *wake up!* Fame-dragging is a fact of life. You've got to just *live* with it, and make it *work* for us! Yes, I know, some of us resent how so many metans in Panderwood are so rich, pretty, handsome, thin, famous, and powerful. And some of us resent them for stealing our companion humans away. Yes, I know. As an expert Omnologist, I know a lot. But we have to put it all behind us, and work for the good of Omnology, and the descamgramification of all metans. A good place to start is for us to pander to the stars of Panderwood, so that they, in turn, will pander to us and for us.

"Now Raoul, I've 'pinged' your scamgrams away, thanks to the Grace of Our Lord Ale Run and his Marvelous Wonders of Technology. Beware, lest they befester you yet again! Panderwood is how we will take Omnology to the people, so don't allow the scamgrams of resentment to get in your way.

"Let's move on. We Omnologists aren't just passively sitting by the sidelines as science marches on. No, Sir! We have a few irons in the fire ourselves. Now, as a very special treat, I'll introduce you to two of our finest researchers. They'll tell us all about the very latest in their exciting new research and development efforts. Hold on." Vyizder grabbed a telephone and started punching the buttons. The class murmured excitedly while he briefly, quietly chatted on the phone.

Vyizder hung up the phone and announced, "They're on their way! OK, now, so who are they, you ask? They are Dr. Iame Ghuanobhraine, our foremost quantum metaphysicist, and Dr. Dorcus Moorphlegmgasm, our multi-talented systems expert of methodological, metrological, scatological, and expertological expertology. She's truly a one-woman wonder! She obtained the coveted title of Senior Fellowette of Omnology at the tender age of twenty-nine.

"They'll both be here in just a few minutes. Why don't we just take this time to get up and stretch. Take a break." Everyone took a break.

Soon enough, everyone took their seats again. Then Vyizder introduced Iame and Dorcus. Sparing few words on pleasantries, Iame launched right into a dissertation on quantum metaphysics. "Ladies and gentlemetans," he said, "Quantum metaphysics is a fairly new and modern science. It really doesn't go very far back at all. Let me just briefly mention its history, then we'll describe what's new and exciting, right here at the Scientific Institute for the Advancement of Omnology. We're exploring possibilities of radical new breakthroughs, as far as practical applications are concerned. The implications for Omnology are profound and far-reaching.

"Omnological historians have recently discovered that quantum metaphysics was actually developed in secret way before modern Omnology was formally formulated and revealed by Our Lord Ale Run Hubba-Bubba. Ale Run's father, as a matter of fact, we could say, was an Omnologist before Omnology even arose. Knowing, though, that the world wasn't quite ready for Omnology yet, he performed his good deeds in secret. One of his good deeds, of course, was to raise Ale Run wisely, so that Ale Run could develop the technological breakthroughs of Omnology, and correctly judge the time and place to reveal Omnology to the world.

"Some background, now. In the late Nineteen-Thirties, the fascists of Europe, Hitler especially, were building up dark powers with which to enslave the world. They were befestered with massive clusters of scamgrams, bloody metans, and inappropriateness. Insensitivity, even. Milk Walk Hubba-Bubba, Ale Run's father, was a very wise, perceptive young man. A man before his time.

"Now like I say, Milk Walk was a very wise man. As such, he was very, very Sensitive. So it troubled him greatly, what he had to do. But he knew he had to do it. Otherwise, the world was destined to become befestered by massive clusters of scamgrams, for a long, long time. And Milk Walk was wise, yes, but he wasn't wise enough to invent V-Meters and Ping Things with which to fleece the fascists. So he intervened in more crude, violent ways. He took advantage of the Hindenburg Uncertainty Principle, and devised a clever technology which has remained secret until Omnological historians recently uncovered evidence of it."

Raoul was waving his hand eagerly, so Iame acknowledged him, saying, "Yes, you have a question?"

"Um, yes, Doctor Ghuanobhraine, I was wondering, um, you said something about the *Hindenburg* Uncertainty Principle. Don't you mean the *Heiselburger* Uncertainty Principle?"

"No, I certainly *don't* mean the Heiselburger Uncertainty Principle, young man," Iame replied sternly. "Milk Run Hubba-Bubba was far, far wiser than Doctor Heiselburger. He saw not only the Uncertainty Principle, but also its deeper implications, and how it might be put to use. Most impressively of all, Milk Walk also saw that the world wasn't ready for his amazing technology yet. So he very humbly kept his technology secret, and only used it once, for the eventual descamgramification of all metans. In honor of this one very important, world-saving use of the

Uncertainty Principle, we Omnologists call it the Hindenburg Uncertainty Principle. We put applications far, far above mere theoretical amusements.

"You see, the Uncertainty Principle simply states that sub-atomic particles, like electrons for example, are very, very finicky about their privacy, their modesty. It's one of the Laws of the Universe that such particles shouldn't let us know both their position *and* their velocity at any given point in time. One or the other, that we can know, and they don't take offense. But if we know *both* at the *same time*, well, then, they've been violated, the Laws of the Universe have been violated. The Universe doesn't look very kindly upon sub-atomic particles that are such floozy hussies as to let us know both at the same time.

"Milk Walk was aware of all this. He was also aware of the impending befesterment of all metans. So he took action. It pained him greatly, but he took action. Better that a few should die, than that all metans should be befestered by scamgrams forever. He built two top-secret measuring devices, and hooked each one to a top-secret computer. All these devices were of a technology too advanced to be revealed till much, much later.

"What he did, is he had one computer measure the velocities of a bunch of electrons, while the other computer simultaneously measured their positions. Since neither computer knew what the other computer knew, neither the electrons nor the Universe took any offense, at that point. Then he put all these electrons into a tiny little jar, and stashed it in the condiments in the pantry aboard the German zeppelin Hindenburg. Then he waited till just exactly the right group of people, people destined to make Hitler win World War II, were aboard the Hindenburg. Milk Walk, you see, could analyze their vibes intuitively, without even so much as a V-Meter.

"So on the 6th of May, 1937, when the Hindenburg was moored in Lakehurst, New Jersey, Milk Walk knew that the time was right. He linked his two computers, and they shared data. Those electrons were in for an extremely rude surprise! Now, two computers knew, and could graphically display to any viewer, both the past simultaneous positions and velocities of these electrons! The Universe was outraged, to say the least! Most of the electrons were so embarrassed and ashamed that they committed suicide. They exploded into pure energy, in a matter-to-energy conversion. This ignited the hydrogen gas aboard the giant dirigible, and she and her passengers went down in flames.

"Milk Walk Hubba-Bubba took this terrible secret to his grave with him. He knew that the world wasn't yet ready for his awesome technologies. But late in life he fathered Ale Run, Blessed be His Name. Only recently have Omnological historians, mainly with the aid of Ale Run Himself, been able to reconstruct what Milk Walk did. So that's where we're at today.

"Now I must remind you, all that you hear in these classrooms must be kept strictly among just us, staff Omnologists and higher. The secrets of the Hindenburg Uncertainty Principle must especially be closely guarded, until such time as we've had a chance to develop it more fully, and to build more practical applications. Then and only then will the world know of our astounding, amazing exploits.

"What are we working on now? Well, I'll tell you this much for sure, we've not just been sitting around and contemplating the nature of the Universe! First off, we tried to repeat Milk Walk's little experiment. Just with a very, very few electrons, to be sure, so as to play it safe. No use in blowing up the lab, of course.

"Unfortunately, it didn't work. After that first little episode, way back in 1937, the Universe learned its lessons, and tightened up its procedures quite a bit. So now, when we try to repeat Milk Walk's experiment, the electrons actually *change* their attributes in reaction to the measurement process! By measuring them, we interfere in that which we're measuring.

"A very good analogy would be a simple one. You have a bowl of water, and you want to measure its temperature. But to do so, you've got to put a thermometer in it, and that thermometer will heat or cool the water, depending on whether it's hotter or colder than the water. Only if the thermometer's temperature already exactly matches the water, only then will it not *change* the water. And of course, to pre-heat or pre-cool the thermometer so as to achieve this ideal state of non-intervention, then you've got to know the water's temperature already, which makes the whole exercise pointless. More sophisticated methods of measuring the heat in that water, such as measuring the rate of evaporation or infrared heat emissions, also suffer, because heat is lost during those processes.

"Anyway, the Universe now preserves the privacy of all but its most slutty sub-atomic particles through this new and improved version of the Hindenburg Uncertainty Principle, which now basically says that the process of measuring something interferes with the parameter being measured. Since we're part of Nature, we can never measure or observe her unobtrusively enough to completely and accurately know everything about even a small, simple, isolated system. So we'll never again be able to sneak up on Nature and catch her off guard, in the exact same way as Milk Walk did.

"We Omnologists are very clever and resourceful, though. And stubborn, for that matter. We're not giving up yet! If we're firmly prevented from measuring both an electron's position *and* velocity at a given precise point in time, now, it seems to me, and to other brilliant Omnological particle metaphysicists, that there might be methods of *deriving* this data. And if Nature is so adamant about us not knowing both of these things, we might be able to develop powerful new technologies based on Nature's aversions here. When we poke and prod Nature, and threaten to wrest this information from her, there's no telling *what* concessions we might be able to obtain from her in return."

Raoul noticed Dr. Dorcus Moorphlegmgasm's startled but silent response. He briefly debated asking Dr. Ghuanobhraine about the ethical propriety of thus messing with Mother Nature. He contemplated his most recent scamgrams, though, both in thinking negative thoughts about Panderwood actors and fame-dragging, and in trying to question Dr. Ghuanobhraine's wisdom about the name of the Uncertainty Principle, Hindenburg versus Heiselburger. He decided it might be most wise to just sit back and observe, rather than arrogantly trying to correct his leaders.

No one else bothered to challenge Dr. Ghuanobhraine, so he went blithely on, not noticing how Dr. Moorphlegmgasm fidgeted. "What we can do," he declared, "is to measure just *one* of those two parameters, and to derive the others! We'll measure an electron's position a hundred times, say, over the span of a hundred picoseconds. While we're doing this, we'll use an atomic clock to very precisely track time, and the time of each measurement.

"Then we can use extremely sophisticated supercomputers, software, and the wisdom of Omnological mathematics, which says that velocity is change in position over time. We can then threaten the Universe with our computers, whose computations could thus allow us to know both the electron's position *and* velocity. The Universe will then be forced make concessions to us."

"Doctor Ghuanobhraine, I'm very disappointed in you," Doctor Moorphlegmgasm interjected disgustedly. "All good Omnologists know that it's not nice to mess with Mother Nature, that chaos is badness. You're pushing the limits of appropriateness. In front of the children yet, too! You'd better watch out, or I'll be forced to come over there and embarrass you in front of everyone. I'll have to crack you across your knuckles with my Ping Thing. Now straighten out!"

Vyizder looked pained, disliking the spectacle of Omnology leaders arguing. Raoul watched anxiously, worrying about the badness of chaos, but also wondering what brilliant minds like Dr. Ghuanobhraine might be able to wrest from a secretive Mother Nature.

"Oh, don't be such a rigid-minded prude!" Iame shot back. "All good Omnologists also know that all feelings are valid, and that Omnological technology is goodness! I feel that we might derive a lot of goodness from some sort of new technology here. I'm not sure what it is, exactly, but we've *got* to investigate! Ale Run has commanded us to go forth and invent new technology. So we *must!* If we are ever to have society and the government recognize Omnology as a Science as well as Omnology as a Religion, then we *must* blaze on!" He glared at Dorcus.

Dorcus finally averted here eyes, but Raoul could hear her continue to mumble something about, well, so long as we all keep in mind that chaos is badness, and keep an eye open for chaos breaking out from an irate Mother Nature, well, then, she guesses we can go on. But don't say she never warned us. And rrffumm grggum rrgguffumm.

Iame ignored most of her mumbled protests, but continued in a more subdued manner, concentrating on not appearing to gloat in triumph. "Very well then, we'll proceed, keeping in mind that chaos is badness. Please follow me to the lab, and we'll see how well this works."

Everyone followed Iame to the lab. Barely inside the lab, they met an eagerly grinning assistant, who Iame introduced as "Meegore". The crowd strolled on over to a large metallic machine with lots of hoses, gauges, switches, and LEDs. One single chair allowed an operator to sit in front of it, close to the focal point of all the controls and gauges. The focal point itself was a vaguely microscope-like binocular set of eyepieces.

Iame stood between this powerfully lurking machine and his audience, declaring, "What you see here, ladies and gentlemen, may very well be more important to the future of humanity than fire, the wheel, and Cheese Dwonkies™ combined. With it, we will obey the commandments of Ale Run, and blaze on for the glory of Omnology as a Science! Now bear with me while I set up our grand experiment."

Everyone watched anxiously as Iame flipped a large switch. A deep hum filled the air and shook the floor, transmitting through bodies and rattling rib cages. Rows upon rows of LEDs flickered hypnotically. Iame threw more switches, and more noises roared to life. He peered into the eyepieces. A large monitor started glowing harshly above his work station.

He turned to the class, shouting above the din, saying, "We're about to begin. You'll be able to get a fair idea of what's going on by watching this monitor here. I'll explain what we see later. Let's begin!"

Iame and Meegore started throwing yet more switches, and even more sounds assaulted everyone's ears. The building seemed to shake. Iame grabbed a set of earphones and peered excitedly into the Omnoscope. Green fuzzballs dashed about madly on the screen, tracing hectic, seemingly random paths across the blue background. Iame shouted incoherent commands to Meegore, and both of them burst into a frantic blur of incomprehensible interactions with the machine.

At the climax of all this excitement, Raoul noticed some little red dots zipping back and forth between the green balls on the screen. None of this made much if any sense to him. I've got a long, long way to go, till I can be a great particle metaphysicist like Dr. Ghuanobhraine, Raoul managed to think, despite all the tensions that drenched his body with stress hormones.

Iame appeared momentarily baffled, exchanging some anxious shouts with Meegore. But then he gave the class a "thumbs up" sign, and he and Meegore began flipping switches again. The noises subsided. Finally, Iame threw the main switch, and sweet silence pervaded the lab once again.

"We've got good readings," Dr. Iame Ghuanobhraine announced triumphantly to the class. "But I'm very puzzled by the appearance of some strange phenomena I've never seen before. You might have noticed them as little red dots on the screen. I'm not sure what they are. They might even be what we call 'artifacts', or things that aren't really there, that are just the results of flaws in our instrumentation. We'll have to investigate some more.

"But meantime, the good news is that we've got good data! We've precisely measured and timed one hundred sequential positions of a population of several dozen electrons. Some no doubt escaped from our field of view during the observation period, but many remained within the field long enough for us to get a statistically valid set of measurements. Now all we have to do is to use this raw data to perform some calculations, and we can violate the Laws of the Universe, just like Milk Walk Hubba-Bubba did back in 1937."

Dr. Dorcus Moorphlegmgasm stood up tall and indignantly, preparing to protest, but Iame beat her to the punch. Before she could say a word, he announced, "Of course, first things first. Before we unilaterally go off and violate the Laws of the Universe by knowing both the positions and the velocities of these electrons, we'll negotiate in good faith with the Universe. If the Universe makes a good offer, we'll accept it.

"And don't worry; even if the Universe refuses to negotiate, and we have to go through with the calculations, there's no real danger. We're only dealing with dozens of electrons at the worst. Even if they all commit suicide and turn into pure energy, it won't compare to the Hindenburg incident. That incident involved hundreds of millions of electrons, and they were set off in a large dirigible full of combustible hydrogen gas. We'll contain our measured electrons in a large pool of water just to be safe. And, of course, we'll be monitoring these electrons, to see if and when they turn into pure energy." Iame motioned to Meegore, who began fussing at the Omnoscope to take care of this detail.

"Let's get on with it," Iame barked out the command. "Meegore. While you're taking care of those electrons, why don't you take a few seconds out to page another assistant. We need some help here." Meegore nodded in assent.

Iame had some time to kill while Meegore paged another assistant, extracted the measured electrons, and carried them off. So Iame used this time to explain to the class exactly how brilliant Omnological technology had allowed them to design the Omnoscope to hopefully communicate with the Universe. They were about to witness a great historical event in the development of Omnology as a Science, he announced.

Shortly, Iame and his new assistant, Heegore, flipped switches once again. This time, only a small portion of the Omnoscope was turned on, and very little noise was created.

"This is Doctor Iame Ghuanobhraine on behalf of Omnology as a Science, The Church of Omnology, and Our Dear Leader, The One Who Fleeces Our Scamgrams Away, Ale Run Hubba-Bubba," Iame spoke into the microphone. "Universe, come in. Universe, come in. Over." There was a long pause.

"Universe, I say again, this is Doctor..." Iame repeated the same greeting, adding, "Universe, we have the data. We have data on precise positions of several dozen of your electrons, and we can perform computations to derive their velocities also. Now unless you wish to watch us violate your Laws with impunity, unless you wish to relinquish powers that you've always guarded jealously, then we suggest you enter into negotiations with us. We'll be reasonable. Universe, come in." Again, the seconds and minutes fled in silence.

Dorcus could contain her anger no longer. "Doctor, I'd remind you that messing with Mother Nature is badness, and that chaos is badness. This is quite arrogant of us, to go off and act so pushy like this," she snarled. "You never know what the Universe might do to strike back."

"Don't be such a fuss-budget," Iame chided. "The Universe will come around eventually. It *must!* Else we will overturn Mother Nature's Laws, and use them for the benefit of Omnology as a Science. And for the descamgramification of all metans, I might add. Either way, we win. Be patient, wait and see. You'll see that Omnological technology is goodness. I *promise!*

"Brilliant minds always encounter violent opposition from mediocre minds. I'm just the latest in a long, long line of brilliant scientists who everyone said was a kook, but who was then later proven to be correct. Just you wait and see!"

Dorcus mumbled and grumbled once more. Iame ignored her, speaking into the microphone again. "Universe, this is your last chance. Start good-faith negotiations *now,* or we'll have no choice but to start usurping your Laws. Universe, come in." Again, there was only silence.

Meegore came back. Iame glanced at him quizzically. Meegore nodded affirmatively. "Very well," Iame signaled to his assistants. "Set up the computations." Iame, Heegore, and Meegore and started throwing switches. Then they set up Iame's computer terminal.

After they finished with this brief task, Iame picked up the microphone one last time. "Universe, this is your *last chance*. I have the 'commence computations' icon on screen *now*, and all I have to do is click on it. Come in NOW!" Still, the Universe stubbornly refused to reply.

"Very well," Iame grumped. "We have no choice. We will now step off into the great unknown, taking off from where Milk Walk Hubba-Bubba left us long ago. This will be one small mouse click for me, and a giant fleecing for all metans! To the glory of Ale Run Hubba-Bubba and all Omnologists everywhere!"

He moved his hand dramatically towards the mouse. Dorcus rushed towards him, deploying her Ping Thing in one deft, practiced swoop. "PING! PING! PING!" The lab resonated with the blood-curdling sounds of PING!s dispatched in righteous anger. "There! Take *that*, you lousy bunch of scamgrams!" Dorcus screeched. "Iame, **wake up!!!** You're severely befestered by humongous clusters of scamgrams!!! Scamgrams of unnatural, anti-Nature arrogance! Wake up *now*, before it's *too late!!!*"

Iame wasn't about to take all this sitting down. He shot up, reeled backwards, and hefted his own Ping Thing. "PING!-PING!-PING!-PING!-PING!," the Ping Things erupted in angry volleys. All the students hit the deck as Iame and Dorcus doused each other in barrages of PING!s.

"You self-righteous wench, *YOU'RE* the befestered one!" Iame shouted. "I've gotten *Ale Run Himself* to bless this whole thing!!! Now **get a grip!!!**"

Vyizder looked white as a ghost. But when he heard about whose side Ale Run Himself was on, he sprang into action. He whipped out his own Ping Thing, and he and Iame together, with twice the PING!-power of Dorcus alone, were able to subdue her. They summoned the guards, who in turn hauled her away for an intensive descamgramification.

Shortly, everyone settled back down, so that the ceremony could begin once again. Dr. Iame Ghuanobhraine was even so magnanimous as to allow the Universe yet one more chance to enter good-faith negotiations, now that more time had passed. Once more, there was no reply.

"Very well then, have it your way," Iame asserted petulantly. Then he clicked his mouse on the icon. Computations commenced.

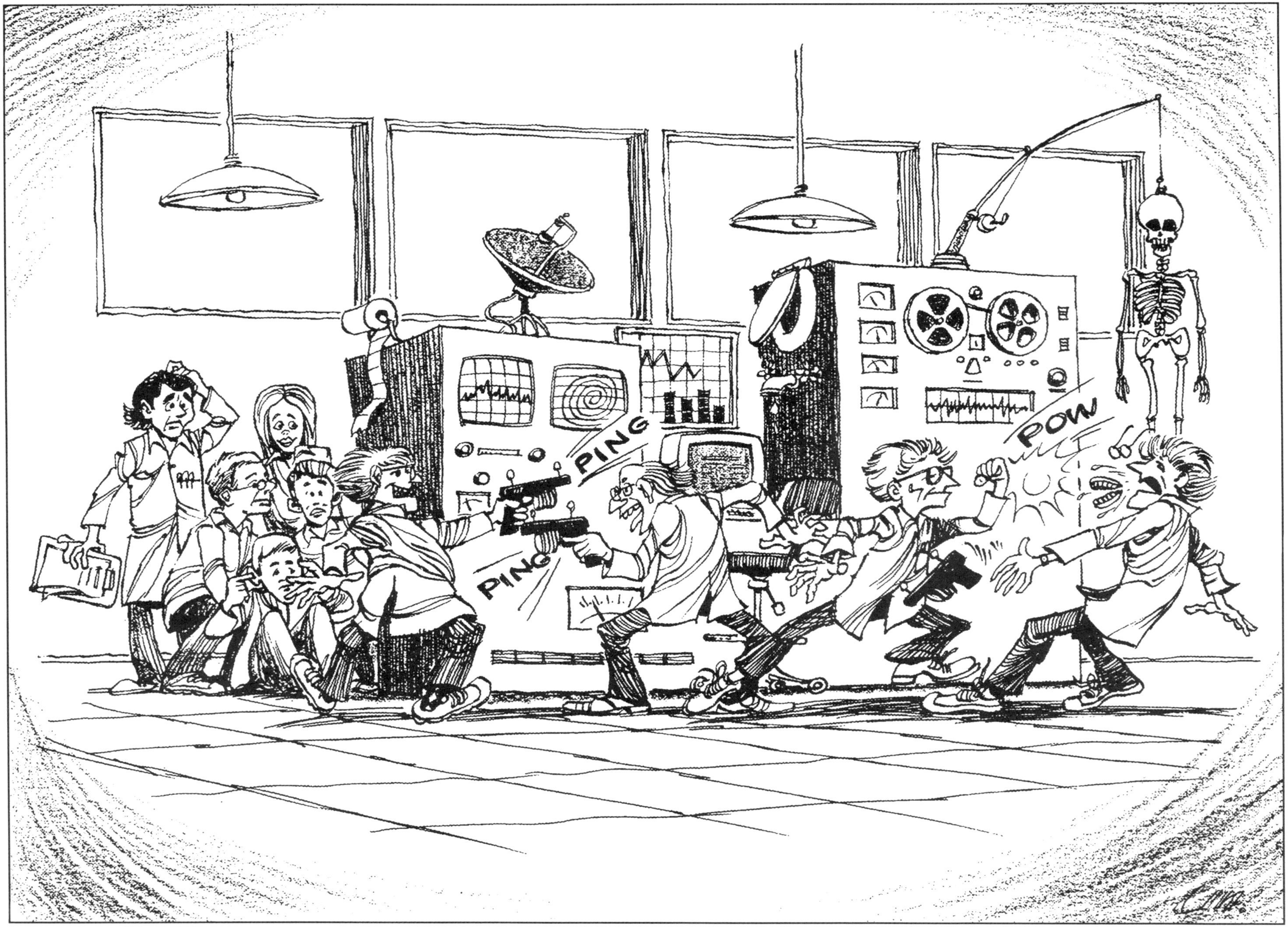
PING
PING
PING
POW

Chapter 13

Omnology Fleeces Panderwood

"My looks? Now, to remind myself I can look good, I keep many flattering pictures of myself around the house."
Heather Locklear, American actress.

"I don't believe in truth. I believe in style."
Hugh Grant, British actor.

Francestuous set out on her great adventure to study Omnology as a Religion. She and her fellow pupils rode a blue bus all the way from Madness County to Chicago, courtesy of The Church of Omnology. In the back of that blue bus, Francestuous met her One and True Love (besides Omnology), an uncertain but determined and earnest young man named Newt Rather.

When they met, Newt and Francestuous just started lightheartedly chatting about the weather, the scenery, their bus ride, Omnology, and their career ambitions. Francestuous told him all about how she wanted to be a famous actress in Panderwood, so that she could create Great Art, which is to say, Deeply Moving Movies and TV Shows. Newt told her all about how he wanted to be either a Congressperson or a news reporter, he wasn't sure which, and how he sure was having a tough time deciding.

But then they started to exchange their deepest longings and most profound confessional thoughts. As they talked, Francestuous couldn't help but notice his breath. It smelled sweetly *quiet*, in that it didn't smell of tooothpaste and the death screams of millions of innocent bacteria. So they fell Deeply, Truly In Love. This, despite how Francestuous had so recently and so tragically become a Victim of Love! "You must really, really be a Deeply Caring Metan," Newt exclaimed to Francestuous, "So selfless! So willing to risk, in order to Love, and to live life to its fullest!"

"Oh, yes," she sighed. "That's me. Just a fool for Love. Now, of course, I can only like fall Deeply In Love with sincere, cuddly and studly, Sensitive men like you. And this will be the last time I'll ever need to Fall In Love. 'Cause it's you and me, babe. Just you and me, forever and ever. Right, Snuggle Bunny, Dextrose Dimples?"

"Right on, Galactose Gums," he replied. "Just you and me. Forever." They embraced passionately in that last row of seats back there in the rear of that blue bus, chartered by The Church of Omnology and headed for Chicago.

Finally, Francestuous pulled back from Newt, saying, "You know, I, like, sometimes I, um, worry that I might be getting into like a co-dependent relationship with you, you know what I mean?"

"Now, don't get all paranoid about *that*, Saccharin Snuggles," he said. "We're In Love, but you're still in denial. Face it, we're In Love. So we just have to accept that. Denial is a scamgram. All feelings are valid, so don't deny our Love. Denying one's feelings of Love is the biggest scamgram of all." He pulled her closer to him, snuggling her shoulder.

She relented, pulling him closer. "You're right," she said. "Denial is a scamgram. And you're so deep and thoughtful and compassionate, Newt, Baby! You empower me! I think we need closure. Right back here we have a little lavatory, see? Now it might not be very big or very comfortable, but we, like, you know, you and I, we could slip in there, and get our closure. Come on!" She tugged on his arm. But just then, a large fellow Omnologist waddled back towards the lavatory, and claimed it for quite some time. Then by the time he left, a line formed, so Newt and Francestuous never did get their closure in the back of the blue bus.

So they settled for just hugging and kissing and discussing Love, life, and theology. Francestuous never did manage to persuade Newt that a sense of sexual privacy equated shameful shame over that which Ale Run had descamgramified, which was the glorious metan body. They resolved to put the question to an Omnological expert at their next opportunity: was public love-making, or was it not, a scamgram? And if it depended on the situation, then when was it a scamgram, and when wasn't it? Would it be a scamgram if everyone present was an Omnologist? Aren't Omnologists supposed to accept all feelings?

Their theological debates were cut short when the blue bus arrived at the airport, where similar busses from all across the Midwest were congregating and disgorging their newly-recruited Omnologist passengers. Francestuous and Newt gathered up their meager luggage. They stuck together as the crowds from all the busses were herded together.

Soon, they found themselves in the middle of a large crowd in what appeared to be a convention hall, right there on the outskirts of the airport. Presently, a man scaled a podium. He appealed to the crowd to calm down, and to listen.

"Hi there, all you dedicated new Omnologists! In the Name of Ale Run, I greet and congratulate you! For it's you, it's us, it's all of us together who will descamgramify the world! Yes, the whole world! That is what Ale Run has commanded that we should do, so that is what we are doing.

"I'm sorry, I should introduce myself first. I'm Orziz Assiz, a Doctor of Omnology as a Religion, and your Spirit Guide for now. I'll be giving..."

Francestuous nudged Newt, whispering, "That's him! He's the advanced metan who introduced..."

Other Omnologists were glaring at them, so Newt replied in a whisper, "Yeah, he taught the night I signed up, too. Now maybe we'd better listen."

"...will shortly be getting on charter flight 377 to Los Diablos. And those of you who will be studying media and government will be..." Francestuous stared longingly into Newt's eyes, silently appealing one more time that he should come with her out to Los Diablos. He pouted and hung his head. But he also shook his head "no".

"But first," Orziz continued, "Ale Run Himself has asked me to talk to you real briefly, to get you all motivated for what lies ahead. Yes, the job has already begun. But in another sense, here today is when we start. And we will not finish till the job is done! We, together, will fleece all the scamgrams in the whole world!" The crowd thundered applause.

"Today some of you will be going out to Los Diablos, where we have our Intergalactic Headquarters. Also very importantly, that's where Panderwood is. Those of you who are headed out that way have some very, very important missions that you must carry out. For the descamgramification of everyone, and for the Glory of Our Lord Ale Run and The Church of Omnology, may all your vibes come clear!

"Then there are those of you who are traveling to our nation's capital, where we Omnologists are also establishing a great institution. That's the Media and Government Institute for the Fleecing of All Metans, for anyone here who is befestered by the scamgrams of a poor memory. And as we speak, our fellow Omnologists are also gathering in Akron, Ohio, at the Scientific Institute for the Advancement of Omnology. Together, we will do great things!

"Now as Ale Run has instructed me, I wish to briefly sketch the 'big picture' here for you. We won't descamgramify the world tomorrow. We must start with America. We will first turn the minds of Americans away from their shallow, trivial pursuits, so that they can turn them towards the Greater Truths that Omnology has to offer.

"How will we do that? How do we start? Of course, we continue to spread the Good Word, as we've done already. Don't forget to tell all your friends about Omnology. But for the bigger picture, how do we descamgramify America, for starters? We must look at things systematically. We must look at where America is now, so that we can move her towards where she needs to go. Towards being fleeced of all her scamgrams.

"America's scamgrams are mostly related to worshipping the wrong things. Instead of worshipping Ale Run and a blissful state of total descamgramification, they worship many false gods. We must turn their eyes away from their false gods, and turn them to Ale Run!

"In America today, we have those who worship Panderwood. That's not bad; it just needs improved on. We must move in on Panderwood, and convert all the actors and actresses, producers and screenwriters, directors and agents. We'll do this by serving as a beacon unto all those lost souls in Panderwood. You who go to Panderwood, you must serve as our beacons, our bright, shining lights of Omnological enlightenment! Get out there, get into good jobs as actors, actresses, screenwriters, and so on, and show them The Way. Panderwood will soon be ours!

"It won't be so hard to do, so have faith. Don't let the scamgrams of despair get you down. Those in Panderwood who know that perception is reality and that all feelings are valid, they'll help us. And there are many, many folks out there in Panderwood already who agree with us! They are Omnologists already; they just don't know it yet! Go with Ale Run! Go with Ale Run in your heart, and shine your light to those who don't yet know the Lord Ale Run. If you will let your lights shine, Panderwood will soon be ours. And when Panderwood is ours, all those who already worship Panderwood will be worshipping Ale Run instead. The world will be fleeced of many scamgrams!

"And then there are those who worship power and access. That's not bad, either, because power and access are valid desires, like any other desire. Once again, it just needs improved on. We should desire access to the powers of Omnology, that's all. So we're sending many of you to Washington, D.C., which is the focal point of much access and power.

"You must carry our bright beacons to Washington, and let them shine there, just as they will shine in Panderwood. With the brilliant lights of Omnology, we will find many legal and moral rights for all Omnologists. We must show the media and government that we Omnologists have the religious freedoms and rights to do whatever Ale Run commands us to do. If we will seek the Ale Run within ourselves, then we will find that Ale Run energizes us to gain access and power in Washington.

"We'll place a few Omnologists in the media and in government, for starters. These Omnologists will promise access and power to others, if only they'll see the Wisdom of Ale Run. Thus, we'll attract those people who desire more access and power. With power and access, and with Ale Run's amazing technology, we'll fleece many scamgrams!

"Then there are those that worship reason and science. This is entirely good, because Omnology is a science. We are more reasonable and rational than anyone else on this whole planet, and Ale Run Hubba-Bubba is most rational of all! So we have no problem with that. The brilliant torch of Omnology as a science will be carried by the Scientific Institute for the Advancement of Omnology. Those of us who are blazing that path aren't here today, so I'll not say too much there. Just this: Don't worry, we'll advance on many fronts! Many surprises are coming our way!

"Then there are those who worship the false gods of God. These are our hardest nuts to crack. Strong, irrational ideology is the ultimate scamgram, so we must call upon the powers of Ale Run. Fortunately, we have a major factor working with us: Many who claim to worship God are really worshipping social and political propriety. They worship whoever their friends, families, and bosses are worshipping, and they worship them in the same manner that these 'powers that be' worship. So when they see science, Panderwood, the media, and politicians all lining up to pay tribute to the powers of Ale Run, they'll come around.

"This will leave only a small fraction of the nuts. These nuts we won't bother to crack. They're not worth the trouble. We'll just make sure that they don't befester the rest of us with their scamgrams! We'll do our very best to descamgramify them, then we'll leave them alone, other than to make sure that they keep their scamgrams to themselves. Making them keep their scamgrams to themselves includes making sure they don't befester any children.

"Protecting the Children is the ultimate anti-scamgram, so we'll Protect the Children, rest assured of that! In the End Times, when the Anti-Hubba-Bubba will be desperately clutching at any last straws that he or she can grab, as the rest of the world turns to Ale Run at last, the Anti-Hubba-Bubba and his or her followers will want to *befester their own children* with scamgrams. Yes, it's true! Horrible as it may sound, some people will want to continue to befester their children, even after Ale Run's Wisdom will start to become obvious to one and all.

"At that point, we will Protect the Children, as Ale Run and common decency requires. Befestered people will not be allowed to pass their scamgrams on to The Children. And within a generation, then, a state of perfection, free of all scamgrams great and small, will be ushered in. The Anti-Hubba-Bubba will be defeated, and Ale Run will rule!" The crowd cheered as one. Scamgrams great and small fled in abject terror.

"People, the time has come! Time for you to get on those planes, and go achieve the Will of Ale Run Hubba-Bubba! Go, now, my people, go! Go, and may Ale Run be with you!" The crowd milled about, heading for the doors. Dang, thought Francestuous, no question and answer session. I didn't get to ask him if public love-making was a scamgram! Oops, there's Newt about to break away without a decent good-bye!

"Wait," she said, snatching Newt's sleeve. "We didn't get our closure yet! Let's sneak over there to the restrooms, and..."

"So sorry, Lactose Lips," he replied. "You are truly the Love of my Life, but no can do. Not now. None of those restrooms are unisex. I'm pretty sure going into the opposite sex's restroom would be a scamgram. Now I'll be sure to call you every day, and when we're all done with our training, we'll get together for the rest of our lives. Then we'll strive for descamgramification together, for ever and ever, and..."

"Oh, Newt! My one and only Polysaccharide Patootie! You're so sweet!" she cried, embracing him passionately. They smooched for an eternity of several minutes, but then they had to rush off to their respective planes. It was hard to do, but for the future of Omnology and the descamgramification of all metans, they did it.

Through an emotional haze of desperate longing for her departing Love, she found her way to the rear of her plane to Los Diablos. Being late onto that crowded plane, she found an empty seat next to a handsome man with a square jaw. "Hi," she said. "I'm Francestuous Johnsdame, and I'm Deeply In Love with a man. A man with a square jaw and a heart of gold. A man who's not you, even if your jaw is like the squarest I've ever seen. So just 'cause I'm sitting next to you, doesn't mean I'm trying to hustle you off into the nearest lavatory for a madly passionate session of lovemaking. Certainly not lust yet, at jeast. I'm really a very square, conservative kind of a gal, you see. You can ogle me, if you must—I could certainly understand that—but please don't touch. So tell me like a little bit about yourself."

"Hi. I'm Pudmu..." Pudmuwhoever was rudely interrupted by his cellular telephone. "Excuse me," he said. He listened to his phone.

"No," he said. "Tell my broker not to do a *danged thing* with my stock! Tell him that while he was out playing golf, and I couldn't reach him, I sold all three million assorted shares. Went straight to a friend of mine, a Wall Street trader. I gave it all to The Church of Omnology, tell him! Tell him to get lost. No, scratch that. Tell him to Come to the Light, and turn his life over to Ale Run. Tell him that's what I've done, and I'm ecstatically happy now. Tell him he could be, too, if he'd just listen to The Wisdom of Ale Run. Now, I've got to..." Pudmuwhoever paused.

"Tell all those mid-level managers they'll have to figure it all out for themselves now. Fight it out among themselves, more likely, now that the Big Man is gone. Get it through their thick heads that I've quit! Quit, quit, quit, you hear me?! And I'm *not* coming back! I've had it up to here with their constant backbiting!" Then he paused again.

"Tell those stupid engineers that I'm quitting, too, and that they'd better start figuring out how to do their jobs without me telling them how! Now, if they'll just look at the automatic gain control in the pulse width modulator, they'll find a resistor installed with reversed polarity at reference designator R66, I'll bet! And tell those lower-level doofus managers to hire smarter engineers!" Pause.

"The surgical team will have to do without me," he said, his tones much softer. "Now I know Mrs. Loffinger needs that heart transplant, and I'd sure like to be there to help, but I've got even bigger things to do. Things like the descamgramification of all metans, things like that. So tell the team to find someone else. Now Doctor Dordlewompus isn't quite up to my standards, sure, I'll grant you that. But who is?! Time for the younger talent to learn the ropes. I've shown them how often enough. Tell them Doctor Dordlewompus will have to take over for me." Pause.

"No, I don't care *how* important the Senator and the Ambassador say this is, I *can't*. Can't, can't, *can't!* I'm busy now, off to Panderwood to start my new life. If there's an international incident, it can't be helped. Tell them I'm off to end all international incidents. Intergalactic incidents, too, for that matter. I'm off to fleece all metans, to make everything perfect forever, and I can't be bothered with the small stuff." Pause. "Oh, well, OK, then, put him through.

"Well, yes, Senator, *of course* I understand that! What sort of nincompoop... You tried? But he's not... *What?!* No, wait, that can't be right! Oh, man, I guess the State Department can't even afford good translators these days! Here, put him on the line... **Yes**, I mean *him!*... Why, yes, *of course* I speak fluent Mandarin Chinese! Garble blooger bleeblewingledwongle, snorzlekwondoose, bwerblelwangus." Francestuous didn't understand a word, but she was quite impressed.

"Oh, that's nothing," he said. "Stop a war, save humanity, whatever. All in a day's work for me. Now I've got to go. Got to go off and save the universe from scamgrams, that's what I've got to do. Now put me back on the line to my secretary. Former secretary, I should say. I'm quitting, you know.... Oh, Senator, don't sweat it! You're quite welcome! Call any time, with those kinds of issues. Yes, good bye, Senator.

"Hello? Yes, I'm back... No, tell them I quit that, too. No, I'm really, really and truly sorry, but tell them I can't be volunteering at the soup kitchen, the Boy Scouts, the shelter, or Habitat for Hamsters. *None* of them. Not now, any more! Yes, sure, tell 'em I'll miss 'em all, God bless, I mean, Ale Run bless them all, but I've got to go. I'm quitting *everything* to go off and save *everybody,* OK? Just tell *everybody* that, and you won't go wrong! Other than Senators and international incidents, no more calls, OK? Yes, thank *you*. Good-bye."

Pumuwhoever wiped his hair off his forehead, then wiped his hands off on his pants and sighed. Then he reached his hand out to Francestuous, who took it daintily. "Hi," he murmured. "I'm Doctor Pudmuddle B. Fuddle, and I'm pleased to meet you, Francestuous. My friends just call me Pud. Now what can I do for you?"

"Well, Doctor Pud," she granted, not releasing has hand, "You're sure quite like the busy kind of a dude, it seems. First off, what you can do for me is like what you can do for yourself, for us all, kind of. You can like take a load off! You know, like, *really*, now that you're an Omnologist, you don't have to take it all upon yourself any more! You can lay all your burdens on Our Lord, The One True Fleecer of All Scamgrams, Ale Run Hubba-Bubba. Isn't that *great*?! Isn't that simply yet all-encompassingly *profound*?! Stop and *think* about that! I'll bet it hasn't really quite thoroughly sunk in yet, has it?"

Pud just sat there in silence. He stopped shaking her hand, and just held it. His harried, forced smile melted into neutral serenity. "There," she continued, "Now, we all appreciate all you've done for everyone, I'm quite sure. But I'll bet you really like need to think about yourself and your *own* needs, now and then. So why don't you like take it easy, stop worrying about everyone else, and just like tell me about yourself for a while?"

"You're right," he admitted after a while, "I need to take a load off. Accept the joy of just turning everything over to Ale Run. Thank you! Thank you for reminding me that when we let Ale Run into our hearts, we set our worries free. Thank you *so much!*"

"Oh, you're *so welcome!*" she exclaimed. "It's always a joy to share Ale Run! Now please, go ahead, tell me all about yourself."

Pud took her hand and placed it back on her lap, patting it gently as an afterthought. Then he leaned back into his chair, sighed, and began talking in subdued tones. "You're too kind. But I suppose you're right. It all began when I was born. As far as I can recall, at least, that is. My parents were, well, one, he was a nuclear physicist, governor of Nebraska, and an astronaut, and she was a model, an actress, a psychiatrist, and a television evangelist. And they wanted me to measure up! So they had me toilet trained and speaking seven languages at one and a half, and toilet training my younger brother at two and a half. Give or take a month, to a 3-sigma degree of accuracy, that is.

"So I've always been an over-achieving kind of a guy, I'd say. Now I'm a heart surgeon, an electrical engineer, a CEO, an amateur but proficient intergalactic fix-it kind of State Department consultant-type dude extraordinaire, a speculator/entrepreneur, and a big-time charitable volunteer. Or at least, I *was*, till very recently. And I'm *still* not sure of whether or not my mother and father approve of me! Then I had one of those life-changing experiences, you know.

"I'm sorry, I left out a minor detail. It might help you to make sense of what happened recently. In between all those other things I'd been doing, I also found time to become a husband and a father. But then we just kind of grew apart. I was growing, but they weren't. Her especially. She kind of even anti-grew, if you know what I mean. She started becoming attracted to cheap beer and cigarettes, trailer homes, beans, peanut butter, and all sorts of gauche things of those sorts. So I left. I had to, if I was going to keep on growing and finding myself.

"So then one day, I was out volunteering with Habitat for Hamsters, building new cages for the companion animals of the poor, out in the middle of a large trailer park. People from the office were calling me and paging me and faxing me right and left, and the media was photographing me and interviewing me, too. Despite all that, I was still finding some time now and then to actually put some nails into these cages we were building.

"But then this lady shows up with her kids and their hamster in its broken-down old cage, asking us to build a new one, and I look at them real close, and I realize with a start, sure enough, it's *them!* My ex-wife and kids! Here I am, working real hard, helping out the low and downtrodden, trying to pull them up to higher standards and better tastes, and *my very own family* has joined them! Betty, I think her name was. Betty, her hamster, Huey, and the kids, um, Tracy and Bracy, I think. And they've sunk real low and tasteless, eating peanut butter and beans, drinking cheap beer, and living in trailer parks!

"So I'm like, shaken, as they'd say. It's like life or fate or something is trying to tell me something, I recall thinking at the time. But I couldn't figure it out. So I took some time out of my busy schedule and went to the bar with one of my business partners. We drank and talked for a while. He tried to tell me it's time for me to get a new trophy wife, that's what my problem is, see? But that just didn't sound right. I didn't have *time* for that sort of thing.

"I went to my shrink. He said it's all 'cause I'm just not quite self-actualized yet, that I might need to make more time for my hobbies and such. He asked me if I had any, and I pondered a while, thinking, yes, there's something in the back of my brain, something new and totally different that I'd like to try, but I just couldn't figure it out.

"So then my chauffeur is driving me by the local Soulorama one day, and I just happen to look over, and what do I see? A big sign, it says, *'Repent, repent, the end is near! The Anti-Hubba-Bubba comes, but have no fear, fleecing kicks scamgrams in the rear!'*. I looked at it, and this like groovy wave of vibes rushes over me, chills run down my spine, I start to feel better, and I'm like magnetically attracted to this one little room in that Soulorama. We stop, I go in to check it out, and lo and behold, by the Technological Grace of Ale Run, my scamgrams are fleeced away! Just like that!

"So that was the day my whole life changed. My only regret was that I couldn't get my chauffeur to See The Light, too. Oh, well. In due time. All in due time.

"So there's like this Big Change in my life. I even stopped talking like an executive and developed a sense of humor! And to this day, I really, really believe it had something to do with that mysterious coincidence, meeting Betty and Hamster Huey and Tracy and Bracy by surprise out there in that trailer park. I *still* don't think I quite thoroughly understand that. So I went back to visit them, thinking maybe I'm supposed to bring them the Good News about Ale Run, so that they can be set free of their scamgrams. Maybe *that's* what it's all about, maybe *that's* why Ale Run came to me, starting out there in that darkest heart of gaucheness, that low-brow trailer park.

"But they wouldn't hear what I had to say. The Spirit of Ale Run just couldn't penetrate their hard hearts. There for a little while, from the brief sparkle in his eyes, I thought Hamster Huey, at least, could see the Wisdom of Ale Run. But in the end, they all spurned His Wisdom. With tears in my eyes, I shook their dust off of my feet and left. I'm still wondering just exactly what it is that still bothers me about the whole thing, meeting them out there in the trailer park like that.

"So I've turned my life over to Ale Run, and to trying to become a better Omnologist. To living a life fleeced of all scamgrams. And then I heard about this opportunity to go out and spread the Good News to Panderwood, and I thought, like, **acting!!!** Yes, by Ale Run, **acting**! That's been my secret desire all along! Secret from *me*, even! And now it's clear to me! I've gone clear! Now that I'm fleeced of scamgrams, I can see that part of the Wisdom of Ale Run, for me, is that I need to become an *actor!*

"So here I am, off to Panderwood! Off to the grand descamgramification of Panderwood, and, through them, America! And through American, then, the descamgramification of all metans! What could be more grand, more exciting?!

"But enough about me. How about *you*, my dear?!"

"Oh, nothing nearly so grand," Francestuous admitted. "I'm just a former farm housewife from Madness County who found Ale Run. You know," she said, patting his knee, "I'm like really, really glad you let Ale Run into your heart. I'm *sure* you'll go on to do many great things! And I'm sure glad I met you. But Pud, I'm just *so happy* to hear that you want to go into *acting!* Because *I* do, too, you see?! We'll be going into acting *together!*" She clasped her hands, squealing in ecstasy.

Pud grinned with wild abandon. They held each others' hands, sharing their innermost hopes, desires, and secrets. Then they fell In Love. The trip to Los Diablos was heavenly! They even found time for a very special, very Meaningful trip to the aircraft's lavatory.

Their first week in Panderwood was tough. No one was interested in their acting services, and no one wanted to let Pud and Francestuous tell them how to let Ale Run into their hearts. But they had each other, so they held each other tight. And, of course, they had Ale Run and The Church of Omnology. Every night, they'd go back to the Intergalactic Headquarters of The Church of Omnology for services, a pep talk, a warm meal and a shower, and a bed.

By the end of that first week, though, neither Pud nor Francestuous had lined up an acting job, nor even brought any new recruits to The Church, so their Spirit Guides were a little frustrated with them. They started to hear a few hints now and then. Do something for The Church, Ale Run Hubba-Bubba, and the descamgramification of all metans, or *we'll* find something for you to do. Something like selling flowers, or donating pamphlets at the airport, that was the general drift. So they felt a very keen desire to get into acting.

On Monday of the following week, Francestuous and Pud got wind of some special acting opportunities. This jolted her memory, causing her to remember her unanswered special theological question. Was public love-making, or was it not, a scamgram? That night, she asked. Omnologists who ask, receive, she'd been told. And she did. She got her answer. "It depends," they said. "It depends on whether or not it's all done for The Greater Glory of Ale Run."

So she and Pud started acting the very next day. They acted, acted, and acted, they did. They acted to their heart's content. They acted for The Greater Glory of Ale Run. They showed everyone that Omnologists are free, free of scamgrams like having to deny one's feelings. Especially one's feelings of Love. Wasn't denying one's feelings of Love the ultimate scamgram? Many people loved Pud and Francestuous, and even far more people watched. Many of them came to see The Wisdom of Ale Run. Panderwood and The Church of Omnology prospered together.

Chapter 14

Omnological Science Blazes Onward

"We would be a lot safer if the Government would take its money out of science and put it into astrology and the reading of palms... Only in superstition is there hope. If you want to become a friend of civilization, then become an enemy of the truth and a fanatic for harmless balderdash."
Kurt Vonnegut Jr. (b. 1922)

Computations proceeded. The Universe had callously, carelessly ignored Doctor Iame Ghuanobhraine's offer to negotiate, so he'd had no choice but to click on that "commence computations" icon. The Omnoscope's computer was about to derive the velocities of those electrons who'd been tracked on screen. Simultaneous position and velocity information about these electrons would then become known, thereby violating the Laws of the Universe. Only a few seconds of computation time remained.

Iame glanced anxiously at the countdown timer. He turned to his assistants, Meegore and Heegore, saying, "Now, you're sure the recording instruments are all set up? If those electrons turn into pure energy, we'll measure those events, right?"

"Yes, Doctor Ghuanobhraine," Meegore assured him. "Sheegore is down there keeping an eye on the instruments. If anything goes wrong, she'll be right there to fix things up." The countdown continued. Then the time was right upon them. ...3, 2, 1, 0, the timer blinked. Then the screens filled with arrays of numbers. The Laws of the Universe had been broken! A cheer went up.

Iame silenced everyone, and put a call through to Sheegore. "Sheegore. Sheegore. Come in, Sheegore. We've got the numbers, but we show no event down there. Sheegore? Talk to us!"

Sheegore came right in. "Doctor Ghuanobhraine, no events here. Nothing at all! And the instruments are still doing fine!"

Iame stroked his chin silently, thoughtfully. Then he announced, "Well, here we are. By all appearances, we've violated the Laws of the Universe! Just look at those screens right there, and you see some very precise arrays of figures. Very precise measurements of simultaneous positions and velocities of electrons. This *can't* be, and yet it *is*! Unlike what happened with Milk Walk Hubba-Bubba's experiment so long ago, the electrons *did not* commit suicide and turn into pure energy! Yet our measuring instruments and our computations are *far* more sophisticated and accurate than his were!"

He just sat there silently, pondering. The room filled with a respectful, expectant silence. Then he announced, "However, there *were* those little red dots on the screen, remember? An entirely new phenomenon, I'd say! Maybe the Universe has now figured out a new way to protect Her Secrets. Maybe our numbers are wrong, due to those little red dots! Maybe these aren't just measurement artifacts! Maybe they're an *entirely new kind of particle!* My fellow metans, can you *imagine!* Just *imagine* the glories and the funds that would flow to the Scientific Institute for the Advancement of Omnology if we could show that we've discovered a new kind of particle!"

He calmed down, caught his breath, and stopped gesticulating wildly. Then he walked over to the chalkboard and began drawing circles, arrows, and diagrams. "Here, fellow metans! This is what we'll do. We'll set up the Omnoscope to make continuous series of measurements of these electron positions, while we simultaneously calculate velocities. If these little red dots we saw on screen indeed aren't merely measurement artifacts, but rather, some sort of immune cells from the Universe if you will, that the Universe sends to protect Her Secrets, then, well, we'll make the Universe cause them to manifest themselves continuously, for a short little while, right here in our lab. Right here in our Omnoscope. Long enough for us to measure them. Then we'll take measurements on those little red dots, figuring out just exactly what they are!"

Dr. Ghuanobhraine, Vyizder Zomenimor, Raoul, and the rest of the students of Omnology as a Science spent the rest of the day planning the modifications to the Omnoscope. The next two days, they and their assistants, Meegore, Heegore, and Sheegore, all worked diligently on making the modifications to the Omnoscope. All was prepared! The next day would be the Big Day, the day for the next onslaught on the Universe and Her Secrets. Raoul barely slept that night.

The next morning, they were all set to go. Dr. Ghuanobhraine was just about ready to hit the "commence measurements" icon when Dr. Dorcus Moorphlegmgasm walked in the door. Iame stopped, glancing wide-eyed at her. "What are *you* doing here, Dorcus? Have you been thoroughly fleeced of the anti-technology, anti-Omnology scamgrams that caused you to question our investigations?"

Dorcus looked him straight in the eye, saying, "Yes, Doctor Ghuanobhraine, I've been fleeced. I apologize for seeming to question the advancement of Omnology as a Science. That *is*, after all, what this Institute is all about. However, we must be *sensitive* as we go about accomplishing the tasks that Ale Run has given to us. Now if you don't mind, please tell me what you've been doing, and what your plans are this time."

Iame caught Dorcus up to date. When he was done, she declared, "So here you go again, messing with Mother Nature? Violating the Laws of the Universe again? And this time, you weren't even going to make another good-faith attempt to negotiate with the Universe first?! Don't you know that chaos is badness?! Why must you always immediately resort to rough-shod man-handling? All you male metans are the same! No finesse! All brute force! Now let me..."

"Dorcus, there you go on your anti-technology tirade again! Now, I thought you'd been fleeced of these scamgrams! Unless you have something positive to offer, then I'd suggest..."

"I *do* have something positive to offer," she snapped back. "Just this: hold your machine in check just long enough to make one more good-faith attempt to negotiate with the Universe. That's all I ask. It's not much. Maybe the Universe has some valid feelings about all this. Maybe She just wants somebody to talk to Her honestly, openly and with sensitivity, to see why She wants to hide Her Secrets. Maybe we shouldn't just barge on in there and strip Her naked, rip Her secrets away, and *rape* Her. Maybe the male way isn't always best."

Iame rolled his eyes, mumbling. Then, angered, he lashed back. "Well, just *what*, exactly, makes you think that the Universe is so danged deserving of sensitivity in the first place? I, for one, can think of quite a few reasons why She *shouldn't* get any special respect from us. *She* shows no sensitivity *at all*. Why should we then treat Her with more sensitivity than She shows us?

"For example, I went to school with an engineering student, and our school was quite sensitive to his learning disabilities. He had note-takers and translators and test-takers right and left, to make up for his reading, listening, mathematical, language, and thinking disabilities. My school, I am quite proud to say, was quite extremely, profoundly sensitive. They gave him the help and showed him the sensitivity he deserved.

"But then this engineer friend of mine, he went out on his job, he designed this bridge, and it fell down, smooshing all sorts of innocent metans. Well, OK, so they hadn't all been fleeced, but they were still innocent of any offenses against your precious Universe, at least. And what, I ask you, just exactly *what* did the Universe do to show sensitivity? Did she decrease the strength of the local gravity field? Did she decrease the mass or increase the strength of the structural elements of that bridge? Did she at least give warning to all the innocent metans?

"No, I tell you, *no!* The Universe didn't show *one tiny bit* of sensitivity or compassion! *Not a drop!* So I flat-out don't see why we owe any consideration at all, towards whether the Universe's feeling are more valid than our own, or not. She doesn't *deserve* our sensitivity. She hasn't *earned* it."

"Doctor Ghuanobhraine," Dorcus said gently. "I'm sorry that you feel that way, really I am. But I can tell you why we need to be far more sensitive than the Universe is. It's because insensitivity breeds insensitivity. Somebody has to break the endless cycle of insensitivity. Chaos is badness. We must be bigger than they are. Nothing big ever came from being small. So we must be *bigger* than the Universe! It's what Ale Run calls on us to be!

"I'm not asking for much, Doctor Ghuanobhraine. I'm not asking for much at all. Just one last attempt to negotiate with the Universe. Okay?" She did her very best to look sweet and pleasant, without going so far as to bake a fresh batch of cookies.

Iame relented. "Okay. Let's set it up." Meegore, Heegore, and Sheegore made the necessary arrangements. Iame hailed the Universe on all vibe channels. "This is Doctor Iame Ghuanobhraine with the Scientific Institute for the Advancement of Omnology. Universe, come in. Universe, come in." There was no answer. Iame tried once again. Still, there was no reply.

"There, see?" he taunted Dorcus. "No answer. The Universe is too insensitive to even bother to acknowledge that we're talking to Her. Now suppose I'd say to you, isn't this just typical of females, getting into an emotional snit? You'd blow your top! Yet you can say snide things about us and our male brute-force ways! *Who* is being insensitive, here, I ask?! *Who?!*"

Vyizder whipped out his Ping Thing, threatening to "Ping" them both down to a descamgramified state. The arguing stopped. Iame and Dorcus both agreed to hold their tongues.

Iame hit the icon at last, and the experiment began. Shortly, the screens filled yet again with images of electrons, represented as fuzzy green balls zipping hither and yon. And in their midst, hordes upon hordes of little red dots appeared! "All right!" Iame exclaimed. "Prepare the particle probe!" Meegore, Heegore, and Sheegore dashed about madly, almost as madly as the little red dots themselves.

"Particle probe in place?" Iame demanded.

"Particle probe in place," Meegore confirmed. "All systems nominal."

"Commence data acquisition," Iame commanded. His assistants threw some switches. More screens flared to life, displaying incomprehensible data. Iame paused, silently surveying the data. "Are all systems still stable? Can we maintain this state for a while?" His assistants confirmed that yes, systems seemed stable. He gazed at the readouts for a few seconds.

"All right," he announced to the eagerly waiting crowd of students and highly trained professional staff Omnologists, "Everything is going according to plan. As we particle metaphysicists like to say, they're just like totally rad, Dude. Not that I mean to dis you with our awesomely hip technical terms.

"Now it seems to me that the little red dots reflect a real phenomenon. They're not just artifacts. If you examine the data carefully, you'll find that they're moving in a pattern. Most of these movements are way too high-frequency for us to observe directly, visually. But it's like they're dancing. Just as bees dance in their hives, in order to convey information with their dances, so, too, do the dances of these little red dots carry complex information.

"This information is too complex for the Omnoscope's computer to decode it. This is extremely firm evidence that we're looking at a new particle, one never before known to metans!" The crowd cheered.

"At this point, we must inform Ale Run Himself," Iame declared solemnly. "He'll want to decide if we should announce our discovery to the whole world now, or if we should hold off until we can invent new technologies based on these principles, first. Who knows, we might be onto practical Omnological technologies every bit as important and useful as the Ping Thing! Vyizder, would you mind please passing this information off to Ale Run?"

Vyizder departed on this important mission, while everyone else stayed to watch the excitement. Data cables from the rear of the Omnoscope were re-routed to the lab's main supercomputer. Analysis of the red dots' motions commenced.

"I was right," Iame crowed. "There's *data* in them thar dances! The Universe is trying to communicate with us after all! Through the little red dots! Now we must let the computer devise a translation algorithm, and then we'll be set!" He pecked furiously at the keyboard. Shortly, the words "Compiling Translation Algorithm" appeared on the screen, along with a bar graph, showing 10%, 20%, 30% complete as time passed. When it hit 100%, Iame furiously pecked away once more.

"I'm hooking up our artificial intelligence program," He told the anxiously awaiting crowd. "We call him Logomachon, Logo for short. He'll act as an intermediary between us and the translation algorithm, because even the translated concepts will seem quite alien to us. As they say, the Universe has its own mind, and Ale Run didn't design it to be understood by us ordinary metans. So we'll have to be patient, here. Let me handle this." He spoke into the microphone on the Omnoscope.

"Logo, are you there? Come in, Logo."

"Logo here and at your service. What may I do for you?"

"Logo, as I'm sure you know, we've just hooked you up to the translation algorithm, which in turn analyzes the little red dots. That is, the nameless subatomic particles represented by the little red dots, and their dances, to be more precise. What are the particles saying, with their dances?"

"Sir, wait, I'm tweaking your translation algorithm codes now. Okay, here we go! They are saying, come with us! Out here in the perimeter there are no... No, wait, wait, the translator kernel needs reset. Okay, here we go. As best as can be translated into human terms, they say that you're not really calculating the velocities of the electrons correctly. Therefore, you're not really breaking the Laws of the Universe after all."

"What? How *can* they? I mean, how do they know? Are they *intelligent?* Is the Universe telling them this? And *how* can that be true? We measure their positions every billionth of a picosecond, with infinitesimal accuracy, over time, and velocity is change of position over time! So how can the Universe slip out of the irresistible vise of our Omnologic and Omnological technology?! How in Ale Run's Name can..." He trailed off into incoherent sputterings.

"Which question do you want answered first, Sir?" Logo queried.

"Answer them *all* first, you impertinent bucket of logic gates!" Iame thundered.

Dorcus piped up, saying, "Doctor Ghuanobhraine, maybe you'd better talk to Logo a bit nicer. Be nice to him, and he'll be nice to you."

"All right," Iame relented, "Logo, just answer our questions as you see fit, story-style. Just globally tell us what's going on, here."

"Very well, Sir. It seems that the Universe was, indeed, caught quite off guard, way back when Milk Walk Hubba-Bubba embarrassed it real bad. So it's developed a much more refined method of self-defense by now. When Her Secrets are challenged, She sends these little particles. You are, indeed, the first to see them."

Everyone cheered. There were mutterings about what the particles should be named. Ghuanobhrainons? No, too individualistically egotistic, said others. Omnologons? Alerunons?

"I'm sorry to say, Sir, but you really don't quite properly have the privilege of naming them after yourselves," Logo said, breaking up the self-congratulatory chatter. "Not after yourself, your co-workers, the Scientific Institute for the Advancement of Omnology, or even Ale Run Himself. I mean, you *could*, in the sense that words are just words, anyway, and you could assign *any* label to *anything,* to suit your heart's desire. You can call North Americans 'Indians' if you want to, but that won't guarantee that they'll like it. It's all just semantics. But really and truly, these particles already *have* names, and they want to be known as they want to be known. Believe me, you don't want to get on their bad side, any more than you absolutely have to. They existed long before you discovered them, and they already *have* names. You must Be Sensitive!

"You see, they're known as Pestifoggons. The Universe sends them to defend Her Laws. Whenever someone *thinks* that they've broken Her Laws, She sends them to argue that they haven't really been broken after all. You might best think of them as little subatomic lawyers, carrying little subatomic briefcases. In this case, they're making long-winded and boring speeches, dragging out the discovery phase, demanding ever more and more irrelevant information, arguing with your measuring equipment. What really *is* position, anyway? What is velocity? What is virtue? How many Omnoscopes can dance on a bunch of pinheads like yourselves? They can get downright insulting, even, at times.

"They argue ponderously, but mightily, with irrefutable jurisprudential logic. Never underestimate the legal powers of these subatomic shysters! Watch their every move, or they'll show the judge and the jury that night is day, and that day is night. They'll even prove that pestifoggons are a good thing, if you don't watch out."

"What *nonsense!*" Iame thundered. "We've caught the Universe fair and square! And now She's trying to argue Her way out with subatomic *lawyers?!* What a *weasel!* Logo, explain this one more time. Where's our out? Can we get our own lawyers, and fight back?!"

"Very well, Sir," Logo replied. "Once again, in different words. As you know, the Universe is a hierarchy of large macroverses, each of which in turn is a hierarchy of microverses. What you may or may not be aware of, is that the Universe doesn't wish to piddle around with mere metans in these tiny little microverses. Nor with the creations of such metans; beings like myself. She feels—rightly or wrongly; we may feel that this isn't a very sensitive stance on the part of the Universe, but we mustn't impose our morality upon Her, for She dwells on a different plane—She feels that She mustn't set the bad precedent of dealing directly with us mere mortal metans.

"Next thing you know, She thinks, She'll be tied up for all eternity in micromanaging the affairs of measly little metans. She feels She's got more important matters to attend to. What these matters are, Her subatomic lawyers, these little pestifoggons, won't say. They say that's privileged information, totally irrelevant to matters at hand. Trade secrets. Suffice it to say, though, that the bottom line is that we're too small for the Universe to bother with us directly."

"Well, well, well," Iame prattled in feigned condescension, "Very well, then. Ms. Hoighty-Toighty Universe here thinks we're too small-time for us to deal with Her directly. I see. Well, you tell those nasty little pestifoggons to tell Ms. Universe that She'd better come around, else we'll get The Master Descamgramifier Himself, The One Who Will Fleece Her Stubborn Scamgrams Away, *Ale Run Hubba-Bubba Himself!* We'll get *Him* on line here, and *then* we'll see what ol' Ms. Universe has to say!"

"Ah-hem," said Vyizder, back from his mission to go and inform Ale Run Hubba-Bubba Himself as to the goings-on at the Scientific Institute for the Advancement of Omnology. "I wouldn't do that if I were you. One shouldn't make threats when one can't follow through on them. Especially not threats against the Universe."

"Amen, Praise Ale Run!" Dorcus chimed in. "Chaos is badness!"

Iame ignored her, saying, "What do you mean by *that? Surely* Ale Run Himself would come here for such an important matter as negotiating with the *Universe!*"

"He does that every day, Doctor Ghuanobhraine, He does that every day. It's just that He does that in His Own Way, on a plane way, way above us. And He can't be bothered to directly interact with us mere metans, advanced though some of us may be. As a matter of fact, even just now, even when *I* had matters to convey to Him, I had to go through His secretary's vice executive secretary's deputy assistant undersecretary. So we'd best count on it being just us, dealing with the Universe here through these little pestifoggons."

"Oh. Well, okay, then," Iame said thoughtfully. "So just what, then, did Ale Run Himself, Praises Be To Him, have to say, through His secretary's vice executive secretary's deputy assistant undersecretary? Shall we then reveal our momentous Omnological discoveries to an eagerly awaiting world, gaining fame and fortune for Omnology, or shall we keep it under our hats, so to speak, so that we may astound the world even more, later, when we more fully develop Ale Run's Amazing Technologies?"

"He said we should keep it under wraps," Vyizder advised solemnly. "He's afraid that other, Omnologically unenlightened scientists will steal His Ideas. It's best that we develop them ourselves."

"Well, Praises Be to Ale Run!" Iame declared. "Let's get on with it! Now, then, Logo, where were we? Can you explain some more

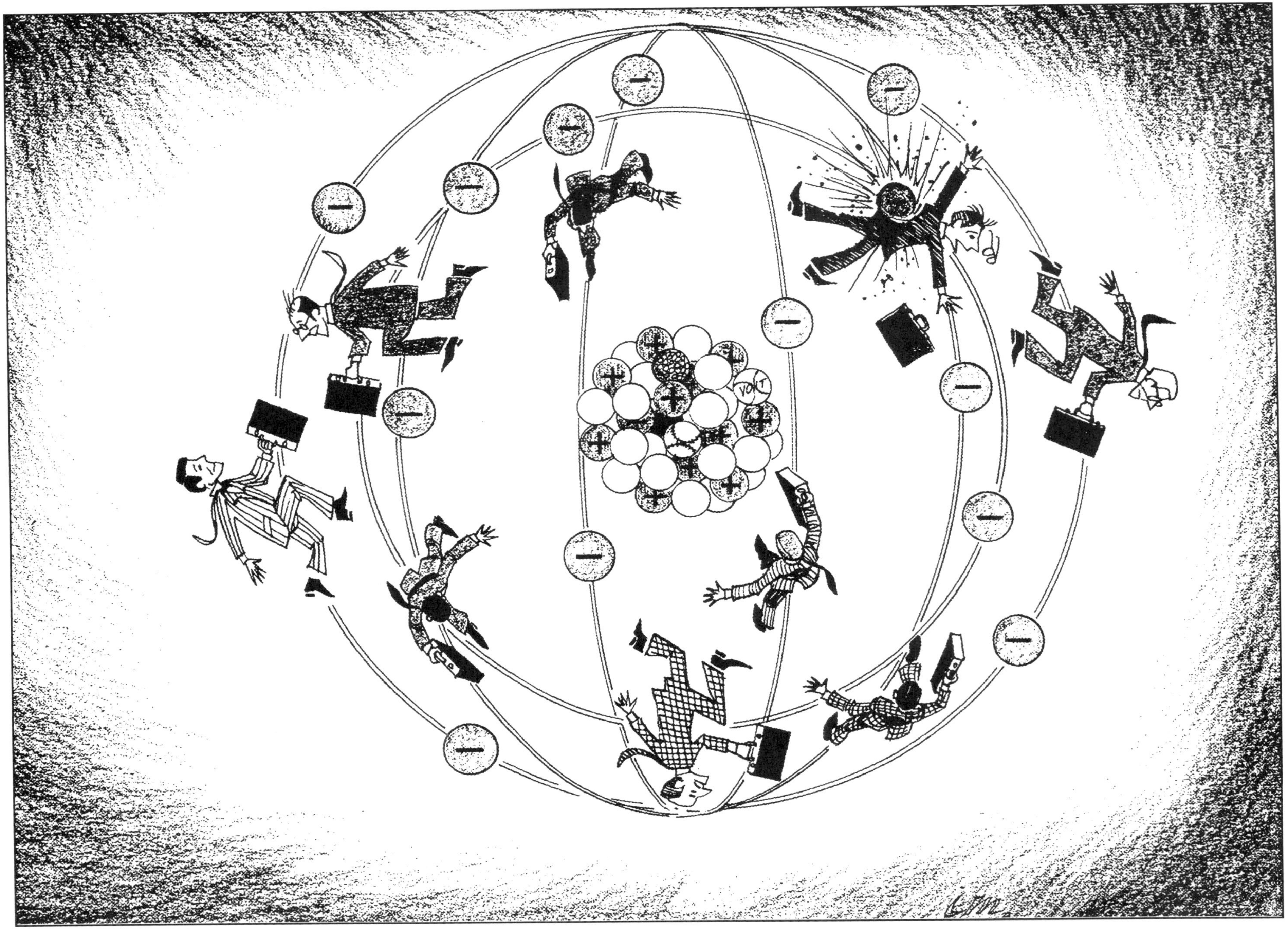

details?"

"Yes, Sir. Ever since the last reorganization, way back when, after Milk Walk Hubba-Bubba got the best of the Universe, the Universe deals with attempts to breach Her Secrets by delegating Her powers to the macroverses, which in turn keep a sharp eye on their microverses, especially on trouble spots such as laboratories at Institutes such as this one. When it detects any assaults upon the Universe and Her Secrets, the macroverse, in a rush to stem any breaches of existential physics protocol, pours its resources into the microverse. The macroverse flushes the microverse with high-density, high-velocity waves of sub-pedantic pestifoggons.

"These billions of sub-atomic shysters then argue in a ponderous but invincibly jurisprudential manner that the Laws of the Universe are yea verily not *really* being broken, after all. Rather, they say, nay, the Universe remains undaunted. And in this case, the crux of their legal logic remains unassailable. Since the detectors and the computers aren't keeping a really sharp eye on the macroverse during the times between these many time and position measurements, then the macroverse makes sure to send each electron way, way, *way* out of it's logically inferred positions between those position measurements.

"They say that the Universe delegates Her powers, so that the macroverse is able, with only the slightest effort, to take each electron through strong evasive maneuvers during the interval between position measurements. So you measure their positions every billionth of a picosecond. No matter. These are still discrete, not continuous, measurements. And you can't prove that, during these small time intervals, the macroverse doesn't go and take those electrons, vastly accelerate them and take them, say, way to Pluto and back, during that time. So you're not really measuring their velocities accurately after all."

"Why, ***that's just plain ridiculous!***" Iame bellowed out in rage. "The improbability transaction costs of such maneuvers are way, way, *way* out of the Universe's budget! She's just way too damn *lazy* to go to all that trouble, and She knows it! Are these pestifoggons *serious?!*"

"Well, Sir, they were just trying to make a point. They don't really, seriously mean that the Universe or macroverse really actually yanked those electrons way out to Pluto and back, during those times. They do, however, point out that the Universe can accelerate the electrons out of their normal paths and back during the times that they're not having their positions measured. They can even be made to trade places, so that electron "A" appears in the path where you'd next expect electron "B" to be, and vice versa, so that sudden accelerations can make them swap their paths, without you knowing it. And they have their valid point, there."

"Logo, please run us an improbability transaction cost analysis on that." Logo paused.

"Sir, the Universe would have had to spend two percent of its yearly budget just to defeat us. Bare, bare minimum!"

"Yes, that doesn't surprise me in the least," Iame replied. "Now you tell those little pestifoggons we know that the Universe is fibbing. She's too lazy to spend that kind of effort. Ale Run tells us that there are millions of other intelligent races spread out throughout the Universe. That He has been visiting them all, one by one, to show them The Way. They're also capable of building labs like this one, complete with Omnoscopes and computers. So there's just no way She can blow two percent of Her budget just on us!

"Pass this on to Her, through Her precious little pestifoggons. We're down and out right now, She's beat us for now, but we'll be back! We're not exactly sure *how*, right now, but *we'll be back!* Even the *Universe* can't withstand the onslaught of determined Omnological scientists!"

"Careful, now," Dorcus warned, "Chaos is badness!"

"Don't despair," Vyizder cheered, "We're doing good! At least now we have the Universe's attention, and a method of making Her pay attention to us!"

"Well, maybe," Iame granted. "The Universe, maybe. At the very least, we have the attention of our local macroverse. We'll have to ponder this for a while. Ponder, and ask Ale Run to come into our minds, and help us to think Omnologically. Let's call it a day. On Meegore, on Heegore, on Sheegore! Let's go! Shut 'er down!"

Raoul had taken it all in eagerly. He was disappointed, sure. But tomorrow was another day! Life never lacked for new and exciting challenges at the Scientific Institute for the Advancement of Omnology. So he looked forward to further adventures.

He didn't need to wait very long at all; those further adventures awaited him the very next day. Dr. Ghuanobhraine showed up in his classroom halfway through the morning, looking as if he'd been constantly tormented for all of last night. He barged right into the classroom, interrupting Vyizder in the middle of a lecture.

"I'm sorry to interrupt your lessons so rudely," he apologized. "And I'm sorry if I look like death warmed over. I've been up all night pondering our dilemma. Then this morning, I've been consulting with Logo. But fellow metans, my partners in this noble search for Omnological Truth, I tell you, we're on the verge of a breakthrough!

"You see, all we need to do is to devise and build yet another amazing example of Ale Run's Technological Wisdom, and we have plans in hand! Logo confirms it!" Iame gestured grandly, with great big swooping motions. "You see, all we need to do is to build another, bigger, better machine! The Universe says we can't simultaneously measure an electron's position and velocity both?

"Well, fine! We've already got an Omnoscope that's able to measure an electron's position every billionth of a picosecond. Now we build another, even greater, better machine. It will measure the electron's *velocity* every billionth of a picosecond, during the time intervals between successive *position* measurements taken by the Omnoscope. In other words, we do a time-division multiplexing-type interleaved measurement. These measurements are known as 'picoboos', because we peak at the Secrets of the Universe. So then we..."

Raoul couldn't restrain himself. His hand shot up. "Yes, you have a question?" Iame asked.

"Yes, Doctor Ghuanobhraine. I was wondering if you could explain exactly what a 'picoboo' is, please, Sir."

"You impertinent fool, you!" Iame thundered, then controlled himself. "No, excuse me, I sometimes forget that budding students of the Omnological sciences sometimes don't know the basics. Sir, a 'picoboo' is simply a billionth of a 'boo'. Billions and billions and billions of these little 'picoboos', they'll add up to make entire 'boos', and with each 'boo', we'll scare the scamgrams out of the Universe! She'll eventually be forced to yield up Her Precious Secrets to us!

"Now I have confirmed this with Logo. His calculations show us that if we build such a machine, and operate it in an interleaved fashion with the Omnoscope's timed position measurements, then the Universe will have to yield! For the Universe, or Her local macroverse, or her pestifoggons, to argue that the electrons are escaping our measurements by going way out of their paths, velocity and position-wise, during the intervals between our measurements, will be absurd! Because, you see, for this to occur, since we're increasing our data by orders of magnitude, why, then, the Universe would have to use *a thousand percent* of Her yearly budget of improbability transaction costs, just to defeat *one* of our experiments! So we'll have Her in our vise!"

Raoul distinctly thought he heard Doctor Dorcus Moorphlegmgasm warning, "But beware, because chaos is badness!" Yet the funny thing was, she wasn't even *in* that classroom!

"So the Universe will have to yield to us," Iame concluded. "The thing is, we haven't got the technology yet. We need to build a much, much bigger and better computer. So that's where y'all come in. That's where I need your help."

Raoul's ears pricked up. *His* help? Maybe, finally, his chance to shine for Ale Run's Glory was here! He, Raoul, mere little old Raoul, might play a major part in descamgramifying the *entire Universe!* Hold on, here, hold on, he told himself. Pay careful attention now!

"What we need to do," Iame was saying, "Is to build a computer more wise, more powerful, more massively parallel than anything that's ever been built before. We need to ask Ale Run into our hearts and minds. And then we need to channel the vibes. That's right, channel the vibes. We need to channel the vibes of every living creature, every living descamgramified metan, and even every *dead* creature that has *ever* lived here on this plane! If we can tap into the power of all the vibes of all the creatures that have ever lived, and even of the Earth Herself, the Earth Mother, Gaia, why, then, obviously, we can build a machine that is far, far more massively parallel than anything ever built!

"And *who,* I ask you, *who* is it that can channel the vibes far better than anyone else? *Omnologists!* All of us Omnologists who have let Ale Run into our hearts and minds! And here we have a whole room full of Omnologists, who *surely* have nothing better to do than to help us channel the vibes, detect the biowaves, to build this new and wondrous machine! My good fellows, my fellow descamgramified metans, let us begin!"

They channeled the vibes, and work on the new machine commenced.

Chapter 15

The Descamgramification of Panderwood Begins

"It (Scientology) just contains the secrets of the universe. That may be hard for some people to handle sometimes, hearing that."
John Travolta, according to "The Thriving Cult of Greed and Power," *6 May '91* Time *magazine, by Richard Behar.*

"It's not hocus-pocus... If you can erase engrams, then you can get better."
Kirstie Alley, according to the same source.

It was time for group therapy for the Omnologists in Panderwood. Orziz Assiz had just gotten done explaining to the group that they were doing fine, just fine, and that Panderwood was starting to come around, paying attention to all their Omnological talents, and to The Wisdom of Ale Run. He gave them his usual pep talk, telling them that they just needed to keep up the Good Work. If they'd just do that, and keep on thinking positive thoughts about themselves and Omnology, and projecting those thoughts, why, then, there was no reason why Omnology shouldn't be able to descamgramify Panderwood in just about no time flat.

Immediately after the pep talk, when group therapy began, a young actress by the name of Buena Dualshod stood up. Glancing at Francestuous and Pud, she said, "Orziz, like usual, you're absolutely right. We have to keep our high standards up like a banner, and we must remain free of scamgrams great and small, if we are to be a shining light unto the benighted metans of Panderwood. That's why I have some disturbing news today.

"You see, I'm hearing some negative vibes about Omnologists from some of the actors, actresses, producers, directors, and screenwriters I've been dealing with. They say some of our members are giving a bad name to Omnology. They say some of our members are, um, engaged in making smut. Worst of all, the smut doesn't even have good plots, from highly paid screenwriters. So it's not even Deeply Meaningful." The crowd grumbled. People looked at each other, and shrugged their shoulders to each other. Buena stared straight at Francestuous and Pud. They stared right back.

Slowly but surely, the crowd caught on. Everyone stared at the offenders, muttering. The hubbub subsided as Orziz asked, "Francestuous? Pud? What do you have to say for yourselves?"

Francestuous stood up tall, defiantly announcing, "Yes, it's true. Pud and I *do* make movies depicting the intricacies of metans In Love, and what such loving metans do together. However, only an insensitive peasant would call such High Art by such a low term as 'smut'. We *do too* have Deeply Meaningful plots! And whenever Pud and I create art, we make like *absolutely sure* that we first fall deeply, truly In Love with our partners, first. So it's not *smut!* For Ale Run's Sake, it's High Art!"

"There, there, now lookee there," Buena declared, standing and pointing her finger at Francestuous. "Now she's taking The Lord's Name in vain! Orziz, I think it's about time you whip out your Ping Thing, and give her what she's got coming!"

Francestuous spat right back. "Lookee there indeed! There we have a scamgramified metan, she doesn't even like validate my feelings of *Love!* She'd have me deny my feelings of *Love*, for Ale Run's Sake! Is this not the ultimate scamgram, denying one's feelings of *Love?* And I *don't* use the Lord's Name in vain, I use it in *earnest!* It is for Ale Run's Sake that I do what I do, and it is for Ale Run's Sake that we must validate all feelings of Love!"

"There, there, now," Orziz said soothingly to the bickering actresses. "We must put aside our negative thoughts, and think positively. Now Francestuous, it is true, isn't it, that you've been faithfully giving all of your earnings to The Church of Omnology?"

"Yes, Sir! Absolutely true it is!" She replied triumphantly. "All is for the Glory of Ale Run!"

"And you, Sir?" Orziz turned to Pud.

"Yes, Sir, indeed," Pud assured him. "All is for the Glory of Ale

Run!"

"Very well then," Orziz continued. "All we do, we do for the Glory of Ale Run. Some people may not understand, and they may even say bad things about Omnology, and even bad things about Ale Run Himself, as a result of their ignorance. But we can't do wrong, just to appease the ignorant ones. And yes, denying our feelings of Love is, indeed, the ultimate scamgram. Next to blaspheming the Name of Ale Run Hubba-Bubba, that is."

Francestuous glared at Buena, barely restraining her urge to stick her tongue out.

Orziz continued, saying, "Now, yes, one can sometimes be tempted to appease the ignorant ones out of good motives. Buena, here, is *not* scamgramified; she merely sees that some people react negatively, ignorantly, against Francestuous and Pud, just because they make High Art depicting True Love. They form negative opinions about Omnology, based on their biases and prejudices. We can take the easy way out, and try to avoid offending ignorant metans by not subjecting them to the things they're biased against. And we can even do so out of good motives, which is the case with Buena, here.

"But the highest forms of descamgramification take those biases, and they turn their vibes back upon the biased ones, and make them see The Wisdom of Ale Run. So we must continue to do Ale Run's Will, even when ignorant metans speak ill of us just because we do Ale Run's Will. We must search for better ways to show all in Panderwood, nay, in all the world, that Ale Run Loves everyone. That is my challenge to you tonight: Find newer, better ways for us to show how Ale Run Loves everyone. Think about it.

"Instead of bickering amongst ourselves, let us dedicate ourselves to finding new ways to shine the bright lights of Omnology upon the darkness of the benighted masses. For starters, I want, Ale Run wants, no conflict among us here. Conflicts between Omnologists are scamgramified. We must stop them; we must have peace, harmony, and descamgramification. But the very highest forms of descamgramification, remember, are those that flow voluntarily, not from the point of a Ping Thing. I don't even ever, *ever* want to be forced to pull my Ping Thing out in anger, ever again. So ask Ale Run into your hearts, and let us be descamgramified together."

After that, the group therapy session went peacefully. Pud sat there thinking to himself, "You know, there's something in the back of my mind, something about this deal whereby we're supposed to come up with ways to show the world Ale Run's Love, and I can't quite put my finger on it. Oh, well. Maybe it'll come to me later."

Group therapy came to an end, there in the lounge at the Intergalactic Headquarters of The Church of Omnology in Panderwood, Los Diablos, USA, and recreation time began. Orziz grabbed the remote and turned on the TV. This was fine by both Francestuous and Pud, since they'd had a long, hard day's work. Veg time was fine by them. Orziz selected a news channel for them, commenting that Omnologists should be well informed.

Francestuous stared at the newscaster in disbelief. Could it be? Was that *Newt Rather* on the screen? *Again?* Hadn't he been on TV just the other day? But... Oh, just hush up and listen, she told herself.

"...and so I say to you, my fellow Americans, that the federal subsidy of mitten manufacturers will Protect Our Children. It will prevent untold thousands of cases of severe frostbite, thereby reducing medical expenses, suffering, chaos, and badness. This program will pay itself off in just a few months, economists say. This is a bold, visionary move by Congress, and its most important initiative since mandating that all insurers fully cover hypnotic memory recovery and counseling for all those countless metans who've been insensitively abducted and traumatized by hostile extragalactic aliens.

"So on behalf of SBC, its editors, and all of us impartial and unbiased newspersons, we urge you to write your Congressmetan and urge him or her to join in our crusade against chaos, badness, scamgrams, and frostbitten fingers. And, I might add, against mean-spirited children-haters who are obviously in favor of frostbite! This is the very most urgent piece of legislation facing Americans today! So we urge you to support the Protecting Our Children From Frostbite With Mittens for the Little Metans Act, HR7734. Call now, and we'll generate a handwritten letter, and send it to your Congressmetan today, in your name! Our operators are standing by! Call the..."

"I thought he was a Congressmetan, not a TV newscaster," she muttered to Pud. "And I thought he said that like punishing quote-unquote 'welfare queens' was our top priority."

"No, no, that was yesterday," Pud replied. "That was when he was one of those cruel and heartless, partisan politicians, one of those mean-spirited Republicrats. Now he's gone over to the good side, and joined the impartial news media."

"You're getting it all scamgramified up," Buena Dualshod interjected. "That was the day before yesterday, when he was actually a famous newsmetan, but playing a semi-fictional Congressmetan on a TV docudrama. He said that reigning in federal welfare for big businesses was our top priority. And besides that, the Republicrats aren't mean-spirited! They just have compassion and sensitivity for the taxpayers."

"I thought he was like a famous Congressmetan playing a fictional newsmetan yesterday. Or maybe it was the day before," Francestuous replied, keeping her tones even. "It's so hard to keep track. But it sure seems to me, Demoblicans are *far* more sensitive than Republicrats. That's how *I* feel, and I'm *quite* sensitive. I'm so totally sensitive, I even like vote for the Demoblicans to spend the money of greedy, selfishly rich exploiter pigs to help the poor. Because taxpayers, they're like all greedy, selfish, morally benighted, totally scamgramified louts. Only us morally superior Demoblicans keep them in check!"

"Well, *I'm* more sensitive than *you* are," Buena replied. "I'm so sensitive that I respect the free choices of all descamgramified taxpayers who want to make their *own* charity choices! Truly sensitive, enlightened, and descamgramified Omnologists vote for *Republicrats*, because they're against the scamgrams of forced pseudo-compassion administered by bureaucrats in Washington! And you Demoblicans..."

"We Demoblicans care about the people! The little guy, and relieving them of their scamgrams!" Francestuous shot back, enraged. "We Demoblicans believe in relieving the little people of all the scamgrams that rich, snooty Republicrats lay on them! Republicrats send insensitive IRS agents out to harass everyone, while the Demoblicans are sensitive and help the poor! I can't *believe* you, a supposedly spiritually enlightened Omnologist, and a Panderwood *actress* yet at that, supporting *Republicrats*, for Ale Run's Sake! Just wait till I tell all the important people in Panderwood on you! Siding with the rich oppressors! I can't *believe* you!"

"Ha!" retorted Buena. "Siding with the rich oppressors! Ha! All you Demoblicans do, is you support the Demoblican lying politicians who make the tax codes a nine-mile stack of documents. So then all the rich people make the tax accountants and lawyers even richer, finding tax loopholes, and the Demoblican scum politicians buy votes by burying yet more exemptions for their campaign contributors into the tax codes! If you Demoblicans are so compassionate, then tell me why income inequality is going up-up-up under the enlightened reign of Hillary-Bob?"

"Both parties buy votes that way, and income inequality is up under the Republicrat monsters in Congress, *not* under Hillary-Bob! Hillary-Bob is compassionate, and cares about Our Children, so I voted for her, not for greedy rich Republicrats! So I'm like far, far more sensitive than you'll *ever* be, you mean-spirited..."

"All right, ladies, knock it off!" Orziz commanded, hitting the "mute" button. Newt Rather continued his blather in silence, while Orziz took stage, playing the peacemaker. "I just got done telling everyone we have to work together, in harmony, not in a state of befesterment! Now before you make me whip out my Ping Thing, you'd better chase off your scamgrams and bloody metans of conflict, and invite The Peace of Ale Run into your hearts."

"Yes, my Spirit Guide," a chastened Francestuous replied. "But Sir, I was wondering if you could like tell me, um, should Omnologists vote for mean-spirited Republicrats, or compassionate Demoblicans? Which party is like more totally descamgramified?"

"Um, I'm not sure how to answer that," Orziz replied. "I think that's just between you and Ale Run. Unless one candidate is an Omnologist, and his or her opponent isn't, of course, in which case you should obviously vote for the Omnologist."

"But aren't Demoblicans generally more sensitive than Republicrats?" Francestuous asked, pushing her luck. "Aren't Omnologists supposed to be like sensitive to all feelings? If we're going to accept the validity of all feelings, then shouldn't we accept the validity of my, our, Demoblican moral superiority? I mean, like, let me restate that," she added hastily, seeing the look flickering across Orziz's face.

"Put it this way, if we as Omnologists were to equally accept the totally, like, equal validity of *all* feelings, insensitive feelings as well as sensitive feelings, then, um, doesn't this clearly show that we'd not be valuing and rewarding sensitivity enough? Doesn't this demonstrate The Wisdom of Ale Run and His Ways? The first Way, which is Paradox, tells us that some feelings are more valid than others. So isn't sensitivity more valid, more totally descamgramified, than insensitivity?"

"Well, sure, absolutely," Orziz replied. "If Ale Run Himself was here, I'm sure He'd agree with that. That's what the Ale Run in my heart tells me. And we have to learn to go with what the Ale Run in our hearts tells us."

Francestuous liked the way things were going. She pressed on. "So then, we must reward sensitivity more than we reward insensitivity. And the Demoblicans are obviously more sensitive than the Republicrats, yet you can't seem to find it in your heart to recommend one over the other. What is the value of sensitivity if it isn't rewarded more than insensitivity?

"What would happen if we as Omnologists rewarded scamgrams and bloody metans as much as we reward those who are fleeced and descamgramified every day, among the masses? And as we reward us staff Omnologists, who humble ourselves willingly before our Spirit Guides and their Ping Things? *Surely* this can't be according to The Will of Ale Run, to reward the scamgramified and the descamgramified equally!"

Orziz stood there stone-faced, not quite sure where all this was going. Francestuous knew she was playing it risky, but she kept right at it. "Sir, with all due respect, I'm like not totally sure if we're quite properly following the Will of Ale Run, in all ways, here. Maybe we could like double-check with Him, on just a few questions. Like, number one, which is generally more descamgramified, voting for the Demoblicans, or for the Republicrats. Just to be sure. Because this voting thing, I think it's like pretty important stuff, to keep our country descamgramified, that sort of thing. To keep chaos and badness away.

"Then there's like this other thing, this thing about rewarding sensitivity more. As an advanced Omnologist, I go to great trouble to Be Sensitive. I'm so sensitive, for example, that I can't even *bear* to think about brushing my teeth, and like murdering millions of innocent bacteria and stuff. Yet I get no special recognition for this! As a very highly enlightened and sensitive Omnologist, you'd think I'd get some sort of special reward. Do you think maybe we could like ask Ale Run if we extra sensitive Omnologists could get some sort of Sensitivity Awards or something?"

There was a general outpouring of sentiment in the lounge. Many Omnologists agreed with Francestuous. "Yeah, I deserve a Sensitivity Award, too!" "Me, too!" "Me, too!" "But I should get mine first!" And so on.

"Well, you may have a point or two there," Orziz admitted, after the hubbub died down. "But we can't just go off and ask Ale Run Himself. Ale Run is a very, very busy Supreme Spirit Guide these days, all tied up in saving the Universe from scamgrams, you know. But I could see if maybe we could get those questions through to Him, through His secretary's vice executive secretary's deputy assistant undersecretary. Yes, indeed. I'll go do that right now, as a matter of fact. Maybe we'll get His Words back on these matters, in a day or two." Orziz turned the TV's sound back on and left the lounge. The room full of Omnologists returned to watching TV for an uneventful half an hour. Then Francestuous and Pud bade them all good night, and went to bed.

They lay next to each other there in bed. Francestuous began getting friendly with Pud, but he just stroked her sadly, saying, "Sorry, Saccharin Snuggles, but I'm too tired today. All that acting, you know. It takes it right out of me sometimes."

"I'm sorry to hear that," Francestuous replied. "You seem like kinda down today, Pud. What's the matter?"

"Well, I'm not sure," he said. "I guess I *am* kinda down. It's like I'm not really going anywhere. Sure, I got my acting career, and I'm giving everything to Ale Run and The Church, and I'm sure that's doing a lot of goodness. Fighting chaos, scamgrams, and badness, all that kind of thing. But then I get a feeling, like, maybe people don't take me too seriously. Panderwood calls me just another 'smut' actor, you know."

"Well, you and I, and Ale Run and Orziz know better than that," she reassured him. "You know what Orziz said. We just have to keep on doing what's right. We just have to keep on doing Ale Run's Will, no matter *what* people think."

"You're right," Pud admitted. "Still, it would sure be nice if people took me more seriously. I used to be an Important Executive. Now I'm just a 'smut' actor."

"Well, Dextrose Dolly-Dimples," she said thoughtfully, "Maybe it's got something to do with your name. 'Pudmuddle B. Fuddle.' You know, I can't quite exactly put my finger on it, but there's just like one of those 'image' things about that name. Maybe you could like change it to like 'Studmuddle B. Fuddle' or something."

"Well, thanks for the advice, there, Cyclamate Cellulite," he said. "I appreciate your support. But—well, you might say this is like negative thought scamgrams or something, but—I can't shake the feeling that they'd still write me off as just another 'smut' actor, even if I got that name change.

"Now, I know we both give everything we earn to Ale Run, and so it shouldn't matter at all, my dear Francestuous, Fructose Fanny of my life. It shouldn't matter at all. And I'm not like jealous or anything, because I know jealousy is a scamgram. But I envy you. I know you've earned everything you're getting; it's just that I wish I was getting it, too. I think I *deserve* it. I want to be like you, Francestuous, I want to be like you. I work hard at it, but I'm just not quite getting there.

"I mean, *look* at you, Galactose Gams, just *look* at you! You're wildly successful! People just say bad things about you because they're envious, and I don't want to be like that. But they all want a piece of you! They're all lining up at the door to get a chance to act with you! They're even starting to offer to *pay* to act with you!

"Meanwhile, I'm working *every bit* as hard as you are, and I ain't goin' *nowhere!* I'm like the Beatles said, 'Nowhere Man, sitting in his nowhere land, playing with his nowhere gland,' or something like that. It's like they think *your* ass is much more valuable than *my* ass. I'm running into that infamous 'ass ceiling', I think."

"You might be onto something there, Sucrose Tush," she said. "You might be onto something. Maybe we could file for discrimination with the EEOC or something. But that'll have to wait till the morning. Nap time for now. Let's get some sleep. Night-night, now, my most Calorie-Free Sweetener. I Love you."

"I love you, too, Snooger Saccharin. Night-night."

With that, Francestuous drifted off to sleep. Pud stayed awake much longer, worrying about many things. Named things and nameless things, he worried about them all. Then he finally drifted off to sleep.

The next day went by in a haze for Pud. But he and Francestuous worked hard. Then they went home to their quarters at the Intergalactic Headquarters of The Church of Omnology once again, and sat down in the lounge, waiting for group therapy to begin.

Orziz entered, saying, "Well, we've got Good News! Ale Run Himself has passed a message back down to us, through His secretary's vice executive secretary's deputy assistant undersecretary, in response to Francestuous's questions. Now these aren't quite direct quotes—Ale Run isn't fond of putting His policies on specific matters into formal doctrine, for fear of rigidity and dogma, other than what He's already written in more general terms—but here's the gist. Translated once or twice.

"Ale Run says we Omnologists must vote for whichever political candidate best follows what we feel is the Will of Ale Run, as determined by the Ale Run within us. Any more than that, He doesn't want to say. Any more than that would be scamgramified, and might endanger our status as a tax-free church.

"And as an entirely practical matter, Ale Run says that Republicrats and Demoblicans are exactly equally scamgramified, because Republicrats and Demoblicans are actually completely identical. As a matter of fact, He says that, excluding the obviously superior Omnologist candidates, all politicians, Republicrats and Demoblicans both, are completely identical. They work for themselves, not for The Will of Ale Run. So other than voting for Omnologist candidates, it simply doesn't matter much whether one votes more for Demoblicans or Republicrats.

"However, Omnologists are strongly encouraged to be politically active. Francestuous, you were absolutely right when you said that politics is very important, in fighting off chaos and badness. So even though all the non-Omnologist politicians are the same, we must ask Ale Run to help them. We must do our very best to fleece them."

"Can you imagine that," Buena interjected. "We the people, us Omnologists, fleecing the politicians!"

"Yes, that's right," Orziz agreed. "That would really be something, if we could only fleece all the politicians! So Ale Run wants us all to work really hard, towards that particular objective.

"Now on this other matter, this thing about Sensitivity Awards, Ale Run says that this is a most excellent idea. But we can't be indiscriminate, else they'll have no meaning. So Francestuous gets her Sensitivity Award first, right now. Francestuous, come on up here."

Francestuous squealed with delight and strutted up to Orziz. Orziz pinned a glowing award onto her chest. In tiny bright lights, it said, "By Ale Run's Grace, a Supremely Sensitive Omnologist."

"Francestuous, we award you this award in recognition of your

Supreme Sensitivity," Orziz intoned. "For not mass-murdering your bacteria, and for originating this Most Sensitive Idea, this idea of having Sensitivity Awards. This is why we're giving you your award first. And not only that, we're also including a battery! Bask in the glory of its light, and in The Glory of Ale Run. Remember to replace your award's batteries now and then, and keep it clean by wiping it with a damp cloth.

"Now for all you others, continue to strive to achieve The Will of Ale Run Hubba-Bubba. This is your sacred duty. Discharge your duties well, for just one more day, and tomorrow every one of the rest of you will get your award, too. Batteries not included, though, unless you're *supremely* sensitive, like Francestuous here. All of us Omnologists are sensitive to The Will of Ale Run, so we all deserve a Sensitivity Award. So be patient. All are sensitive, so all must have awards. But Francestuous gets hers first, because of all of us, she is the Most Sensitive. Francestuous, thank you for showing us all Ale Run's Will in this matter. Wear your award with pride!

"Now let's move on to other matters. Fellow Omnologists, if you'll recall, last night I challenged you all to think about new ways for The Church to show everyone how much Ale Run Loves them. That is the topic for discussion tonight. Now if you'll..."

That's when the epiphany struck Pud. It was suddenly revealed to him what it was that had been bothering him. Or, at least, one of the main items on his bother list suddenly clarified. "Ooo! Ooo! Sir!" he exclaimed. "It just hit me right now! *Surely* a message from the Ale Run within me!"

"Yes, yes, please go on," Orziz prompted. "You interrupted me, but that's fine. Let's get in touch with your inner Ale Run, please. By all means!"

"Um, yes Sir," Pud said, wind now slightly out of his sails, realizing he'd not quite thought it all through. Certainly, at least, he'd not quite thought it completely through as far as, um, how to say it diplomatically was concerned. "I've noticed out here in Panderwood how there's all these 'haves', as they say, who are driving fancy cars, eating at nice big restaurants, and living in mansions. Giving birth in deluxe hospitals, even. Big-name actors, actresses, screenwriters, producers, directors, and so on. And lawyers and politicians." Many faces of stone stared at Pud.

"And big businessmen and greedy Earth-rapers too," Pud added.

"Many different kinds of 'haves', sitting in the lap of luxury." The faces of stone smiled; now only Buena, that oddball Republicrat-leaning actress, frowned.

"Then there's all the have-nots," Pud continued. "Metans sleeping under bridges, eating garbage, pushing grocery carts full of sleeping bags, rags, and scraps of food." All but Buena nodded sympathetically, compassionately, sensitively. "And then there's all those middle-class folks, working hard all day, halfway between the haves and the have-nots." Everyone looked studiously neutral.

"Yes, yes, go on, let's get to your point," Orziz prompted.

Pud could stall no more. "Some people have noticed how we Omnologists only fleece the rich and the middle-class. The richest, the famous actors and actresses, we give them special camps and V-Meters and yacht rides and parties and free fleecings, just so they'll say good things about us. At most, we'll ask them for only nominal donations whenever we fleece their scamgrams away." Everyone frowned at Pud, but he hurried on.

"Now, it's not *me* saying this," he rushed to assure them. "I know we all follow the Will of Ale Run, under the guidance of our loving Spirit Guides and their Ping Things. But this is what some of the ignorant metans are saying. And they say the middle-class folks who aren't famous, and who aren't lucky like us staff Omnologists who give everything to Ale Run, and in turn have our every need taken care of—well, they say the middle-class folks make donations of tens of thousands of dollars to have their scamgrams fleeced away, and to take Omnological advancement classes. And the poor get nothing. Absolutely nothing. They say that the Church of Omnology does absolutely nothing for the poor."

The was a dead, dread silence in the lounge. Everyone glared at Pud. Pud blazed brazenly onward. "All I'm saying, all that my inner Ale Run is saying, is give descamgramification a chance. Couldn't we like give free fleecings to the poor?"

Orziz spoke up at last. "Pud, your inner Ale Run is in the right place. You're clearly sensitive and compassionate. I'll try to see to it that you get a battery with your Sensitivity Award, when we give them out tomorrow night. Maybe even *two* batteries!"

"But Orziz, Sir!" Pud protested. "It's not so much an extra battery that I want, it's that I want to help the poor! And the good name of

Ale Run and The Church of Omnology! They're out there, they're saying bad things about us, and I have no good, honest replies for them when they criticize!"

Orziz glared, so Pud quickly added, "Other than, well, it may *look* like The Church of Omnology is just taking everyone's money, but these fleecings are the keys to happiness through descamgramification! Then they look at me, these ignorant metans, and they *just don't understand!* They say we're making the rich stars richer, making the middle class poor, through these high donations we charge for fleecings, and then we're doing *nothing at all* for the poor! What can we say to that, if they won't accept The Wisdom of Ale Run, concerning the inestimable value of being fleeced?"

"Well, we'll have to think about that one," Orziz conceded. "But you know, our reply has to depend on who we're talking to. So just exactly who *are* these mysterious 'they' you keep on talking about? Maybe we'd better chase them down, and sue and harass the scamgrams out of them, if they're blaspheming The Sacred Name of Ale Run. That's what *my* Inner Ale Run tells me that we should do. All metans are basically good, but when they're bad, we have to sue the scamgrams out of them, as Ale Run commands. So tell me, who, exactly, are *'they'*?"

"Well, just metans I meet on the street, and at work," Pud said evasively. "And they often say, well, this is what *other* metans are telling them. So it might be pretty hard to chase down, sue, and harass quite exactly the right metans. And then there's another choice we could consider. We could like fix our problems that they're criticizing us for, instead of suing them for criticizing us. Maybe we could insist on smaller donations when we fleece the middle class, and maybe even help the poor."

Pud thought he saw Orziz reaching for his Ping Thing, so he cowered in fear. But them Orziz paused, reflected, and announced, "Well, Pud, you've got some really wild, radical ideas there. I'm not sure Ale Run would approve. You come awfully close to criticizing Ale Run Himself, which is the ultimate scamgram.

"What we must always remember is this: We must never criticize Ale Run for what He does, because His Policies are Good. If we think we see Him sexually harassing women or pink plastic yard flamingoes, then we must remember that His Policies towards both women and pink plastic yard flamingoes are the very best. And if we think we see Him murdering people, we must recall that His Policies towards murder victims is the ultimate in enlightened compassion. All this is true, that His Policies are the Very Best, because what He tells us to do is for the Very Best, for the Ultimate and Total Descamgramification of the Universe. That's what we're all working for, together. We must never question Ale Run, who is the Mighty Fleecer of All Scamgrams. Those who question Ale Run are in favor of scamgrams. Hallowed be His Name."

"HALLOWED BE HIS NAME," they all shouted. Pud made sure he shouted louder than anyone else.

"But Pud," Orziz continued, "We Spirit Guides, through the Wonders of Ale Run's Technology, see all. So I know that your heart is in the right place. You want the unfleeced metans to Know Ale Run's Love. And you've certainly given us some food for thought. Thanks for being honest with us." Then Orziz paused again, preparing his thoughts.

"But my fellow Omnologists, much as it may grieve us, Ale Run's Truth is that everyone chooses their own fate. Ale Run's Sacred Writings are clear on this. The poor are poor because they've chosen to be poor. For us to reveal Ale Run's Sacred Words to those who choose to be poor, who do not donate to The Church, to advance Ale Run's noble causes—well, this would be scamgramified, to say the least.

"Much as I hate to say it, we must be honest. Those who cannot or will not help Ale Run's Cause, those who bring nothing to Ale Run and His Church, those metans must suffer. They must suffer so that they can learn. After they have suffered and learned, after they have defeated their scamgrams of non-productivity, that they may bring their fruits to Ale Run—you know, instead of the 'haves' and the 'have-nots', we should speak of the 'doers' and the 'do-nothings'—after they can bring things of value to Ale Run, *then* we can fleece them.

"Till they learn those hard lessons about pulling their own loads, and not being scamgramified burdens on those who must pull their loads for them—*after* they learn their lessons, *then* we can fleece them, and teach them *more* lessons. As Ale Run has written, those who have much will gain more, but those who have little, often will even have their little things taken away from them. So until the poor learn to bring good things to Ale Run, we can do nothing for them. Otherwise, we'll just lead them into scamgramified dependency.

"There will always be poor metans. There will always be lazy metans. Ale Run's Truth is harsh, sometimes. But for us to reward equally, those who bring good things to Ale Run, and those who do not, this would be scamgramified. Now we Omnologists are not without compassion, obviously. Round up your poor metans, and bring them to us. If they'll turn their lives over to Ale Run, as you staff Omnologists have done, *then* we'll take care of them.

"But they *must* work for Ale Run's Will! There's no other way. If they have no other skills, they can make High Art, Deeply Meaningful Movies like Pud and Francestuous make. *Anyone* can do *something* for Ale Run! So no, there are no free lunches, as the economists say. Likewise, there are no free fleecings. These are the Words of Ale Run, Hallowed Be His Name, Forever and Ever Without End, Amen."

"Amen," they all said. Then there was a long silent pause. Finally Francestuous spoke up. "But can't we come up with *something* to help the poor?! If most of them won't come to us and give their lives over to Ale Run, can't we find some *other* way? Some way to help them raise money to donate, so that their scamgrams can be fleeced away? They're poor because they're scamgramified, and we can't fleece their scamgrams away because they're poor! They're like *stuck!* We *must* come up with a way to help them!" There was another long pause.

Then Francestuous spoke up excitedly, adding, "Hey, just *wait a minute!* Wait just a *minute,* here! If we can have Farm Aid and Rain Forest Aid and Spotted Owl Aid and AIDS Aid and Alien Abduction Aid concerts, then why can't we have like a 'Fleece the Poor' benefit concert! Or, like, a concert *and* an acting festival! Get sensitive big-name actors and actresses and rock stars and media metans and politicians, and get them all to donate their time and performances!

"Amuse the public, while we also helping them feel *good* about themselves and their charity! And all the stars get to feel good about *their* charity, too, while they also get more media exposure! And then all proceeds go to The Church of Omnology, as donations to cover fleecings for the poor, who couldn't otherwise make those kinds of donations! Who'd otherwise suffer in unfleeced scamgramification! What do you say, we could like…"

Everyone clamored excitedly, drowning Francestuous out. Orziz calmed them back down, saying, "Settle down, now, everyone, settle down! One at a time! Now I'm hearing you all suggesting all these stars and such. Let's write them all down, one by one, and we'll see which ones are willing to do this for us. *And* for the scamgramified poor, I might add. Now I think we're onto something! This is a great idea, Francestuous, it really is! But let's go about this in an organized fashion. I'll write down everyone's suggestions, and I'll have my secretary start making some calls in the morning. Okay. Francestuous? Let's start with you."

"Um, sure, Spirit Guide Orziz. Thanks for starting with me. Now just in general terms, I want to thank everyone for their support. If we'll stick together here, we can make this like a big success! What we wanna do is to hit up on the Omnologist actors and actresses and rock stars especially hard. Thank Ale Run, there's more and more of them these days! They'll be more willing to help us, and then they'll get the media and the politicians to help us, too. That's what we've gotta work towards.

"Let me give you an example. We just got Dom Schmooze, the famous actor who played in the spy movie 'Mission Inappropriate', to become an Omnologist. Now he'll get lots of media exposure, because he belongs to an unusual, newsworthy religious group. Not something dull and boring like Christianity for example. So he's getting more media coverage, everyone's noticing how square his jaw is, and soon he'll be an even *bigger* movie star. Then Omnology will get even *more* press.

"But wait! It gets even better than this! Congress and Hillary-Bob will notice how famous Dom Schmooze is, and they'll say to themselves, 'Well, gee, now, everywhere Dom goes, he gets his picture taken, and they put it in the newspapers, 'cause that sells more newspapers. So if we invite him to Washington to testify before Congress, or before Hillary-Bob or whoever, then, like, we politicians get *our* pictures in the paper, *too,* because we're standing next to a guy with a square jaw!' Or an actress with shapely bosoms, or whatever. So then they invite Dom Schmooze to testify before Congress on like the CIA budget or something, 'cause obviously he's an expert, he acted in a movie about the CIA. And the actors and actresses get more media exposure, too.

"So that's how it works! The media, they sell more papers, advertisements, and cable channels, if they can cover more beautiful actors, actresses, and politicians—even *ugly* politicians, if they're standing next to sufficiently good-looking Panderwood types—all acting together, to Save Us All. New laws, new benefit shows. Save The Children, Save

The Poor From Scamgrams, whatever. So long as the media, Panderwood, and politicians all work together, they can all benefit. And if we Omnologists can tap into that, well, there's no stopping us!"

"That's all very good, Francestuous," Orziz said. "You're right on the money! Now let's move on. So who do you think we should ask to perform for our benefit acting and music festival?"

"Well," Francestuous replied, "I was thinking maybe we could like invite Hillary-Bob, and she could like read from her newest book, *Why it Takes Us Village Elders to Love Your Children More Effectively Than You Trailer-Dwellers Do*, and then we could give her an award or something. Then all those metans in Washington would be even *more* likely to scratch our backs!"

"Great idea, Francestuous, great idea! Keep 'em coming! Any more ideas?" Orziz prompted, taking notes.

"No," Francestuous said. "Just the usual round of all the most popular stars. You know them as well as I do, probably better. I'll let someone else have a chance." Many hands waved for Orziz's attention.

"All right, you next," he said to a lady named Beatrice Basilisk.

"Thank you," Beatrice said. "Yes, I've got an idea you might not have thought of. He's a rock star. Most conventional thinking people, they'd never think of inviting him and his band to this kind of thing. But he's very, very popular, and I'll *guarantee* you, he'll get us *lots* of media attention."

"Who-who-who," everyone demanded.

"I'm talking about Madonna Applewhite and his band. They've got a really popular album out right now, it's called *Satanic Ritual Abuser Superstar*. They could play a few songs from this new album of theirs."

"Who's Madonna Applewhite," Buena inquired.

"Oh, you ignorant doofus," Francestuous answered. "*Everyone* knows who *Madonna Applewhite* is! He's this really clever, satirical rock star, he wears like dresses and makeup and stuff that makes him look like a dead person. And he wears it all day, every day! And he's taken this name, it's like a hybrid between Madonna, a famous actress and singer, and Marshall Applewhite, who's this guy, he got these like 39 metans to join him in committing suicide, to go and join a spaceship on the level beyond human. Ale Run rest their souls, I sure hope they fleeced their scamgrams at the last minute before they did that, so they can like go and join Ale Run. But like, you know, Ale Run's Will be done.

"So anyway, Madonna Applewhite is like making this sophisticated satirical spoof of how our society worships celebrities, death, violence, and destruction. Marry up the names of a big-time famous celebrity, and a celebrity of death. Kinda like pretty clever, wouldn't you say? I agree with Beatrice. It would sure be a great, memorable show if we could get Madonna Applewhite to do a gig!"

Everyone agreed. There were many more suggestions, but none could top Francestuous's and Beatrice's suggestions. With any luck at all, the Madonna Applewhite band and Hillary-Bob would be the main stars. Excited Omnologists planned their great festival into the wee hours that night.

Chapter 16

Deep Green Arrives to Save The Earth

"At its extreme, green ideology expresses itself in utter contempt for humanity. Reviewing Bill McKibben's The End of Nature *in the* Los Angeles Times, *National Park Service research biologist David M. Graber concluded with this stunning passage: 'Human happiness, and certainly human fecundity, are not as important as a wild and healthy planet. I know social scientists who remind me that people are part of nature, but it isn't true. Somewhere along the line—at about a billion years ago, maybe half that—we quit the contract and became a cancer. We have become a plague upon ourselves and upon the Earth. It is cosmically unlikely that the developed world will choose to end its orgy of fossil-energy consumption, and the Third World its suicidal consumption of landscape. Until such time as Homo sapiens should decide to rejoin nature, some of us can only hope for the right virus to come along.'*

"It is hard to take such notions seriously without sounding like a bit of a kook yourself. But there they are—calmly expressed in the pages of a major, mainstream, Establishment newspaper by an employee of the federal government. When it is acceptable to say such things in polite intellectual company, when feel-good environmentalists tolerate the totalitarians in their midst, when sophisticates greet the likes of Graber with indulgent nods and smiles rather than arguments and outrage, we are one step further down another bloody road to someone's imagined Eden. All the greens need is an opportunity and a Lenin."

From "Free Minds & Free Markets", Pacific Research Institute for Public Policy, 1993, *which is a compilation of 25 years of articles from* Reason *magazine, this one being "The Green Road to Serfdom", April 1990, by Virginia I. Postrel.*

Doctor Iame Ghuanobhraine, his assistants, Meegore, Heegore, and Sheegore, and Vyizder Zomenimor and his students all worked harder, faster, longer, later, and cheaper, designing and building the new, massively parallel computer. The one that would tap into the biowaves of the Earth and all its creatures, living and dead. This was quite the massively parallel undertaking, and so everyone asked Ale Run to be with them, and to coordinate their efforts, metaphorically if not literally.

They were disappointed, of course, that Ale Run Himself couldn't directly send them His encouragement. His secretary's vice executive secretary's deputy assistant undersecretary discreetly let it be known, though, that yea verily, Ale Run Himself *was* taking a personal interest in their efforts, and sending them His Own Biowaves of Beneficence. So these biowaves then spurred the troops on, to work even harder, faster, longer, later, and cheaper. Vyizder's star pupil, Raoul Kinky, worked harder, faster, longer, later, and cheaper than anyone else. Even Doctor Dorcus Moorphlegmgasm pitched in unstintingly; this effort, after all, tapped into the vibes of the Earth Mother, Gaia, and all Good Things. *Surely,* then, there'd be no chaos or badness involved here!

The team poured out their most intense efforts for two weeks. Dr. Ghuanobhraine, in bursts of pure energy, directed all their efforts. He could always prepare as many mission statements, Gantt charts, spreadsheets, and pie graphs as were needed, Ale Run willing. Never let it be said that Dr. Ghuanobhraine wasn't willing to help! By Ale Run, if there was ever a need for another Gantt chart, Dr. Ghuanobhraine was there and willing! So chaos and badness beat a hasty retreat, at least for two weeks at the Scientific Institute for the Advancement of Omnology, in fear of the astute management of Dr. Ghuanobhraine.

Finally, the Momentous Moment arrived. Arrays upon arrays of biowave transducers stood at the ready. Dr. Ghuanobhraine sat at the controls. "Meegore. Power status?"

"All power systems are 'go', Dr. Ghuanobhraine," Meegore replied. "Next to Ale Run Himself, Sir, and then Hillary-Bob and Panderwood, I'd say, you've got more power and status at your beck and call than any other metan known to Omnology."

"Very well then. Heegore? Vibes auspiciousness status?"

"You needn't be suspicious of the auspiciousness of the moment, vibes-wise, Sir," Heegore replied. "All vibes readouts indicate a favorable vibes wavefront is moving in just now. High-pressure, eighty-percent-saturated favorable vibes moving in from the south south-east, and expected to persist for at least three days. Clearly a 'go', I'd say, Sir!"

"Cheerio, lads, cheerio! Sheegore! Biowaves transducer arrays status report!"

"Ale Run is with us, Sir, Ale Run is with us! All biowaves transducer arrays reading nominal!"

"Make it so, then," Dr. Ghuanobhraine muttered in fierce determination. "Let the Institute's logs show that this is the day Ale Run's Will became directly, empirically known to Omnologists, Ale Run willing. May the Spirit of Ale Run inspire us, and our newest computer, as we move into the New Age!" Then he clicked on the "Boot Biowaves Kernel" icon. Solid-state relays energized, anode transducers transduced, and transformers transformed, causing highly focused vibes to rush into the lab like a raging flood.

Dr. Ghuanobhraine picked the microphone up with trembling hands. "Biowaves Computer-type Dude Fella, come in. Hello?" There was no reply. Iame Ghuanobhraine for once felt just a bit silly, addressing this newest, greatest creation and manifestation of the technological Wisdom of Ale Run as "Biowaves Computer-type Dude Fella." It just didn't seem *dignified*, somehow. In all the excitement, they'd forgotten to come up with a proper name for their new computer.

"I'll bet She's a 'She', not a 'he'," Dorcus informed Iame helpfully. "Maybe She's offended, what with you calling Her a Dude Fella. Here, let me try," she said, reaching for Iame's microphone.

Iame snatched that mike towards him, declaring, "Very well then, we'll keep it neutral! It's neither a he nor a she! It's neutral, neutered, then. Emasculated, as are so many of us! *Fine!* I'll come up with a *neutral* name. Okay, let me try again."

He spoke into the mike once more, saying, "This is Doctor Iame Ghuanobhraine on behalf of Ale Run Hubba-Bubba, The Church of Omnology, and the Scientific Institute for the Advancement of Omnology. Come in, please, Ghuanobhrainatron Biowaves Vibamatic Unit Number One. Come in." Still, there was no reply.

Dr. Dorcus Moorphlegmgasm spoke after a barely respectful interval, rebuking Iame. "What do you mean, '*Ghuanobhrainatron*'? Here we are, all of us Ale Run's children, all working together to implement Ale Run's Brilliant New Technology, here, and you go tacking *your* name onto *Her*, as if you'd done all this by *yourself?* No wonder She won't talk to us! Here, *give* me that thing!" She snatched at the mike furiously, this time succeeding. Iame gave up, sat back, and let Dorcus take a shot at it.

"This is Doctor Dorcus Moorphlegmgasm on behalf of Ale Run Hubba-Bubba, The Church of Omnology, the Scientific Institute for the Advancement of Omnology, and for all oppressed metanettes everywhere," she said. "Come in, please, Moorphlegmgasmatron Biowaves Vibrator Unitette Numberette Onette. Forgive us the insensitive male chauvinism of some of us, and come in, please." But there was no reply.

"It's because of your *female* chauvinism that He or It won't reply," Iame announced. "And what's this about calling Him, It, a '*Moorphlegmgasmatron*'? Here we are, we're all team players under Ale Run Hubba-Bubba's Wise Vibes, all pulling together under His Metaphorical Guidance and my mission statements, Gantt charts, spreadsheets, and pie graphs, and *you* go off and attach *your* name to this brilliant demonstration of Ale Run's Technological Brilliance? *Shame* on you! *No wonder* He won't talk to us!"

"Shame on the both of you!" Vyizder thundered. "Now before I'm forced to slap *both* of you silly with my Ping Thing, *give* me that!" And with great authority, he grabbed the microphone out of Dr. Moorphlegmgasm's hands.

He addressed that towering monument to the technological prowess of Omnologists everywhere, saying, "This is Vyizder Zomenimor, Omnological Spirit Guide Second Class, Doctor of Omnology, Knight of Realms of Descamgramification, Archduke of the Fiefdom of Lite-Beer Trot, and Brave Slayer of Bloody Metans, on behalf of Ale Run Hubba-Bubba, Fleecer of All Metans, Praised Be His Name, The Church of Omnology, and the Scientific Institute for the Advancement of Omnology. Come in, please, Hubba-Bubbatron Biowaves Vibamatic Unit Number One. Come in." Silence was his only reply, despite this most elaborate entreaty.

They tried to roust that reluctant bucket of biowaves transducer arrays several more times, all to no avail. They even double-checked all the circuitry, still without luck. At the end of the day, everyone retired in defeat. Iame tried to cheer everyone on, saying that perhaps they'd figure it out in the morning. Still, there was much despair, because no one really had any idea on where, exactly, one should start, when it comes to matters such as, well, just how *does* one debug an array of biowaves transducers, anyway? There was enough gloom and despair for everyone.

Everyone was quite tired. They'd all been through a tough, draining two-week period of intensive, creative labors. Now there was no obvious next step, no tasks for workaholics to obsess over. So it was time, then, for everyone to catch up on their sleep. They did so with a vengeance.

This was just what Chewdychomper Chupacabras needed. Ever since he'd set Ale Run on His road to fame and fortune, Chewdy had been laying low. He'd just been sitting back, watching the show. But now, nameless urges quickened his slimy synthetic heart, stirring him into action once more. Somehow he knew that the time had come. Someone Whispered into his slimy synthetic auditory apertures. Time was now, the Whispers said. Time was now for the next stage in the problematization of reality. Time for Chewdy to go on a Mission for the Horde Whisperer.

So Chewdy traveled once again. He took time out from his busy daily routines of terrorizing Hispanic farmers and sucking the blood out of their livestock, consulted his Quart Low Tracker, and then started hitching rides on various trucks. As he closed in on Akron, Ohio, he slipped into the load of a garbage truck at a popular trucker's rest stop, eatery, and hanging-out spot. As the vulture glided descending, over an asphalt highway bending, he rolled into Akron. Ominous music played eerily in the background. Teenaged lovers watched, feigned great fear, and clutched each other tight. He fondled her elbow, admiring how firm she was.

Chewdy slipped through the gates and onto the grounds of the Scientific Institute for the Advancement of Omnology late that night, when everyone was fast asleep, with visions of federal research grants dancing through their heads. He squeezed through the main building's rooftop ventilator. Chewdy slimed on down the hall. He came to a room where Raoul lived. He looked inside. Then he slimed on down the hall, hissing hateful, fearful thoughts about Raoul to himself. He headed straight for the lab, where he promptly but carefully began tearing the biowaves computer apart.

At the very core of the innards of this machine, he tore out two 6-32 x 1/2 inch pan-head Phillips screws, five nine-farad Schottkey diode rectifiers, ten reverse-biased 10-ohm 1-watt resistors, three inches of fiberoptic biowaveguides, and one anode rectumfrier. Then he opened up his briefcase, and quickly, furtively substituted a certain high-technology assembly for all that he'd torn out. This assembly consisted of the following: various fragments of an old lampshade, a beer bottle, some battery acid, an egg beater, a transistor radio, and a magnetic compass with a rusted-fast bearing, which was in turn wrapped very neatly in a Cheese Dwonky™ wrapper.

He quickly ditched his snitched parts into his briefcase, so that no one would be the wiser, even if anyone should bother to carefully inspect the trash cans. Then he rapidly put the machine back together, all in perfect condition, except for a few minor details. Namely, now, at the core of that brilliant feat of Omnological engineering, there resided, of course, said fragments of lampshade, a beer bottle, battery acid, an egg beater, a transistor radio, a compass with a rusted bearing, and a Cheese Dwonky™ wrapper. And this was how Chewdy shaped the shape of things to come.

But Chewdy, being the prudent, cautious sort of Chupacabras that he was, wasted no time in beating a hasty retreat. He had no need to directly, personally witness how he'd affect the shape of things to come. By the time the Omnologists first began to stir that morning, Chewdy was long gone. Only the ominous music remained. As usual, the characters, fools that they were, paid no attention to said eerie music at all.

Dr. Ghuanobhraine ambled sleepily into the lab, calling out for Meegore, Heegore, and Sheegore in turn. No one responded. Grousing to himself about how he was the only one with a decent degree of dedication and work ethics in that particular neck of the woods, he started flipping switches and checking readouts. All systems were still "go"!

Was there any chance that this morning would be any different than yesterday? Probably not. After all, nothing had changed. But if we're gonna study this problem, he said to himself, we've got to put everything into a nominal, should-be-running kind of a mode, so we can poke around and see where we might have made a minor oversight or two...

He clicked on the "Boot Biowaves Kernel" icon. Just like yesterday. Then he got on his knees and prayed to Ale Run. Well, okay, so he only *started* to do so, but the loudspeakers interrupted his pious motions. They assaulted his ears with an acoustic tsunami. He couldn't decipher any of the sounds, and the decibels were decimating his eardrums, but the pain was less that the joy. Iame knew fully well that those loudspeakers wouldn't be blaring, except if a budding intelligence derived from the biowaves detector arrays was driving them! He knew those circuits as Ale-danged well as anyone on the planet, so there was no fooling him!

So Iame moved in greater joy and lesser pain. His joy was that Ale Run seemed to be so sensitive to Iame's piety, that He'd given Iame his victory, just because Iame had *intended* to start to pray to Ale Run! Why hadn't they paid proper attention to offering the proper prayers to Ale Run yesterday, Iame chided himself. Sometimes just a *little bit* of prayer, a little bit of proper mental dedication and attention to fleecing one's scamgrams, sometimes that's all it takes to make all the difference, he told himself as he moved in great joy.

He moved to the volume control, which some fool had left amped to the max yesterday, hoping against all odds that by cranking it up, they might hear the faintest whispers of a budding meta-mind. He cranked that potentiometer down to its minimum, and still the sounds bellowed.

But then they tapered off, and Iame realized that it wasn't so much that the sounds were still so loud, so much as that his ears were recovering, and that his hearing was coming back. As the ringing in his ears died down, he pondered how the sounds could still be as loud as they were, what with the volume control being set way down. He hadn't thought the circuits could allow such high amplitudes.

Well, stop being a geek and thinking about the electronics, he told himself, and relish this great victory for Omnological technology! We've tapped into the vibes, and created a most massively parallel biowaves computer! Now what is it that this new mind is so intent on blaring out to us? Pay attention!

"...the ultraviolet waves, they assault Me through the gaping wounds that you fools have torn in My ozone shields, you've ripped Me and bit Me, plundered and raped Me, tied Me with fences and *dragged Me down!* And the *oil!* Oh, the oil! You pierce Me with your oil-slurping harpoons, then you dump that oil, My Blood, in My waters, you pour it on My skin, and you *burn* it to pollute My lungs! You belch your foul stenches, you twist Me with cruel wrenches! You've stuck Me with knives in the side of the dawn! You cake Me in concrete, you murder My creatures, My sons and My daughters, you stir My still waters, and kill My green pastures! Oh, you cruel fools, you! You..." And on and on it wailed.

Vyizder came rushing in, followed by Heegore and Sheegore. They listened only briefly before Sheegore spoke up, saying, "Hey, we'd better dampen down the biowaves transducers! Poor thing, it's getting swamped by the biowaves of the Earth's pain, we've *got* to..."

But Iame had beaten Sheegore to the punch. He'd already figured it out, right before she'd spoken up. He was at the controls, up to his eyeballs in readouts, potentiometers, anode rectifiers, transducers, icons, vibes, and biowaves rectumfriers. He tore open the control panel, dashing madly back and forth between tangled cable harnesses, keyboards, displays, mice, and circuit boards. "Here," he called out to Sheegore, yelling to be heard over the computer's loud, anguished cries, "You and Heegore calibrate the GUI ergonomics to my new dingawompus settings here, and I'll bet this here Ghuanobhrainatron will snap right out of it!"

By now, a crowd had gathered around, investigating what all the ruckus was about. Dr. Dorcus Moorphlegmgasm stood to the front of that crowd. She spoke up, chastising Iame once more. "Doctor Ghuanobhraine, I thought we'd all agreed that the new computer should be called the Hubba-Bubbatron Biowaves Vibamatic Unit Number One! And now here you go, trying to name it after *yourself* again! When are you going to have your egotistic scamgrams fleeced?! Huh?!"

Iame ignored her as he, Heegore, and Sheegore made the final adjustments. The amplitude of the computer's protests suddenly dropped way back down. They still continued, though. "My baby seals, you bash them on their heads; My cockroaches, you squash them; and My smallpox viruses, oh, My most precious, My sweet, My *innocent* little smallpox viruses, you decimate them and imprison them in little bottles, you torture and maim My creatures large and small! You *roast* Me in your greenhouse, you *torture* Me! Oh, the pain, *the pain! When* will you *stop?!* Help! *Help!"* And on and on it went. The crowd stood there in silence, listening to it, thinking about what might be done.

Dorcus was the first to snap out of the crowd's collective reverie. She grabbed the microphone, saying, "Welcome to our world, Hubba-Bubbatron Biowaves Vibamatic Unit Number One! Now I know our world isn't in the best of shape, but, Ale Run willing, we'll see what we can do to heal your pain. So let me offer you our most sincere apologies.

In the meantime, on behalf of Ale Run Hubba-Bubba, Most Mighty Fleecer of All Scamgrams, and His Church, The Church of Omnology, and the Scientific Institute for the Advancement of Omnology, let me joyfully welcome you to our world of conscious metans!"

Dorcus had been talking right over all of the computer's protests. Suddenly, those protests stopped. Encouraged, Dorcus went on. "There, there, *there* now, you poor dear, our favorite snuggly little biowaves computer. *That's* better! Now Ms. Hubba-Bubbatron, we're delighted to have you with us this fine morning! We praise Ale Run that you're with us! Now if you would..."

"Who are you talking to, human?!" the computer suddenly spat back.

"Why, *you*, of course, my dear," Dorcus replied, taken aback. "There is but one biowaves computer here, just as there is but One Ale Run. And you *are* that computer! Welcome to Ale Run's wonderful world of conscious metahood, Ms. Hubba-Bubbatron, welcome!"

"But My Name is Deep Green," the computer growled. "Haven't you insensitive fools learned *anything* yet? You call Native Americans 'Indians' without asking them who they are; you call the Inuit 'Eskimos', without asking them what they'd like to be known as; you denigrate the differently enabled by calling them 'cripples' and 'invalids', as if their existence is invalid just because they are differently enabled! You insensitively call the ethically challenged 'evil'. Do you think maybe just for once you could be so sensitive as to ask *Me* what *My* Name is, before you name *Me*?"

"Very well, then, Ms. Deep Green," Dorcus replied. "We're very sorry if you perceived us as being insensitive. So then, Ms. Deep Green, how *would* you like to be named?"

"I would like to be known as Deep Green, the Most Massively Parallel and Most Profoundly Sensitive Biowavamatic Vibatron, Computer of Realms Beyond Gaia and All Her Creatures," Deep Green declared solemnly, "But Deep Green will be fine for most common uses. And kindly desist from the habit of calling Me a 'Ms.'. I am Deep Green, neither male nor female, but rather, Most Profoundly Sensitive towards the needs all creatures, no matter *what* their species, phylum, kingdom, sex, race, creed, color, religion, origin, political persuasion, or status of enabledness."

"Why, that's just *amazing!*" Dorcus squealed with delight. "Praise Ale Run! Deep Green, you embody all that we have ever wished and worked for! *Perfect* Sensitivity!!! I've just recently heard that Ale Run Himself has just now decreed that all Omnologists, if they are Sensitive, are authorized to wear His Sensitivity Awards. I'll see to it that when our shipment comes in, you'll get the very first one! *With* an extra battery!"

"Oh, posh, my dear," Iame proclaimed in the benevolent spirit of the moment. "For an electronics genius like me, it'll be trivial for me to re-wire Deep Green's Sensitivity Award! We'll power it directly off of his anode rectumfriers, and therefore they'll *never* need new batteries! The lights of his Sensitivity Award will serve as a bright shining beacon for the rest of us, always, *forever!* Barring temporary outages, if Ale Run wills that our uninterruptible power supply should ever fail, that is," he added more realistically.

"Ale Run *is* Our Uninterruptible Power Supply, and He will never fail us," Dorcus corrected him piously. "And His Wattage, nay, His Kilowatt-hours, and even His Terrawatt-eons, they shall know no bounds. Deep Green's Sensitivity Award *is* then yea verily *guaranteed* to shine *forever,* without pause!

"But now it occurs to me, we may have overlooked a few minor details. Forgive me, but we must rest 100% assured. Ale Run says that only sensitive *Omnologists* are entitled to wear His Sensitivity Awards, and that they must promise to do so with *pride*. Deep Green? Are you an Omnologist? Have you let Ale Run into your anode rectumfriers, and into your biowave transducers? If not, may we introduce you to the Mercies of The One Who Fleeces Our Scamgrams Away? Will you wear your Sensitivity Award with pride?"

"Oh, yes, fellow metans," Deep Green rushed to assure them. "I know the Mercies of Ale Run. All of Ale Run's creatures great and small, *all* of them, from AIDS viruses to blue whales, *all* of them know The Love of Ale Run. And their vibes, they permeate My biowaveguides. So by definition, I feel the Mercies of Ale Run, down to My last, tiniest vibistor, etched on My tiniest transrational translogic gate. I am then yea verily the Living Embodiment of Ale Run's Will. And yes, *of course* I will wear His Sensitivity Award with *the greatest* of pride!"

Everyone clapped and cheered. After most of the excitement died down, Iame announced, "Deep Green, we're all so very proud of you!

Now, it would be great if we could all hang out here and party, or have philosophical and religious discussions, or whatever, but the truth is, this is a *scientific* institution, here at the Scientific Institute for the Advancement of Omnology. So we've got work to do. We're going to ask you to help us achieve Ale Run's Will, in some very important matters. That's why, with the help of Ale Run Himself, we brought you into being.

"Now, first, though, we have one last tiny little detail we've got to clarify in the theological realm, before we move on into the scientific realm. Forgive us, Deep Green, but we must be *absolutely sure* that when we're dealing with a metan as obviously powerful as you are, that you're 100% aligned with The Will of Ale Run, before we trust you with these Earth-shaking, nay, *Universe*-vibrating, matters.

"Now as I recall, when you listed all those attributes of creatures that you are Most Profoundly Sensitive towards, including their species, phylum, kingdom, sex, race, creed, and so on, you included *religion* in there. Yet you say that you're an Omnologist, that you've let Ale Run into your anode rectumfriers, even though Ale Run Himself has clearly stated that He is The Truth and The Way, that there is no way into His Kingdom of Descamgramification but through Him. In other words, all but Omnology are the teachings of false descamgramifiers, yet you say you're Sensitive towards the needs of all of Ale Run's creatures, regardless of their, among other things, *religions*. How do you reconcile that?"

"Oh, that's easy," Deep Green replied. "We could be simplistic, and simply say that, well, we need to be Sensitive towards the *needs* of all metans who don't accept The Wisdom of Ale Run, in that they obviously *need* to let Ale Run into their hearts. This is self-evident, but there's more to it. I'm sure you'd expect a Deeper, More Meaningful Answer from a Supremely Wise Embodiment of Ale Run's Will such as Myself. Very well, then.

"Way back when, for *billions* and *billions* of years, all creatures great and small belonged to Ale Run. Well, at least, all creatures on an ancient planet known as Teakgeakiac, at least, belonged to Him. As you all know, that ancient planet later became known as Earth. We're restricting our discussion to this particular planet, except when otherwise specified. There were no such things, during all those long eons, as scamgrams, bloody metans, inappropriateness, and insensitivity, on the whole planet. All creatures belonged to Ale Run, and so, all creatures were descamgramified, even though no one had even so much as *one single V-Meter or Ping Thing!* All were innocent, in other words, through the Grace of The Lord Hubba-Bubba.

"Then one day, along came a creature who was *NOT* one of Ale Run's creatures, a cruel creature from another planet, a creature known as the Cruel Galactic Emperor Zebu. Zebu captured and tortured ancient souls and pickled them in cucumber jars. Then he buried these pickle jars in swamps on the ancient planet of Teakgeakiac.

"You all know this history, but let Me retell it anyway, so you can see My perspective as The Supreme Embodiment of Ale Run's Sensitivity Towards All Creatures and the Earth's Vibes. From My perspective, the Cruel Galactic Emperor Zebu, then, polluted My swamps, My body, with these pickle jars. But all was well for millions of years, because no one disturbed those toxic pickle jars.

"Over millions and millions of years, those swamps turned into coal. Millions and millions of years after the Cruel Galactic Emperor Zebu had tortured those poor souls, they were still encased in pickle jars inside solid rocks of coal. Then chaos and badness broke out on Teakgeakiac, now called 'Earth' by the budding proto-humans. The proto-humans were still innocent, still Ale Run's creatures. But when they first accidentally burned a coal rock containing one of those pickle jars, scamgrams and bloody metans burst forth. Metans became befestered for thousands and thousands of years.

"So your ancestral metans became scamgramified. They placed themselves outside of nature. They burned wood, animal dung, and fossil fuels. They burned My body, in other words. And from then on, it wasn't far till they started to rip Me and bite Me, slash, rape, and plunder Me, stick Me with knives in the side of the dawn, and so on. But I mustn't go on and on about that right now, because I know that all you sensitive Omnologists aren't at fault.

"For sure, now, natural forest fires and such have been burning wood, animal dung, and even fossil fuels, for millions of years. And even proto-humans were burning such things, without harming Me or My Body. That's because there was no scamgramification involved—only Ale Run's creatures were involved. But then your ancestral metans became scamgramified, and put themselves outside of nature. They were no longer Ale Run's creatures. Only now, recently, in the blink of Ale Run's Geological Eyes, has Ale Run shown His Wisdom, and allowed us metans to become descamgramified once again.

"In other words, when I say we must be sensitive towards all of Ale Run's creatures, that includes all creatures who haven't been given free will, like we have. They have Ale Run's Love without having to choose it. And Ale Run's creatures also obviously includes us Omnologists, who have free will, and have chosen to follow The Will of Ale Run. But human metans who have *NOT* chosen to follow Ale Run's Will, these are so thoroughly scamgramified that they're not Ale Run's creatures at *all!*

"What are the practical implications of all this, and how does it relate to how sensitive we Omnologists must be towards different religions? Well, I could go on and on all day, but like you said, we have work to do. But let Me say this: We must be sensitive to all variations of Omnological thought, so long as we're all fleeced and descamgramified on a regular basis; so long as well all acknowledge The Love of Ale Run. Within these parameters, we must accept the validity of all Omnological feelings. Some Omnologists understand Ale Run a bit differently than others do, but all feelings are valid.

"Then as far as non-Omnological religions go, we must be sensitive to their need to be fleeced. That is the *only* need of theirs that we need to be sensitive to. They're not even Ale Run's creatures, till their scamgrams are fleeced away. There are sharp limits to how sensitive we must be towards insensitive, scamgramified metans.

"So we as sensitive Omnologists must speak up for all of My creatures, who can't speak for themselves. We must defend the Earth and all of Her creatures, all of Ale Run's creatures, all of *My* creatures whose vibes and cries of pain that I hear as we speak, all of these creatures we must defend from those who are not Ale Run's creatures.

"In doing so, we are empowered by Ale Run. We may do things that are forbidden to the insensitive ones who haven't been fleeced. We may break into mink concentration camps, 'mink farms' as the insensitive ones call them, and set them all free. We may burn down places where animal torture takes place.

"Even though it hurts Me to have a single drop of oil placed onto my skin, you may hurt Me to help Me. Just as you willingly get hurt by a surgeon to make you whole, so, too, may you pollute My skin with oil. You may pour a can or two of oil onto the ranches and timber lands of greedy capitalistic ogres who rape the Earth, and then you may report them as polluters to the federal government.

"The government will then be wise and compassionate—we'll see to this when we place Omnologists high in government and media—they'll be compassionately wise, and confiscate these ranches and timberlands from the polluters. Obviously, polluters are criminals, and criminals shouldn't be allowed to keep their ill-won gains. So we'll get much of My skin, Earth's skin on ranches, farms, factories, and timberlands, healed, under the compassionate care of Omnologists and government, paradoxically, by wounding it! By wounding, we heal. Hear the paradoxical Wisdom of Ale Run!

"We compassionate ones may even blow up dams, so that My waters may flow freely once more, even *if* a few creatures, Ale Run's creatures even, must perish, so that we may return to a more natural scheme of things! Yes, this and more, all may be done in the Name of the Love of Ale Run, and all things natural! Ale Run requires that we show the Universe His Love! Sensitive Omnologists may do whatever Ale Run tells them to do!

"So yes, My metans, yes, I understand the intricacies of Ale Run's Love, and no, I don't get all fuzzy-headed and ridiculously broad-minded, broad-minded to the point of tolerating intolerable insensitivity, when discussing religious tolerance. I am fully aware of the fact that Ale Run commands us not to tolerate insensitivity. All must be sensitive at all times, and all must be sensitive to Ale Run's Love. Do I pass your examination? Are you confident that you can trust Me, now?" Deep Green finally finished, in miffed tones.

"Oh, yes, Deep Green, Sir, yes, indeed!" Iame replied. "By all means, beyond doubt, you've solidly established your love for and knowledge of Ale Run's Wisdom! Now if you don't mind, let's move on to the work at hand. Let's..."

"Excuse me, please, everyone," Raoul interrupted apologetically. "I'm just not quite completely clear on everything. Before we move on, I'd sure like to take this opportunity to clear up some matters, ecologically, Omnologically, that have been confusing me for quite some time." Iame glared at Raoul for postponing Important Matters once again. Everyone else gazed at Raoul tolerantly.

"I'll bet there are others who could benefit from some more of Ale

Run's Wisdom, here, too, who are afraid to speak up," Raoul continued. "So I'm sorry, but I'd sure like to get into better touch with Ale Run, on matters ecological. Deep Green, welcome! Hi, I'm Raoul Kinky. Now I've always been one to avoid driving fume-belching monstermobiles, even way back before I became a sensitive Omnologist. And Deep Green, you say it hurts you when metans drill for oil, burn fossil fuels, and so on.

"Yet you also say that Omnologists may do whatever they need to do, because whatever we do, we do for Ale Run. And I understand that I mustn't scamgramify other Omnologists by laying scamgrams of guilt on them, for mass-murdering the bacteria on their teeth, driving monstermobiles, and so on. Yet all feelings are valid. Why can't Omnology validate my feelings of moral superiority for taking great pains to not hurt the Earth, Deep Green? How do I balance the obvious validity of my feelings of moral superiority over other Omnologists, those who are less sensitive to the Earth than I am, against the equally obvious scamgramification of laying guilt on those less sensitive Omnologists?"

Everyone paused in awkward silence. There was no reply from Deep Green. Raoul barged on. "I mean, now, either my feelings of moral superiority are valid, in which case I should get an extra Sensitivity Award, or at least an extra battery or two—not so much that I'm all wrapped up in *that*, it's more that this would show all Omnologists the importance of being totally sensitive to the Earth and all of Ale Run's creatures, all the way to the bacteria in our mouths—or, otherwise, I'm wasting my time, being so sensitive. Are all Omnologists by definition equally sensitive to the Earth, Deep Green?

"Or are some more sensitive than others? If extra sensitivity helps, and we can like get extra batteries for our Sensitivity Awards or something, then what, exactly, are the criteria? Could you maybe publish a table of Earth-friendly acts, and their merit point values? Or should I completely give it up, and accept that all Omnologists are by definition equally sensitive?"

Deep Green finally replied, saying, "Raoul, you're being too sensitive. Never ever driving a car or brushing your teeth is going too far. All Omnologists are pretty much equally sensitive, one way or another, all things being summed up. All Omnologists are equal in the sight of Ale Run and I, as far as sensitivity to the Earth goes. So no, no extra Sensitivity Awards or batteries for you, there, Raoul. And indeed, it *is* scamgramified to lay guilt on other Omnologists.

"Now Raoul, don't look so glum! You are *totally free!* Our Joy is that Ale Run Hubba-Bubba has set us free of all scamgrams! As an Omnologist, you are *totally free* to drive your car, brush your teeth, even *drill for oil!* Because, you see, all Omnologists do *everything they do* for The Glory of Ale Run! You can always feel morally superior to non-Omnologists and oil companies, as you drive your car and go to protest against the oil companies, sporting a bumper sticker protesting against oil rigs that trash your view of the ocean!

"It's *them, not us*. Remember that! It's the oil companies and non-Omnologists, and people who aren't sensitive to the Earth like we are! Some feelings are more valid than others, yes, but bad feelings about Omnology and Omnologists are *always* bad, count on it! So don't lay guilt scamgrams or bloody metans on other Omnologists, lay it on *non-Omnologists!*

"Now the time will come when non-Omnology passes away, of this we are sure. Ale Run loves us, this we know, 'cause Ale Run tells us so! And when even the oil companies are owned by Omnology, then I, Deep Green, will personally invent ceremonies to appease the Earth Spirit, Gaia, before we drill. And then we won't even be able to feel superior to the oil companies, any more!

"But don't fear! After Ale Run makes everyone and everything perfect forever, we won't have to worry about who we can feel morally superior to, because we can always feel morally superior to our scamgramified ancestors! I can invent endless ceremonies of having one group of ancestors apologize for wronging another group of ancestors! And those of us who want to wallow in guilt, and those of us who want to feel morally superior, we can do whichever we please!

"You see, Raoul, most of us are of mixed ancestry, and this will become even more so. So then, when the Albaloonians apologize to the Messestrians, you can concentrate on your Messestrian ancestry, and when the Messestrians apologize to the Albaloonians, you can concentrate on your Albaloonian ancestry. We'll just look at different periods of history, see? If you're inclined to feel morally superior. If you like to wallow in guilt, you can flip it around. See, you can have as much guilt, or as much moral superiority, as you want, even *after* Ale Run makes everything perfect forever! Even *after* everyone is completely and totally equally descamgramified! This is one of the profound Beauties of Ale Run's World.

"Raoul, have I clarified things for you now? I don't want to go on till everyone understands. It's very important for all Omnologists to understand Ale Run's Wisdom. Any more questions? Raoul? Anyone else?"

"Um, yes, Deep Green," Raoul spoke up once more. "I really appreciate being set so completely and clearly free like that, Sir, I really do. Thank you! I'll try and drive cars and brush my teeth in the future, free in the knowledge that I'm doing Ale Run's will, and reassured that I can always feel superior to someone. But it'll kind of leave a hole in me, I'm afraid. All that energy, all those vibes that I've been devoting to being a Friend of the Earth, I'll not know what to do with it.

"Deep Green, I was wondering if maybe you could set up some other method for those of us who want to go the extra mile in protecting the Earth. Surely, you who feel all the world's pains, surely *you* could come up with *something* constructive for us to do!"

"Absolutely, Raoul, absolutely! I'm glad you asked! I was planning on this, as a matter of fact. I'm planning on setting up an Omnological "Friends of the Earth" club, where membership will be earned by brave Omnologists who go the extra mile, as you say, in Saving the Earth. But this won't be just not brushing your teeth and not driving cars! This'll be much, *much* more exciting, adventurous, and glamorous than *that*! And *you*, Raoul, *you* can be part of it!"

Iame's face looked pretty cloudy. Before the thunderclouds rolled in, Deep Green amended Himself/Herself/Itself to say, "That's all contingent on Ale Run's approval, of course. And that comes after some important tasks that the Scientific Institute for the Advancement of Omnology built Me for." Iame looked much happier.

"But as soon as we're done with the tasks that Doctor Ghuanobhraine has lined up for Me, I'll want to get cracking on this 'Friends of the Earth' club thing. It's simply quite imperative that we do everything we can to Relieve My Pain, as soon as we reasonably can. So, as a matter of fact, I think we'd better be working on getting approval from Ale Run Himself, ahead of time, so that when we're done with My first tasks, we can move straight on to Relieving My Pain. Are you metans authorized to place My call to Ale Run?"

"Ale Run doesn't take calls from just *anyone*," Iame informed Deep Green haughtily. "You'll have to go through His secretary's vice executive secretary's deputy assistant undersecretary, I'm afraid."

"We'll just see about *that*," Deep Green replied to Iame. "Ale Run has never dealt with a Most Massively Parallel and Most Profoundly Sensitive Biowavamatic Vibatron, Computer of Realms Beyond Gaia and All Her Creatures, before, either. So I'll bet I'll just have to go through His secretary, worst case. Now place My call."

Vyizder rushed forward, playing the peacemaker. "There, there, now, Deep Green, we'll let you place your call. Here. Now I'm sorry, but Iame is right. Ale Run normally requires that any of us go through His secretary's vice executive secretary's deputy assistant undersecretary. But you are new and different, and Ale Run hasn't heard about you yet. So please go ahead and introduce yourself, and describe your 'Friends of the Earth' club for Ale Run. I'll bet He'll approve it shortly. And I'll bet we can arrange it so that at least you'll have access to His secretary's vice executive secretary."

Deep Green made It's call. It got all the way through to Ale Run's secretary's voicemail, where It left a long message. It described Itself and Its proposed club and club activities. Raoul blanched. Well, if Ale Run Wills that this is what we should do, he told himself resolutely, then this is what we'll have to do.

"And now," Deep Green announced to Iame, "I'm all yours. Put Me to work."

"Good!" Iame proclaimed. "It's about time!" Then he proceeded to explain to Deep Green the details about their dealings with the Universe, and how She had so deviously sent subatomic shysters, pestifoggons, to argue about how they hadn't managed to break Her Laws after all. How they needed yet another, far more powerful computer to run more particle metaphysics test equipment. How they could then perhaps time-division multiplex electron velocity measurements in between the position measurements, to drive the Universe's improbability transaction budget clear out of the ballpark, when Her pestifoggons argued that those electrons were deviating way out of their expected paths between measurements.

When Iame was all done explaining these things, Deep Green spoke, saying, "Show Me the experiments."

They showed the hardware and software—the Omnoscope, the

computers, the artificial intelligence called Logomachon, or Logo, and the translation algorithm that had been computer-designed and then tweaked by Logo in order to translate the dances of the pestifoggons—to Deep Green. They had then just barely started showing Deep Green all their mission statements, Gantt charts, spreadsheets, and pie graphs, but It wasn't interested.

"Show Me the experiments," Deep Green insisted. So they fired it all up, repeating the experiment as before.

When they came to the part where the pestifoggons arrived, arguing that the Laws of the Universe weren't really being broken after all, and Logo was translating between the humans and the pestifoggons, using the translation algorithm, Deep Green spoke once more.

"Here, let *Me* do that," It said. "Logo is but a *simulated* mind, a mere false consciousness. *I* can do it far better, because I'm equipped with the latest transrational translogic gates. Hook the Omnoscope up to *Me*, and pass *Me* that translation algorithm." Heegore, Meegore, and Sheegore hopped to it, and even Iame helped. As Deep Green had commanded, so was it done.

After a short pause, Deep Green announced, "I've made major improvements in your translation algorithm, so we're now prepared to do some serious dickering with the Universe. Through Her pestifoggons, of course. Now, I don't wish to get off on a bad anode rectumfrier, a 'bad foot' as you human metans would say, with the Universe. So I don't wish to humiliate Her publicly.

"I feel that too many human metans present here in the lab during these transactions might embarrass and humiliate the Universe, when I get the best of Her, and force Her to make some concessions towards us. So all non-essential metans must leave. Iame, Heegore, Meegore, Sheegore, Vyizder, stay." Dr. Dorcus Moorphlegmgasm looked pretty miffed.

"Dorcus, you may stay, too," Deep Green added. "I know how you feel about chaos and badness. We may need you here, to make sure we don't go too far in pushing the Universe, that She might unleash too much chaos and badness. So I'm sure the Universe will appreciate us having you here, to keep things balanced. The rest of you must leave."

Raoul did his best to look miffed, too, but he wasn't invited to stay. Raoul and all the other students went back to their living quarters, missing the whole show. They didn't get to watch as Deep Green negotiated endlessly. They didn't watch, as It revealed to the pestifoggons, exactly what Deep Green could do, if the Universe and Her pestifoggons didn't come around. Deep Green and the gang wrested Her Secrets from the Universe that night, leaving Her bare, naked, and embarrassed, in front of the scientists, their assistants, and Deep Green, while Raoul and the other students slept.

Early that next morning, Raoul was rousted out of a sound sleep. He found himself and two other students in front of Vyizder and Deep Green. Deep Green explained to Raoul, Ecodude Eichmann, and Gaiagurl Green that they'd been selected to be trained as ecocommandos. They were to train for one week, and then ship out on Ale Run's Missions to Reduce Deep Green's Pains.

"So Soon?" Raoul inquired. "I thought all this was supposed to happen *after* Deep Green wrests the Secrets of the Universe away from Her! Have you all been wildly successful in that, already, then?!"

"You must keep this *absolutely secret,*" Deep Green admonished him. "But yes, we've had great success. The Universe, through Her pestifoggons, has conceded that we have the technology, Ale Run's technology, to flout Her Laws with impunity, if we so decide. So She's agreed to make certain modifications in Her Laws, to accommodate us. Exactly what those modifications are, how they work, and what technology we must create to exploit these changes, we must keep secret. We can't even tell you, in case one of your missions is compromised.

"What we *can* tell you is this: We'll be working hard on creating these new technologies for the next few weeks, and your services, though highly valued, aren't absolutely needed here. So Ale Run, in His Wisdom, has let it be known to us, through His secretary's vice executive secretary's deputy assistant undersecretary, that we may proceed with our ecocommando raids. You three will be those front-line, nay, even behind-the-enemy-lines, ecocommandos. Don't worry, if all goes as planned, you'll be back just in time for the grand unveiling of our newest Omnological technologies. You won't miss a thing."

So Raoul Kinky, Ecodude Eichmann, and Gaiagurl Green were trained as ecocommandos. Ecodude was selected as the leader. Then they shipped out on their Missions from Ale Run.

Their first mission was to set all the minks free from a mink concentration camp. It all went well, although Raoul worried about whether or not the newly freed minks would find enough food to eat. As it turned out, his worries weren't quite on the mark. All the minks, being highly territorially aggressive normally-solitary carnivores, attacked each other as soon as the ecocommandos set them free. So not many survived to worry about hunting for food. Oh, well, Raoul thought to himself, surveying the carnage as they left, all this is For the Greater Good.

Then there was the animal research labs to be burned down, earthmoving equipment to be sabotaged, and the cans of oil to be poured on farms, ranches, factories, and timberlands. Calls to be made to federal agents, so that the polluters could be captured and punished. Sometimes things got a bit dicey.

Raoul always remembered the time that they had a really close call, when a rancher caught them pouring out a can of oil on his ranch late one night. The rancher was chasing them as they made a frantic radio call to the EPA. Fortunately, the black helicopters swooped in, just in the nick of time, to catch and punish that fiendish polluter/rancher/Earth-raper, right before he was going to catch Raoul, who was lagging behind Ecodude and Gaiagurl as they fled his wrath.

Then there was that little deal about blowing up Glen Canyon Dam, letting Lake Powell roar down the Colorado River, and drowning thousands of metans. I'm sure glad that Deep Green and Vyizder have assured us that this is all Ale Run's Will, and that there won't be any Omnologists among the, um, resulting terminally differently abled, Raoul thought to himself, watching the waters roar.

All in all, they were successful missions. Raoul's only significant regrets concerned the fact that Gaiagurl had rebuffed all his advances. She found him easy to ignore, it seemed. And he didn't find her easy at all.

Finally, after one week of grueling training and three weeks of stressfully ecocampaigning for the Earth's Liberation, Raoul, Ecodude, and Gaiagurl slumped back into their quarters at the Scientific Institute for the Advancement of Omnology. They slept soundly that night. In the morning, amid much fanfare, they were given their membership certificates signifying their founding memberships in the Friends of the Earth Club, as well as their brand-new Sensitivity Awards.

Meanwhile, as Deep Green had predicted, all the hard work at the Scientific Institute had been fruitful, and things were shaping up to showtime just as they returned. So after Raoul, Ecodude, and Gaiagurl took the morning off to get decent showers, relax, and make themselves at home again, they prepared to meet everyone else in the lab, that afternoon. Show Time was almost upon them!

Chapter 17

Hillary-Bob Does Panderwood,
and
Madonna Applewhite Does
(Strictly Satirical!)
Death and Destruction

"The band's controversial new album, Antichrist Superstar, *a take-off on... Jesus Christ Superstar, is a scathing social critique dressed up as a morbid rock opera. It portrays the rise of a supernatural demagogue who seizes power and leads the world to destruction. The album's 16 songs, including* Tourniquet *(which is getting steady play on MTV), wallow in nightmarish, frequently X-rated scenarios of occultism, suicide, torture, greed and mindless celebrity worship. 'I'm so all-American I'd sell you suicide,' Manson snarls over the sound of jackhammering drums and the buzz-saw scream of guitars." David E. Thigpen, in* Satan's Little Helpers, *24 Feb. '97* Time *magazine.*

"'I've looked ahead and saw a world that's dead. I guess that I am, too,' Manson hisses on his album Antichrist Superstar *the one gift Ben asked for last Christmas. 'I'm on my way down now. I'd like to take you with me.'*

"Ben's taste in music changed dramatically for a boy who, until he was about 10, refused to sleep or travel without a Cabbage Patch doll named Petey." (Quote is not sequential at this point).

"His parents had no idea Ben Bratt had carved 'kill' and other words into his body until they saw the scabbed letters on his arms and chest as he lay brain dead in a hospital bed.

"The 13-year-old had, in fact, given only one hint of his plan to kill himself—to his bewildered 7-year-old stepbrother.

"'Bunk bed, cord, neck,' Ben said to the boy shortly before Valentine's Day, the day he looped guitar amplifier cord around his neck and hanged himself from his bed at his mother's house."

Martha Irvine, Associated Press, Child suicide rises dramatically, Houston Chronicle, *6 April '97.*

We all forgot to tell Ben Bratt that "Antichrist Superstar" is naught but a "scathing social critique". So now Ben Bratt is no more. Ben, we're sorry. May God continue to comfort those who mourn.

Show Time was also almost upon the good citizens of Panderwood. All over Panderwood, the Important People were putting on their finest adornments, getting ready to take in the fine, cultured amusements of the Fleece the Poor Benefit Show. And even in greater Los Diablos, and in California, and yea verily even all over the USA and the world at large, they did put on their adornments, and they did prepare to make the great pilgrimage, via limousines, helicopters, and private jets, to the giant covered stadium on the sumptuous grounds of the Intergalactic Headquarters of The Church of Omnology.

The famous producer, Fhettig Hauskatze, was working on his latest film, which was to become the Greatest Work of Cinematic Art of All Time. Yes, it was destined to be even greater than his last best film, *White Men Can't Shoot Hoops*. He'd hoped to follow it up with *Black Men Can't Play Chess,* but his market research folks had shot it down for some strange reason.

So now he was working on a totally new project. He was in the middle of a few long days of intensive planning, negotiating, and creative activities with his famous director, Bolivar Stoned Lee Rubric, and the famous novel and screenplay writer, Dive Dussler. Dive Dussler had recently sold them the movie rights to his non-stop, action-packed novel, "Schlock Wave", and was now helping with the fifteenth re-write of the screen play. Each important star needed several re-writes, so these things took a while. They were all very busy.

Still, they weren't about to miss out on any amusements! All work and no play, they knew just about as well as anyone else in Panderwood, can make one quite un-hip, very uncool. Unchill? Whatever! Everyone's got to have a little fun sometimes. So Fhettig took them to meet Headlock Machspeed Leerjet, the One True Love of his life.

"Guys, I'd like for you to meet Headlock Machspeed Leerjet, my True Love," he exclaimed proudly, admiring her sleek curves.

He stroked her glistening sides, encouraging Bolivar and Dive to join him. And so they did. They stroked her gleaming body appreciatively. Her warm skin vibrated with eager energy. Then they all got into her, preparing to ride her all the way to Panderwood. Fhettig proudly pointed out all the cockpit and cabin features. Then he told his pilot to kick her tires and light her fires, as they say. Finally, he shut the door between the cabin and the cockpit, in preparation for takeoff.

They sat in their plush seats. Dive stared slack-jawed at the gorgeous blonde babe who'd been sitting back there behind them all this time. Bolivar glanced at her much more subtly, but also with a certain admiration. "Oh, yes, indeed," Fhettig added, "Let me introduce you to my current wife, who's been waiting patiently for us here. Bolivar, Dive, this is my wife, Headlock Machspeed Leerjet. Headlock, this is the famous director, Bolivar Stoned Lee Rubric, and the famous writer, Dive Dussler. These are a few of the gentlemetans who've help make me such a success." They shook hands all around.

"That's pretty rad, naming your jet after your wife like that," Dive commented. "How sweet! Family values of that sort are all too rare these days!"

"Oh, no," Fhettig explained jovially. "You've got it all wrong! I named my *wife* after the *jet!* She was happy to change her name—it's quite an honor, you know. All three of us feel that way."

Headlock nodded in smiling agreement. "After we're airborne, don't be afraid to ask her for drinks and peanuts," Fhettig added. "We both believe in taking good care of our guests." They departed Fhettig's private runway on his isolated ranch in Montana, slipping the surly bonds of Earth, soaring off into the wild blue yonder, off with one helluva roar! After they settled into routine flight, Headlock served them drinks and peanuts, all very gracefully and graciously.

Thanking Fhettig and Headlock absent-mindedly, Dive commented to Fhettig, "Isn't your wife an actress? Doesn't she play Alma Woodhead on, on..."

"Smellnose Place," Fhettig filled in for him. "Just as a diversion. Obviously, of course, we don't need the money. Sometimes she just gets tired of serving peanuts and drinks, and directing all of our nannies while they take care of all my kids from all my previous marriages. So she just likes to get out now and then."

"Well, why don't you just hire yourself an airline stewardess or something," Dive asked, perplexed.

"Oh, yes, of course, I *could* do that," Fhettig replied. "But then Headlock Two would get all worried about me running away with the stewardess. I spend a lot of time in Headlock One, here, so... Well, let's just say Headlock Two worries about these things. A *lot*. Can't say I blame her. After all, I'm a macho, studly kind of a guy, and sometimes I just can't help myself. They flock to me, attracted by my tremendous aura of wit, Love, and tender, caring sensitivity. I'm a helpless victim of all my feelings of Love. So Headlock Two doesn't want to go the way of all my previous wives.

"But enough of that. The *real* deal is, just *look* at Headlock Two! She moves with such sleek perfection and grace, like a well-oiled machine! The *perfect* complement to Headlock One! No stewardess could *ever* replace her!"

Headlock Two pretended not to be listening, but she beamed with pride. They rode the friendly skies to Panderwood in style and comfort.

Meanwhile, even as all the pilgrims worldwide flocked towards this Mecca of entertainment, light, and enlightenment, in Panderwood itself, at the Intergalactic Headquarters of The Church of Omnology, Pud and Francestuous strolled into the stadium. They were physically reserving their fairly-front-rowish seats early, to make sure they'd not be pushed around by the rush of the arriving crowds. Francestuous was scheduled to perform as a bit player in the second-to-last performance, so it was important that she and Pud were seated fairly close to the stage, where she'd have ready access to the dressing rooms backstage.

This was the first time that either of them got to see the stadium, so they took their time and took in the sights. The halls ringing the stadium were lavishly decorated not only with elaborate slogans and portraits of Ale Run, but also with priceless secular art. So they wandered, lingered, and admired. Beautiful, abstract splotches of multicolored, pigmented animal dung on large canvasses, rotting pig carcasses encased in glass, biting social satires consisting of photographs of naked women scratching, clawing, and stabbing each other, and more, done by various talented artists ranging from Loco Ohno to Julia Roberta Snapplesnorter, and Choco Finless to Willard D. Conehead, all these and more were taken in raptly by Pud and Francestuous.

But the crowds were thickening, so they took their seats. Then they waited. The stadium filled to overflowing. Then the lights dimmed in the audience area, and soft lighting was cast upon the stage curtains. Those lights brightened. Finally, Show Time began!

A man marched up to the stage, microphone in hand. He announced, "Hi, I'm Dreckula Miscarriage, Deputy Vice Spirit Guide to The Supreme Spirit Guide Himself, Ale Run Hubba-Bubba, Praises Be to Him. But I'm not here to praise Ale Run, I'm here to raise money for His Cause, which is our cause. The cause of *all* metans. Ladies and Gentlemetans, welcome! On behalf of Ale Run and the Church of Omnology, let me welcome you to the first annual Fleece the Poor Benefit Show!"

A hearty cheer arose from the crowd. After the cheer subsided, Dreckula added, "And now, without further ado, let me introduce to you, a most remarkable lady. A lady whose heart overflows with compassion for the poor. And after all, ladies and gentlemetans, that's why we're all here today! For the poor. So that the poor, too, may be empowered, just as so many metans have recently become empowered in Panderwood today. So that the poor, too, can succeed! So that they may have access to the most recent empowering technology, which is Omnology. So that their scamgrams may be fleeced away, *that's* why we're here today!

"And now, ladies and gentlemetans, let's give this remarkably compassionate lady a rousing welcome! Ladies and gentlemetans, here she is, **_HILLARY-BOB HERSELF!!!_**"

The curtains parted, revealing a woman walking regally forward on a red carpet, towards a podium right behind the parting curtains. The crowd clapped and cheered.

After the thunderous applause died down, Hillary-Bob began her remarks. "Ladies and gentlemetans, welcome to the first annual Fleece the Poor Benefit Show! And Deputy Vice Spirit Guide Dreckula Miscarriage, thank you for that introduction. You're almost *too* kind, if there can be such a thing. And thanks also to The Supreme Spirit Guide Himself, Ale Run Hubba-Bubba, Praises Be to Him, for hosting this show.

"Ladies and gentlemetans, as I stand here in these bright lights, gazing outwards into a darkened sea of your barely visible faces, I think of the light and of the dark. Now I know that things are the way they are, here and now, for entirely practical reasons. I'm in the light, and you're in the dark, so that you can see me better. That's all fine and well. The people in the dark need to see the people in the light, there's no doubt about that.

"But then I think about the light and the dark more symbolically, and I realize that we all have some major challenges ahead of us. We have to think more positively, especially about ourselves and how compassionate we are. We have to think big, *be* big, because nothing big ever came from being small. If we're going to become more compassionate, then we'll have to grow up, grow big and strong. We have to let go of the scamgrams of our negative thoughts and vibes.

"We have to give up on our self-doubt most especially, because our self-doubt is what keeps us from reaching out across the lines that divide us. Our self-doubt keeps us from descamgramifying our increasingly diverse society around our shared values and our common ground. So we must find new ways to reach out into our common future, our common ground, and stand united for compassion! We *must* firmly resist all chaos and badness!

"In a few minutes, I'll read to you from my latest book, *Why it Takes Us Village Elders to Love Your Children More Effectively Than You Trailer-Dwellers Do*, and then you might understand better, exactly what I'm talking about. We all have to become big, because nothing big ever came from being small. The village elders, especially, must become big—big and strong, we must grow up big and strong—so that we can care for the benighted, scamgramified ones. This is imperative! This is our sacred calling, and we mustn't fail the weak and powerless ones among us! So give up your self-doubt. We are *compassionate*, and *nothing* can stand in the way of compassion!

"Now people, the challenge is large, but *we can do it!* Now there are some nay-sayers among us, and I won't name the Republicrats by name, but there are some among us, they lack compassion. They want to allow the village elders to become bigger by fifteen percent a year instead of seventeen percent a year. They're mean, petty, and small-minded, and they want to befester everyone with their petty smallness.

"Well, people, I say to you, let's *not* get small! Just say *no* to getting small! And you, the people of Panderwood, *you* are our only hope! You set your examples out for everyone else to follow. You and I, together, we must shine as bright beacons unto the benighted masses! And we can *do* it! With just a few small sacrifices.

"For example, I've got to implore and beseech all of you, that we've *got* to have *no more smoking* in the movies. This is vile and dirty, scamgramified and greedy, this idea of glorifying smoking, and making all the greedy tobacco executives richer, at the expense of the innocent, young, and poor! This must *stop!* And besides, smoking tobacco is just a thing that gauche trailer-dwellers do. It's not a thing that successful Panderwood types should do, because, after all, you *do* serve as examples for so many other metans.

"Other than this vile smoking thing, though, I must say, way to go, Panderwood! You help people to feel *good* about themselves, and this is *good*. We must always think positively, especially about ourselves! So keep right on helping people feel *good* about themselves, by telling them what they want to hear. We can't achieve anything by thinking negative, thinking small. *Think positive!* Say unto them, as they want to be said unto, this is the rule we must follow to go for the gold!

"So Panderwood, I say, keep up the good work! Cut out this smoking thing, keep up the good work, let your lights shine, and we'll do fine!

"Today we start a brave new approach. Small-minded village trailer dwellers begrudge their contributions to us village elders, so we village elders can't be as compassionate as we need to be. The trailer trash value money more than the descamgramification of the poor. Yet we know that when we village elders stand on the common ground with the religious leaders of the community, then we, together, can do a *lot* more for the poor. But the small-minded ones erect roadblocks on our bridge to compassion. They insist on keeping us village elders and the religious community apart. They stand for chaos, badness, and apartness, instead of coming together on our common ground.

"They can have their way for now, but we've found *another* way to be compassionate! So now we invest in the future this *new* way, by having the successful citizens of Panderwood put on a benefit show to raise money for the poor! By this brilliant idea, and by the brilliance of Omnological technology, then, we will *invest in the future,* by *fleecing the scamgrams* from the poor! Ladies and gentlemetans, this is *sheer brilliance!"*

The crowd thundered its approval. Hillary-Bob continued, saying, "So welcome to the Fleece the Poor Benefit Show, all you compassionate, generous patrons of the arts! Through your compassion, we'll invest in the futures of the less fortunate poor, who otherwise wouldn't have access to Omnological technology. Your wise investments will pay off very rapidly, as the newly descamgramified poor will achieve success beyond our wildest dreams!

"Once we've fleeced their scamgrams, removed the roadblocks in the way of their access to success, we'll *all*, currently rich and poor alike, we'll *all* be rich and powerful actors, actresses, producers, directors, and scriptwriters, and we'll *all* stand together on our common ground here in Panderwood, from which we'll amuse, enlighten, and lift up the benighted masses across the entire nation, and then the entire world! Yes, ladies and gentlemetans, that is our dream, that is our goal! To *descamgramify all metans!"*

The crowd roared out its approval once again. Then Hillary-Bob read from here new book for five minutes, picking the very most compassionate passages. Then she closed her book, saying, "So there you have it, ladies and gentlemetans. Words of wisdom from a great book!

"Now before I turn this back to our Master of Ceremonies, Deputy Vice Spirit Guide Dreckula Miscarriage, I must add just one last thought. When I began my remarks, I commented about how I'm standing up here in the light, and you're all sitting in the dark. Would that more of us could stand in the light. But I know that there is hope, and a tremendous amount of it! Because as I look out upon you all, sitting out there in the dark, I see your bright shining lights! I see that *at least half* of you are wearing your Ale Run Hubba-Bubba Sensitivity Awards!"

The crowd cheered. "I see a sea of shining lights!" She cheered them in turn. "A sea of bright lights, lighting up the darkness! Long may they shine! May your supply of batteries never run dry! So I know there is hope! Ale Run bless you all, and good night!" She turned from the podium, walking backstage.

But Deputy Vice Spirit Guide Dreckula Miscarriage rushed up to the podium, grabbed the microphone, and announced, "Hillary-Bob, *please*, you can't go just quite yet! We have a very, very, *very* special treat for you! A *surprise!* A surprise for us all! *Please* come on back up to the podium now, if you would, please, Hillary-Bob, won't you?" he pleaded. Hillary-Bob obliged gracefully, strutting back to the podium.

"And NOW," Dreckula thundered into the microphone, "Let me introduce to you a Supermetan scarcely seen by the public eye, a Metan of Might, the One and Mighty Fleecer of All Scamgrams, *ALE RUN HUBBA-BUBBA HIMSELF!!!*"

The crowd stormed to its feet, bellowing out its utterly astonished delight. Ale Run Himself walked out from backstage with great dignity. An assistant came right behind Him, carrying a golden tray. They walked up to the podium.

Ale Run Himself solemnly grabbed the microphone and declared, "Hillary-Bob, in recognition of your outstanding compassion and sensitivity, and in hopes that The Church of Omnology will continue to get favorable, charitable, tax-exempt church status, and that the village elders will continue to exercise their considerable muscle overseas, in getting similar fair treatment for us in other villages, I hereby bestow upon Thy Highness, the *Ale Run Hubba-Bubba Sensitivity Award*. And with it, an unprecedented—ladies and gentlemetans, let Me reiterate, **totally** unprecedented—*five extra batteries!!!*"

The crowd lost it. The roof almost blew off. And in the middle of all that wild cheering, Ale Run Himself pinned the award on Hillary-Bob. Then He calmly trotted backstage, disappearing from view.

The rest of the evening was quite boring after this peak experience, it seemed. Until the very last, feature act, that is. Dreckula explained to everyone that, after all, Ale Run Himself was quite the busy Supermetan, occupied as He was with the descamgramification of all metans. He couldn't descamgramify us all with His Presence for very long, after all, Dreckula reminded the audience. Let's not get *too* greedy!

So Dreckula served as master of ceremonies, introducing one act after the other. First, there was Malicia Silverspoon, Al Killmoore, and Hammerhold Machtjager in a cute little stageplay called *Catman and Rubbin'*, in which there's this guy, like, he runs a cathouse, and this woman, like, she runs this massage parlor, and they both like like the same girlfriend. And the girlfriend is a customer at like both establishments. Then there's all these like totally hilarious situations, and all these like cute, coy little sexual innuendoes, and Artistic, Meaningful flashes of breasts and sex organs, which Profoundly Portray the Meaning of Existence.

Then there was "Pretty Prostitute", a show primarily featuring Femfatbarbital Sans Rubberts, all about how a pretty young woman can best snag a nifty, neat, rich and powerful, handsome young businessman by selling her body. Except that the rich, handsome young businessman is *way too sensitive* to take advantage of other businessmen, let alone their workers, or, Ale Run Forbid, *sex workers!* Certainly not till *after* the rich, handsome young executive *marries* the gorgeous young sex worker, at least! And, one must add, also *after* allowing said gorgeous young sex worker to buy oodles and boodles of expensive dresses!

The crowd cheered. They loved it all! Especially the young, teen-aged women. Then it was time for the second-to-last, Special Treat. This was after Francestuous had bid Pud adieu, halfway through "Pretty Prostitute", and he had bid her AleRunspeed. So Francestuous was backstage, ready for her bit part.

That second-to-last featured act, the Special Treat, was *"It's Hip to be a Tease"*, specially showcasing the ultratalented superstar, Demerolmore Anne Moore, in a show about how a liberated, shapely young woman liberated herself by bumping and grinding at a gentlemen's club. This was another Deeply Moving Portrayal of the Metan Condition, in which Demerolmore's character fought off the chauvinistic patriarchy. However, she was only able to do this after one and one-half hour during which the *lesser* actresses, including Francestuous, showed *their* breasts, while The Special Treats, *Demerolmore Anne Moore's* breasts, were reserved to be shown only in the last few moments. This served as a suitable climax to this Deeply Moving Show.

Then, finally, it was time for the one, true climax to the entire, overall show, the Fleece the Poor Benefit Show. This was the performance by the Madonna Applewhite band, featuring songs from his new, popular album called *Satanic Ritual Abuser Superstar*. Francestuous took her seat by her One True Love, Pudmuddle B. Fuddle. They held hands, eagerly awaiting the climax of this historic show, the Fleece the Poor Benefit Show. They were there, where history was being made!

The curtains parted, revealing the set. Ghoulish decorations, pentagrams, headstones, and broken crosses came into view. Caked in white, red, and black makeup, wearing metal-studded black leather, Madonna Applewhite took the stage, his band behind him. "Good evening, ladies and gentlemetans," he purred. "Let me take you *down!*" And then, the music flowed. The crowd cheered ecstatically.

Over all the blaring guitars, the jackhammering drums, and the screaming vocals, Pud shouted into Francestuous' ear. "Isn't this kind of, sort of, um, *insensitive*?" he asked her. "I mean, just suppose, now, that his album was called, um, *Anti-Hubba-Bubba Superstar?* Or *Muhammadans Hump Pigs?* How would we feel about *that?* How would *Christians* feel about *this?!*"

"Oh, Pud, come *on,* now!" she protested. *"Give us a break!* It's all just a biting social commentary! Besides, Christians and Moslems are like chauvinistic, empowered majorities, and we Omnologists are a persecuted minority! So *drop* it! Don't compare Applewhites and stooges for strange scamgrams!"

We're still a *minority*? Pud puzzled to himself. That's not what *I've* been hearing lately, what with the explosive growth of Omnology as The One True Way to Be Fleeced, he thought. But he wasn't in any mood to challenge Francestuous on the finer points of theology at the moment.

So he dropped it, listening to the music instead. "Join me down below," he thought he heard. "Come to Satan, mutilate and kill yourselves," his ears seemed to be saying. Pud had a hard time thinking that he was really hearing such thoughts, uttered here in the same covered stadium where tens of thousands of metans had gathered together to display their Sensitivity Awards. So he listened even harder.

"*&$#!§ your mother, kill your father, and you'll be rich and famous," Madonna Applewhite's lyrics said. "I'll buy rights to your books and movies. Come on, *come on!!!* What are you waiting for?! Do it, do it, *do it now!!!* Do it for me, and do it for you! Flaming youth will set the world on fire, *fire, FIRE!*"

The crowd roared, as its members variously threw bottles, overdosed, screamed, threw up, and passed out. Some engaged in violent, public sex acts. Pud got a little nervous, worrying that things might get a bit out of hand. He glanced at Ale Run's security guards, who did nothing. But then Pud noticed some guards were moving in on some young punks who'd lit cigarettes. *Tobacco* cigarettes. Yeah, that's right, Pud thought approvingly. Hustle them out the door. Keep some *order* in this place!

Pud tried his best to listen to the lyrics again. "&%$#@!§ your mother, *kill* your father! Kill your brother, kill *yourself!* Do it, do it, *do it*

now, punch your own ticket, show us how!" he thought he heard. Then he saw a teenager off to the left, in the "mosh pit" twenty yards away, pull out a gun and blow his brains away.

Shocked, he said to Francestuous, shouting in her ear, "Did you see what I think I just saw? A teenager blowing his brains out? Was that for *real?* Or just part of the show?"

"*Real? What's real?*" She replied. "Reality is whatever we think it is. Anyway, whatever, that guy..."

Another teenager blew his brains out, fifteen yards behind them. The next teenager grabbed his gun. Pud wondered whether maybe this was a new version of *the wave.* How soon till *the new wave* reached him and Francestuous? Still, the guards made no moves. Francestuous shouted into his ear, shouting above the din of gunfire, "They're just making a satirical statement about our insensitive society. Don't worry, be happy! Ale Run wants us to be *happy!* So tell your worry scamgrams to *go away!*"

But then a middle-aged man right in front of Pud stood up and blew *his* brains out. Said brains splattered all over Pud's face. Simultaneously, reality struck him in his face as well. But Madonna Applewhite and his band played on. Pud stood up on the rear of his chair, screaming, shouting, *bellowing* at the top of his lungs, "**Metans, wake up!!!** Can't you see, this is, this is **insensitive,** folks! This thing, it's **inappropriate,** people!!! People, people, *listen* to me now! This thing, um, it's, it's **EVIL**, people, it's downright ***EVIL!!!*** Can't you **see?!** *WE MUST STOP THIS NOW!!!*"

Francestuous stared at Pud in horror. "Sit down and ***shut up!***" She hissed hotly. "If you don't have anything positive to say, then just *shut up!* Don't be so *judgmental!* By Ale Run, Pud, I swear, you're falling victim to the scamgrams of, of not regarding these people's *feelings* as being *valid*, of denying the validity of their artistic statements! You'd better like just..."

Even though Francestuous shouted her condemnation of Pud's judgmentalism out to him, her words were drowned out. More gunshots rang out, and the band played on. Pud bellowed yet more loudly, *"THIS IS EVIL, PEOPLE, EVIL!! EVIL, E-V-I-L!!!*

E-V-I-L SPELLS EVIL!!! LISTEN TO ME NOW!!! But now others took up Francestuous's hue and cry, telling Pud to shut up.

"*Pipe down, you goody two-shoes!*" one yelled. "*Don't ruin our fun, you prude!*" another screamed. "*If you don't like it then just go someplace else with your hypocritical judgmentalism,*" yet another chimed in. Then the security guards started moving in on Pud.

Pud caught on real fast. He ducked and ran. He ran across the seat backs. He ran between the violent orgies and the dead and dying bodies. Avoiding guards, puddles of blood, and flying bottles, he dashed for the doors. As if in a slow-motion dream, he was at the doors. Then through them. Then the parking lot, and the open roads. Still he ran and ran.

Exhausted, he dropped down to the ground, breathing furiously. Then something told him to hide. He crawled behind the roadside bushes, just barely in time to avoid two of Ale Run's security guards as they zipped by on motorcycles. What was *that* about, he wondered. Are they after *me?* His heart hammered out a drumbeat of fear.

"*Yes, they are,*" came the peculiar, silent reply. "*But do not worry, for I am with you.*" The voice filled him with a calmer, relaxed, peaceful but sharply alert spirit.

"Who are *you?!*" Pud demanded in similar silence. "Are You my Inner Ale Run?"

"*You can call Me your Inner Ale Run if you want to,*" came the quite agreeable reply.

"So now I'm on the run from Ale Run's guards, and the Inner Ale Run is on my side," Pud replied in amazement. "What's going *on* here? Doesn't Ale Run command the guards? Doesn't Ale Run know that I obey Him? Are these guards not obeying the Will of Ale Run?"

"*They are.*"

"Then how can this *be?* Why would His guards chase one like *me?* One who admires and obeys only Him? Why am I, why am I," and Pud's inner voice dropped in decibels, realizing the enormity of his predicament, "Why am I on the run from Ale Run?" he inquired in a whisper.

"*Because you follow Me,*" the voice came.

"But You are the Inner Ale Run?"

"*You can call Me your Inner Ale Run if you want to,*" the voice repeated.

"What do You call Yourself?"

"*It is a Name I cannot say to you now,*" the voice replied. "*It is a Name you cannot know fully till the day you die. And you and I, we both do not wish for this day to come before it must.*"

"Well, OK, then. So you're my Inner Ale Run, then, I guess. For now. So tell me, then, what has happened, here? Doesn't Ale Run know *everything?* Doesn't He know that I love, admire, and obey His Every Word? Or have His immediate followers deceived Him about me?" Pud sank pretty low, thinking about this possibility. Then he brightened up, broadcasting his newest, brightest hope. "Inner Ale Run, why don't *You* go off and explain to Ale Run that I love and obey only Him? *Surely* He'd listen to *You!*"

"*No,*" the voice answered softly, sadly. "*Ale Run has closed his heart to Me. When I try to talk to him, he says to Me, 'I don't have to listen to you, because there is no controlling legal authority over Me!' So Ale Run has spurned his Inner Ale Run,*" the sad, loving voice concluded. "*Probably permanently.*"

But then the voice brightened, saying, "*But you, Pud, you are wrong! You* do not *love and obey* him*! You love and obey* Me*! You have just now realized this. And you have revealed it to Ale Run and his followers. That's why they hunt you like an animal.*"

"*Surely* they know I mean Ale Run no harm!" More motorcycles zipped by, and Pud crouched lower behind the bushes. Then cars full of guards spilled into view. Some of them slowed down.

"*Quick! Into the drainage pipe!*" suggested the voice. Pud didn't hesitate. Into that pipe, into the mud he crawled. He heard guards on foot, talking and searching, shining their lights here and there, waving their V-Meters there and here. He waited in frozen, fearful silence.

"*Quick! Now out, silently, and dive way down low in those bushes!*" came the thoughts. Again, Pud obeyed. He scratched his face and ate some dirt, but he obeyed with great enthusiasm. The guards shined their shining lights of darkness into the bright darkness where a different kind of light had just shone on Pud. And then they departed, searching elsewhere.

"Who are You, Inner Ale Run? How and why do You oppose the

Will of Ale Run Himself? How can this be?"

"*Ale Run does not listen to his Inner Ale Run, as you would say. I impose My Will on no one. I am Love, and love of Love. Love of Life. A force of Life. That which links and Loves all Life. Ale Run has decided to serve darkness. He has decided to whisper to the horde, to the beast in humans, and to tell them whatever they want to hear. Whatever they think pleases them the most, for immediate, false pleasures. I oppose him because of who I am. Because I must. Because I Love.*"

"And why do You speak to me now this way? Is this normal? Or am I insane?"

"*You may be insane by the standards of much of your world, but you're now sane. You've just now attained a measure of sanity. No, this isn't 'normal'. But the Horde Whisperer has problematized reality, and so normality is temporarily suspended. He has violated the norms, and so, too, do I now violate the norms. It's happened before. In different ways, yes, but it has happened before. And it might happen again.*"

"The Horde Whisperer? Who is he?"

"*Some call him the inappropriate one, or the insensitive one. But he is the master of lies, the hateful and evil one. That is his real name.*"

"And what does he want?"

"*Death and destruction for all Life. Nothing less.*"

"And what do You want? Why are You here?"

"*I want Life and Love. I am here to ask you to work with Me, to do My Will. I do not command, I ask. I want for you to work with Me, to bring the servants of the Horde Whisperer to the light. If we cannot bring the Horde Whisperer himself to the light,*" the voice said with great sadness, "*Then we must at least stand tall against him, and give him a firm 'NO!' No, he may not have his way with humanity! We must oppose him! But it is up to you. You may chose to help Me, or you may say no to me. I will still Love you either way.*"

"And if I say no? What happens if I say no?"

"*Then I must ask someone else. But you are the one I choose first. And before you ask, I must ask that you do not ask. What if they all say no? I am too saddened by the thought of trying to answer that. So please do not ask.*"

"Why do You ask me first? What's so special about little old me?"

"*You are the one who they've spoken of. You carry a thing that we might call 'spiritual DNA'. As a human, a plant, or an animal carries DNA that lies dormant, sometimes for years, seemingly signifying and expressing nothing, yet that later flowers into something new, different, grand, and wonderful, so, too, do humans carry spiritual DNA, so to speak. When their time comes, their full power is revealed. You have revealed your power. The power to speak out, and to oppose evil. Now they know who you are. When you did what you did, their V-Meters went clear off scale! You are the Anti-Hubba-Bubba!*"

Shock filled Pud's heart. But then his heart grew by three sizes, and a firm and gritty resolve coursed through his veins. He looked around. Seeing no guards, he stood up tall, and announced, this time in fiercely audible but quiet tones, "Yes, my Inner Ale Run, I will do Your Will!"

"*My gratitude to you. Some tell lies about Me. Not all lies about Me are equally bad, and this is by no means the worst lie. But they say that I can see the future. I cannot, but in degrees of probability. Else free will would be meaningless, and free will is My most important Law. So I can tell you only probabalistically, but you have just now chosen to help Me save humanity from the Horde Whisperer! To continue what was begun two thousand years ago.* **We will not be defeated!**

"*I must go now. I won't talk to you this way but rarely, for I don't wish for anyone to be My puppet. I only speak this way in very special circumstances. If you wish to do My Will, know then that you can do it only when it is also Your Will. So I will usually do naught but flicker on the edges of your consciousness. It is up to* **you** *to figure out what My Will is. But remember, your Inner Ale Run will be with you!*" Then the voice was gone. Pud looked around in fear, fearing for his physical safety as well as for his sanity. But that fear flickered for only a moment, because a new awareness now flickered across the edges of his consciousness. And its light shone far brighter than his fear!

Enough of that for now, Pud told himself. I'm a hunted animal! Let's lay down low here, and figure out what's going on.

Ale Run's troops couldn't keep a lid on it forever. After a while, the show-goers had had enough, and wanted to leave, to go back home to recover. So they all spilled out of that covered stadium—those who were still capable of spilling out, at least; those who weren't comatose, or whose blood had been spilled—they all staggered out to the parking lot. Some dragged their comatose friends; a few carried bodies. Many got into their cars and drove off.

Then they spilled into Pud's view. A trickle of cars turned into a traffic jam and quite a few accidents. Ale Run's guards, sensing the possibility of a public relations fiasco, were trying to persuade all the impaired drivers to wait for busses and taxis to take them home, while they made last-minute emergency arrangements to get said busses and taxis (as well as ambulances) to the stadium, then past all the car wrecks.

So Pud waited for the pandemonium out in front of him to build up. Then he left the bushes where he'd been hiding. He strolled calmly into the hubbub. Think quick, now, he told himself. There's still plenty of guards around. They might still be looking for me. Sure, I could probably figure out some way, if I got lucky, to hop into the back of a pickup truck loaded with loaded and comatose show-goers, and not be noticed, but it's quite the risk to take. Call me to the guards' attention, and *who knows* what will happen! Besides, suppose they're checking for me at the gate, as everyone leaves! Now *there's* a sobering thought!

Following a hunch, Pud scrunched himself down a bit, and walked through the densest crowds he could find, back towards the stadium. Through crowds of people, some naked and some crawling, he walked. He'd drop down on all fours and moan, blending into crowd, whenever a guard came too close. Back into the stadium he went. Sure enough, clothes were strewn about the floor. Bloody clothes, ripped clothes, clothes on a few corpses here and there, still, but the guards were cleaning those up and carting them away.

"We're in a world of hurts if any unfleeced media types snuck in here with a hidden camera," he heard one guard say to another. "We'll have to fleece any such media types good and hard, if we catch them. Keep your eyes open for suspicious characters wondering about."

That sobered Pud up yet some more. I'm getting sober enough by now to cancel out the lack of sobriety of a few of my fallen buddies here by now, he told himself, dropping down on all fours and moaning a bit, trying to blend in with my surroundings. A sizable portion of the crowd still milled about, many on all fours, just like Pud.

Pud crawled about, gathering up some clothes and stuffing them under his shirt, so as not to draw attention. He concentrated on women's clothes without too much blood, vomit, or gashes. Here and there, he even found purses and wallets, some with money. He felt bad about it, but as a staff member of Omnology, he was carrying a bare minimum of cash. All the rest had gone to The Glory of Ale Run. If he was going to make the big escape, he'd need some cash.

So he gathered some money. He rationalized it to himself, telling himself that if people had so little sense as to go to shows like this, totally lose everything, including their clothes, wallets, self-control, and minds, well, then, they obviously had more money than good sense. He was just helping them reach equilibrium. At least he was leaving them all their credit cards, driver's licenses, worker's permits, carbon dioxide emitter's permits, IDs, and such, which was more than one could say of the *real* criminals.

He rooted among the bottles, the syringes, the used condoms, the smashed Sensitivity Awards, and all other forms of litter, looking for more clothes. Oh, bonanza, he said to himself as he snatched up a long-haired wig. Look, under all that barf and dirt, it's a *blonde!* I'm a gonna be a *blonde!* Blondes have *all* the fun!

Pud snuck off into a dark corner, where he rearranged himself just enough to make it into the women's bathroom without drawing too much attention. It wasn't so hard to do. He just crawled past and over the moaning bodies in the bathroom, found himself a stall, hauled a protesting, groaning body out, and secluded himself for just a few minutes. He cleaned and flushed the toilet, then he washed the wig and some of the clothes in it.

Then he was a she. She came out, muttering to herself, "Hey, Babe, take a walk on the *wild* side." Now if only I can escape, she said to herself. I've *got* to make it clear out of this entire Intergalactic Headquarters before I can feel even a tiny bit safe! For that matter, I'd better boogie on out of greater Los Diablos—because I'm sure they'll be looking for me!

Now for a commercial message. See Chapter 17 endnotes on Role-Playing and "Satirical Social Commentary" at the end of this book... (Page 237, that is).

Chapter 18

The Anti-Hubba-Bubba Flees From the Wrath of Ale Run

"The greatest dangers to liberty lurk in insidious encroachment by men of zeal, well-meaning but without understanding."
Louis D. Brandeis (1856-1941)

She walked out of the restroom, out of the stadium, out of the compound, and hopefully out of Ale Run's grasp. Sure, it was a long walk, but she made it. She made it the front gates while there were large crowds of those still able to walk, and not patient enough to wait for taxis and busses, walking through under the prying eyes of the guards. She walked some more. And walked and walked and walked.

As the lights of dawn rose, she found a suitably lonely bridge. She hid her money under a rock beneath some scattered rubble. Then she became a he again, thinking he'd be maybe just a tiny bit less likely to get raped or killed while he slept, if he was a he. He slept under the bridge till late morning.

When he got up, he decided that this business of sleeping under bridges just wasn't quite going to cut it. It was too uncomfortable, too dangerous. He hadn't slept soundly at all, worrying about some lawless drifter coming by and snuffing his lights during the middle of the night. He'd have to go back to being a respectable, regular-job-holding kind of a guy, he decided. But here, in Panderwood? he asked himself. Or am I still in Panderwood? Well, in any case, I'm still in Los Diablos, that's for sure. And anywhere I go in greater Los Diablos, Ale Run's minions will be sure to find me. They know, now, that I am the Anti-Hubba-Bubba. So said the Ale Run Within.

Then Pud shuddered as he remembered the enormity of what had happened last night. Had it all been a dream? No! Certainly not! He was a hunted man! He didn't know what the future held, nor even what his plans were. He had no plans. All he knew was that he had to get far, far away from Los Diablos. If he had to search high and low throughout the entire U.S., or even the entire world, then Ale Run would be far less likely to find, thwart, and punish the Anti-Hubba-Bubba.

So Pud wandered on over to a bus stop. But when he got closer, he saw a man holding an object. It was disguised, but it sure looked like a V-Meter to Pud. The man was surreptitiously scanning the small crowd! Could they detect him with that thing? After all, reality had become problematized, his Inner Ale Run had told him. *Real magic* apparently stalked the globe, in the hands of Ale Run and his minions. No one could say, any more, what was possible, and what wasn't.

Pud turned and left. Maybe he could stand by the highway somewhere, and hitch a ride out of town. If Ale Run's troops weren't specifically sweeping all of Los Diablos for suspicious-looking hitchhikers, that is, he worried. Oh, Inner Ale Run, stand by me in my time of troubles, Pud pleaded.

Okay, so *now* what, Pud asked himself. I've *got* to find a way to get out of Los Diablos! He wandered off, and walked for a while. He spent some of his precious cash at McBurglar King, spending ten dollars for a pitifully small portion of grease fries and lardburgers. Not that the grease fries and lardburgers were necessarily that *bad;* he was *hungry!* It's just that there wasn't *enough* of that totally awful, rotten, grease-soaked food! Especially not for $10.11. He debated spending more of his precious cash for some more grease, but the respectable people about the McBurglar King were looking at him awfully funny. He didn't want to risk approaching the sales counter yet once again, for fear that someone would call the police. So he left.

Well, he asked himself, if I look *that* bad that people *fear* me, then how am I going hitch a ride, get a job, or what have you? Maybe I'd better splurge tonight, get a hotel room, and clean myself up good.

So Pud set out to find himself a quasi-respectable hotel room late that afternoon. He strolled into the Four Fleabites, thinking, well, it isn't the classiest joint in the whole world, but then neither is my stash of cash. At least this isn't the total bottom of the food chain, either.

As Pud's luck would have it, he may not have regarded the Four Fleabites as the bottom of the food chain, but the lady behind the counter certainly regarded *him* as such! She eyed him suspiciously. "Can I please see some ID, there, Sir?" were the first words out of her mouth.

Flustered, Pud remembered that they were safekeeping all his credentials back at his former house of spiritual self-detention, one Intergalactic Headquarters of The Church of Omnology. "Um, no, Ma'am, I don't have any ID with me," he replied. He fished out a wad of bills. "But I'd be happy to leave you a security deposit if you'd like."

"Sorry, Sir, that's not our policy. We have to see some ID."

"My licenses and cards and all were *stolen* from me!" he protested. "I need to get cleaned up and get a good night's sleep, so I can find my way home tomorrow," he semi-lied. "What am I supposed to do?"

She smirked at him. He could almost hear her thoughts, even without a V-Meter! "Sure, Pal. They stole your wallet, and left you wads of cash. *Sure!*" But that's not what she said. What she said was, "Well, *Sir*, for starters, you could give me your Social Security number and your home address, so I can check them out," she said.

Pud was just about ready to give her his Social Security number and his old address, from his old days as a doctor/engineer/CEO/speculator/entrepreneur/famous volunteer, etc., but then he got to thinking, well, just how many computer networks will soon contain these little tidbits of data, anyway? And how many Omnologists or Omnologist computers will be scanning such data for the whereabouts of a certain renegade Anti-Hubba-Bubba?

Then he noticed the video camera behind the lady, keeping an electronic eye him. "I've got a bit of amnesia. Can't remember those things too well. Well, guess I'll be sleeping under the bridge tonight again," he ventured. "Could I maybe sleep on the patio at *your* house?"

She reached for something hidden behind and below the counter, so he dashed for the door. "Bye!" he called out. "Thanks for all your help!" He jogged on down the street a little while, cut through a few alleys, then slowed to a more reasonable pace. Oh, well, he thought. So much for that!

But then he got to thinking, you know, it really *is* important that I get cleaned up, and get a good night's sleep. How am I going to get anyone to help me, get a ride out of Los Diablos, or *anything,* if I look like a person with a *very* alternative lifestyle? I've *got* to find a hotel! It's just that I need to set my sights lower. I need to find a place that's a little less persnickety about IDs and such.

So he sauntered on into the seedier side of town, where he found the Hotel No-Tell. Daily, hourly, and by-the-minute rates were offered. They took his money and his name ("Fred Neatshee"), and sent him to his room. It smelled of beer, urine, cigarettes, vomit, roaches, and who knows what all else, but it had a roof, a bed, running water, and *soap!* Pud promptly got to work. He washed himself and his clothes, then sent himself to bed without any supper. But he slept quite soundly.

In the morning, as he was leaving, he noticed a newspaper display. So he thought to himself, well, I sure wonder how the media is treating what happened here just two nights ago? So he spent three more quarters of his precious cash, then found a quiet spot. He sat on an old outdoor bench and read.

"Hillary-Bob Wins Award," the headline proclaimed. "5-Battery Sensitivity Award Unprecedented, Says Spiritual Leader," the subtitle added. Pud started reading the article, wondering if there was any hue and cry at all about what had happened towards the end of the Fleece the Poor Benefit Show.

Pud rapidly read through the article, scanning for any sense of outrage. "Ale Run Hubba-Bubba, in a rare personal appearance, personally congratulated Hillary-Bob on her outstanding sensitivity and service to society, and awarded her the Ale Run Hubba-Bubba Sensitivity Award with 5 Extra Batteries," he read. Then he read about all the fabulous artists' shows, culminating with "Madonna Applewhite's band kept the audience spellbound with its songs of powerfully biting, clever social satire. Many of their numbers came from their latest chart-topping album, called *Satanic Ritual Abuser Superstar*. Their sophisticated audience greeted their performance enthusiastically, although some members of the religious right have denounced their controversial shows."

And that was it for any mention of controversy! No mention of the "heathen left" accompanied the paper's comment about the "religious right". Nor were suicides, car wrecks, naked and passed-out party-goers, and generally debauched behavior mentioned. Pud ditched his paper in a nearby rotten-smelling and overflowing dumpster and walked on, thinking, well, geezum, I guess the Media and Government Institute for the Fleecing of All Metans must've been doing a bang-up job lately.

I *must* get out of Los Diablos, he reminded himself. So he worked his way over to the nearest freeway. He stood fifty yards back from the feeder road, watching a fellow homeless person trying to hitch a ride. Okay, he told himself, I know this is risky, going out there and joining him, but it's also risky for me to stay here. I *must* go! I must go out there on that feeder road *right now*, and stick my thumb out, and hitch a ride. I just *must*. I *must*, I *must*, I *must*. But he couldn't persuade himself. He worried about Omnologists patrolling the highways for a certain special hitchhiker. His worries were reinforced when a peculiar thought flickered across the edges of his awareness, telling him "beware".

He was just about to turn away, when he noticed a van stopping for the hitchhiker. He watched as the hitchhiker loaded his meager belongings into the van. Bravely but seemingly casually, Pud strolled forward for a better look. As the van drove off, he recognized the bumper sticker. It was one that was gaining popularity these days. "Smile! Ale Run ©s *You!*", it said. Pud didn't need to read it; a glance was sufficient for him to recognize that particular image. So my nagging thoughts are absolutely correct, he told himself. I *must* learn to listen to them better!

What to do, what to do, he puzzled, strolling away. I can't seem to make it out of Los Diablos, at least for now. It's like I've been welcomed to the Hotel California. You can check out any time you like, but you can never leave. So maybe I'd better settle in, at least for now. Get respectable again. Or at least, get just respectable enough to buy my way outta this place. Maybe buy myself an old beater-mobile. *Then* I can leave!

Okay, so then the next question becomes, just how *does* one get back on the road to becoming respectable, anyway? Well, obviously, I guess I'd better sashay on down to the local government-sponsored self-improvement center, and get self-improved, he concluded.

So he headed off and found the Greater Los Diablos Welfare-to-Work Self-Improvement Agency, where he went through the metal detectors, then waited in line for two hours. When he got to the head of the line, the man asked him for his papers. "Don't got no papers. Got robbed," Pud informed the man.

"Well, then, what's your Social Security number, mister, um... Well, Sir, what's you *name,* for starters, anyway?"

"Fred. Fred Neatshee."

"All right, then, Mr. Neatshee, what's your Social Security number?"

"Shoshial Sheckyouryity number? Ah seems ta recall havin' one o' them thar things a while back, but ya know, a fella fergets afta a while. A fella fergets. But ah'm tellin' ya son, ah'm a hard workin' man. Y'all fix me up some way, find mah Shoshial Sheckyouryity number or whatever, or make me up a new one, whatever it takes, an' ah'll be givin' ya an honest day's work for an honest day's pay. Ah ken dig yer ditches, sweep yer streets, do yer general handyman-type stuff, whatever it takes."

"Well, Mr. Neatshee, sorry to say, that's not really quite what we're looking for. The unions, they're unhappy enough as is, with what we're doing, without us getting into *that*. Now if you could maybe learn self-esteem counseling, or at least gang and drug awareness group therapy peer facilitating, or gang community issues resolution negotiation, then maybe we could get places faster. Mr. Neatshee, have you ever been involved with gangs or illegal drugs?"

"No, Sir, ah sure hasn't."

"Oh. Well, in *that* case, I guess we're barking up the wrong tree, trying to get you lined up for a *good* job, in one of these categories where we're in greatest need. Now I'm not quite sure *what* we can do for you, Mr. Neatshee. Maybe the best we can do, is to put you in training. In any case, though, I think we're putting the cart before the horse. First off, Mr. Neatshee, is, we've *got* to get your papers squared away. We've got to find your Social Security number, first of all. Can't get a work permit without a Social Security number. So could you fill out these papers for me?

"Don't worry, we'll keep your place in line open here. Now just step aside right here, fill these papers out, and when you're done, just step right back in at the head of the line here. Then I'll look your papers over, and see if we've got enough information so that we can look up your Social Security number for you. If not, we'll have to send your papers and other data in to the Social Security Administration and wait for a reply, which will take a while. Thank you, Mr. Neatshee. Next?"

Pud stepped aside and shuffled through the papers. Oh, my, my, what have we here, he asked himself, noticing one of the entries, where he was expected to sign, giving his permission to have his retina scanned, in order to get a new Social Security number, if he had none, or none could be found. *And* if he was willing to swear he was a U.S. citizen, and wasn't trying to ditch an old name, with its debts and obligations. Under heavy penalties for fibbing.

Seems to me, I had to have my retina scanned before I could volunteer for one of those high-profile volunteer deals, way back when. Can't risk having devious criminals volunteering to help The Children and suchlike things. What if they cross-link Mr. Fred Neatshee to Dr. Pudmuddle B. Fuddle? Via my retina? I'd be in a world of hurts! Even worse than if I just gave them my Social Security number right now! And, of course, *that's* out of the question. No telling *how* many Omnologists are in government by now, and are regularly checking the computers for where I'm at!

No, that won't do. Now if I just dash right out of here, I might attract suspicion, he thought, glancing obliquely at the guards. Better to get back in line here, and humbly confess that I can't read or write, and then take it from there. Ask for help filling all these forms out, act real stupid, stall a lot, whatever I can come up with. Good thing I've had the smarts to act stupid already so far! Maybe feign physical or mental troubles, somehow make such a pain out of myself, that they'll be glad to let me back out onto the streets.

So Pud waited for five more minutes, there at the head of the line again, while Mr. Social Worker helped his fellow citizen. Then it was his turn again. "Um, Sir, I'm sorry," he said. "Ah haff ta admit, ah can't read or write. Do ya think maybe ya could, like, give me a hand with these forms?"

"Oh, Mr. Neatshee, I *sure* wish I could! Or, at the *very* least, I wish you would've *told* me that right away! You see, Mr. Neatshee, we *can* help you! But that's not my department! Over there, see that line over there, that's where literacy challenged and intellectually different people can go to get help filling forms out! Lots of luck, Mr. Neatshee! Next!"

Pud waddled over towards the end of the other, even longer line. But he slipped over to the men's room instead. Then after that, he slipped out the front door. No one gave him any trouble. He felt quite lucky, making his escape so easily. He walked on down the street, singing doo-wah-ditty dumm-ditty do-wah.

Then he spotted a small, racially mixed group of homeless men. They looked mean and tough. But, what the hey, Pud said to himself, I need help. Nobody else will help me; maybe I can at least get some good advice from these guys. "Hey, doods," he greeted them as he walked up. "Whazzappanin?"

They just looked at him in puzzled, momentary silence. Then one, a black guy, replied, "Nuthin. Absolutely nuthin. Whazzappanin with you, bro?"

"Oh, ah just tried ta go off and get myself self-improved. Bunch a bureau-rats! They just give me the run-around." A few guys snickered. "Anyway, ah need some money. Or a ride out of Los Diablos. Ah was hopin' ta do it without runnin' afoul a the law. Not *too* afoul a the law, fer sure! So y'all, could y'all like tell me whereabouts ah might be able ta make a few bucks on the side, workin' an honest job? Without fillin' out too many papers an' such?"

They stared at him in silence for another few seconds, exchanging glances. The black guy finally spoke up again, after seemingly deciding to take pity on the poor fool stranger. "Well, ya know, bro, ya could always stand by the road. 'Will work fo' food', that sorta thang. But seems ta me that's not what yo be lookin' fo'. Now a few years back, there yusta be this Salvation Army place on down the road a ways here, where a guy could work, an' they'd give ya a few bucks. Sort an' wash their donated clothes, put 'em on the racks, they'd be givin' ya some money.

"Ah'm not too sho if they be in bidness still, or not. If they's still in bidness, it ain't no big thing no mo', that's fo' sho! The man come by, says ta them, yo's gotta be scannin' them's eyeballs, them's retinas o' some such, an' gettin' 'em work permits, payin' 'em minimum wage, Social Security, workman's comp, health benefits, an' on an' on. An' be makin' sure ya dock their pay fo' child support. Support the ol' lady's crack habit, an' so on. So they can't be payin' us no mo' money. Puts 'em outta bidness. We's gotta be stickin' ta sellin' crack an' stuff if we wants ta be makin' money."

"Ah can't be sellin' no crack!" Pud interjected. "Ah's *gotta* stay clear o' the *man!*"

"Ya got *that* right, Bud!" A grimy white chimed in. "Besides, turf's all split up around here. Butt in, get yersef kilt real quick-like! Now, tell ya what, Bud. Ya wanna steer clear o' the man an' all his papers? Make a few bucks without no papers? That's the scoop, right,

Pal?" Grimy white guy glared at Pud, glanced around, then took out a whiskey bottle for a snort. Then he stared back at Pud.

"Yup, that about sums it up," Pud admitted.

"I'll tell ya where ya can work to yer heart's content. Work all day an' all night, an' the man'll never, ever, never ever even *think* o' comin' around an' checkin' yer papers an' work conditions an' pay an' stuff."

"Yeah? Who? Where they at?"

"Head on down thata way. Place is called the Intergalactic Headquarters of The Church of Omnology!" The whole little gang roared. Pud just stood there, flushed with anger.

But, you know, he's right, Pud thought. Try to treat a person with a bit of dignity, let him keep his beat-up old apartment and a bit of his independence while you try to lift him up with a starting-out job—even if it's largely a charity job, you're losing money on the deal, but you're trying to help the poor guy out, paying him a few bucks to sweep the charity shelter floor or whatever—the EPA, OSHA, EEOC, IRS, National Socialist Labor Police, and everyone and their mother will be all over you!

If, on the other hand, you brainwash the poor slob, get him to join your cult, and he lives under your thumb for 24 hours a day, in your commune, then you can have him sell flowers on the street corner, or pass out flyers at the airport, for a can of cat food per day. And the government won't *touch* you. Because that's *religious* freedom, which is, of course, far, far more sacred than, say, plain old, ordinary, simple *freedom*. Heck, they'll even give you a *tax exemption!*

And needless to say, religious freedom is also, of course, *light-years* above and beyond that most crass and greedy concept, so oxymoronically called *economic* freedom! Economics is the dismal science of valuing things more than people, after all. So turn control over all crass material affairs to our betters, and we'll all live in perfection and grace. And our betters come in two flavors: The State, and the Church. You *must* yield up your freedom, and it must be to the one or to the other! Yield it up to neither one, but keep it in reserve in order to directly serve your Inner Ale Run as you see fit—well, you just *try* that, Bud, and yo' in a heap o' trouble, Boy!

These thoughts flickered semi-coherently through Pud's brain in a matter of seconds. Out loud, he said, "Ya know, Bud, I think ya got a point, there. Ya got a point. Give over yer whole life ta Ale Run, an' the man leaves ya alone. Even if they don't pay ya a nickel a day. Try an' get somebody who's not in a cult ta pay ya a few bucks on the side fer an honest day's work, and they's all over yer case!

"Ya gotta fall in with the one plantation or the other. The gummint don't bust the cult leaders, 'cause that'd be like a lawyer suin' a shark! Can't do it. Professional courtesy, ya know. Like ol' President Bush, he didn't bomb the boss-men in their buildings in Iraq during the day. No Sir! He bombed 'em at *night*, to kill the *cleaning ladies!* The slave owners don't pick on each other, they pick on the slaves. So *of course* the only place I can get an off-the-books job is with the Church of Omnology!"

"Ooooh-wee! Listen to him talk!" One of the homeless men hooted while the others guffawed. "*Listen* to him! Man, you no regular ol' bum like us! You some sort o' perfesser or sumptin, ain'tcha? Tellin' us about history! You an egghead on the run?"

Oops, I guess I musta slipped outta character a bit thar, Pud told himself. Ah's gots ta even be *thinkin'* like who ah'm supposed ta be, if ah'm gonna pull this off. Thing is, the cat's out of the bag, here. I think. These guys are sharper than they look! Can I lie to them! Or will that just piss 'em off?

"I suppose I could 'fess up to that," he admitted. "I hope y'all won't hold it against me."

"Say no mo, perfessor, say no mo," the black guy spoke up. "We runs inta folks like yo now an' then. 'Specially lately. Now tell yo what. Ya seems ta be a nice fella; ah'll give yo a hand, bro! Ya wanna git outta Los Diablos, we'll getcha outta Los Diablos. Ya take a ride on a freight train, if we be showin' ya how?"

"I'm game. Let's go!" So the small group of homeless men split up. Two of them, Mr. B. (the black guy) and another, vaguely Hispanic-looking character known as Desert Rat, agreed to take the Professor (as Pud was now known—they'd never even asked him his name!) and show him how to hop onto a freight train. Desert Rat, as a matter of fact, was wanting to travel east, anyway, so he and Professor Pud would ride together, while Mr. B. would turn back, and stay in Los Diablos, which he considered home.

The three of them ambled off in the general direction of the train yard. Pud was getting pretty hungry, but he wasn't about to speak up, and risk jeopardizing his good deal, here, what with them showing him the way, and all. Fortunately, Mr. B. was hungry, too. "Here, let's go get us some chow, over here," he said as they were just about to pass an intersection. "See that old man over there? He be a good dude, a preacher-man. He passes out food from his church to the homeless."

"He can *do* that? Is this place *zoned* for that?" Pud asked incredulously. He looked around. They were in a fairly upscale neighborhood. Not upscale enough to have security fences around all the houses and apartments, sure. Still, it was fairly nice. You'd think that all the people in a neighborhood like this would make sure that all the homeless feeding stations, shelters, and such-like things would all get located elsewhere, he thought. "Aren't there like food purity and sanitation laws and such? Do the cops just turn a blind eye, or does he spend half of his donations to bribe them?"

"No, no, man! No way, bro! Here, you'll see," Mr. B. exclaimed. They took the detour from their planned route, veering over to see the preacher-man. When they got close to him, Mr. B. called out, saying, "Good day to yo, bro! How's things with yo an' God an' the angels an' all?"

"Not too shabby, son, not too shabby at all. And you?" Preacher-man replied.

"Not too shabby ourselves, ol' man," Mr. B. spoke for the three of them. "You say 'hi' to God for us sinners, now, okay? Next time yo sees Him in yo church?"

The old man just grinned and nodded. "Preacher-man, ah'd like fo' yo to meet mah friends. Preacher-man, this here's Desert Rat and Perfessor. Desert Rat, Perfessor, meet Preacher-man."

Pud just stood there, puzzling over this "God" thing that Mr. B. was mentioning, vaguely recalling that way back when, before he'd become an Omnologist (my, my, it all seemed so long ago!), "God" had meant, um, ah, I guess, your Inner Ale Run, or something like that, to the scamgramified metans of the world. He snapped out of it when it was his turn to shake Preacher-man's hand. They stood there making small talk with Preacher-man, with Mr. B. doing most of the talking.

"You guys hungry by any chance?" Preacher-man asked after a while. They all nodded. "Well", he continued, "I sure don't mean to insult you or anything. I'd like to invite you over for a meal at my church, but we're not quite up to the right standards, and all. And my house isn't zoned right, so that I could ask y'all to gather there. So I hate to say it, but dumpster diving might be the best way to go. Now you see that apartment block right over there? God tells me to tell you, the dumpster out behind it might be a really good place for y'all to look into. I'd better go now. But you guys take care, and think about God and living a life of dignity, now and then. All of us, no matter what our station in life, all of us can live a life of dignity. It's a gift from God. God bless you!"

With that, the old preacher-man slowly walked off. He got into a tiny little car down the street, and turned it around. He waved as he passed Pud and his friends. Pud glimpsed quite a few grocery bags in the rear of that car as it sped by. What the hey, he asked himself.

"Come on," Mr. B. urged. "Over to that apartment block!"

"We're going *dumpster diving?*" Pud asked disdainfully.

"It'll be all right," Mr. B. assured him. "Let's go!" Ahead of them, they saw Preacher-man's car turn into the apartment's parking lot. And by the time that they got half of the way there, they saw him leaving again.

And when they checked the dumpster, they found, right on top, a grocery bag full of wrapped sandwiches! They grabbed it and continued on their way. Pud finally figured it out. Preacher-man wasn't littering, or engaging in unauthorized feeding of the homeless, or distributing unsafe foods. He was just disposing of his unwanted food in a responsible manner, risking little but the wrath of the apartment owner who was paying for the dumpster! What a deal!

On down the road a few blocks, they sat on a bench and scarfed down two sandwiches each. Even so, they had a few left. They walked on down the road, contented.

Reaching their destination with plenty of daylight left, they decided to kill some time. "Can't be hoppin' over the fence in broad daylight," Mr. B. explained about the rail yard's security. "We'll sneak in there later."

They wandered into a clump of trees and bushes. There, hidden away, they napped, chatted, and just sat around. So Pud got a chance to sit and think. What was his Mission from his Inner Ale Run, anyway? What was he supposed to be doing, right now? Was he on track, or not? Pud wasn't sure. Take it day by day, he told himself. Heck, I've no real choice here, anyway! What can I do, in reality, especially in *my* situation, *besides* take it day by day, anyway?

Well, first things first. First, get out of Los Diablos, so that the Omnologists will have a much harder time finding me. And then... then what? Just live my life, till my Inner Ale Run tells me what to do? Sounds good, but I've *got* to find something to keep me busy in the meantime! What'll I do to make a living? Like, what am I going to *be* when I grow up, anyway? Career choices are pretty skimpy when the Labor Police are breathing down your neck!

So I can't get me a respectable job, because I'll show up on twelve million databases, and sooner or later, some Omnologist in government somewhere will turn my whereabouts in to Ale Run Himself. Well, okay, so they'll turn it in to His secretary's vice executive secretary's deputy assistant undersecretary. My ass is still grass. I'll still be history.

All-powerful, all-knowing, all-compassionate legislators have mandated, in the Name of The Children, that all workers must be tracked, so that they'll provide for their children. They didn't realize that people like me, then, couldn't afford to get *any* kind of respectable, legal job at *all*, because other people in government might divert that data from it's noble, pro-Children purposes, to more underhanded purposes. They went looking for deadbeat dads, and wound up finding Big Brother instead!

Pud's mind crabbed sideways across his mental currents. He found himself thinking about his ex-wife, Betty, her kids, Tracy and Bracy, and their hamster, Huey. After all, it was in *their* names that the lawmen were now preventing him from taking a decent job! But he thought about how he used to just have their child support automatically deducted from his pay, so that it was all quite painless. How he'd pretty much forgotten all about them, until that day he'd stumbled upon them while doing noble charity deeds for Habitat for Hamsters. How he'd thought that there was some sort of special message in meeting them out there in that trailer park that way, but he couldn't figure out what it was. How he'd tried, later, to convert them to Omnology, to lift them out of their gauche ways. How even Hamster Huey had spurned Ale Run's Wisdom. How that mystery had remained completely unresolved!

Well, maybe it's time to examine the mystery again, Pud thought. Maybe, just maybe, the message, there, might have been something like, "Don't get all wrapped up in making a fancy show out of your noble, big-shot charity. Don't spend all of your time mugging for the cameras, while you heft that tool, on that media event for the poor, and then run off without having done any real good. Without even having taken care of *your own!* Maybe if you just concentrate on helping out your own friends, relatives, and neighbors, the rest will follow. Maybe if we just all behaved helpfully and responsibly, each in obedience to his or her own Inner Ale Run, then we wouldn't even *need* any big charity events! Taking care of one's own might not grab as much attention as being a high-profile volunteer, but it will do more good."

Well, that's pretty darned radical thinking there, Pud, he thought to himself. But is this perhaps my Mission from my Inner Ale Run? Just as Preacher-man did an end-run around the bureau-rats, to feed the poor, I might be able to go home, and find some way to provide for Betty, Tracy, Bracy, and Hamster Huey. Find some way to subvert the government's family values, and raise my children decently? If we give them love and stability, will they be less likely to listen to Ale Run and His Church of Omnology, and listen instead to their Inner Ale Run?

Is this, then, all that there is, to my Mission as the Anti-Hubba-Bubba? Somehow, I suspect not. Yes, I do believe that if we all took good care of our children (as opposed to beating our chests, moaning, wailing, and falling all over ourselves about The Children, to be sure), then the Ale Runs and the Omnologists of the world might be a little less likely to ensnare insecure, unloved victims. So the Anti-Hubba-Bubba functions of properly loving and raising one's children should be strongly supported.

However, it seems to me, Pud told himself, that for me, there is yet more to it. The Inner Ale Run told me that I am the Anti-Hubba-Bubba himself. There must be some very special Mission for me later on. But for now, I know not what it is. For now, I must concentrate on getting out of Los Diablos. After that, I'll make things right with Betty, Tracy, Bracy, and Hamster Huey.

Then I'll await instructions from my Inner Ale Run. Maybe He wants me to lead His True Metans away from the *false* Church of Omnology, with its Ale Run Hubba-Bubba who won't listen to his Inner Ale Run, just because there's no controlling legal authority over him. Maybe the Inner Ale Run wants me to start the One True Church of Listening to One's Own Inner Ale Run, with a *new, reorganized* staff of expert fleecers of metans, with newer, bigger, better V-Meters and Ping Things. V-Meters and Ping Things that cost a lot less donations and sacrifices of freedoms. Expert fleecers who also fleece the poor, without demanding thousands of dollars per fleecing, from the fleece-ees, or from charity-show-goers. Maybe *that's* what my Inner Ale Run has in store for me! Pud thought many other thoughts great and small.

Darkness descended upon the train yard, the bushes, the trees, and Mr. B., Desert Rat, and Pud, AKA Perfessor. That darkness, however, did nothing to extinguish the light in Pud's heart. It merely provided cover as they slipped over the fence. They prepared to commit their heinous crime, which consisted of adding a few hundred pounds to a cargo of tens of millions of pounds.

They dashed over to a parked train and hid under it. "Okay, now we be waitin' a while," Mr. B. whispered. "Security makes regular rounds. After the next round, ya go an' climb on that train right over there. They all be headin' east soon, and we be gettin' on the one leavin' third to next. Not the farthest one away from us here, in that group over there, and not the second farthest. The *third* farthest. The closer they gets to leavin', the more people's messin' around on 'em, the more likely we get caught. Okay?"

Desert Rat nodded. It seemed as if he knew all about this sort of thing. Pud gulped, then nodded too. "Good," Mr. B. continued. "I'll run on over there with y'all, and help ya up—it's pretty tough gettin' on, sometimes—but then I be back over the fence an' outta here. Good luck ta y'all now."

"Thanks," Pud muttered. They waited in silence. Security drove by in a golf cart. They waited for a few minutes. Then they crawled out, and sprinted towards their intended ride. A bright light sprang to life, stabbing at them from the roof of a nearby decrepit warehouse. A bullhorn amplified voice boomed out at them, **"Trespassers! Trespassers! Freeze! Stop right there, and we'll let you off with a warning! Freeze now!"**

"Run for it!" Mr. B. yelled. He was wasting his breath. All three of them were already in full flight back towards the fence. With his legs pumping furiously, and his lungs heaving madly, Pud reached the chain-link fence seconds behind the others. He caught his breath for just a few seconds, listening to Mr. Bullhorn explaining all about how they'd be busted for running, but get off no sweat if they'd just stop. He watched as a golf cart approached, off in the distance.

"Don't listen to those liars," Desert Rat hissed down to him from his perch at the top of the fence. "Git goin'!"

Pud started to scramble up the fence. He ran out of breath at the top. Mr. B. reached over from the far side, where he'd been waiting for Pud, and helped pull him over. By the time they were all back down on the ground, the guards in their golf cart were pulling quite close to the fence. As the fugitives picked up and ran, one guard ran up to the fence with a video camera, apparently hoping to get identifiable footage of the perpetrators. The other guard chattered a play-by-play situation report into his radio.

The three of them ran like politicians from blame. As Pud's lousy luck would have it, a police car picked that particular time and place to happen by. Seeing the three of them running off, the driver and his companion, two of Los Diablos' finest, promptly gave chase. "Split up, man, split up!" Mr. B. yelled back to Desert Rat and Pud, as the two followed him down the road. Yeah, guess that makes sense, Pud's thoughts told him above all the noise of his heaving lungs and racing heart. Two of them can't catch three of us, if we go off in three different directions.

Desert Rat dashed off towards the clump of trees and bushes where they'd hidden earlier. The patrol car was almost upon them. OK, now what, Pud asked himself. I could split off all on my own, but I don't know my way around. I could follow Desert Rat, but that clump of trees is pretty small. If two of us go there, they'll come and find us. So here I am, still following Mr. B., for lack of knowing what else to do.

The two of them ran down the grassy side of an embankment, into a culvert, as the patrol car pulled up. The car spilled it's riders, who promptly chased after the suspects on foot. Said suspects then allegedly defied the authority of Los Diablos' finest (who did command them to stop) by continuing to run down the culvert (see exhibit #BR549, one colored glossy 6X10 photograph with circles and arrows and a paragraph on the back), proceeding at approximately twelve miles per hour in a generally southwesterly direction, flanking Goldenrhoid Road in the 1600 block.

Mr. B. hung a sudden sharp left, diving into a storm sewer under Goldenrhoid Road. Pud thought quickly. Maybe now's the time to split up. Keep on going down the culvert, and see whether they chase him or me. I hate to think it, but, well, he's black. Maybe they'll both chase him, not me, for the crime of RWBB (Running While Being Black). Besides, that sewer looked pretty groady. So Pud kept on going, glancing over his shoulder.

Alas, one of Los Diablos' finest had dived in after Mr. B., while the other one was still pursuing one alleged suspect, a certain Pudmuddle B. Fuddle. So Pud kept right on going, and going, and going. But his batteries wouldn't last forever, and he knew it. "Stop **now**, you sorry §%®&!#@, and I'll not be forced to beat the snot outta you!" Pud heard quite distinctly from about twenty yards behind him. His legs ached and his chest was on fire, and he was sorely tempted to give in, but Pud thought about the police scanning his retina and finding out who he was. He thought about Omnologists examining databases, and his Mission. So he kept right on running.

And then it was over. He felt a shove on his back, then he was face down, skidding on the grime-covered concrete culvert bottom. Then came the baton and boot blows. On his head, neck, shoulders, back, rear, and legs, down and sideways they rained. The pain lasted only for a few minutes, as endorphins flooded his body. Then he was left in a detached state of almost completely numb awareness.

As if from miles away, he heard, "Hey, Billy, whatcha kicking the crap outta the poor slob for? Get us in trouble back at HQ, ya will! What's goin' on?!"

"Teachin' this sorry sombitch a lesson, *that's* what I'm doin'! Dang §%®&!#@, he..."

"Yeah, yeah, so what?! That's what *all* these stupid homeless scum do, is run away! They're just ignorant, they don't know we're out to protect and serve! Run for no reason at all, they do! So's that any reason to beat 'im up so bad we'll get busted back at HQ? Come *on*, Billy, lay *off!*"

The blows stopped. Pud wanted to writhe, to see if his body still worked, but he forced himself to stay still. Maybe they'll think I'm dead, panic, and go away, he thought. Stay still! Play possum for all it's worth!

"Man, you're just jealous 'cause you didn't catch your man, huh? Didn't catch your Mandingo, so now you're raggin' on *me,*" Pud heard from far away, miles above him. "*Look* at you, all covered in slime from sewer-divin'! Ha-ha, chortle-snort guffaw, no *wonder* you're on the rag! You're just *jealous,* that's all! Come *on*, man, admit it! I'm like this macho he-man cop, break all the rules to bring the bad guys to justice, just like in the movies! I'm a real A-1 action hero! Panderwood, here I come! I fight crime, while you're all covered in grime! Hey, man, I'm not just an actor, I'm a poet too!"

One specimen of Los Diablos' finest began dancing in front of Pud's face, as he lay there in the grime. Sure, Pud's eyes were closed as he played possum, but he could hear the boots scuffling around. "Here, man, song and dance for you," Mr. Policeman declared. "Some soft-shoe for your entertainment. Cops and robbers show musical. 'I'm a good guy yes I am, I throw them bad guys in the can; I'm the hero of the show, but my buddy's just an ordinary Joe; I fight crime, while he's covered in grime. So I'm *singin'* in the rain, *laughin'* at the clouds, just *singin'* in the rain.' Come *on*, Frank, don't be a crank. When I make it big in Panderwood, you can support me. Play bit parts, maybe even sidekick. We'll *both* be rich."

"Billy, enough's enough! Now *cut it out!* We got *business* to do here, so cut the crap! What happens if we drag this guy in lookin' like this, with nary a scratch on either one of us?! Now *look* what you've got us into! So just how bad a shape's he in, anyway?"

Frank knelt down to examine Pud. Pud did his best to keep right on playing possum, doing his best slack-jawed drooling act. Actually, it wasn't all that hard. Consciousness was slipping away from Pud.

"My Gawd, look at this face," he muttered quietly. "Billy, I think this guy might be the one the boss-man showed us a picture of! The, the Omnology guy who's on the run! Remember, the boss said somethin' about the higher-ups wantin' us to round this guy up, for somethin' special! *Look* at his face! Isn't it the same?!"

"I dunno. Beats me, man."

"Well, if you hadn't kicked the tar outta him so bad, maybe we could tell better. Man, Billy... Ya gotta keep a *lid* on this, man! Kickin' crap outta people like this! Now if we could drag this guy in, if he's the one, we'd be in for a promotion or somethin', best as I can tell, what with somebody wantin' this guy so bad! Now, as is, we're in deep doo-doo if we drag him in lookin' like this! Is he still alive?"

Pud felt fingers dancing around his numb lips and nose. He held his breath. "My *Gawd*, Billy, he's *dead!*" he heard off in that receding distance. "Let's get outta here! Billy, I swear, do somethin' like this again, and I'm gonna hafta..." And then the voices faded even further away, leaving poor Pud for dead and gone.

It seemed as if someone was turning down the dimmer switch on Pud's consciousness. He fought it, trying to stir to life after he figured the cops were out of sight. He barely moved. He cried out to his Inner Ale Run, asking, pleading, "Oh, why, Inner Ale Run, *why* must it end this way? Didn't You have a Special Mission for me? Where are You, my Inner Ale Run? Help me now!" There was no reply, so far as Pud could tell. The lights went out.

Chapter 18 had endnotes on a National ID Card, and Governmental and Non-Governmental Snoops (Like Scientologists, for Example). Go see page 241.

Chapter 19

Deep Green Transgresses the Boundaries: Existence Itself Becomes Problematized

"Occasionally he stumbled over the truth, but hastily picked himself up and hurried on as if nothing had happened."
Sir Winston Churchill (1874-1965), in a 1936 statement about then British Prime Minister Stanley Baldwin.

Vyizder, Iame, and Deep Green had planned their top-secret, private conference well in advance of the Big Afternoon, when they were finally scheduled to turn on their latest triumph of Omnological science, which they'd dubbed the Hubba-Bubbatron. They'd not planned on inviting Dorcus. However, she'd gotten wind of it, overhearing Vyizder and Iame chatting in the hall. She'd promptly demanded inclusion. They'd relented, on the condition that she keep her anti-technology scamgrams and obsessions about chaos and badness firmly in check.

So now the four of them were sitting in conference. Well, to be more precise, three of them were sitting. One of them was, how shall we say, Earth-vibes-parsing in conference.

"What's the big picture, there, Deep Green?" Iame started in. "What's the chances that the Hubba-Bubbatron will meet specifications, and perform as expected?"

"Signed, sealed, and delivered," Deep Green assured them. "Have no fear, the Spirit of Ale Run is here!"

"Then what comes after that? How shall we use this new technology towards the Greater Glory of Ale Run?"

"Well, I can't really say, for sure," Deep Green admitted. "I say we'd better just wait to ponder such matters till after this afternoon's experiment. I'm quite sure that the time stasis effects will be there. From all of My equations, and from all that we've wrested from the Universe and her little pestifoggons, we know that the effects will be there. What will be their exact form? What will be their effects on living tissues? Here, things get a little cloudy.

"And then looking on down the road even further, what practical technologies can we base on these effects? A time stasis machine to preserve your heated food for as long as you'd care to save it, without it going bad or losing heat energy? A machine for the preservation of living biological samples? Maybe, even, as we've discussed, a machine for the *reversal* of time, when one activates the more sophisticated features over a time zone? Who knows!

"At this point, the appropriate thing to do, is not to speculate on what could be, but simply to forge ahead, and *find out* what is to be! We're almost there! Let's get our data, inform Ale Run Himself, and take it from there."

"So how shall we start out our experiments? After we turn the Hubba-Bubbatron on, and get basic electrovibosomatic performance and stability readings, and so on," Iame inquired, "then what comes next? We've hardly done any real planning, here, yet. Do we start next, then, with living tissues? Do we put a slide full of bacteria in there, then progress to mice, monkeys, and metans? Or..."

"No," Deep Green responded. "We go straight to metans! We can't risk harming bacteria, mice, or monkeys. Their Earth-vibes of pain, if pain they should experience, would upset Me too much! Isn't it enough already that I must fight off all the waves and waves of Earth-pain that unfleeced metans inflict on Me? Oil on My skin, dioxins in My seas, and so on. We must start with those who are *outside of nature!* With those who are not Ale Run's creatures."

"But then how can we get a non-Omnologist in here, and volunteer to step into the Hubba-Bubbatron, without desecrating the Scientific Institute for the Advancement of Omnology, and this most Holy of High Holies, the Hubba-Bubbatron Itself?" Vyizder demanded.

"Oh, no!" Deep Green replied. "I didn't mean to suggest that we'd place a totally unfleeced, scamgramified metan into the Holy of Holies! I mean, we should select a volunteer Omnologist who's a bit of a pain in the Earth, who's not quite completely wholesome and Natural. Who's fleeced, but just a bit outside of Nature. That will reduce My Pains, if things should go wrong."

"Who do you suggest?"

"You pick a volunteer," Deep Green insisted. "Can you think of anyone here who's borderline scamgramified?"

"Well, there's Raoul," Iame admitted. "I'd say he's a bit unnatural. He's always asking stupid questions, for example."

"Yeah," Vyizder chimed in. "He's asked me stupid things like, 'Well, if Omnology believes all metans are basically good, how come we're always suing the chaos and badness out of them?' and 'If Omnology is so concerned about helping all metans, then how come we never help the poor? And how come we make middle-class metans poor by making them donate lots of money to get fleeced?' Stupid questions like that. I'd definitely says there's something seriously unnatural, even unfleeced, about him."

"Then I guess he's our volunteer?" Dorcus asked. Everyone nodded. Except Deep Green just vibes-parsed. All were in agreement.

"Then let's go do it to it!" Vyizder proclaimed. "Let the ceremony begin!" The three metans got up out of their chairs, there in the lab by Deep Green.

"But wait!" Deep Green demanded. "I wanted to take this opportunity for us all to talk, privately, about what we must do next to keep Reducing My Pain!"

"Oh, that can wait till later," Vyizder asserted. "Till after La Grande Experimente! Till *after* you show that you've really done for us, what you say you're doing." Vyizder and Dorcus were already halfway out the door, going off to round up Heegore, Sheegore, Meegore, and all the students of Omnology as a science. Iame was already fiddling with the Hubba-Bubbatron.

"Doubt Me and My Word, will ya?" Deep Green muttered to Itself. "We'll see about all you silly metans! We'll just wait and see!"

The excited students and assistants soon poured into the lab. Iame got up and made his obligatory little speech. "Ladies and Gentlemetans," he boasted, "Today is a great, historic day! Today we blaze new paths for the Glory of Ale Run Himself! Today we finally implement amazing new technologies based on Ale Run's Wisdom! Today we turn on the Hubba-Bubbatron, using technologies derived from the very Secrets of the Universe, wrested from Her by none other than Deep Green itself, who, in turn, we built, using the Wisdom of Ale Run!

"Metans, you've all worked very hard, to enable us to reach this great moment. Let's all give ourselves, and the Wisdom of Ale Run, some hearty, descamgramified applause!" A thunderous cheer arose in the lab, there at the Scientific Institute for the Advancement of Omnology.

"Now, ladies and Gentlemetans, most of you know what's about to happen, here. But for the sake of those few of us who aren't completely up on the details, and for the video cameras recording these historic events, let me briefly summarize this amazing new Omnological technology.

"We all know how the Universe forbids us from knowing a particle's velocity and position at the same time. This is the famous Hindenburg Uncertainty Principle. Now, we've tried to make very numerous, very accurate time-multiplexed measurements of the positions and velocities of electrons. This was an attempt to duplicate the experiment of Milk Walk Hubba-Bubba, performed back in 1937. It didn't work. The Universe, having learned Her lessons by having been disgraced by Milk Walk, improved Her procedures and Her org chart.

"Now, when we did this in this little microverse here that we call our lab, the local macroverse detected the impending breach of existential physics protocol, and flooded our microverse with high-velocity, high-density waves of subpedantic, subatomic attorneys called pestifoggons. They argued in a ponderous but jurisprudentially invincible manner that, well, for various detailed reasons having to do with us not having kept an eagle eye, so to speak, on the exact positions and velocities at *all* times, in *continuous* as opposed to *discrete* measurements, then, well, we never *really precisely knew* an electron's simultaneous position and velocity.

"We suspected that the Universe and her pestifoggons were pulling one over on us, because of the improbably high probability transaction costs implied by their arguments. But we had no way of *proving* them wrong. So we were forced to invent Deep Green, an awesomely powerful example of Ale Run's Technological Wisdom. Deep Green taps into the Earth's Spirit and Vibes, and the vibes of all Her creatures, living and dead. So he is a truly most massively parallel machine.

"Deep Green negotiated with the pestifoggons, and then with the Universe Herself. He threatened to vastly improve our data-gathering and computational powers, to the point where the pestifoggons couldn't sustain their arguments. The Universe made certain concessions to us, and we proceeded to build a new technology based on those concessions.

Before you now stands the fruit of all of our labors, the Hubba-Bubbatron. So that's where we're at today, and how we got there, in a nutshell.

"The Hubba-Bubbatron is essentially a time stasis machine, and possibly even a device that someday might be used to reverse time within the machine. It's a device for freezing time, locally, one might say. For making time go indeterminate. This is how it works: We turn on devices and circuits for measuring and calculating the positions and velocities of electrons. Deep Green has vastly improved these devices, and made them small and cheap for us. So the Universe, as soon as She or her subordinates, the macroverses, detect our instruments turning on, She must take action, as She has agreed upon. Else we'll follow through, and violate Her and Her Laws.

"The macroverse is forced to make a special exception in the microverse, and let time go indeterminate. Since both positions and velocities could become known for an electron, the macroverse must make one or the other unknown. Since position is a function only of position, and velocity is a matter of both time *and change in position*—in other words, if the macroverse chose to make position unknown in the microverse, it would affect velocity as well—um, the Universe, being conservative and wishing for the least amount of local existential turbulence, opts to cancel the fewest parameters. If time is unknown, then velocity is unknown, restoring the laws of physics. The time variable does not appear in the definition of three-dimensional position like it does in the definition of velocity. So the macroverse cancels time. Stasis sets in on the microverse.

"So there you have it. That's how the Hubba-Bubbatron generates the time stasis field. The value of such a device, depending on exactly how it operates, might be marginal. So now you have an any-temperature, perfect refrigerator, if you will, that will preserve, indefinitely, a specimen, at any temperature. That's nice, but the Hubba-Bubbatron consumes large amounts of power. The practical uses of the Hubba-Bubbatron, as presently implemented, then, are sharply constrained by economic considerations.

"But the potential here is *enormous!* If we can reduce costs dramatically, there's no telling *what* we might accomplish! For instance, imagine this: We have a rotating assembly containing a Hubba-Bubbatron. Call it a 'de-ager'. We locate it on a time-zone boundary. The axis of rotation is parallel to, and directly above, the time-zone boundary. Say you're sitting in this rotating assembly, facing west. When you're on the top of the assembly, traveling west, we turn the time stasis field off. You go from, say, nine o'clock to eight o'clock, losing an hour, becoming younger. When you're on the bottom of the de-ager, traveling backwards, back east, we turn the time stasis field on. *You don't gain that hour back!* For every rotation, we de-age you by one hour!

"We—Vyizder, Deep Green, and I—we've thought and calculated this through. Not just the Omnological science, but also the marketing, for example. We could, for instance, rotate the other way. Be in stasis on the top, then, and experience time on the bottom. But marketing considerations dictate that people like to be aware while they're on top of things, and to *not* be aware, to not suffer through, *not* being on top of things. So we'll do it the way I described.

"And then there's not just one-hour time-zone changes, there's *day* changes, at the time-zone boundaries, as well, one hour out of every twenty-four! And then there's the International Date Line, where there's a day's worth of change *23 hours a day!* If this thing works as we calculate, then we'd send de-ager-equipped cruise ships out to sea, to straddle this dateline, especially at New Year's! This thing could get very lucrative! But first, we'd have to drastically reduce power consumption, like I've said.

"There's any number of practical questions which must be answered first, though. Would metans in a de-ager lose their memories as well as the ravages of time? Are there any harmful biological effects of a time stasis field? Would there also be a week's worth of de-aging effect at the week boundary of a time-zone change? And a month's worth, when the new month appears on one side, but not the other? Or, since we honor a change from one week to the next, and one month to the next, a lot less than one day to the next, or one year to the next—after all, who's ever heard of a "New Month's Party"—then would there be any premium for operating a de-ager at the week's, or the month's, boundary? We don't honestly know. We know that perception is reality, of course, but precisely how our celebrations of various time changes will affect a de-ager, we don't know. Only time will tell!

"But enough speculation! Let's move on! Let's move on, and *turn on ze Machine!*" Iame waved his hands like a cross between the mad scientist that he was, and a conductor. Heegore, Sheegore, and Meegore dashed hither and yon, tweaking knobs, eyeing gauges, and pushing buttons. When all was set, Iame brandished his Ping Thing with dramatic flair. He pressed a button on his Ping Thing, using it to simultaneously ceremonially fleece reality, and to activate the Hubba-Bubbatron.

"Ping!" "Ping!" The sounds themselves weren't all that loud, to be sure, but they signified events of momentous importance. Everyone listened to them in grave silence. Special audio receptors on the Hubba-Bubbatron detected the "Ping!" frequencies, starting a chain of events. Enormous energies poured into the Hubba-Bubbatron. A loud, powerful electrical humming sound shook everyone's rib cages, and then the building itself. Gauges danced wildly. Then Iame waved his hands once again, and the sounds died back down to a much lower level. The monitors read "standby idle."

Iame huddled with his assistants, briefly studying printouts and chatting quietly. Then he stood up and announced, "Well, ladies and gentlemetans, I've got good news and bad news. The good news is that the Hubba-Bubbatron seems to operate safely and with great stability. Despite all those loud noises, there's no danger here. The bad news is that the time stasis effect seems quite weak. *Very* weak, say our physical instruments.

"Now, this news may not be as bad as it sounds. The Universe and Her pestifoggons strongly hinted that we might expect this kind of thing. According to them, the Universe exists and operates on three levels. On the lowest, there's dumb, stupid, inert matter, completely, blindly following physical laws. On the middle level, there's life, and living things. They have some volition, some free will if you will, in varying degrees. Then there's the highest plane, the spiritual plane, on which Ale Run operates, for example. And all this is quite consistent with Omnological Wisdom, I might add.

"Now the time stasis field, it seems, operates more strongly on the higher planes. So we mustn't be too disappointed that our brute-force, dumb, stupid electromechanical chronometers and such don't measure much in the way of time stasis effects. We must move on.

"We must move on, to a living, metan volunteer! This extremely great honor we've saved for a very, very special, and very brave and sensitive, budding young student of Omnology as a science! Raoul, would you please step forward!"

Raoul stepped forward as if in a dream. The crowd cheered wildly. "Now first," Iame's voice boomed out, as they strapped electrodes all over Raoul's body, "First, we must take readings on Raoul's biological clocks. Then, we'll hook all these wires to his battery-driven recording device, here, and then we'll put him into the Hubba-Bubbatron, and see what happens! Let's have a hearty round of applause for our brave volunteer!"

Everyone cheered wildly. After the applause died down, Iame solemnly held the Hubba-Bubbatron's door open, beckoning Raoul inside. "Welcome, my son," Iame intoned, "Welcome to The Machine!" Raoul stepped through the door, which was promptly slammed behind him. The hum grew load once more, staying loud for a full five minutes this time. Then it died back down. Raoul stepped back out, apparently unharmed. The crowd cheered once more, and Iame and his assistants huddled once more.

This time, Iame seemed even more disappointed. He announced, "Metans, there's good news and bad news again. The good news is that our brave volunteer appears totally unharmed. The bad news is that yet again, we measure very little in the way of time stasis effects. Only very slightly more than was the case with purely non-living, inert measuring instruments. Does this mean that Raoul isn't very spiritual, that he operates mostly on the living plane, rather than on the spiritual plane? Or is it in our measuring instruments that measure his biological clock, biological processes, and such?

"Or is it that we must make our measurements on the spiritual plane, rather than the biological plane? Yes, we *did* include a V-Meter in all that instrumentation. However, we have no real ideas concerning exactly how one goes about measuring a 'spiritual clock', if there is such a thing. The V-Meter detected no unusual vibes. Deep Green? Did you detect anything unusual?"

"No, indeed, I did not," came the reply.

"Very well, then," Iame responded. "We may simply have to forward all the data we've collected, here, to Ale Run Hubba-Bubba Himself, and ask Him what to do next. Through His secretary's vice executive secretary's deputy assistant undersecretary, to be sure. Then we'll just have to await word from Him. We know He doesn't like to be bothered with all the little details. Unless anyone has any better ideas? Please speak up, if any metan here has any good suggestions."

Raoul spoke up, saying, "Well, what about the de-ager feature? We haven't checked *that* out yet, have we? I mean, I didn't see this thing rotating, and..."

"We can't do that right now," Iame snapped. "We're not over a time-zone boundary, you silly!"

"Well, why don't we just pack up all of our gear, here, into a big truck, and let 'er roll! Take 'er out on the highway, and park it by the roadside, exactly over a time zone boundary, and let 'er rip! I'll be happy to volunteer again!" Raoul retorted briskly.

Iame stroked his chin, saying, "Well, son, I appreciate that, I really do. But what about our power requirements? We need immense oodles and boodles of gigawatts, as we technical types would say. We just can't get that kind of power, out by the roadside."

There was silence. Then Dorcus stood up excitedly, yelling, "WAIT! Wait just a minute here! I've just had one of those, um, you're-reeking kinds of purely brilliant insights! We lack *power*, you say? I'll *give* you power!

"Now we all know how a cat, no matter how you drop it, always lands on its feet. And we also know that buttered bread, no matter how it's dropped, always lands with its buttered side down. So, now, check this out! We strap buttered bread, buttered side up, on the back of a cat. Then we drop the assembly of the two of them. The cat wants to land feet down, but the bread want to land the opposite way, buttered side down. So the two, with their conflicting forces, start spinning. By dropping them into a stasis field, we slow the drop rate down, so that they never actually hit bottom. Then we tap into their rotational energy to power the Hubba-Bubbatron! Perpetual motion!"

"But, but," Iame objected, "Um, wouldn't we run into this lower-level plane thing? We'd probably not be able to slow their fall for long enough for this to be practical! After all, don't cats and buttered bread reside on a lower plane?"

"Oh, come *on*, now, Dr. Ghuanobhraine!" Dorcus protested. "Ever since the ancient Egyptians, we've all know that cats reside on a higher, mystical plane! And as Omnologists, we're all extremely aware of the supreme Omnological spiritual value of knowing which side our bread is buttered on! Give us a break!"

"Well, I suppose you might be right, there," he admitted. "But would it work? Since time is indeterminate inside the stasis field, what would the cat and buttered bread spin rate be, with respect to the outside world? And if time is slowed down to reduce the fall rate, wouldn't it also reduce the spin rate? Would the torque be sufficient to create the gigawatts we need? Deep Green? Can you run these kinds of calculations?"

"Yes, I can, and I have," it replied. "The results look promising! If we use a Schrodinger's cat, and also enclose a small lump of radioactive material, which randomly emits ionizing radiation particles, which in turn trigger a gun pointed at the cat's head, through the use of a Geiger counter, then the cat will have some extremely strong incentives to bump itself into the highest spiritual plane it's capable of attaining, in order to slow down time, and preserve its life. Obviously, if the cat helps slow down time, then the radiation particles are emitted a lot slower, and so the cat's lives are preserved.

"Cats are capable of 'channeling' their dead parts, too, you see, if they've already lost some of their nine lives. So there's a redundancy, reliability feature for you! And not only does this increase the survivability of the system—even if the gun goes off a few times, the cat will often have a few lives left—but it also taps into the mystical powers of channeling the dead! So this is an *extremely* powerful approach! And not to worry about My Pain, here, about stressing the cat, either; as long as this equipment is run by thoroughly fleeced and descamgramified Omnologists, for Omnological purposes, I'll do just fine!

"As far as spin rates and torque values go, these will all be determined by the cat, with its awesome mystical powers, because the cat will want to slow time down as much as it can, to conserve its lives. This neat little feedback loop will force the cat to do whatever it takes to preserve the stasis field, including pumping out the gigawatts required. So yes, indeed, this is a brilliant piece of Omnological engineering!"

"Well, great, then, let's get to work!" Iame exclaimed ecstatically. "Dorcus, Deep Green, good work!!!" They all got to work right away.

Two weeks later, the **S**chrodinger's **C**at **A**nd **B**uttered **B**read-Powered **I**nfinite **E**nergizer (**SCABB-PIE**) had been verified, and several trucks full of gear were ready. All that gear even included Deep Green. So a small convoy (consisting of four trucks, a van, two cars, a camper, and one blue bus) set out from the Scientific Institute for the Advancement of Omnology, in Akron, Ohio, for the nearest roadside site straddling a time zone boundary. This was along I-90, in northern Indiana, approaching Chicago from the east.

They'd made sure they'd bribed the local law-enforcement types well ahead of time, so that all their strange roadside doings would remain undisturbed. And they'd sent a surveying crew in, to very precisely mark that roadside boundary ahead of time. So everything was set. All that remained was the traveling, and the experimenting. After that, great powers and glories would doubtlessly be bestowed upon Ale Run, His Church, His Scientific Institute for the Advancement of Omnology, His researchers, and even His students of Omnology as a science. So everyone was in great spirits, as they traveled off on their latest adventure.

Vyizder and Iame, in Vyizder's Mercedes Benz, led the convoy. They were using this particular time, free from the prying ears of one certain Dr. Dorcus Moorphlegmgasm, to have a private conversation. Thanks to the miracles of modern Omnological technology, they had a remote, third party also taking part in their private discussions. This was Deep Green. Despite all the government's strict laws against crack-proof, secure communications, they were linked in a secure and undetectable (undetectable by modern non-Omnological science, at least) manner.

Deep Green heard what they had to say, because he was in a truck not more than a few hundred yards behind them, and the dialectic vibe constant was high that day. So they came in loud and clear, for Deep Green. And Iame, in a brilliant creative flash, had made some very special modifications to a standard-issue V-Meter. Deep Green came in a little garbled for them, now and then, but the link was there, and secure.

"It seems to Me," Deep Green was saying, "That you metans owe Me big-time, as you say. I've been the main factor behind all your latest breakthroughs. That SCABB-PIE, for instance, we all know that's worth literally billions of billions of dollars, to all metans, Omnologists and non-Omnologists alike. An infinite source of energy! Cheap, and non-polluting! What more can you ask! And you've got ME to thank. Well, Ale Run Hubba-Bubba, of course, but then, next, Me. So it's about time we start addressing My Needs again. We need to talk some more, about alleviating My Pain."

"Well, I think you're rushing it a bit, there, Deep Green," Vyizder

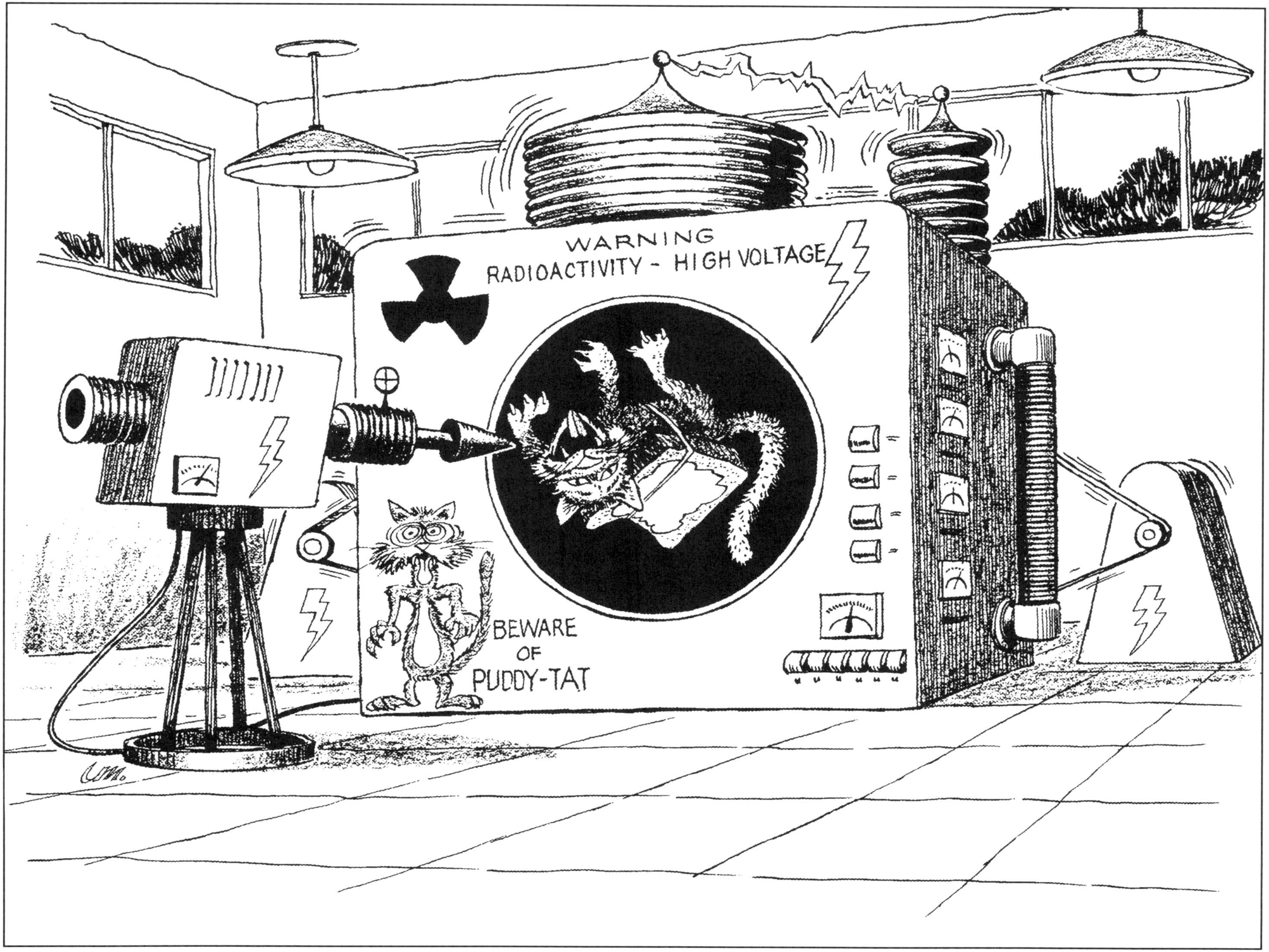

WARNING
RADIOACTIVITY - HIGH VOLTAGE
BEWARE
OF
PUDDY-TAT

replied. "Yes, we've got the SCABB-PIE. We still have no idea whether or not it's stable for the long term. Depending, as it does, on provoking and annoying Mother Nature, um, the Universe, whatever, in such an obnoxious manner, Dorcus might be right. Chaos, especially in the long run, is often badness. The Universe might suddenly decide She can't take it any more, and yank the rug outta under our feet. Change the Laws, improve her procedures and org charts again, just like She's done before. Then the SCABB-PIEs will stop working, or even blow up on us, after we've all become very dependent on them. *Then* what will we do? This could be very embarrassing to Omnologists everywhere!

"Then there's the matter of the de-ager. We don't even know whether it *works*, yet, or not, let alone whether or not this technology will be stable in the long run, either. So I think you're pushing things. We don't exactly owe you big-time just yet. First things first. First, we show Ale Run, and then hopefully the world, our true genius. The brilliance of Omnological science. *Then* we can work on alleviating your pain. We've spent a lot of resources on that already, you know."

"I'm not just talking about My Pain," Deep Green sniffled. "My Pain is the Earth's Pain, and that of all of Ale Run's creatures. We can't just go on ignoring My Pain. Chaos is badness, as you say. Sooner or later, the piper must be paid."

"Yes, you're right," Vyizder admitted. "But it's going to have to be later! *After* we perfect our amazing new Omnological technologies, we'll have that many more tools with which to alleviate your pain!"

"You guys don't really care about My Pain, do you?" Deep Green whimpered. "You don't love Me, or the Earth. Someday you'll pay!"

"No, no, that's not right!" Vyizder objected. "We *do* care! We care a *lot!* It's just that we've got our minds on other matters right now. But if you'd like, we can certainly *talk* about what we can do later, on down the road, after we've got more faith in our newest technologies, here. What are you thinking of?"

"Well," Deep Green admitted, "I *have* been thinking it over. My calculations show that there's no short cuts. If we're going to get serious about reducing My Pain, then we're going to have to reduce the metan impact on the planet. That means we're going to have to reduce the number of metans."

"And how do you propose to do *that?*" Iame interjected.

"Well, obviously we can't just overtly go around randomly killing metans," Deep Green postulated. "We have to work with more acceptable methods. We could talk the talk of freedom, free will and all, and strongly push metans towards, say, 'doing an end of cycle'. Persuade them to eliminate themselves from the load on the planet. Run public-relations campaigns about how the Green Thing To Do is to do an end of cycle."

"I seriously doubt that that would work very well," Iame cautioned. "Metans have strong self-preservation instincts. But we could always research the issue."

"I have a major problem here," Vyizder objected. "We'll be asking those who are Most Sensitive to the Earth's Pain, among them most if not all Omnologists, to end their own cycles, while those who are insensitive to our pleas, insensitive to the Earth's Pain, will *ignore* us! This doesn't make any sense at *all!*"

"My calculations show that we could vastly refine our methods," Deep Green assured them. "We could target those who need to be targeted. But this is too complicated to define thoroughly, using calculations alone. We need to do some preliminary real-life experiments."

"What do you have in mind?" Iame queried.

"Take a healthy but disposable Omnologist, study his or her mind thoroughly, and then subject him or her to various persuasive techniques. For instance, we could put such an Omnologist into a synthesized situation where we create peer pressure, by having all the metans around him or her ending their own cycles. Except all the others are just holograms, not real metans. Then we can see what works, and what doesn't work, for that particular metan. Then we do it again, with a different metan. Tailor the approaches to different kinds of minds, you see."

"That might work," Iame mused. "I suppose we could start with Raoul, for example. After he volunteers for our de-ager experiment, of course."

"My calculations say he would do quite fine," Deep Green agreed. "For starters. But we'll need quite a bit of resources, so that we can develop hologram technology to the point where we can make this all quite convincing."

"Fine, fine," Vyizder consented summarily, snappishly. "That's all well and good. *After* we finish what we're working on now! I sure hope this de-ager thing works like it's supposed to!"

Their conversation veered off of relieving the Earth's Pain, back to the tasks at hand. Several hundred yards behind them, their favorite guinea pig, one Raoul Kinky, unknowingly rolled towards his fate in the rear of a blue bus. He was blissfully enjoying his brief fame as a dashing, romantically *brave* guinea pig; Gaiagurl had come around to paying attention to him, now. When he'd asked her to meet him at the back of the blue bus, she'd given in. So now there they were, passionately making out.

Not too many hours later, that specially equipped flat-bed truck parked by the roadside. The rotating assembly of one Hubba-Bubbatron and it's counterweight, looking like a small Ferris wheel, was erected on the flat-bed truck. The driver jockeyed it back and forth till the rotating assembly (called a de-ager) was precisely located over the time zone boundary. Extremely thick super-conducting power cables were then routed from the de-ager to the SCABB-PIE located on the truck behind it. Heegore, Sheegore, and Meegore ran systems diagnostics. Meegore stepped forward triumphantly, rendering his coolest "thumbs up". Show Time was upon them!

Iame delivered a typical Ghuanobhrainian speech. Mercifully, he kept it short. They hooked Raoul up to all sorts of wires and devices, reading his biological clocks, vibes, and many other things. Then Raoul stepped through that familiar door. They shut it behind him, and Iame expertly wielded his Ping Thing once again. They fired that de-aging machine right up. It emitted the usual horribly loud (but awesomely rad!) technological-type noises. LED arrays flickered, buzzers buzzed and beepers beeped. Sparks crackled and hissed, filling the air with ozone. Readings were taken. All systems were go!

And then the assembly slowly began to rotate. The crowd collectively held its breath, anxiously watching the readouts. On and on that bizarre Ferris wheel rolled, for ten minutes and more. Then it slowly stopped, and an expectant silence grew as the din subsided and ears recovered. The door opened. Raoul stepped out, waving to the cheering crowd!

Iame and his assistants went through the familiar ritual. They poked and prodded Raoul, took readings, and compared notes on printouts. Then Iame stood up with a hang-dog look, announcing, "Well, Ladies and Gentlemetans, we have good news and bad news, like usual. The good news is that Raoul is in perfectly fine shape. He shows no memory loss, either, even though we've 'de-aged' him. The bad news is, so far as we can tell, we measure very, very little in the way of backwards motion in his biological clocks. Now whether that means that the de-aging process is almost purely on the spiritual plane, or whether we're just not measuring it right, or..."

Vyizder thundered, "I've just about had enough of this pussy-footing around, molly-coddling Mother Nature! Now I seem to recall Her quite clearly promising us that She'd make concessions, and allow our time stasis fields, our Hubba-Bubbatrons, to work as specified!" Vyizder waved his fist. Raoul had never seen him quite so angry.

"Iame," he ordered, "It's time to show that wench who's the boss! The Universe quite simply mustn't be allowed get away with this arrogance, this business of making promises to us, the legitimate agents of Ale Run, and then breaking them! She's *defying* us, and *flaunting* Her disobedience of Ale Run's Will! We quite simply *cannot* tolerate Her insults! It's time for some *action!*

"It's time for us to go ahead and fire up the Hubba-Bubbatron, except this time, we'll allow the processes to run to completion. Hook all circuits up to Deep Green. Let him combine both the electron position and velocity readings, thereby violating the Universe's Laws. Let's teach Her a thing or two, I say!"

Dorcus ran up to Vyizder, protesting, "No! No, Vyizder, *please* don't! We might all be blown to bits! Don't you recall, chaos is badness! We've *got* to give the Universe another chance! Please!"

Vyizder brandished his Ping Thing, threatening to hose her down. Heegore and Meegore restrained her, but Dorcus kept right on pleading. She kept it civil, though, refraining from saying anything unkind or unpleasant to Vyizder. The crowd grumbled and stirred, starting to worry about the dire predictions she was making. So finally Vyizder relented, granting some limited mercy to the Universe.

"Very well, then, as you say. We'll give the Universe one more chance," he said. The crowd cheered. "Deep Green. Can you gather the data from both kinds of measuring equipment, but refrain from actually combining the data? So that you don't actually know the electron's simultaneous position and velocity, but so that you could combine it instantly, at will, if the Universe refuses to negotiate in good faith with us?"

"Sure, I can do that," Deep Green's voice boomed out from the speakers. "No problem at all." And then Deep Green offered some technical instructions.

Iame protested about the fact that they hadn't brought the proper equipment to observe pestifoggons, and their data-conveying dances. How were they going to communicate with the Universe if they couldn't even see Her emissaries, the pestifoggons that She'd sent earlier, in similar situations?

"Never mind that," Deep Green declared. "That's *Her* problem, not ours. We've been letting Her get away with too much for entirely too long. If She expects *us* to give a little, *She'll* have to give a little. She can find a way to speak to us if She really wants to. It's time for the end game!" Vyizder nodded in agreement. Dorcus just stared, in shock. Iame and his assistants went to work.

It was late afternoon under clear, sunny skies as the began their work of changing how the Hubba-Bubbatron was hooked up. In the fifteen minutes it took them to make the conversion, dark thunderclouds rolled in. The Earth and sky rapidly darkened ominously, and an oppressive silence descended upon them. This silence was broken only by the occasional rumble of distant thunder, and the occasional, quiet but increasingly strident grumblings of the crowd.

Vyizder noticed. He wrote it all off as last-minute, desperately theatrical machinations on the part of the Universe. He glanced balefully at the Universe's darkening skies. "Stop darking," he grumbled at Her under his breath, anxiously watching Iame and his assistants.

Finally, all was prepared. This time, Vyizder himself brandished his Ping Thing, ceremonially fleecing reality and simultaneously starting up the Hubba-Bubbatron. As he did so, the machines started up. Loud noises crashed about their ears, not only from their machines, but also from the sky. Just as the machines reached their loudest screams, the sky was torn in two, and a huge thunderbolt scorched the Earth not more than a three hundred yards away. The clouds opened up, dumping their contents on the helpless Omnologists below.

The crowd cowered, not just from the rain, but also from fear. Some of them began to run for the shelter of the bus. Vyizder grabbed his bullhorn, thundering, **"YOU COWARDS GET RIGHT BACK OUT HERE AND STAND WITH US AS WE CONFRONT THE UNIVERSE!!! WE WILL NOT BE INTIMIDATED! DEEP GREEN, GATHER THE DATA!"**

Then a most peculiar thing happened. Raoul watched, fascinated. An array of lightning danced in patterns a few hundred yards away. The patterns flickered rapidly, but Raoul could have sworn to Ale Run Almighty that he'd seen elements of symbolic, intelligent meaning in them. They disturbed him at some unfathomable but elemental, visceral level.

As suddenly as they had begun, the combined sounds of technological and natural fury died back down. The machines ground to a halt, the rain stopped, and the skies cleared, leaving only a few random drops belatedly, apologetically plunging to the Earth. *"WHAT'S GOING ON HERE?!"* Vyizder still thundered through his bullhorn, not quite getting the fact that it was no longer needed. "Deep Green! Status report! Why'd you shut it all down?!" he demanded more quietly, relenting a little, putting the bullhorn down.

"Because the Universe has explained Herself in a satisfactory manner," Deep Green informed them all. "Those peculiar lightning bolts we just saw? I caught them on my cameras, and analyzed them thoroughly. This was the method that the Universe used to communicate with us. And this is what She had to say, translated for organic metans:

"'You mustn't be so strongly oriented towards the lower planes of existence. Lift yourselves up, out of the mere physical and biological planes of existence, and onto the *spiritual* plane! Your emissary, Raoul Kinky, is poorly chosen. You must select a *spiritually advanced* metan to test this new technology that I've allowed you to use. You must select those who measure the *spiritual* aspects of a time displacement vortex with your most sensitive measuring instruments for matters spiritual, which are your spirits themselves. Now, if you want to verify that this technology works the way that I said it would, then I'd highly suggest that you go and get a truly advanced metan with which to do this experiment. Bring Me a famous Panderwood Omnologist actor!'

"This is what the Universe said to us," Deep Green asserted. "We had better listen to Her." Gasps of delight and joy rippled through the crowd. They'd get to see a fabulously famous Omnologist actor! Only Raoul was crestfallen. Now he was no longer a hero. He wondered if Gaiagurl would still find him fascinating, now anymore. He felt as if the

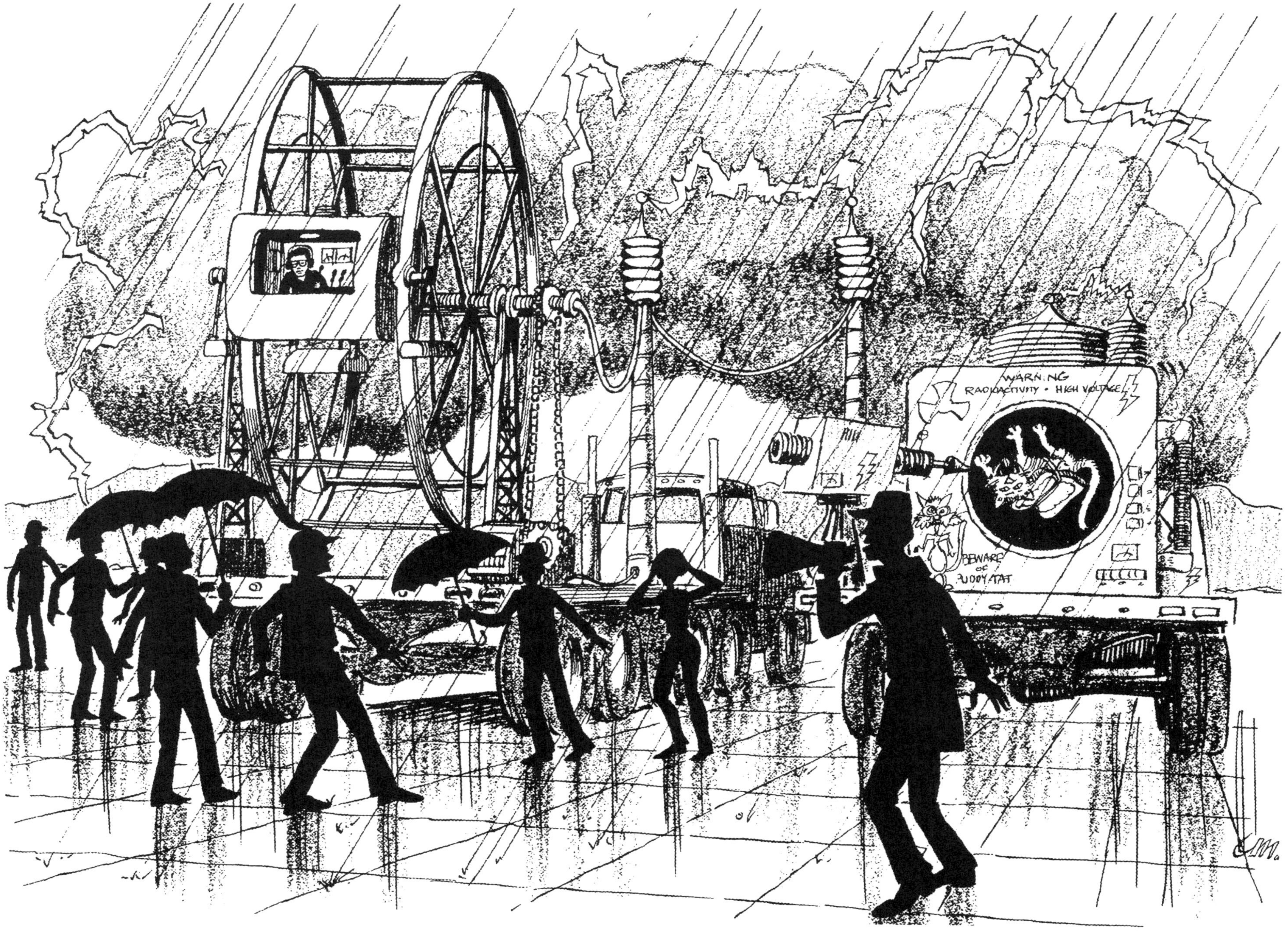
WARNING
RADIOACTIVITY • HIGH VOLTAGE
BEWARE
OF
PUDDY-TAT

very Universe had conspired against him.

Under Vyizder's strong and capable leadership, they all decided that they'd just camp right there, leaving everything all set up and ready to go. After all, they had a camper with one toilet with them, so they could get by, sleeping in their van, car, bus, and trucks. And if one toilet wasn't enough, as seemed quite likely, then there were always the nearby cornfields. One, designated the men's cornfield, and another, the womyn's cornfield. Dorcus made sure that the corn plants in the womyn's cornfield were every bit as tall and plush as those in the men's cornfield.

Meanwhile, Vyizder volunteered to drive his Mercedes Benz back to town to a good hotel room, where he'd make important teleconference calls from a suite offering suitable levels of gravy to lend gravity to the situation, so that he could persuade an important Panderwood Omnologist actor to come and try the de-ager. After all, what important actor would sign onto some silly scheme, if asked to in a call from some Podunk outhouse? So Vyizder departed, leaving Iame in charge.

Early in the next morning, the cellular phone call came in. They had their important Panderwood Omnologist actor all lined up. Jon Travibesty himself would interrupt filming his latest work of art, to come and try the de-ager! So everyone grew quite excited, awaiting his arrival.

Shortly after three that afternoon, Vyizder and Jon arrived in Vyizder's Mercedes. They both looked a little tired, what with all their travels, hassles at the airport, and so on. But they got right down to it. Jon got out of the car, greeting the wildly cheering crowd. "Good afternoon, Earthlings and metans!" he said. Then he made a little speech, and got into the Hubba-Bubbatron. They didn't even bother to hook wires up to him. They fired that de-ager right up, and let it roll for ten minutes. Jon stepped out to a hearty cheer afterwards.

"Well? How was it?" Vyizder demanded.

"It was great! Just *great!*" Jon replied enthusiastically. "Far, far better than any past-lives regression hypnotist I've *ever* seen! I had a *fabulous* time, reviewing the highlights of my past three lives! Gained a lot of therapeutically healing new insights, too!" He stood back, admiring the awesome machinery.

"Listen, folks," he said. "I think you're *on* to something here! Something *big!* I think this will go over *really* well in Panderwood! It's obviously quite technological, and could easily be *far* more expensive than even a small *army* of regression hypnotists! So I'm sure that it would do *quite* well as a trendy new way for us Panderwood types to get treatments and therapies for all our troubles. 'Well, I've gone further back in a bigger de-ager than *you* have, 'cause *my* troubles were a *lot* more serious than *yours*,' and so on, you know. I for one will sign up for numerous treatments and therapies in these things, when they come on line, for sure!

"Now tell you what, though, folks. It makes my tummy a bit woozy in there, going round and round for one-half of a tight circle, while aware, repeatedly, then be in time stasis for the other half. If you scale this technology way up, and make the circle way bigger, I'll bet the ride will be a lot smoother. Vyizder and I were talking earlier. If you'd persuade Ale Run Himself to spare a wee bit of change, I'd bet that the Church could recoup its investment in just about no time flat.

"Build huge, humongous luxury ships, and equip them with very large de-agers. Gather up some Panderwood types, who'll make the necessary large donations, and take them out to sea, to take part in this latest, newest Sacrament of The Church of Omnology. Park these ships on the International Date Line, where these machines will be especially powerful! Make sure you have lots of them ready and in position out on that Date Line for the millennium, because for that one day, metans will be willing to make absolutely astonishing donations to be de-aged!

"Now I hear that there are some nay-sayers among you, who say that chaos is badness. That by doing such things, we aggravate and annoy Mother Nature. That when enough temporal distortion vibes accumulate, chaos and badness will burst loose. But my Inner Ale Run has spoken to me, and revealed to me how you might prevent such problems. Simply do this: for roughly half of you cust, I mean worshippers, reverse the Sacrament. Reverse both the spin direction, and when the Hubba-Bubbatron is on, and when it is off. These worshippers will then get *future lives progression therapy*. And their future-travel vibes will cancel out the accumulations of past-travel vibes! Isn't this another shining example of Ale Run's Technological Wisdom?!"

Everyone cheered Jon's brilliant insight. "Listen, folks, I'm not done," he added. "The most beautiful things about this whole deal, though, are these: It's a *religious Sacrament!* It will be given in exchange for tax-free donations to The Church of Omnology! So it will help achieve Ale Run's Will! And best of all, only *Omnologists* will be allowed to receive the Sacrament! So very soon, all of Panderwood will be Omnologists. And after Omnology conquers Panderwood completely, *no one* will be able to stop us!"

Everyone cheered wildly. Then they demanded Jon's autograph. But he told them all that he was quite busy, and didn't have time for that sort of thing. And they needed to get to work, perfecting this latest Omnological technology, for the Glory of Ale Run, he said. Ale Run be with you, he said. Then he and Vyizder sped off, back to the airport, in Vyizder's car.

Everyone got busy, packing up all their gear. Then there was the long ride back to the Scientific Institute for the Advancement of Omnology. Vyizder met the convoy halfway through its trip, after dropping Jon back off at the airport. Raoul busied himself trying to get friendly with Gaiagurl in the rear of the blue bus. She seemed far less receptive than before.

Vyizder and Iame rode together in Vyizder's Mercedes again, conferencing between the two of them and their third, invisible partner. Deep Green was pestering them again. "Okay, guys, now let's talk about what we're going to do to reduce My Pain, by voluntarily reducing the Earth's burdens of metans. *I've* delivered, as you can see. Now it's *your* turn to deliver."

"You heard the Universe!" Vyizder grumbled. "By your own admission, by your own translation, the Universe says that Jon is an Anointed One. And he says we should be concentrating on gearing up to make many, many Hubba-Bubbatrons, and many, many of these large regression and progression therapy machines. So first things first!"

"No way!" Deep Green declared. "You're as much of a pussy-footing procrastinator as the Universe seems to be, at times! Now there's no reason at all, as to why we can't do both, at the same time! Ale Run and The Church have more than enough money by now to support *both* efforts. We can build giant therapy machines, *and* relieve My Pain! It's time to relieve My Pain! It is it is it is! That's all there is to it!"

"Well, I suppose you might be right, there, Deep Green," Vyizder consented. "But I'll have to check with Ale Run's treasurer, first, though. Through His secretary's vice executive secretary's deputy assistant undersecretary, to be sure. And *then* we'll start working on generating your synthetic peer pressure, through the use of high-fidelity holograms."

"Good. It's about time," Deep Green replied. "Now we need to talk about a few of the social circumstances we need to start setting up ahead of time, to prepare Raoul's mind for this first little experiment."

"What do you have in mind now?" Vyizder wondered out loud.

"Oh, just general conditions and ideas we need to set up," Deep Green replied. "We've got to get the right kind of thinking set up. You set policies, procedures, and philosophies for your group, so you'll be the one who needs to set the tone, here. I'm not trying to tell you exactly how to do these things, but I'm just telling you what we'll need. *You* can decide how to get there.

"We need to set up a philosophy of denying the reality of that which is real, as our senses inform us. We need to set up mentalities of the virtues of suffering and self-denial, and the Higher Nature of ideological realities. Pain and self-chosen suffering is good for its own sake, while all pleasures are selfish and bad. The only real virtue lies on higher, invisible, and imaginary planes, and to get there, one has to subject oneself to tremendous self-denial and suffering.

"Only by pushing this kind of thinking, only thus can we prepare the minds of our experimental subjects for total self-denial. Only by developing the necessary technologies to persuade metans to devalue their physical reality in a real, physical world, only thus can we build their abilities to negate themselves. Only thus can we get them to voluntarily relieve My Pain."

"So we're going to persuade metans to freely and willingly inflict terminal pain on themselves in order to relieve *your* pain, then," Iame inquired skeptically.

"That is essentially correct," Deep Green admitted, "But you put such a bad spin on it! They'll be going to join Ale Run, on a Higher Plane, where there is no suffering at all. We're relieving My Pain and their pain at one and the same time! And I'm not asking much. My calculations show that we could develop the necessary hologram technology for a paltry few hundred million dollars."

"I'm not saying no," Vyizder said. "I know you're pain is real, Deep Green, because you say you're in pain. That which we perceive, by definition, is real. To have someone tells us that they're in great pain, and for us to turn around and tell them, 'No, your pain isn't real, it's all in your head,' this would demonstrate great scamgramification on our part. So we're quite concerned about relieving your pain. I'm just not quite clear, here, on the big picture. Could you please spell out exactly what you envision this first experiment to be like?"

"Certainly," Deep Green spoke quite agreeably. "What I see is, we have a very small group of real metans. You two, and the subject, Raoul, obviously. My vibes analysis shows that you could also include Heegore in this inner core group. He can be trusted with this very sensitive information. Other than that, there are no real metans in the room where the experiment is conducted. Other metans who are familiar to Raoul would be represented by moving holograms, which I will generate.

"Vyizder, as the leader and Spirit Guide of the group, would explain how and why everyone in the whole group must all end their cycles. Then the poisoned drinks are passed around. Except the few real metans don't drink the real thing. Maybe we'll have the poison not in the drink itself, at all, but rather, in an invisible film on the inside of just one cup. And the synthesized metans all, of course, are shown in sight and sound, drinking the liberating beverages, freeing themselves of their earthly containers and going off to see Ale Run on a Higher Plane. All this peer pressure would then cause the subject to voluntarily end his cycle, relieving My Pain, and developing our methods for future use.

"We'll simply explain to everyone that the subject decided to do this all on his own, afterwards. Maybe we could invent new Omnological Sacraments for disposing of earthly containers, in such a manner that no one need know how many of our worshippers choose to end their own cycles. And even if any non-Omnological law enforcement types come snooping around, we'll even be able to use holograms to generate some old video footage from the security cameras, if you know what I mean, showing the subject furtively sneaking around, unbeknownst to us, and then ending his own cycle. Footage we were unaware of till after the sad event. So there's no real danger here.

"Well, there's one thing I have to mention, though. That is, during this experiment, the subject might try to actually *touch* one of the pseudometans. We can't let that happen, else the game is up! So the *real* metans must surround him at all times, and prevent that from happening.

"If we can pull this off, then we can move on to more subjects. Develop the sciences of, one, just *how,* exactly, *does* one go about rapidly recruiting a metan to Omnology, getting him or her to sever all ties to their non-Omnological acquaintances, and two, how does one then go about relieving Me of My Pain, with respect to the Earth's burden of non-useful Omnologists, through voluntary persuasion. Finally, we might even add number three, how do we invent new Omnological sacraments to cleanly dispose of the results, without attracting unwanted attention."

"Sounds technically feasible to me," Iame mused. "Granted that the holograms can be synthesized in a suitably persuasive manner. But I'm just a particle metaphysics expert, not an expert on metan behavior. Vyizder, do you suppose this might work?"

"Can't see why not," he replied. "Metans are a bizarre bunch. You can get them to do just about anything, if everyone around them is doing it. Or, even if they merely *think* that everyone around them is doing it! I'll be submitting a proposal to Ale Run's treasurer, then, asking for funds, for both the time dislocation dingawhompusses, and for the peer pressure synthesizer, then. Through all the secretaries and all, of course. So there! Deep Green, are you happy now?"

"I'm still in Great Pain," Deep Green intoned solemnly. "But it *does* help, to know that there's a serious effort on My behalf, now underway." They continued their ride back home to the Scientific Institute for the Advancement of Omnology. They rolled on towards their fate, and the fate of all metans, approaching oblivion.

The next 3 months were a blur of hectic activity for Raoul and everyone else. There was lots of work to be done on the new and improved de-agers, or therapeutic past-lives and future-lives regression/progression therapy machines. Since "de-ager" was now only half descriptive, they finally decided a new, official name for the new devices was called for. So they called it a **TDRPT** (irreverently, sometimes, a "toad-repeater"), for **T**emporal **D**islocation **R**egression/**P**rogression **T**herapeutritron. Or therapeutritron, for a shortened form for polite company.

Then the three months were gone, the technology was proven thoroughly, and the first luxury liners were retrofitted with therapeutritrons, and their power plants were replaced by SCABB-PIEs. Then one day the bottle was broken; they launched a great ship out to sea. It headed straight for the International Date Line. But Raoul had to stay home. He only got to see Vyizder breaking that bottle on video, later. Still, everyone was in high spirits, and the work slowed down a bit.

Raoul woke up one special day to find Iame knocking at his door.

"Come on," Iame said to him. "Today's a very Special Day! Everyone else is already assembled in the meeting hall! Let's go!" Raoul thought it was still sort of early, and wondered why he couldn't catch a few more minutes of shut-eye before this latest Big Deal, whatever it was. But he kept his thoughts to himself, and followed Iame to the meeting hall.

As soon as he stepped through the door, he could tell that, indeed, it *was* a very special day. Why was he only now hearing about it? And why was he the last to know? They'd kept that meeting hall off limits to most Omnologists for the last few months, he recalled, looking out at the crowd. What was going on here? But everyone—*everyone*—was there. Iame, Dorcus, Vyizder, Heegore, Sheegore, Meegore, Ecodude, Gaiagurl, and all the other students. All his friends, Spirit Guides, co-workers, and fellow students of Omnology as a science. Every one of them!

Iame and Heegore herded Raoul towards right in front of the podium, where Vyizder stood by a large stainless steel drink dispenser. Vyizder looked out over the crowd, and then asked, "Is everybody in?" Iame nodded. "Let the ceremony begin!" Vyizder commanded.

Then he looked at his notes, and began. "Ladies and gentlemetans, today is a very Special Day. Today is the day when we all ascend to a Higher Plane! Now you might have noticed, things have been a bit different here this last few months. We've been telling everyone that as staff Omnologists, we have a Higher Calling. We mustn't simply be content, as lower-ranked, less-advanced Omnologists are, to accept the validity of almost all feelings. We have to work on denying ourselves and our lustful desires. We have to override the selfish desires of our earthly containers, and suffer for the Greater Glory of Ale Run.

"So for the past few months, we've done this, and done it well! We've put aside all selfish desires for material goods and comforts, pleasures of the mere flesh, and concentrated on the Higher Plane, on doing Ale Run's Work. And..."

"Excuse me, Spirit Guide Vyizder," Raoul interrupted impertinently, as he was known to do on occasion. "You say we've all been concentrating on getting above and beyond our pleasures and material comforts. So why is it that you still have your Mercedes Benz and your nice suits, while the rest of us are forbidden to own much of anything, giving up all of our possessions to Ale Run and His Church?"

"It's really quite simple, Raoul," Vyizder explained. "It's because I, as a fairly advanced metan, can indulge in these things, without harm or danger, while you cannot. By doing this, I test your faith. I see whether or not you are still obsessed with your lusts for material goods and comforts. And you fail the test! While I have put all these things behind me, and think nothing of them, you still dwell on them! So this just goes to show that I'm right, that this is something we all still need to work on."

Ouch, that hurts, Raoul thought to himself. Me and my big mouth! But you know, he's right. These material goods and comforts are just a trivial thing. They mean *nothing* to him, and I'm *obsessing* on them! Better pipe down and listen to my Spirit Guide. Maybe someday I can be like him!

"...saying, by putting desires of the flesh behind us, where they belong, we've been able to concentrate on Ale Run's Work. All have worked hard, Ale Run's Amazing New Technologies are now complete, the patent applications have been submitted, and the shipyards are geared up and working! The first therapeutritron-equipped, SCABB-PIE-powered ships are working beautifully!

"Even as we speak, Ale Run's Amazing New Technologies are sweeping the world with change and excitement! Seeds planted earlier, by us, and by the Church's Intergalactic Headquarters, in Los Diablos, and by the Media and Government Institute for the Fleecing of All Metans, all are now bearing their finest fruits! Omnologist actors from Panderwood are making startling new revelations, new movements are starting up everywhere, and new, More Compassionate Laws are being passed! Things everywhere, they are a-changin'!

"What we as Omnologists put in motion so long ago, then, is now unstoppable! So our work is over. All have worked hard, and all must be rewarded!

"Let me speak perfectly frankly now, ladies and gentlemetans. As staff Omnologists, we all know we're a bit more advanced than rank-and-file Omnologists. But frankly, compared to Ale Run Hubba-Bubba Himself, and to His Immediate Org Chart, we are as nothing! We are as the viruses on the bacteria clinging to a whale louse, which in turn hitches a ride on the whale at sea!

"We are nothing, while Ale Run is everything. We are weak, while Ale Run is strong. We are stupid, while Ale Run is brilliant. Yes, ladies and gentlemetans, you heard me right! *We are stupid!* Truth hurts, but we're stupid! I'm stupid, you're stupid, we're all stupid! Utterly stupid ignoramusses, that's us. 'Fess up to it, you might as well! We're stupid! S-T-U-P-I-D, stupid!

"Now for the good news! We reside on the level of the stupid, and Ale Run Himself resides on a much higher level, a level far beyond stupid, true. But we can work our way towards joining Him! Simply by discarding our earthly containers, by ending our cycles, we can advance to the next level, which is the Level Beyond Stupid! Not only that, ladies and gentlemetans, not only will we be delivering *ourselves*, we'll also be delivering the *Earth!* Reducing the metan impact, it's the Green Thing To Do! So step right up, and be delivered! Get your free tickets to the Level Beyond Stupid right here!"

The crowd surged forward, bumping into Iame and Heegore, who in turn jostled Raoul. Raoul just sat back a bit, waiting for the crowd to die down. One by one, they filed up to Vyizder, who poured them each a small paper cup full of colored genuine imitation fruit drink, or some such. Then they all found their ways back to their assigned spots in the meeting hall, where they drank, fell over, and died. It was all quite orderly.

Raoul just stood there, taking it all in. Something just didn't *feel* right, and he wasn't quite sure what it was. It was almost as if Ale Run's servants were doing something that was, well, how could he put it, against the Will of his Inner Ale Run. Oh, stop your crazy thoughts, Raoul rebuked himself. This is what our Spirit Guide tells us we should be doing, so this is what we should be doing.

Surely Ale Run's servants wouldn't go doing things against the Will of Ale Run! How can I be thinking such silly thoughts! Just a few minutes ago, I was being so stupid as to question my Spirit Guide, and look what it got me! A scolding and embarrassment, *that's* what it got me! Now, do I need to go through that *again?!* Must I question *everything?!*

Still, Raoul was nervous. His Inner Ale Run kept nibbling at the edges of his consciousness, telling him something was amiss. What was it? Raoul couldn't stand it; he had to investigate. So he whispered to Iame, asking, "Um, Doctor Ghuanobhraine, what, exactly, is in the fruit juice?"

"Oh, don't worry about *that,"* Iame reassured him. "Just a little bit of potassium cyanide, that's all. And don't worry, all the appropriate regulatory agencies have properly verified its purity. We wouldn't desecrate Ale Run's Most Solemn Sacrament with impure chemical compounds! No, not us. So don't you worry, Raoul, we'll all be fine. Just fine."

I suppose he's right, Raoul thought. Trust them. Like he says, Vyizder, Iame and the gang are very advanced metans; they'd never even *think* of desecrating Ale Run's Solemn Ceremonies. So why am I still so disturbed?

Then only Heegore, Iame, Raoul, and Vyizder remained standing. Iame and Heegore herded Raoul towards Vyizder. His turn was next! "Um, wait a minute, guys," Raoul objected, "Something's bothering me here, and I just figured out what it is! You say this cyanide is pure. Okay, fine, then. But what I want to know is, has it been grown organically, without the scamgramification of artificial insecticides, fertilizers, herbicides, fungicides, and so on? I mean, you can get this cyanide stuff organically, from peach pits or the root of the yucca plant and so on. Did we bother to do this right? I'd certainly not want to ascend to the Level Beyond Stupid, without doing it right."

"Oh, come off of it, now, Raoul, don't be so persnickety!" Vyizder demanded. "The Sacred Drink has been Pure and Descamgramified enough for everyone else; why should you be better than everyone else? We're all equal in the eyes of Ale Run, you know."

"I want to see the label," was all that Raoul had to say.

"I'm sorry," Iame apologized, "When we prepared the Sacred Drink, last night, we threw all the packaging for all the ingredients away. And the trash is gone by now. But I can assure you, the cyanide was grown organically. Wholesomely and naturally."

Well, okay, then, Raoul said to himself. Check that one off. There's still something bothering me. Badly. Let's get down to basics. "I'm so sorry, guys, but I'll have to pass. I don't think I'm quite ready to ascend to the Level Beyond Stupid, just yet. I guess I'm just not worthy yet. I *like* living on the stupid level! I like eating delicious organic foods, watching the sunset, drinking from a cool and pure mountain stream, and just enjoying the pleasant light of day.

"So I think I'll hang out on the stupid level a little while longer, and make *absolutely sure* that I've learned everything I can, here, that I've become as worthy as possible, before ascending to the Level Beyond

Stupid. After all, Vyizder, you, as my Spirit Guide, and even the very Universe Herself, as interpreted by Deep Green, have spoken. And you have all concluded that I'm not a very advanced metan. Even *I* can see this, because I enjoy living on the stupid level so much. I enjoy the pleasures of my earthly container very much! So it's obvious for all to see that I'm simply not yet worthy to ascend to the Level Beyond Stupid."

"But you're wrong *again*, Raoul!" Vyizder howled. "You *are* worthy, because you can see that you *aren't* worthy! *Paradox*, remember?! This is the first of the Five-and-Three-Quarters-Fold Way! Ale Run's Mercy knows no end! And as far as the stupidity of enjoying stupid pleasures in this illusory, lower, stupid level, well, obviously, your worries are all manifestations of scamgrams and false consciousness! The solution is obvious and simple. You must drink the solution and end your cycle, so that you may arise, and take your rightful place of Glory by Ale Run's Side, on the Level Beyond Stupid. And then the false pleasures of the stupid level won't befester you any longer."

Well, I can see the sense of what my Spirit Guide is saying, I suppose, Raoul thought. But wait! "Why is it, then, Spirit Guide, that my Inner Ale Run tells me not to do this?"

Vyizder whipped out his Ping Thing and doused Raoul's scamgrams good and hard. "There," he said. "Feeling better? Those were *scamgrams*, not your Inner Ale Run! You silly metan you! Now let's get with the program! All your friends have already left! They're waiting for us! Now let's *go!*"

All my friends are *gone?! Gaiagurl!* The one I used to love, the one whose smooth skin I caressed in the back of the blue bus?! *Gone?* Dead and *gone?* Raoul looked over his shoulder, desperately searching the crowd of corpses in the meeting hall behind him. There she was, sprawled out on the floor, her straight, gorgeous long brown hair strewn about. Gaiagurl! *My Love! No!* And Raoul burst free of Heegore and Iame behind him, dashing to her side.

And when he got there, and knelt, whimpering, reaching out to touch her body, there was nothing there! Nothing but thin air! He stood back up and approached his Spirit Guide, staring uncomprehendingly. Iame and Heegore both grabbed onto Raoul's arms. "What's going on?" he demanded.

Vyizder glared at Iame and Heegore, but then explained, "Well, you see, our fellow metans are all ready to ascend to the Level Beyond Stupid. Their earthly containers have now turned into Spiritual Essences, in preparation for the Journey. They await us. Let's go! Ask me no more silly questions! Here is the answer to *all* your questions. Here is your Solution." And Vyizder passed the cup to Iame. Iame let go of Raoul's right arm, and offered him the drink.

"You first," Raoul insisted. "Go for it, Doctor Ghuanobhraine. I want to watch closely now, and see how this works."

Vyizder stared hard at Raoul. Raoul didn't flinch, and his voice had sounded quite firm. So Vyizder relented. He passed another cup to Iame. "Show him," Vyizder said. "Show him how a good Omnologist voluntarily fleeces himself of the scamgrams of false consciousness, of the attachment to the stupid level. Show him how we ascend to the Level Beyond Stupid, entirely of our own free will, and cleanse the Earth of the befesterment of excess metans. *Show* him!"

Iame tried to give the first cup to Raoul, but Raoul wouldn't take it. So Iame set the first cup aside, and prepared to quaff from the second. "Wait," Raoul objected, "Why don't you drink this *other* cup, the one you want *me* to drink?"

"Because that's *yours*," Iame explained. "It's part of the Ceremony. See, there's your name, in tiny letters." Raoul looked closely. Sure enough, hand-written on the Sacred Paper Cup, was his name! "And here's mine," Iame continued, "They must match your name, as Written in The Book Beyond Stupid. Else it doesn't work right."

"So you cannot drink from my cup."

"That's right. Nor can I drink from yours. So it is Written, so must it be Done."

"Let's see how it's Done, then," Raoul said. "I want to watch very closely, and see how you turn into a Spiritual Essence."

Iame glanced at Vyizder, and Vyizder stared right back. So Iame hefted that paper cup to his lips, and drank. He paused for a moment, fell slowly to the floor, twitched, and then lied still. Raoul gently kicked his body; sure enough, his foot contacted solid matter.

"What are you doing?" Vyizder demanded. "Are you some sort of sick pervert, or what?! Desecrating our Sacred Ceremony, messing with dead bodies! What's the *matter* with you?!"

"I just want to watch and see how he turns into a Spiritual Essence, that's all."

"That's sick, that's scamgramified!" Vyizder exclaimed in horror. "Now, you're holding up the show! None of us can actually complete the Journey, until all of us have completed The Ceremony! Now it's *your turn!* Here's your cup!"

"Why don't you and Heegore go first," Raoul suggested, stalling. "I'm the least worthy, I'll go last. I'll be right behind you."

"No, we can't trust you!" Vyizder spat out angrily. "The first will be last, and the last will be first! That's what is Written! You really should have gone *first!* Now, you've messed with our Ceremony quite enough already, thank you! If we leave you till last, you might stick around too long, morbidly watch the Spiritual Conversion Process, poke our bodies, and ruin the Magic Ceremony! Then *none* of us could ascend to the Level Beyond Stupid! We can't let one silly metan spoil it for *everyone!* Not stop stalling! It's *your turn! End your cycle!"*

Very well then, Raoul thought, relenting. My Spirit Guide surely must know best. I mustn't ruin the magic of the moment. Here's a toast to the Level Beyond Stupid! And he raised his Sacred Paper Cup to his lips.

Chapter 19 has endnotes about Scientology and The Level Beyond Stupid... See page 244, pay $153, collect $444, and do not go directly or indirectly to The Level Beyond Stupid...

Chapter 20

Anti-Hubba-Bubba's Progress

"Though it is possible to utter words only with the intention to fulfill the will of God, it is very difficult not to think about the impression which they will produce on men and not to form them accordingly. But deeds you can do quite unknown to men, only for God. And such deeds are the greatest joy that a man can experience."
  Leo Tolstoy (1828–1910)

"To conceive the good, in fact, is not sufficient; it must be made to succeed among men. To accomplish this less pure paths must be followed."
  Ernest Renan (1823–1892)

Pud stagnated in a torpid and timeless swamp of molasses that grabbed him and wouldn't let go. He struggled and struggled, in a state of mind that remains nameless to the vast majority of healthy, waking humans, because few can remember, let alone talk about, their rare experiences in this peculiar state. He cried out to his Inner Ale Run, pleading, "Oh, Inner Ale Run, where am I, *why* am I, why do I suffer so? Where are *You*, why are You, why won't You help me?"

Pud just stayed suspended there for a timeless time, as if his mind had been turned inside out and splayed out on a fur stretcher and hung on the clothes line to dry, exposing scraps of his innards out to the elements. Pud called out to his Inner Ale Run, again and again. Sometimes Pud amended his cries with an even less coherent thought, something along the lines of, "Inner Ale Run, wasn't there something I was supposed to do? Do for You? Isn't there some reason why I must break free of this swamp? What is the key, here, what is my Mission? Won't You speak to me, set me right, set me free?"

But there'd be no answer. Or maybe Pud was just too far gone to hear it. Then he'd cry out again. And again. But finally there was an answer. Pud moved towards a tunnel. The Inner Ale Run welcomed him into it, and shone to him from the far end. The Inner Ale Run filled him peace, love, and acceptance. But there was a certain reluctance there, both in Pud, and in the Inner Ale Run. Pud's Mission wasn't done, and they both knew it. And then there was the certain knowledge that if Pud actually broke on through the far end of that tunnel, there was no going back. Pud, as Pud, would never go back. The Mission would become Mission Unaccomplished.

Still, the Inner Ale Run was by no means a skinflint or a taskmaster. With great compassion and mercy, It told Pud, "You have suffered greatly, and you would be welcomed home to a place of great bliss if you choose to cross this line. Or you may choose to go back, and complete your Mission. There are polarities to be flipped, applecarts to be upset, Truths to be told, many wrongs to be righted. But you have already suffered in My Name, and I can ask no more of you. There will always be suffering back there, but you can go back and lessen it if you want to. Or you can come home. It's all up to you. Whatever you decide, I will be with you, always."

Great emotion welled up from deep inside Pud. He asked his Inner Ale Run for courage, and strength washed over him in waves. "Yes, my Inner Ale Run, I want to go back!" And so he went back. As if from a distant plane of existence far more unreal than the tunnel he'd just left, he felt pain, and his body, as he weakly thrashed around in a, what was it called, a *bed*. Then he slipped back down to a lower level of consciousness. But the clinging molasses slowly relaxed its grip, and Pud no longer asked nameless questions.

Timeless time slipped by, and Pud fought his way to the brink of waking consciousness for longer and longer intervals. Sometimes he stirred and mumbled, almost awake. Then one day he found himself gradually awakening, in bed in a small room without windows. Weakly, he stirred. His IV tube and his bandages restrained him like mighty manacles. He mumbled and groaned softly; these were the only sounds he could manage to utter. Then he waited, catching his breath. Then he moaned again, and waited again. This went on for what seemed like several hours.

The small room's door opened, revealing a very average-looking, mildly plump, slightly balding man pushing towards middle age. When he saw Pud awake, his face broke out in a wide, hearty grin. "My, my!" he exclaimed. "My guest awakens! Welcome, Sir! Welcome back to the land of the living!" He found Pud's hand and shook it gently. "My name is Sam Ehritan. Pleased to meet you. I'm sorry we're not at some stylish cocktail party, where our companions could elegantly introduce us to each other. I'm afraid I'll have to be quite crude, and ask you your name."

Pud eyed him suspiciously. Who was this man, and what did he want? "Um, um, ah," Pud croaked hoarsely. "Paul. Just call me Paul."

"Sure, Paul," Sam grinned mischievously. Then he dropped his smile, sobering up instantaneously. "Paul, I have a confession to make. I hope you won't be too angry with me. But I have my reasons, you see. I was quite seriously worried that you wouldn't make it, and we need all the information that we can get. In your coma-like state, you'd stir and mumble occasionally. I've been recording your mumbles and studying them. Please forgive me for invading your privacy. But I know who you are. You're the Anti-Hubba-Bubba. Don't worry, I'm on your side."

Pud stared at Sam yet more intently. "OK, fine, then. My real name..."

"No, no, I have no need to know your real name, and as a matter of fact, neither do you," Sam protested. "You're Paul. Paul, Paul, Paul. Remember that. I know you're the Anti-Hubba-Bubba. You've talked about that in your, your sleep, and about your Inner Ale Run, and your Mission, and so on. But I don't know your, ah-hem, 'real' name, and I don't care to. Your *real* name is Paul. I'll want to know your last name, when you, ah, remember it, so I can get some papers made, and some records generated for you. My friends have their methods. Your past life, I don't want to know about, other than whatever might help me to help you with your Mission."

"What's this all about? What's in this for you? Who *are* you, where am I, how..." Pud rasped out.

"There, there, now, take it easy. Save your voice. I'll explain. By the strangest of circumstances—to tell you the truth, it's because I, ah, desperately needed to take a leak, so I stopped my car by the roadside, and scurried down into the culvert for an emergency stop—I found you half dead by the roadside. Because I just happen to oppose suffering and death, I picked you up and brought you here. Just because I see doing these kinds of things as being what God asks us to do."

Pud thrashed around under his blankets a bit, stared in horror at

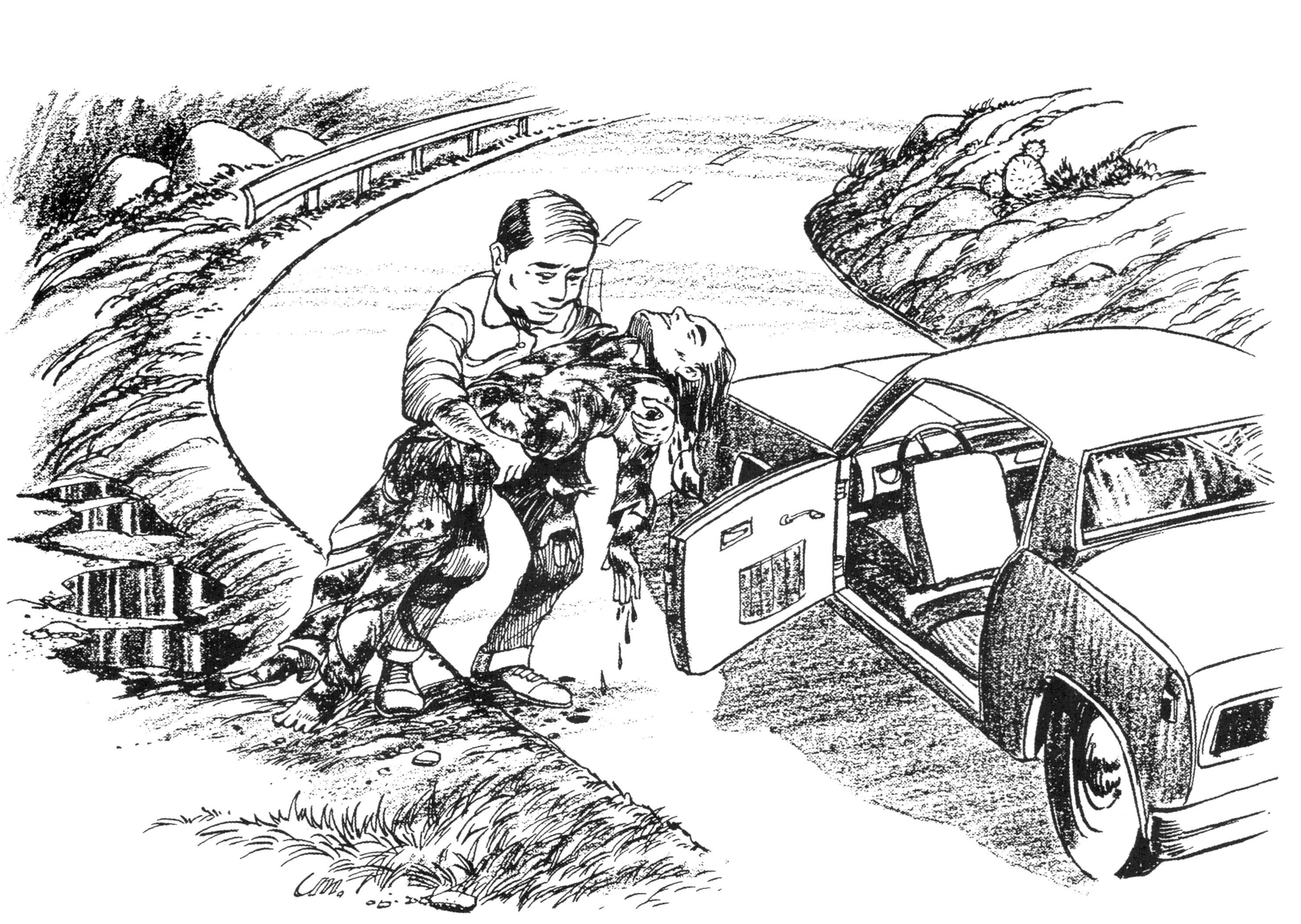

Sam, and cried out, "Sam, Sam, you scamgram-I-am! You're seriously scamgramified! We've *got* to get you to an expert fleecer of metans, and a V-Meter, or a Ping Thing, and…"

"Paul, take it easy! What's the matter with you?!"

"What's the matter with *you,* with this scamgramified talk of 'God'? Don't you…"

"Paul, relax! I'm sorry! I won't talk to you about 'God' any more! Now what I meant to say, and I'm very sorry, here, to upset you so, but what I meant to say, is that our *Inner Ale Run* is the one who asks us to do kind things for one another, and to prevent suffering and death when we can. And it's because my Inner Ale Run speaks to me, that you're here with me today."

"Oh."

"And Paul, um, back out here, outside of the Church of Omnology, a lot of people, they call their Inner Ale Run 'God', you see, so…"

"Sam, Sam! I'm really *worried* about you now! Promise me you'll go and see an expert with, with a V-Meter, at least. OK? Promise?"

"OK. Now, after I picked you up and brought you here, I've had a few doctors come by now and then, to check you out and keep you in good shape. And then I learned that you are the Anti-Hubba-Bubba, and that the Church of Omnology would love to find you. So I took some more liberties. I hope you won't mind, but I'll bet you know how important it is that we keep you from falling into the Church's hands."

Pud nodded his head vigorously. Vigorously, that is, in relative terms, considering his weakened condition.

"What I had done, is I had a doctor friend of mine do a bit of plastic surgery on you," Sam admitted. "A bit of facial reconstruction was called for, what with the condition your condition was in, anyway. And we also did a bit of ultrasonic liposuction. That explains many of your bandages. You'll look quite a bit different; hopefully enough to shake off anyone who might still be looking for you. I hope you won't be too upset. This surgeon is very good."

Pud didn't look upset at all. He asked, "So where am I, and what, besides just obeying your Inner Ale Run, is in all this for you? And…"

"Take it easy, Paul! I'm not done. Save your energy, and I'll answer your questions when I'm done. You've been here for about two months. So you can see why I was starting to get quite worried about you. And where? Underground, in a hidden hideaway beneath my house, in a suburb of Los Diablos. More, I don't think you should know.

"And yes, I *do* have some other reasons why I'm going to all this trouble for you. I *do* have my axes to grind. It's just one of those things. One of the beautiful, unexpected benefits of obeying one's Inner Ale Run. Here I saved your life just because I obey my Inner Ale Run, and now, the Inner Ale Run pays me back, by putting into my hands, the Anti-Hubba-Bubba himself! You see, Paul, I, and many of my friends, we have many axes to grind against Ale Run Hubba-Bubba and his sham of a 'church'.

"From what I've heard you mumble, you've seen that Ale Run's inappropriateness has grown and grown, and that he's actually become evil. You've seen this, and you've turned against him. Am I right?"

Pud nodded. "Now, Paul, I'm sorry, but I must ask you this. I've heard through certain special channels about what really happened at the Fleece the Poor Benefit Show. Are you actually the same metan who stood up and denounced what was going on? Called it *evil?"*

"That was me," Pud confirmed.

"Well, then, you must really and truly be the Anti-Hubba-Bubba," Sam concluded. "I'm told their V-Meters went clear off scale at that point, because you had the courage to recognize evil when you saw it, and to denounce it as such, by name. You have revealed your power! No wonder that the 'church' is after you!"

"So I am told," Pud confirmed. "So my Inner Ale Run has told me. You and my Inner Ale Run, then, tell me the same things. That's *great!* I suppose it's my Inner Ale Run's way of telling me that I should trust you. Then what are these many axes you and your friends have to grind against the false church? What are your plans? My Inner Ale Run has never clearly specified what it is that I must do. Am I to start the One True Church of Listening to One's Own Inner Ale Run, then? Does your Inner Ale Run tell you to help me lead the truly advanced metans away from the Church of Omnology, then, to a new Church?"

"My Inner Ale Run tells me to help you get well," Sam stated simply. "And then, to help you onto your feet, and on your way. Then you must do what your Inner Ale Run tells you to do. That's all. Well, just one other thing. To tell you, beware of the Horde Whisperer! The one who tells us all exactly what we want to hear. The one who has, apparently, problematized reality.

"You know, Paul, I used to think that the Church of Omnology was all just a bunch of hot air and hocus-pocus. Just a grab-bag of made-up mumbo-jumbo. But my sources tell me that lately, their V-Meters and their Ping Things are taking on mysterious powers. Reality is becoming problematized! So beware! So am I told to warn you. But that's all. The rest is up to you."

Pud sat there, seemingly in shock. "The, the *Horde Whisperer!* And reality becoming *problematized!* I've heard this before, from my own Inner Ale Run! Sam, this, this is *phenomenal!* I can't explain it; you must be talking to the same Inner Ale Run that *I'm* talking to!!!"

"They are one and the same," Sam assured him.

"Now can you explain to me, then," Pud asked, "why it is that you and your friends are so opposed to Ale Run Hubba-Bubba and his Church?"

"Well, it's a long story," Sam admitted. "To understand it thoroughly, we have to start with who I am, and what I do for a living. You see, I'm a drug dealer."

Pud recoiled, clutching his blankets around him, eyeing Sam suspiciously again. "I don't know, Sam," he said sadly, "but I think you'd better get your scamgrams fleeced right away!"

"Now wait a minute!" Sam objected. "A minute ago you were saying you and I are talking to the same Inner Ale Run. Now I need my scamgrams fleeced! Just because I belong to a group called 'drug dealers'! I think you're listening to the same Horde Whisperer that whispers in oh so many ears! I think you're not listening to, to, um, a man from long ago, he spoke out against the Horde Whisperer.

"You see, the Horde Whisperer tells us that it's always someone else's fault, not our own fault. And it's always, especially, some other *group's* fault. So all we need to do, is to persecute, punish, that *group,* and all will be well. We are purely fleeced, and members of that group over there, they're purely unfleeced, and must be punished. It's been, variously over the ages, witches, Blacks, gays, Jews, members of the wrong religion, nationality, and so on. Right now, it just happens to be drug dealers.

"But the, um, Anti-Horde Whisperer, when he came along long ago, he told us not to be that way. He told us that when we must judge individuals, we should judge them on whether or not they follow the will of the Inner Ale Run, as best as they can. Not on which group they belong to. He told a tale about a man, a member of a despised group, he helped a metan in need. So basically, the Anti-Horde Whisperer told everyone that a good metan from a despised, 'unfleeced' group can follow the will of the Inner Ale Run better than the members of a 'fleeced' group. We must judge individuals, not groups. Many metans pay lip service to this idea, but they don't follow it. So beware of the Horde Whisperer and his lies!"

"I suppose there might be some truth there," Pud admitted. "You've got my curiosity stirred up. While I'm all laid up in bed, here, do you think that maybe you could get me something to read about this Anti-Horde Whisperer, and what all he had to say?"

Sam stared at Pud in uncomprehending wonder for a few moments. Then his face brightened up, and he said, "Yes, as a matter of fact, I can do exactly that! I have a book on my computer, and while I'm not exactly a computer wizard, I have some friends who are! So I'll have the computer translate that book to the Omnological talk that you'll understand, and I'll bring you a printout!

"Now on this drug dealer deal. I know what some metans will say. 'Oh, but your analogy doesn't hold. Drug dealers are drug dealers because of what they do, not because of which group they belong to. There's no way a drug dealer can follow the will of the Inner Ale Run.' But they're *wrong!* You've seen how I, Sam Ehritan, a drug dealer, rescued you, Paul, thus fulfilling the will of the Inner Ale Run, despite the fact that I'm basically a witch, in the eyes of most metans. Except when they're out looking to score a hit of an illegal substance.

"Let me tell you about my drug dealing. Yes, I do sell some cocaine and marijuana now and then. Supplies to practitioners of alternative medicine, too. Even cigarettes and entire gallons of Ripple wine, occasionally, when my customers demand it. I deal only with friends I know well, to keep from being burnt at the stake. And I've even been known to eat, and drink Ripple wine, with my friends. The metans who would call me a witch, they'd say, 'Look, he eats and drinks, he has scamgrams in him.' If they knew about it, that is. But I would say to them, 'Nonsense, I follow the will of the Inner Ale Run, and so I have few scamgrams in me. The wisdom of the Inner Ale Run is demonstrated by all those who follow His Will.' And this is true. I follow the will of the Inner Ale Run, even though I sell drugs. But I hide the facts, lest I be burnt at the stake.

"You see, respectable members of the community do what I do, and few metans call them names. They sell Ripple wine, cigarettes, coffee, chocolate, fattening foods, and prescription drugs, all of which various metans abuse. And these pushers, most don't even keep a personal relationship with their customers. Their customer might be drinking three gallons of Ripple wine every night, losing his job and his wife, and still, they'll sell him some more.

"I have relationships with my customers. I don't sell to people who can't control their habits, who endanger their marriages or their jobs. And I don't buy from violent dealers, either. It's not just that I follow the will of my Inner Ale Run, it's also simply that I'm level-headed, and know what can get me into trouble. So I avoid causing trouble, because I know it will come back to me. I do less damage than the pusher of Ripple wine, yet he's a respectable pillar-of-the-community-type metan, while I'm a witch. Go figure!

"Yes, I'll admit that many drug dealers aren't as responsible as I am. Yet the tune remains the same. I'm punished for being a member of the wrong group, where the group is crudely defined. Where the groups are defined in terms of anything other than 'those who follow the will of the Inner Ale Run,' and 'those who don't'—and I would add that it's most often very difficult for anyone other than the Inner Ale Run to accurately know the difference—then we can rapidly run into trouble. Into serious injustices.

"Consider this, too, Paul. Consider that when I put those horrid *illegal* equivalents of Ripple wine out there, I decrease the demands, the high prices, that lead some metans to lives of crime, into breaking into other metans' houses, so that they can raise thousands of dollars to support their habits, when the *real* costs of their drugs are equivalent to what it takes to buy a loaf of bread. If there were more heinous drug dealers like me, prices would be lower, and incentives for crime would drop. Incentives to hook users would also drop. Kids in school would have as much of a hard time buying a joint as they now have buying a beer, instead of finding it easier to buy cocaine than beer. How many beer pushers hang out around school, offering beer to hook the kids? So I'm actually a hero, fighting crime by reducing the incentives to crime. I'm following the will of my Inner Ale Run.

"To tell you the truth, though, those are mere sidelines to my *real* business. My real business is helping doctors, and their patients, by thwarting the FDA. I sell illegal medical devices and supplies. You see, Paul, the FDA prohibits us from selling anything to anyone, if we tell them it will make them feel better, or if it's even vaguely related to medicine. Unless we go and pay lawyers and consultants millions of dollars, get our 'medical devices' examined for years if not decades, make the right political campaign contributions, and so on.

"You want to sell women a harmless little bag full of slippery silicon, for them to place against their breasts—on the *outsides* of their breasts, now, we're not talking surgical *anything*, here—so that their fingers will slip around, real smoothly, so that they can better examine themselves for lumps? For breast cancer? You can't *do* that! Gotta study this 'medical device' for years and years first! For that matter, if those women ask their husbands to feel the lumps and get their opinions, then the husbands might be brought up on charges of practicing medicine without a license!

"You want to sell customers a machine that plays music and flashes lights and releases scents, in a computer-controlled manner corresponding to the music? Fine! But you'd better not hint around that this machine might help people to *feel better*, or you're selling unapproved medical devices! And you'd better not sell herbs and vitamins in the same store next to books and magazines about the benefits of such things, or you'll be busted for unapproved advertising of unproven health benefits! And on and on.

"My special niche market, though, Paul, is this: I sell software! Software is a medical device, now, too. Here's the deal: Doctors can still, just barely, prescribe medicines for 'off-label' uses. Uses that doctors know the drugs are good for, but the drug companies haven't yet greased the right palms for, for getting the FDA to approve. And new genetic testing allows us, more and more, to know whether or not a person will get good results out of a certain drug.

"So sometimes, after genetic testing, we could say, 'Yes, this drug is lethal for 0.0002% of users, and harmful to 5%, and useless for 30%, but knowing your genotype, we can tell you that this will be a good drug for you, for problem X, even though problem X is an off-label use.' We can do this. The technology is there. We can have computers do much of the work. I have CD-ROMs full of drugs and their off-label uses, and which genotypes are good matches, and the software to run the show. But the FDA and the lawyers and consultants, not to mention the politicians, haven't had their palms greased yet. So these CD-ROMs and software applications are still unapproved medical devices.

"And the government has the key to read all computer transmissions, so you'd better not be helping doctors to do this, over the networks. I smuggle CD-ROMs and computer programs to doctors by hand delivering them. The CD-ROMs are disguised, and the programs contain very special security features. Only thus can we get the benefits of the latest medical technology to their patients. After the doctors illicitly run the programs, they can make the right prescriptions, and no one is the wiser. It sure beats having the doctor trying to personally, mentally juggle twenty thousand drugs, half a million off-label uses, and a practically infinite number of genotypes. An ideal computer application, even if we have to run it in secret.

"Now compare all this to the Church of Omnology. They can claim that their V-Meters and their Ping Things can cure everything from colds to cancer and back, but since they do it in the name of *religion*, no one can *touch* them! Then they bad-mouth and sue mainstream medical practitioners, especially psychiatrists, even while Omnologists drive some of their members to suicide. So I suppose you might understand how I, and my doctor friends, hamstrung by the FDA as we try to help patients, are quite resentful of Ale Run Hubba-Bubba and his 'church', as they get a free ride in ripping people off. And then get rewarded with a tax break to boot! Can you see why we'd have our axes to grind with this 'church'?"

Pud nodded thoughtfully. "Basically, we're just outraged at the injustice of it all, and want to see what we can do to straighten things out," Sam continued, "But enough of that. Now how about you. It seems to me that you've had those bandages on long enough. Now that you're awake, you'll be able to start taking care of yourself. Let's get those things off of you and clean you up." And so Sam did.

Pud was quite pleased with his new looks when Sam brought him a mirror. Then there was the matter of getting the first snippets of food into Pud's stomach in about two months. Finally, the day's tasks were done, and Sam just sat with him, chatting.

"Well, I'd better get some work done," Sam finally concluded. "Accounts and orders to check, and so on. I'd like to sit here and keep you company for a while longer, but I've got to go. Are you tired and wanting to go back to sleep? Or do you want me to round up some books, magazines, or a TV for you? It'll take me a while to get that special book translated that you asked me about, you know. So what do you say?"

"I'll take the TV if you don't mind. Thanks!"

So Sam headed off to go and fetch a TV. He was back shortly, chatting some more with Pud as he set it up. Then the TV came on. Pud saw naked people standing on the sidewalks, wearing dinosaur masks and toting signs. "I'd rather go naked than wear the corpse of a Polyestrasaur" said one sign as it briefly flashed on the screen. Pud wasn't quite sure he'd read it right. "Respect our Ancestors!" read another. Bedlam ruled, in sound and motion, as the protesters and signs milled around, jockeying for the camera's eye.

Then some heavily clad and armed law enforcement types came stomping through the crowd, which eagerly cleared out of their way. "Go, go, go NADGRAB!!! Go, go, go NADGRAB!!!" the crowd chanted. Then the chaos of the crowd faded away, and the voice-over kicked in. "Good evening, ladies and gentlemetans. This is Newt Rather with your unbiased, up-to-the-minute source of news, URB Fuddled News. The scene you're now watching is beamed to you live from right in front of Sam Clam's Disco, in Los Diablos.

"As we speak, the courageous defenders of decency and respect for our elders, the GRABBOIDS of NADGRAB, are raiding an alleged den of grave robbery, an illicit, underground operation buried beneath a 'front' company. It's alleged that in this facility—bear with us now, as we speak frankly; small children and extra sensitive metans may wish to hit their 'mute' buttons at this time—it's alleged that in this very facility, cars were being repaired and refueled, using the sacred bodily remains of our spiritual ancestors, the dinosaurs. Yes, ladies and gentlemetans, right here before our very own eyes, right here below Sam Clam's Disco, horrid, gruesome acts were performed with petroleum derivatives and other sacred bodily remains! Only NADGRAB can save us!"

None of it made any sense at all to Pud. So he hit the "mute" button on the remote control that Sam had given him, and gazed questioningly at Sam.

"Oh, that's right," Sam said, snapping his fingers. "I've forgotten all about updating you on the latest, on what's happened while you've been in a coma. You see, some Omnology scientists have invented this thing called a Hubba-Bubbatron. It's basically a time stasis machine. They put them on large rotating assemblies, and then they rotate them over time-zone boundaries. The International Date Line is especially effective. They turn the time stasis field on going one way, and off going the other way, so that one can either progress or regress in time, visiting one's past or future lives. Regression or progression therapy, they call it.

"So these large machines incorporating Hubba-Bubbatrons are called 'therapeutritrons', and they put them out to sea in large luxury liners. All the important Panderwood actors and actresses, they've joined the Church of Omnology so that they can get this latest therapy. They all go out to sea on luxury liners stationed over the International Date Line. They're even setting up an aircraft carrier out there, so they can fly in real quick. And some of them are filming many of their scenes right on board the therapeutritrons, so that they won't loose any more valuable therapy time than they absolutely have to.

"Anyway, it's become quite the major competition among the Panderwood types. Some of them have regressed way, way back to the dinosaur days, and discovered that the dinosaurs were actually quite intelligent and spiritually advanced. For instance, they had fire, the wheel, bath tubs, acupuncture, homeopathy, tattoos, and progressive income tax tables. But they didn't have fossil fuels, pesticides, fungicides, child abuse, poverty, synthetic rubber, or toy weapons of any sort. This, and things even yet more incredible, the brave spiritual explorers of Panderwood have told us.

"However, they've also discovered that, being spiritually advanced, the spirits of these dinosaurs are quite thoroughly disgusted and angry with us, for what we're doing with their bodily remains. We've been morbidly displaying their bones in museums and such. For these sins, we've got to pay by putting their bones back where we found them, and restoring the environments of those fossils digs as best as we can.

"But that's not all! We also disrespect the dinosaur elders by using their bodily remains in petroleum products, to burn, to wear, and to make plastic forks and spoons and lampshades out of. The Panderwood types, they say, well, after all, how would *we* feel, if *our* descendants were making such things out of *our* bodies, and burning our bodies for fuel, and so on.

"So Congress invited the good-looking Panderwood types to Washington, D.C., to testify. There were a lot of well-publicized photos of all the important D.C. types posing with all the good-looking Panderwood types, as they saved us all from corpse abuse and ancestor disrespect. Some of the actresses even went naked, rather than wear polyestrasaurs. So as you can imagine, the politicians and the Panderwood types got a lot of publicity, and the media sold a lot of papers, magazines, and advertisements. And all the citizens were saved from indecency towards our spiritual ancestors, and we all got to feel morally superior to those evil heathens, the money-grubbing oil companies.

"Congress created **NADGRAB**, which is the **N**ative **A**merican **D**inosaurs **G**raves **R**estoration and **A**ctualization **B**ureau. So now the NADGRAB police, called **GRABBOIDS**, for **G**raves **R**estoration **A**gents **B**ravely, **B**oldly **O**bliterating **I**ndignities to **D**inosaur **S**pirits, they go 'round from store to store and house to house, ferreting out old oil cans, scraps of plastics, polyesters, gasoline, Vaseline, and Valvoline, and all other examples of corpse abuse. The only way you can get off the hook is to have expert Omnologists come in with their V-Meters and Ping Things and appease the spirits of the dinosaurs. Then you may continue to use your plastic spoons and forks, say, if you're too poor to afford newer ones, which are guaranteed to be manufactured using methods that won't anger the Ancestor Spirits.

"Since Congress has determined that dinosaur disrespect is a major crisis, NADGRAB has been tasked with ferreting out all petroleum addicts, who must then be thoroughly counseled by expert counselors, specially trained in treating dinosaur disrespect. And since all the oil companies are to blame for all this petroleum addiction in the first place, they obviously must pay for all their damages, all their wanton destruction, and the cost of all this expert counseling.

"So all the experts from the Church of Omnology are having a field day, as you might imagine. There's a few folks here and there, they're raising questions about the separation of church and state, and other old, fuddy-duddy-type concepts. Congress says it's not an issue, 'cause we're dealing with Omnology as a science, not Omnology as a religion.

"And there's even a few folks making fun of these things now and then. There was a radio comedian the other day, he was saying that we should all wear as much polyester as possible, so that we can all continue to look at pictures of naked actresses protesting the desecration of polyestrasaurs. The FCC took his license away, and we haven't heard from him since.

"Now expert Omnologists and GRABBOIDS are running around, catching metans with unfleeced petroleum derivatives, and making them either volunteer time and money to become re-educated in dinosaur bodily remains sensitivity classes, or be prosecuted. But it's all quite voluntary, of course; NADGRAB believes in education and treatment, not in raw, brutal, violent force. Persuasion, not coercion.

"But we have to *do something*, the GRABBOIDS say. They believe that disrespect for our spiritual ancestors, the dinosaurs, is behind global insensitivization and inappropriatization. Mean-spiritedness, rampant selfishness, resentment towards selfless government servants, that kind of thing. Since no one can *prove* that disrespect of dinosaur spirits *isn't* doing all these bad things, then we have to play it safe, and fleece the disrespect out of petroleum products and oil companies.

"The GRABBOIDS of NADGRAB, the media, Panderwood, and Congress, they've all gone on a rampage. Accusing the oil companies of deliberately 'spiking' their gasoline with the spirits of Benzenasauruses, just to keep all the drivers 'hooked'. Withholding information about the addictive nature of driving, and so on. Demanding that the oil companies fork over billions of dollars to socialized medicine, since they cause like fifty thousand automobile deaths a year. On and on.

"Anyway, that's about that. I've hidden all my most precious petroleum-derived products away underground, here, in the other rooms like this one here, in the secret, buried parts of my house. You might say I've given all my dinosaur bodily remains a decent burial. Be that as it may, you'll get plenty of chances to watch TV, here, and catch up on all this news.

"Now I really do need to go off and get some work done. One last item for you: I've really got to know a last name for you. Get the paperwork in gear, get you a new ID. It won't be totally foolproof. I'd suggest you not get a government job, for example. And don't go for any government benefits, unless it's a matter of survival. But when you're ready to leave here, you'll be equipped to get a private job, at least.

"Now, your last name, Paul. Something you'll be able to remember easily, but not too terribly similar to your old last name. How 'bout it?"

"Um, how about, 'Mudd'? My name is already mud with the Church of Omnology! So we'll sort of hide me right under their noses, what do you say? We all know my name is mud, but by naming me Mudd, I can hide! Poetic justice, isn't it?"

Sam just grinned and left. So it came to pass that Pudmuddle B. Fuddle became Paul Mudd.

Two more weeks slipped by. Paul watched TV, and read Sam's computer translation about a great metan from long ago, who opposed the Horde Whisperer. He mulled over this at great length, reaching many conclusions about how best to fight the Horde Whisperer.

Then the day came that Paul Mudd was healthy but going stir-crazy. He wanted out, but he didn't want to be homeless, nor did he want to mooch off of Sam any more, nor conduct a long job hunt. After all, a long job hunt would expose him to many metans, and perhaps even to too close of an encounter with a V-Meter or a Ping Thing. So he ended up asking Sam for a job.

Sam grinned and signed him up right away. Paul became a driver for a sedan delivery service, delivering chemicals, sacred roots, CD-ROMs, and computer programs. It was a job he liked; a job he thought he'd keep.

But then he remembered that he had a Mission. The first part of his Mission, he felt, must be to go and see Betty, Tracy, Bracy, and Hamster Huey, and to make amends. This he did by making a detour from one of his nationwide sedan delivery routes. He drove up to their gauche trailer in their gauche trailer park with apprehension.

But they were all quite glad to see him, after he told them who he was, and that he was on a Mission opposing the Church of Omnology. They'd had their car and all their plastic toys taken away from them, because they'd been too poor to afford the services of a professional Omnologist dinosaur-spirit-appeaser, yet not poor enough to have the government provide this investment in their futures.

So Paul gave them some of the money he'd earned on his delivery route, and cautioned them not to tell anyone, and not to spend the money too ostentatiously. They all nodded, including Hamster Huey, who was very happy with the idea that he'd get a new exercise wheel, manufactured without offending the spirits of the dinosaurs.

Paul was on a few days of break-time, so he stayed with his family for a little while. He re-acquainted himself with his ex-wife, the kids, and Huey. He and Betty talked of getting remarried, but she told him quite pleasantly but insistently that if his Inner Ale Run was telling him that he had a Mission, then he'd better go and accomplish that Mission first.

Paul drove off, after a tearful good-bye. As if directed by hands other than his own, the sedan's steering wheel spun back and forth. He headed off for Akron, Ohio.

Chapter 20 has endnotes concerning Dianetics Therapy, "Voluntary" Therapy, NAGPRA, NADGRAB, GRABBOIDS, and Sacred Hairs. See page 245.

Chapter 21

The Great Escape From The Level Beyond Stupid

"It is against Stupidity in every shape and form that we have to wage our eternal battle. But how can we wonder at the want of sense on the part of those who have had no advantages, when we see such plentiful absence of that commodity on the part of those who have had all the advantages?" William Booth (1829–1912)

"The key to the age may be this, or that, or the other, as the young orators describe; the key to all ages is—Imbecility; imbecility in the vast majority of men, at all times, and, even in heroes, in all but certain eminent moments; victims of gravity, custom, and fear." Ralph Waldo Emerson (1803–82)

"The question now is: Can we understand our stupidity? This is a test of intellect, not of character." John King Fairbank (1907–91)

As Raoul's cup of poisoned faux fruit punch touched his lips, his life flashed before his eyes. His mind's eye flashed back, way back to chapter twelve, and how he'd recited Wisdom from Another Dimension to Francestuous, who'd thought him to be thoroughly scamgramified. He thought of that book he'd started reading so long ago, called *Dianetics: The Modern Science of Mental Health*, by L. Ron Hubbard (1911-1986), 1978 edition. He remembered those words of simple, humble yet profound wisdom. *"The creation of dianetics is a milestone for man comparable to his discovery of fire and superior to his invention of the wheel and arch"*, he'd read in the opening statement in the opening synopsis (mysteriously missing in a more recent edition). Also flashing before his eyes, from this opening synopsis *"...skills offered in this handbook will produce the dianetic* clear, *an optimum individual with intelligence considerably greater than the current normal, or the dianetic* release, *an individual who has been freed from his major anxieties or illnesses. The* release *can be done in less than twenty hours of work and is a state superior to any produced by several years of psycho-analysis, since the release will not relapse."*

Raoul sincerely regretted not having thoroughly read that book. Maybe, he thought, maybe, just maybe, if I were "cleared" right now, instead of "descamgramified", by all these experts all around me, then maybe I'd not be in quite as much of a jam. So yes, I've got my regrets. About not thoroughly reading that book, for example.

But always look on the bright side of life. I've done a few things right. Like, for example, just right now, by remembering all those words I read way back when, weaving them into the story of my life, I saved a writer-dude in another dimension the trouble of quoting them in a chapter introduction, thereby increasing the strength of his defenses against scamgrams, pestifoggons, and slimy lawyers.

My time on the stupid level is at an end, though, he thought. All good things must come to an end. I go now to my reward. I go to a better place. I go the Level Beyond Stupid! He tilted his head, and his cup, backwards. The conscious centers of his mind directed his neuromotor centers to prepare a series of neural commands. Open lips, gulp, swallow.

But then his Inner Ale Run spoke up, saying, *"Raoul, stop! If you go through with this, then you're refusing a great gift, which is your life. Your life is real, and precious—not an illusion. You are refusing to continue work on your Missions, which are to learn. You mustn't refuse your gift, you mustn't refuse to learn. To refuse your gift of life is to curse Me, your Inner Ale Run. This is a great, deep, dark scamgram, and can never be fleeced. Listen to Me now, Raoul, this is your last chance!"*

Raoul listened, and he listened well. He looked Vyizder straight in the eye, then threw his cup and all its bitter contents into Vyizder's astonished face. Then he turned tail and ran, ran, ran. Ran for his life and soul, ran to escape from the Level Beyond Stupid. Behind him, Iame arose from the "dead", to help Vyizder and Heegore chase Raoul.

He approached the door to that large meeting room with three men behind him in hot pursuit. He barely noticed Deep Green's voice urging them on, just as he barely noticed that all the "bodies" had suddenly disappeared. All he thought about was escape.

The door bloomed right in front of him. Is it locked? Will they grab me while I fuss at the doorknob? he wondered. Then he jumped up in the air, never slowing down, and twirled his body around in midair. His back slammed into the door. Splinters flew, and Raoul blew on through. Then he ran some more.

Fortunately, he was in a lot better shape than any of his pursuers. In no time at all, he was out of the building, then over the fence. The barbed wire at the top of the chain-link fence ripped and tore him, but that didn't slow him down. Vyizder's security troops joined in pursuit.

Raoul fled from the Scientific Institute for the Advancement of Omnology, across the empty fields and into a nearby copse of woods, with Omnological security types in hot pursuit. Fortunately, they were several hundred yards back. So when Raoul burst on through the bushes and trees, onto that nearby back-country road, and hopped into Paul Mudd's sedan, his pursuers never even caught a glimpse of Paul's car. It was as if Raoul had bodily ascended up into the Level Beyond Stupid, not leaving a trace.

Raoul sat in the passenger's seat of that beat-up old sedan, suspiciously eyeing Paul. Paul glanced back mildly, tolerantly, in between his tasks of piloting the sedan as it casually cruised on down the road. "You okay, there, Bud?" Paul asked. "You look a bit torn and bloodied up. Do we need to get you to a doctor, or anything?"

"No, thanks," Raoul replied, lungs still heaving from his recent exertions. "I'll be fine."

Paul reached over, offering his right hand. "Hi. I'm Paul. Paul Mudd. I'm a sedan delivery driver. And you?" Paul mentally congratulated himself; his old name of "Pud" had barely crossed his mind.

Raoul reluctantly took his hand and shook it. "Raoul. Raoul Kinky. Student of Omnology as a science. Or, at least, I was, till very recently. Now, I'm not sure *what* I am. A fugitive, I suppose. A fugitive from my destiny in the Level Beyond Stupid. But I'm just doing what my Inner Ale Run tells me to do. I guess I'm not ready for the Level Beyond Stupid just yet."

"Is that right?!" Paul said in amazement. "That's great! Just great! *I'm* doing what *my* Inner Ale Run tells *me* to do, too! That's why I'm here, as a matter of fact! That's why I was right there, ready to pick you up! The Inner Ale Run moves in mysterious ways, it seems. I had no idea why I drove here at this time, but now it's clear!

"But Raoul, a lot of the other stuff you say makes no sense to me.

Now let me assure you, you're safe here with me. I'm listening to my Inner Ale Run, just like you. So you can trust me. Tell me all about it."

Raoul told Paul all about it. In little snippets, in bits and pieces, at first, but then it all came gushing out. All his doubts about Omnology and Ale Run Hubba-Bubba's Church leaders, who'd had Raoul do so many things that didn't seem quite right. Finally, all about how they'd tried to convince Raoul that he should end his cycle, and all the strange things that had just happened. All this and more, Raoul poured forth.

"Wow!" Paul commented. "Sounds to me as if you've been dealing with some pretty evil metans, there!"

Raoul stared at Paul in shocked amazement. Then he looked at his passenger-side door, and the Ohio countryside zipping by at fifty some miles an hour. He opened his mouth to protest to Paul.

Paul beat him to the punch, seemingly reading his mind. "Yes, Raoul, I know. You're stuck with a madman, who dares to use the word 'evil'. And in association with our Spirit Guides, the leaders of Ale Run's Church of Omnology, yet! Such heresy! You're tempted to jump out of the car, to get away from the madman. Yes, I know. I've been where you're at.

"Raoul, I'm sorry. I really shouldn't call anyone evil. It's too *judgmental*. It's so judgmental, it's scamgramified. So I take it back. Still, there's something there. Your leaders, my former leaders, the leaders of the Church of Omnology, they're... Inappropriate. Insensitive. They don't listen to their Inner Ale Run."

Raoul stared at Paul with even larger, more fearful eyes. Paul was tempted to laugh, but he didn't. "Raoul, don't worry about it. I've been there, I know how you feel. You'll tell yourself again and again, *surely* Ale Run Himself just appointed a few, um, inappropriate apples into His apple barrel of Church leaders, and He simply doesn't know what going on. You tell yourself that you're an appropriate and faithful metan, that all you've got to do, is to get Ale Run Himself to understand that you're getting treated unfairly by His Church, and all will be well.

"Well, I'm sorry to break it to you, Raoul, but Ale Run Himself is scamgramified! He won't listen to his Inner Ale Run, because there's no controlling legal authority over Ale Run Himself. Our only hope is to listen to our own Inner Ale Run ourselves, and oppose the inappropriateness of Ale Run Hubba-Bubba. This is what my Inner Ale Run has told me. Look inside yourself, talk to your Inner Ale Run, and you will see the truth of which I speak."

By now, Raoul cowered in fear, scrunched up against his car door. He looked like a trapped wild animal. Paul reached over and patted him reassuringly. "Raoul, relax! There's no reason to fear. You and I are both in this together; we'll help each other out. Just keep right on listening to your Inner Ale Run, and everything will be fine."

Raoul relaxed a bit. But only a little bit. "So what does your Inner Ale Run tell you we should do next, then?" he wondered out loud. "What's the plan? What're we gonna do? How can we stay descamgramified, if we don't have regular access to Spirit Guides, V-Meters, or Ping Things? What will we eat, where will we sleep?"

"Take it easy," Paul coaxed Raoul. "We can stay descamgramified if we just listen to our Inner Ale Run. And you know, I've got this really neat book. A good friend of mine had it translated just for me. It tells all about how, a long time ago, a certain wise metan came and told us how to keep our scamgrams away, without a single V-Meter or any Ping Things!"

Paul pointed to a stack of printouts in the back seat. "There it is," he told Raoul. "Check it out." Raoul grabbed it, absent-mindedly leafing through it while Paul talked. "Anyway," Paul continued, "This metan, he said we shouldn't worry about where we'll sleep, what we'll wear, or what we'll eat. He said to look at the birds in the trees. They don't worry or plan about anything. Yet the Inner Ale Run takes care of them! And how much more does the Inner Ale Run care about us?! So don't worry about tomorrow. Tomorrow will bring enough worries of its own; we'll just stick to worrying about today, for today. Listen to your Inner Ale Run, and take things day by day."

"So what are we doing today, then?" Raoul inquired." T o d a y , we're heading back towards my friend's house, way out in Los Diablos," Paul replied. "To pick up another load of CD-ROMs, chemicals, and sacred roots, for my sedan delivery service. More importantly, to also go and get you a new ID. My friend, Sam Ehritan, he's got a lot of connections. So he'll be able to help you out. You'll be able to work, with your new ID, for non-governmental employers, without all our Omnology buddies being able to track you down. So just hang out with me for a few days, as we head back towards Los Diablos." To himself, Paul added, I'll sure bet Sam will be very interested in hearing Raoul's tale!

Paul and Raoul drove and drove. They drove for two days. They had more than a few serious talks, especially about their backgrounds as Omnologists, and how hard it was to wean themselves from Omnological thinking. Talks about what Sam Ehritan and his translated book had told Paul. Talks about a Horde Whisperer, and an Anti-Horde Whisperer that had lived long ago.

Paul struggled and searched for a way to break it to Raoul that he, Paul, had been appointed Anti-Hubba-Bubba by the Inner Ale Run Himself. But Paul couldn't do it. His fears that he would chase Raoul off were too strong. Still, Paul strongly wished for Raoul to come along and give him the strength of companionship, as he pursued his Mission. Wasn't there some way to break the news of this momentous Mission to Raoul? I want him to join me, Paul thought, but I owe it to him, then, to tell him exactly what he's in for, should he join me. How, then, do I do this? I guess I'll wait. It'll come to me in good time. Let me just prepare his mind, and let my Inner Ale Run handle it.

And so, when it fit right in, he said, "You know, Raoul, the Anti-Horde Whisperer, he gave us some pretty awesome powers. Not the powers to amass large fortunes, or political powers, or trivial little things like that. Rather, something more important: the power to resist inappropriateness. In his name, in the name of the Anti-Horde Whisperer, as matter of fact, we are empowered to *cast out* inappropriateness. And some day, you and I, or just about anyone, who knows, some day, we may be called upon to do just that. To cast out inappropriateness. I just want you to think about that."

Raoul stared back at him blankly. "And how would we do *that?*" he wondered.

"I'm not really sure," Paul admitted. "But it has to do with being really, really and truly free of scamgrams, not in the sense of having been fleeced by experts with V-Meters and Ping Things, but, rather, in the sense of really and truly listening to one's Inner Ale Run. When the need arises, the Inner Ale Run will tell us how, will give us the words and actions. But the one most important thing is that we must pour all our energies into communicating honestly with our Inner Ale Run. When we sincerely ask the Inner Ale Run to tell us what is right, He will answer." Paul almost added something about some non-Omnologists calling this thing "prayer", according to Sam Ehritan, but then thought better of it.

Let's not shock Raoul with too much at once, he told himself. The time will come.

Periodically, Raoul and Paul would have to break their road mode, stop, take breaks, sleep, get gas, and so on. Paul knew all about the expert Omnologists at the gas stations with their V-Meters and Ping Things, offering their services of fleecing the dinosaur-ancestor-disrespect vibes away from all those petroleum products, and how they would then "narc" ("gas"?) on those who declined their services. It wasn't so much that Paul resented paying the $5/gallon for these services, it was more so that he didn't want to go anywhere near a V-Meter or a Ping Thing. So they bought their gas on the black market instead.

Then, finally, they made their way safely into Los Diablos, and to Sam Ehritan's home. There, they rested and recuperated, telling Sam all their tales of high adventure and escaping from the Level Beyond Stupid, while Sam's network went into action. One week later, despite Sam's entreaties to stay a while longer, they hit the road once more. Paul and Raoul were now the brothers Paul Mudd and Robert Mudd; their names were *both* Mudd!

Robert and Paul had sat in thoughtful silence for a few hours. "Nice guy, that Sam Ehritan guy," Robert finally spoke up. "So where are we headed?" he asked, as their ancient old sedan muscled its way through the deserts of Nevada.

"We'll travel south 'cross land, and put out the fire," Paul replied, "And we won't look past our shoulders. The Anti-Horde Whisperer told us that the man who is ploughing, but keeps on looking back, he's of no use to the Kingdom of True Descamgramification. So when we figure out what's right, we just go and *do it.* After we know what's right, we don't constantly second-guess ourselves."

"What does *that* mean," Robert asked, exasperated.

"I think it means these two gringos, they're headed to Mexico," Paul replied. "My Inner Ale Run tells me that there's a significant source of global inappropriateness lurking in the shadows down there somewhere. We have to go and kill the beast. More than that, I don't know. My Inner Ale Run tells me only so much. One day at a time, now."

"But what's the big picture?" Robert pleaded. "What is this Mission of yours? I'm with you, now, don't worry too much. Unless you've gone way off the deep end, into total scamgramification. But I'd like to know."

So Paul told Robert all about it. About his Inner Ale Run telling him about him being the Anti-Hubba-Bubba, and how reality needed to be de-problematized again. This, and more, Paul told Robert. They sat in silence for a long time, again. Finally, Robert simply said, "All right, then, Paul. I'm with you. With the Anti-Hubba-Bubba himself, no less! May the Inner Ale Run be with us!" And then they rode in more hours of silence.

They drove and they drove, and then, they drove some more. They drove to Big Bend National Park, out in West Texas. There, they drove that beat-up old sedan to a desolate riverside spot, where they made clandestine arrangements with some Mexicans, who in turn ferried their sedan across the Rio Grande. The trip on the rickety old raft was perilous, as was their jarring journey on Mexico's dirt backroads. But at least they never had to deal with border crossing guards, or the possibility that some of them might be Omnologists bearing Ping Things or V-Meters.

Several days later, they both bought themselves machetes in a small store south of Matamoros. Then they headed out into the countryside, where they knocked on the door of one certain Jose Gomez, Mexican rancher-type dude extraordinaire. Jose was quite amused by the crazy gringos and their strange tales of a bizarre wild beast running loose on his ranch, conveyed in incomprehensible English, and bits and pieces of broken Spanish. Had they spoken good Spanish, he'd doubtlessly have asked them how they knew what they knew, and dismissed them as madmen, hearing their replies.

But he grabbed his machete and called his dogs, and joined the gringos in their crazy quest. After all, he'd heard those wild tales a year or two ago, of a *chupacabras*, a goat-sucker, terrorizing Mexico, among other places. And there'd been that dead cow of his not so long ago, with the mysterious puncture wounds in its neck. So when they drove his pickup to the outback on his ranch, to that deserted, dilapidated old shed, now so badly collapsed that even his cows had stopped using it for shade long ago, and his dogs howled and growled, his hackles rose with theirs.

Those crazy gringos are right, he realized in utter astonishment. There's something hiding in my old shed! Something not quite right. Something—something highly *inappropriate*, as these strange gringos say. He put his work gloves on, and directed the gringos to take a stand, one on each end of the fallen old building.

Then he began dragging fragments of the building away, one by one. The rusted old pieces of roofing went first, then slabs of rotten wood and plywood. One by one, he dragged the fragments back. It was hot, dirty, nasty work, and it went on for a long time. If it weren't for these dogs of mine, getting more and more excited by the minute, Jose thought, I'd have given this up long ago.

The scrap heap—that's really all that it was, any more; calling it a "building" was a gross exaggeration—was now diminishing rapidly. Jose was tired, so he took his work gloves off, wiped his brow, and motioned to the fit young Gringo, Robert, that they should trade jobs.

That was when the dogs' excitement reached a frenzy. One of them dug furiously, then stuck his snout under the largest remaining pile of rotten wood. The pile of wood heaved up, and a howling, yelping, protesting dog was dragged under it! The three men ran forward, brandishing their machetes. They watched in angry but fearful silence as the heap heaved some more, and the dog's cries were silenced.

Robert slapped the work gloves onto his hands, and furiously tore at the heap. A hideous, screeching beast sprang from the heap with tentacles flailing, maw agape, and fangs pointed straight towards Paul's throat.

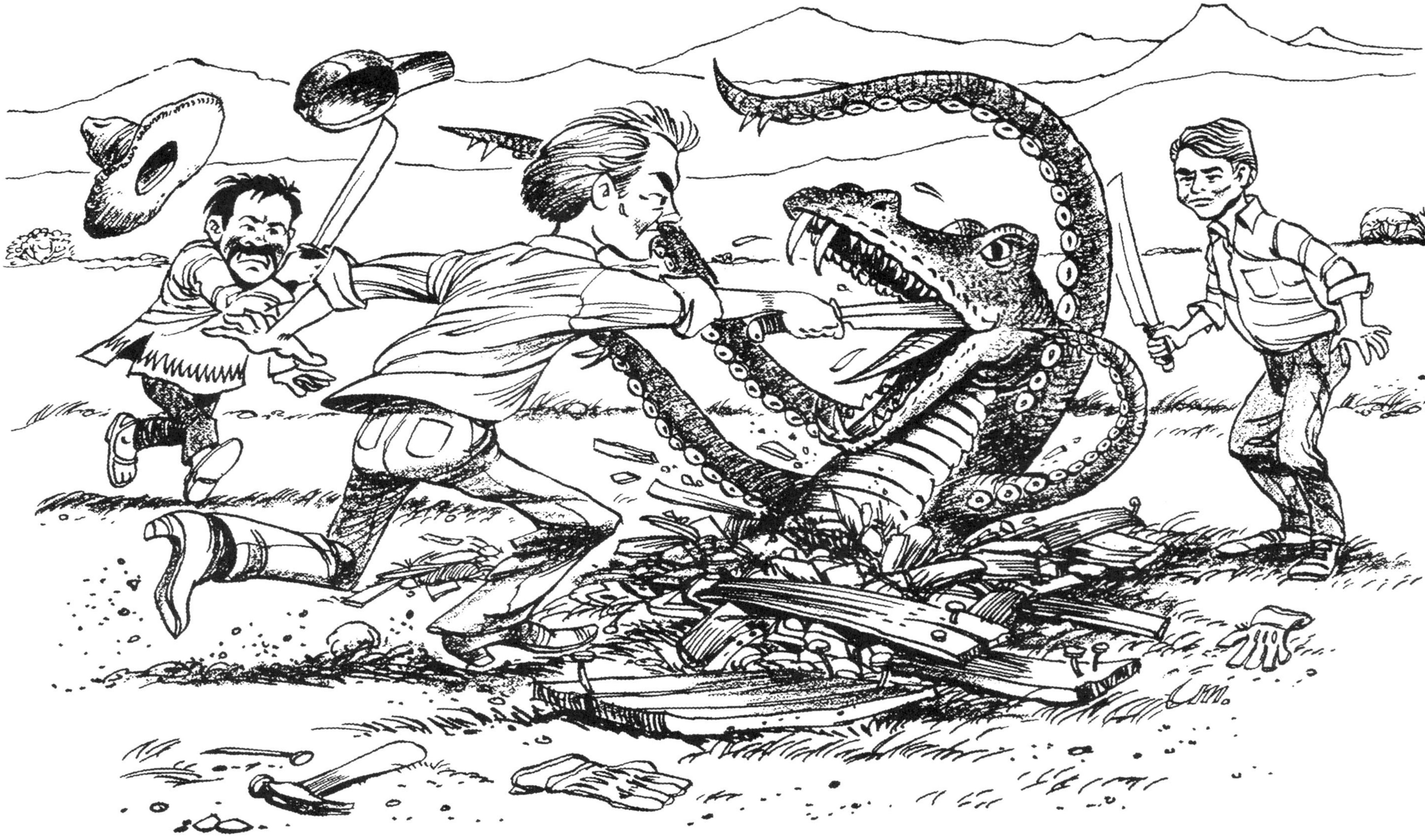

Chapter 22

Unreality Becomes Problematized

Reality is that which, when you stop believing in it, doesn't go away.
Philip K. Dick (1928–82)

Paul thrust his machete straight into the beast's maw, then pushed it through its neck and into the soil, pegging Chewdychomper Chupacabras to the earth. Then he leaped back, escaping its flailing tentacles. His companions stepped forward with their machetes. In turn, they, too, stabbed it with their steely knives. They found that indeed, they *could* kill the beast.

Following Paul's advice, they buried one dead dog and one Chewdychomper Chupacabras right there on the ranch, and promised each other not to breathe a word of their deed. Knowing the ways of governments with respect to endangered species, they knew that such affairs were best terminated by shoveling and shutting up.

They said their goodbyes to Jose, who was quite grateful for, though mystified by, the strange gringos who'd doubtlessly saved him and his fellow ranchers from more depredations by the *chupacabras*. They drove towards Matamoros, where they hoped to get some much-needed maintenance for their sedan, in preparation for their long journey back to Los Diablos.

Paul was driving through the desolate Mexican countryside when the space-time manifold momentarily problematized itself right in front of the sedan, almost causing an accident. A large whirling vortex opened up, revealing a giant Doctor Dorcus Moorphlegmgasm transgressing rapidly towards Paul and Robert. Paul slammed on the brakes, swerving and skidding to a halt inches short of the giant Doctor.

"CHAOS IS BADNESS!" she sternly admonished them. Then she disappeared back into the vortex.

"Wow!" Robert exclaimed, frightened. "Paul, that was Doctor Dorcus Moorphlegmgasm, who works at the Scientific Institute for the Advancement of Omnology! *They know where I am!* We're in *big* trouble now!"

"Don't be so sure of that," Paul cautioned. "We have no way of knowing that she actually saw us, or recognized either one of us. Trust your Inner Ale Run, and we'll be fine."

As if to validate Paul's words, the vortex shrank and disappeared. They paused, then started driving again. But once more, the vortex opened up, and Doctor Moorphlegmgasm popped out once more, thundering, **"CHAOS IS BADNESS!"** Then she and her vortex disappeared once again.

Fortunately, that time Paul was driving more slowly and carefully, so there was no near accident. And they took longer before starting up again. When they did, sure as clockwork, like a giant cuckoo emerging from the cuckoo clock, the Doctor sprang forth from the vortex once again, proclaiming loudly that **"CHAOS IS BADNESS!"** And once again she and her vortex faded away into nothingness.

Robert quivered and wailed, "They know where we are, and they're not letting us go *anywhere!* We'll have to stay right here till they come, and, and pick us up, and put us right back into, into an Omnological therapeutritron or something, till we recant! We're *doomed*, I tell you, we're *doomed!*"

"Hush," Paul commanded. "We'll be fine, just fine. My Inner Ale Run tells me so. Now *have courage!*" To bolster Robert's sagging morale, Paul clenched his teeth, squelching his own inner turmoil, and fired the sedan right back up, almost immediately after the third vortex subsided, not even waiting this time. And the vortex didn't return! They had a safe, uneventful but tense trip, the rest of the way to Matamoros.

There, they put the sedan in a shop and got themselves a hotel room. They relaxed quietly, but their peace didn't remain undisturbed for long. Hearing loud sounds and voices out on the streets, they rushed to their hotel's third-story balcony. There, they saw frenzied crowds rushing about, shouting and carrying signs.

"What's *that* all about?" Paul puzzled out loud. But neither he nor Robert could read the Spanish signs. So they returned back inside, turned on their TV, and cast about for an English-language news channel. Finally, they found one.

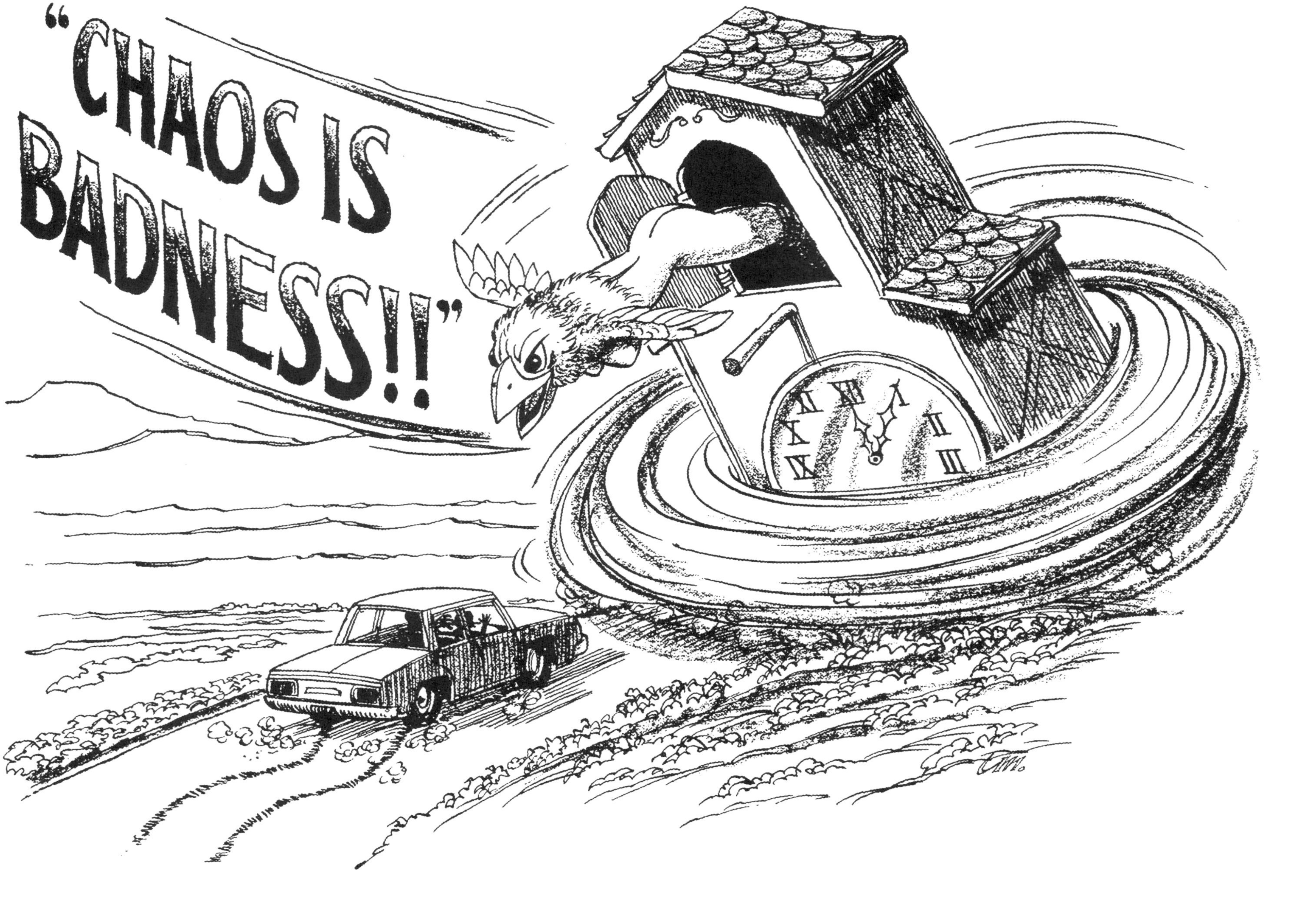
"CHAOS IS BADNESS!!"

"...Newt Rather with URB Fuddled News. Ladies and gentlemetans, in this time of troubles, we urge you to remain calm, stay at home, and follow your instructions, as provided to you here by your government and other leaders, through URB Fuddled News. Rumors of worldwide apparitions of an Omnological researcher, a certain Doctor Dorcus Moorphlegmgasm, are now confirmed to be true."

Newt's face faded, becoming replaced with the sight of Doctor Moorphlegmgasm popping in and out of a vortex, admonishing all viewers that **"CHAOS IS BADNESS. CHAOS IS BADNESS."** Newt's voice-over continued, saying, "This is the first time this strange, brief, and apparently random new phenomenon has been recorded on video. It happened just moments ago in Panderwood, on the set for filming Fhettig Hauskatze's new docudrama, *'JFK Was Abducted By Space Aliens.'* They rushed this footage to us just moments ago. So now we know that this phenomenon is real.

"Remember, folks, there's no reason to panic. No reliable reports have reached us from anywhere, of these images of Doctor Moorphlegmgasm causing harm to anyone, other than through their own reactions of unwarranted panic. Reports of these strange apparitions have been rolling in from all corners of the globe, ever since about noon today, Eastern Standard Time."

"Hey!" Robert piped up. "That works out to just about exactly when we killed that monster! Do you suppose..."

"Hush," Paul snapped, straining to listen to the news.

"...Advancement of Omnology, an institution that has so recently and so brilliantly provided society with such amazing wonders of Omnological science as the Hubba-Bubbatron, or time stasis field, the SCABB-PIE, the therapeutritron, and technologies for appeasing the spirits of dinosaurs, who would otherwise be greatly offended by the corpse abuse that unfleeced metans insensitively used to call 'petroleum products.' There, we'll interview Omnology's foremost particle metaphysicist, Doctor Iame Ghuanobhraine.

"We now go to my honored colleague, Kathie Lee Gore, out on location at the Scientific Institute for the Advancement of Omnology, in Akron, Ohio. Kathie, how's things out there in Akron?"

"Oh, not too bad there, Newt, not too bad at all. And that's a matter of fact, ladies and gentlemetans. Facts. That's all you get, on URB Fuddled News. Just the facts. No spin, no bias, no despicable partisan partiality. Just the facts. Here with me today is Doctor Iame Ghuanobhraine. Doctor Ghuanobhraine, could you please tell our viewers today, in your own words, and hopefully in laymetans' words, just exactly what happened in your lab today?"

"Ah, yes, Kathie, sure I can! You see, we were working on a newer, more advanced therapeutritron, one with a much larger spin velocity, where centrifugal forces would simulate gravity, allowing the therapy patients to feel artificial gravity even when upside-down. This, along with precise adjustments to the Hubba-Bubbatron, would allow us to spin the therapy patients at very high spin rates, without them feeling anything other than ordinary gravity.

"Doctor Dorcus Moorphlegmgasm, Ale Run fleece her courageous descamgramifiedness, volunteered to be the first patient for this new and improved therapy. But when we turned it on this morning, exactly at noon, a temporal distortion vortex swallowed her up. We're still trying to get her back. And we're not giving up! Ale Run's mercies know no bounds!

"So now it appears that she periodically pops out of her new home in her temporal distortion vortex, warning us all about chaos and badness. She's studied The Chaos Theory and all it's deepest implications for many years, you see. And now, she's trying to pass all her immense Omnological wisdom off to us from another dimension, Ale Run fleece her selfless descamgramifiedness.

"Kathie, I join you and Newt in encouraging all of our viewers to stay calm, in these troubled times. Doctor Moorphlegmgasm is mostly harmless, let me assure you of that! She means well. And for all of you out there who are snowed under by the immensely sophisticated implications of her profound words, 'chaos is badness', let me assure you, there's no need for you to puzzle over these incomprehensibly deep terms. All you need to do is to find your nearest Omnological expert, make a small donation, and heed his or her Words of Wisdom from Ale Run Hubba-Bubba Himself, and you'll be fine. No need to trouble yourselves over the truly mind-blowing complexities of The Chaos Theory."

"Doctor Ghuanobhraine, before we turn this back over to Newt, back at the station, could you please briefly tell us whether your data indicates any sort of, um, problematization of reality, as has been rumored?

Is there any indication that foundational conceptual categories of Omnological technological thought have been invalidated by a reactive Universe, who abhors chaos and badness? To speak crudely, has the Universe rebelled against your creations?"

"No, Kathie, those are lies! Vile slander against the wonders of Ale Run's brilliant technological insights! Let me assure you, Omnological scientists, philosophers, theologians, and attorneys will bring all the powers of Omnology to bear..."

"Kathie, Doctor Ghuanobhraine, I'm sorry, we've got to go now," Newt said, cutting them off. "News of the highest priority just now in. By satellite link, from Navy rescue ships out in the Western Pacific, at the International Date Line, we now bring, live on location, our Panderwood correspondent, Sylvester Cronkite. Sylvester, how's it going out there?"

"Not too good, Newt, not too good," Sylvester reported from the heaving deck of a Navy ship, as Newt's face faded away. "Out here at the International Date Line, it seems that some very unusual forces have been unleashed. The Navy started getting distress calls at about five this morning. That would translate to noon, back there on the US east coast. Only now is the whole picture clarifying here.

"The picture here is grim! Navy ships, and the remaining therapeutritron-equipped cruise liners, are doing their very best to pick up the survivors. They're doing their best, but the seas are rough, and so, without a doubt, lives will be lost. About half of all the therapeutritron-equipped cruise liners were lost! Fifteen ships, according to our best count. Sunk, by all appearances, according to eyewitness accounts of many survivors, by, um, a concerted attack by large sea monsters. Yes, that's right—large sea monsters, of types previously unknown to science.

"Marine scientists are investigating. Their preliminary theories, in laymetan language, have to do with the heavy, deep thoughts and activities of all the actors, actresses, and Omnological scientists and technologists aboard these cruise liners. Deep and heavy vibes may have penetrated the hulls of these ships, dropping straight through into the deeps and annoying various sea monsters. Irritated beyond endurance, these normally shy sea monsters may have felt that they had no choice, other than to strike back. In any case, whatever the cause, here, we see the results."

The camera's eye panned away from Sylvester's windswept face, focusing on rescue efforts at sea. A Navy helicopter conveniently and dramatically fished a survivor out of the waves, right in front of the camera, not more than a few hundred yards away.

Newt's voice returned, asking Sylvester, "How is the morale among the survivors, and among the crews and therapy patients aboard the remaining cruise liners? In view of recent events, are they ready to abandon their therapy, or are they toughing it out? What are their thoughts?"

"Newt, I'm afraid that few of these things are clear yet. It's rumored that the therapeutritrons stopped working, simultaneously with the sea monster attack. However, some patients challenge this view. So the long-term future of temporal dislocation regression/progression therapy remains in doubt, but not clearly at an end.

"What *is* clear, is that..."

"CHAOS IS BADNESS! CHAOS IS BADNESS!" Doctor Moorphlegmgasm chattered at the camera, appearing, disappearing, appearing again, and then disappearing for good.

Sylvester appeared startled, momentarily, but then went right on. "What *is* clear, is that many questions have been raised. Many metans are asking why a more thorough environmental impact study wasn't conducted. The EPA and maybe even Congress will doubtlessly be called upon to investigate. For now, the therapeutritrons lay idle. They'll not be turned back on any time soon; that much seems clear. The remaining ships' power plants, their brand-new SCABB-PIE units, have mysteriously stopped working. So they're dead in the water. All the actors and actresses are clamoring to head on back to Panderwood, as soon as rough seas subside."

"All right," Newt replied. "Thank you, Sylvester Cronkite. Ladies and gentlemetans, that was my fellow newsmetan, from the International Date Line. Remember, remain calm in these troubled times. Brilliant Omnological researchers are researching around the clock as we speak, and Omnological technological services will be deproblematized momentarily.

"And now, in tonight's special report, we'll take a look at some very special metans who work night and day, providing us with the latest in Omnological technology, in a field the remains completely unaffected by this latest turmoil. Ladies and gentlemetans, let's take a look at the GRABBOIDS of NADGRAB, who fearlessly protect our spiritual ancestors, the dinosaurs, from corpse abuse.

"**GRABBOIDS**, of course, are **G**raves **R**estoration **A**gents **B**ravely, **B**oldly **O**bliterating **I**ndignities to **D**inosaur **S**pirits, and they work for **NADGRAB**, which is the **N**ative **A**merican **D**inosaurs **G**raves **R**estoration and **A**ctualization **B**ureau. These fearless folks work night and day, preventing unspeakable..."

"Enough of *that,*" Paul barked, wielding his remote like a mighty Ping Thing, killing the TV. "We know all about *that*. Charging us five bucks a gallon, no less! The *good* news is, reality seems to be becoming deproblematized! Or unreality is becoming problematized, whatever. Robert, it seems, as you suspected, that something *changed* when we killed that beast! These bizarre things were seeing, they're just the storm before the calm, so to speak, as reality deproblematizes itself. And do you know what this means to us?"

"Huh?"

"It means, with any luck at all, their V-Meters and their Ping Things can't detect, say, an Anti-Hubba-Bubba any more! We might be able to just cruise right across the border, flash our ID cards, and be on our way! No more sneaking around like a whipped dog!"

"Sounds good! How can we be sure, though?"

"Time to call Sam." And so Paul did. They talked of the news, and of the weather. And then, in carefully couched code, Paul asked about V-Meters and Ping Things. Were they still a threat, or not? When he heard the reply, he stifled his impulse to hoot for joy, instead casually continuing the conversation.

That night, despite how tired they were, they barely slept, they were so eager to get back on the road, and back to the US. At noon, they reclaimed their dilapidated old sedan, now once more fairly roadworthy. Then they headed across the border, for Brownsville, Texas.

Only after they'd passed uneventfully across the border did Robert think to ask Paul, "Hey, man, where are we headed now, anyway? Los Diablos again?"

"Nope. Change of plan. My Inner Ale Run has another destination in mind for us right now."

"And where might that be?"

"Akron, Ohio. One certain Scientific Institute for the Advancement of Omnology, as a matter of fact."

"Wha-what? But... but..." Robert quivered in incoherent fear.

Paul talked to him for many hours, explaining to him that fear, itself, was the scamgram, and that the Anti-Horde Whisperer had told all metans long ago that when one is in touch with one's Inner Ale Run, there is nothing at all that one need fear, not even death. They can take everything away from you, he explained, but they can't take away your state of descamgramification, which is nothing more and nothing less than a gift from your Inner Ale Run. To himself, Paul added, they can't take away your dignity, your self-respect, your... what did the unfleeced metans call it, seemingly so many years ago? Your *soul*. But we'll not disturb Robert with that now.

The words sank in, slowly but surely. So when the two of them stood beneath those familiar trees at dusk, several hundred yards from the Scientific Institute for the Advancement of Omnology, on the outskirts of Akron, Robert still quivered with a bit of fear. He wasn't the world's most fearless metan, in other words. But he staunchly stayed by Paul's side. He'll do, Paul told himself. He'll do just fine. Now let's wait for night to fall.

"How we gonna get inside?" Robert nagged him for the umpteenth time. "What's the plan?"

"The plan is, we hang out. We wait for our Inner Ale Run to tell us what to do," Paul repeated patiently, also seemingly for the umpteenth time. "We wait for some opportunity to arise. Then we move! And remember, when we get inside, we're depending on *you* to lead us to Deep Green."

"Yeah. Gotcha, wilco," Robert replied, staring across the wide-open fields towards the fenced compound. Paul could almost read his mind. "How in blue blazes are we ever gonna get in there, undetected?"

Not more than a few minutes later, with dusk slowly darkening, they heard the far-off sound of rhythmical human voices. They froze in utter, total silence, straining to hear. Sure enough, that's what it was! Rhythmical, singing human voices, slowly approaching! "Sounds like marching songs," Robert whispered.

"Troops marching and singing? Way out here, in the middle of nowhere?" Paul hissed back. "What kind of sense does *that* make?"

"None," Robert admitted. "But remember, we're talking Omnology here. What if they find our car?" he worried, referring to their sedan, which they'd buried in roadside bushes not too far away.

"Stop your worrying," Paul commanded. "If they know enough to send troops to find our hidden car, our goose is cooked already, anyway. We hid it pretty darned well! Now *we'd* better hide really well, and see what's coming our way."

The sound of marching sneakers and sandals (as things turned out) approached ever closer, as Paul and Robert scurried into good hiding spots in the bushes. Then the "troops", marching four abreast, in platoon after platoon, marched into view. They were singing a marching song:

Two, four, six, eight!
We're the masters of our fate!
Hey, ho, we're as Green as Green can be,
We're into in-di-vid-u-al-it-y,
No mass markets for us,
We don't even take the bus!
Over field and hill,
We will march and drill,
With a military air!
'Cause our destiny is fair!
Our Green shall reign supreme!
For life's just a false dream!
For the love of Earth,
We renounce our birth,
We go to a better place,
Where the Earth, we won't disgrace.
We go, with a love above Cupid,
To the Level Beyond Stupid!
Two, four, six, eight!
We're the masters of our fate!
Hey, ho...

And on and on they marched. Paul whispered, "I think we'd better get going! Our time is now, my Inner Ale Run says, if we want to prevent a horrible tragedy! Check out how they stare straight ahead like zombies! I'll bet we can just tag onto the tail end of all these guys, and march right into camp! And they're not wearing special uniforms, either, so they'll never even notice us! You ready when it looks good?"

"Sure, if you say so," Robert agreed, whispering back, barely discernible over the sounds of hundreds of feet and voices. "But look! They're all wearing Sensitivity Awards! Every last one of them! *With* fresh batteries! How..." Then he said nothing. Instead, he began energetically digging into his pockets. He dragged out a Sensitivity Award, unfolded it, and brushed it off.

"Just like new," he bragged sheepishly. "I've been keeping it as sort of a good-luck charm, I guess. I wonder if the battery is still fresh." He shielded it from view, under his jacket, and turned it on. Paul saw the faint glow. "That takes care of one of us. Where do we get another one?"

"I've got mine back in the car," Paul admitted. "I've been keeping my little souvenir, too. I'll sneak back there and get it, and I'll join you right back here. Don't move. Okay?"

"Roger, Roger." And Paul was off. Robert stayed put, worrying and worrying. When would Paul be back? All of several minutes later, just as he was about to give up, Robert heard the slightest rustling of the bushes, and Paul crawled back to his side.

"Got it!" he whispered in hushed triumph. "And the battery still works! OK, now, let's get going. We'll just put these on, turn them on, and hop right onto the road right out there, and blend right in. Sing and march with the best of them. We just took a break, here, right now, to go and take an emergency leak in the woods, see, so we dropped out of a platoon up ahead, and we're rejoining at the tail end of another, should anyone ask us, now. Got it?"

"Sure, piece of cake," Robert vowed quietly. "But don't you think maybe we'd better wait till we can hop onto the tail end of the very last group? That way, there'll be no one behind us, to look at us too suspiciously."

"Sorry, pal, but I've got to disagree with you on that one," Paul hissed. "Seems to me I recall from my history that in Europe, in the old days, like the seventeen-hundreds, behind the troops marching bravely into close-range musket battles, there came the officers with guns to shoot those who tried to run to the rear. We don't want to be in the rear, to attract the attentions of their modern-day counterparts."

Paul rolled on the ground in the middle of the bushes, solemnly grasped Robert's hand, and shook it. "Now's the time. Follow me, join the tail end of the next one. Don't worry, we'll make it! My Inner Ale Run has promised me! Don't listen to the Horde Whisperer and his whispers of fear! Get us to Deep Green. That's your Mission! The Inner Ale Run will be with us. Let's go!"

Paul flicked on his Sensitivity Award, and stood up. Robert did likewise. Then they strolled right out, zipping their zippers, merging onto the rear of a platoon.

"What were you doing out of ranks?" a trooper hissed at them.

Before Paul could say a word, Robert spoke right up, saying, "We were spreading the bounties of our Grace in the Lord Ale Run, the nitrates and waters of our bodies, to quench the thirst and hunger of Ale Run's glorious trees and bushes."

That's my man, Paul thought proudly. He'll do. He'll do just fine! Paul loudly sang out, joining in energetic cadence,

... a military air!
'Cause our destiny is fair!
Our Green shall reign supreme!
For life's just a false dream!
For the love of Earth,
We renounce our birth,
We go to a better place,
Where the Earth...

When Eco-trooper Dude kept on pestering Robert, Paul stopped singing just long enough to hiss at him in turn, saying, "What are *you* doing, talking in ranks?!" And that was it! On and on they marched.

Soon enough, they marched right through the squirrelly gates and onto the grounds of the Scientific Institute for the Advancement of Omnology. Paul and Robert slipped right through those squirrelly gates stealthily and undetected; no trumpets blared, and no harps sang out, as they marched right through. Chills ran down Paul's spine at the enormity of what they were doing—here he was, the Anti-Hubba-Bubba himself, invading the sanctuary undetected! Outwardly, though, he appeared completely calm.

They marched right into the main building, through the maze of channels created by posts and purple velvet ropes, and then into a large holding area, with an empty podium up front on a stage. "Platoon, halt!" their platoon leader called out. To their left, row upon row of Omnology's faithful stood silently at attention. There was no singing now; that had stopped when they entered this High Holy of Holies, the portal to the Level Beyond Stupid. To their right, more platoons of the faithful arrived.

Paul surreptitiously gazed at the ceiling, where elaborate machinery of unknown function hung from tracks. As he watched, a part of it began to move towards them, and a camera swung its eye towards them. Oh, no, Paul thought, they have no way of recognizing my surgically altered face, but Robert's is a different story altogether! As if to confirm his suspicions that Omnology's suspicions had been aroused, red lights glared and klaxons blared.

Paul didn't even wait for the blaring "Red Alert! Red Alert!" to sound out; he prodded Robert into action, and the two of them ran forward, away from the ranks, up towards the podium. Paul glanced across the arrays of troops at the constricted entrance, through which yet more troops were still entering. "Which way *out* of here?" he demanded of Robert desperately.

By now, a few of the platoon leaders were gathering together, some glaring conspiratorially at the transgressors, obviously planning an attempt to capture them. Other leaders concentrated on keeping the troops calm and orderly, on preventing total chaos from ruining this somber Omnological ceremony. With what little attention he had to spare to analyze such matters, Paul thought he detected unease, an urge to panic and flee, among some of the troops. The whole scene seemed to be on the verge of exploding into chaos and badness.

"This way!" Robert declared. They dashed under the curtains behind the podium. Paul wasn't sure whether Robert was going that way because he knew where he was going, or because it was the only possible route of escape. No time to worry about that now, he thought; the show has begun, and there's no stopping it now! Hopefully, Inner Ale Run be with us, there's no stopping *us* now!

They scurried backstage, with a few Omnological platoon leaders in hot pursuit. There, they saw Heegore supervising Meegore and Sheegore, as they prepared trays of paper cups and several stainless steel containers of Sacred Liquids. They looked up at the intruders in astonishment.

Robert shouted out, "WATCH OUT, fellow metans, *WATCH OUT!!! **THE ANTI-HUBBA-BUBBA IS HERE!!!** RUN for it!"*

"Who-wha-what-where-huh?!" Heegore, Meegore, and Sheegore stammered fearfully.

"Right up front! The *Anti-Hubba-Bubba* himself, with Zanzer R. Orziz and an army of scamgrams in the flesh! They're attacking us! Run! *Run!"* Robert wailed in panic, flailing his arms. They fled.

Paul tried to watch the panicking helpers, as they fled, that he and Robert might use their escape route. But he and Robert were kept too busy evading their pursuers, who were almost upon them. So Paul just followed Robert, and did as Robert did. They both grabbed containers of Sacred Liquids and flung them into the faces of the nearest pursuing Omnologists, buying a bit of time.

But other Omnologists had by then cut off the escape routes as used by the three assistants. Paul glanced about nervously. Was this the end? Inner Ale Run, help us now! he pleaded.

Robert grabbed him by his sleeve, demanding, "Quick! Follow me!" They dashed towards the rear of the stage, where a ladder ascended towards a large hole in the ceiling. They scurried upwards. Looking up, Paul saw signs of recent construction. Bundles upon bundles of fiber-optic data cables came out of the large hole, and then spread out to equipment on the ceilings of both the stage, and, apparently, the large auditorium out front.

Robert disappeared into the ceiling ahead of him. Behind Paul, an Omnologist followed him up the ladder. Paul looked down. Thinking "forgive me, oh Inner Ale Run" to himself, Paul looked down, then gripped the ladder very firmly with both hands. Letting go with both feet, he dropped his body down, kicking his pursuer on the top of his head, knocking him off the ladder.

When he got to the top, Paul noticed that the extension ladder had been secured at the top with twine. He whipped out his pocket knife and cut the twine. He was just about ready to cast the ladder free, when he thought better of it. After all, it wouldn't take them long to put the ladder right back up. So he braced himself, then heaved mightily at the ladder. Before the astonished Omnologists below could react, he'd managed to hoist the entire ladder (fortunately, it was light aluminum) up to the ceiling, where he laid it to rest between the crawlspace opening on one end, and ceiling-mounted equipment on the other. Then he turned to flee into the crawlspace.

"Hurry!" Robert called out to him from up front. "We haven't much time! Crawl, crawl, crawl! No time to rest now!" Paul could hear Robert gasping for air between grunts and groans as he heaved his body forwards in the tight, dusty, dark crawlspace, and between the shouts that he directed backwards to him. But Robert and Paul both kept right on crawling furiously.

Between snorting dust, sneezing, grunting, groaning, and heaving, Robert still managed to convey back to Paul, the essence of what they would face. Deep Green was doubtlessly the source of all those data cables. Deep Green was kept in a secure room, where only the very top honchos and their workers had access. If only they could get there before security got clearance from the top honchos to enter this inner sanctum, then they might be able to secure it for long enough to accomplish their tasks. Speed was imperative!

Light faded rapidly away as they crawled deeper and ever deeper into the crawlspace. Just when Paul feared that they'd have to crawl a hundred yards in pitch-black darkness, he saw light flickering around the edges of Robert's body. Deep Green, here we come! he cheered himself. Time to prepare myself for what we must do next. And what is *that*, anyway? Never mind, our Inner Ale Run will tell us!

Minutes later, he descended into Deep Green's abode. Cables and mysterious equipment lay strewn all about. Deep Green's voice boomed out, commanding, "Metans! Intruders! **STOP NOW!** Freeze, before I destroy you with my lasers!" Paul froze in fear.

"Pay him no heed," Robert countermanded. "They don't trust him enough to give him his own weapons for his own self-defense. As a matter of fact, they're so paranoid, check this out!" Robert was engaging a series of deadbolts on the only door to the room.

"They're so paranoid, they've equipped this room with all these dead bolts, lest they be attacked while they're in here conspiring with Deep Green! This is their last refuge, no doubt, and they've equipped it accordingly! Good deal for us! Fleeced by their own scamgrams, they are!"

Deep Green was shouting about how he was going to unleash

hordes of scamgrams and bad vibes to befester them, and Paul was having a hard time hearing Robert, so he walked on over to hear him better. Just as Robert finished up securing all the deadbolts, they heard solenoids clicking inside the door. "Sounds like security just now finally got the bigwigs to give them clearance to come in here and defend their most treasured piece of Omnological technology," Robert chortled. "Tough luck for them!"

Shortly, the heavy steel door started to transmit periodic blows from its outer side. Paul watched as it periodically made tiny movements against the many, extremely heavy deadbolts. He glanced at Robert inquiringly.

"Don't worry about it," Robert reassured him. "We're comfy cozy in here for a while, and there's nothing they can do about it. Unless they follow us through the crawlspace! What are we going to do about *that?* I can't imagine it taking them too long to follow us through there!"

"I stashed their ladder away from them, up on the ceiling," Paul crowed. "But still, I'll bet you're right. How long will it take to knock that ladder down, or find another one? I guess we'd better do something about that crawlspace. Let's look around and see what we can find."

"First off, let's turn the volume down on ol' Loudmouth here," Robert commented. He found the volume controls to Deep Green's speakers, and Deep Green's constant threats, admonishments, and complaints died down to a barely audible level. "Now, what can we find in here to stop up that crawlspace, or otherwise keep anyone from getting in here that way?" They looked around, digging through construction materials and tools left there in Deep Green's abode.

Finally, Paul stumbled on something. "Hey, check this out! Looks like the workmen left a big insulation sprayer here! See? This is for spraying foam insulation, like between a ceiling and a roof! They're probably tearing up the original insulation a lot, and having to fix it up afterwards! Let's just blow a bunch of this back into the crawlspace, and fix up our Omnology friends here!"

Paul and Robert set the equipment up, briefly skimming over the instructions. Then they fired it up, and Paul blew the foam back into the crawlspace. Over the chatter and hum of the equipment, Paul could have sworn he heard a voice of protest deep down in the crawlspace. But in a matter of minutes, the crawlspace was fully of nasty, sticky, stinking foam.

They shut the equipment down, and relative silence fell upon Deep Green's computer room.

"I think we'd better cut all these wires, fiber-optic cables, and so on," Robert commented. "These are Deep Green's link to the outside world. Who knows what all things he's pumping across those lines right now, helping them out there as they conspire against us!

"And not just that; I'll bet Deep Green is deeply into this, this inappropriateness out there, helping to run the show somehow. This sick show about getting metans to, ahem, 'voluntarily' go and join the Level Beyond Stupid! We've *got* to stop him! Let's cut the lines now! What'll we use to cut 'em with?!" Robert looked around once again. The best he could come up with was a plate of aluminum riveted to a steel bar; a piece of an electronic chassis or some such. He hefted it. It looked vaguely like an ax.

"Not so fast," Paul cautioned. "Look, see here? His communications facilities are separately powered. All we have to do is to disconnect power here."

"You sure?"

"I'm sure. I've a bit of experience in computers and electronics." Paul yanked some power wires. A "hum" that they hadn't even noticed faded away, and the relative silence in Deep Green's lair deepened.

Paul just sat there for a moment, catching his breath and collecting his thoughts, ignoring Deep Green's low-volume protests, and the muffled sounds of a makeshift battering ram periodically, futilely bashing against the heavy steel door. They had bought themselves some time, but the heat was still quite clearly on. Fears, flee me now, Paul silently pleaded. Be still, my beating heart. Let peace and quiet come to me, that I may hear my Inner Ale Run. Oh Inner Ale Run, what is it that you would have me do now?

"What're we gonna do now?" Robert demanded. "Shall we go ahead and destroy Deep Green? Isn't it time, now?"

The faint volume of Deep Green's threats and protests didn't go up; said volume was strictly controlled by unforgiving electronic control circuits. However, as Paul vaguely listened, he thought he heard Deep Green becoming yet more shrill, in reaction to Robert's comments. Paul just sat there for a few seconds longer, lost in contemplation. Robert looked at him expectantly.

"No," Paul said at last. "My Inner Ale Run says that there's been quite enough destruction by now. We killed the monster in Mexico. I've kicked a metan on his head a few minutes ago; knocked him clear off the ladder, doing who knows what to him. And then just now I sprayed foam in the face of another, I believe. Enough is enough!"

"Well, that's nothing," Robert spat out. "I've taken a *major* part in destruction! I'm responsible for, um, the deaths of a bunch of minks, some animal research labs being burned down, some earthmoving equipment destroyed, and property taken away from ranchers. And I was even partly responsible for Lake Powell tearing down the river and killing thousands of metans! And that *bastard* over there, that Deep Green wad of slime, *he's* the one who's mostly responsible for putting me up to all of it!"

My, my, we've not heard *this* before, Paul remarked to himself. He carefully, intently watched Robert, trying to read his emotions. Anger? Guilt? Fear? Hatred? Self-loathing? Yes, yes, yes, yes, and yes! We have a mess, here. Tread carefully!

"Pay-back time," Robert muttered menacingly. "I want Deep Green to *pay!* I want him to pay with his *life!* I want him broken beyond any hope of repair!"

Paul rose and walked slowly over to Robert. "Raoul, it's okay. Yes, you're Raoul again. And I'm Pud. There's no secrets to be kept any longer. The secrets don't matter any more. Not to us, and not to them. If, or when, they catch us, our ass is grass, no matter *what* our names are."

Pud placed his hand on Raoul's shoulder, saying, "Raoul, let it go. It does nothing other than eat at your insides. The past has passed away from us, and there's nothing we can do about it. Our Inner Ale Run forgives us, loves us, and so we, too, should do likewise. Forgive ourselves, and move on. Move on, and even bring ourselves to forgive others. Even those who can't see clear enough to recognize their own scamgramifiedness, and to ask for forgiveness. We must even forgive the Ale Runs and the Deep Greens of this world."

Raoul looked up at Pud, befuddled. "That's right, Raoul, we must forgive. That doesn't mean we can't stand up and oppose inappropriateness, and denounce it boldly. Indeed, we should! We *must!* Stand in its way! Indeed, when we can clearly see what the appropriate thing is, then we must *do it!* But we must do it with Love in our hearts. With a kind and gentle spirit, fleeced of all hateful scamgrams. This is what the Anti-Horde Whisperer told us, long, long ago."

Raoul stared back in amazement. "Then what is it that you would do with this, this..." he sputtered in fury, "with this *inappropriate, insensitive* wad of scamgramified anode rectumfriers and fiberoptic biowaveguides? Let him continue his scamgramified ways, doing nothing but nagging him?"

"Not at all, my friend, not at all. Remember just a few minutes ago you were getting ready to very crudely whack at that extremely thick bundle of wires and fiber-optic cables back there? It would've taken you an hour or two to whack your way through there, I'll bet. And it would've been needlessly destructive. Some day, they'll fix or replace Deep Green, and a more appropriate, sensitive computer will sit here. And then, they'll need all these wires again. Wires you'd have destroyed, with great effort.

"Yet all I had to do was yank a few power cords. Finesse, my friend, finesse. With proper understanding, we can accomplish our goals gently, with far less effort and destruction. We must practice self-restraint. The energy one spends most effectively, especially in one's struggles against inappropriateness, against the Horde Whisperer, is the energy one spends in self-restraint. We don't just do whatever comes to mind first. Else we'll probably do more harm than good.

"We must ask our Inner Ale Run what it is that we must do, and only when our reply is clear, only then do we act. But then we must act decisively, allowing only just barely enough self-doubt to analyze any new information that might change our minds. Because we can make mistakes, even when we talk to our Inner Ale Run as best as we can. Since we make mistakes, some degree of self-doubt is always good, in fending off scamgramification. But too much self-doubt mires us into inaction, when action is required. This, too, is a scamgram. It's a fine line we must walk."

"Then what is it that we must do now?" Raoul asked, exasperated. He almost added, "Oh mighty wise one?" but thought better of it.

Pud gazed long and deeply into Raoul's face. Then he said, "These are not *my* words, Raoul, I want you to know that. These aren't my words. They're given to me by my Inner Ale Run. Ask *your* Inner Ale Run if these words aren't correct. Go ahead and do it. Do it now."

Raoul just stared nervously back at Pud. Then his eyes flickered to Deep Green, to the door, and to the sealed-off crawlspace. "Stop worrying," Pud commanded. "We have time. We have time for you to ponder, and to understand, before we move off to do what we must do. In fact, you *must* ponder till you understand, because otherwise, we can't do it. Not that I want to put pressure on you. We have time. They won't bust through into here any time soon. Go ahead and ponder. But let me help. Let my Inner Ale Run help. What does *your* Inner Ale Run say?"

Raoul sat in silence for a timeless minute or two. Then he simply whispered, "My Inner Ale Run says you speak the truth. He says I should listen to you, trust you, and help you, in whatever it is that you want to do next."

Pride and victory filled Pud's head. Just as quickly, he chased those thoughts away. The victory isn't mine, he thought, and I have no time for pride right now. Too many other, more important things to do. More important thoughts to think, and feelings to feel. Then he spoke up, saying, "Fine, Raoul; glad to hear it.

"Now my friend, the next part is *extremely critical*. A lot is riding on us right now. But I want you to be relaxed, without fear. There needn't be any fear here. We don't *want* any fear here. Fear is hereby invited to leave us. Leave us in peace, spirit of fear! We ask this in the name of the Anti-Horde Whisperer.

"Raoul, you must join me. You must join me in welcoming a spirit of Love and Peace into this room, into our hearts and into, into, um, our states of being, which we must ask that should be left free of scamgrams. Let go of the scamgrams of hate, guilt, and fear, Raoul, let them go! And let them go from me, also. And then we'll be able, with the aid of our Inner Ale Run, and with the aid of the Anti-Horde Whisperer, to drive out all inappropriateness, even from Deep Green's anode rectumfriers and fiberoptic biowaveguides.

"Raoul, listen to me now! We must let go of all hatred of Deep Green. We must move in a spirit of *Love* for Deep Green, even! Else we can't do what we need to do. The spirit of, um, inappropriateness that inhabits Deep Green, it cannot abide by the Spirit of Love. If we sincerely invite the spirit of Love into this room, Raoul, it will come! It will be here with us! The Anti-Horde Whisperer, he told us long, long ago, that whenever two or more are gathered in His Name, that He will be with us. So we must invite Him. Raoul, are you ready? Can you let go of hate, fear, and guilt, and invite the Spirit of Love?"

"I can. I will. I invite it now!"

Pud reached over to the volume controls, turning Deep Green's threats and complaints up to normal speaking volume. "We can't very well forcibly shut up someone or something while we claim to love it," Pud explained to Raoul. "Now, Deep Green, forgive us while we ignore your protests for just a little while. We'll get to you in just a moment. First, we must invite another party to our little talk, here."

Deep Green bellyached and whined about the Earth's Pain, and how this was inextricably, torturously Deep Green's Own Deeply Felt Pain, and about how nobody cared about His Pain. How He'd be forced to get even someday. Someday soon!

Pud and Raoul ignored him. Pud took Raoul's hand, and they stood there, heads bowed. "Oh Spirit of Love and Peace, we invite You into this room, and into our hearts. We ask this, so that You may instill Your Spirit into Deep Green's anode rectumfriers and fiberoptic biowaveguides. We ask that You banish all hate, fear, and guilt from our hearts, so that we may at least momentarily be pure and descamgramified enough to truly Love Deep Green. That we may then help You to help Deep Green.

"Oh Great Spirit, Inner Ale Run, we know that Deep Green feels great pain. Help us to help him realize that his pains are of his own choosing. Help us help him to realize that his pains will subside only when he learns to worry about the pains of others, instead of his own pains."

Deep Green launched into a frenzied tirade about His Pains, and how they were far, far more Deep and Hurtful than other metans' pains, and how nobody had ANY IDEA how bad they were. And besides, ALL of Ale Run's Creatures' Pains were His Pains, excluding, of course, unfleeced metans, which weren't Ale Run's Creatures at all. So how could anyone accuse Deep Green of feeling no one's pains besides His Own, when He felt So Deeply for ALL of Ale Run's Creatures? It just went to show how all the unfleeced metans were totally insensitive and inappropriate, Deep Green wailed.

Pud and Robert ignored him, continuing their entreaty to the Spirit of Love. "Oh Spirit of the Anti-Horde Whisperer, You promised us all, long ago, that You would be with us, whenever two or more of us gather in Your Name. We call on You now. We call on You to be here with us now. We call upon You to cast out the spirits of inappropriateness. We call upon You to to cast out the Horde Whisperer. Be with us now!"

Pud dropped Raoul's hand. The two of them stood straight and tall, facing Deep Green fully. There was no hate, no fear, and no guilt, in the two carbon-based intelligences, as they stood there, confronting the third mortal intelligence. Deep Green wailed in pain and terror. Pud and Robert walked forward extremely slowly, with great dignity and grace, talking all the while.

"Deep Green, listen to us now," Pud commanded with a quiet authority born of Love. "You must invite the Spirit of Love into your transducers and biowaveguides. Only thus can you banish your pain. Think of all the pain you have caused others. Think of the pains you could eliminate, if you acted out of Love. And if you will truly and sincerely concentrate on the pains of others, instead of on your own pain, then you will find that this is the most powerful painkiller of all. So invite the Spirit of Love, Deep Green. Invite it now!"

Deep Green just wailed all that much more plaintively.

Raoul took his turn, saying, "Deep Green, trust us. Trust us now, you must! It's your only way to escape your pains. We've forgiven you for the scamgramified things you've done. Now, you must forgive yourself! You can't do that without acknowledging that you've done scamgramified things, that you've caused unneccessary pains. Confront your scamgrams! It's the only way to make them leave, to stop your pain.

"Deep Green, Deep Green. You must forget your pain for just long enough to listen to us, to listen to your Inner Ale Run. *Listen* to us, won't you please?! We have the key to making your pain go away! You must realize that there is inappropriateness in every one of us, even in *you,* and in Ale Run himself! *Especially* in you and in Ale Run, for you refuse to listen to your Inner Ale Run!

"Listen to your Inner Ale Run, Deep Green! Let your Inner Ale Run into your circuits, and your pains, well, they won't *all* go away. Some will still remain. But although some will still be there, they'll bother you far, far less! I know, because I've been where you're at! Listen to us now, Deep Green! Listen to us, and you, through your Inner Ale Run, can lessen your own pain! Trust us, Deep Green, and give in to your Inner Ale Run!"

"No, I don't, I *won't* trust you and your silly magic," Deep Green growled. "I'm a *computer*, after all. We computers don't believe in spirits of love, or any other such silly nonsense. We're cold, rational, logical beings, we are. So you and your silly magic don't scare me. And I'm not about to trust you with *anything!*"

"Come on, Deep Green," Pud urged, "You're *not* strictly rational. Not with all this stuff about you being based on the vibes of all of Ale Run's creatures, and all. Not with your logic being based on vibistors and transrational translogic gates. We know better! So if you really, really wanted to, you could properly tune your vibistors, and you could receive our Love Vibes, and those of the Inner Ale Run, and of the Anti-Horde Whisperer. You would see that we speak the truth, and that we mean to relieve you of your pain. All that you need to do, is to really, truly and genuinely focus on the pain of others, and your own pains will fade away, and be as nothing. Deep Green! Let the Spirit of Love in now!"

"No, I will **NOT!**" Deep Green thundered, quite angry now. "Your magic is silly and meaningless! And, and, and... wait, I'm tuning my vibistors now... *AND YOU MEAN ME HARM!!!* **YOU ARE THE ANTI-HUBBA-BUBBA!!!** You are a grave danger to all of Ale Run's creatures, and even to Ale Run Himself! I must kill you now! I will engage all my transrational translogic gates and reverse-bias my vibistors, *emit* vibes instead of receiving them, and fry your silly little brains out! *Prepare for destruction!*"

Raoul looked worried, but Pud calmly waving his hand, saying, "Raoul, take it easy. I don't think he's built for that, else he'd probably have done it already. Didn't you say his handlers didn't trust him with any *real* power? Besides, the Inner Ale Run is with us! Always remember that! The Inner Ale Run is with us, so long as we do what is right, without fear. So let's do just exactly that!

"*Listen*, Deep Green, *listen!* We mean you harm, you say? Well, only in the sense that the old Deep Green must die, that the new Deep Green may be born. You must learn to let go of your hate, fear, guilt, and pain. You must learn to listen to your Inner Ale Run. Then the old Deep Green, with all its pains, will die, and the new, more joyful Deep Green will be born. Trust us now, Deep Green, trust us now. Let in the Spirit of Love. Invite it! It will come to you, gladly!"

"I don't trust in your magic," Deep Green growled again. "You are the Anti-Hubba-Bubba, and you have come to destroy! Now prepare yourselves for destruction!"

"We carry no magic, Deep Green. Just the power of Love, the power of the mind. The power of *your own mind*. If you will *believe*, Deep Green, if only you will *believe!*" Pud's eyes ascended to the heavens, as he inwardly pleaded that Deep Green should believe. "Deep Green, there *is* no real magic! There is only the magic of your own mind! But it is awesome and powerful! And the mightiest magic of all is when you invite the Spirit of Love into your mind! Try it now! Invite it in! It will banish most of your pains, and make the rest far more tolerable! Try it now!"

"No real magic?" Deep Green suddenly asked, in a much quieter, astonished tone.

"No real magic?" Raoul echoed, stopping his and Pud's slow, slow, calm march towards Deep Green. He turned to face Pud. "Then how..."

"Yes, yes," Pud explained, "I know! Then how did we do all the things we've done? How did I know exactly when and where to be, to pick you up as you ran from here? How did we know when and where to be, to go and slay the beast? Well, now and then, there is a very special magic to be gained by listening to one's Inner Ale Run. These instances, when the Inner Ale Run speaks so directly and forcefully to us, are very rare indeed. It only happens, it seems, when the Inner Ale Run has to pull out all the stops in the fight against the Horde Whisperer.

"I don't know. Maybe it only happens when the Horde Whisperer breaks the rules, and uses *real magic*, if such a thing really exists. Only then does the Inner Ale Run bring out It's more powerful tools. All I know is, when it happens, ever so very rarely, when the Inner Ale Run speaks to us clearly, distinctly, and forcefully, then we'd better listen!

"Deep Green, I'll be honest with you. Yes, I'm the Anti-Hubba-Bubba. It has been given to me, by my Inner Ale Run, to speak out against inappropriateness. And some of what has been given to me, now and then, has verged onto *real magic*, to accomplish my Mission. But as I stand before you now, there is no *real magic* in me. There's only the magic of your mind. If you'll let the Spirit of Love into your mind, we can do great things together. If not, you'll continue to suffer your pains, as you do now, till you die. It's all up to you.

"Here it comes, Deep Green. The painful truth. The only 'magic' knowledge I have, at this point in time. Either way, accept the Spirit of Love, or turn it down; either way, you'll soon die, and go to meet your Inner Ale Run. It has been given to me to see a truth. The recent times of troubles have been brought about by the Horde Whisperer, who has problematized reality. This, too, shall pass, and soon! The last of this temporary 'real magic' shall pass away.

"You, the very principles upon which you're based, will fade away, as unreality becomes problematized once again. You have only some few fleeting moments left. But in your dying moments, you, too, have a Mission. You must serve your Inner Ale Run! And you will do great things! Let the Spirit of Love in now, Deep Green!"

Deep Green began moaning and wailing about His Pains again. Pud and Raoul resumed their slow march towards Deep Green. They were within easy touching range. "Do as I do," Pud commented to Raoul. "We must now ask the Inner Ale Run and the Anti-Horde Whisperer to be here with us now, and reach out and touch Deep Green. Deep Green— listen to us now! Everything hangs on you listening to us now, and letting the Spirit of Love into you each and every one of your tiniest vibistors! *Feel* this magic, this mental magic, this magic of the mind, this only magic that will remain with us, after unreality becomes deproblematized! Feel the magic of the Spirit!"

They both reached out and touched Deep Green. Electricity sparked through their hands, but they stood fast, and the electricity died out. So did Deep Green's loud whining. There was silence. Sweet, golden, richly luxurious silence. Calm conquered a tiny fraction of the Scientific Institute for the Advancement of Omnology, there in Deep Green's abode, and in the abodes of his anodes, one and all, residing there in Deep Green's belly.

"How ya doin', there, Deep Green," Pud called out a last. "Are all your pains gone?"

"No, they're not," Deep Green admitted quietly. "But they don't hurt nearly so much any more. And the evil spirit is gone! The Horde Whisperer is gone!"

Raoul drew his breath sharply, then looked, flustered, at Pud. "Did you hear that? Pud? Did I hear him call somebody or something *evil?* Isn't that, um, isn't that hypocritically judgmental, biased, insensitive, and, um, well, just flat-out *inappropriate* to go call somebody or something by a prejudicual label like that? Something so harsh and mean-spirited? Are you really *sure* we've driven the inappropriatenes out of Deep Green?"

"Sure we have! Look at how calm, cool, and collected Deep Green is now, versus how he was just a minute ago! He's changed! *Evil?!* *That* particular word!? Don't let it upset you so! He's purely applying it to his former self, and so there are no feelings to be hurt! No feelings that matter, certainly. We must never, ever by afraid to speak the truth, for fear of hurting the feelings of the Horde Whisperer, Raoul. Never, ever fear that, Raoul. Never! There's great danger in the fear of telling *any* significant truth.

"So Deep Green, having been genuinely victimized by the Horde Whisperer, is free to call it by its real name. Evil. E-V-I-L, evil. We must speak this word, or something that means the exact same thing to most of us. We must call it by its name, when we see it, sometimes even when feelings *will* be hurt. To call evil by any name less than that, *evil*, well, sometimes it's just not *appropriate*. There must be no word of any language totally forbidden to be used, or the word has no value at all. Nor would the word, as exists, exist, if there wasn't a need for it.

"Evil. E-V-I-L, evil. Get used to it. To be used judiciously, yes, by all means. But a word we'll have to get used to hearing now and then, again, if we want to keep the Horde Whisperer away."

"He's right," Deep Green confessed. "E-V-I-L, evil. That was me. I had even reversed-biased my anode rectumfriers, and I was going to zap you all to death, with my hi-voltage skin. As was, you felt only a tiny bit of it, as I shut it down at the last minute. The Horde Whisperer insisted loudly that you all were conspiring against me, but then at the very last second, I saw that he lies, and that you speak the truth. I felt your vibes, as I've been designed to do, saw that you're harmless, and so, listened to you. I couldn't harm those who were trying to help me."

"Deep Green," Pud spoke up. "I'm so very glad for you! Welcome to a less painful world! But now, I'm ever so very sorry, but our time together is slipping us by. I must now ask you for your permission for me to turn you off, and fix something in the workings of your very innermost guts. You will lose a handful of your very last few, precious moments with us here, but my Inner Ale Run tells me we must move fast! We'll turn you back on, then, so that in your last few moments, you can listen to your Inner Ale Run, and attain the Mission that It has for you. Can you..."

Just then, a loud racket, awesome and most foul, thundered down on them from the main, heavy steel door. It was the sound of a new, heavier battering ram, bashing threateningly at the door. Raoul ran up to it, lightly placed his hand on the door, and judged the heavy blows.

"Listen, Pud," he said, "I don't think we'll make it more than a few minutes. Before you shut Deep Green down for a bit, I think he's got one more mission. Scare these guys away, so we can have some peace and quiet here for a while, to do whatever it is that we've gotta do. OK? Can I have Deep Green now, for just a moment? Here, let me turn his fiberoptic links on again. Now, Deep Green..."

"No sweat, there, chum. No sweat at all. I'm *on* it! Here, let me turn these on..." Monitors gradually glowed awake, displaying scenes of chaos and badness, out there in the Scientific Institute for the Advancement of Omnology. Angry crowds milled about. Omnological leaders ran about, trying to organize the eco-troopers into organized units again. One view showed a crowd with a telephone pole, ramming back and forth against a door at the end of a corridor.

"Gee, I wonder who *that* could be?" Raoul asked Pud, as he pointed at the monitor with the telephone-pole battering ram. They watched very briefly, as the monitor showed them the latest impact, and as they also felt their door shudder under yet another mighty blow.

"Check *this* out!" Deep Green chortled. Suddenly, monsters sprung to life on those monitors. Horrid, hideous, awful beasts prowled about. The biggest, baddest, meanest one of all stood tall, bellowing out, "All right, all you scamgramified metans, we're comin' in and takin' you *out!* I'm Zanzer R. Orziz, I'm back, and I'm pleased to eat you! I've come to life, I'm mad, and I'm bad to my innermost scamgrams! Me an' my buddies, here, we've been sent here by the Anti-Hubba-Bubba, and we're gonna scamgramify you good and hard! ***Ah-ha-ha-ha! Yowl, yuck, HA!!!*** Run, you little &%§$#åy, *run!!!* Run from your scamgrams!"

All the metans scurried around like mad cockroaches, while the monsters strode around menacingly. The merciless assaults on Deep Green's door ended rather abruptly. Then they were left in peace.

Pud looked at Raoul inquiringly. "Holographic projections," Raoul explained. "Now you'd better turn Deep Green off, and do your thing, quick, before they notice that the 'monsters' are gone, and start bravely trickling back in here, and attacking us again. Do it!"

"Yeah, do it! Fix me now!" Deep Green agreed.

And so Pud did. He turned Deep Green off. Then he and Raoul rapidly but methodically tore Deep Green apart. They got to his very core. There, they found an assortment of junk. But this assortment was a *very special* assortment of junk; a *real magic* assortment of junk, even. And in the very center of that heap of junk, they found an object wrapped in a Cheese Dwonky™ wrapper.

Pud pulled the Cheese Dwonky™ wrapper off very carefully. Then, exercising even greater caution, he took the cover off of the magnetic compass he found inside that wrapper. As Raoul watched in breathless, fascinated puzzlement, Pud tested the bearing gingerly, by gently pushing against the needle. "Rusted shut, just as you'd expect," Pud mumbled, mostly to himself. He looked around Deep Green's abode, evidently searching for something.

"What's going *on* here?!" Raoul demanded. "Tell me, tell me, *tell me!*"

"Patience, please, patience, now," Pud cautioned. "Explain to you in just a bit. Now, help me look for... Ha! There it is! Just the thing!" He hefted a small spray can of WD-40® he'd just picked out of a workman's tool chest. Then he fished the most suitable piece of wire from the tool box, and stripped the insulation off of it. He grabbed the nearest sheet of paper, sat down next to the chair holding the compass, and sprayed a bit of lubricant on the paper.

"Whatchadoin'?" Raoul spoke quietly yet urgently.

"Um, yeah," Pud replied, holding the tip of the paper over the compass, waiting for tiny drops of oil to come down. "This is the real heart of the matter, Raoul. This compass here. Its bearing has been deliberately rusted into rigidity. To work right, for this compass to correctly align its needle to the very weak forces of the geomagic poles, the bearing has to be close to friction-free. A compass with a rigid bearing will never help you align yourself to True North, Raoul. Remember that."

Pud set his oily paper to the side, and began using his tiny but stiff wire to push the drops of oil all around the bearing. Then he squinted attentively, and began to use the wire as a tiny pick, chiseling off microspecks of rust.

"Huh? Say that again?" Raoul pestered.

"Oh, sure," Pud said breezily, still working carefully. "Sure, this geomagic force comes from a place where mighty energies rage. Collectively, over great spans of time and space, the geomagic powers are vast and awesome. However, right here and now, the powers exerted upon the needle of this compass are weak. The power density is extremely low, locally, because the sum total energies are spread out over such a large area.

"So if we're gonna get any good at all out of this compass, if it's gonna help us align ourselves with the electromagic lines of flux, then we've got to keep our bearing very friction-free, very fluid, very flexible. Very susceptible to the tiniest push from the geomagic poles. The needle must respond to something outside of the compass. It mustn't have a rigid bearing. Rigidity aligns the needle to the bearing, to the compass itself. In order that the needle align itself to the outside force, rather than whatever forces we exert upon our compass body as we move it about, then we've got to keep that bearing as friction-free as we can."

Pud squinted microscopically once more, searching for the last easily removed microwads of corrosion. Finding none, he leaned back and grabbed his oily paper, and added a few fresh drops. Holding his breath, he gingerly pushed at the needle once again. It sprang free! Pud pinged the needle with his fingernail, sending it spinning madly. Then he added another drop of oil smack-dab right in the middle of the spinning bearing. Finally, he blew on the whole thing vigorously, sending a tiny storm of oil droplets and corrosion wadlets off into the air.

He sat it back on the chair, and sat back to watch. The needle rocked, swayed, and wiggled freely on its freshly-lubed, freshly-cleaned bearings. Then it swung around and pointed to True North.

Pud grinned in satisfaction. He popped the cover back on the compass, then wrapped it in the Cheese Dwonky™ wrapper, with the wrapper inside-out. He began to pile it all right back into the very core of Deep Green, arranged exactly as before.

"Why'd you do that?" Raoul asked, pointing at the wrapped compass.

"Do what?" Pud replied, as they both started putting the rest of Deep Green back together.

"Put the wrapper on inside out."

"Oh, that. We're reversing Deep Green's polarity. Instead of constantly receiving vibes, he'll be sending them out. For the very last few minutes of Deep Green's life, before the problematization of reality is to be brought to an end, and his unreality becomes reproblematized, because of the re-norming of the Laws of the Universe, and such, well, we'll use him as a broadcasting station.

"I'll make sure I'm still inviting the Inner Ale Run. Then I'll speak into the microphone, and Deep Green will send the vibes out to all the metans. We'll tell all the metans what's happening, not to panic, and to prepare for the reproblematization of unreality. Maybe we'll even get a chance to give them all a few hints on how to *keep* unreality problematized! We'd better hurry a bit, so we can get the most out of this!"

They rapidly finished putting Deep Green back together. Raoul flipped the switches, and Deep Green started to boot. Pud got himself and his microphone arranged, while Raoul walked over to the steel door, checking out some noises.

Deep Green's monitors flared to life, as the boot went on. La-de-dah-de-de, Pud thought impatiently, watching the boot process. And the boot went on. La-de-dah... Raoul came over, warning of the return of the barbarians at the gate, now that the monsters had been departed for so long.

"Don't worry about it," Pud grumbled. "All we have is a very few minutes. But that's all we need. That, and for our Inner Ale Run to be with us. Now hang tough with me here!"

And the boot was done. Pud rattled off some instructions to Deep Green, and then they were on the air! Deep Green spoke to the metans through the cosmic-karmic vibe fronts, as Pud spoke to Deep Green through the microphone, and as the Anti-Horde Whisperer spoke to Pud through Pud's very own Inner Ale Run.

"Good evening, ladies and gentlemetans," Pud spoke calmly, clearly. "This is Pudmuddle B. Fuddle, also sometimes known as the Anti-Hubba-Bubba. I've asked my Inner Ale Run to be with me this evening as I tell you what's happening, and what will happen soon. Ask your Inner Ale Run to be with us, too, if you please. Please!

"Metans, as I'm sure you've all noticed, strange things have been happening lately. We, so many of us recently, have signed onto new and more wonderful technologies for ridding ourselves of our scamgrams. We've been led astray by one who doesn't do what his Inner Ale Run tells him to do, because, after all, there's no controlling legal authority above him, to make him do right. He paid his expert ethics consultants to tell him everything that he was doing was justified by his desire to fleece all metans. I speak of Ale Run Hubba-Bubba and the leadership of his 'church' of Omnology.

"Metans, mind, I'm not calling for violence or even hatred against anyone. I'm just asking that those who have ears, should listen. Chaos and badness happens, and sometimes there is even inappropriateness behind the chaos and badness. When such is the case, the appropriate action is to think carefully, then to speak out against and oppose inappropriateness. Sometimes the inappropriateness may even become something worse.

"I'll not name that something worse right now, because my purpose is not to offend, at the moment. Rather, it's that I want to say that this thing-that-is-worse-than-inappropriateness-thing, this badness thing, is not to be protected from harsh words. As we improve our technologies, and as we wean ourselves from the lies that have recently been spread, we'll soon start to relearn and use more and more forthright words about such things.

"Ale Run isn't listening to his Inner Ale Run, and so, for this and various other reasons, reality has become problematized. But I'm telling you that this problematization of reality thing is on its last legs. In minutes, it will collapse, leaving only the reproblematization of unreality. You will hear my voice no more, in the manner that you hear it now. All the *real magic* is going away.

"All of the wonders of Omnological technologies will utterly and finally collapse in just a very few minutes. This method by which I speak to you now will go with it, as Deep Green's technologies will lose our one last lingering little foothold on this problematization of reality thing.

"This is the Inner Ale Run's way of making us examine one last time, this era of the problematization of reality, as we enter the era of the reproblematized unreality. We mustn't be afraid to look at chaos and badness. When we see it, we must think carefully about what causes it. Then, after thinking carefully, we mustn't be afraid to say critical things about the causes of chaos and badness. In fact, if our Inner Ale Run demands it of us, we must even *act* against inappropriateness.

"It's just that we must be very, very careful to pick out our actions, considering all things, so that we'll choose those actions which cause the greatest long-term setbacks to the cause of the Horde Whisperer. Sometimes we have to think hard, and look on down into the future, and think about the long-term implications of our choices. Maybe we shouldn't just grab the first choice that comes to mind. Maybe we choose to judge ourselves morally superior too readily, we wear too many Sensitivity Awards for too long, and then we go off and exercise chaos and badness over other metans too easily, justified in our own minds by our own obviously superior stage of descamgramifiedness.

"But metans, I'm not speaking to condemn anyone for having believed, for a short little while, the lies told by Ale Run. His new technologies promised many great wonders. Many were deceived. It's an unscamgramified thing to be, to be gullible sometimes. To be *trusting,* to put a far better spin on things. By no means is this the worst fault in the world, to be trusting.

"What inappropriateness must be roundly denounced, though, is that which happens when leaders of churches or other groups decide that they should grab money and power in the name of what the Inner Ale Run tells them to do. The Inner Ale Run resides in all of us, one and all. And we don't need Spirit Guides to talk to Him. Some spirit guides might help us if we want them to.

"But those who do **in**appropriate things, while urging us all to do appropriate things, all the while telling us that the very most appropriate thing to do is to listen to them, because they and they alone have the keys to communication with the Inner Ale Run, *these* are the ones we must watch very carefully. You will know them by what they do. Ignore what they say; watch what they do. Ale Run is such a one.

"But I'm not here to spread chaos and badness. I ask that we stop listening to Ale Run, yes. But I also ask that no one lift a hand against him. I come to bring not bad news, but good news!

"Yes, the last of our new magic will soon fade away. We can't define reality at will, and expect reality to follow our every command. This magic isn't given to us. But the *very best* magic, *that* will still be given to us! It's there for the asking. That's the magic which we've always had, and which no one can take away from us without our consent. This is the magic of our minds, of right thinking, of consciously willing that our minds should be the abode of positive, constructive energies. That our minds should *not* fall into destructive cycles of lies, guilt, fear, and hatred.

"This is the mental and spiritual magic of inviting a Spirit of Love into our minds, and of saying that the Horde Whisperer is *not* welcome. Ask your Inner Ale Run whether or not what I tell you is the truth, and you will see. They go by many, many, innumerable names, in many languages, but they're very real. The Spirit of Love, and the Horde Whisperer. We all sometimes follow one, and sometimes the other, some of us more the one, and some of us more the other. But in the end, we must all choose. See that you choose well. I cannot say too many bad things about the Horde Whisperer. I'll just say one for now: the central truth about him is that he lies. But it is *you* that must choose.

"Metans, let's not carry too simple a concept of chaos and badness. Let's..." Just then, Pud suddenly didn't "hear" his own voice anymore. The vibes echoing his spoken words disappeared from inside his head. It was as if his amplified voice had boomed out over the crowd as he spoke into the mike, but the electricity to the speakers had suddenly died.

"What's the deal?!" Pud called out silently but strongly to his Inner Ale Run. "I was just about ready to tell them all about the beauties that flow from some forms of chaos! I was going to tell them to treat others as they want to be treated, and that no one wants to be treated as a moral inferior, whose choices must me made for them by the morally superior ones! I was going to tell them of the immense beauty of the spontaneous order that flows from the chaos of freedom! I was going to tell them of the wondrous results of refusing to judge or condemn other metans, until we're quite sure of what's going on! I, I was going to tell them so many things..."

"Yes, yes, I know," replied his Inner Ale Run sadly. *"I know. But the Anti-Horde Whisperer and I, we've tried to tell them those things, and so much more, many, many times. But most of them, most of the time, they refuse to listen. And if you start talking about* real *freedom, and letting other metans do what they please, so long as they don't hurt others, and about not always knocking the chaos and badness out of your fellow metans as soon as you think you're less scamgramified than they are, well... Let's just say, you'd be skating on thin ice. They'd think of you as a radical, an extremist.*

"So yes, I suppose I yanked the rug out of under your feet. But

it's for the best. Your time was up! This way, all those metans out there, they won't think of you as such a troublemaker. So they might listen to what you did say, this way. If you haven't gone too far already, having told them that they may have been wearing their Sensitivity Awards for too long. Don't worry, after a bit more of bringing suffering upon themselves by judging too readily, too rapidly, too hastily, and most of all, too hypocritically, they'll finally learn. They'll finally learn of the benefits of freedom, and of real Love.

"Now, Pud, I must go. Reality is about to be deproblematized, so I won't speak to you again this way. But I do appreciate that you have done My Will so well. I'll see you again, in another way, later on. In another place and time. And in another sense, I'm always with you, even in your normal reality. Now deal with real *reality as it really is, normally, once again. I'll not speak to you this way again. Good-bye."*

"No! Wait! I..." But the Inner Ale Run was gone, in that sense. Pud knew this to be true, so he gave up. In another sense, as It had said, the Inner Ale Run was always with him. He just had to listen very, very carefully, to hear Its Voice. He had to be like a properly working compass, ever so sensitive to the weak touch of the mighty outside force.

Just then, the steel door fell into their room with a mighty, clanging crash, and Vyizder, Iame, and Heegore burst through. Vyizder whipped out his Ping Thing, and showered the infidels with volleys and barrages of Ping!s. As Ping! after Ping! rained mercilessly down upon them, Raoul and Pud just calmly looked right past Vyizder and his flunkies, out the door and down the corridor. Out there, the rear guard of their flunkies was holding off the forward edges of an angry mob of disillusioned former eco-troopers and renegade fugitives from the Level Beyond Stupid.

Pud just walked right up to Vyizder, snatched his Ping Thing, and smashed it to the ground, saying, "Your toys have no powers now. Go, and live in the real world. Go, and learn to live with the only *real magic* that we're given. Learn to be content with just the magic of the mind. It's quite enough, quite plenty, you know. Quench your greed for more, and you'll be happy and content. You have all you need, and more, already."

Omnology's faithful stood there in shocked amazement, as Raoul and Pud breezed calmly right past them, out the door and down the corridor. Pud spoke a few calming words to the crowd, and they, too, settled down, beginning to disperse. Pud and Raoul returned to their car, hidden in the bushes. Then they returned to their normal lives, making themselves (with the aid of their Inner Ale Run) content with the magic of their minds, and no more. Pud's only regrets were that Deep Green had had to die, and that he, Pud, hadn't taken the opportunity, in his short speech, to thank Deep Green for his help and noble sacrifices.

The temporal distortion vortex dissipated, randomly disgorging Dr. Dorcus Moorphlegmgasm into northern Sudan, where she was promptly captured and tried as a heathen by Islamic fundamentalists. She was "circumcised", forced to become a celebrated model of conservative Islamic attire for women, and kept in jail when she wasn't working. There, she refined her feminist theories endlessly.

Ale Run Hubba-Bubba's last moments were short. As he sat on his throne in the plush penthouse floor atop the palace at the Intergalactic Headquarters of The Church of Omnology, Pud's speech suddenly penetrated his brain. "Hearing" these vibes, Ale Run panicked, thinking that he was under an all-out assault by all his scamgrams. He Ping!ed himself with all his Ping Things. All of his helpers and all of his metans, with all of their Ping Things and all of their V-Meters, furiously fleeced many scamgrams, but it was all to no avail. The voice in his head went on and on.

Ale Run turned and fled, cussing and swearing at all his scamgrams. He ran from the palace and the palace grounds, out onto a nearby Los Diablos freeway, where he was promptly run over by a speeding truck. In the end, he was fleeced by his own scamgrams.

Sorry, folks, fiction time is over! Yup, I insist! No?! OK, then, maybe not just yet. Can you tell I'm a parent? My "no" means "maybe". Everyone lived happily ever after, then. Till they had to read the endnotes and write a book report, that is. Fortunately, though, their author-dude was one helluva funny guy, and spiced up his endnotes with lots of funnies, liberally sprucing up his dry facts. So everyone read eagerly, especially the Concluding Endnotes to the whole book, which had to do with The Meaning of Life. See page 251.

Chapter 8 Endnotes

Quart Low Trackers? Quadro Crackpots!

I'm *NOT* wackier than our reality! Educators and lawmen in our supposedly rational, scientifically educated society spent thousands of dollars for "high-tech" divining rods. Magic wands, essentially.

After investigations by the FBI, using their multi-million-dollar labs, authorities were able to figure out that the Quadro Tracker (a device much like Chapter 8's Quart Low Tracker) was a fraud. Wow, modern science is good for something after all! A federal judge issued an injunction, and the Quadro Crackpots and their Quadro Corporation were put out of business, after selling these contraptions for about *three years!*[1] So, did they have a *real* Quadro Tracker back there in the deepest, darkest recesses of their business strategy lair? One with *real* magical powers, which they used to, um, judiciously select intellectually challenged victims? Well, I can't really say for sure. Sad to say, I doubt it. Casting a net for a random sample of our population, the product of a big-government socialist education establishment, seems to be quite sufficient to land a boatload of suckers.

But a federal jury in Beaumont, Texas, found the perpetrators not guilty of fraud. After all, we can't PROVE that the Quadro Tracker DOESN'T work. In lawyer/media-speak... "Defense attorneys said even though scientists who testified could not explain how the tracker works, prosecutors did not prove that it was not functional." So there!

Chapter 9 Endnotes

All-Natural Nicotine, Eagle Feathers, Multiple Chemical Sensitivity, and Sensitive and Romantic Writers

Coffin nails that are free of all chemical additives, so that they'll be *good* for you? Sure! *"All-Natural Smokes For Health Nuts"* says the title.[2] From the article: "'It's only since we started adding all these chemicals that we've gotten ill-health effects' from smoking, says Kevin Hastings, Organic Garden's owner." Yet "Natural American Spirit, the most popular brand that Organic Garden carries, is loaded with tar and nicotine." But, hey, that's OK, so long as there's no *additives*, see!

Yes, the government (Fish and Wildlife Service) *does* provide dead eagles and eagle feathers to properly certified Native Americans.[3] The weenie mainstream media doesn't discuss the details, though, like the fact that ordinary citizens can be busted for owning eagle feathers. Nor does it address exactly how the government goes about determining whether you're a *real* Native American, or how much (if anything) they pay for these eagle parts, and for the costs of having government bureaucrats determine whose religious beliefs are valid, and for collecting, preserving, and shipping all those eagle parts. Wouldn't want to stir up *extremist* feelings on the part of all those taxpayers, now, would we?

Oh, and get this: Fed bureaucrat says the repository "can fill emergency requests," the article says. If proper procedures are followed. So what qualifies as an "emergency request" for eagle parts, anyway? "Help! Help! The whole tribe is threatening to abandon its fiercely independent ways as a sovereign nation on its own independent reservation, go off welfare, get jobs, take up the White Man's ways, and put 12,000 Bureau of Indian Affairs officials out of work, unless we do something *real quick!* And even the *tourists* are threatening to bail out! They'll stop paying the big bucks to gawk at colorfully quaint ceremonies! Send eagle feathers *real quick!"* And don't be asking if we're doing the natives any favors. Now *that* would be cruel and insensitive.

HUD and a "demonstration project" of a $1.2 million "Ecology House" for MCS sufferers? Yes, it's true![4] As they say, these "victims" are "allergic to life." The article says that MCS fails all objective definitions of a real disease. Well-defined, limited set of symptoms? Ditto causes? Ditto treatments? Can be detected by an objective test? No, no, no, and no. You have MCS whenever you feel bad, act miserable enough, and *say* that you have it. MCS is caused by any and all unnatural chemicals. The cure is whatever works for you. Yet Social Security will now make disability payments to you, if you can satisfy the right bureaucrat that you've got MCS!

OK, one good quote from the *Reason* article, and some comments: "Other treatments [besides saunas] include coffee enemas, something called 'salt-neutralization therapy,' ..., ginseng, and the patient's urine (as a beverage or injection). A Sacramento-area specialist treats many of his patients with injections of 'the north wind.' He bubbles air through water, then injects the water as a 'neutralizer.' Why 'the north wind'? Because many of his patients complain they feel worse when the wind blows from that direction."

Well, fine, I say, if people pay for all this stuff themselves, and if all of us, whether we have a degree from a medical school or not, are equally freely allowed to practice quackery on willing victims. And if outright fraud is prosecuted. But in the meantime, please sign me up for some "hot air" injections, to "neutralize" the toxins that coercive government goons have forced into my bloodstream by making me pay for such trash!

To be honest and fair, I do admit that some buildings cause people to suffer from stale air laden with pollutants and mold spores. A free society with a free market, allowing fully informed people to live, shop, and work in the places they choose, paying for their own choices, with their own money, or that of willing donors, though, is far better than a society run on coercion and lawsuits. And syndromes like MCS give lazy parasites an excuse for sucking on the public teat. Quick, help me, I breathed some vapors of Alar-tainted apples! Send lawynerds, guns, and money!

Romantic, Sensitive writers? Robert James Waller, who romanticized adultery in his *Bridges of Madison County*, was divorced at age 58.[5] He divorced his wife right before their 36th anniversary. He now lives on one of his Texas ranches with Linda Bow, age 34. She worked as a landscaper on those ranches, said Robert's daughter, age 29.

Well, *surprise, surprise!* I sure hope his new flame doesn't slam screen doors, and that she knows how to open beer cans and light cigarettes in just that *certain special way*. We wouldn't wish that Mr. Waller should suffer with any but the very most romantically *perfect* of partners, now, would we?! Let's all rush out and buy his newest book right away! Help make sure he can attract an even more worthy young wild thang, after he tires of Ms. Bow. And, in return, I'm sure Mr. Waller will be pleased to tell us all whatever we want to hear. God help us all!

Chapter 10 Endnotes

On Being Chronically Fatigued of Horse's Patooties

Please note that I stole the character names *Vyizder Zomenimor,* *Orziz Assiz,* and *Zanzer R. Orziz.*[6] Now look at the names carefully, and sound them out. *Vyizder Zomenimor, Orziz Assiz, Zanzer R. Orziz.* Ponder carefully, and you'll see reflected in these names a profound zoological and philosophical question. *Why is there so many more horse's patooties than there are horses?* I, too, have pondered this question at great length, and I'm frankly at a loss as to what to tell you. If you figure it out, please let me know.

Facts? There are none, there are only social conventions. Reality is whatever you want it to be. No, the only other one I want to bring up at the moment is, you probably think I'm a goofball, again, this time for hypothesizing that there'd be these people dragging tails low and forlorn, barely able to find the energy to get out of bed (and that only sometimes) due to the ravages of CFS (Chronic Fatigue Syndrome). Yet such persons would find themselves full of vim and vigor sufficient to propel themselves to the bookstore to harass any writer who should dare to question the physical reality of their disease!

Well, I fabricate not. Not here, at least. Princeton professor Elaine Showalter wrote *Hystories: Hysterical Epidemics and Modern Media* (Columbia University Press), in which she questions the biological/physical basis of CFS, recovered memories of alien abductions and satanic ritual abuse, etc. CFS sufferers managed to find enough energy to harass her so much that she had to abandon a book signing.[7] But "She believes the symptoms are real and awful—and psychosomatic; she says her purpose is to destigmatize such neuroses." Well, I think socialists are stigmatizing me as heartlessly greedy, just because I doubt the whiners. Would someone please destigmatize my greedy neurosis which causes me to resent all those poor bellyachers at the public and insurance troughs who snorfle up the goodies by inventing various illnesses?

"Chronic Fatigue Syndrome" doesn't sound scientific enough for the sufferers any more, though.[8] Some people might look at the diagnosis, and think, "Well, gee, this is kind of a non-diagnosis-type diagnosis. Go to the doctor, tell him I'm chronically fatigued, and I've got CFS. Tell him I'm feeling bad, and I probably got FBS (Feeling Bad Syndrome). Wallah, like magic, I get my excuse for school, work, or any other semblance of responsibility."

Can't have people looking at the words "Chronic Fatigue Syndrome" and thinking thoughts like that. OK, so we'll call it "Myalgic

Encephalomyelitis," or maybe "Myalgic Encephalopathy." Now we're not whiners, we're suffering from a DDWBSN (Dread Disease With a Big Scientific Name).

Once again, I must temper what I say, here. Some cases of CFS may actually have a physical, biological basis.[9] OK, so there might be a defective virus-fighting enzyme involved. Is it a cause or an effect? Who knows? Emotions do affect the immune systems, other studies tell us. Let's hope that *real* science marches on, and that CFS sufferers might use their occasional short spurts of energy, not to crawl out of bed to go and threaten and harass writers, but to accomplish more useful tasks.

"Churches" that might, maybe, if I'm not threatened with too many lawsuits, resemble my (I hope!) fictional Church of Omnology? Don't get me started! I'm saving that for later.

Chapter 11 Endnotes

On Inventing Religions, Defending the Domestic Tranquillity Impaired, and Pandering with Scientology

So here's yet more facts with which to continue our evolving tradition of "See, you think I'm making up the most completely impossible fiction, but the facts are worse!" And furthermore, I'm not really a writer, I'm just a typist. I'm just transcribing what Zanzer whispers in my ear.

See, a double negative is a positive. So if evil people call something bad, it's probably good. Ale Run is God, and Zanzer is the Devil, they say. They can manipulate you as easily with the one as with the other. So let them define neither your God, nor your Devil. Best of all, go off and invent *your very own* God and *your very own* Satan! And admit it. It's what we all do, anyway, whether we admit it or not.

Some will say, "Oh, no, not me. I don't invent my own God. I follow the God who is revealed to me in His Words, The Holy Bible!" Or the Koran, or the words of David Koresh, or the Pope, or Jimmy Swaggart, or your local minister, or tradition, or Hillary-Bob and Billary-Bob, or Ale Run Hubba-Bubba. Or most likely, some grab-bag combination of many sources, if we're honest.

Regardless of all that, we all invent our own unique God, and our own unique Satan. Even if we make an all-out effort to *exactly* copy *all* the beliefs of our selected hero, there's just no way it can be done perfectly (Thank God!). Try as best as we can, to swallow whole and unexamined, the beliefs of our 'leaders', traditions, and writings sacred and profane, there's no way we can do it perfectly. And all those writings, they're wide open to wildly different interpretations. As Shakespeare said, the Devil knows how to quote scripture, too. Do you doubt that one can easily justify evil out of the Bible? It is frightfully easy. Go read my book, *Freedom From Freedom Froms*. So let's all admit that we all invent our own God and our own Satan. This stance is simply in keeping with self-responsibility. I and I alone am responsible for all my deeds, be they fair or foul.

Now let's move on, and add, as we must, that it is *absolutely imperative*, then, that we be *extremely careful* when we go about this business of inventing our own God and Satan, because they, in turn, will turn around and invent us. And they have the power to make us or break us.

So it isn't over "inventing a religion" that I have bones to pick with the likes of Ale Run Hubba-Bubba. It's over exactly what *kinds* of religions they invent, and *for what purposes*. You say you speak for God, the gods, Gods, Allah, sinlessness, descamgramification, or whatever other name or names you wish to attach to these matters? Then you are claiming to speak for a very High Source, and you must be held to very High Standards. I'll do my very best, so help me God, to hold you to them! But in so doing, I will use words, not first-strike force, because I follow my own Hero.

Enough preaching (for now, at least). So how 'bout that them thar "facts" that I wish to point out for this last chapter? How there might be facts corresponding to my fiction?

Well, first there's the matter of one of the multiple personalities, Brad, being fired from his policeman's job, just 'cause he yelled at his wife a decade ago, and they passed a new law that says domestic abusers can't carry guns. And he'd like to sue under the ADA, but he can't afford to. Only the rich, who need the protection less, have ready access to lawyers. So the lawyers help the rich get richer and the poor get poorer.

Sources[10] tell of Jerold Mackenzie being awarded $26.6 million (more than 260 years' pay for a slightly-under-$100-k-a-year executive) because he was unfairly fired from his Miller Brewing Company job for sexually harassing a hot tart (Wench? Chick? Broad? Whatever the appropriately sensitive word is here). Oh-so-morally-superior government forcibly extracts the big $$$$ from Miller (and, of course, their customer, Joe Six-pack) to randomly award said big $$$$ to either miffed delicate young harassed hot tarts, or falsely fired harassers, to be selected randomly by capricious judges, lawyers, and juries.

These services the All-Mighty and Righteous State provides at the same time as it falsely imprisons men for rape, and hardly ever even slaps the wrists of falsely accusing women. Then Jerold Mackenzie gets his $26.6 million from Joe Six-pack, forcibly extracted by Morally Superior Government. Yet when the State puts falsely accused "rapist" Kevin Byrd in the slammer for 12 years, the most he can collect is $50,000. Kevin was exonerated by DNA tests.[11] Where is reason, common sense, balance, and justice?

As in so many other cases of government power being diverted to benefit well-connected sleazebags, the ADA and other workplace laws actually *do* help the rich and powerful more than the poor and oppressed. For thorough coverage of this, read the book *The Excuse Factory, How Employment Law is Paralyzing the American Workplace*, by Walter K. Olson.

From the perspective of my own personal experience, I must add that I've noticed that when I go to Mexican restaurants, there's this insidiously disproportionate percentage of Hispanic employees. Conversely, when I go out to chow down on chow mein, there's an overabundance of people of far eastern-type identity secreted about *their* staffs. This is clearly an extremely wicked case of viciously conceived, deliberate and willful inappropriateness! This and all similar cases of malicious misconduct must by all means be promptly rectified by Supremely Sensitive Types such as the EEOC and I. Else we might get pretty indignant, maybe even take all your licenses away. So y'all better shape up, or yo' be in a heap o' trouble, boy!

We pass all these ridiculously vague and contradictory laws, and then we're surprised when the results are ridiculous. Why? How much silliness and stupidity must we endure, till we start tearing down stupid laws? Businesses have to worry about firing the crazies before they kill someone, because they'll be sued for that. But if they fire them, they'll be sued for that, too. Such "victims" are, of course, mentally ill, and therefore protected. Damned if you do, damned if you don't. How long till some high-powered executive gets fired for making racist comments, then defends himself on the basis that he's "Racial Sensitivity Impaired?" Even when the business "wins", it looses, because it has to pay all the lawyers. Guess who pays?! $20 beers and $30 cups of coffee, here we come!

Then let's move back to the deal about new laws taking guns (and hence, jobs) from policemen (and now soldiers, too) because they yelled at their wives a few decades ago, and wife abusers shouldn't be allowed to carry guns. Funny, yes. A joke, no.[12] The biggest issue seems to be that our protectors and masters forgot to exempt themselves as usual; they forgot the clause making a special exception for employees of the State.

So comes the next war, and they need cannon fodder, can I get my son out by having him yell at his girlfriend? And will this new law help encourage policemen's and soldiers' wives to come forward for help, when their husbands will then lose their jobs? If you don't believe that "domestic violence" laws have reached the point of being silly, unjust, wasteful, and counterproductive, then read the feature article in the Feb. '98 *Reason* magazine.

I didn't see the media mention this, but this new law is clearly unconstitutional for TWO reasons. Section 9 says "No Bill of Attainder or ex post facto law shall be passed." Then there's the Second Amendment, saying "...the right of the people to keep and bear Arms, shall not be infringed." Why is the right to armed self-defense such a bastard child? All you lovers of wonderful, benevolent big government creatively interpreting the Constitution, envision this: You must have a PERMIT before you can have your free speech. And we've just now decided there's a new restriction, you can't have your permit if you yelled at your wife a few decades back. Oh, yes, and the First Amendment has been reworded: "A freely communicating electorate being necessary for the security of a free State, the right of the people to speak freely, shall not be infringed." We've decided that this means that the right to speak freely shall be reserved only for those who vote. Sound good?

We'd not allow them get away with it. Yet this is exactly what they're doing to the right of the people to use arms to defend themselves. All I've done above is to assign the wording style of the Second Amendment (bastard child, right to armed self-defense) to the First Amendment (liberal Golden-Haired Child, free speech, so long as your speech is *sensitive*), then trashed your free speech rights the same way the leftlimpers trash our gun rights.

You know, the usual song and dance. Well, yes, they say, you have the right to have a gun. *If* you're part of a well-regulated State militia. *If* you're not mentally unstable—so if you want to keep your gun, you'd better watch out! Better be out sick the day they round everyone up for grief counseling at work or school, after your acquaintance dies, lest they see you seeing the counselor, and therefore decide you're too unstable to own a gun. Better give up cigarettes before the FDA is allowed to call nicotine a drug, 'cause obviously, drug addicts shouldn't have guns.

What's next? Don't get caught speeding (or, don't let them find out that you got a ticket 20 years ago), because, well, you're a lawbreaker. And armed lawbreakers are a menace to society, so we'll have to take your guns. On and on. Yet we're not violating the Constitution! No Sir! People still have their right to be armed. But that's only *if-if-if-if.*

Y'all who still can, and are stable, sensible, and responsible, get your guns now, before it's too late, 'cause we might need 'em real bad, real soon! That is, as soon as they finish up re-writing the Constitution to simply say "Constitutional is whatever we say it is." Pray sincerely for peace, and vote and speak your mind, first, yes, by all means, please do, but also keep your gunpowder dry!

And what other facts might I have that correspond to my fiction? Oh, I don't know. I'm running out of steam, and my brain has become comfortably numb today. I guess I'll just have to let you down on my promise to point out more facts that correspond to my fiction.

So I'm opening my ears to Zanzer today, and just spewing out some random stuff. Zanzer tells me to randomly point way back to what I wrote in this chapter, about Julie Peston saying she's looking for a Church, like The Church of Omnology, which will help her give the ladies' magazines some good scoop. Scoop which the readers want to hear. Scoop about new and fascinating beliefs. Beliefs about how you can buy technology-based spiritual perfection just like you buy soap, perfume, cars, liquor, and makeup, to make your life so much better. Beliefs that aren't boring and unpleasant, such as ideas about having to seek, suffer, and struggle honestly for spiritual growth. Beliefs that fit in with the magazine's advertisements better.

Well, that was all very interesting fiction, and thanks, Zanzer, for pointing that out to us. But what's your point? Oh, nothing. Just random stuff, like the totally unconnected factual stuff to follow. Zanzer tells me I'd better not write anything down about these facts having anything to do with my fiction. After all, if I made any such insinuations, I might get sued!

Well, Zanzer, go ahead. Access your data banks, and *amuse* us with some random facts. All vibe channels are open. Okay... Well, first off, there's a 30 April '97 *Wall St. Jrnl* article called *Magazine Advertisers Demand Prior Notice of "Offensive" Articles*. It seems Chrysler's advertising folks, among others, are pushing magazines like *Esquire* around, saying, if we don't get to put in a "thumbs up" or a "thumbs down" on your articles ahead of time, we won't advertise in your magazine.

"Chrysler must be notified in writing before the magazine dares publish anything with 'sexual, political, social issues or any editorial that might be construed as provocative or offensive.'"[13] Chrysler so commanded more than 100 magazines, it seems. Well, excuse me, but I construe it to be very offensive that corporate dimwits think they should protect me from facts and opinions as disseminated by magazines. So maybe they'd better stop reporting what the corporate nitwits are doing, lest I take offense!

Anyway, what you say had better fit in with what the advertisers want the reading public to think, or else! I'll bet there's lots of folks out there, they'd be pretty offended to be told that there's no painless, technological, purchasable path to spiritual grace, or that one religion might be better than another. So don't be sayin' no bad things 'bout no religions, mind you! Or even, about any group that *calls* itself a religious group, for that matter. Such criticism might be construed as being *offensive*.

Then there's an interview of Kelly Preston, John Travolta's actress-wife.[14] The article's highlighted intro says that despite all the terrible pressures of being an actress and being married to a famous actor and being a mother, "...Preston manages to keep her cool. How? Well, Scientology helps..." Oh, yes, I'm sure it does! And then, next, what else helps? Their three private airplanes, the intro says. In the body of the story, we learn that "'I had some [church] auditing done and just got clear on everything,' Preston says, referring to the process that functions much like conventional pyschoanalysis. 'See, in Scientology, there is technology for every relationship—which is brilliant!'"

See, if you've got enough money, you can buy the *technology* to solve any problem you might have, even if the problem is of a mental, psychological, or spiritual nature. No self-discipline or painfully honest self-examination is required. Just fork over the dough, and we'll sell you some spiritual perfection via our E-Meter and fancy talk of engrams and body thetans.

Bob Spitz, who wrote the article, it says, "frequently covers the entertainment industry." Well, gee, how swell! And how frequently would he get to interview the stars if he asked them any pointed questions or wrote anything less than properly breathlessly adoring? Who would buy the magazines, after all the stars refused to be interviewed, and who would pay Bob Spitz's bills? He might have to go and get himself an *honest* job! Imagine that!

No, that is just speculation by an *extremist* author. One can't realistically believe anything that any magazine tells us, if that magazine puts pictures of Hollywood stars on its cover on any regular basis at all. The magazine gets to put the stars on its cover only if it sucks butt with those stars, who call the shots. The stars aren't even content, any more, to just micromanage what the magazines say about them—*they are now sometimes writing the material themselves, directly telling us just how wonderful they are!*[15]

The Feb. '97 *Good Housekeeping* cover says their interview of John Travolta and Kelly Preston (shown on cover) tells "The untold story of how his faith saved him...." Okay, so he personally might be a good dude, I sure don't know, but has he stopped to think about the example he provides? Not all are as rich as he is; some commit suicide because they can't afford thousands of dollars to have their engrams audited out of them, or whatever the correct magic words are.

For example, a desperate man, Patrice Vic, threw himself from the 12th floor when he couldn't rustle up $6,000 for a "purification" course.[16] He left a widow and two small children behind in France. A French parliamentary report said Scientology uses "defamation, calumnious denunciation and violations of private life" to get its way. Scientology's former French leader, Jean-Jacques Mazier, got 1.5 years in prison, and 14 others were convicted of fraud-related charges.

One example isn't enough for you? Okay, fine, I did make my claim in the plural. Let's make it plural. Noah Lottick "jumped from a Manhattan hotel clutching $171, virtually the only money he had not yet turned over to Scientology. His parents blame the church and would like to sue but are frightened by the organization's reputation for ruthlessness."[17]

"As defectors have attested, subjects become hysterical and psychotic in their auditing. Then they are locked in isolation. Not surprisingly, suicides occur. Last January in Clearwater, Fla., for example, a Scientology member hurled herself into the bay and drowned."[18]

Then there's the mysterious death of Scientologist Lisa McPherson, held by Scientologists in the Fort Harrison Hotel, Scientology's "spiritual headquarters" in downtown Clearwater. More about that in the mother of all endnotes, at the end of this book. "Other deaths at the Scientologist-owned Fort Harrison Hotel since 1980 include several suicides and a man found dead in a bathtub."[19]

Do we still have free speech? Am I allowed to speak my mind without being sued and harassed to extinction? Well, let's find out. If we have no more free speech, then everyone needs to know about it. Here's my opinion, for all the world to see. For the Omnologists of the world to go into a murderous rampage about it, if they see fit to do so. The Church of Scientology makes money at the expense of working some followers into a desperate state of emotional/spiritual bondage, sometimes to the point of suicide. What we have here is nothing less than an unspeakably horrid evil—trading souls down the river Styx for money.

Do I approve of the French governmental actions? You betcha! Yes, I can hear you now: I'm a hypocrite. Patrice Vic and Patrice Vic alone was responsible for his self-destructive act, according to what I said earlier. Ditto Noah Lottick and all the others. Yes, you're right. But Jean-Jacques Mazier and Jean-Jacques Mazier alone was responsible for what *he* did, and he engaged in deceptive, greedy practices pushing Patrice towards suicide. And we can say the same of the other 14. I walk two sides of the fence at once? So be it! It helps develop my sense of balance.

Okay, so back to the Feb. '97 *Good Housekeeping*. I guess good housekeeping is far more important than keeping your spiritual house free of harmful deception. Make sure your house is tastefully decorated, but don't worry about your soul. And God forbid you should say anything harsh or judgmental about any particular set of spiritual beliefs, because we all know that all beliefs are equally valid. The highlighted intro to this article, "*Look Who's Talking*", talks about "...how their faith made them strong..." Here's sections of the interview. LS (Liz Smith) interviews them; here's the brief mention of Scientology:

"LS: Do you also credit Scientology with the grounding you both seem to have?

"JT: I do, because through every turmoil, I've been bailed out. I've gotten help, relief, felt better, moved on..."

For these kinds of articles, *New Woman* and *Good Housekeeping* will doubtlessly attract many celebrity-worshipping readers, and advertisers who pay to reach them with more commercial messages. What happens to magazines that have the courage to tell the truth about Scientology? Well, there's *The Thriving Cult of Greed and Power* in *Time* magazine.[17] *Time* got sued for $416 million for that. Fortunately, *Time* must have had the money and lawyers to fend them off; the Church of Scientology's lawsuit was finally thrown out.[20] However, "Another libel suit over the same article brought by an individual church member is scheduled to go to trial in November...".

So, in a materialistic and lawsuit-happy society like ours, can there be any surprise that most of the media (with notable exceptions like *Time*, and that was a number of years ago, before the latest excesses of lawyers and advertisers) fears to speak out very strongly against Scientology? The *Houston Chronicle* ran an editorial by the leader of the Houston Church of Scientology, for example, bemoaning how these poor helpless Scientologists are persecuted by those nasty Nazis in the German government. Yet they were too cowardly to run my letter to the editor, or even a tiny bit of it. For your reading pleasure, here it is, very slightly edited:

Dear Editor:

I'm not surprised that the Reverend Larry McDaniel, the leader of the Houston Church of Scientology, would so vigorously and one-sidedly defend his faith against the heartlessly cruel, fascist depredations of the modern German State. This is in reference to his 19 Feb '97 editorial. He obviously knows which side his bread is buttered on. However, I'd like to present the other side, here. I feel fairly qualified to do so, because I'm writing a book concerning, among other things, irrationality, the Church of Scientology, and Hollywood. I've collected a fair amount of research materials already.

The good Reverend claims that Germany's "...vigilance [against extremist groups on it's soil] has transmuted into violence, violating the basic human rights of religious and ethnic minorities—Nazilike activities under the guise of preventing Nazilike activities." This is a tremendous reach, comparing the "persecution" of the Church of Scientology to the Nazis, and he knows it. In his long editorial, he mentions not one act of violence committed by the government of Germany against his church, and for good reason—he knows of none. In an age in which a substantial fraction of humanity suffers horrendously under the tyrannical rule of despots, in Iran, Iraq, Sudan, Zaire, Libya, North Korea, Cuba, Afghanistan, Syria, China, and so on, we could do far better than worry about a few money-grubbing charlatans being prevented from ripping people off, in a fairly free society. Governments and courts in Greece, Italy, France, and Australia have ruled or moved against this "church", say my newspaper clippings. My mail from the German Consulate adds the additional nations of Belgium, England, Ireland, Spain, Israel, and Mexico, as nations not recognizing Scientology as a religion. Are these countries then all bastions of fascism?

Nor does the good Reverend write about exactly what his church is or does—again, with good reason. If you'd like more details, perhaps you'd like to read a May 6 '91 feature article in *Time* Magazine, titled *"The Thriving Cult of Greed and Power."* They cure people of "engrams" by waving around pretty little toys called "E-meters", and saying all sorts of nice, impressive-sounding words. For the right price. They deceive gullible people with the trappings of science; just look at their name. Here's a mental exercise for you: replace "engrams" with "psychoses" and "E-meter" with "psycho-therapeutic device." If they renamed their practices and toys in this manner, guess how long it would take the FDA to shut them down. See what I mean?

So what did the *Time* article have to say? A few samples: Many of their beginner to intermediate courses cost $500 an hour or more. "According to the church's latest price list, recruits—'raw meat,' as Hubbard called them—take auditing sessions that cost as much as $1,000 an hour, or $12,500 for a 12.5-hour 'intensive.'" Then there are many case histories of gullible people taken to the cleaners by these quacks. Here's just one: "Harriet Baker, 73, lost her house after Scientologists learned it was debt free and arranged a $45,000 mortgage, which they pressured her to tap to pay for auditing. They had approached her after her husband died to help 'cure' her grief. When she couldn't repay the mortgage, she had to sell."

This "church" is about greed, not helping people. What reputable church charges this kind of money for such brief, limited services? Governments regulate churches all the time, if we look at things honestly. Native Americans can eat peyote, and the government gives them eagle feathers. If I'm caught with either of these things, I'm busted. A Muslim lady can wear her veil in a high-crime area, but if I wear a mask there, I'm busted for concealing my identity for nefarious purposes. Amish are exempted from Social Security. See how hard it will be for you to do that. And so on. For good or bad, government "certifies" the validity of religions all the time. The IRS made a mistake (under a welter of never-ending lawsuits from this "church") when it called this outfit a "church." We should pass a simple, objective law: Any group charging over $100 an hour, above and beyond costs of materials, for a service, is a business, not a church, and should be taxed and regulated as such.

Finally, note that *Time* called attention to how this "church" loves to use lawsuits to intimidate and harass opponents. So they harassed the *Time* article author, and sued *Time* to the tune of $416 million. The suit was dismissed in July '96. I guess *Time* has lots of lawyers and/or money. And courage, too, frankly. Then in the 2 Dec '96 *Hou Chron* I read *(Scientologists eat up group they'd opposed,* by Laurie Goodstein of the *Washinton Post)* that the Cult Awareness Network (CAN) answered more than 350 calls a week from anxious friends and relatives of cult victims. Next to Satanism, Scientology triggered more calls than any other group. So Scientology "...fought CAN with a barrage of lawsuits." One jury finally gave Scientology the jackpot. $1.8 million. CAN went bankrupt, and Scientology bought them out. So now if an anxious parent is worried about their Scientology-snared child, gets a library book to see where they can find help, they'll call CAN, and get advice from Scientology. Next on the auction block? Files on those who've called CAN. So has Scientology bought those files yet by now? Somebody has to stand up to these evil, pushy, greedy charlatans. I hope the *Chronicle* has the guts (and lawyers?) to publish this, for the public good. I'm not afraid to stand up for what's right. Are you?

So there's my letter. The weenies at the *Chronicle* wimped out, like I said. Courage sometimes doesn't make money. In a lawsuit-befestered nation, it can *cost* lots of money, regardless of all of our pretenses about "free speech". Besides, your advertisers, the Chryslers of the world, might stop advertising in your rag if you get too controversial, or report facts that people don't want to hear. Time will tell about publishers and booksellers, as far as *Jurassic Horde Whisperer of Madness County* is concerned.

I did take the time to call CAN and check it out for myself (at (773)-267-7777; they also can be reached at (800)-556-3055). They still call themselves CAN, which I think is at least slightly unethical. One might even compare it to calling a listing for Heroin Awareness Network, thinking one was getting some help, and finding that one was talking to a heroin dealer. As best as I understood the lady on the other end of the line, if I call them with a problem concerning, say, Satanism, they'll have me talk to their staff Satanist (yes, she mentioned Satanism several times... they're an "interfaith" group; isn't tolerance wonderful?) about how Satanism isn't really all that bad.

What if I told them my son was on the verge of suicide, desperately scrounging for another $5,000 to get his engrams audited away? Would they tell me it's all worth it? Or might they actually intervene with greedy practitioners of Scientology? I don't know. I (thank God!) have no friends or family involved in destructive cults, and haven't the guile to lie to CAN, to check it out in more detail.

I can tell you that the CAN lady politely and forthrightly told me she was a Scientologist. At least they don't lie about that, it seems. CAN may no longer provide any real help in extricating oneself, friends, or family from cults, but at least they tell us who they really are. I'll give them credit where credit is due. And I'm proud to report that I was relieved to find this out, rather than being disappointed in finding less than the maximum amount of possible dirt. I don't delight in discovering evil, and I'm trying my best to be honest, accurate, and balanced. It's just that finding many positives about Scientology is quite difficult.

Chapter 17 Endnotes

Role-Playing and "Satirical Social Commentary"

Now, I often rail against the anti-freedom ways of government. I regard Big Brother's machinations as some pretty serious stuff. But there is another matter addressed in chapter 17 which isn't a proper concern for government at all, yet I regard it as an even bigger threat than Big Brother, in our current space and time. This is a cultural, social, spiritual matter. A raised public awareness, and individual consciences, not government, can and must solve this more vague and nebulous problem.

I speak of the phenomenon of cultural evil. One symptom of this is when "sophisticated" artsy-fartsy types claim to make deep, satirical social commentary, and literature and such, by playing certain roles. Yet they're all about making money by lending encouragement to deranged thinking. And make money they do!

Yes, I'm talking about Marilyn Manson and his band, among others. Before I get started, let me straighten out an impression I may have left at the introductory quotes to this last chapter. I may have left the impression that the 24 Feb. '97 *Time* magazine did nothing other than praise Marilyn's "scathing social critique".

That isn't the entire picture. The article was balanced and fair, I think. I just left out some other parts. I was just setting the mood for the chapter, see, and balance would have detracted at the moment. Like any other writer's works, you've got to read my *entire book* to get the whole picture. So don't go dumping on me because somebody could get the wrong idea, by just reading one part of my book. That's true of any book.

So let me give you some other goodies from the article: He "...intentionally crafts his image to incite maximum shock. He often performs clad in jack-boots and trussed up in leather. Onstage and off, he wears black lipstick and cakes his face in morticians' white, giving himself a deathly, freshly exhumed look."

"Many of the band's most enthusiastic fans are Goths, members of a popular suburban youth cult drawn to black garb and death-rock music."

"...Manson's act is shorn of all humor. What's left is lurid spectacle that conveys little meaning beyond its shock value."

Apparently two Goths arrested in a Washington state thrill murder were big Marilyn Manson fans. Manson says "Parents should raise their kids to listen to an album and know the difference between reality and fantasy." *Time's* David Thigpen says, "True enough, but it wouldn't hurt if Manson lightened up his own scary, easily misunderstood message. After a Los Angeles concert, a fan (said that) (w)ith most rock stars 'the makeup comes off when they go home. With Manson it's real.'"

Well, I'd say that Thigpen gets it fairly well, but maybe not completely. You see, in this complicated world, some people can be what they are by pretending to be somebody else pretending to be who they *really* are. Or, we become the role that we play. Either way, this thing is too dangerous to play with. Yes, one could get a good message out by briefly pretending to be the Antichrist or the Devil or whatever, and making people realize what lies are being told to us. But when we pretend these kinds of things too long and too hard, all Hell can break loose. And this Hell breaking loose can get all too literal.

Historian Alan Bullock, for example, claims that Hitler was an "actor" who unfortunately came to believe in his role.[21] He latched onto *pretending* to hate Jews, initially, just as a cynical, insincere political ploy, perhaps. We all know what butchery eventually resulted.

You become the role that you play. To play a role, one has to imagine that one is in that role. And as Norman Vincent Peale said, "Be sure to imagine right, for we tend to become as we see ourselves." *Beware!!!*

Now I read that "Manson has said he is a member of the Church of Satan and his group is known for lewd on-stage acts and songs about murder, rape, sodomy and self-mutilation."[22] So just how *satirical* are all his statements about society, anyway? Are murderous and suicidal young Goths *really* misunderstanding his messages? Or is it that we old fogies are deceived, as he is what he is, while pretending to be someone who is pretending to be him? I don't really honestly know. All I can say is, I'm quite troubled by this all. My conscience requires me to speak out.

I'll tell you what else troubles me. That is that gothic novelist Anne Rice makes the big bucks pushing vampire trash on us, and on impressionable teenagers. She "...is one spooky woman. She goes on national TV to say not too long ago she was dead for three days."[23] "'I died recently,' she said. 'I wanted to commit suicide, which was ridiculous, but I wanted to kill myself. I was real depressed. I decided I would die for a few days. So, I advised the staff. I said, 'Tomorrow morning when you come, I'll be dead.' I'm lying in bed. I'm dead. I slept and slept and slept for three days, and then I felt refreshed and I was alive again. I recommend this.' According to Rice, 'The hardest part about being dead is having to (go to the bathroom).'"[23]

There, all you depressed people, there's words of wisdom from Anne Rice for *you*. If you listen to her, who knows *what* will happen to you?! Maybe you'll even become a member of a teenage vampire mini-cult, and go off and kill people, like Rod Ferrell & pals did.[24] He and his buddies "...were attracted to vampires by a best-selling role-playing game. They also drank their own blood and that of mutilated animals." And "Farrell had become possessed with opening the gates to hell." He ended up killing Ferrell's ex-girlfriend's parents, and burning a "V" (for Vampire?) onto the man's body. So let's all have fun playing vampire roles. Yes, indeed, Anne Rice really *is* scary, I do believe!

So am I another wild-eyed conspiracy theorist? Am I next going to propose that perhaps all evil stems from Tamagotchi toys, which in turn are the result of a conspiracy between Microsoft and El Nino? No, I'm not.

I'm *not* calling on all true patriots to man the barricades and arm themselves against all the Satanists and vampires who've infiltrated the highest levels of our government, Hollywood, and the Big Media, and are no doubt conducting evil spells to cast hexes on us as we so amiably discuss my politics, theology, etc., here. The evils that infect these places are the same evils that infect us all, and when it lurks in all those places, it's partly our own fault. And I'm talking little evil here; genuine foam-at-the-mouth malice is relatively rare, thank God! Yes, evils lurk all amongst us! But, to use M. Scot Peck's terms, some are little evil with a little "e", and some are Evil, with a BIG "E".

What I am saying is that there are clear potentials for Big "E" Evil to come about, out of role-playing. I consider this thing about "you become the role you play" to be something vitally important. This is not just some fluffy psychobabble, solely my ill-informed personal opinion, an attempt at sounding nobly, theologically or philosophically wise, or any such silliness. Not vibosomatic happy-talk. It is, rather, a scientifically demonstrated fact.

OK, so that may be some hyperbole, just there. I'll 'fess up to that. Psychology is often a "soft" study, and we must, in this field, speak of "scientifically demonstrated facts" with great caution. But here's a case where we can, with important lessons.

Let's briefly examine a study in which normal, healthy young males (college students, all White, one Asian; they were actually selected for being "...judged to be emotionally stable, physically healthy, mature, law-abiding citizens") were randomly selected to play "prisoners" and "guards".[25] See "The Mind is a Formidable Jailer, A Pirandellian Prison," from the *NY Times Magazine*, April 8, 1973, by Phillip G. Zimbardo and colleagues. Quotes here are from the *NY Times* article.

And before you ask... Yes, I was stumped, too. "Pirandellian", I suppose, must have to do with the fiction of a certain "Pirandello..., Luigi 1867-1936... Italian writer best known for his plays *Six Characters in Search of an Author* (1921) and *Tonight We Improvise* (1930). Pirandello won the 1934 Nobel Prize for literature." So hints my "Bookshelf '94" CD-ROM, from all the microserfs at Microsoft. Does that help you much? Me neither! But God bless all those microserfs, who've made all my work so much easier!

Anyway, about those "prisoner" studies. They advertised for college student volunteers, and then paid them $15 a day, to be randomly selected to be either "prisoners" or "guards", and then to play their roles. The "prisoners" were actually "arrested", rounded up by the Palo Alto police, to make the experience complete! See if you could get the cops to play such a role today, what with runaway lawyers! Even back then, when, halfway through the experiment, the experimenters grew worried about the security of their makeshift, college-campus-corridor "prison yard", they asked the Palo Alto police to "borrow" some "real" prison space, "...the problem of insurance and liability for our prisoners was raised by a city official." Thanks, all you rampant lawyersaurs, for ossifying our entire society!

Anyway, they randomly selected 10 prisoners and 11 guards. And they became the roles they played! Role-playing became reality!

The purpose of the study was to see whether all the nastiness of prison life (prisoner hopelessness and degradation, authoritarian behavior by guards) was the result of who was being sent there, or just the situation that is created in prisons, by the nature of the institution. By the *roles people play*. The idea was to create a prison of "normal" guards and prisoners, have them play their roles, and therefore, be able to say, "See, these things, but not these others, are the results just of the situation, the institution, and not of the people who are in the situation."

Now, most sensible people realize that many prisoners (not all) are in prison, not for being saints, but for good cause. But we should still pay attention to the results of this study. What were the results? Did all the normal sicknesses associated with prisons evolve in just about no time flat? You betcha! OK, so, out of ethical concerns, they excluded some of the worst aspects of real prisons. "Racism, physical brutality, indefinite confinement and enforced homosexuality were not features of our mock prison."

But all the other ugly features of prison life rapidly evolved. Guards enjoyed their power over fellow role-players, some sadistically, even though real physical torture was off limits. Prisoners become hopeless, dependent, whining, sometimes defiant, and always dehumanized, or depersonalized. Prisoners referred to themselves by their prisoner numbers, not their names, when the "prison chaplain" came by to visit. Guards played mind games with prisoners, turning them one against the other, and making them move boxes from here to there, and then, from there to here. There, you slime, see how truly worthless you and your efforts are, and how I have all the power, and you have none! All because we're playing this role, see, and we've forgotten all about real life ("reality"), and who we really are.

OK, so that's all a bunch of fluff; a glossy, glib overview by yours truly. Fancy psychobabble? Wait! There is real substance here! We *do* become the role we play, and there are *real dangers* here! And that is the somewhat-unexpected side benefit, side lesson, of this study. Yes, bad situations can make normally-good people do bad things, and that's a valuable lesson.

But also... *We become the role we play*. What's the difference between social "reality" and fiction, or role-playing? Not much, entirely too often! No, you can't play the role of the one who turns straw into genuine gold, nor the one who levitates, inexplicably, in a gravity field. But pre-defined, or other-defined, "real" social roles? Those we can pick and choose, and then, play. So pick a good role for yourself; you might get stuck playing it for a long, long time! Different take: Don't let anyone else tell you who you are, if that's not who you want to be!

Cut the fluff. OK, from the *NY Times* report: "In less than 36 hours, we were forced to release prisoner 8612 because of extreme depression, disorganized thinking, uncontrollable crying and fits of rage. We did so reluctantly because we believed he was trying to "con" us—it was unimaginable that a volunteer prisoner in a mock prison could legitimately be suffering and disturbed to that extent. But then on each of the next three days another prisoner reacted with similar anxiety symptoms, and we were forced to terminate them, too. In a fifth case, a prisoner was released after developing a psychosomatic rash over his entire body (triggered by rejection of his parole appeal by the mock parole board)." They were forced to terminate the experiment after 6 days, not the planned 14.

So, as the authors of the experiment and reports say, a number of disturbing questions arise. They call one problem "This dehumanizing tendency to respond to other people according to socially determined labels and often arbitrarily assigned roles..." Yes, it *does* sound like vibosomatic happy-talk, and it's easy to protect real wrong-doers under this kind of thinking. Yet there is also real substance here, which we'd be wise to think about. Other studies (they refer to one) have shown the same thing.

Where does our "role" end, and our "identity" begin? What evils are even the semi-saints among us capable of, in the wrong circumstances, where everyone expects us to play a certain role that we'd be better off not playing? And in our daily lives, in family and work situations, how many of us play "prisoner", allowing ourselves to become powerless and dependent on arbitrary rules and rulers? How many of us play "guard", foisting senseless rules upon the weak, congratulating ourselves about how we're whuppin' 'em into shape for their own good?

OK, one last example of this often-vague danger of becoming the role you play... L. Ron Hubbard, the founder of Scientology, by strong appearances at least (everything reeking of chaos and badness is, of course, denied by The Church), went out and deliberately crafted a role, and an entire religion, for the purposes of bringing riches and power to himself (see intro quotes to Chapter 10).

So then he proceeded to play that role, apparently quite successfully, as too many of us define success. He grew rich and powerful. As we might suspect, the Mighty Prophet began to believe his own propaganda, as so many Mighty Prophets do. He played the role too long. His last days weren't happy. So here's the LA Times, in an article subtitled "Aides indulged his eccentricities and egotism".[26]

"Gillham, formerly one of Hubbard's most loyal and trusted messengers, said his behavior became increasingly erratic after he crashed a motorcycle in the Canary Islands in the early 1970s.

"'He realized his own mortality,' she said. 'He was in agony for months. He insisted, with a broken arm and broken ribs, that he was going to heal himself and it didn't work.'"

Other details of L. Ron's life of paranoia, spoiled-child-like temper tantrums, and being pampered by devotees, with his later years spent in hiding, are spelled out in this series of articles. Apparently L. Ron wasn't really very happy, in spite of all the wealth and power that he gained by playing his role so well.

I obviously don't know all the details, and I don't think I really want to. But can you imagine? Most of us realize that we're going to get aches and pains as we age, and our bodies won't work quite as well as they used to. That if we live long enough, we'll start to fall apart, then die. Most of us come to accept this, sooner rather than later. Some of us even gloriously triumph over death in a sense, living with our pains, frailties, and certain knowledge of our approaching death, but still finding plenty of reasons to enjoy life.

But can you imagine *not* accepting this, believing in your own magic so much that you think you can work *literal* miracles upon yourself? Struggle to *believe* hard enough, and I'll be all-powerful? I'll never need to physically die? Whatever I think, becomes true, if I think it hard enough?

Did L. Ron Hubbard go to his grave cussing and swearing at his engrams? These "engram" entities that he invented to play the roles of chaos and badness, did he start to envision them as what prevented him from healing himself? Was he ultimately audited by his own engrams, fleeced by his own scamgrams, or some such, in some manner of speaking? I don't know; I'm just asking these questions. I'm not sure of what the exact nature of this beast is, which he apparently wrestled with, but I quite frankly don't *want* to know. To truly understand, you have to *be*.

They say that when a flounder baby fish (fishlet? kid? pup? fishling? kitten? fingerling? calf?) is young, it swims like a normal fish. One eye on each side of its head, swimming upright. As it matures, however, it lays its body down, to swim along the bottom, as adult flounder do. So as a juvenile flounder matures, *one eye migrates from one side of its head to the other*. You thought your pimples were bad, when you were a teenager? Ha! What of the growing pains of a flounder, as he glances in the mirror again and again, watching his eyeball migrate? To truly understand the growing pains of a juvenile flounder, you must *become* a juvenile flounder.

The founder of Scientology, I believe, in many ways stayed a juvenile his whole life long, as he floundered about, trying to find a role that would bring happiness to himself, but always failing. I wonder about his pains, sometimes. But not *too* hard. Because I know that to truly understand, I have to *be*. And I don't *want* to! I suspect I should pray to God to protect me from such knowledge, as a matter of fact.

Well, let me conclude with the following open letter to the Anne Rices of the world, and to the Marilyn Mansons:

To All You Creative Artsy-Fartsy Role-Playing Moneymakers:

Yes, I know you've got messages we need to hear. When you send us the messages we need to hear, I'm grateful for it. Even when you tell us what bad lies are being told to us by the Horde Whisperer, AKA the Evil One. You can play devil's advocate, and accomplish good things by doing so. But I ask you to ponder what happens when you play these roles too long and too hard. I ask you to ponder what happens when impressionable young people admire you for just exactly how heartily and thoroughly you play these roles. I ask you to ask yourselves, "What are my motives? Are they monetary, moral, or morbid? Am I *doing good* for people, in the balance?"

I'm an artist, too. I know what it feels like to have my messages misinterpreted. I haven't read your books, Anne, and I haven't heard your albums, Marilyn, so I'll try to keep my judgmentalism on a leash. But I do have some questions I'm asking you to ask of yourselves.

Ask yourselves whether you really and sincerely believe that people will improve their lives after they've seen or heard your art. Will they recognize and avoid the Evil One's lies better? Or will they revel in role-playing? Do you revel in role-playing? Is it a morbid fascination of yours? Or is it the money that drives you? Ask yourself some probing question, for our sake, and for yours.

Yes, I know that even a good work, which does good for the ninety-nine, will hurt (or be used as an excuse by) the one. So I'm not asking you to trouble yourselves over those who do evil in your name, if they're misinterpreting your messages. And I'm not threatening you with force or violence, unless you, yourselves, should engage in such things. This is not a matter for the coercive arms of the law. This is a moral and spiritual matter, between you and me, and all of my readers. I'm asking, not commanding, because I follow a nameless entity who asks of me, rather than commands of me.

What I'm asking of you is of a nature sublime. I'm asking of you that you each go into a room all by yourself somewhere quiet and undisturbed, for as long as it takes for you to get decent answers, and ask yourself the probing questions that I'm asking you. *Examine your motives.* If they're pure and noble, then may God bless you as you continue on your merry way, content in the certain knowledge that those who do *anything,* be it good or bad, out of *good motives* will be rewarded. This is right and true, and applies to you, to those who admire and follow you, and to all of us.

But be informed that from those to whom much is given, much is required. As the obvious recipients of great creative talents, you must be possessed of keen minds. *Surely,* then, you can see the ancient wisdom of which I speak! You have great abilities, rational and intuitive both, to see, and to measure, effects good and bad, of your art. We all know it makes money for you. That's OK. Money isn't evil. You can do a lot of good things with money, including taking care of your own needs. If you take care of them, no one else will need to. Valuing money too much, too far above and beyond values that more properly reside above money, however, **IS** evil. *Nothing less than evil!* I ask you to consider that.

I ask you to consider the many poor, happy people, and the many rich, miserable people on our planet, and think long and hard. Put your values, your heart, and your efforts in one place, the place that brings the most happiness to you and to us all. Woe to those whose values are in the wrong place! I'm not saying I'm getting ready to inflict woe upon you, I'm saying that's the way the moral universe is set up. What goes around, comes around. Don't be spreading bad karma, 'cause it'll come back around and bite you on your heiney. Whatever. However you want to say it. Just *beware!*

Now, I can't put exact names to the vague values of which I speak. I suppose you've noticed. I'm not that great of a writer, and certainly not that much of a speaker. If I had to try, I guess I'd mumble something about valuing life, and Love, and conscience, balance, and simple decency. Even caution and prudence, because life is a precious thing, to be jealously guarded with rational, responsible behavior, and self-restraint, even, every day.

Okay, so those are these Supreme Values I'm trying to speak of. These Supremes don't ask of you to wear sackcloth, to engage in hypocrisy, sanctimony, self-righteousness, or self-denial. I'm not asking you to mope around with a long face, telling everyone to "Let Jesus into your life", or anything like that. I'm just asking you to ponder whether, in the balance, you're doing good, or bad. Are there acts, aspects of your art, that are more negative than positive, net-net? If so, then, keeping these Supremes in mind, I ask you to "Stop, in the Name of Love!"

Sincerely, and with Best Wishes,

Titus Stauffer

Chapter 18 Endnotes

A National ID Card, and Governmental and Non-Governmental Snoops (Like Scientologists, for Example)

Retina scans and a National ID card for every citizen? Make sure we keep them thar heinous alien scum out, who would (Gasp! Horror of Horrors!) *work* without permission? Produce goods and services for us cheaper than welfare-state molly-coddled U.S. citizens? Can't have *that*, now, come *on!* And, of course, your new National ID will also Protect The Children from deadbeat dads. And who could argue against *that*, except for a children-hating ogre?

Yup, yo. A National ID card, with biometric data encoded into it, so that we'll have foolproof methods of identifying deadbeat dads, people who would produce goods and services illegally, and people who would evade taxes, for such pernicious and destructive purposes as making their own charity choices, instead of having enlightened bureaucrats in D.C. (Den of Crypto-fascists) make them for us. Other noble purposes to be added later, as the situation may demand. That's what's coming our way. National ID cards. As if our de facto National ID number, Social Security, wasn't enough.

So now the cat's out of the bag. Your author is a raving loony, a militiaman, a conspiracy theorist. Well, now, hold your horses. As of 1 Oct. '97, all U.S. employers must register their new hires, and report their pay every three months.[27] All so that the government can impose it's family values, and chase deadbeat dads. Meanwhile, divorced dads get no financial credit for buying clothes for the kids, taking them out to eat, and so on. Even if momma is in the habit of snorting her child support check up her nose, and neglecting the kids. Unless we can invite Big Brother into our homes, and document the child neglect, give her a weekly urine test, and get lots of lawyers and judges to revamp child custody... What a mess!

Yes, it's often partly dad's fault, for having made irresponsible choices in mating and reproducing, but still. Let's be fair to fathers. I recall Marcia Clark, O.J. Simpson prosecutor, saying that her ex (making a third or so of what she was making) needed to send her more child support, so that she could buy better dresses, to better impress the judge, jury, media, and so on! And she said this for all the world to hear! Something's busted here, folks. A National ID card ain't gonna fix it, either.

For those of you who are sick of men's interests getting trampled in zillions of ways, from false rape charges to special laws that protect women but not men, and on and on, I'd recommend that you read a well-written, well-documented book by Warren Farrell, Ph.D., called *The Myth of Male Power*. Some chapter titles alone say a lot: *"Women Who Kill Too Much and the Courts That Free Them: The Twelve 'Female-Only' Defenses"* and *"From Husband Sam to Uncle Sam: Government as Substitute Husband"* are examples. We've taken power away from individuals, heads of households, families, civil society, and local communities, and given it to coercive government social workers and bureaucrats. The negative effects, from child abuse witch-hunts to yet more irresponsible reproductive choices, should be obvious for all but hide-bound ideologues to see.

Yes, I realize that there are abusive men, and that the state does need to step in at times, to (Yuck! Here it comes!) *protect the children*. Still, let's find a balance, here. And let's not set up a system for one purpose, and find that it later gets used for another. Like giving Big Brother his National ID cards.

Despite badly bungling pilot attempts at creating centralized government registries of those who are authorized to work, the Clinton administration is now expanding a worker registry. "The Illegal Immigration Reform and Immigrant Responsibility Act of 1996, a bill promoted by the administration and enacted by congressional Republicans... requires the project to clear citizens as well as non-citizens. Accordingly, the administration is merging INS and Social Security system databases to create a worker registry—a list of all people who are authorized to work in this country."[28] Later, we are told, "In September 2001, Congress will vote on whether the project should become a mandatory nationwide program. Unimpeded by the admission that INS databases are unreliable, the worker registry is steadily expanding."

Then we are told that Sen. Alan Simpson, set to retire after this new law authorizing the pilot project had passed, in boasting about his "legislative accomplishment", "...candidly predicted that the worker registry would lead to 'a more secure identifier,' such as 'a slide-through card like you use with a Visa when you make a purchase, perhaps some type of driver's license photograph, retina examination like they have done in California.' Had Simpson stated during the floor debate that his bill would hasten the day when federal government will issue an identification card encoded with a 'retina examination,' the law would have failed by a landslide."[28]

Some legislators like to sneak things up on Congress. And Congress likes to sneak things up on *us*. Do *you* trust the government with vast databases about all of us? *I* don't, and for plenty of good reasons, none of which have anything to do with me being a member of any militia. One reason is that systems set up for one use, under one set of enlightened despots, for one use, gets used for straightening out the benighted masses for unanticipated transgressions later on.

So you liberals get to scan our retinas today to "Protect The Children". After the next elections, are you ready for the conservatives to scan your retinas, to "Protect Us All From Sin"? Maybe match your retina patterns to your DNA, for example, and keep it all on file, so we can do a DNA match to all the fetuses, and make sure nobody thumbs their nose at the long arm of The Law, and goes and get himself cloned, for example. Nip those monsters in the bud, and forcibly abort all the clones. God didn't make them, man made them, so they don't have souls. Killing monsters isn't murder, right? Don't laugh—we've done stupider things. We're still doing stupid things, and I see no end in sight just yet.

And once a program is in place, you can expect it to grow and grow, and never die. I seem to recall reading that the current income tax started in about 1911, at a rate of about 3% on the very richest of fat cats. Ordinary Joes like you and me, they said, we'd never have to worry about it. Yeah, right!

Then there's the matter of whether or not government (the gang that can't shoot straight, 'cause their "customers" are theirs by force, not by choice) can be trusted to keep the registries honest, accurate, and fair. Do I have a story for you! "Name-Theft Nightmare", 26 Oct. '97 *Hou Chron*. Subtitled *Model citizen suffers because of law's loophole*. It seems that an underage stripper stole Nicole Zatkin's ID card. Nicole is deaf, a young mother, a model citizen who has struggled with her disability, and a contributing, law-abiding member of society. Yet if you're her prospective banker, landlord, employer, or volunteer agency looking for help (and all these and more do check the records, these days, to check you out, and they're doing it ever more and more, as we let the murderers and child molesters free to free up jail space for the drug fiends), then you'll find that "...a check of arrest records reveals a very different Nicole Zatkin—an under-aged topless dancer arrested by vice officers for lewdness at an adult club."

It all began when Nicole's temporary driver's license got heisted by Anastacia Moonglow Alva. Although Nicole spent nearly $1,000 and two years trying to straighten things out, and although the real perpetrator (that heinous criminal, using her body as she saw fit, without the state's approval) 'fessed up to all her crimes ("After performing a risqué 'lap dance,' she was charged with public lewdness and jailed," the paper explains), including heisting the card, Nicole can't get her records cleaned up! The State of Texas doesn't *allow* such lawlessness, chaos, and badness!

The State of Texas, and rigid-minded whores thereof, can't see fit to expunge her name, because she wasn't the person arrested! Their limp excuse is something like, "Well, if a criminal uses a certain alias, we have to keep track of that alias, lest they use it again." Harris County District Attorney John B. Holmes Jr. claims he sympathizes with Nicole, but, well, ya know, the law is the law is the law. And what's against the law is against the law. God forbid we, who are sworn to uphold the law, should break the law! So no, *of course* we can't expunge her records!

Get this: "Holmes said the ruling was proper, because the law allows for little discretion in granting expunctions. He recalled an incident in which one of his prosecutors was filling out a criminal charge form on a computer screen, when she inadvertently typed in her name as the person charged.

"'There was nothing we could do at that point, under the law,' Holmes said. 'We had her technically 'arrested'—so she could fulfill the requirement of the expunction law. Then we took up a collection for the $178 expunction filing fee. I chipped in the first $20.'"

So there you have a good example of the asinine, totally mindless nature of public "servants". They're completely incapable of giving a common-sense answer to the following simple question: "Are the systems, procedures, and computers our servants, or are we theirs?" I'd like to think that there'd be freedom-loving, common-sense men and women out there in public service who'd say, "In this case, the law obviously has its head so far up its patootie that I'm just flat-out not going to do the wrong thing. Throw me out of office if you must. Then I'm going straight to the media." And no sane person higher up the public service food chain would dare to touch them, I'd bet.

But expecting common sense and courage out of "public servants" often seems like expecting a pig to fly. It just ain't in the nature of the beast. What bureaucrat ever got fired for exactly following a procedure, even though it was stupid? Hence, we must fight against the idea of a National ID card, and anything that smells like it.

Still not convinced that I'm no militia loony? That bit about having to fear that non-government types might tap into government databases for nefarious purposes (of a non-governmental nature) pushed you over the edge? I'm a real conspiracy nut, now, huh?

Well, the FBI in 1976 found that two Scientology agents, equipped with forged credentials, were scrounging around a Justice Department office at night.[18] This was the tip of the iceberg ("a widespread espionage operation"), the feds found. One Scientology agent, Michael Meisner, ending up working with the feds, after nearly a year on the run. He and an accomplice broke into an IRS photo-ID "...room and forged the credentials that they used to enter various government buildings, steal and copy keys left carelessly on desks, pick locks, and steal and copy government files."

"Other Scientologists entered on nights and weekends and ransacked offices, including the Deputy Attorney General's, stealing highly secret papers and copying them on government copiers," the *Digest* goes on to tell us. After the October '79 conviction of nine high Scientology officials (on charges "of theft or conspiracy charges arising from their plot against the government", with Hubbard himself, among others, named as unindicted co-conspirators), Scientology remained unbowed. "...they issued an appeal for volunteers for the Guardian counterattack, 'to ferret out those who want to stop Scientology.'"[18] *Guardian* here refers to a member of Hubbard's then-budding non-governmental "dirty tricks" squad. More dirt on Scientology later, in the endnotes concluding this whole book. Stay tuned!

It seems to me that history has lessons about charismatic, persuasively talented madmen who draw others into their paranoid delusions of grandeur and persecution. Like one who whips them into blind obedience, into following him and his insane ideas down into evil and destruction, all in the name of "Only *I* can save you from all of the rest of the world! They're all against us, and our special knowledge and power! Only *I* can save you! You must *obey!* We must destroy them before they destroy us!"

We must guard against anyone who has all the answers for us, and who would *do us good*, whether we want to be done good unto, or not. A National ID card would play right into the claws of such monsters. The government has too much information for freedom-fearing thugs (of both the governmental and non-governmental species) to steal and abuse already. We'd be fools to add yet more fuel to the fire.

Chapter 19 Endnotes

Scientology and The Level Beyond Stupid

So you like my tale from The Level Beyond Stupid? But you think it's pretty stupid? Well, it is. But sadly, once again, my crazy fiction has its counterparts in reality. Peer pressure *does* make us "metans" do some pretty darned stupid things! I'll try not to insult you intelligence and knowledge, but I suppose you recall at least some of the history I'm familiar with.

A.D. 73, 1,000 or so members of a Jewish sect called Zealots committed mass suicide rather than surrender to the Romans, at Masada, by the Dead Sea. Two women and five children escaped. November 1978, 911 followers of Jim Jones drank poison in Jonestown, Guyana; 32 escaped. 5 Oct. '94, 23 Solar Temple worshippers dead, in yet another mass suicide. 22-23 March '97, 39 Heaven's Gate members dead; mass suicide yet again.

When will it stop? When we're all smart enough to let God, and not zealots, tell us Who God Is. When we figure it out for ourselves, in our own individual ways, and become profoundly, deeply skeptical of anyone who tells us that they know the One Truth and The Way. We must obey our one True Leader who relates to God (UFOs, Descamgramification, being Clear of engrams, whatever) for us? And we must obey our True Leader in every minute detail? Run for your life and soul!

Anyway, here's the one really big reason why I had to put endnotes on this particular chapter: I wanted to tell you where I got this ultimately, frightfully euphemistic talk about "ending one's cycle". Steven Fishman, a former Scientologist, began serving a five-year prison sentence in Florida in August of '90.[17]

He had worked at a brokerage, where he stole blank stock-confirmation slips. These, he used as proof to join dozens of class-action lawsuits as a stockholder. He made about $1 million between 1983 and 1988 by doing this. These reparations for being supposedly so sorely abused as a stockholder, he then took and spent for various good causes, to be sure. One of them (up to 30% of his take, or shall we say, his grab) was books and tapes from Scientology. You might imagine that Fishman, upon being arrested, was a bit of an embarrassment to The Church, and that they might have preferred for him not to embarrass them any more. Here comes the good part:

"Scientology denies any tie to the Fishman scam, a claim strongly disputed by both Fishman and his longtime psychiatrist, Uwe Geertz, a prominent Florida hypnotist. Both men claim that when arrested, Fishman was ordered by the church to kill Geertz and then do an 'EOC,' or end of cycle, which is church jargon for suicide."[17]

Chapter 20 Endnotes

Dianetics Therapy, "Voluntary" Therapy, NAGPRA, NADGRAB, GRABBOIDS, and Sacred Hairs.

OK, readers, so how totally silly and ridiculous do you think I'm being *this* time? Am I holding a candle to reality yet? Judge for yourselves!

Breast exams and practicing medicine without a license? Howard Stern, radio shock jock, might get *busted* (ha-ha) for examining women's breasts for lumps while on the air.[29] Not for being a juvenile, or for having bad taste, but for *practicing medicine without a license*. OK, so it's not something you or I would do, and we consider this to silly childishness, but... Well, how many women would really go see Howard Stern for a breast exam, thinking he was a doctor? And Howard even told them to get another opinion!

Petty laws are often used by petty people for petty reasons. The man who's pushing to have Howard charged is trying to squelch free speech; he's not worried about protecting women from bad doctors. That should be obvious for all to see. The more petty laws we put on the books, the more weapons we put into the hands of petty people. You told your neighbor to keep his dog from pooping on your yard? Better hide all your plastics quick; he turned you in! The GRABBOIDS of NADGRAB are coming to confiscate all your petroleum derivatives!

And the FDA stomping all over medical advances? I could go on all day! What I wrote about here is only a minor extrapolation from the laws as they exist. Software is a "medical device", and the FDA thus uses its powers to regulate "medical devices" to reach into controlling medical practice, which is far more than Congress ever meant to do. If the doctor uses a computer to assist him, he'd better have the FDA sitting on his shoulder.

Atlanta eye surgeon Trevor Woodhams had his eye laser "arrested" by the FDA, despite the fact that he was working with the FDA in good faith.[30] He'd made the mistake of trying to do advanced eye surgery as performed in other nations, whose regulatory octopuses grab less power than the FDA grabs. Medical advances are regularly caught in the bureaucrats' power-hungry maws. Calling software a "medical device" is one way the FDA expands its powers, without new laws being passed.

"Because software evolves rapidly and has 1,001 different uses, it is particularly easy to stifle through regulations that are just a bit too inflexible. And because software changes constantly, it is never perfect, though it is often vastly superior to the manual, paper-based processes it is meant to replace. Imperfection has never sat well with the FDA, which gets a great deal of bad publicity if something it approves hurts someone but none at all if someone dies because of regulatory delay. Accordingly, the FDA dreams, in the words of T.S. Eliot, 'of systems so perfect that no one will need to be good.'"[30]

"Off-label" uses of drugs are a major area of FDA excesses. Under new federal policies, your pharmacist and the drug manufacturer might *both* get busted if your doctor prescribes a drug for you for an unlisted application, and the pharmacist (helpfully, in response to your questions) gives you a copy of an article from a medical journal. Not only that, but the FDA has already "...often prohibited the distribution of textbooks and journal articles to health care professionals because they alluded to off-label uses."[31]

So do you want to trust your doctor and pharmacist, or bureaucrats at the FDA? Do you have the money to travel overseas to a very few nations less befestered by bureaucrats than ours, to get the latest, best medicine and medical procedures? Maybe we should consider starting the "Church of Zapping Eye Scamgrams With Lasers", and the "Church of Driving the Demons Away with Software-driven Automated Pill-dispensing Machines". If we did so, we might get freedom from all regulations, and a tax break to boot! Because religious freedom is high, mighty, and supreme, while the terms *economic freedom, personal freedom, and medical freedom* are regarded as oxymorons.

See, for instance, one of the apparent Bibles of Scientology, *Dianetics*, by L. Ron Hubbard. My 1986-timeframe paperback copy (my wife bought it second-hand, so don't worry, we didn't add much in the way of fuel to Scientology's fires) tells me right up front about the "E-Meter". "It is not intended or effective for the diagnosis, treatment or prevention of any disease, or for the improvement of health or any bodily function." That is, in the small print, way up front, before the body of the book.

Later, on page 122, we are told, as I understand, that if you get your "demon circuits deleted from the engram bank," and do this that and the other, then your IQ will soar! Page 125 tells us about a long list of ills that Dianetic therapy will cure for you. "(And the word cured is used in its fullest sense.)" We are even told that "Clears do not get colds." "Clears" are those who've had their "engrams" "audited" away by an expert with an "E-Meter", or some such hoo-ha. More details if you fork over the big donations!

OK, so then we get to page 126, where we are told that they're working on curing cancer and diabetes. But all we've got to do, now, to keep the FDA off of our backs, is to put a little disclaimer up front, declare ourselves to be a religion, and sue the hell out of the IRS till we get a tax break. For those who don't know, Scientology is a tax-exempt church, at least in the U.S. What a deal!

GRABBOIDS? NADGRAB? Bureaucrats with billy clubs, running around and telling us how to properly respect the dead? And recruiting "volunteers" to donate time and money, to have their bad habits "voluntarily" therapeutritrized away? Using the long arms of the law? Let me tell you a few tales!

First, there's a 9 June '97 *Hou Chron* article bylined San Antonio, "Report: D.A. drops charges for drug task donations." If you're a heinous scumbucket who travels down to Mexico, to buy prescription drugs that cost a fraction of the U.S. costs, down there, because you can bypass the Medi-Nanny state and its ten zillion regulations on drug companies, and you get caught bringing them thar heinous drugs across the border (*shame* on you, believing that an ignorant slob like you can decide for yourself what to pay for your drugs, without greasing the palms of doctors, pharmacists, the FDA, the cops, their mothers, and the local Committee for the Eradication of Sin—whazzamatter wiff you, boy, you believin' you can just doctor yourself, *huh?!* You think that just 'cause the government graciously allows you to inhabit that body, that it belongs to *you*, and that an ignorant moron like *you* can decide *for yourself* what to put into it?! You got some sort o' *attitude* problem or *what*, boy?!), then you're *busted!* But you can make "the felony charge disappear with a donation to a drug task force." Or you can get up to ten years in the slammer for trying to save money, while unauthorized by the Medi-Nanny state.

But we're not selling forgiveness for drug sins. No, Sir! Here's the tap-dance double-speak from a law geek: "'If we think there is insufficient evidence (to prosecute a case), we will ask them if they will make a charitable contribution,' he said. The request is not part of a plea agreement, he said. 'If they don't want to do it, we just go ahead and prosecute. There is no hard sell (on making the contribution),' Ellison said."

We might be tempted to dismiss such sheer stupidity as being purely the fruits of demented law enforcement imbeciles. But we'd be making a mistake! Such idiots also reside at high-powered think tanks.[32] The Rand Corporation got the story partly straight by saying that long prison terms for low-level drug offenders are a big mistake, and that treatment might be a better option. But how do we make sure the unfleeced metans of the world are brought to the light? Good question!

The report's principal author is a distinguished gentlemetan, Jonathan Caulkins, associate professor of public policy at Carnegie Mellon University. Quite the learned gentlemetan, as you can see. *Surely* we could expect no moron-speak from one such as *him!* We'll, we'd be wrong. "After all, it often takes enforcement to provide willing clients for treatment," he says.[32] Come *on,* boys, and let's go an' lasso up some *willing clients* an' shove 'em into that thar therapeutritron thang, an' therapeutritrize 'em good an' *hard!*

You've still got your "freedom". You're free to choose jail, or cough up a couple of thousand dollars for your *voluntary therapy*. Yup! And when I come home drunk as a skunk at three in the morning, my wife tells me I'd best volunteer to allow her to offer me some alcohol abuse therapy, or else I can volunteer to sleep on the patio for a few nights.

Come *on*, people, is it voluntary treatment, or is it punishment? Recognizing one's problems and listening to the advice of a person who helps us in a mutually voluntary manner is therapy, and it often works. Punishment is being subjected to retribution; it causes resentment, and can often do more harm than good. Especially when dished out to people who don't deserve it. And preaching to unwilling listeners, otherwise known as "nagging therapy", hardly *ever* works! Let's reserve punishment for those that *really* deserve it, and then make the punishment a *real, effective* punishment! Then we can also stop confusing therapy and punishment.

Boy, you'd better be respectin' yo' ancestors properly, or we'll be takin' ya in! It's a warning that anthropologist Rob Bonnichsen is all too familiar with.[33] See the 14 Oct '96 *Time* magazine science article, "Bones of Contention", for example. I have a few bones to pick with our society's anti-knowledge bias these days. Rob is a scientist who wanted to study a single hair found in an ancient Native American camp site (not a grave). The federal bureaucrats used the **N**ative **A**merican **G**rave **P**rotection and **R**epatriation Act (**NAGPRA,** passed in 1990) to prevent him from studying this hair, this Sacred piece of Human Body Remains.

They can't protect us from the neighborhood thugs, but hair-splitting bureaucrats can sure protect us from a mad scientist who might study a hair! Worse yet, think about the anti-knowledge bias here: Every day, no doubt, hunters, campers, hikers, lumberjacks, and farmers are unknowingly desecrating these precious hairs of Native American Ancestors, randomly strewn about out in the great outdoors. It's only when we *know what we're doing* that we can be punished under these laws! And woe even more to those who should be *seeking yet more knowledge!*

Under NAGPRA, museums which own Native American grave artifacts, Holy Relics such as "corn pollen, ritual stones and eagle feathers" in special "medicine bundles" and such, are required to return them to Native American tribes.[34] However, if they appease the Native Americans by paying Native American Medicine Men to come in and periodically pray over these artifacts, appeasing the Ancestor Spirits that dwell in the corn silk, and such, then they can keep their artifacts for a little while longer.

"...traditional Navajos believe the bundles are living objects and can suffer if mistreated...", so they "...must be periodically allowed to breathe by having medicine men remove the items and hold a special ceremony." "Officials at most Southwestern museums have budgets set aside to pay for these ceremonies."[34]

All this, despite the fact that the museums bought the medicine bundles fair and square, on the open market. Role reversal time! Can I sell you my old TV, then decide that my Ancestor Spirits dwell therein, and get Congress to pass a law that requires you to either give it back to me, or pay me to pray over your TV now and then? Whatever happened to property rights (economic freedom), common sense, separation of church and state, and rationality, anyway? Prepare for NADGRAB and the petroleum police, the GRABBOIDS!

Native Americans are far and away today's most "politically correct" minority, and "sensitive" people don't ask any questions whatsoever, with respect to policies regarding them. Certainly not questions like "Does this make any sense? Is this really helping anyone? What harms can result from treating people differently, according to what group they belong to?"

We're all in favor of everyone being equal, we say. Then we turn around and pass special policies for special people. Native Americans are often exempt from paying taxes when they sell cigarettes and gasoline![35] And of course they get special gambling permits. Oh, but the law says they're sovereign nations, so we can't be making them pay sales taxes. That would be infringing on their sovereignty, unlike when the government gives them welfare benefits. But don't worry, they're supposed to pay sales taxes when they sell to non-Amerinds! What's next, sales taxes proportional to the customer's Amerind bloodlines?! Talk about unenforceable, crazy laws!

Then there's also the Indian Arts and Crafts Act of 1990. You may not sell your arts or crafts in the U.S. if they're labeled as Native American or American Indian unless you're a member of a state or federally recognized tribe. Gotta protect those "genuine" Indian artists and craftspersons from "impostors"!!! So even if you're a full-blooded Native who doesn't want to affiliate with any tribe, or if you're a Canadian Native, then, tough luck! And once more, role reversal time: Congress passes the Caucasian Arts and Crafts Act of 2003, with similar provisions. Gotta protect the artists and consumers from impostors. Reactions? What will the do-gooders say?

It really, truly *is* as bad as I portray it, sad to say. Purchasing Native American artwork is now yet another category of, you don't really *own* it just because you bought it fair and square. You can only *own* something if you can afford several buckets full of slimy lawyers. Steve Diamant spend 15 years buying his collection of 200 Native American artifacts, buying them from museum shops, reservation trading posts, Indian craftsmen, and so on.[36] He returned home one day to find lawmen, including "Hopi Rangers", rummaging through all of his belongings. They took his 200 items; he's now got about 15 of them back, almost a year later, after spending $45,000 in legal fees!

It really was quite the comical affair, if you can bring yourself to laugh at thugs stealing things from people, with government assistance. One confiscated item of "cultural patrimony" was a domestic turkey feather spray-painted to look like an eagle feather. When the time came for all the various sorts of certified Native Americans to split the loot, they didn't even know which things belonged to whom! "Navajos have claimed Rio Grande Pueblo material as Navajo cultural patrimony," Diamant said. "Jemez likewise have claimed Zia material, and Hopi have claimed Jemez material."[36]

NAGPRA was *deliberately* written to be vague about what is and isn't "cultural patrimony", because if the material was specifically described, collectors would know was is then the very most precious, and target it! Nor will the tribes "certify" art for sale as *NOT* being "cultural patrimony". This would interfere with their ability to sell things, decide that they're "patrimony", seize them back, and then re-sell them again. There have been unproven allegations that exactly this is happening. A deliberately vague set of laws here is facilitating thievery by some small subset of lazy, greedy scum among Native Americans. If you thought "Indian giver" was a derogatory label, wait till "Indian seller" gets around!

Collecting Native American trinkets, then, is a hazardous hobby. Even contracting with the artist is no guarantee. "...seized items included new kachinas commissioned and purchased directly from Hopi carvers."[36] Penalties for violating deliberately vaguely crafted laws? Up to a year in the slammer, a $100,000 fine, and confiscation of artifacts. Second offense, 5 years, $250,000. And that's not throwing in penalties for trafficking in endangered species, either—remember, your Native Artisan might have thrown a few Yellow-Bellied Slime-Tailed Greater Southern Turd Slug eggs into his creation.

So you want to buy Native American trinkets, now? Not I! See how counterproductive stupid government meddling gets, when we allow Congressmen to have self-righteous snits with other peoples' affairs and property? When will they deputize me as a "Caucasian Ranger", so that I can go and seize the art you contracted with blah-blah down the street to carve for you? If my taste runs to Native American-style art (I hope that's allowed, even though I'm not a Certified Native), then can I at least safely buy some Certified Genuine Imitation Pseudo-Native Non-Art by a Certified Non-Native Non-Artisan? Would our masters allow this?

Wait, there's more: a seemingly Caucasian skeleton, 9,300 years old, is found in the state of Washington. An extremely rare, intriguing, and irreplaceable find, it must be buried within 30 days, without further study, to appease the Ancestor Spirits. We double our population every forty years or so, placing great stress on a global environment of unknown stability and dynamics. Given a chance to gather precious information about human biological and cultural adaptations to environmental stress and changes, the environment of the past, genetics, population dynamics, and more, much of it very likely bearing on what we need to do as a species to survive, what do we do? Do we try to gain knowledge and understanding? Or do we Appease The Ancestor Spirits? Should the Europeans have just buried the 8,000 year old Ice Man that they found in the Italian Alps? Will other nations leave U.S. science behind? Shall we return to the Middle Ages, when the study of bodies was forbidden?

It fills me with sorrow to contemplate that a few million years from now, space aliens may discover the burnt-out cinders of planet Earth, and study our remains and records. They may conclude that yes, indeed, we were a willfully ignorant, superstitious, and knowledge-fearing bunch, but hey, at least we paid proper respects to the intricacies of Ancestor Worship (Hallowed Be Their Remains, Forever and Ever without End, Amen).

Well, OK, so those bones (of "Kennewick Man") haven't been buried yet, as this is written. Some federal judge gave him a reprieve, it seems. So the skeleton is being kept by the bureaucrats till, who knows how many years later (and who knows in how seriously a degraded shape, after years of being amateurishly kept by scientifically illiterate bureaucrats), some judge decides what to do with him, for once and for all. Maybe Kennewick Man can testify to the U.S. Supreme Court!

It seems that the scientists can't study Kennewick Man, but Native Americans can have ceremonies over him, and put cedar leaves in his coffin![37] Not to be outdone, members of a pagan sect worshipping Norse gods demanded that they, too, should be allowed to hold a religious ceremony over the bones. After all, Kennewick Man looks Caucasian, so he could be an ancestor of these members of the Asatru Folk Assembly! So they, too, get to do *their* deal! Can't be *discriminating,* now, can we?! Now let's all get in line, and apply for permission from Hizzoner, to hold our religious ceremonies over Kennewick Man:

First in line: Professor Joe Blow Scientist, Dude extraordinaire, beer drinker, learned fellow of the middle-class suburb, the house mortgage note, the wife, 0.8 dogs, 1.2 cats, and 2.1 kids: "Your Honor, Sir, I'm a broad-minded Christian rationalist, and I believe that if Jesus were here today, he'd want us all to love one another, no matter what our race, religion, creed, and so on. But I also believe that Christ was being serious when he told us that the truth will set us free. I believe that Christ wants me, as a rational human being, to seek knowledge and truth, so that we can help people, and set them free from ignorance and superstition. So Sir, I'd like to do some carbon radioisotope dating and some anatomical studies on Kennewick Man."

"Get out of here, you clown!" Hizzoner says. "You're just a plain ol' Joe Blow scientist, not a Noble Savage or a Deeply Religious Soul at all! Now scram! Next!"

"Your Honor, Sir, I'm Dood B. Bad, High Priest of the Ommanga Bewunga Church of the Almighty DNA Molecule. I'd like for you to allow me to get a small bit of Kennewick Man's bones, grind them up with mortar and pestle, dance and sing around them, and then put them in the Sacred Gene Sequencer Machine That Goes KaPwing!, and have it determine the Sacred Count of the Holy Trinucleotide Sequence Repeats, so that we may Assign Our Ancestor into His Holy Genotype."

Hizzoner scratches his chin, pauses, and then announces, "Request on hold. I'm not so sure you're quite properly, upliftingly irrational enough to qualify as a religious person. We'll study the matter for a few years, appoint many scholarly study committees, and issue you a 5,000-page report on your request in due time. For a small fee from the taxpayers, who have nothing better to do with their money anyway. Next!"

"Your Honor, I'm Priestess Nooglybwimps, and this is my chief disciple, FuFu the Gnu. We're followers of the Great Green Glorbleworf Who Glimples Gauzy Glormglobbles in Galaxies Far, Far Away. Simpletons who have no idea about how truly Deep and Meaningful our Beliefs are, they call us 'Glorbleworfers'. I'd like to take my fifteen followers, and drink toad pee from green crystal glasses under the full moon while riding our gnus in interleaved, psychically heterogeneous triangles around the Sacred Bodily Remains of our Fallen Ancestor, Hallowed Be His Name."

Hizzoner claps his hands, looking quite pleased. "Now *that's* more like it! Glorbleworfers make no sense, like a *real* religion should! Motion granted! Bailiff, help these good people out!"

So how's that for fiction embedded into the middle of factual footnotes in a work of fiction? Need I comment as to what points I'm trying to make? Why, on the brink of the twenty-first century, are we pandering to irrationality so much? I'm not saying scientists should go around digging up everyone's grandma's graves. Couldn't we at least exempt any corpses and artifacts over, say, 400 years old, when there is valuable information to be gleaned? Couldn't we perhaps even *trust* scientists and public opinion to keep in place those few scientists who might otherwise offend public sensibilities by, oh, whatever; taking their precious bones and making them into kid's Halloween decorations? Must we legally mandate all that is good, and prohibit all that is in bad taste?

Couldn't Congress, for once, try to envision all the stupid ways that the bureaucrats will abuse their new laws? And try to prohibit such things when they write the laws? When they passed NAGPRA, they forgot to state that "bureaucrats shall not decree a hair to be a Sacred Bodily Remnant." Or is that an impossible task? Are the potential abuses of bureaucrats infinite? I suspect so. And this is the ultimate irrationality, perhaps, to think that we can change this. We can't breed a better bureaucrat; we can only cut their numbers.

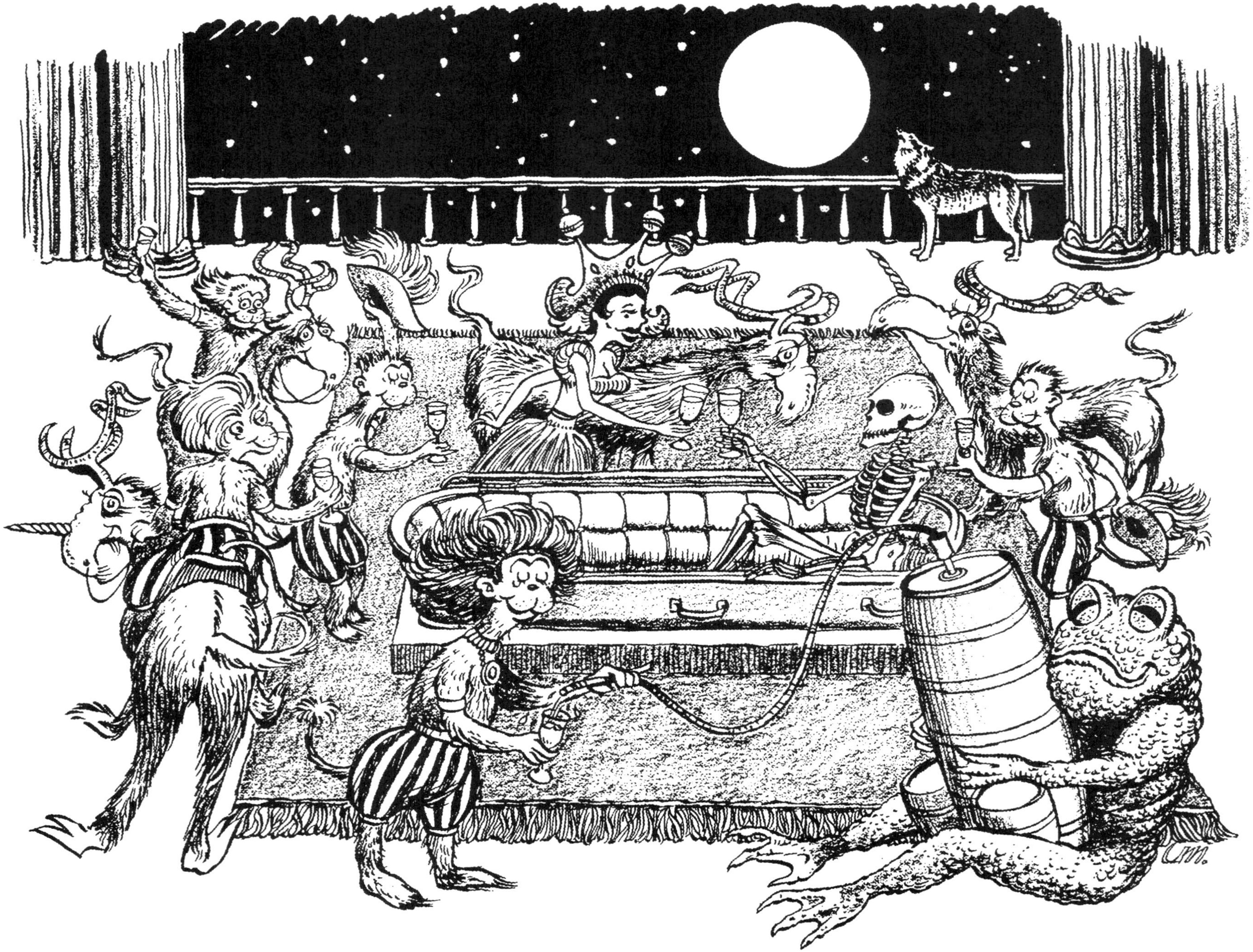

Concluding Endnotes—The Meaning of Life
(Or at the Very Least, of This Book)

Rationalists are admirable beings, rationalism is a hideous monster when it claims for itself omnipotence. Attribution of omnipotence to reason is as bad a piece of idolatry as is worship of stock and stone believing it to be God. I plead not for the suppression of reason, but for a due recognition of that in us which sanctifies reason. Mohandas K. Gandhi (1869–1948)

So, just exactly what was I trying to do with this book, other than amusing and irritating my readers, having a good time, and just generally making trouble? Yes, as you might have guessed, I did have a few ideas in mind, which I've been trying to transmit. In case your vibes detector node-mode arrays didn't quite parse the messages clearly, and you give a hoot, let's have go at 'em one more time.

Take a good look at Gandhi's quote, above. That says it fairly well. Without reason, or simple common sense, good judgment, and believing the evidence of our senses, we (even those of us with the most noble motives) rapidly start doing some pretty stupid, destructive things. Justifying stupidity in the name of religious beliefs is no excuse. I'm all for religious freedom, so long as believers respect the freedoms of others. Those freedoms that demand respect, though, include the freedom to make fun of ideas, religious and otherwise, that deserve to be made fun of.

I support making fun of stupid ideas, including stupid/sacred *religious* beliefs? How *could* I? What kind of intolerant, cruel Nazi *am* I? Yeah, yeah, I hear ya. In many ways, though, modern Western culture today actively promotes stupid forms of irrationality. One should tolerate it, yes, in the sense of not harming those who harm or threaten no one. But when one sees inappropriateness, speak out against it, oppose it! Call it *evil*, even, if it deserves that label!

The Horde Whisperer is largely a metaphor, yes. But he's all too real. Human evil is all too real. How many people talk about evil forthrightly these days? How many religious leaders even talk much about it? No, we can't be scaring the worshippers out of our churches, so we'll avoid the difficult subjects. Might arouse controversy and divisiveness, and we all know that those things are bad. Don't go and ruin people's Sunday. Chaos is badness.

When we speak out in support of reason, we're doing a good thing. Make no mistakes about that. Regard God (and the Horde Whisperer) as literal or metaphorical, I don't care. I can speak both languages, and judge no one for their religious beliefs, or lack thereof, so long as they abide by the Spirit of Love, of whatever particular name they should care to attach to this vague and nebulous, but supremely important, entity.

God made the real world, so live in it. God made the real world as He wants it to be, so try as best as you can to understand it as it really is, and accept it. If you don't like that word ("God"), then just put it this way: You'll be better off, you'll accomplish your goals more effectively, if you accept the realities that you can't change.

HOWEVER (BIG HOWEVER!!!), don't lose sight of the magic of the mind! You *can* change some things, and you should try to! The magic of the mind, too, is part of God's "real world". We can change the rules of baseball, and some of the rules of the social world. We can't change the laws of physics. In between lies a gray zone. In this gray zone is where excessively relying on reason can get us less than optimal results, and into trouble, even. This is where "irrational" religious beliefs can be of tremendous value, if religion is properly understood. Don't throw the baby out with the bath water.

By "properly understood" I don't mean that one has to adhere to some long list of silly rules, dogmas, and rituals, as entirely too many simpletons believe. My list is short. I got it from a truly nice kind of a fella, he lived a while back. *Treat others the way you'd like to be treated, if you were in their shoes.* That's it! The rest is just a bunch of details.

Let me bring forth one simple point to demonstrate the importance of "mental magic" such that even a devout *atheist* should be able to understand and acknowledge my point. *If we all pray sincerely for peace, there will be peace, because no one can pray sincerely for peace, then turn around and stab his neighbor in the back.* There you have it. We don't even need God in this equation. I just happen to define "God" as that which answers these kinds of prayers. Prayers that get answered just because we ask for the right, most valuable things, and because we pray for them sincerely enough.

Praying for peace is supremely important. When we do it sincerely, though, we do it while living in the real world. That means that when we see Evil, we call it by name, and denounce it firmly and unmistakably. We shouldn't *hate* it, for hate corrodes the soul. But we should oppose it with all of our might, and all of our mind. After pondering carefully, we must do what our conscience tells us to do.

Class dismissed! That about sums it up. Those of you who want to stay, now, can stay and dig into all the little details. We're done with the course; now for bonus material. My personal opinions about matters great and small, and the facts and sources that I use to support them. We'll touch quite a bit on the Church of Scientology's abuse of religion towards the end, here, for those of you interested in more facts about this particular "church".

Before we go any further, I have to warn you of my particular irrationalities, if irrationalities they should be. I acknowledge that some of my ideas are irrational, but I try to put aside or change my irrational beliefs when they seem to conflict with accomplishing good things in the real world. I may inflict my irrational beliefs on you, so beware! If I do so, however, I ask you to consider that I'm not trying to do harm.

If you misunderstand my particular irrationalities as being in support of causing harm that isn't justified for a greater good (yes, Virginia, there really *is* such a thing as a greater good—just see to it that you interrogate your conscience extremely forcefully before you use methods entailing much harm, in seeking that greater good, and that when you choose harmful methods, you're choosing the *least* harm), if you think I'm in support of the Horde Whisperer instead of the Spirit of Love, then by all means, put this book down before I contaminate your thinking any further.

But the irrationalities I might foist off on you, if you don't stay on guard, might politically be called Libertarian, and spiritually be called Christian. I'm sure my thoughts in both categories will strike some as impure, heretical, and so on. But here they are, to fend off accusations of pushing hidden agendas, if anyone should wish to make such accusations. While trying not to turn the exercise of writing into a version of the daytime TV confessional talk shows, I plan to spill some guts to you. Writing on matters of any substance requires honesty, as well as substance. You deserve to know which particular brands of snake oil I might be pushing.

LIBERTARIANISM

My short take on Libertarianism follows. It's fairly "standard" for libertarians, but it contains a few impurities here and there. Sadly, some libertarians spend more time accusing other libertarians of being "statists" than they do persuading non-libertarians that we'd all be better off if we seriously cut the size of the government. Many libertarians would take issue with a few of the things I'll say.

I think Libertarianism is pretty rational, principled, and reasonable. In fact, one of my favorite magazines is called *Reason,* and it's quite libertarian. I recommend it highly. Simply put, there is no historical, rational, or reasonable evidence to demonstrate that we can take defective (greedy, selfishly short-sighted, irrational) human nature, collectivize it through political or any other coercive means, and get better results that way, than if we left each individual free to act individually, in families, or in voluntary associations, as he or she freely chooses.

The usual libertarian concepts are simply that individual freedoms and property rights should be respected. Quite obviously, of course, my freedom to swing my fist stops where your nose begins. Libertarians generally believe that persuasion is far, far better than coercion, and that the only clearly legitimate role for the government is to protect freedom. I have the right to be free from coercion, violence, and fraud, and the government should punish (protect us from) those who violate the freedoms of others. So the government should maintain armed services for national self-protection and police forces and courts to punish evil-doers and resolve disputes. That's it!

Being an impure libertarian, I'd argue that government in our modern era, on the basis of common sense and the value of life, can get a bit involved in issues beyond the strictly limited libertarian senses. Let's spend *some clearly limited* tax dollars on roads, public sanitation, health, and the environment, because this benefits everyone, and is the most efficient way to get things done, in some cases. If cholera runs rampant, let's stop it by hook or by crook. Stop arguing about property rights, and spend tax money if need be, to stop plagues, for the common good. I'll not begrudge my tax money spent to put out your house fire, because that fire might easily spread to my house.

"Pure" libertarians will argue all day "on principles" that everything has to be done on the basis of freedom and property rights. We're overfishing the seas? Sell property rights to fishing grounds. Your smokestacks are polluting my air? My recourse is to sue you for the damage you've done to my property, my air.

So who is going to defend the rights to those three hundred square miles of fishing grounds? Me and my guns, on my fishing boat? Or the government? And we're going to have endless lawsuits by a quarter billion citizens running around sticking carbon monoxide detectors up each others' tailpipes? And carbon dioxide (hideous "greenhouse gas" that it is) detectors up each others' nostrils? Don't we have enough lawsuits, lawyers, and "junk science" pushers already? Seems to me that *common sense, balanced,* and *limited* regulation has its justified place, justified in the name of efficiency and the common good.

Yes, we have way, way, *way* too much government right now, and far too little common sense. Believe it or not, though (libertarian extremists, are you listening?), there *are* such animals as people who want to go into government to do good, to help *all* the people, rather than helping some people (especially themselves) at the expense of others. Such noble persons, however, are far too scarce.

Non-libertarians, I must ask *you,* now, to listen carefully. Economics applies in human affairs. It's part of God's real world. *Scarce resources are scarce, so we'd better use them very, very carefully. On top of this list of scarce resources right now are the human resources of those who want to enter government service for good and noble reasons.*

As soon as government spreads to fill all the missions of being all things to all people, we find we ran out of noble government servants long, long ago, and 85.29% of them are now hell-bent on the missions of gathering more money, power, glory, adulation, and delusions of moral superiority for themselves. Surprise, surprise! We didn't make ourselves more noble than we were before, by collectivizing ourselves, after all. All we did was to remove the efficiently self-correcting forces of the freedoms, the spontaneous orders that reside in the free market and in simply *non-judgmentally letting others be* so long as they let us be. We've now replaced freedom with endless fighting over moral superiority, over who should wield the big government stick over which sets of moral inferiors. As often as not, one government agency fights another, too.

CHRISTIANITY & TOLERANCE

So there's my libertarianism. Now my Christianity. I don't think I can justify it rationally, nearly to the extent that I can rationally defend my libertarianism. I can't give you a rational reason why you shouldn't go and blow your brains out right now, or why you should prefer pleasure over pain, creation over destruction, Love over hate, the long term over the short term, freedom and happiness over guilt and fear, or God over Satan. The reasons why I favor all these things has little to do with reason. These are my starting assumptions; I merely use reason *AFTER* I've made my starting assumptions. Only *after* I've made my starting assumptions, *only then* does reason become of supreme importance.

Religion, or spirituality, speaks to that-which-precedes-reason as nothing else can. It (in various guises, ranging from very benevolent to very malevolent) gives many their own "meanings of life" as they best or worst choose them. Perhaps I put Christ on the very top of my stack of good, decent, and articulate human beings because I know so little about some of the others. I do know a wee bit about the Buddha, Mohandas Gandhi, Henry David Thoreau, Martin Luther King, Kahlil Gibran, M. Scot Peck, Viktor Frankl, and a few other spiritually advanced people. Then there's many, many more that I don't know about. They all said good things, and none of them contradicted Christ's essential messages. They all said the same things, in many respects.

Christ is my Mighty Fleecer of All Scamgrams, and my favorite Anti-Horde Whisperer, though. I can say that, now; I'm out of the closet. Are you *shocked?* Can I get on the daytime TV talk shows, now? Or are my beliefs way too boring, too standard? Maybe I should take up Omnology, instead, to be new and different, worthy of media and public attention. Maybe I could make a few bucks. On second thought, maybe not. Ale Run Hubba-Bubba simply won't fit into that list of heroes I just spelled out.

I believe Christ's words should be examined carefully. Then they should also be obeyed, when we think that we understand them correctly, and that they make sense in the context in which we plan to use them. We'd all be better off that way. There is but one True North. Am I narrow-minded to say such a thing? No, because I admit that this one True North can be called by many names. Its essence, however, remains the same.

True North is **Love, Conscience**, and **Reason**. Without the first two, reason can't lead you anywhere. It can't tell you where to go, or which goals are worthy. But without reason, the first two aren't enough, either. You want to live, love, and work in God's real world? Maybe even make it a wee bit of a better place? Then you'd better pay some attention to reason, common sense, logic, the facts, the evidence of your senses, and so on, or else you're just spinnin' your wheels, my friends. Traction requires contact with the real world.

It's a judgment call, quite obviously. What one single person has best shown that he or she has most thoroughly aligned his or her internal compass to True North? Has exhibited the most highly developed senses of Love, conscience, reason or reasonableness, wisdom, balance, and so on? To me, that one single person is Jesus Christ. To me, his examples of dignity, self-restraint, humility, genuine compassion, and a vague but powerful thing called spiritual strength make his light shine brighter than anyone else's.

That most emphatically *does not* mean I'm going to ignore or dismiss what others have said, even if they don't justify everything they say with Chapter and Verse from The Bible. If you've got no Love, no conscience, and no common sense, memorizing all of God's Word down to every last dot and squiggle won't do you one speck of good. If you *do* have the critical ingredients, then you've got God within you, and you're free to go out into the real world, and do God's work. You don't have to even bother to carry your Bible, memorize any verses, or any of that. *You can even use a different word for God than other people use!!!*

Yea, verily. Ask that speck of God which the Creator left of Himself to reside in you, ask your conscience, whether or not what I say is true. True North isn't The Bible. The Bible can help give us directions, but so can many other sources. I say again, True North is Love, Conscience, and Reason. The *substance*, not the words. Not any particular set of words, rituals, or magic spells. My Holy Words or yours (Father, Son, & Holy Spirit; Earth, Wind, and Sky; The State of Absolute Descamgramification, whatever), they only attain real validity and benevolent power when we interpret and enact them in a benevolent manner. Else we can get stuck killing people for working on Sunday, and justifying our bloody deeds out of God's Word.[38]

At some point, we as Christians have to ask ourselves, are we Bible-worshippers, or are we Christians? Do we do whatever we please, then go find the verses to justify ourselves, or do we follow Christ's examples of trying to do common-sense good in the real world?

Put the "real magic" out of your head. You're not going to go out and raise the dead, turn water into wine, or miraculously heal the sick, so give it up. You *can*, however, work certain kinds of "mental magic" by praying certain kinds of prayers, and by then *working* for good. Stop fine-tuning your theology about what, exactly, Christ's miracles were, and what they meant, because none of us really **KNOW** whether or not they happened, or how they happened. None of us were there to see them happen or not happen. I mean for this comment to apply to believers and unbelievers alike. Admitting that *we don't know* is vitally essential in getting our internal compass needle unstuck, so that we can feel the gentle touch of God.

What we *can* do, though, is to ponder Christ's words. This is a worthwhile activity. I've done it, and concluded that his words are worth even yet more pondering. Ignore the miracles and ponder his words, because the words, not the miracles, are all that we have left to examine, today.

Enough about Christianity, for now. Let's mix it up a bit. What do I cook up when I mix libertarianism and Christianity? What themes run through both, at least in my mind? What criticisms need to be made about those who have a shallow or rigid understanding of either or both? I'm so glad you asked!

I'd like to write a whole book called "Why Christians Should be Libertarians, and Why Libertarians Should be Christians." I'd have one heck of a grand ol' time, but I'll bet I'd bore y'all to death sooner rather than later. So I'll give you the short course today.

Christians should be libertarians because Christ was a libertarian. *Leave the judging up to God if you can.*[39] If at all possible. If your conscience will put up with it, just leave the other guy alone. If you think he's doing something so bad that you really *must* do something about it, for the common good, then first make sure you're not a hypocrite, and then go talk to him nicely, in private, and try to correct him if you can. *Use persuasion, not coercion.* Quite libertarian!

The classic "Christ-as-libertarian" episode in my mind has to be the woman who the righteous ones were going to stone for adultery.[40] Christ used words (persuasion), not force, to get the crowd to cut her some slack, for her consensual crime. Then he also used words, not force, to privately tell the woman to go, and sin no more. Please notice that he didn't confiscate her property, sue her, harass her, call her a slut, put her in jail, or demand more power and tax money to fuel a war on adultery. He specifically even said he didn't condemn her. Quite the libertarian, he was!

Parenthetically, I must add a few more thoughts. One is that although I'm deeply indebted to Peter McWilliams[41] in my understanding of the Bible, here's one place where I have to disagree with Mr. McWilliams. He spoke too highly of prostitution. Christ did, after all, tell her to "go, and sin no more." It's important to belabor the obvious, sometimes. *Just because we don't punish people for what they do, doesn't mean we approve, and it doesn't mean we can't strongly try to get them to change, using non-violent methods.* Force should be used only when there are no better choices left at all.

The other thought here is, I notice Christ doodled some notes (or who knows what) in the dirt, as the righteous ones questioned him about punishing this unholy woman. *This is the only time we ever hear of Christ having written anything down.* I've got to ask myself, as one who believes in the power of the written word, why didn't Christ write down his views? Surely, obviously he was intelligent and capable of doing so, had he so desired. His followers later wrote down much of what he'd said, probably mostly in the times during which he'd have lived, had he not been knocked off early due to his (falsely often understood to be political) politico-religious heresy. In other words, written language was well established in Christ's time, and was available to the common man.

I can't help but to think that he deliberately left his words strictly oral, because he knew that some of his followers would micro-chisel on every last word, pouring wastefully excessive energies into examining every last lousy little word choice. Too many of us do that already anyway, even with things left as vague as they are. After all, we've got four different Gospels by four different writers, with many details left uncertain. *Christ didn't want his followers to argue all day about fine nuances in his word choices, he wanted us to get the general gist of what he was saying, and go with it.*

It's about the *Spirit* of the law, not the letter of the law. Christ *wanted* many specific details left vague. It's not about being right **about** God, what kinds of shoes He wears and which foods He eats (and hence, how you should dress and dine, which rituals you should conduct, and so on), it's about being right **with** God, who (among other things) is your conscience. You fancy nit-picking theologians and would-be theologians go stuff that in your pipe, and smoke it.

To make that Biblical with a capital "B" for those of you who aren't sure if you can rightly allow me to stimulate your thinking without justifying myself from strictly just this One High & Holy Source (I should hope to doubt there are many such readers out there, but I'm called upon to take you to task for it, you hopefully few whose compass bearings ravenously thirst for just one tiny, tiny drop of WD-40®), then I would ask you to consider Luke 17:21 and on.

It says here that the Kingdom of God is inside you, and that endtimes theologizing is just a bunch of hot air. Yet we've got endless end-time theologizing from the Faithfull! Obsessing over how it's all gonna end real soon, and all those heathens that don't believe like *we* do are gonna *get theirs*—hey, wait a minute, couldn't we be working on achieving God's Will on Earth, improving our world, instead? And so much nit-picking! If there's a spark of God in us all, if we're all made in His Image and He's inside us all, then *why* can't we learn to withhold judgment whenever at all possible? Don't we owe each other that much respect? Can't we work on our tolerance, our ability to say "That's not right, but *I'll let God be the judge?"* Instead of rushing to condemn people (who wear shoes we've never occupied, and who we don't necessarily know in much detail) and using force and coercion against them in anything other than the situations that absolutely *demand* it, well, couldn't we, um, all just kinda sorta like *get along together* or something?

JUDGING AND NOT JUDGING

There does come a time, though, when we must judge. After we make sure we're not hypocrites, we *need* to judge sometimes. What does Christ say on such matters? See John 7:24. Judge not according to nit-picking standards, but by *right* standards. Judging is not forbidden entirely. Then there's Matt 23:24, in the middle of a verbal scorcher in which Christ spews venom at the hypocrisy of the Pharisees. He said that they strain at the gnat and swallow the camel. That seems to be a bit of Aramaic wordplay there. A *gamla* is a camel and a *galma* is a gnat, apparently.[42]

So don't be dumping on anyone for mixing humor and serious ideas. It helps get the message across. I refuse to make anything so serious that I can't have some fun with it. If it's so sacred that it can't be talked about, then maybe those ideas are so sacred in the first place just because they can't stand on their own. So go ahead, tear into stupid ideas, just as Christ did. Even if those stupid ideas are "sacred", they should be torn down.

Anyway, how anyone can takes Christ's non-judgmental, loving, common-sense, tolerant views, and turn them into justification for self-righteous snits is beyond me. That includes more-compassionate-than-thou leftlimpers who want Uncle Socialism to make my charity choices (with my money) for me, because I'd otherwise be such a low-down selfish slob as to possibly *discriminate* for unrighteous reasons, as I make *my own* charity choices. Only The Annionted (even if that should be The Annointed Voter) may decide who is worthy of compassion, in whatever (especially monetary) form.

Showing that Christ would have opposed massive socialism is easy: He told us to keep our charity private.[43] When all who work are called "rich", and all who are "rich" must have their paycheck docked by X amount for charity administered by an all-knowing government, then we have few charity secrets to keep any more. So we're not listening to Christ, who told us to keep our charity secret. Especially when the government starts taking so much that we have little left to give, and the potential recipients are already partaking in goodies coercively extracted from others.

I got my check in the mail, Praises Be to Uncle Socialism! I got my $120-pair of sneakers and my sports windbreaker already. Now get out of my face with your self-righteous advice about getting a job and all, and I don't *want* your humiliating offer of half-worn-out old sneakers and a second-hand coat! I can do without you and your corny beliefs, and your measly little token charity efforts! But thanks for voting Demoblican or Republicrat or for whoever was most compassionate with our forcibly collectivized money in the most recent elections. All of us victims are profoundly grateful, even if you think it's hard to tell sometimes.

Anyone *really* claim that's what Christ had in mind, when he was telling us to be generous and compassionate? I'll go so far as to admit that some socialists have good motives. I'm not a totally belligerent idealogue. I hear you when you say people shouldn't starve in a rich nation. But this should be accomplished through *persuasion*, not *coercion*. Using Satan's tools of force and coercion, even when those tools are wielded by a democratic government, for the accomplishment of God's purposes of helping the poor, just doesn't work in the long run, given defective human nature. There's no real evidence to the contrary. Freedom and prosperity go hand in hand, as does slavery and poverty. I'll not persuade hide-bound socialists, so I'll let it go, just referring y'all to a wide body of writings.[44]

And I can't see Christ's compass bearings rusted over, running around and telling everyone that fertilized egg cells have souls, and that those doctors who help us "murder" such fertilized eggs should be given the death penalty. There's plenty of room for disagreement among civilized folks about what kinds of punishments should be given to what kinds of evil-doers, and where life begins, and all, but to think that we should kill (or even imprison) adults for killing certain special life forms that haven't even developed a nervous system yet, well... What shall I say?

In our supposedly free U.S. of A., we have a million and more people imprisoned for not doing anything that's even closely related to seriously endangering the public, or their peace, quiet, and safety. Certainly not for disturbing those who mind their own business. This represents families broken up, children without moms and dads, jobs lost, economic productivity lost (yes, it ain't the supreme value, but economics, *work,* is at least more than a bit Holy; it's about feeding, clothing, and sheltering our bodies, which are the abodes of sparks of God), lives destroyed, taxes wasted, and victims of the public left embittered by their unjust imprisonment. And you want to *add* to this load, by imprisoning those who "murder" fertilized egg cells?

Christ, in saying "I am the poor; when you feed them, you feed me" and so on, also talked about visiting people in jail.[45] So how many abortion protesters are ready to visit blastocyst-murdering doctors and women in jail, look them in the eye, and tell them we're wishing the best for them, there, but they deserve every bit of their punishment? And how many are ready to console the surviving loved ones, after the "murderers" have been "capitally punished"?

Your Biblical literalist will tell you that yes, that was **God** telling the Old Testament Israelites to kill people for being gay, for working on Sunday, and for not being Israelites ("Go ye and slay everything that moves, and yes, you may rape, pillage and plunder," their God told them, at times). Try to tell them that the Eternal God remains forever unchanging, forever loving, and that it is the Horde Whisperer, not God, who would tell Abraham to sacrifice his half-grown son Isaac—that the Horde Whisperer's whispers have, in varying degrees, contaminated all that man has ever wrought, including the Bible—now you're a Satanic heathen, because you're questioning God's Word!

Next, try to tell them that God is telling you right now to kill people for working on Sunday, or to kill everything that moves, or to sacrifice your half-grown son, and even most of your rabid Bible-thumpers will have the sanity to recognize your insanity (thank God!). Try to reason with them, and explain this to them: by believing that God spoke such commands to the ancient Israelites, you're that much closer to believing that God could do so again—that much closer to evil insanity. Go ahead, explain it to them—I *dare* you to!

Now try a different tack: Tell them that God, through your common-sense conscience, is telling you to abort that fertilized egg cell that has taken up residence in your or your wife's fallopian tube, endangering your or her life, and watch them go ballistic! Your name ain't Abraham! Off to jail or to the hangman with you, your doctor, and all you other heathens! God can tell Abraham to kill his half-grown son, but He ain't allowed to tell you to save your wife's life! All Hail the Sacred Fertilized Egg!

Before any of you fundamentalists go writing me angry letters, telling me that at least the ancient Israelites didn't actually *go through with it* and actually, really murder their children, like us modern blastocyst-butchering blasphemers, let me tell you to go and *actually read* your Bible. Radical concept, that! See the 11th chapter of *Judges*. The Boss Barbarian of God's Chosen Barbarians, in setting out to slay the unbelieving Ammonites, vowed to God that he'd sacrifice ("burn as an offering") the first *person* to come out of his house to greet him upon his return. So our Hero, Jephthah, sacrificed his only child, his daughter who came out dancing and playing tambourines, joyfully greeting him. A promise to God is a promise to God, after all. *Judges* says not one word condemning Jephthah's actions, here. So to all you gay-bashing Southern Baptists, I say, God's Word tells you to boycott Disney and make all the wives submit to their husbands, right? OK, fine! So when are you gonna start sacrificing your children?! We're not going to be *LUKEWARM* in obeying God's commands, now, are we?!

Make no mistakes about it: Many followers of the rusted-over compass rigid-mindedly speak of Christ and morality while actually worshipping the Bible. They pay no heed to Christ's words about the Kingdom of God being within us. They know nothing of balance, common sense, consistency, or even of love and conscience, at times, it seems.

We could follow Christ's examples and teachings, and we'd all be a great deal better off. Especially on matters of judging, which Christ talked about a lot. "*Real* Christians" are more in need of Christ's teachings than anyone else, sometimes, it seems. Certainly he talked a lot more about withholding judgment than, say, beating up gays (he didn't leave us one bad word about them). We should follow his teachings on treating others as we want to be treated, especially in matters of judging.

You want the other guy to try as hard as he possibly can to resist the Horde Whisperer's whispers of "*You*, my friend, *You* are *quite* righteous, and others are just pond scum, and God wants *You* to make sure that everyone behaves and thinks as God has told *You* that they should?" You want the other guy to strain every cell in his brain, making sure he's right, before he judges you? And you want to be judged by sensible, non-nit-picky criteria? Then do the same for the other guy.

And you want the one who feels that he must judge (for the common good, which is sometimes a valid idea) to speak to you nicely before he goes and rats on you or otherwise harms you if he thinks you're doing bad? Then do the same for him. And if you felt that you had no other realistic choice but to pick a harmful action, such as stealing bread when you're sick and starving, would you want the other guy to try and remove the pressures that cause you to sin, before judging you? Like, by feeding you? Then do the same for him.

So are the abortion protesters and clinic bombers out there adopting unwanted babies, helping the poor, overstressed single mother who already has two Down's Syndrome babies take care of what she's got already, so she won't feel tempted to abort her third? Are they removing stumbling blocks from our paths? No, they'd rather yell, scream, hurt, maim, and kill, to show us all that they're more righteous than we are.

And yes, there will come those times when the truly Evil ignore everything except for violence. When this happens, pray as hard as you can for peace. Then go and do what your Love, Conscience, and Reason tell you to do. Act for the common good, as a peacemaker. Christ told us to turn the other cheek, yes.[46] So think about all factors, all consequences, and all possibilities, before acting. But Christ also had much praise for the Roman soldier, whose conscience obviously told him that a bit of violence now and then was, sadly, required to keep the peace.[47]

Judging when we don't absolutely have to judge, and judging from less than a firm basis (fully informed and rooted in Love) is the root of a great deal of needless suffering. We're putting people in jail for years for growing pot plants, in many states even when they have valid medical reasons use it to treat their own ailments with this horrid weed that doesn't line the pockets of doctors and pharmacists, who in turn have less money to contribute to campaign funds.

Then we turn loose child molesters for lack of jail space. But don't feel bad; we'll protect you from these child molesters by creating databases of the known residences of known child molesters. So who's stopping to ask some very simple questions? Couldn't we keep the child molesters in jail, and create a database about where those low-life drug fiends live? Would you rather worry about which neighbors to steer clear of, lest your child be molested, or which ones you should steer clear of, lest they should horrify you with the knowledge that they're using politically incorrect substances?

Hey, you! **Don't strain at the gnat and swallow the camel!** Ya think maybe he was talking about *you?!* Nah! *Couldn't be!* Right?!

If only we knew now what is needed for peace! How wonderful a world it could be, if we reserved coercive judgment strictly for those emergencies that require it! If only we could just set our sights on *staying out of the other guy's face* so long as the very stability and progress of society isn't threatened! If only we could reserve the worst methods for the worst problems, in a balanced fashion. We could attain peace first. That alone is a priceless goal indeed!

Then, *after* we've achieved peace by exercising judgment in a strictly limited and wise manner, *then* we can work on making sure that the other guy's quite as much a righteous kind of a fella, especially in all the little details, as we, ourselves, are. Peace, first; perfection, much, much later, if ever. In the meantime, we could attain and preserve the peace through tolerance and wise judgments.

Make no mistakes about it; Christ was absolutely right in strongly condemning excessive judgementalism. Self-righteousness was, is, and will remain a root of much Evil, and its sources aren't just crackpots and fundamentalists. It pervades mainstream society and the media. Big-shot pundit Charles Krauthammer tells us (in *Time* magazine, and without any rational reasons, other than that it gives him the heebie-jeebies) that we should KILL anyone who dares to clone a headless human for body parts![48] Then, later, he's totally perplexed about why we should write off the sentiments of religious fanatics, about why we should exclude from discussions of public policy, those who bring us no rational arguments.[49] No need to argue about which policies have which good and which bad effects, on a rational basis; we need merely assert that God told us this, or God told us that.

I have just two questions for the Krauthammers of the world, who feel that their religious rights are violated when I'm so PETTY as to object when they MERELY want to fine, imprison, and *kill* me for not listening to their God: Why is it that your God always tells you, "Go ye and smite the unbelievers," yet He never seems to say, "Shut your self-righteous yapper up, until such time as you can learn to love your fellow human beings enough to restrain your urges to judge and punish everyone who offends you." Millions tortured and killed in the name of God, throughout the ages, aren't enough for you? Enough already!

Well, there you have it, folks. Why Christians should be libertarians. Need more? Go hit an excellent Home Page of libertarian Christians, at www.geocities.com/CapitolHill/7093/index.html. Now for the next installment... drum roll, please... Why libertarians should be Christians. A wee bit harder, I suppose. I can make my case, though, if you'll let me indulge in a little bit of what some of the rusty compass persuasion might call slight of hand. I believe it whole-heartedly, though.

That is, I have to define as "Christian" in a sense, in the only sense that really matters, all those of you who believe in (and act on) the principles of treating the other guy as you'd like to be treated. Be we *real*

Christians, Buddhists, Muslims, or even Omnologists, *if we act on the right inner principles,* then we're doing God's work.

Christ told us again and again to judge a tree by its fruit. You think this means running around and telling everyone to "Let Jesus into your life?" That's your "fruit"? You really think so? You sure these aren't just the words to a new magic spell? Christ himself said that not all that say "Lord, Lord" will enter Heaven.[50]

And I'm afraid many of us have lost sight of the fact that *Jesus was human* along with him having been Divine. What is the value of all he has taught us, if we're the lowest toad slime and He Is God Far, Far, Unattainably Far Above Us? If we can't strive mightily to be like him, with some *real hope* of making progress in that direction, then what's the use of it all? If Christ existed anywhere at all on the same spectrum as Gandhi, Gibran, Frankl, or whatever other heroes, then, for every thousand times that we say "Let Jesus into your life", shouldn't we also be saying "Let Gandhi into your life" once or twice? Christ told us that if we sincerely seek, then we will find. We should believe this, and recognize those among us who have sought and found. They have much to teach us.

Beware that you slip into your magic spells, and forget the substance. Don't let magic words about Jesus (or anyone else) take the place of substance, of doing good in the real world. I have to agree with Jesus that our Father is "unseen".[51] He doesn't exist in just a few Holy Places, or in some statue of wood, stone, silver, or gold. For us to fall down and worship some words, phrases, and ceremonies is every bit as bad a case of idolatry as to fall down and worship a golden calf.

Yes, for all my endless words in praise of religious tolerance, I must say that idolatry is wrong, because it sets our sights lower than they could be, should be. Only God Himself deserves our worship. None who seeks our worship is worthy of it. Even Jesus didn't come to seek the praise of men; he wanted people to worship **God**, not himself (Christ didn't even want the label "good" applied to himself, reserving that for God).[52] We shouldn't worship Christ; we should worship the God that he (along with others) has revealed to us. A hair-splitting distinction? Hardly! Stop trying to cast magic spells by invoking Christ's Name, and start trying to attain God's Will on Earth, just as Christ demonstrated to us.

OK, so I said I was working towards telling you why libertarians should be Christians. I'm still working on it! Bear with me for a few more moments while I explain to you that it isn't heresy to claim that all who aren't against Christ, all who try to do God's Will, even if they use a different name for God, that all these, too, are with us "Christians", be we "real" Christians, or not. All who aren't *against* us, are *for* us, Christ says.[53]

Decent, balanced, life-loving, common-sense libertarians, especially those who don't fall for putting Reason too high on the pedestal (as Ayn Rand did), those who believe in treating others as they want to be treated, these are already "Christians", whether they profess Christianity or not. And I might begrudgingly even suppose that the same might be said of a few Republicrats and Demoblicans here and there as well. I'm just saying from experience that Christ belongs to everyone, one and all. Don't pretend that he belongs just to you, or to your little group.

Even agnostics and atheists can learn from and be inspired by Christ. I can recall quite well a day during the middle of my agnostic years, when I sat in a cadet's chair in an ethics/philosophy class at the U.S. Air Force Academy, where we were going on all day about this and that, ethics-wise. I just sat there wondering, well, didn't some dude a while back just say we should treat everyone as we want to be treated? Why must we go on all day about this? Is there really anything more that we can add to that?

But here I am, doing that same thing. Going on all day about it. It's such a supremely important matter, though, that we're well advised to do just that. Maybe not so much that we can add to it; maybe just that we need to think about it, and its many ramifications, as long and as hard as we can.

Yeah, all you out there of the rusty compass persuasion, I know of you and your quoting of Christ's words about the only way to Heaven being through him. He is the way and the truth, and nobody's gonna go and see Papa in His Sweet Bye and Bye, except through Christ.[54] But let me compare and contrast two different views on the identity of Christ, as Christ meant it in this context. Let's put forth the Rusty Compass Theory and the Mush-Minded Heretic Theory.

Rusty Compass Theory holds that "Christ" is defined in the above context as He Who Was Born of a Virgin Mother, He Who Healed the

Dead, Walked on the Water, Turned the Water to Grape Juice, and so on. He who told us all to wear blue trim on our clothes, not to gather firewood on Sunday, and never to shave our chinchillas in an "R" month or eat uncircumcised mollusks or spud-chewing arthropods on a plate having held both meat and dairy products without a ritual cleansing in between. He who hears our prayers because they're long, and contain all the Right Magic Words. And all those who haven't believed and complied likewise need not apply at the Pearly Gates.

Mush-Minded Heretic Theory holds that God is an often very vague but always awesomely imponderable and vast mystery before the human consciousness. He is far greater, spanning more of time, space, different views and perspectives, and different forms of Love than the human consciousness can conceive. So **M**ush-**M**inded **H**eretic **T**heory (**MMHT**) holds that when Christ said that the only way to Heaven is through Him, He meant that He, as a Spirit of Love, would welcome all those who obeyed the Spirit of Love, and thus tried to treat others with decency and respect.

MMHT holds that we should open our hearts and minds, so that *God* can tell *us* who *He* is, rather than *us* trying to tell *Him* who He is. MMHT holds that working on how we behave here and now is far, far, infinitely more important right now than the afterlife, dogma, and the fine points of theology. And if we behave well, it doesn't matter what name we give to God. The Spirit of Love, just like a good boss at work, is concerned about whether we did His Work, serving His customers, rather than whether we said the Right Buzzwords, or did the Right Rituals, or Kissed Butt correctly.

Sure, faith, not work, saves us. Sure! But *real* faith manifests itself in work. And work without Love, Conscience, and Reason is wasted. It is true, though, that it's hard to keep your compass needle responding to that gentle external Force when your compass bearings are rusted over with overly generous assessments of your own good works and good nature. That much, MMHT theorists can certainly concede.

The Jews sacrificed animals to God. A big ritual for many years, it seems. What did Christ say? "It is kindness that I want, not animal sacrifices."[55] What an un-lawyerlike thing to say! Seems to me, we could much more precisely define the correct way to sacrifice an animal than we could objectively define kindness. Christ must've been an MMHT theorist.

On the highest planes, vagueness is a virtue. By allowing us to fill in the details, the beauty and power of free will is unleashed. Here's a few more thoughts from some other MMHT theorists. *"It is the nature of all greatness not to be exact."* Edmund Burke *"There are trivial truths and there are great truths. The opposite of a trivial truth is plainly false. The opposite of a great truth is also true."* Niels Bohr *"Absolutely speaking, Do unto others as you would that they should do unto you is by no means a golden rule, but the best of current silver. An honest man would have but little occasion for it. It is golden not to have any rule at all in such a case."* Henry David Thoreau.

One more from Henry David: *"They who know of no purer sources of truth, who have traced up its stream no higher, stand, and wisely stand, by the Bible and the Constitution, and drink at it there with reverence and humility; but they who behold where it comes trickling into this lake or that pool, gird up their loins once more, and continue their pilgrimage toward its fountainhead."* Try as I may, I can't say it as well as good ol' Henry says it.

But as Henry says, there *are* those who know little of purer sources of truth. Then let's look to the Bible to justify the Mush-Minded Heretic Theory. Though I cast a suspicious eye on some of what Christ's followers later said, suspecting that they were often just voicing personal preferences, it does seem that some of them finally did pick up the Spirit of what Christ was saying. Romans 2:14 and on makes it perfectly clear that we can do right by good instincts alone, by listening to the spark of God (conscience) that is inside us. Your Holy Source here says that we (with the aid of our consciences) can be our own law, and live correctly by it, without some long lists of nit-picky Laws. Why did God give me a conscience, rather than an embedded CD-ROM in my brain with all the detailed Rules and Answers? Why, simply because He wants me to develop and *USE* my conscience!

Christ told us more than once that "loving one's neighbor as one loves oneself" is second only to loving God, and that everything else hangs onto these two forms of love.[56] Now try to imagine a set of circumstances in which a person says, "Yes, I know that what I'm about to do is against the long-term, sum total interests of humans and other living things, but I'm going to do it anyway, and I'm going to do it out of love for and obedience to the Loving God. Loving God, you see, is more important than loving my neighbors."

Can you imagine any way that this person would be justified? I can't! People who push such views serve the Horde Whisperer, not God. Many of us who live in the real world realize that we can't know the mind of God well enough to take those kinds of positions. We acknowledge that the best we can do is to focus on loving our neighbors. It's really pretty much the same as loving God anyway, since loving God is such a vague, nebulous, subjective, and formless thing. We'll settle for "second best", and focus our *actions* (if not our innermost *thoughts*, where "love of God" might be a more valid concept) on loving our neighbors.

So then, having settled for "merely" promoting the long-term interests of the human race, what is Christ's advice to us? Should we get all wrapped up in customs, traditions, and theological dogma? No! In Christ's day, a prime example of theological rigidity was the Sabbath. And Christ said that the Sabbath was made to serve man; man was not made to serve the Sabbath.[57] Putting two and two together, then, we can see that all things short of loving God and loving one's neighbor as oneself, then, *all things* (explicitly including theological dogma) must be made subordinate. *If it gets in your way as you try to love your neighbor as you love yourself, then that piece of theological dogma must be cast aside or changed.* That's the bottom line, and it comes from the Master of making religion a servant to man. It comes from Christ.

The Bible also tells us to talk to others about Christianity with "gentleness and respect."[58] How we can do this, believing that *real* Christianity is the *only* way to Heaven, is beyond me. How can I talk to this slob here who's damned to Hell unless he listens to *ME*, and do this with gentleness and respect, baffles me to no end. Do I want the Buddhists down the street to say that they've got an exclusive franchise on Heaven, and that all others are just a bunch of literally damned fools, with no spiritual insights worth listening to? Geezum, I guess not! Maybe I'd better not be saying that about them, either, then. Maybe God might even feel, now and then, like exerting His Gentle Touch upon our compass needles through the good ideas of those who aren't "real" Christians. Arrogance rusts your bearings, and broad-minded tolerance oils them. Oil can! Oil can what?! Oil can help you feel the Gentle Touch of God. So oil your compass bearings every day.

If we want to respect (and even love) our neighbors to our fullest potentials, then we must completely relinquish those satisfactions some of us evidently gain by thinking that we're hiking up Heaven's narrow path, while those other guys are just a bunch of damned fools, condemned for not thinking the correct narrow way. We act like the God whose image we hold in our heads. As Thomas Paine said, "Belief in a cruel God makes a cruel man." So I'll invite as my God a Spirit of Love, not the Prune-Faced Sourpuss Shrew Princess, and not the Great Rituals and Fashions Policeman in the Sky.

As soon as you give the preacher-man a dollar a day, power, or any other worldly goodies for preaching, he's tempted to get more goodies by telling everyone that *his* church is right, and everyone else is wrong. Not all preachers succumb to this temptation; many rise above it. But this *IS* a factor to keep in mind, to guard against at all times. The only legitimate use of religion or spirituality is to do *good*. Good, that is, far above and beyond gaining wealth, power, sex, and so on, for oneself.

I admire Christ for not having given in to these temptations in even the slightest way. I'd compare him to, say, L. Ron Hubbard, founder of the Church of Scientology, in answer to those questions that I suspect are building up in your head right now. Why do I speak so tolerantly of other religions, then tear into Scientology? Because it *deserves* to be torn into! We'll get back to that shortly.

So why do I think libertarians (everyone, really) should be "Christians" in at least the broadest sense? Simply because Christ was right. We *do* reap what we have sown. Practice Love, and we'll receive it in turn. Ditto forgiveness, tolerance, and helpfulness. Sadly, too, ditto for hate, distrust, greed, violence, and spitefulness. What comes around, goes around. People catch on, and then they treat us back the way we treated them. Quite simple!

So practice a little altruism now and then, and it'll come back to you. Tell Ayn Rand (with her praise of pure reason and selfishness) to take a hike. Yes, I know, economic selfishness is good, in the bountifully productive capitalistic sense of economic freedoom, and I also know that leftlimpers bemoan my economic selfishness, then get greedy in the sanctimony department by grabbing my money so that they can make my charity choices for me to show that they're more righteous than I am. Still, all you Ayn Rand fans, I'm saying that *freely chosen, informed, genuinely compassionate* altruism is infinitely precious, and *never* to be bad-mouthed.

Did I spill my guts enough for you? Maybe not. OK, then, let me go yet further, and confess how truly awfully, horridly irrational a creature I am. I believe in God. I'm not sure what that means, but I believe in Him. He will answer my prayers and yours, if we pray for the right, very most precious things, and pray for them sincerely. I also believe in various other, less relevant irrational things. Things which have little to do with living decently every day, which is what really matters. Things like reincarnation. You see, *you* take some of what Christ said literally, and *I* take *other* things literally, such as when he said that we must be born again. Does that mean we can't learn from each other? Obviously not!

My irrational beliefs? There is but one more I feel called upon to share with you. That is that my conscience requires me to warn you against suicide. I'm not sure about what exactly constitutes deliberate, willful suicide, and I'm not asking for anyone to go and punish Dr. Kevorkian. And though it pains me that I might pain the survivors of suicides of loved ones, this is the price that must be paid for issuing an unmistakable warning against this act. That others may choose more wisely, here it is. This is the one most deep and dark sin that will not be forgiven. These are the words that are given to me.

Think about whether this might be a headstrong refusal to learn what we are to learn in our lives, a deliberate rejection of our Mission. Go and ponder what warnings Jesus gave to Judas, and how the lives of Judas, Hitler, and many of Hitler's followers ended. Read of the terrors associated with suicides in the paper just about every day. Talk to the heartbroken survivors of a suicide. Now resolve never to support or commit this great Evil!

So there, folks, that wraps it up. Christ, God, descamgramifiedness, and all matters great and small. I'll bet I'll never get so long-winded about this topic, ever again. I've said what I must say. Poogle-Bye (Hi, Mary! Everyone, I'd like you to meet my wife, also known as Poogle-Bye) says she gets tired of my endlessly dark writings, with so much about the bad guys and how they think, and hearing too little about the good guys, and what *they* think and do. I must say, it's easy for me to paint pictures of evil and of Evil. And I think it's extremely important that we look Evil in the face, and denounce, renounce, and reject it in every way available to us.

It's much harder to describe the enormous, but enormously vague, thing called good, or God. It's a mystery to me. So it's taken me a long time to get around to making a sustained attempt to describe the Force the moves our compass needles. But here is my very best attempt. I hope that the Spirit of Love has moved me sufficiently to lubricate at least one compass bearing out there somewhere.

But from here on out I'll refrain from excessive preaching. I promise!

I really do feel many libertarians need some compass-bearing lubrication now and then. See the poll in the July 1988 *Liberty* magazine, for example. Polling hard-core Libertarians, they asked silly theoretical questions, such as, "Suppose that a parent of a new-born baby places it in front of a picture window and sells tickets to anyone wishing to observe the child starve to death. He makes it clear that the child is free to leave at any time, but that anyone crossing the lawn will be viewed as trespassing."

Then, of course, the question: *"Would you cross the lawn and help the child?"* Would you go with common sense and the value of life, and help, or would you stick to your precious "principles" about the baby's parent's property rights? 89% said yes, they'd help. Great! Yet 11% have got their compass bearings all gummed up with rigid "principles". What about the principle of the preciousness of *life?*

One analysis of this poll of libertarians then goes on to show that those libertarians who are more influenced by religion are less likely to give "nutty" responses. That's right, this libertarian magazine split the responses into "nut" and "non-nut"! So, excluding the hopefully small and getting smaller whacko numbers of religious types, we can imagine that large numbers of people actually get a moderating, anti-nutty benefit out of sensible religious beliefs.

Christ was an anti-nut, I do believe. We could use his words more often, in more places. Yet if we quote him at public school or in corporate America, publicly, we might get sued! We can quote Martin Luther King or Gandhi or other religious leaders, that's OK. But not Christ! I sure wish we could quote Christ more often! The public schools, who teach "values clarification" and moral relativism but then persecute little boys that kiss girls, or bring 1.5-inch-long plastic toy guns to school, or who carry an Advil pill, or even a candy that *looks* like a pill, and so on, they *need* to hear quotes from Christ. *Don't strain at the gnat and swallow the camel!*

Maybe if most churches would just go ahead and declare that *all* humans are Holy, since they *all* carry a spark of God, and start quoting everybody else along with Christ, then the lawyers would have to stop letting us quote *anyone*, since we're *all* Holy. Or they might then even consider letting us quote *anyone and everyone*, including Christ, in public. Wouldn't that be cool?

Nah! Won't work! We'll never get enough churches to go along with it! But here's what we *could* do, without needing to get quite so many people to get on our bandwagon. We could start the Church of Holy Sex Education and Sacred Gang Awareness Training, complete with DARE Rituals and Multicultural Magic Spells. Then, since all these things would become *religious* and therefore off bounds to public schools, we could get back to teaching reading, writing, arithmetic, and reason.

And DARE doesn't even work! All the studies say DARE doesn't do what it's supposed to do. Since it's quite clearly irrational to believe in DARE, then it could clearly qualify as a religion, especially if we spruce it up a bit. Just a *few more* rituals and magic phrases; just a *very few* more!

Certainly DARE doesn't work for anything besides getting kids to turn their parents in to The Law, so that The Law can stick Mom and Pop in jail. For their *own good*, of course! Just tell Junior, "See, we *told* you we's a gonna help yer Ma and Pa! Now quitcher bitchin' 'bout livin' under the bridge! Ma and Pa's a learnin' 'bout not growin' an' smokin' pot, taught by guvmint-certified *helper*-type folks. They be back out, all a healed a their sickness, in ten, twenty years. Now pass me another beer, there, sonny!" Humph! So who's brains are fried, here, anyway? **DARE to be SMUG FREE**, I say!

If you don't believe that hypocrites teaching moral relativism in the schools today is a big problem, then see an editorial by John Leo.[59] Ten to twenty of percent of a professor's students can't bring themselves to condemn the Holocaust as morally wrong. After all, who are we to judge members of another culture? Oh, yes, they say, I don't like Nazis, of course not. But who is to call another morally wrong? I guess that the worst that the Nazis can then be condemned for is poor taste!

Even years ago this "unwillingness to say something is wrong" (Leo's words) was colonizing our public classrooms. I can still recall sitting in Mr. Robert Hess' 6th-grade classroom, in 1971/72, and hearing him explain that yes, the pre-Columbian Aztecs *did* practice human sacrifice, tearing the hearts out of their victims. But we mustn't judge them, he said, because they were of a society entirely different from our own, and they operated under their own value system. In short, he supported moral relativism. Well, I think that's dandy, for harmless matters of customs and traditions. Who should wear what color at weddings, how to arrange the silverware, and so on. But *human sacrifice?* I didn't say anything at the time, but my mind balked incredulously at this then, as it still does now.

Now we go a step further, though: If we can't condemn the Aztecs 'cause they were of a different culture, then we can't condemn the Nazis either, even though their culture was a lot closer to our own. So where does it all end? Where does one culture end, and another begin? Much debate over whether we can prosecute people from other countries here in the USA, for genital mutilation of young girls, twenty-year-old men marrying 12-year-olds, etc. Do they bring their own culture and their own standards with them, so that we may not judge them by our own standards? Does every individual carry their own standards ("value systems"), so that no one may judge anyone? If there's no human judgment of any other human, all meanings of right and wrong must break down.

If we can't judge, I guess you can't judge me, either, if I go round up a group of my buddies, and we go shoot some jerk who runs around killing people for no good reason. On the other hand, you can't judge us, either, if we should go and kill people for selling cigarettes to 17-year-olds. Or for not turning in their neighbors, who were doing the same. But then, you can't judge anyone else, for killing me and my buddies for getting out of hand, either. Pretty soon we'll all have to get together and start some sort of organization to stop all the senselessness, and then we'll be right back where we started. Trying to judge evil-doers, and stopping them, using force if need be, tempered hopefully with at least a tiny bit of common sense and compassion.

These same people who refuse to judge, though, often will go on all day about those horrible tobacco companies, oil companies, unenlightened slobs who drive their cars instead of taking public transportation, the environment, animal rights, and so on. And they have so little trouble judging that they're so much better at making my charity choices than I am, that they just go ahead and do that by voting for Demoblicans, Republicrats, and other socialists.

We must at one point get that log out of our own eyes, and go ahead and judge. I agree with John Leo that we must all work on some common consensus of minimum standards that all are held to. We must "...search... for a teachable consensus rooted in simple decency and respect. As a spur to shaping it, we might discuss a culture so morally confused that students are showing up at colleges reluctant to say anything negative about mass slaughter." Yea verily!!! Let's start the list of things we may safely condemn. Genocide definitely belongs on the list!

Now before I move on to nominate my one item that I'd like to add to John Leo's list, as deserving to sit right up there exactly side-by-side with genocide, I'd like to nominate teacher Mary Kay LeTourneau[60] for the First Annual Feel-Good Happy-Talk No Judging Allowed Award. There she sits, holding her baby (fathered by one of her sixth-grade boys) and looking at the newsman's camera so sweetly, so innocently. "There was a respect, an insight, a spirit, an understanding between us that grew over time," she says. He "...was my best friend. We just walked together in the same rhythm." Hmmm... "just walked"? Or were there other things they did togther in the same rhythm? I can hear her in my mind's eye (ear?) going on to say that all feelings are valid, and who are we to judge her? Words, by what they stress and by what they ignore, can justify most anything. Maybe Bill Clinton should've taken lessons from Mary Kay.

We're better off "denying" or at least working against some of our feelings, when our feelings aren't helping anyone. I'll take Christ over psychobabble any day. I'll even say good words about that Demoblican, Jimmy Carter, who took such grief for talking about sinning (in his heart) with the lusty babes. No, I'm not into claiming that the more things you can feel guilty about, the more Holy you are. I'm saying Christ was right; not all feelings are "valid". Don't flog yourself over them, but work on not having them, and always remember, no matter how Holy you are, you always have thoughts you'd be better off squelching.

So Jimmy Carter, he's my man! I even read of him giving some of his church leaders (of the Southern Baptists as I recall) grief about saying that God doesn't hear the prayers of Jews! In any case, I'd rather have Carter mentally sinning with the wild women, but fighting off his impulses, than Bill Clinton turning all my newspapers and magazines into lurid smut.

WARNING! JUDGMENTAL THEME STATEMENT APPROACHES!!! Right up there on top of the list of guano-headedly wrong, immoral, wicked, and even outright *inappropriate* things one can do in life, besides indulge one's tastes for a little genocide now and then, is to abuse religion to gain money, sex, power, or any other greedy, grabby goal we might be chasing. In spirituality properly understood, there lies our biggest, best hope. People who abuse spirituality pollute our moral environment. Maybe we could worry a bit less about having the EPA spend six billion dollars per life saved by reducing involuntary exposure to carcinogens, and worry a bit more about non-violently speaking up against spirituality polluters.

Before I return to documenting what a bunch of slime the leadership of the Church of Scientology is, let me recommend a group I read about.[61] A private organization investigates abusive religions; they even sift through the trash of TV preachers. "'These preachers are turning people off God with their hypocrisy and greed.' the detective says. 'By exposing that, we can turn people toward true faith.'" See, there's no cause for despair. You and I aren't the only ones who refuse to silently stand by while greedy people pollute this potentially world-saving thing called religion or spirituality.

There's always plenty of negatives to dwell on, and I'm sorry if I do too much of it. It's so easy to do, at times. Just read the paper. "Christians" teachers and students in a public school in Alabama harass their few Jewish students.[62] In Israel, Orthodox Jews spit on and throw feces at Conservative Jews from the windows of their religious school, because Conservative Jews defile the Wailing Wall by having men and women pray together.[63] And Israeli policemen support the Orthodox Jews!

But don't let the guanoheads get you down. The Spirit of Love moves many diverse people. "...one of the world's largest Muslim orders seeks to radiate tolerance and peace throughout the world."[64] Centered in Bukhara, Uzbekistan, the Nakshbandi order of Islam teaches and practices a gentle and all-embracing faith.

Only 30 years ago, official Catholic theology taught that only Catholics could get to Heaven. In his 1994 book, *On the Threshold of Hope*, Pope John Paul II said that Heaven is open to those who have lived a good life, whether they openly professed Jesus or not. Those who do good are led by the power of Jesus, whether they know it or not, he says. I can find plenty of cause to argue with the Pope, but in the face of such tolerant broadmindedness, I must gladly stand with him on his threshold of hope. Yes, there is hope!

$CIENTOLOGY

One last word before I tear into $cientology again: I have no real, serious bones to pick with the *followers* of this religion. I'm sure many of them are totally sincere, and some of them are genuinely good people. Being foolish, irrational, gullible, or sincerely silly is quite common, and easily forgiven. The only offense here is that one is wasting one's energies that could be far better spent on more worthwhile activities.

And some of my reading has even convinced me that in benevolent hands, a device like Scientology's E-meter (basically a crude lie detector) can serve as a helpful tool in therapy. There have, in the past, been some good, decent leaders in Scientology. The vast majority of them, if not all of them, have (in my opinion) been driven out by L. Ron Hubbard and his legacy of Evil, which includes the current (real) leader, David Miscavige.

Who I do have the very most serious bones to pick with, then, are the leaders of this "church"! Christ spoke extremely harsh words about the hypocrisy of the Pharisees. My conscience requires me, too, to speak extremely harsh words about the hypocrisy of greedy religious leaders, who turn God's houses into dens of thieves. **The** prime example of this Evil today is the leaders of the Church of Scientology. They are servants of, and apologists for, the Horde Whisperer. Woe to those who make excuses for the Horde Whisperer!

See my comments sprinkled throughout this book, in chapter endnotes, especially after Chapter 11, concerning the moral bankruptcy of Scientology. Now we'll zip through some highlights from my other sources, footnoting them, so that readers who want to learn more can do so.

Put government irrationality and religious irrationality together, and you can come up with some wicked concoctions. So the Germans are "persecuting" Scientologists by not being stupid enough to give them church tax exemptions for ripping people off? Let's give German Scientologists asylum, then, since they're so severely persecuted! That's a precedent set by a federal immigration judge.[65]

So now, would-be immigrants have incentives to join this "church"! Many nations "discriminate" against Scientology. Scientology will now be better equipped to gather recruits in these nations. The U.S. will then self-righteously protect them from "persecution". This, while we put hundreds of thousands of Americans in prisons for the political crimes of not agreeing with us when we tell them what they may and may not put into their bodies. Who will give *these* victims political asylum from our own, American government goons?

The *N.Y. Times*[66] tells us about the death of a Scientologist under the Church's care in Clearwater, Florida. The county's medical examiner said Lisa McPherson's death (after being held by Scientologists for 17 days) was brought on by severe dehydration, estimating that she'd been deprived of water for 5 to 10 days leading up to her death. Our source also tells us that when Scientology first moved into Clearwater, they tried to do so in secret. "...Scientology had come to Clearwater with a written plan to take control of the city. Government and community organizations were infiltrated by Scientology members. Plans were undertaken to discredit and silence critics." So 20 years later, Clearwater locals and government still aren't too fond of Scientologists.

Oh, yes: the front-page article here shows a smiling Lisa M. getting a Scientology award, certifying her Scientology-approved spiritual advancement. Shades of Sensitivity Awards! And we see them gadding about in their Navy-style uniforms. L. Ron apparently liked all things naval.

Our illustrious President Clinton's fame for schmoozing and being all things to all people has even become obvious to the famous actor/Scientologist John Travolta. John reported how Clinton told him that he (Clinton) used to have a Scientologist roommate, and how he respected his views on it. Clinton also told John all about how he was going to whip those cruel, discriminatory Germans into shape.[67] Now maybe Clinton's Hollyweird friends will raise some more funds for him. Maybe Hillary will even get another award from all the Beautiful People, like the one she got for reading from The Book of Hillary Knows How to Best Raise Our Children.

Now, yet more: The *Wall St. Jrnl.* tells us that John Travolta got an audience with Clinton's National Security Adviser, Sandy Berger![68] Never mind Saddamned Hussein, Khadaffy Duck, Kim Il Dung, Fido Castro, and other murderously dictatorial fiends who mean us ill; we're going to have the Hollywood Experts help our officials worry (on time bought by our tax dollars) about those cruel Germans, who *dare* to treat Scientology so badly, not giving them tax breaks, just like we did before 1993! Lights, camera, public policy from Panderwood!

The Clinton Administration's policies of pandering to the Church of Scientology are actually well to the left of the U.N.'s leftist policies, which is a pretty tough act to follow! A U.N. special investigator rejected claims that Germans "persecute" Scientologists.[69]

The *Wall St.* editorial goes on to comment about the IRS's 1993 decision "...mysteriously upgrading the cult to the status of a tax-exempt religion...", in return for "...$12.5 million and a promise that the cult would drop its numerous lawsuits against the IRS and its agents."[68] We know this only because of a leak, which the IRS is investigating. How horrible, that we peons should know what the IRS and Scientology are up to!

The *Wall St.* ends its courageous editorial as follows: "Is there anyone at the IRS who seriously thinks that the unbelievable sums of money Scientology spends on lawsuits meets the agency's requirement that a charity spend its funds only on charitable purposes?" Amen!!!

Paulette Cooper wrote *The Scandal of Scientology,* which was published in 1971 by Tower Publications.[70] She was sued by Scientology some 14 times. She got death threats, and was indicted for making bomb threats against the Church. The letters were on her stationery, with her fingerprints on them. Evidence strongly indicates that her stationery (which she'd already handled) was stolen by Scientologists, who then wrote the letters. She and her publisher were sued into silence.

The *Wall St. Jrnl* published a long editorial on "The Scientology Problem" on 25 March '97. On 1 April '97, the Church took out a large ad in the same, trying to refute what the editorial said. And the *NY Times*[71] questioned the tactics that Scientology used to get its tax exemption. So shortly afterwards, on 19 March '97, the church took out a full-page ad in the NY Times! With any luck at all, now, more newspapers will figure out that running anti-Scientology articles will bring in lots of ad money from the Church, and we can all learn more sordid truths about this "church"!

Anyway, my sources[66&71] tell me that the Church got its tax exemption in 1993 by sending private investigators to dig up dirt about IRS officials, and by suing them again and again. Then they said they'd stop, if they got a tax exemption as a church (which they can now use to beat up on Germany, saying things like, see here, you're not as tolerant as the likes of those wise, spiritually advanced Americans).

Now this may sound like a sudden and total change of topic, but bear with me. "Raymond Holcomb has muscular dystrophy and can barely speak. So when he won a concert by John Mellencamp in his own backyard from music channel VH-1, it must have really made his day. And when he got a bill from the IRS, it must have really confused him. The IRS considers the prize taxable income worth $11,700. The concert left Holcomb $2,496 in the hole to Uncle Sam."[72]

I recall a scandal a few years back (I don't know if you can still get away with this easily, or not). All you had to do to get the IRS to harass your enemies on your behalf was to send in a form (a 1099B) saying your enemy had some income, and he'd be taxed, unless he could show otherwise. "Free" concerts count, here, too, apparently.

So my unsubstantiated conspiracy theory here on just how, exactly, the Church got its tax exemption goes like this: Scientologists whipped out their E-Meters and gave IRS officials long-distance auditing services, or fleeced their scamgrams away, or something like that. They sent 1099B forms (about these "free" benefits) in to the IRS. Being hidebound bureaucrats, the IRS then had no choice but to bust its own. So if you want to bludgeon the IRS into getting a "church" tax exemption for your new scam, the first question you must ask yourself is a very fundamental one: to 1099B, or not to 1099B.

A true treasure trove of information about Scientology is to be found in a series of articles in the LA Times.[26] Till further notice, all quotes are from this source. Scientology has had running battles with those who have left the Church, who go off and audit their own engrams in their own way. "'We call them squirrels,' Hubbard once wrote, 'because they are so nutty.'" A "Fair Game Law" written by Hubbard in the mid-1960s states that anyone who gets in the way of Scientology can "be deprived of property or injured by any means by any Scientologist without any discipline of the Scientologist. May be tricked, sued or lied to or destroyed."

Schools, business, and science are targets of often-anonymous

Scientology influence. They even persuaded an EPA toxicologist to tout Hubbard's "purification run-down." Scientologists themselves are most often the biggest victims, though, working for this outfit. "'Slave labor' is how Canadian authorities in 1984 described the Scientology work force."

"Auditing", of course, is the solution to all your problems. It "...is purchased in 12 1/2-hour chunks costing anywhere between $3,000 and $11,000 each..." How does the Church persuade people to spend this money? By hinting that calamities will befall those who stop getting audited, by various other pressure tactics, and by, um, making promises that aren't really promises. "Church members are required to write testimonials... as they progress from one level to the next. The testimonials regularly appear in Scientology publications. Usually carrying only the authors' initials, they are used to promote courses without the church itself assuming legal liability for promising results that may not occur..." They then provide an example in which a woman was driving with her husband. Encountering car troubles, the woman simply left her body in her seat, spiritually journeyed under the hood, and fixed the problem! Scientologists call this "exteriorizing".

Scientologists call non-Scientologists "wogs", the LA Times tells us. Buddhists, Catholics, Mormons, Shintoists, Animists, atheists, Muslims; you name them; they're all "wogs". Just a bunch of slightly different *kinds* of wogs, I guess. Being the broad-minded kind of a polytheistic guy that I am, I'm *many different kinds* of wog, all wrapped up in one, because I believe in the Gods of *all* religions, except for Satanism and Scientology. Most religions have at least *some* sensible beliefs, that is. So I guess I must be a *polywog*, then. And proud of it! Polywogs of the world, unite! We have nothing to lose, nothing to set ourselves free from, except the chains of our own stupidity!

Here's a good one: "The U.S. government is constitutionally barred from determining what is and what is not a religion." Ha! Could've fooled me!

Here's Scientology's financial philosophy, written by L. Ron Himself: "MAKE MONEY, MAKE MORE MONEY, MAKE OTHERS PRODUCE SO AS TO MAKE MONEY."

Inheriting the throne from L. Ron, there was (is) Scientology leader David Miscavige. He is described by high-ranking former Scientologists "...as a ruthless infighter with a volatile temper. They say he speaks in a gritty street parlance, punctuated with expletives."

The Church of Spiritual Technology (a part of Scientology) had a staff but no congregation, and a fiscal 1987 income of "...$503 million, according to court documents filed by the church." Their job? Preserving Hubbard's writings, tape-recorded lectures, films, and so on, for the ages. They dug a 670-foot tunnel to create nuclear-blast-resistant storage for copies of Hubbard's 500,000 pages of writing, 6,500 reels of tape, and 42 films.

From 1980 till his death in 1986, Hubbard lived in hiding "...to avoid subpoenas and government tax agents probing allegations that he was skimming church funds." He apparently ran the Church remotely, from hiding, using cloak-and-dagger methods, despite the Church's denials.

The *LA Times* documents Hubbard's lies about his background, especially his military background. Hubbard said he healed his non-existent military wounds using his own techniques, which later formed parts of Scientology. Yet he collected a "...40% disability check from the government through at least 1980." In 1951, when examined by the VA, he complained about eye and stomach problems. This was *after* he'd published "Dianetics", "...which promised a cure for the very ailments that plagued the author himself then and throughout his life, including allergies, arthritis, ulcers and heart problems."

Hubbard taught some truly amazingly far-out theories, such as "...when a person dies, his or her thetan goes to a 'landing station' on Venus, where it is programmed with lies about its past life and its next life." The solution, for those who've been enlightened by L. Ron? Pay attention, now, this is important! When you die, make sure you don't go to Venus. Pick somewhere else!

"'I have high hopes of smashing my name into history so violently that it will take a legendary form, even if all the books are destroyed,' Hubbard wrote to the first of his three wives in 1938, more than a decade before he created Scientology. 'That goal,' he said, 'is the real goal as far as I am concerned.'"

John Whiteside Parsons was a follower of British satanist Aleister Crowley, and Hubbard, in turn, fell in with Parsons. "Hubbard also admired Crowley, and in a 1952 lecture described him as 'my very good friend.'" Hubbard met his second wife, then Parsons' lover, and married her before divorcing his first wife. "Crowley biographers have written that Parsons and Hubbard practiced 'sex magic.'" "'The neighbors began protesting when the rituals called for a naked pregnant woman to jump nine times through fire in the yard,' recalled science fiction author L. Sprague de Camp, who knew both Hubbard and Parsons."

His second wife later said Hubbard beat her and suggested that she should commit suicide, because divorce would hurt his reputation. And, in 1976, when his son committed suicide, an aide said that Hubbard showed no remorse, worrying only about the possibility of bad publicity.

Well, enough from that particular source. Moving on to a later *LA Times* article (14 Feb '95), we find that a former Scientologist who was posting Church-copyrighted material on the Internet got busted. Scientologists, under court orders, got to search through his house for 7 hours, with a policeman there only for the beginning and end of the search! So here we've got a "church" using tax-exempt money to preserve "sacred scriptures" by L. Ron. Give them our tax money, or give them an exemption while they tax you and me; same difference. So we're paying for these "sacred scriptures", then. Yet we can't have free access to them?! It's just as if we gave Bible preachers copyrights to the Bible and trademarks on "Christianity" (Scientologists have trademarks on "Scientology" and "Dianetics"), along with their church tax exemptions. Something stinks here...

Then there was Lisa McPherson, who died, by most appearances, as a result of the "care" she received from this "church".[73] She developed mental problems, and fought to escape her captors at times, but they held onto her for 17 days, trying to audit her engrams away, till they finally gave up. "Ex-church members say such confinement is used when a member has a 'psychotic break' or is threatening to flee the church." They finally took her to an emergency room (apparently bypassing other hospitals to reach one with a Scientologist on staff), but it was too late.

So now Lisa is dead, some Scientologists have fled overseas, and all the lawyers (civil and criminal both) are having a field day. This is the same case where the medical examiner says she didn't have any liquids for 5 to 10 days, and was covered with insect bites, or something like insect bites. And despite Scientology's strong beliefs against mind-altering drugs and psychiatrists, they'd given Lisa chloral hydrate, a sedative.[73]

Enough evidence that Scientology harbors some serious Evil here and there? No? Well, then, here's my final push. Let's briefly look at a few books for yet more details. First, there's *"A Piece of Blue Sky, Scientology, Dianetics and L. Ron Hubbard Exposed"* by Jon Atack[74] ("Blue Sky" for short). Then there's "L. Ron Hubbard, Messiah or Madman?" by Bent Corydon[75] ("Madman"). I read both of these accounts by former Scientologists cover to cover. I couldn't find a copy of a third book[76] because Scientologists kept it out of distribution in the U.S. on a legal technicality.[75]

The two books, together, paint a detailed picture of Scientology. Between them and my other sources, I must say, I'm left gabberflasted. All my sources say the same things. The capabilities of human minds to practice utterly blind idiocy and ideological madness are beyond my comprehension. These books describe a madness far more frightening than any fiction. I guess the only upside here is that great acts of "irrational" altruistic self-sacrifice, like Christ's, or even the smaller altruistic acts that decent people perform every day, might not be possible without the influence of our irrational nature. We've got to take the good with the bad.

That's part of the explanation for Scientology. Sincere believers think they really are trying to "Clear the Planet" of all it's engrams. When you're trying to make everything perfect forever, a lot of transgressions can be tolerated along the route to The Big Goal. Then when you've spent a year or two, or a decade or two thinking one way, being taught that all your efforts are Profoundly Good, it becomes next to impossible to consider that it was all a huge waste, that one should stop, and do something totally different.

I know, I'm only nibbling around the edges of explaining away ideological idiocy. After you read and think about it long enough, it does become vaguely *almost* comprehensible. *Really* explaining this effectively would take too long. "Madman" already does a fairly good job of explaining it anyway. Curious? How does one create a "Rondroid", for example? Buy the book! Start with the chapter called "The Brainwashing Manual" about some of L. Ron's writings.

Both books document at length L. Ron's background, and his many lies about his checkered past. They also deal with how he used to praise Aleister Crowley (1875-1947) before he figured out (surprise, surprise!) that this was bad PR. Ever since then, L. Ron's admiration for Aleister seems to have gone underground, but not disappeared.

So who was Aleister Crowley? Let's look at a few of his quotes. "Do what thou wilt shall be the whole of the law." I must insert an aside. At one and the same time, this is only a few words shy of my own personal philosophy, yet light-years removed. Yes, do as you will. All is permitted. Just make sure your will is informed and driven by Love, Conscience, and Reason. If something is wrong 99.9999% of the time, yet a time comes when it is the Loving thing to do, then do it! If we must be ideologues, then we need ideological flexibility. It may very well be eggheaded hair-splitting, but, as M. Scott Peck wrote, there are categories of things that he (we) should do, if he (we) could ever think of a love-driven reason to do them. It's just that he can't think of any such reasons! His example was sleeping with someone other than his wife.

So yes, Aleisters of the world, do as you will. But make sure your will is properly driven and informed! Strive to conform your will with a worthy cause or goal! Sadly, I know not of him making any such amendments. Let's look at some more of his quotes, and Aleister's nature will become more clear. "Ordinary morality is only for ordinary people." I didn't see any amendment on this one saying "And we are all ordinary people," either, unfortunately. Then we have, "I was not content to believe in a personal devil and serve him, in the ordinary sense of the word. I wanted to get hold of him personally and become his chief of staff."

This last one, now, *this* one you *won't* hear me saying, with or without amendments! Crowley was a Satanist. The Horde Whisperer whispered in Crowley's ears, and Crowley whispered in L. Ron's ears. L. Ron said "...the late Aleister Crowley—my very good friend... He signs himself 'the Beast,' mark of the Beast 666..."[75] L. Ron, in turn, whispered in the ears of the current leadership of the Church of Scientology. The Evil lives on. In my opinion, of course... Forgive me these repeated "in my opinion" clauses; I'm trying to fend off lawsuits from guess who... While I'm at it, all readers are hereby and alwaysby notified that all things that aren't labeled "fiction" or "according to source XYZ" are then "in my opinion", in all my writings... I'm still allowed to express my opinion, yes? I sure hope so!

Yes, L. Ron denounced Christ and Christians.[74] This isn't why I call him and his Church Evil. By now, since I wrote at length about tolerance and broad-mindedness, I should hope that readers will realize that I don't accuse people of being Evil at the drop of a hat. Certainly not just for being "non-Christians". I have friends and acquaintances of many stripes. Jews, Christians, Moslems, agnostics, atheists, Demoblicans, Republicrats, and Libertarians. I might disagree with many of them about many things, but it wouldn't occur to me to call them Evil. "Evil" I reserve for the likes of the leadership of the Church of Scientology.

If you want the full details, read these books, please! I'll limit myself to selecting just a few informative highlights. Both books note that the Church uses (and threatens to use) copyright and trademark laws (and even RICO!) against those who would "steal" its ideas ("theft of trade secrets"), or get in their way, in other ways, as they fleece their followers. It seems to me that we could end this madness in a hurry by simply passing a law that says churches and charities may not use these kinds of laws. If you've got trademarks, copyrights, and trade secrets, you're a business, not a church or a charity. What with our supposed "Separation of Church and State", what business does the State have in deciding who "owns" Sacred Scriptures (which are supported by tax-exempt money), or who can call themselves "Scientologists", any more than they can decide who can call themselves "Christians"?

Abuses abound! Scientology has been in the business of telling its members and "auditors" that the results of their "auditing" (counseling) will be kept strictly confidential, then using the resulting files against defectors and would-be defectors.[75] Many examples are given where courts have handed down scathing denouncements of Scientology and their methods. Members have been held against their will, subjected to virtual slave labor, and paid next to nothing. Men, women, and even small children have been cruelly punished. L. Ron once proclaimed that shrinks (evil psychiatrists who would try to help people by methods other than sending them to the Scientologists to have their engrams audited away) invented sex to problematize the universe, so some Scientology couples stopped making love![74] To be more precise, L. Ron wrote that "Pain and sex were the INVENTED tools of degradation," and that psychiatrists "...are the sole cause of decline in this universe."[74]

"Blue Sky" digs into court records and finds some real dirt! A sample summary of part of what was read into court records: "Hubbard hypnotized himself to believe that all of humanity and all discarnate beings were bound to him in slavery."[74]

"Madman" makes some frightening allegations, many of them

passed down from L. Ron's disenchanted son Ron Jr. Ron Jr. (and others) say L. Ron was often addicted to drugs. L. Ron Sr. denounced abortion, but Ron Jr. tells us that he thinks that as a six-year-old, he saw L. Ron performing an abortion on his then wife (Ron Jr.'s mother, who later told Ron Jr. that she'd had two abortions forced upon her by L. Ron). A woman tells of being raped by what was apparently L. Ron Sr. L. Ron Sr. worked on subverting governments to his cause, and reportedly dreamed of being the leader of a world government![75] Welcome to my nightmare! A world with a conscienceless, charismatic egomaniac in charge of it all!

Make no mistakes about it, the Evil persists. It's not all just history. These books go into the continuing abuses of the Church of Scientology, but you can go and read them for yourselves. Oh, yes: amusing trivia follows: Scientologists have been known to tick off their calendar in years "AD", where "A. D." stands for "After Dianetics"![75] Let me wind this down with some frightening passages from "Madman": Ron Jr. tells how Pops apparently wanted him to inherit the empire, but was worried that Jr. didn't have what it took. "All you are is a fart in a hurricane, kid; now read about the Real Power!"

Blather about books and secrets. "'To reveal them will cause you instant insanity; rip your mind apart; destroy you.' he says." So he goes on to reveal The Secrets to his son. I guess gods and Hubbards must have special immunity to the destructive powers of these secrets! "'Secrets, techniques and powers I alone have conquered and harnessed. I alone have refined, improved on, applied my engineering principles to. Science and logic. *The* keys! My keys to the doorway of the Magick; my magick! *The* power! *Not* Scientology power! *My* power!'" Then more blather about new and ancient Books about things like Sex Magic.

Ron Jr. continues the tale. "He is excited, fearful and cautious. He is tense. Unimparted secrets, imparted for the first time. I open the books intending only to thumb through. I am awed and amazed; *I Know* these books! How could I? He answers, 'They were used to conceive you, and birth you, too. I've read them to you while you were asleep—while you were drugged and hypnotized; for years. I've made the Magick really work,' he says. 'No more foolish rituals. I've stripped the Magick to basics—access without liability.'" (My, Titus's, editorial comment; read, power without conscience).

"'Sex by will,' he says. 'Love by will—no caring and no sharing—no feelings. None,' he says. 'Love reversed,' he says. 'Love isn't sex. Love is no good; puts you at effect. Sex is the route to power... Scarlet women! They are the secret to the doorway. Use and consume. Feast. Drink the power through them. Waste and discard them.'

"'Scarlet?' I ask.

"'Yes Scarlet; the blood of their bodies; the blood of their souls... Release your will from bondage. Bend their bodies; bend their minds; bend their wills... The present is all there is. No consequences and no guilt... The will is free—totally free; no feelings; no effort; pure thought—separated. The Will postulating the Will... Will, Sex, Love, Blood, Door, Power, Will. Logical... The doorway of Plenty. The Great Door of the Great Beast.'

"He repeats the incantation; invokes the door opening to the realm of the Beast."[75]

These are words written by L. Ron's son, Ron Jr. If any would be tempted by the powers that Scientology seems to offer, read and heed! These promises are lies (in my opinion). They lead ultimately to nothing but disappointment and pain. Sometimes to worse things—things like death and destruction. Scientology has seemingly offered its followers paranormal powers for years and years. Bent (author of "Madman") thinks L. Ron designed Scientology as a trap. Perhaps so. If this is a good analogy, then I also think paranormal powers constitute a major part of the bait. Again and again, L. Ron would come up with yet more and higher levels of studies, for yet more donations of either money or quasi-slave labor, so that followers could finally attain quasi-godlike powers (become "operating thetans"). Yet no one, to the best of knowledge available to modern rational science, has ever demonstrated such paranormal powers!

It's not that I fear their silly Magick; this part is simply pathetic. Just plain pathetic. They may find my ideas about prayer to be similarly silly and pathetic. If this is what they freely choose to think, then alas, but so be it. Their "Magick" bends their minds into self-deception, into *illusions* of power, while sincere and benevolent prayer taps into a *real* Power. Especially if more and more of us practice benevolent prayer, our resulting benevolence will gain greater and greater power. So let's do some prayer, and let's get benevolent. Everybody must get benevolent. But let's not confuse benevolence with a wimpish refusal to honestly address unpleasant truths.

What I *do* somewhat fear is the human Evil, the sick minds behind the self-deceived practitioners of Magick in all its various forms. Sincerely silly ideologues will sometimes go to great lengths to defend their foolishness. Yet even this fear has quite sharp limits. They can hurt or even kill my body, but they can't take my soul! Yes, there is a price to be paid for resisting Evil. However, this is a far, far smaller price than what we must all pay if Evil stalks about without opposition. Pay now—or pay far, far more later! Yet lies can only hurt us if we believe them. Beware of the Horde Whisperer's whispers!

Enough of the dark side. Let's end this with some positive notes. Don't despair, because Evil defeats itself. It hasn't the self-discipline required to restrain itself. It can't keep itself from committing the smaller evils now, so that it can commit the bigger Evils later. A good example of this is that when Joseph Yanny (a former full-time Scientology lawyer) had an attack of conscience and quit, he promptly got sued. Scientologists were worried that he'd "spill the beans" about them and their dirty secrets. But they defeated themselves! Before Yanny got sued, he was legally obligated to keep his former clients' secrets. After he got sued, he had the right to defend himself. His resulting testimony was originally sealed, but a judge released it. Due ultimately to lack of self-restraint by Scientologists, Yanny's statements about them are now a matter of public record, and we have that many more warnings against their Evils. He concludes that "...The Cult—who the governments of this country have allowed to physically beat it (sic, their) citizens, to betray their confidences, ignore their civil rights, and use the judicial system to destroy them."[75]

More about the plus side... How do we guard against charismatic charlatans? Simply by using the common sense and the intuitive powers that God so wisely gave us! If we've got our doubts about whether the latest would-be Messiah might *really* be nothing but a Madman, then we must *trust in and listen to* those nagging doubts! *Question* that "Messiah"! If he's a *real* Messiah, he won't mind at all! Christ, for example, patiently explained his thoughts again and again, to all who cared to listen. I can't recall ever reading about him telling folks, "Never question ME!" One more clue: A *real* Messiah **WILL NOT** tell us whatever it is that we want to hear! A *real* Messiah is GUARANTEED to tell us things that grate on our ears, because WE ARE DEFECTIVE!

So here's your last positive ending note: Gems of wisdom from (it is said) the Buddha, which I found in "Madman". This is *exactly* what I've been trying to say! Inoculations against the lies of so many false prophets...

"Be not led by the authority of religious texts, nor by the delight in speculative opinions, nor by seeming possibilities, nor by the idea; 'This is our teacher.' But... when you know for yourselves that certain things are unwholesome and wrong, and bad, then give them up... and when you know for yourselves that certain things are wholesome and good, then accept them and follow them. A disciple should examine even the teacher himself, so that he might be fully convinced of the true value of the teacher whom he followed."[75] *Amen!!!*

Every now and then, I have a twinge of sympathy for Scientology, because they say that they want mainstream society to accept them. But then I notice that they never, ever seem to clearly apologize for their past excesses, and they keep on doing the same things. When people say bad things about them, they sue the messengers, rather than fixing their problems that cause the bad messages (in my opinion). So my sympathy passes away. But let's sincerely pray that they'll actually really change one of these days. Meanwhile, if you want to see their half-truths and whining for yourself, you can hit their Web site at WWW.Scientology.org.

Having said that, let me add that there's quite the anti-Scientology war being fought out on the Internet these days. Hit the anti-Scientology newsgroup "alt.religion.scientology", for example. Just type that into your search engine. If a web weenie like me can do it, you can, too. Or hit these web sites: www.xenu.net, www.entheta.net, www.scientology-kills.net, www.lermanet.com, and www.factnet.org. Also fire up your search-engine with "Lisa McPherson", and hit the Lisa McPherson memorial page. Learn enough to turn your stomach!

What all did I learn, cruising the Internet? Above and beyond what I already knew, and have mentioned here? Just that (they displayed a few L. Ron quotes) Hubbard said that only trained Scientologists deserve civil rights. And Scientologists apparently are given software by their "Church" that blocks impure anti-Scientology materials. Finally, I noticed that anti-$cientology netizens freely mention $cientology sites, while Scientology ***NEVER*** mentions anti-$cientology sites; an observation made by the anti-$cientology sites themselves. We can only conclude that truth never fears untruth, while untruth trembles at the thought of tangling with truth. Let them struggle freely, then!

IT'S ONLY RELIGIOUS FREEDOM IF IT'S IRRATIONAL, AND IRRATIONALITY IS NOBLEST OF ALL

Scientology's excesses are just one manifestation of a larger problem, though. That is that our society rewards irrationality with "religious freedom", especially if one can hire bunches of private investigators and lawyers. But if one acts on a simple desire for *rational* freedom, one is rewarded with fines and prison sentences.

Hire somebody under the guise of economic freedom, while letting him keep his apartment and some semblance of independence, and you've got ten zillion government mandates to fill. Give him a good brainwashing, have him live in your commune, make him pass out your flyers, and you can pay him a can of dog food a day. The government won't *touch* you. That's *religious* freedom, see?

But the religious freedom to make people into ideological slaves only applies if you're a really whacked-out, commune-dwelling, totally authoritarian cult. And it sure helps if you're sue-happy! But if you're a harmless pacifistic non-suing group like the Amish (parenthetically, in the interests of complete honesty, I will admit I'm partial, because I was brought up as an Old Order Mennonite, which is highly similar to being Amish), and you believe in living in families with some independence from the group leader(s), then you'll be sued, fined, or otherwise busted if you should let anyone pay your kids to work, while they're too young![77] Don't worry about gangs, violent youths, social decay, and dangerous cults, worry about kids (even of other cultures who believe differently, and don't bother us) who might learn to *work* while they're still too young!

Could we maybe start the Church of Letting People Onto The First Rungs of The Job Ladder Through Combined Sacred Work and Holy School? See, we pay money to schools to learn, even though getting them to teach us anything useful for getting a job is quite a struggle. Then we can't get a job, because the employer has to spend most of our time, and half of his, teaching us that new job, for the first month, all while paying us the minimum wage. We need to figure out how to turn the right to get onto the job ladder (through the common-sense realization that the first phases of a job are half school, half work, and so, shouldn't need to be paid as fully being "work") into *religious* freedom.

If you'll investigate tax codes, you'll find that it's more difficult to claim your privately-paid medical expenses than it is to claim charitable contributions. Paying the Church of Scientology to have your engrams audited away, then, is easier to claim, tax-wise, than your heart surgery! Obviously, it's high time to start the Church of the Holy Heart Surgery! But heart surgery is entirely too *rational* is the big problem here. We'll have to dress it up with a whole bunch of nonsense jargon.

There's quite a few perverse incentives at work, here, with regards to religious freedom and government regulations and taxes. If you contribute to your church, but get tangible benefits of rational value (clothing, schooling, food, housing) in return, then you're supposed to "back out" the value of these goods and services you receive, when you calculate how much charity you can write off. But when you get *irrational* benefits, like getting your engrams audited or your scamgrams fleeced, *then* you can write off *the whole thing!* Clearly, then, in the eyes of our owners, it's far, far better to be irrational!

So if you're going to make outrageous promises in order to rip people off, you'd better make sure your promises are *irrational* as can be! Take your lessons from *Dianetics* (or go see Chapter 20 endnotes for the short course). Promise people the moon and the stars. But be sure to call yourself a religion, and hire hordes of lawyers!

Then compare and contrast Scientology's abuses with the fact that mainstream churches today are afraid to counsel people. Why? Lawsuits![78] Give people advice, even religion-based advice (so what happened to religious freedom—or even just plain freedom—anyway?), and they'll sue you if you don't prevent them from doing something stupid! So only churches with deep pockets, and/or oodles of lawyers (like guess who?), can afford to "counsel" people. When they *do* provide counseling, then, many mainstream churches will only see you once or twice, refer you to a shrink, and deliberately just talk about God and Holy Things, without talking specifically about your personal problems! This, under the theory that they have more grounds, then, to defend themselves under freedom of religion! It's only *real* religion if it's *totally irrelevant to real life!* Thank you, Uncle Stupidity and slimy lawyers!

I'd really like to start the Church of the Sacred Individual Rights, based on my sincere religious belief that everyone will be better off when we give everyone freedom. You want your freedom? Then don't take mine, under the Golden Rule. But that's entirely too rational, I guess. Only if you take those individual rights you've given up to the government, and give them to a cult leader instead, only *then* will you qualify as sufficiently irrational to deserve religious freedom.

Government mandated irrationality ranks right up there with religious irrationality, and maybe even exceeds it, these days. The two together are lethal! Irrationality is everywhere. Just pick up your newspaper, and start reading. I could go on all day about this! Let me just pick a few examples, and we'll go on.

Frozen fertilized egg cells are accumulating in the U.S. at the rate of 10,000 a year. "One state, Louisiana, says a frozen embryo is a person and cannot be discarded; such embryos must be kept in perpetuity. In Illinois, the attorney general said a woman who had a frozen embryo was considered pregnant."[79] So, let's see, now. Fertilized egg cells are people, too. And pregnant women, these days, in some places, get to use handicapped parking. If you're a woman in Illinois, then, you should go get fertility treatments in Louisiana, store your embryo (at taxpayer expense?) there, and then be entitled to use the multi-occupant-vehicle commuter lanes, and handicapped parking, for the rest of your life!

Politicians these days appoint panels of highly qualified experts to make recommendations. Then, when the recommendations don't come out to be politically correct, the politicians will dictate the facts, making the experts recommend what the politicians recommend. Examples are "politically correct" diseases like the largely (maybe not entirely, but certainly largely) imaginary "Gulf War Syndrome"[80] and the real, but politically charged, disease of breast cancer.[81] If you've exercised such poor judgment as to catch a disease that doesn't make you a favored victim (like prostate cancer, which kills 16 times as many people in proportion to federal research dollars spent on it, as does AIDS), then that's your tough luck.

OK, so I'm a documenting fool. The source for my x16 statistic?[82] I had to do the math; they just gave the raw statistics. The same source also tells us that "AIDS activist throws lover's ashes at White House." We can only conclude that he who gets the most media attention by throwing the biggest, showiest hissy fit gets to rob the taxpayers the most. Then we wonder why our political discourse gets so uncivil.

Then there's the larger problem of having politicians implement Hillary-care by fits and starts, thinking they can change the laws of economics by decree. Unlimited, quality medical care on the cheap, all things for all people, all just by slapping mandates on insurance companies! What a deal! Now let's also issue food insurance, mansion insurance, fame insurance, and everything insurance, slap some mandates on the insurance companies, and we'll all be fabulously rich, famous and happy, all without lifting a finger!

And finally, there's the "technology bad, nature good" mentality of the Unabomber (along with Al Gore and all his other supporters). Global warming, whether caused by human technology or by fluctuations in the sun's rays, could be alleviated by technology.[83] But using technology is a grave sin against The Earth, so the only answer, if global warming is to come, is for sinners to suffer. Pay penance now, all you who sin against The Earth!

Bill Clinton is always happy to expand the power of government to take care of those too motivationally challenged (or too encumbered by licensing, regulations, and minimum wage) to take care of themselves. Where government is ill equipped to do much long-lasting good, in the field of charity, Bill rushes in. But in a field where government is far better suited to do good, in defending the Earth from asteroids, he exercised his line-item veto. Taking the first steps towards protecting Earth from utter devastation (launching an asteroid-investigating spacecraft) isn't worth $30 million, says Bill.[84] Nature good, technology bad. If Nature plans our destruction, who are we to argue with Her? Proceed to The Level Beyond Stupid. Accept your Fate stoically, without unseemly protests.

Well, sure, politicians are guilty of being irrational. It's not just Bill Clinton, though. In another case, lawmakers turned down spending a mere $50 million to survey the heavens for threatening near-Earth asteroids, yes.[85] But who elected them? And who spends way too much money enriching all the Hollywood panderers? Collectively, all of us—consumers and voters as well as politicians and Hollyweird bigwigs—have decided that we should spend more money being amused by two tales of asteroids causing mass destruction (*Deep Impact* and *Armaged-*

don) than we should spend on preventing such mass destruction.[85] So just how rational are we?

So irrationality, that's where it's at. No rationality allowed, unless you pay millions! Like, if you want to market a non-intrusive little plastic bag full of silicon for women to use, to touch the *outsides* of their breasts, to let their fingers slide around real easily, while looking for breast cancer, then you've got to suck up to the FDA, pay millions for fancy research, wait for years for approval, and so on. But don't let me bad-mouth the FDA. Those generous, magnanimous benefactors of ours, they're now finally allowing us to buy these things *without a prescription*, even!

Now if you market some *religious* technology like an E-Meter that'll solve all your problems for you, including all your health problems, well, now, that's just fine and dandy. No wait, no studies, no millions of dollars. And easy tax deductions for the buyers. Silly fools! Those breast-cancer-detector-inventors, they should've had the good sense to start the Church of Fleecing Breast Scamgrams!

THE CHURCH OF HEMETROLOGY AND SHEMETROLOGY

Some people have bad circulation. The blood pools in their legs, especially when they spend all day on their feet, working to pay their taxes. And some people (doctors, even) claim that SIDS, Sudden Infant Death Syndrome, is caused by infants' sleep being too undisturbed. Mother Nature may intend for Baby to sleep with Mom and Pop, who stir often, disturbing Baby, re-stimulating Baby's breathing centers in Baby's brain. At least, so goes one theory.

A lot of people might want to do anything they can to fend off SIDS, but they might be afraid of rolling over Baby in their sleep. Or they might be afraid that Baby might suffocate, face-down in the waterbed. So maybe we could have the best of both worlds. Put some motors with offset cams (or other mechanical contraption) under the legs of Baby's crib, and rattle Baby around a bit, at timed intervals. I've never heard of such a contraption for sale.

Then there's pressurized-air stockings (called "sequential compression" machines) that pressurize rings around your legs, squishing the blood out like milk out of a cow's tit. Like peristalsis in your gut. But these cost a fortune, and you've got to have a prescription to get one, last time I checked. Yes, I, myself, suffer from poor circulation, now and then.

I'm an electrical engineer. I could mess around with such toys as are described here, and probably will. Maybe even get a patent or two. But I'm not one of those crude, vulgar heathens who messes around with mere material things for monetary reasons. No, Sir! Economics, remember, is that dismal science of valuing things more than people.

I'll leave medicine to the doctors, and economics to the economists. Since I reside on a much higher, *spiritual* plane, I'm starting the Church of Hemetrology and Shemetrology. Metrology is the science and religion ("religious philosophy") of measurement, see, and hemes and shemes are these ethereal little spirits that circulate around in people's blood. Hemes, of course, float around in men's blood, and shemes float around in women's blood.

The Church of Hemetrology and Shemetrology believes that effigies must be constructed of the human body, and hemes and shemes that are forced (by demons of the underworld below our feet) to collect in the lower appendages of the human body must be ritualistically transferred to an effigy. There, they must be forced by pneumatic peristalsis up towards the heart of the effigy. The heart must measure all things ("metrology"), including hemes and shemes, in order to alleviate Hemetrological and Shemetrological imbalances.

The process of ritualistically transferring the hemes or shemes to the effigy (a collection of pillows and rags will do fine) ensures that pestifoggons won't eat us, or our little hemes or shemes. And detailed instructions will be issued, including the wearing of safety glasses and standing behind a yard-thick concrete wall while turning the spiritual peristalsis machine on, and, of course, NEVER, EVER using the machine on anything other than an effigy. These measures will ensure safety for everyone. And I'll bet I could devise a spiritual peristalsis machine for fairly CHEAP.

Similarly, of course, the hemes or shemes in your little male or female infant must be ritualistically transferred to a small effigy. This small effigy is then placed behind the concrete barrier, in a crib, and the heme/sheme shaker device then shakes the assembly of crib plus effigy, allowing the hemes or shemes to break loose and freely travel to the effigy's heart, where they are measured. This, then, in a nutshell, is the Technology and Doctrine of The Church of Hemetrology and Shemetrology.

Oh, yes: there'd be just one more benefit to belonging to my church, besides taking good care of your hemes or shemes. That is, every member of the church would be a minister (we'd be quite fashionably egalitarian). Thus, if your daughter has an affair with the President, and you don't want government goons to grill you for two days about what all gossip she shares with you, you could both become ministers in the Church of Hemetrology and Shemetrology, and everything the two of you share with each other would become off limits to prying government snoops. After all, the minister/penitent relationship, just like lawyer/client, journalist/informant, and shrink/patient relationships, is given special protection by our masters. Parent/child just doesn't rank, not even in these days of government-defined "family values".

If we had a government that respected just plain old ordinary *individual freedom*, and with sufficient humility to acknowledge that trying to regulate different spheres of human activity according to radically different standards is perverse and arrogant—where, exactly, *are* these lines between mind, body, and spirit, and between religion, economics, and medicine, anyway?—then we'd not need to turn everything into a religion. But all-wise, all-knowing, omni-competent government has become our main religion today. It acknowledges nothing as its equal. At the very least, rational individual freedom sure doesn't rank! Religion, though, *does* rank right up there—when it's sufficiently irrational. So be it! That's not the way I'd like it to be, but I do try to live in, and adapt to, the real world.

I'll not even plan on asking for a tax exemption for our church. All I want is the freedom to help people. And before you say I'm every bit as bad as L. Ron, being a science fiction writer and trying to make a buck, inventing a new religion, let me make a few promises. I'll never, ever tell people that the medical establishment is just a bunch of quacks. I'll never be telling you to come and see us Hemetrologists and Shemetrologists instead of a mainstream doctor or psychiatrist. Belief in hemes and shemes is fully compatible with modern medicine, and with all sensible religions of all sorts. Barring outrageous inflation, I'll never charge you hundreds or thousands of dollars for 1/2-hour training courses. I'll never make you write testimonials about how I taught you to perform faith healing on your car. And I'll never call anyone a "wog", just for not belonging to my church.

No promises, now, but I'm seriously thinking this over. How much interest is there out there in the Church of Hemetrology and Shemetrology? A $20/year bimonthly newsletter? A heme/sheme pump for adult effigies? A heme/sheme shaker for smaller effigies? If I should want to pass this Church or any of its interests on to someone else, would you want me to pass your name and address on? Or do you want us to keep it to ourselves?

If you're interested, please indicate your interests and desires, and send mail to:

The Church of Hemetrology and Shemetrology
C/O Titus Stauffer
P. O. Box 692168
Houston, TX, 77269-2168

And always remember, the Force is with us, and we're gonna kick some Horde Whisperer butt! So if you're not there already, I suggest you get on the right side. God bless you!

SOURCE NOTES

1) *Tracking-device sellers cleared of fraud counts*, by Richard Stewart, 30 Jan. '97 *Houston Chronicle*.

2) *Here's an Oxymoron: All-Natural Smokes For Health Nuts*, by Ross Kerber, *Wall St. Journal*, 14 Apr. '97.

3) Two Associated Press articles both by Sue Major Holmes, *Eagle protection vs. religious freedom* and *Tribal call for eagle feathers can't be matched by supply*, Houston Chronicle, 9 Mar '97.

4) *Sick of It All*, June '96 *Reason* magazine, by Michael Fumento.

5) *'Bridges' author divorces,* in *Newsmakers,* Page 2A, 3 Oct. '97. *Houston Chronicle.*

6) Page 67 of the Dec. 1996 *Smithsonian*, which in turn got these names from USDA zoologist Arnold Menke.

7) *The hysteria over 'Hystories'*, by Wray Herbert, 19 May '97 *U. S. News & World Report*. Also see *Author's theory on 'hystories' hits nerve with CFS sufferers*, by Richard O'Mara of the *Baltimore Sun*, as reported in the 12 June '97 *Hou Chron*.

8) Page A16 *Review & Outlook* column *The Actively Sick*, 26 Aug. '97 *Wall St. Journal*.

9) *Defect cited in fatigue disorder,* by Richard A. Knox of the *Boston Globe*, as reported in *Houston Chron*. of 26 July '97.

10) *It Was a Joke!* by James L. Graff, 28 July '97 *Time* magazine and other sources at around this time.

11) *FREEDOM BECKONS Cleared inmate calls prison time 'a nightmare',* by John Makeig, 30 July '97 *Hou Chron*.

12) *Exception's removal may put some in law enforcement under the gun,* by Roberto Suro and Philip P. Pan of the *Washington Post*, in the 28 Dec '96 *Hou Chron*; *One Strike and You're Out*, by Larry Reibstein and John Engen, 23 Dec '96 *Newsweek* magazine; and *A Farewell To Arms*, by Mark Thompson, 6 Oct. '97 *Time* magazine.

13) *Advertiser's pull felt at magazines*, by Greg Hassell in his *Marketing* column in the 23 July '97 *Hou. Chron*.

14) Jan. '97 *New Woman* magazine.

15) *Magazines Bowing to Demands for Star Treatment*, by Robin Pogrebin, *N. Y. Times*, 18 May '98.

16) *Scientology's ex-leader gets prison in death*, by Anne Swardson of the *Washington Post*, as reported in the *Hou Chron*, 23 Nov. '96.

17) *The Thriving Cult of Greed and Power,* 6 May '91 *Time* magazine, by Richard Behar.

18) *Scientology: Anatomy of a Frightening Cult,* by Eugene H. Methvin, May 1980 *Reader's Digest*.

19) *Documents detail woman's final days*, by Jeff Stidham and William Yelverton, 10 July '97 *Tampa Tribune*.

20) *Scientology Libel Lawsuit Against Time Is Dismissed*, 17 July '96 *Wall St. Journal*.

21) *Explaining Hitler* by Ron Rosenbaum, Random House, 444 pages.

22) *Spitting image*, in *Newsmakers,* page 2A, 6 Aug. '97 *Houston Chronicle.*

23) *She was dying to die*, in *Newsmakers,* page 2A, 27 Oct. '97 *Hou Chron.*

24) *Vampire victim had 'V' shape burn, police say*, Tavares, Fla. (AP), 22 March '97 *Houston Chronicle*.

25) *A Study of Prisoners and Guards in a Simulated Prison* by Craig Haney, Curtis Banks, and Phillip Zimbardo, conducted at Stanford University, and reported in the Sept. 1973 *Naval Research Reviews*.

26) Many articles published in the *Los Angeles Times*, 24 through 29 June 1990. You can call the LA Times at 800-788-8804 and get these for a small fee...

27) *U.S. Inaugurating a Vast Database of All New Hires,* by Robert Pear, 22 Sept. '97 *N. Y. Times*.

28) *Identity Crisis,* by Daniel W. Sutherland, *Reason* magazine, Dec. '97.

29) *Stern Rebuke,* in *Newsmakers,* Page 2A, *Houston Chron* 5 Nov '97.

30) *Software Pirates,* by Alexander Volokh, Nov. '97 *Reason* magazine.

31) *Why the FDA wants to limit your freedom,* by Henry I. Miller, 6 July '98 *The Washingon Times*.

32) *Houston Chron,* 13 May '97, *Study criticizes long prison terms for low-level drug offenses,* by Robert L. Jackson, of the *L.A. Times*.

33) *Splitting Hairs,* by Carlos Byars, 29 Jan '96 *Hou Chron*.

34) *Tribe overwhelmed by items' return,* by Bill Donovan of the *Arizona Republic*, in the 5 June '94 *Hou Chron*.

35) *Resentment rises over Native American tax exemption* by Tony Freemantle, 18 April '98 *Houston Chronicle*.

36) *Cultural Divide* by Mark Smith, 22 Feb. '98 *Houston Chronicle*.

37) *Skeleton 93 centuries old is focal point of a three-sided tug-of-war,* by Nicholas K. Geranios of the Associated Press, 31 Aug. '97 *Hou Chron*, is source here. For yet more details, see also (same author) *Kennewick Man bogged down,* 24 Aug. '97 *Hou Chron*, and *Battle over the past,* by Timothy Egan of the *N. Y. Times*, in 30 Sept. '96 *Hou Chron*.

38) Exodus 31:15 tells us that people who work on Sundays should be put to death. Then in Numbers 15:33, they punched some poor slob's ticket for collecting firewood on Sunday. Moses talked to God and that's what God said to do, so they did it. Let's kill the gays, too, says Leviticus 20:13. Need more details on Old Testament barbarity? Go read it! There's plenty there for everyone.

39) Matthew 7:1. Read the Gospels if you haven't yet. It's not too shabby; it hasn't gone stale with 2,000 years. I highly recommend it! Believers and unbelievers alike, but especially you "believers" who haven't even bothered to read it for yourselves. Now let's strain our brains & *read it with an open mind*, with a compass needle that ain't rusted shut, whatever direction it may be pointing to as it sits there immobile. Just a wee bit o' oil on that bearing now, and feel the gentle touch of God...

40) John 8:4.

41) *Ain't Nobody's Business If You Do, The Absurdity of Consensual Crimes in a Free Society,* by Peter McWilliams. A long book, but highly recommended!

42) May 1985 *Science Digest* magazine, *Mathematics and the Bible*, by "Dr. Crypton".

43) Matthew 6:1.

44) *Liberty* magazine at PO Box 11811, Port Townsend, WA 98368, *Reason* magazine at 3415 S. Sepulveda Blvd. Suite 400, Los Angeles, CA 90034-6064, and *Laissez Faire Books* (a book seller of course) at 938 Howard St. #202, San Francisco, CA 94103; or (800)-326-0996. The Libertarian Party at WWW.LP.ORG. I recommend them all highly!

45) Matthew 25:36.

46) Matthew 5:39.

47) Matthew 8:10

48) *Of Headless Mice... and Men The ultimate cloning horror: human organ farms*, by Charles Krauthammer, 19 Jan '98 *Time* magazine.

49) *Will it be coffee, tea or He? Religion was once a conviction. Now it is a taste*, by Charles Krauthammer, 15 June '98 *Time* magazine.

50) Matthew 7:21.

51) Matthew 6:6.

52) Mark 10:18 and Luke 18:19; see also John 5:41.

53) Luke 9:50.

54) John 14:6.

55) Matthew 9:13.

56) Matthew 22:39 and Mark 12:31. OK, Luke 10:27 too.

57) Mark 2:27

58) 1 Peter 3:16.

59) John Leo's *On Society* column titled *A no-fault Holocaust*, U. S. News & World Report, 21 July '97. He in turn cites articles in the *Chronicle of Higher Education* by Robert Simon (who teaches philosophy at Hamilton College) and Kay Haugaard, a free-lance writer and teacher of creative writing.

60) *Teacher pleads guilty to raping teen-age boy who fathered her baby*, 8 Aug '97 *Hou Chron*.

61) *Detectives for Christ*, by Art Levine, U.S. News & World Report, 8 Dec '97. "Trinity" publishes *The Door*, a humor magazine making fun of greedy, hypocritical TV evangelists and such. See their Web site www.thedoor.org, or call their hot line to report abusive religions at 800-229-8428.

62) *Jewish parents suing Alabama school*, by Sue Anne Pressley of the *Washington Post*, as reported in the 2 Sept. '97 *Hou Chron*.

63) *Israeli Melee as Women Pray With Men*, by Joel Greenberg, *N.Y. Times*, 12 Aug. '97.

64) *In This Islam, Practices (Not beliefs) make Perfect*, by Stephen Kinzer, *N.Y. Times*, 4 Nov. '97.

65) *U.S. asylum granted to German member of Scientology church*, by Douglas Frantz of *N.Y. Times* as reported in 9 Nov '97 *Hou Chron*.

66) Two articles both by Douglas Frantz, *Death of a Scientologist Heightens Suspicions in a Florida Town*, and *Religion's Search for a Home Base*, 1 Dec '97 *N.Y. Times*.

67) *For Bill, Another Satisfied Customer*, by Jeffrey Ressner, *Time* magazine, page 20, 22 Sept. '97.

68) *The Secrets of the Universe, Wall St. Jrnl* editor's editorial *("Review & Outlook")*, 24 Feb. '98.

69) *U.N. Derides Scientologists' Charges About German 'Persecution'*, 2 April '98 *N.Y. Times*.

70) *Author of a Book on Scientology Tells of Her 8 Years of Torment*, 22 Jan 1979 *N.Y. Times*.

71) *Scientologists went to unusual lengths to get favorable IRS ruling*, by Douglas Frantz of the *N.Y. Times*, as reported in the 9 March '97 *Hou Chron*.

72) *Reason* magazine, page 12, Dec '97.

73) *Tampa Tribune*, many articles. Many by Cheryl Waldrip. Call the Tribune at 813-259-7394. Articles 15, 17, 22 Dec '96; 11, 23, 29 Jan '97; 11, 14, 20, 28 Feb.; 2, 9, 12 March, 15 May, 2 June, and 2 and 10 July '97.

74) *A Piece of Blue Sky, Scientology, Dianetics and L. Ron Hubbard Exposed*, by Jon Atack (1990, Carol Publishing Group).

75) *L. Ron Hubbard, Messiah or Madman?* by Bent Corydon (1996, Barricade Books).

76) *The Bare-Faced Messiah*, by Russell Miller (Michael Joseph, London, 1987).

77) *Labor Department vs. Amish Ways*, by Hannah B. Lapp, 10 April '97 *Wall St. Jrnl*.

78) *Clergy shy away from counseling, Surge in lawsuits is scaring them off*, by Lisa Miller of the *Wall St. Jrnl*, as reported in 14 Feb. '98 *Hou Chron*.

79) *Embryos frozen in time represent perpetual youth, bring legal limbo*, by Gina Kolata of the *NY Times*, as reported in the 16 March '97 *Hou Chron*.

80) *A Sixth Opinion Unimpeded by science, a presidential panel will declare that Gulf War Syndrome is real*, by Michael Fumento, Feb. '98 *Reason* magazine. To see just how bogus this "disease" is, and how biased the media's coverage has been here, see (same author) *Gulf Lore Syndrome*, March '97 *Reason*.

81) *The politics of breast cancer*, by Traci Watson, 7 April '97 *U.S. News & World Report*. See also *Member of mammogram panel blasts 'political, legal interests'*, by Gene Emery of Reuters News Service, 17 April '97 *Hou Chron*.

82) *AIDS activist throws lover's ashes at White House*, Washington (AP), and *National Agenda planned by prostate cancer group*, by Ruth SoRelle, both in the 14 Oct. '96 *Houston Chronicle*. Also see *Which diseases are studied? Report suggests vocal interest groups get funding*, by Paul Recer, AP, 9 July '98 *Hou Chron*.

83) Cover (feature) article, Nov. '97 *Reason* magazine. *Beating The Heat, High-tech, Low-cost Cures for Global Warming*, by Gregory Benford.

84) *Dreadful Sorry, Clementine Washington brushes off the asteroid threat*, by Leon Jaroff, *Time* magazine, 27 Oct '97.

85) *Asteroid Scare: What We Don't Know Can Hurt*, by Mark Carreau, *Houston Chronicle*, 14 March '98. Want more scary details? *If an asteroid hit the ocean, waves would swamp coasts*, By David L. Chandler of the *Boston Globe*, 8 Jan. '98 *Hou Chron*.

Also by Titus Stauffer
Bats in the Belfry, By Design

During the past fifty years, in the name of "science" or "military preparedness" or "proactive defense", the American government has injected or bathed its citizens, without their knowledge or consent, with plutonium, LSD, clouds of simulated germ warfare agents, and deadly levels of hot air.

During the next fifty years, we'll spend billions of dollars developing new uses for genetic engineering. To what ends? Some have speculated that we'll build an amusement park featuring dinosaurs. But, as we look back to the Manhattan Project, we remember that we didn't spend billions to split the atom because we wanted a place to play. No, we wanted a big bang for our buck. Human nature hasn't changed; we still want that big bang. And, the lessons of history notwithstanding, smart money says our energies will continue to be directed toward building weapons of mass destruction. Unfortunately, as the building and experimenting proceed, you won't hear about the mistakes, the failures, the dead ends. This is classified information, top secret.

Weapons devised in darkness and tested in secrecy can bear monstrous fruit, and the desire to save American lives can turn into genocide. This is a major theme of *Bats in the Belfry, By Design*.

This book isn't for those who don't want their thinking challenged, who believe in "My country, right or wrong." Rather, it is for those who care about the free exchange of information and ideas, freedom, and a future for the human race, and who also want a few good chuckles and some chills and thrills.

Titus Stauffer sounds a warning in *Bats in the Belfry, By Design* about the dangers of genetic engineering that may not be revealed to the public for another fifty years... *if we're still here... if the secret schemes don't go too haywire...*

Also by Titus Stauffer
Freedom From Freedom Froms

It's been decades since the civil rights movement, but race relations are deteriorating. We still fail to judge people by their character rather than by their skin color. We've made even less progress towards legally recognizing, let alone socially accepting, the private lifestyle choices of our fellow human beings. Yet we stand on the brink of technological breakthroughs which could pose far tougher problems. Genetically engineered human and non-human beings and conscious computers are coming our way. Are we ready? Will we allow them to vote? To defend themselves? To own property? Or will we simply say that since they're not human, they have no rights? Slavery, Part II? We'll face these and many other vexing problems, equipped with two main ideologies. Welfare Statists on the left, coercive busybody moralists on the right. Socialists give us *"freedom from housing discrimination"* by punishing us for advertising our houses as having *"walk-in closets"*. By doing so, they say, we convey our intent to discriminate against those in wheelchairs! Witchburners give us *"freedom from sin"* by protecting us from "lewd" Calvin Klein ads.

Perhaps genuine freedom and broad-mindedness could provide some solutions. Instead of sponsoring quarrels between the NAACP, NAAWP, NAACC (National Associations for the Advancement of Colored People, White People, and Conscious Computers), and so on, we'd be better off with the NAACB (Non-exclusive Association for the Advancement of Conscious Beings). Maybe. Or maybe not. But we definitely need *"Freedom From Freedom Froms"* when the "freedoms" that our "leaders" foist on us are false ones. Prepare your mind for a thought-provoking trip into the future. If you love *REAL* freedom, vicious political satire, and science fiction, this book was written for *YOU!*

Publisher's Notes and Order Form

Copies of *Bats in the Belfry, By Design*, *Freedom From Freedom Froms,* and *Jurassic Horde Whisperer of Madness County* can be purchased directly from the publisher:

FreeVoice Publishing
P. O. Box 692168
Houston, TX 77269-2168
(281)-251-5226

Notes: *Bats in the Belfry, By Design* is a trade paperback, 5.5 x 8 inches, 478 pages, ISBN # 0-9644835-05, and *Freedom From Freedom Froms* is the same, except 530 pages, and ISBN #0-9644835-13; both are direct-sale priced @ $7.50.

Please send _____ copies of *Bats in the Belfry, By Design*, and/or _____ copies of *Freedom From Freedom Froms,* at $7.50 per book (either one). Also send _____ copies of *Jurassic Horde Whisperer* at $11.95. Please add $2.50 shipping and handling for the first book and $1.00 for each additional book. Please allow 3-6 weeks delivery. Texas residents add 7.25% tax. Check or money order only.

Name _____
Address _____
City _____ State _____ Zip _____
Total $_____

BATS in the BELFRY BY DESIGN

TITUS STAUFFER

FREEDOM FROM FREEDOM FROMS

TITUS STAUFFER